Sabrina the teenage witch
the magic within
book 2

SABRINA THE TEENAGE WITCH: THE MAGIC WITHIN 2
Published by Archie Comic Publications, Inc.
325 Fayette Avenue, Mamaroneck, NY 10543-2318.

FIRST PRINTING.

ISBN: 978-1-936975-54-9

Printed in Canada.

PUBLISHER/CO-CEO: Jon Goldwater
CO-CEO: Nancy Silberkleit
PRESIDENT: Mike Pellerito
CO-PRESIDENT/EDITOR-IN-CHIEF: Victor Gorelick
CFO: William Mooar
SENIOR VICE PRESIDENT, SALES & BUSINESS DEVELOPMENT: Jim Sokolowski
SENIOR VICE PRESIDENT, PUBLISHING & OPERATIONS: Harold Buchholz
VICE PRESIDENT, SPECIAL PROJECTS: Steve Mooar
EXECUTIVE DIRECTOR OF EDITORIAL: Paul Kaminski
PRODUCTION MANAGER: Stephen Oswald
DIRECTOR OF PUBLICITY & MARKETING: Steven Scott
PROJECT COORDINATOR/BOOK DESIGN: Duncan McLachlan
EDITORIAL ASSISTANT/PROOFREADER: Jonathan Mosley
PRODUCTION: Suzannah Rowntree, Kari Silbergleit, Vincent Lovallo

FEATURING THE TALENTS OF:

STORY & PENCILS **Tania del Rio**

INKS **Jim Amash**

LETTERS **Jeff Powell**
with **Ridge Rooms**
Teresa Davidson

COVER COLORS, RENDERING **Jason Jensen**

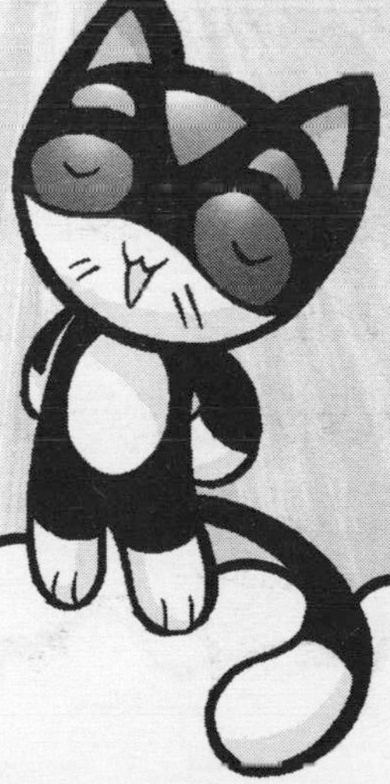

Characters

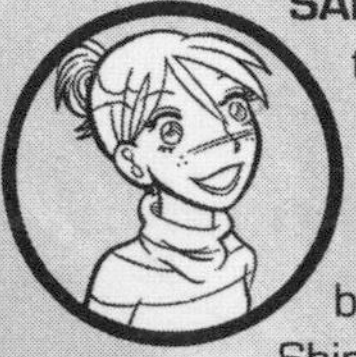

SABRINA's life is still pretty complicated—but things do seem to be getting better! She managed to impress the Magic Realm's leaders by capturing an evil sorcerer, and she's even passing Charm School there, too! Back in the Mortal Realm, she's finally going steady with her crush Harvey. But he's been awfully distant recently . . . and she still has feelings for Shinji. Being a teenager isn't easy—even for a witch!

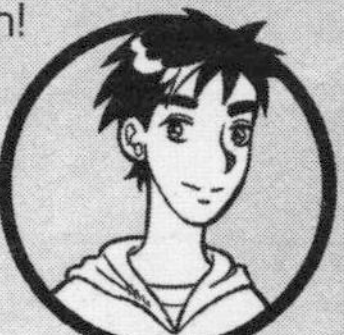

HARVEY is Sabrina's mortal boyfriend . . . but he has no idea that she's a witch! He and Sabrina have been friends since they were little kids, and have always been in love. So why is he acting so strange now that they're *finally* dating?

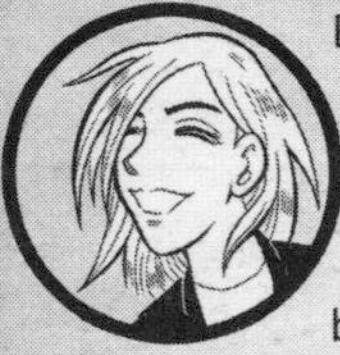

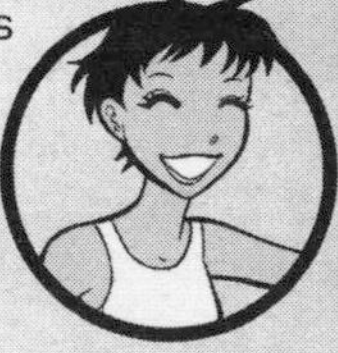

Blue-haired wizard **SHINJI** attends both high school and Charm School with Sabrina . . . and he has feelings for her, too. This makes things a bit awkward, considering he's now dating her best friend **LLANDRA**, who also splits time between realms (but at a different mortal high school than them). Can Sabrina and Llandra's friendship survive all the changes that high school (and magic) throw at them? And just what kind of secret is Shinji hiding, anyway?

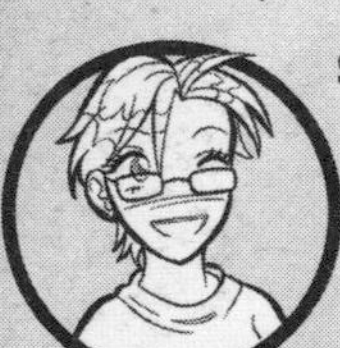

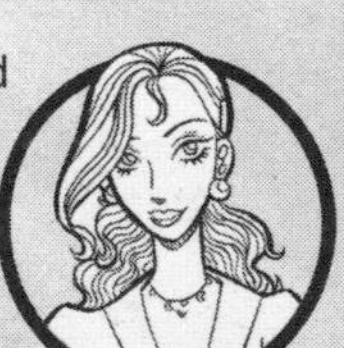

Sabrina's aunts and legal guardians, **HILDA** and **ZELDA** are doing their best to raise Sabrina to be a capable young witch while living in the Mortal Realm. Hilda recently achieved a personal dream—an appointment to the Ministry of Magic, the Magic Realm's government!

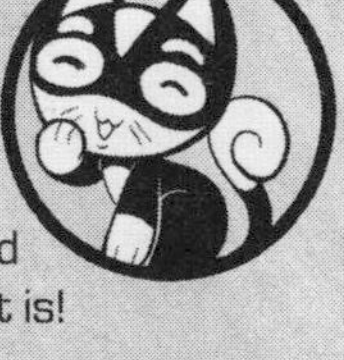

SALEM is Sabrina's pet cat and familiar. He may look cute, but it's worth noting that he was once a dangerous and powerful wizard, transformed to his magicless feline form as punishment for trying to conquer the entire Magic Realm! He's mellowed a *lot* now, though, and he always has Sabrina's back . . . as long as he isn't distracted by his reflection, that is!

Chapter 1

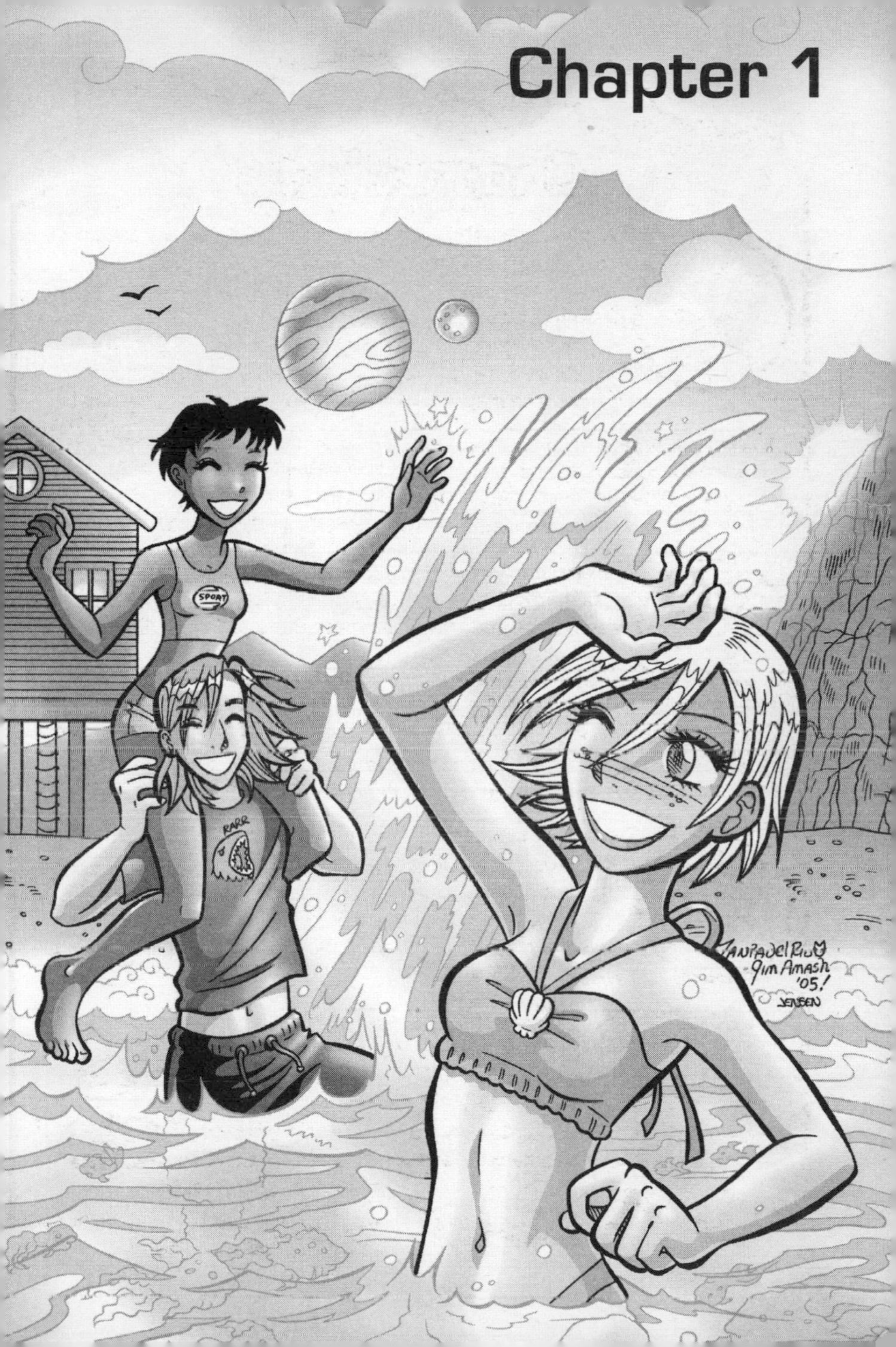

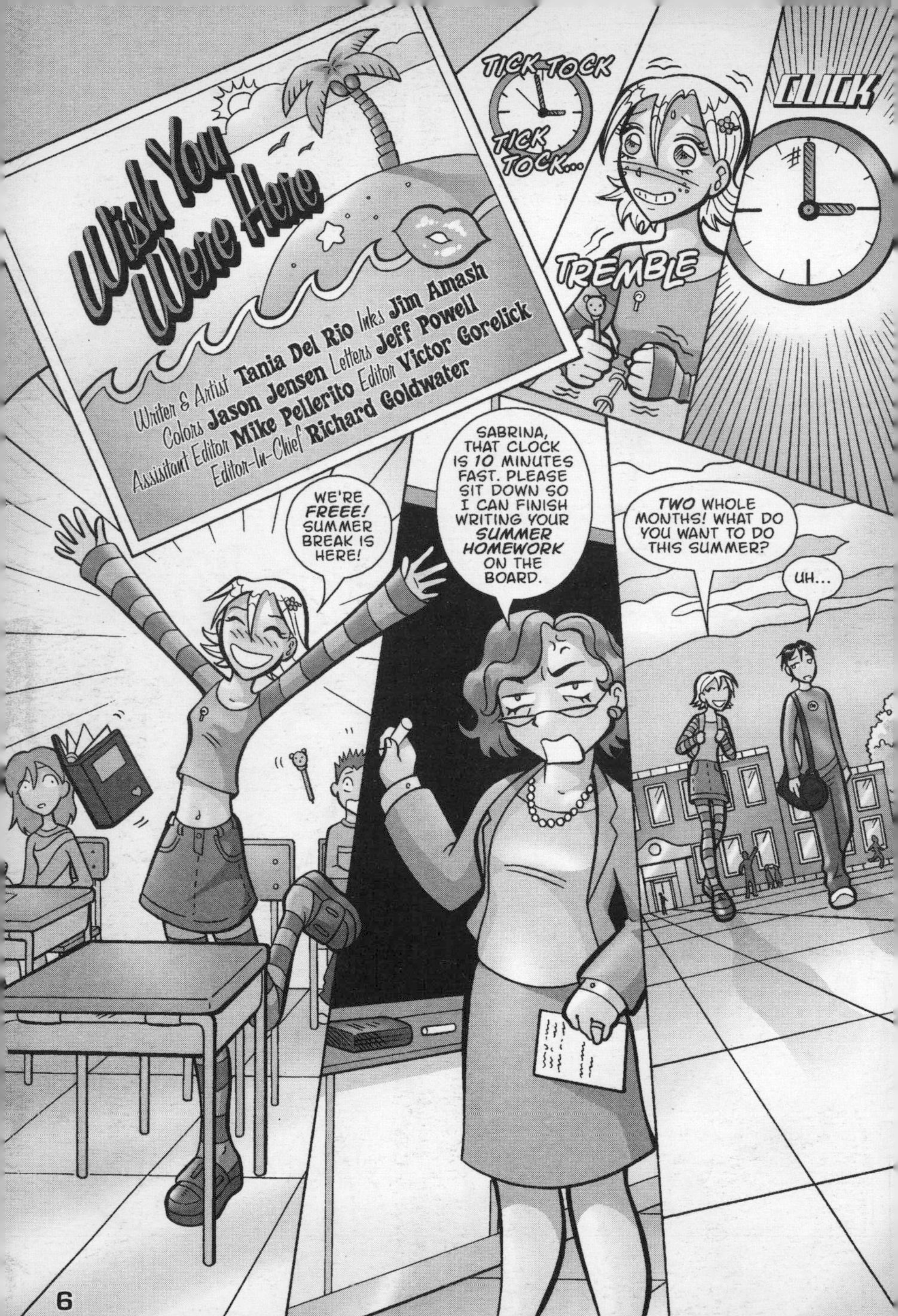
Wish You Were Here
Writer & Artist Tania Del Rio Inks Jim Amash
Colors Jason Jensen Letters Jeff Powell
Assistant Editor Mike Pellerito Editor Victor Gorelick
Editor-In-Chief Richard Goldwater
TICK TOCK
TICK TOCK...
TREMBLE
CLICK
WE'RE FREEE! SUMMER BREAK IS HERE!
SABRINA, THAT CLOCK IS 10 MINUTES FAST. PLEASE SIT DOWN SO I CAN FINISH WRITING YOUR SUMMER HOMEWORK ON THE BOARD.
TWO WHOLE MONTHS! WHAT DO YOU WANT TO DO THIS SUMMER?
UH...

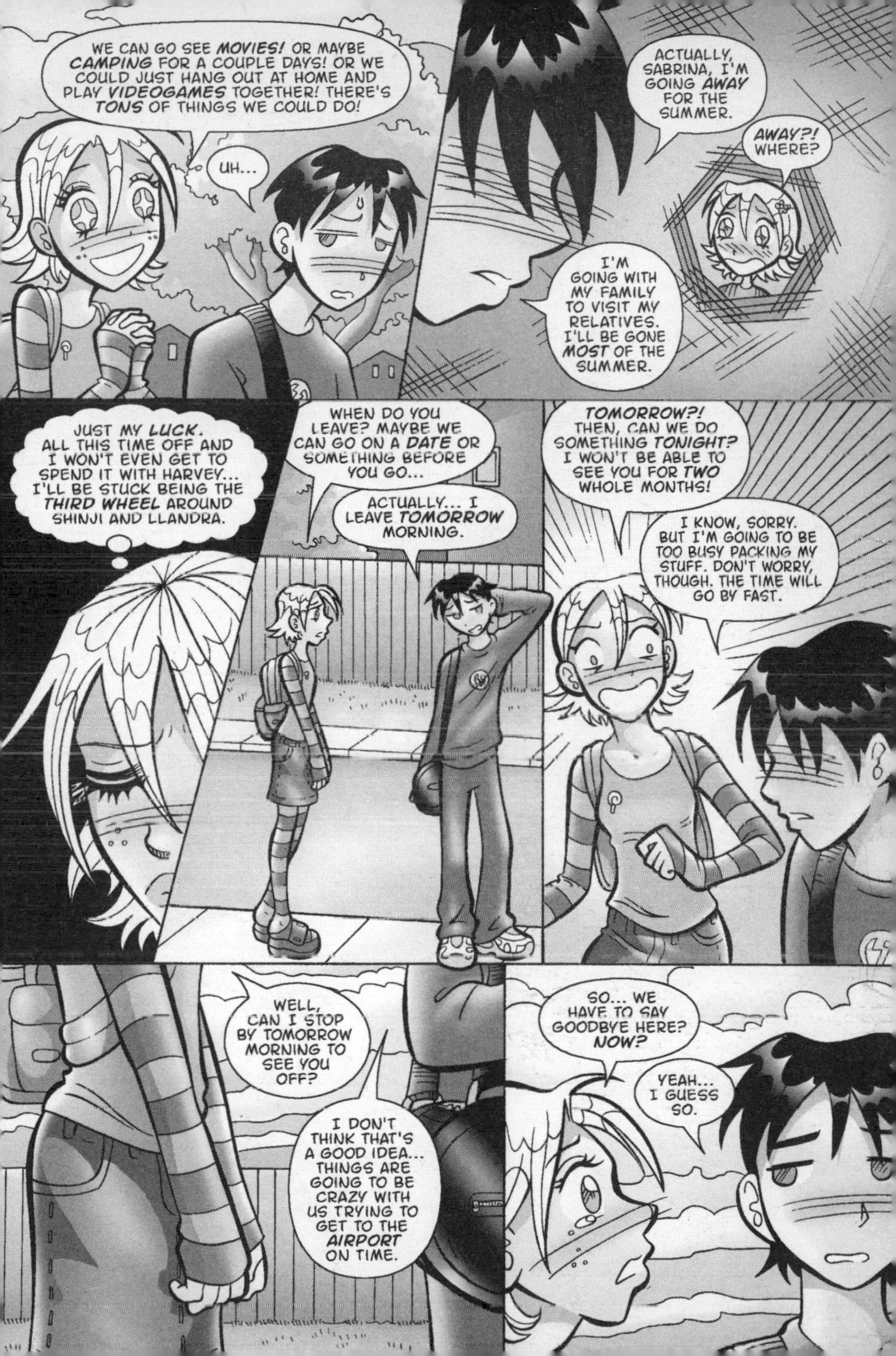
WE CAN GO SEE **MOVIES!** OR MAYBE **CAMPING** FOR A COUPLE DAYS! OR WE COULD JUST HANG OUT AT HOME AND PLAY **VIDEOGAMES** TOGETHER! THERE'S **TONS** OF THINGS WE COULD DO!
UH...
ACTUALLY, SABRINA, I'M GOING **AWAY** FOR THE SUMMER.
AWAY?! WHERE?
I'M GOING WITH MY FAMILY TO VISIT MY RELATIVES. I'LL BE GONE **MOST** OF THE SUMMER.
JUST MY **LUCK.** ALL THIS TIME OFF AND I WON'T EVEN GET TO SPEND IT WITH HARVEY... I'LL BE STUCK BEING THE **THIRD WHEEL** AROUND SHINJI AND LLANDRA.
WHEN DO YOU LEAVE? MAYBE WE CAN GO ON A **DATE** OR SOMETHING BEFORE YOU GO...
ACTUALLY... I LEAVE **TOMORROW** MORNING.
TOMORROW?! THEN, CAN WE DO SOMETHING **TONIGHT?** I WON'T BE ABLE TO SEE YOU FOR **TWO** WHOLE MONTHS!
I KNOW, SORRY. BUT I'M GOING TO BE TOO BUSY PACKING MY STUFF. DON'T WORRY, THOUGH. THE TIME WILL GO BY FAST.
WELL, CAN I STOP BY TOMORROW MORNING TO SEE YOU OFF?
I DON'T THINK THAT'S A GOOD IDEA... THINGS ARE GOING TO BE CRAZY WITH US TRYING TO GET TO THE **AIRPORT** ON TIME.
SO... WE HAVE TO SAY GOODBYE HERE? **NOW?**
YEAH... I GUESS SO.

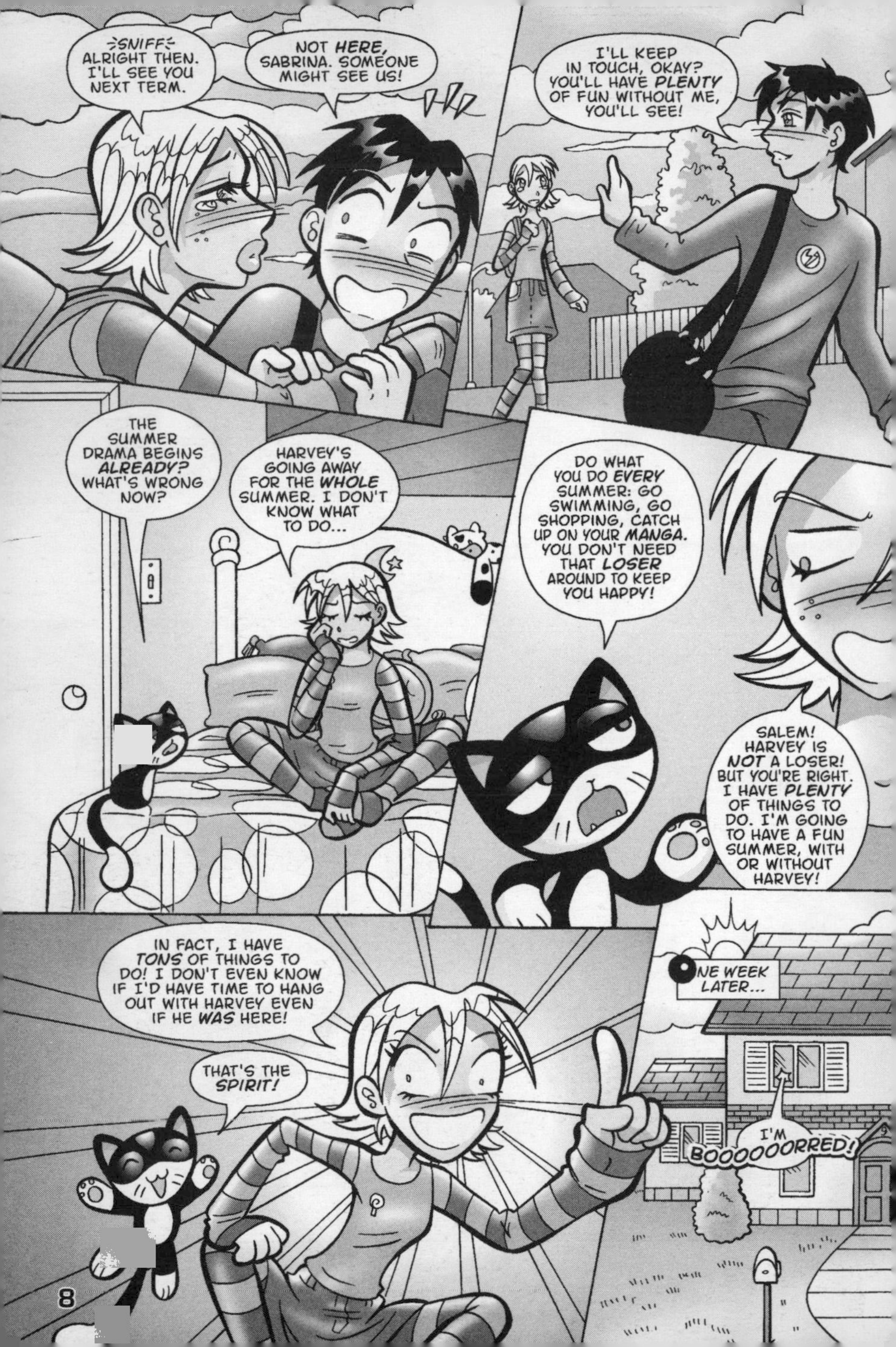

-SNIFF- ALRIGHT THEN. I'LL SEE YOU NEXT TERM.
NOT HERE, SABRINA. SOMEONE MIGHT SEE US!
I'LL KEEP IN TOUCH, OKAY? YOU'LL HAVE PLENTY OF FUN WITHOUT ME, YOU'LL SEE!
THE SUMMER DRAMA BEGINS ALREADY? WHAT'S WRONG NOW?
HARVEY'S GOING AWAY FOR THE WHOLE SUMMER. I DON'T KNOW WHAT TO DO...
DO WHAT YOU DO EVERY SUMMER: GO SWIMMING, GO SHOPPING, CATCH UP ON YOUR MANGA. YOU DON'T NEED THAT LOSER AROUND TO KEEP YOU HAPPY!
SALEM! HARVEY IS NOT A LOSER! BUT YOU'RE RIGHT. I HAVE PLENTY OF THINGS TO DO. I'M GOING TO HAVE A FUN SUMMER, WITH OR WITHOUT HARVEY!
IN FACT, I HAVE TONS OF THINGS TO DO! I DON'T EVEN KNOW IF I'D HAVE TIME TO HANG OUT WITH HARVEY EVEN IF HE WAS HERE!
THAT'S THE SPIRIT!
ONE WEEK LATER...
I'M BOOOOOORRED!

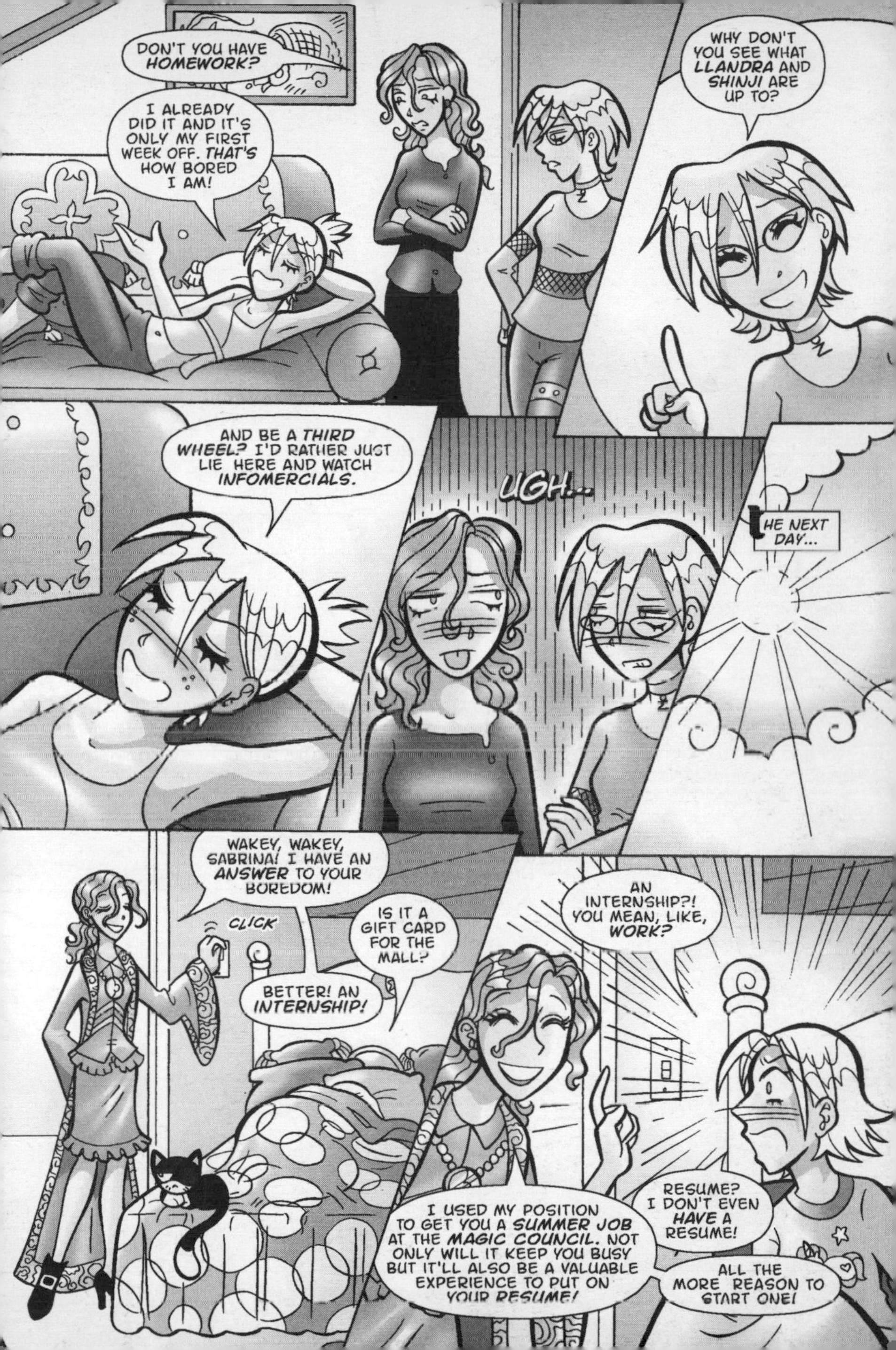
DON'T YOU HAVE HOMEWORK?
I ALREADY DID IT AND IT'S ONLY MY FIRST WEEK OFF. THAT'S HOW BORED I AM!
WHY DON'T YOU SEE WHAT LLANDRA AND SHINJI ARE UP TO?
AND BE A THIRD WHEEL? I'D RATHER JUST LIE HERE AND WATCH INFOMERCIALS.
UGH...
THE NEXT DAY...
WAKEY, WAKEY, SABRINA! I HAVE AN ANSWER TO YOUR BOREDOM!
CLICK
IS IT A GIFT CARD FOR THE MALL?
BETTER! AN INTERNSHIP!
AN INTERNSHIP?! YOU MEAN, LIKE, WORK?
I USED MY POSITION TO GET YOU A SUMMER JOB AT THE MAGIC COUNCIL. NOT ONLY WILL IT KEEP YOU BUSY BUT IT'LL ALSO BE A VALUABLE EXPERIENCE TO PUT ON YOUR RESUME!
RESUME? I DON'T EVEN HAVE A RESUME!
ALL THE MORE REASON TO START ONE!

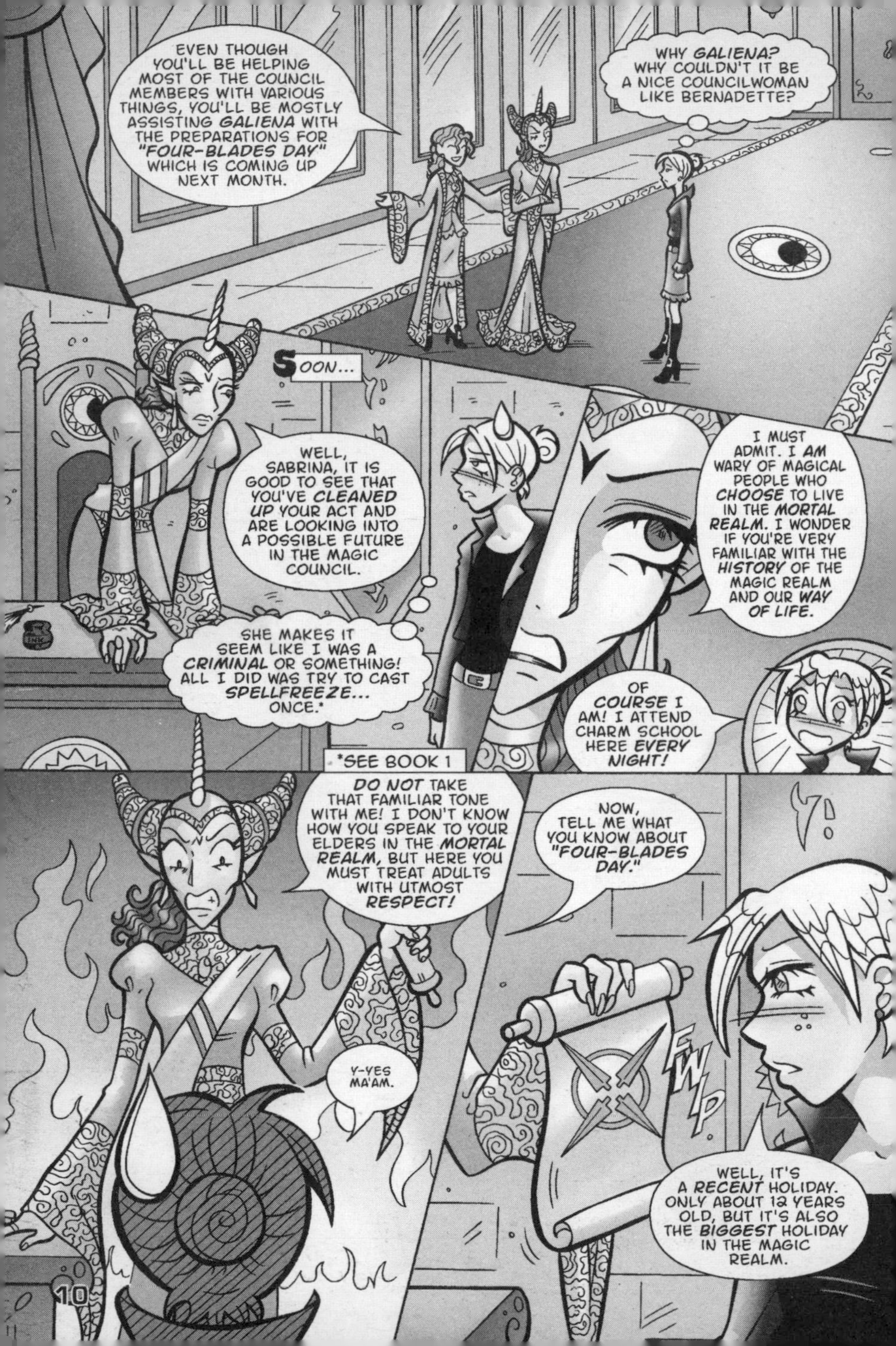
EVEN THOUGH YOU'LL BE HELPING MOST OF THE COUNCIL MEMBERS WITH VARIOUS THINGS, YOU'LL BE MOSTLY ASSISTING *GALIENA* WITH THE PREPARATIONS FOR *"FOUR-BLADES DAY"* WHICH IS COMING UP NEXT MONTH.
WHY *GALIENA?* WHY COULDN'T IT BE A NICE COUNCILWOMAN LIKE BERNADETTE?
SOON...
WELL, SABRINA, IT IS GOOD TO SEE THAT YOU'VE *CLEANED UP* YOUR ACT AND ARE LOOKING INTO A POSSIBLE FUTURE IN THE MAGIC COUNCIL.
SHE MAKES IT SEEM LIKE I WAS A *CRIMINAL* OR SOMETHING! ALL I DID WAS TRY TO CAST *SPELLFREEZE...* ONCE.*
*SEE BOOK 1
I MUST ADMIT. I *AM* WARY OF MAGICAL PEOPLE WHO *CHOOSE* TO LIVE IN THE *MORTAL REALM*. I WONDER IF YOU'RE VERY FAMILIAR WITH THE *HISTORY* OF THE MAGIC REALM AND OUR *WAY OF LIFE.*
OF *COURSE* I AM! I ATTEND CHARM SCHOOL HERE *EVERY NIGHT!*
DO NOT TAKE THAT FAMILIAR TONE WITH ME! I DON'T KNOW HOW YOU SPEAK TO YOUR ELDERS IN THE *MORTAL REALM*, BUT HERE YOU MUST TREAT ADULTS WITH UTMOST *RESPECT!*
Y-YES MA'AM.
NOW, TELL ME WHAT YOU KNOW ABOUT *"FOUR-BLADES DAY."*
FWIP
WELL, IT'S A *RECENT* HOLIDAY. ONLY ABOUT 12 YEARS OLD, BUT IT'S ALSO THE *BIGGEST* HOLIDAY IN THE MAGIC REALM.

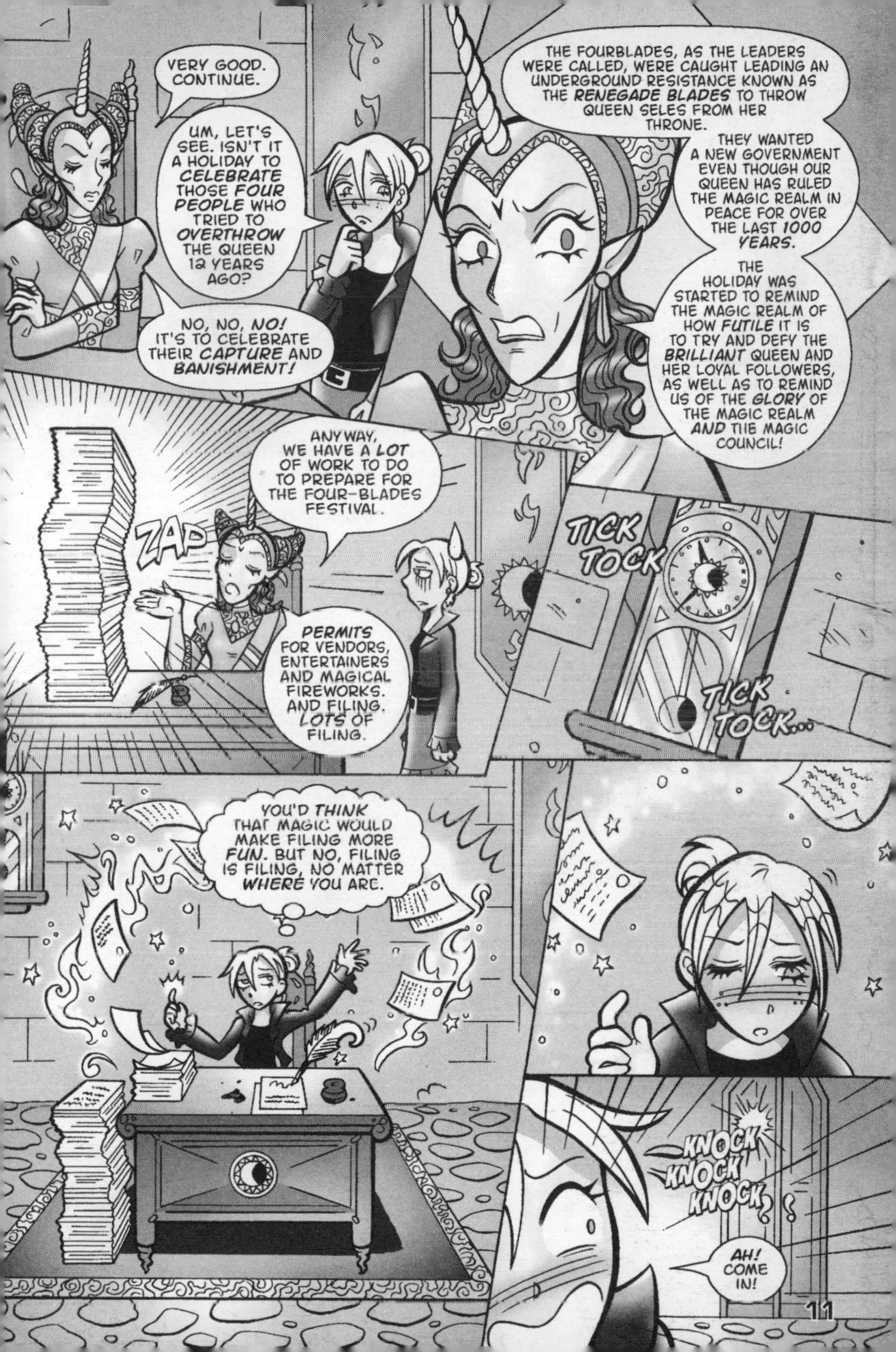
VERY GOOD. CONTINUE.
UM, LET'S SEE. ISN'T IT A HOLIDAY TO CELEBRATE THOSE FOUR PEOPLE WHO TRIED TO OVERTHROW THE QUEEN 12 YEARS AGO?
NO, NO, NO! IT'S TO CELEBRATE THEIR CAPTURE AND BANISHMENT!
THE FOURBLADES, AS THE LEADERS WERE CALLED, WERE CAUGHT LEADING AN UNDERGROUND RESISTANCE KNOWN AS THE RENEGADE BLADES TO THROW QUEEN SELES FROM HER THRONE.
THEY WANTED A NEW GOVERNMENT EVEN THOUGH OUR QUEEN HAS RULED THE MAGIC REALM IN PEACE FOR OVER THE LAST 1000 YEARS.
THE HOLIDAY WAS STARTED TO REMIND THE MAGIC REALM OF HOW FUTILE IT IS TO TRY AND DEFY THE BRILLIANT QUEEN AND HER LOYAL FOLLOWERS, AS WELL AS TO REMIND US OF THE GLORY OF THE MAGIC REALM AND THE MAGIC COUNCIL!
ZAP
ANYWAY, WE HAVE A LOT OF WORK TO DO TO PREPARE FOR THE FOUR-BLADES FESTIVAL.
PERMITS FOR VENDORS, ENTERTAINERS AND MAGICAL FIREWORKS. AND FILING. LOTS OF FILING.
TICK TOCK
TICK TOCK...
YOU'D THINK THAT MAGIC WOULD MAKE FILING MORE FUN. BUT NO, FILING IS FILING, NO MATTER WHERE YOU ARE.
KNOCK KNOCK KNOCK
AH! COME IN!

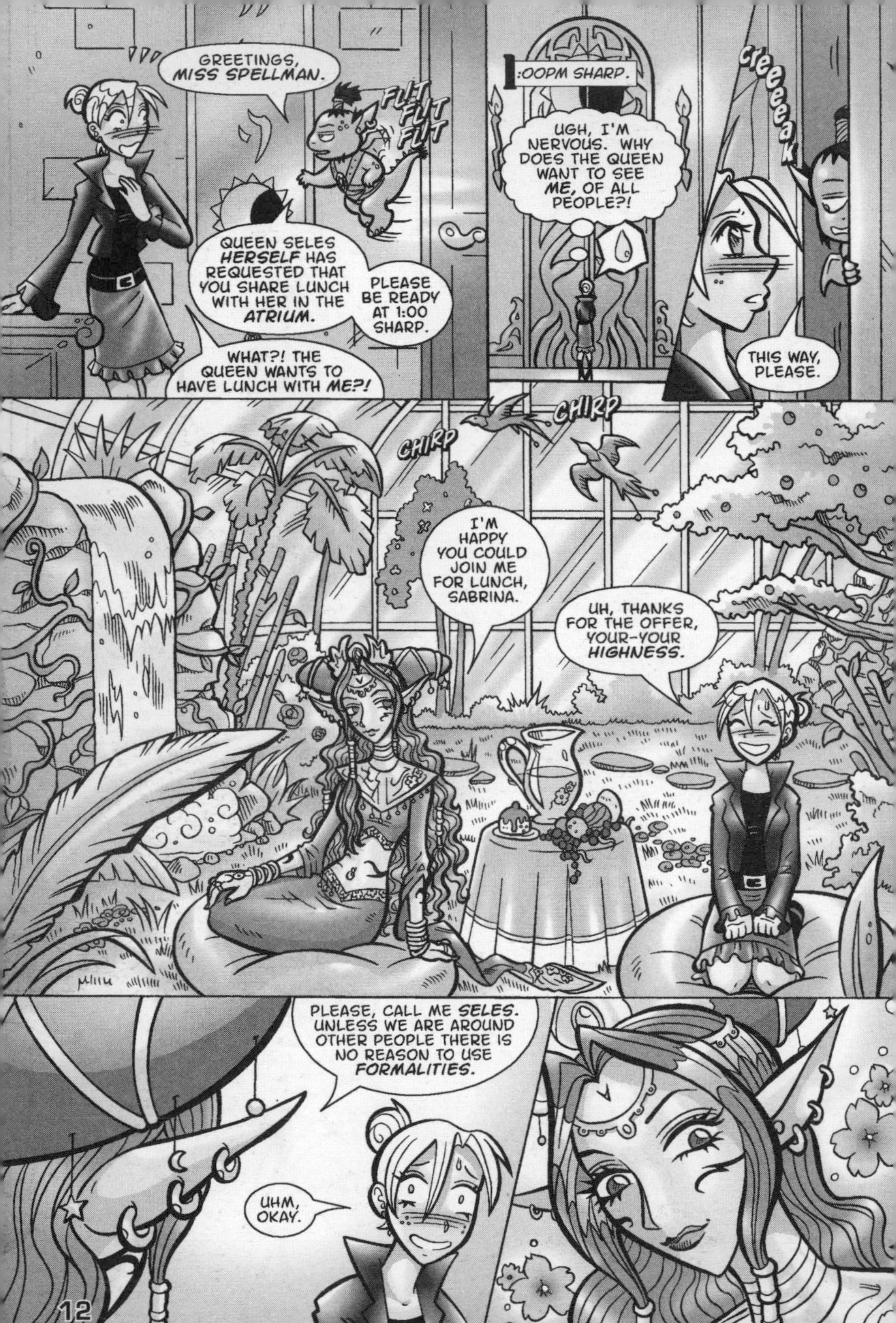
GREETINGS, MISS SPELLMAN.
FLIT FLIT FLIT
QUEEN SELES HERSELF HAS REQUESTED THAT YOU SHARE LUNCH WITH HER IN THE ATRIUM.
PLEASE BE READY AT 1:00 SHARP.
WHAT?! THE QUEEN WANTS TO HAVE LUNCH WITH ME?!
1:00PM SHARP.
UGH, I'M NERVOUS. WHY DOES THE QUEEN WANT TO SEE ME, OF ALL PEOPLE?!
creeeeak
THIS WAY, PLEASE.
CHIRP
CHIRP
I'M HAPPY YOU COULD JOIN ME FOR LUNCH, SABRINA.
UH, THANKS FOR THE OFFER, YOUR-YOUR HIGHNESS.
PLEASE, CALL ME SELES. UNLESS WE ARE AROUND OTHER PEOPLE THERE IS NO REASON TO USE FORMALITIES.
UHM, OKAY.

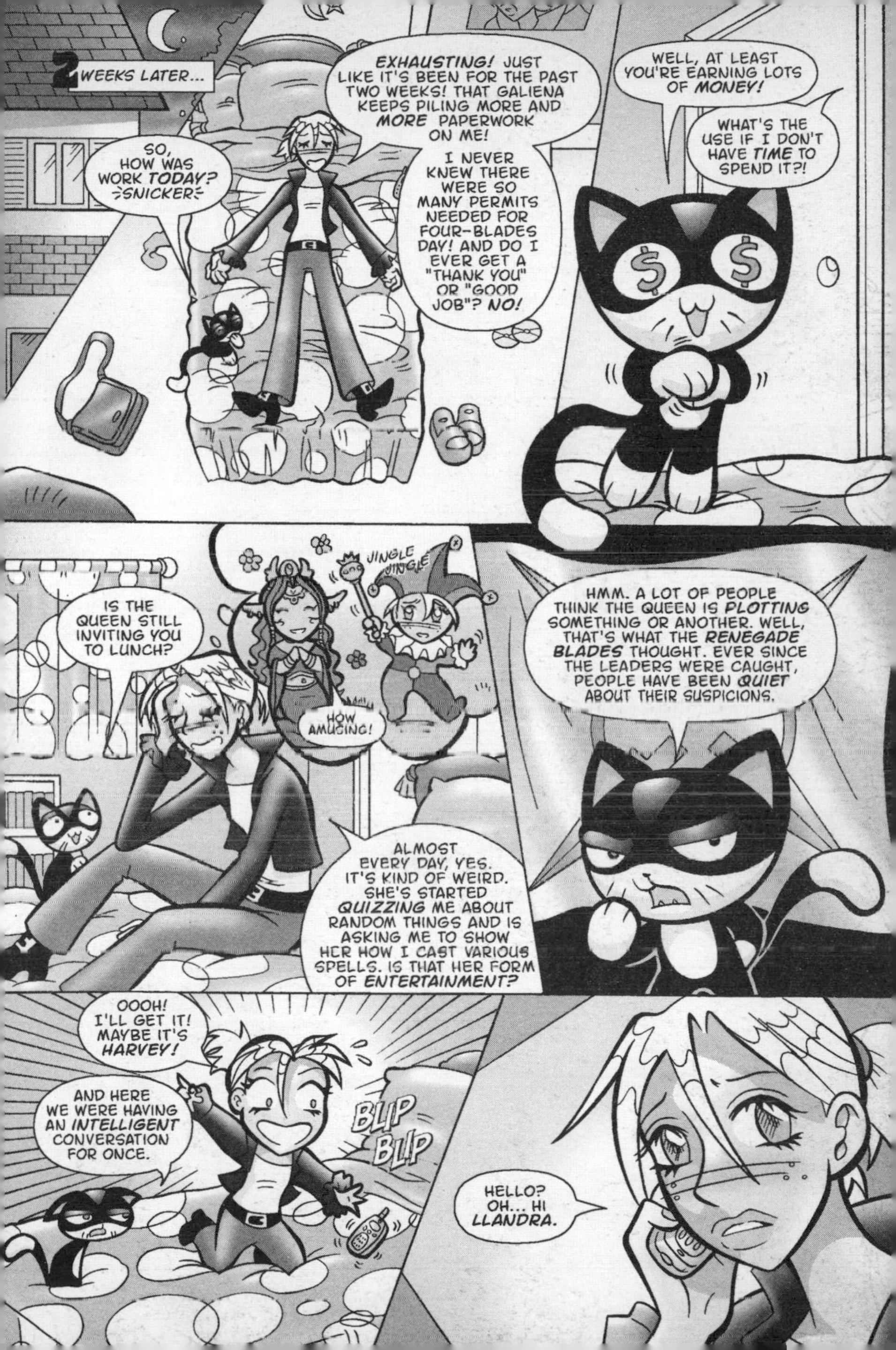
2 WEEKS LATER...
SO, HOW WAS WORK TODAY? SNICKER
EXHAUSTING! JUST LIKE IT'S BEEN FOR THE PAST TWO WEEKS! THAT GALIENA KEEPS PILING MORE AND MORE PAPERWORK ON ME!
I NEVER KNEW THERE WERE SO MANY PERMITS NEEDED FOR FOUR-BLADES DAY! AND DO I EVER GET A "THANK YOU" OR "GOOD JOB"? NO!
WELL, AT LEAST YOU'RE EARNING LOTS OF MONEY!
WHAT'S THE USE IF I DON'T HAVE TIME TO SPEND IT?!
IS THE QUEEN STILL INVITING YOU TO LUNCH?
JINGLE JINGLE
HOW AMUSING!
ALMOST EVERY DAY, YES. IT'S KIND OF WEIRD. SHE'S STARTED QUIZZING ME ABOUT RANDOM THINGS AND IS ASKING ME TO SHOW HER HOW I CAST VARIOUS SPELLS. IS THAT HER FORM OF ENTERTAINMENT?
HMM. A LOT OF PEOPLE THINK THE QUEEN IS PLOTTING SOMETHING OR ANOTHER. WELL, THAT'S WHAT THE RENEGADE BLADES THOUGHT. EVER SINCE THE LEADERS WERE CAUGHT, PEOPLE HAVE BEEN QUIET ABOUT THEIR SUSPICIONS.
OOOH! I'LL GET IT! MAYBE IT'S HARVEY!
AND HERE WE WERE HAVING AN INTELLIGENT CONVERSATION FOR ONCE.
BLIP BLIP
HELLO? OH... HI LLANDRA.

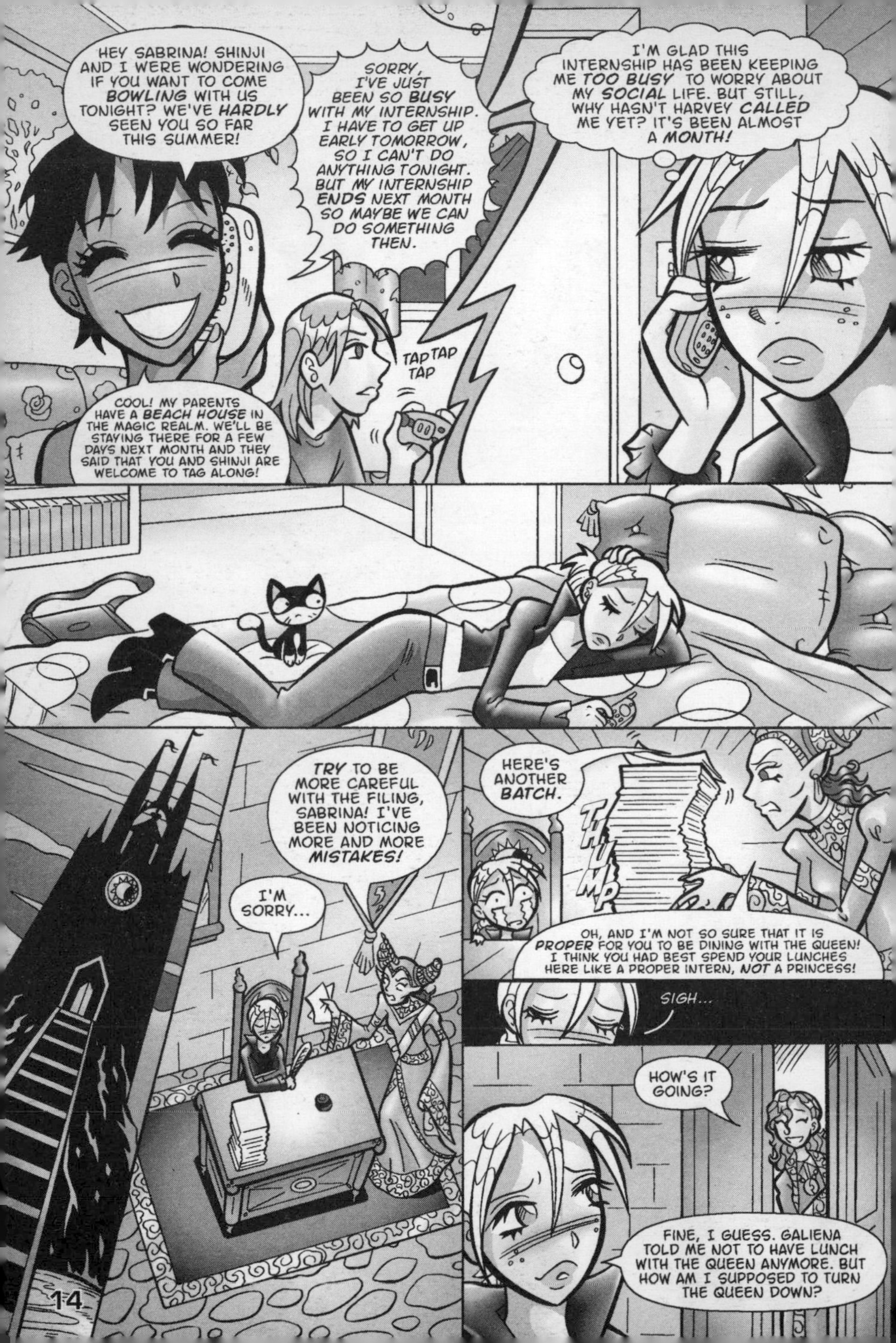
HEY SABRINA! SHINJI AND I WERE WONDERING IF YOU WANT TO COME BOWLING WITH US TONIGHT? WE'VE HARDLY SEEN YOU SO FAR THIS SUMMER!
SORRY, I'VE JUST BEEN SO BUSY WITH MY INTERNSHIP. I HAVE TO GET UP EARLY TOMORROW, SO I CAN'T DO ANYTHING TONIGHT. BUT MY INTERNSHIP ENDS NEXT MONTH SO MAYBE WE CAN DO SOMETHING THEN.
TAP TAP TAP
COOL! MY PARENTS HAVE A BEACH HOUSE IN THE MAGIC REALM. WE'LL BE STAYING THERE FOR A FEW DAYS NEXT MONTH AND THEY SAID THAT YOU AND SHINJI ARE WELCOME TO TAG ALONG!
I'M GLAD THIS INTERNSHIP HAS BEEN KEEPING ME TOO BUSY TO WORRY ABOUT MY SOCIAL LIFE. BUT STILL, WHY HASN'T HARVEY CALLED ME YET? IT'S BEEN ALMOST A MONTH!
TRY TO BE MORE CAREFUL WITH THE FILING, SABRINA! I'VE BEEN NOTICING MORE AND MORE MISTAKES!
I'M SORRY...
HERE'S ANOTHER BATCH.
THUMP
OH, AND I'M NOT SO SURE THAT IT IS PROPER FOR YOU TO BE DINING WITH THE QUEEN! I THINK YOU HAD BEST SPEND YOUR LUNCHES HERE LIKE A PROPER INTERN, NOT A PRINCESS!
SIGH...
HOW'S IT GOING?
FINE, I GUESS. GALIENA TOLD ME NOT TO HAVE LUNCH WITH THE QUEEN ANYMORE. BUT HOW AM I SUPPOSED TO TURN THE QUEEN DOWN?

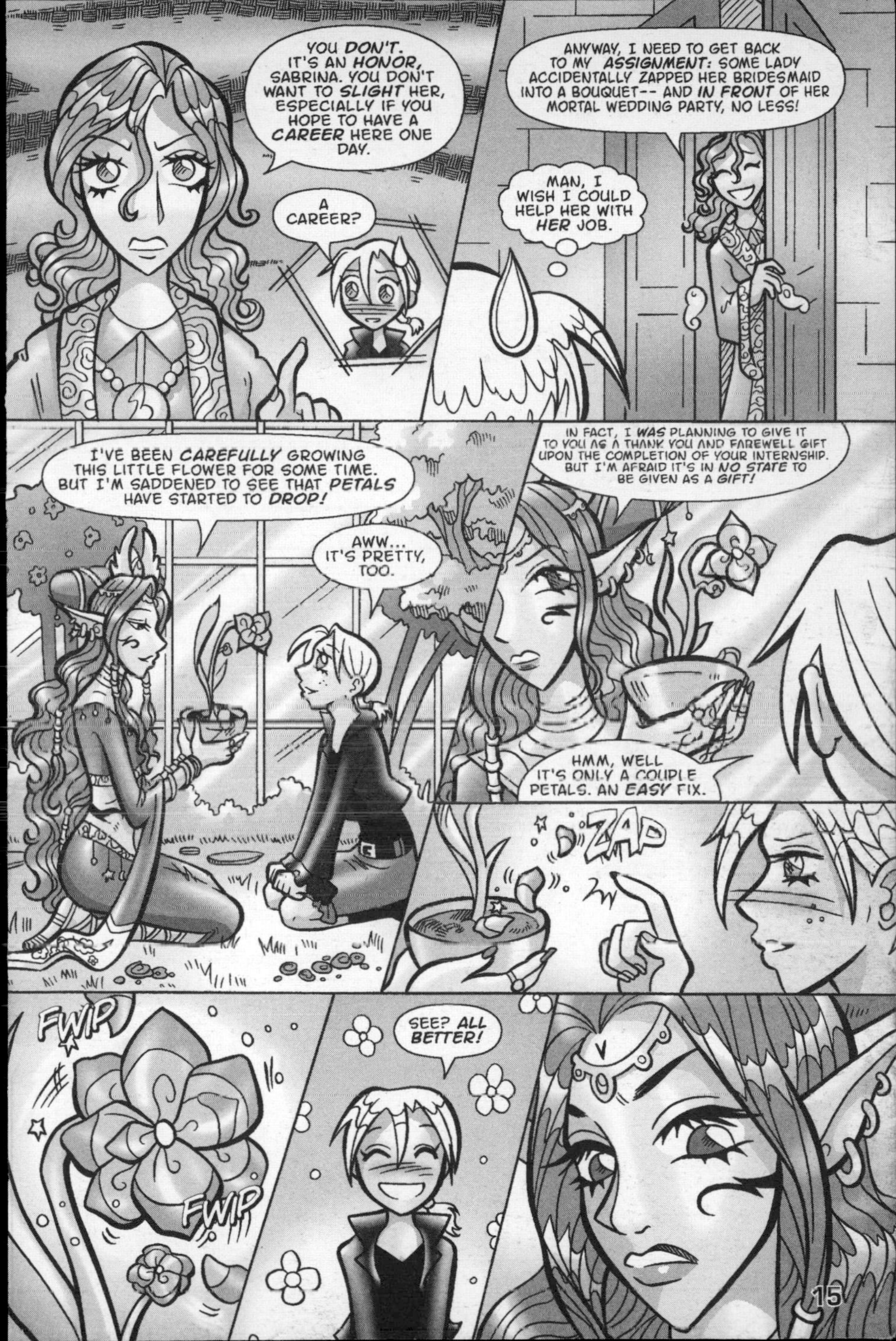
YOU DON'T. IT'S AN HONOR, SABRINA. YOU DON'T WANT TO SLIGHT HER, ESPECIALLY IF YOU HOPE TO HAVE A CAREER HERE ONE DAY.
A CAREER?
ANYWAY, I NEED TO GET BACK TO MY ASSIGNMENT: SOME LADY ACCIDENTALLY ZAPPED HER BRIDESMAID INTO A BOUQUET-- AND IN FRONT OF HER MORTAL WEDDING PARTY, NO LESS!
MAN, I WISH I COULD HELP HER WITH HER JOB.
I'VE BEEN CAREFULLY GROWING THIS LITTLE FLOWER FOR SOME TIME. BUT I'M SADDENED TO SEE THAT PETALS HAVE STARTED TO DROP!
AWW... IT'S PRETTY, TOO.
IN FACT, I WAS PLANNING TO GIVE IT TO YOU AS A THANK YOU AND FAREWELL GIFT UPON THE COMPLETION OF YOUR INTERNSHIP. BUT I'M AFRAID IT'S IN NO STATE TO BE GIVEN AS A GIFT!
HMM, WELL IT'S ONLY A COUPLE PETALS. AN EASY FIX.
ZAP
FWIP
FWIP
SEE? ALL BETTER!

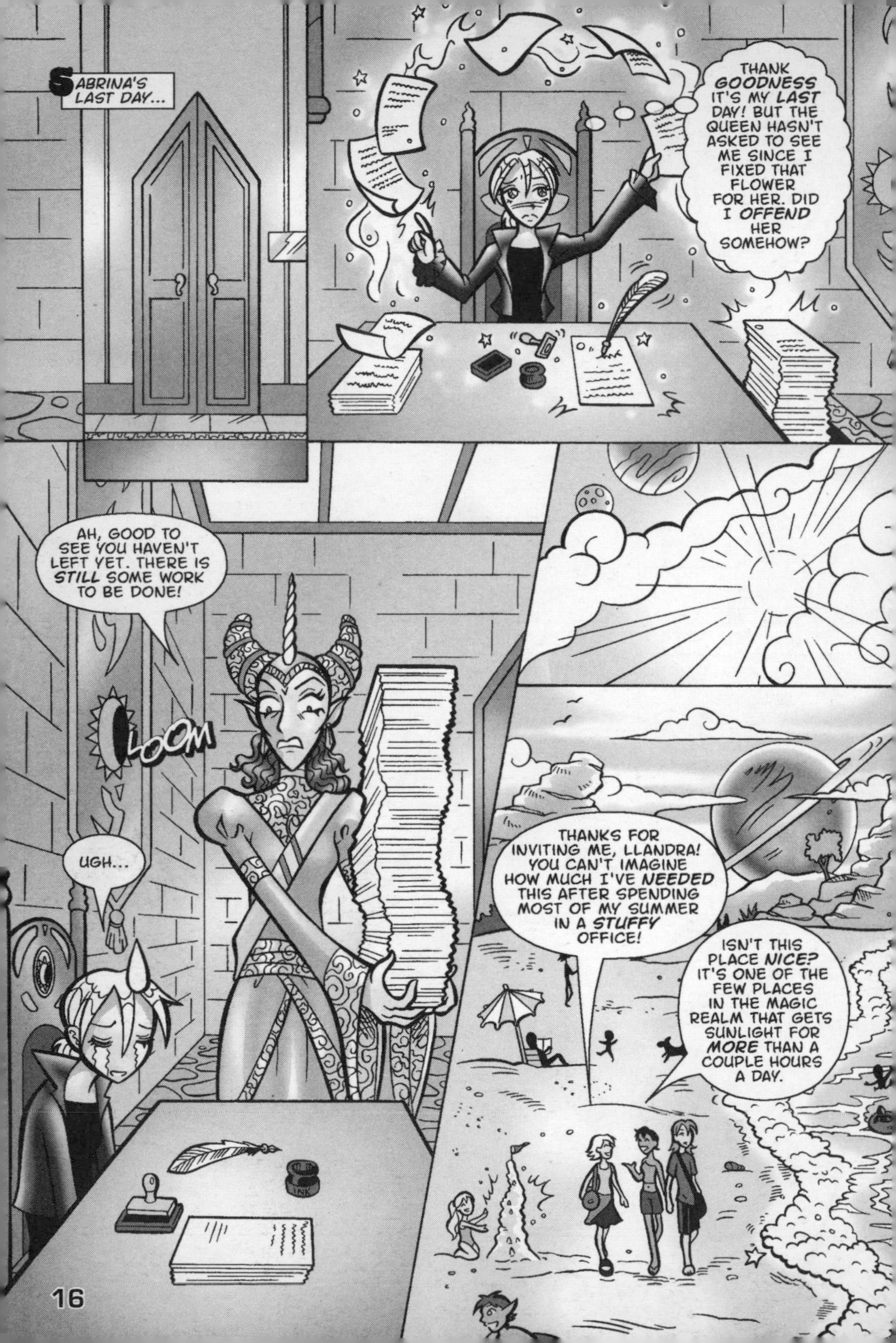
SABRINA'S LAST DAY...
THANK GOODNESS IT'S MY LAST DAY! BUT THE QUEEN HASN'T ASKED TO SEE ME SINCE I FIXED THAT FLOWER FOR HER. DID I OFFEND HER SOMEHOW?
AH, GOOD TO SEE YOU HAVEN'T LEFT YET. THERE IS STILL SOME WORK TO BE DONE!
FLOOM
UGH...
THANKS FOR INVITING ME, LLANDRA! YOU CAN'T IMAGINE HOW MUCH I'VE NEEDED THIS AFTER SPENDING MOST OF MY SUMMER IN A STUFFY OFFICE!
ISN'T THIS PLACE NICE? IT'S ONE OF THE FEW PLACES IN THE MAGIC REALM THAT GETS SUNLIGHT FOR MORE THAN A COUPLE HOURS A DAY.

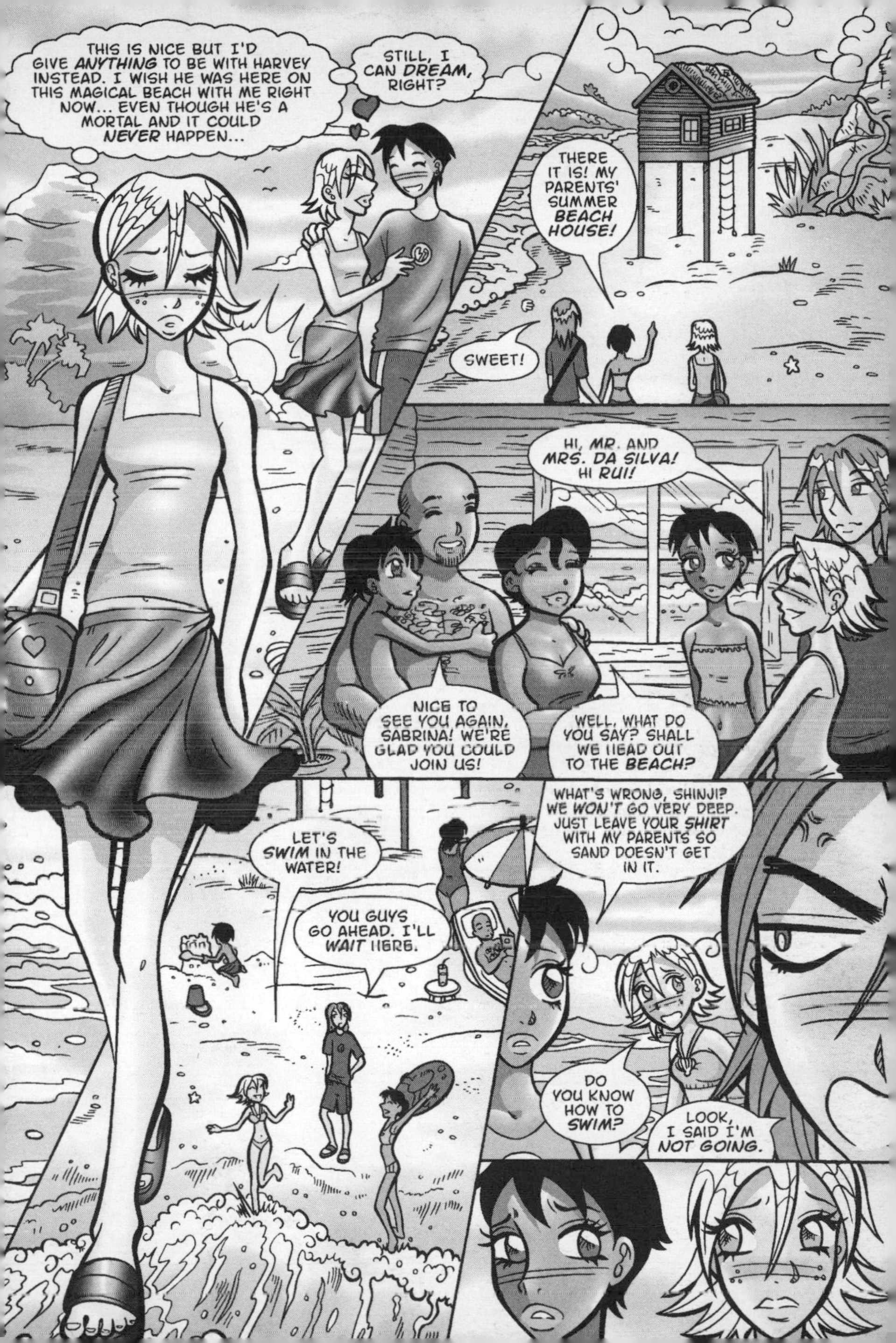
THIS IS NICE BUT I'D GIVE ANYTHING TO BE WITH HARVEY INSTEAD. I WISH HE WAS HERE ON THIS MAGICAL BEACH WITH ME RIGHT NOW... EVEN THOUGH HE'S A MORTAL AND IT COULD NEVER HAPPEN...
STILL, I CAN DREAM, RIGHT?
THERE IT IS! MY PARENTS' SUMMER BEACH HOUSE!
SWEET!
HI, MR. AND MRS. DA SILVA! HI RUI!
NICE TO SEE YOU AGAIN, SABRINA! WE'RE GLAD YOU COULD JOIN US!
WELL, WHAT DO YOU SAY? SHALL WE HEAD OUT TO THE BEACH?
LET'S SWIM IN THE WATER!
YOU GUYS GO AHEAD. I'LL WAIT HERE.
WHAT'S WRONG, SHINJI? WE WON'T GO VERY DEEP. JUST LEAVE YOUR SHIRT WITH MY PARENTS SO SAND DOESN'T GET IN IT.
DO YOU KNOW HOW TO SWIM?
LOOK, I SAID I'M NOT GOING.

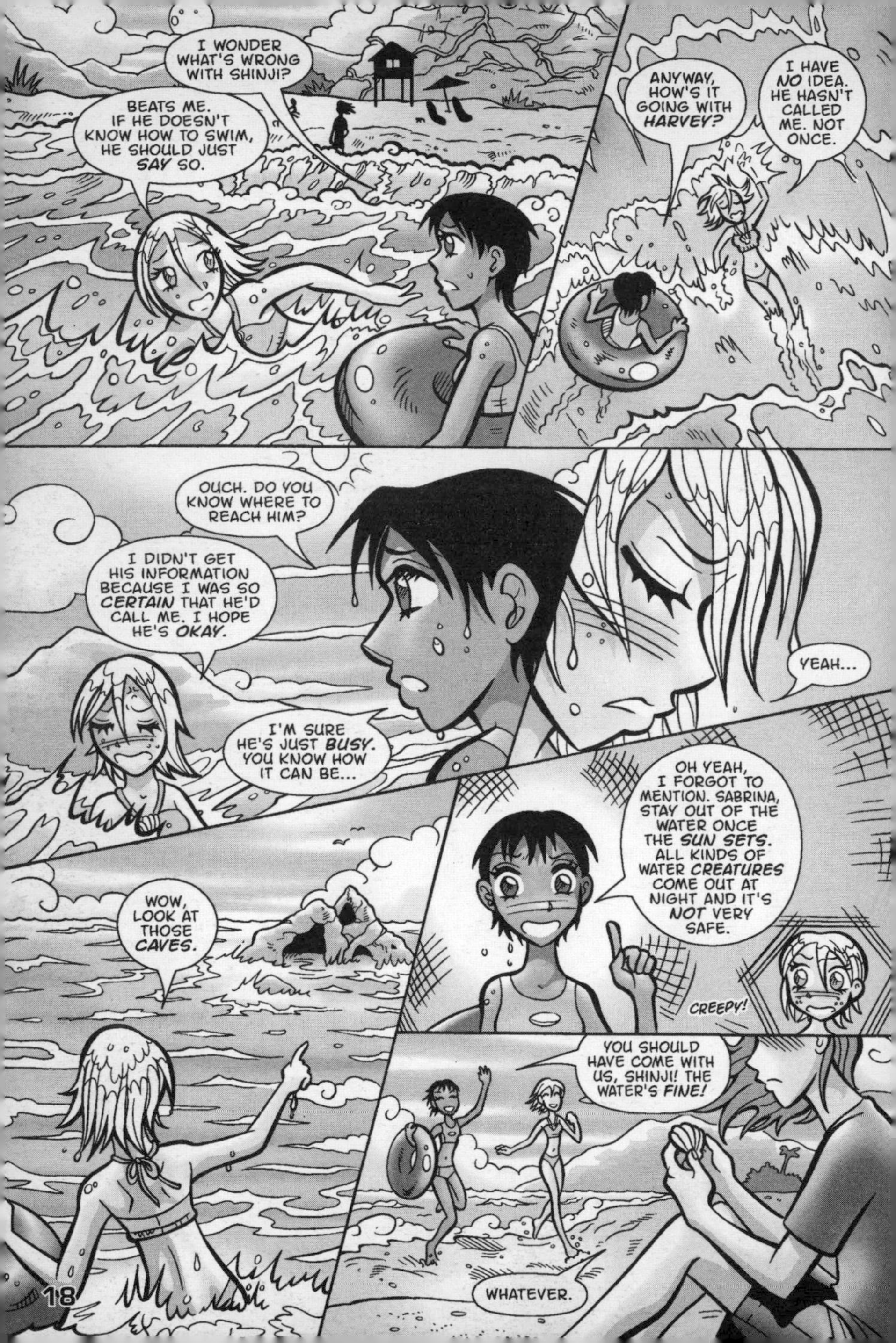
I WONDER WHAT'S WRONG WITH SHINJI?
BEATS ME. IF HE DOESN'T KNOW HOW TO SWIM, HE SHOULD JUST *SAY* SO.
ANYWAY, HOW'S IT GOING WITH *HARVEY?*
I HAVE *NO* IDEA. HE HASN'T CALLED ME. NOT ONCE.
OUCH. DO YOU KNOW WHERE TO REACH HIM?
I DIDN'T GET HIS INFORMATION BECAUSE I WAS SO *CERTAIN* THAT HE'D CALL ME. I HOPE HE'S *OKAY*.
I'M SURE HE'S JUST *BUSY*. YOU KNOW HOW IT CAN BE...
YEAH...
WOW, LOOK AT THOSE *CAVES*.
OH YEAH, I FORGOT TO MENTION. SABRINA, STAY OUT OF THE WATER ONCE THE *SUN SETS*. ALL KINDS OF WATER *CREATURES* COME OUT AT NIGHT AND IT'S *NOT* VERY SAFE.
CREEPY!
YOU SHOULD HAVE COME WITH US, SHINJI! THE WATER'S *FINE!*
WHATEVER.

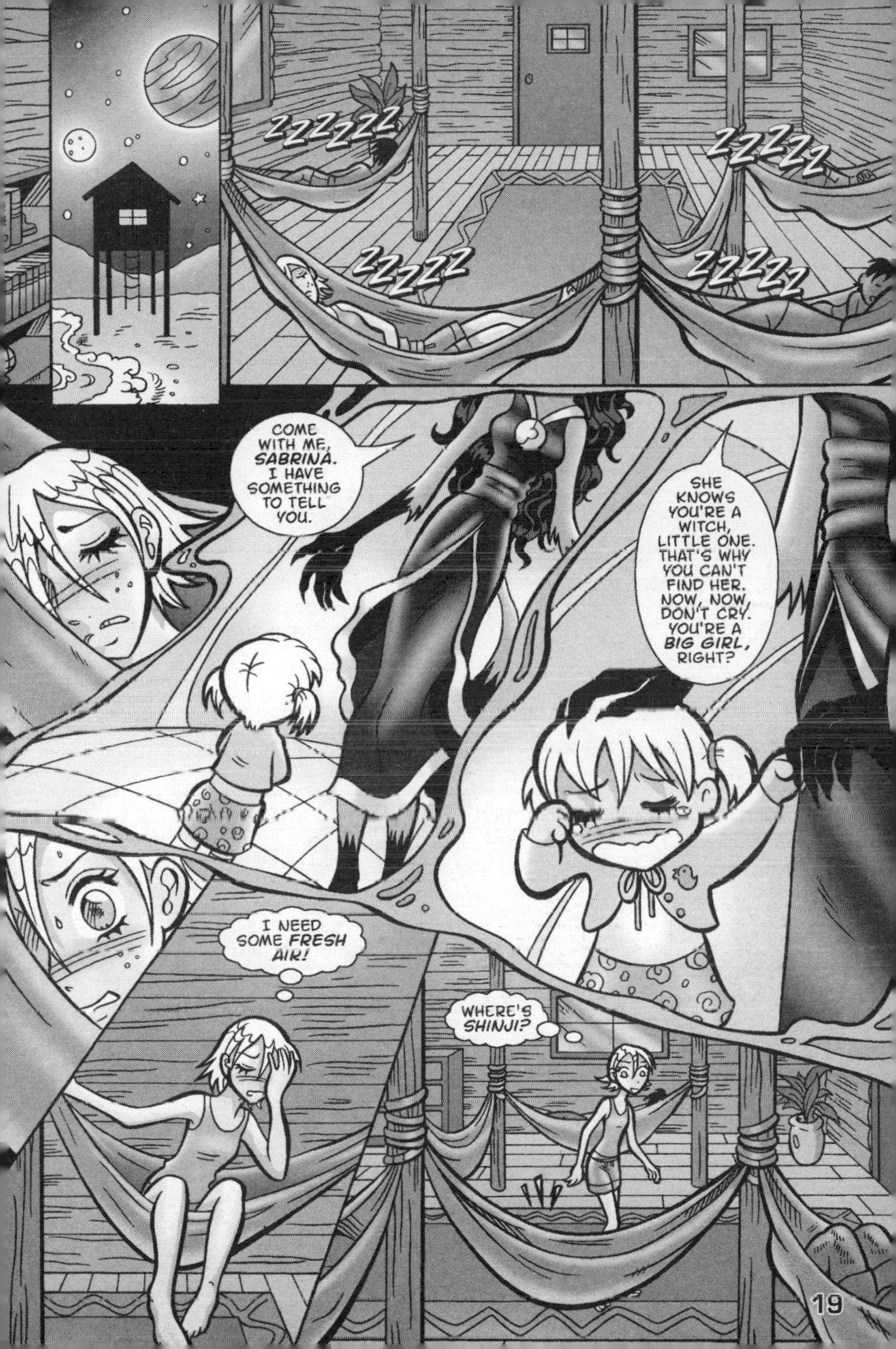
ZZZZZZZ
ZZZZZZ
ZZZZZZ
ZZZZZZZ
COME WITH ME, SABRINA. I HAVE SOMETHING TO TELL YOU.
SHE KNOWS YOU'RE A WITCH, LITTLE ONE. THAT'S WHY YOU CAN'T FIND HER. NOW, NOW, DON'T CRY. YOU'RE A BIG GIRL, RIGHT?
I NEED SOME FRESH AIR!
WHERE'S SHINJI?

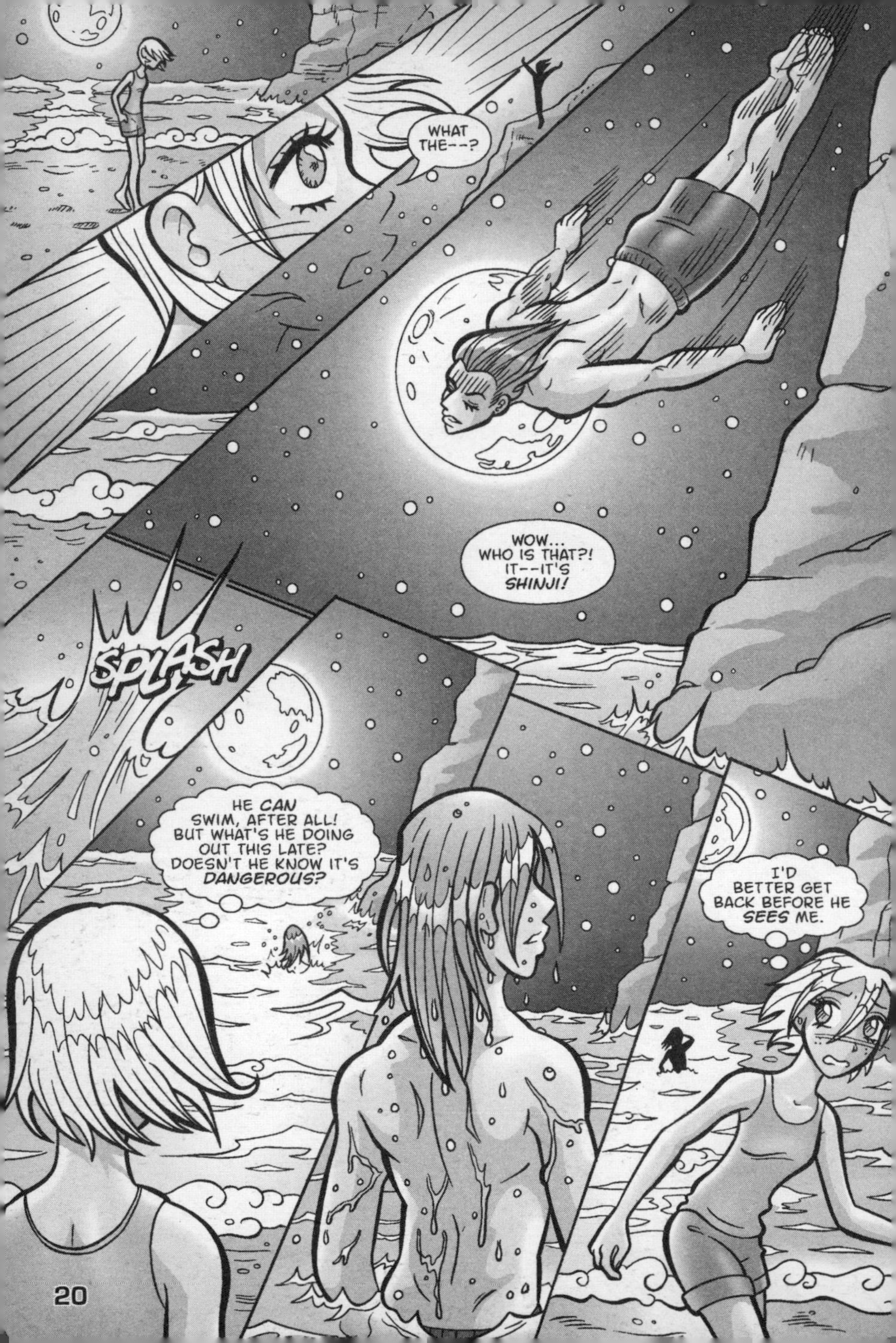
WHAT THE--?
WOW... WHO IS THAT?! IT--IT'S SHINJI!
SPLASH
HE CAN SWIM, AFTER ALL! BUT WHAT'S HE DOING OUT THIS LATE? DOESN'T HE KNOW IT'S DANGEROUS?
I'D BETTER GET BACK BEFORE HE SEES ME.

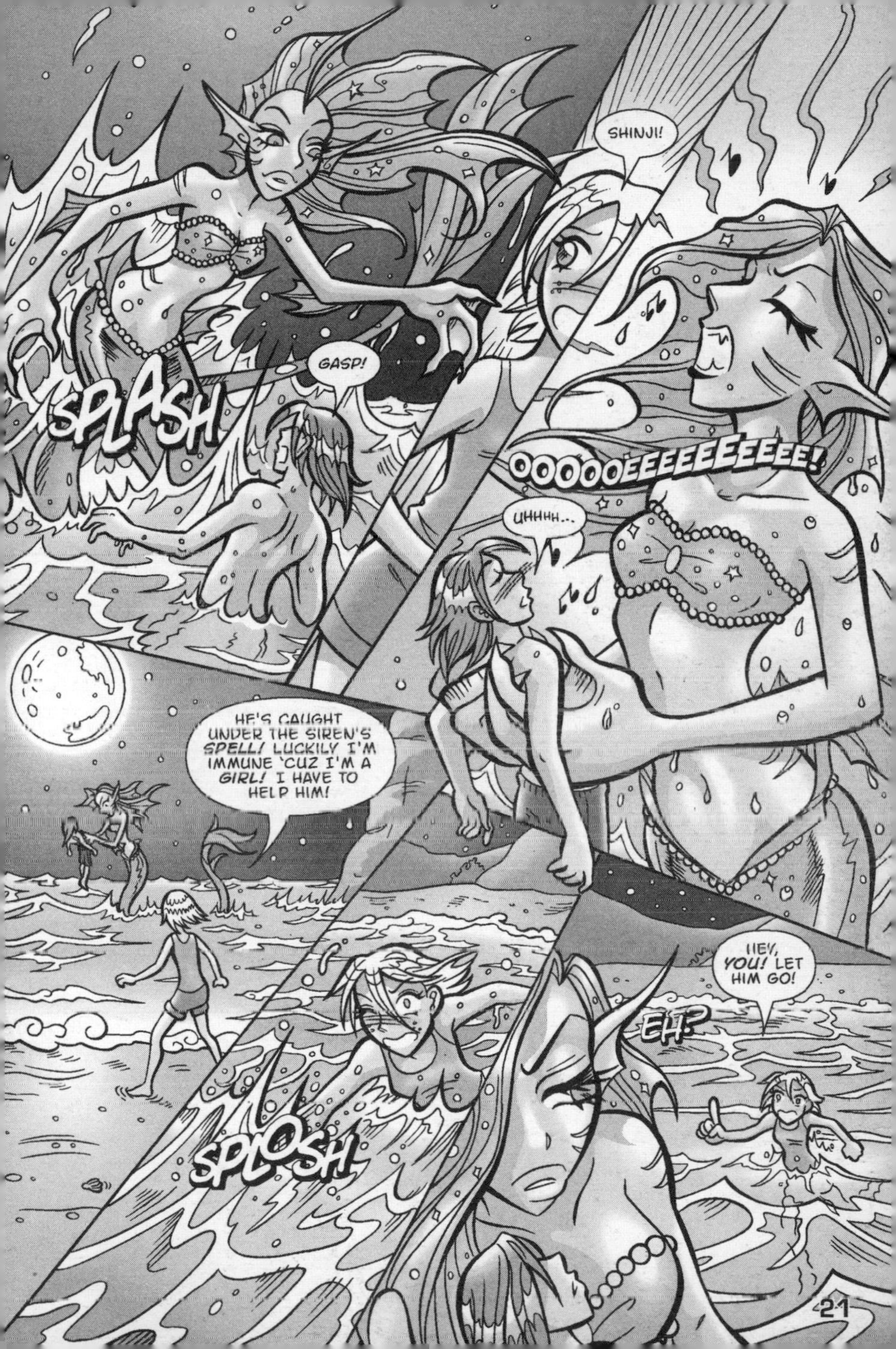
GASP!
SPLASH
SHINJI!
OOOOOEEEEEEEEEE!
UHHHH...
HE'S CAUGHT UNDER THE SIREN'S SPELL! LUCKILY I'M IMMUNE 'CUZ I'M A GIRL! I HAVE TO HELP HIM!
SPLOSH
EH?
HEY, YOU! LET HIM GO!

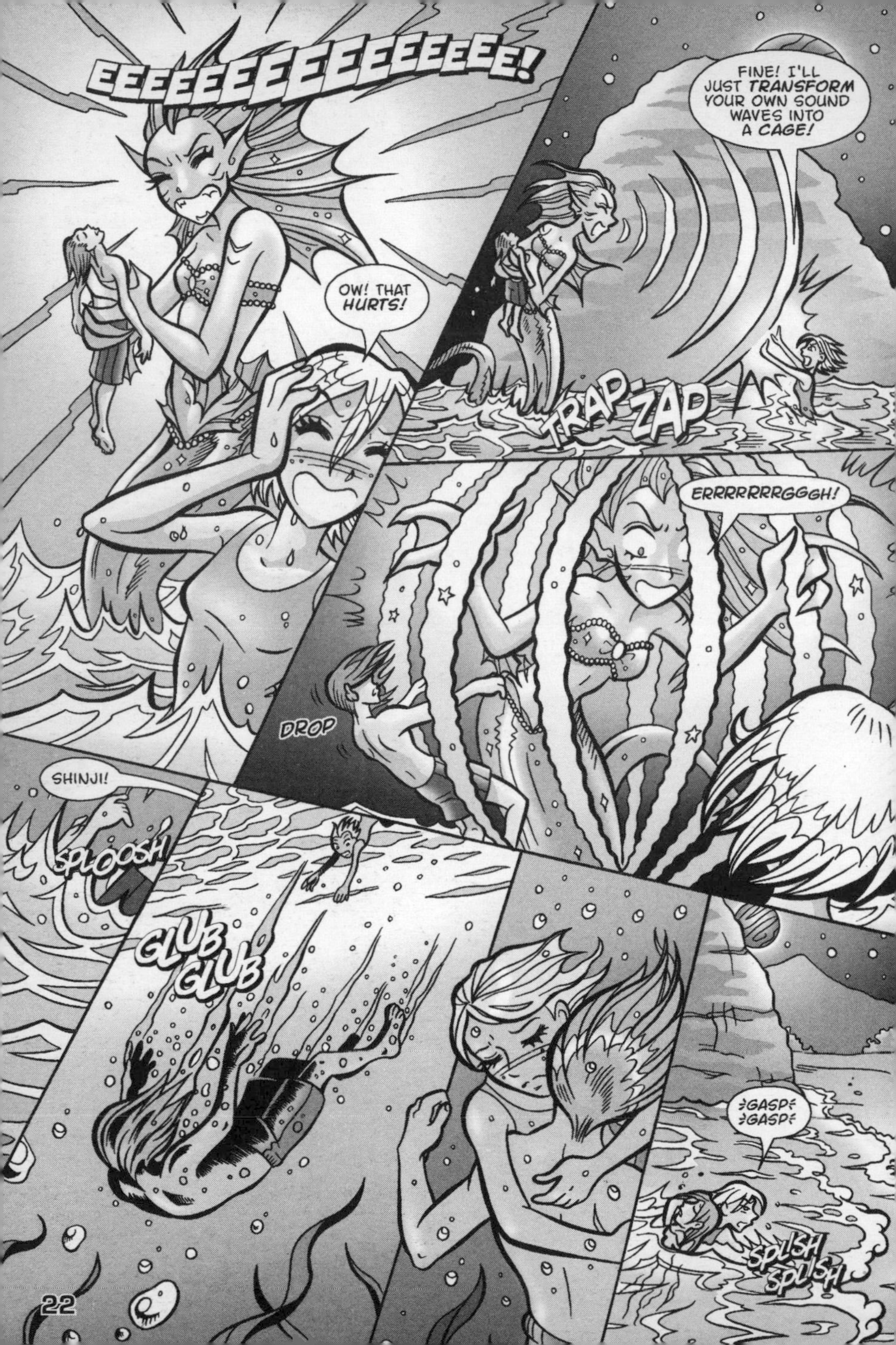
EEEEEEEEEEEEEEEE!
OW! THAT HURTS!
FINE! I'LL JUST TRANSFORM YOUR OWN SOUND WAVES INTO A CAGE!
TRAP-ZAP
DROP
ERRRRRRRGGGH!
SHINJI!
SPLOOSH
GLUB GLUB
GASP GASP
SPLISH SPLISH

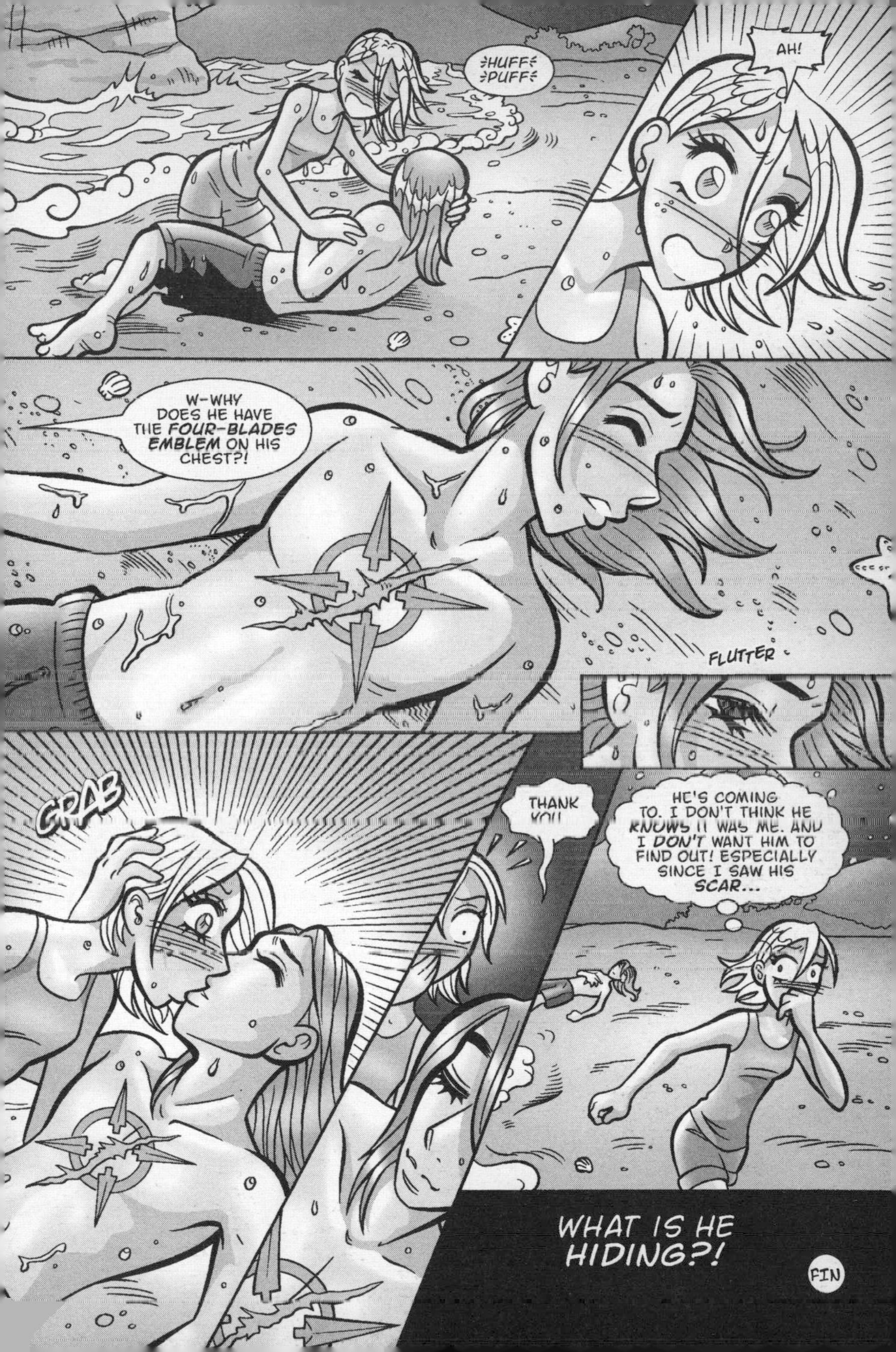
HUFF PUFF
AH!
W-WHY DOES HE HAVE THE FOUR-BLADES EMBLEM ON HIS CHEST?!
FLUTTER
GRAB
THANK YOU.
HE'S COMING TO. I DON'T THINK HE KNOWS IT WAS ME. AND I DON'T WANT HIM TO FIND OUT! ESPECIALLY SINCE I SAW HIS SCAR...
WHAT IS HE HIDING?!
FIN

Chapter 2

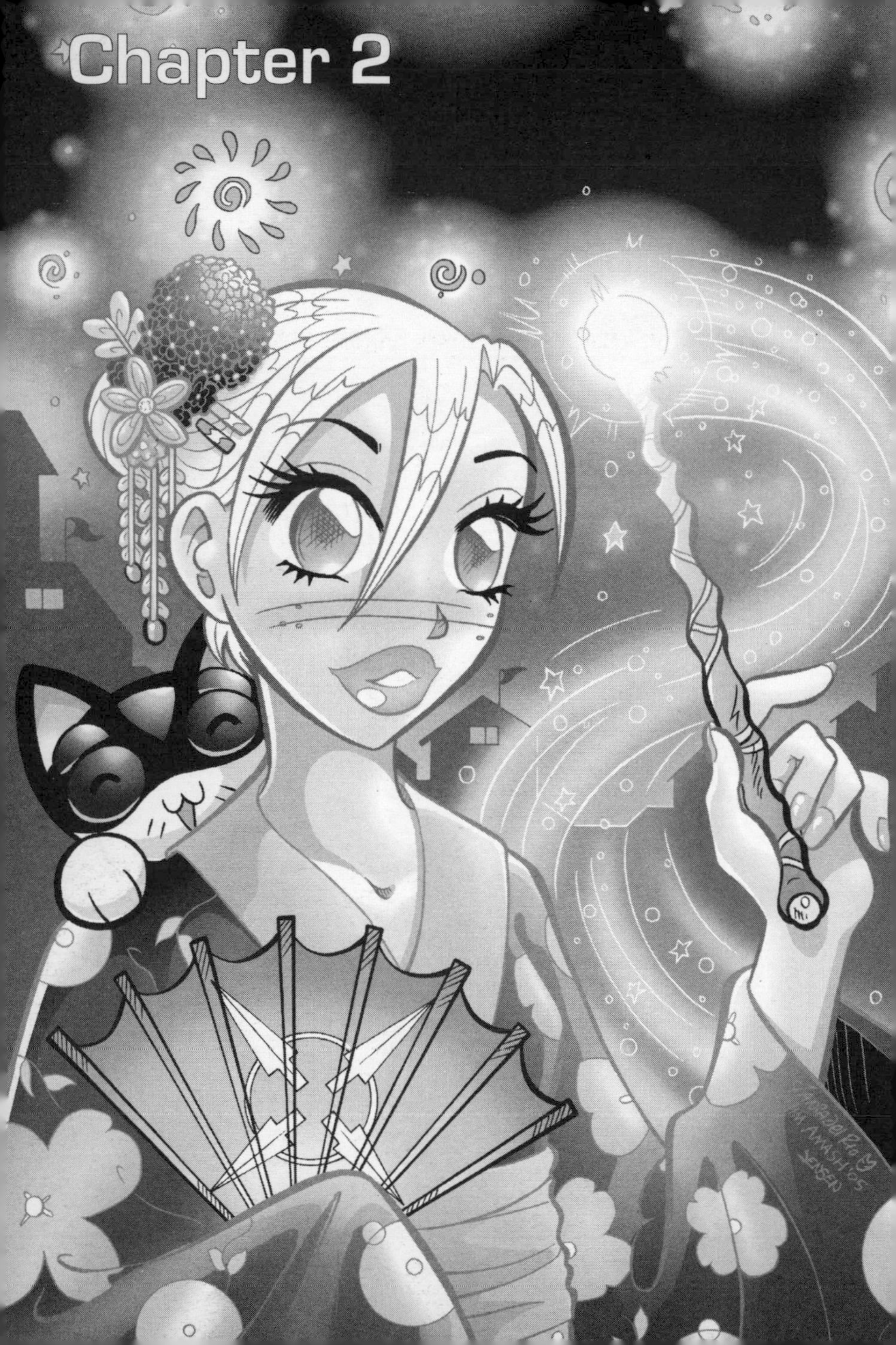

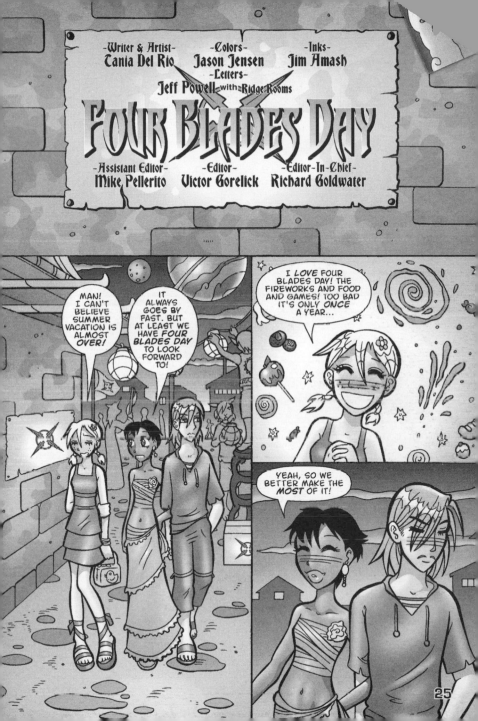

-Writer & Artist-
Tania Del Rio

-Colors-
Jason Jensen

-Inks-
Jim Amash

-Letters-
Jeff Powell with Ridge Rooms

FOUR BLADES DAY

-Assistant Editor-
Mike Pellerito

-Editor-
Victor Gorelick

-Editor-In-Chief-
Richard Goldwater

MAN! I CAN'T BELIEVE SUMMER VACATION IS ALMOST *OVER!*

IT ALWAYS GOES BY FAST. BUT AT LEAST WE HAVE *FOUR BLADES DAY* TO LOOK FORWARD TO!

I LOVE FOUR BLADES DAY! THE FIREWORKS AND FOOD AND GAMES! TOO BAD IT'S ONLY *ONCE* A YEAR...

YEAH, SO WE BETTER MAKE THE *MOST* OF IT!

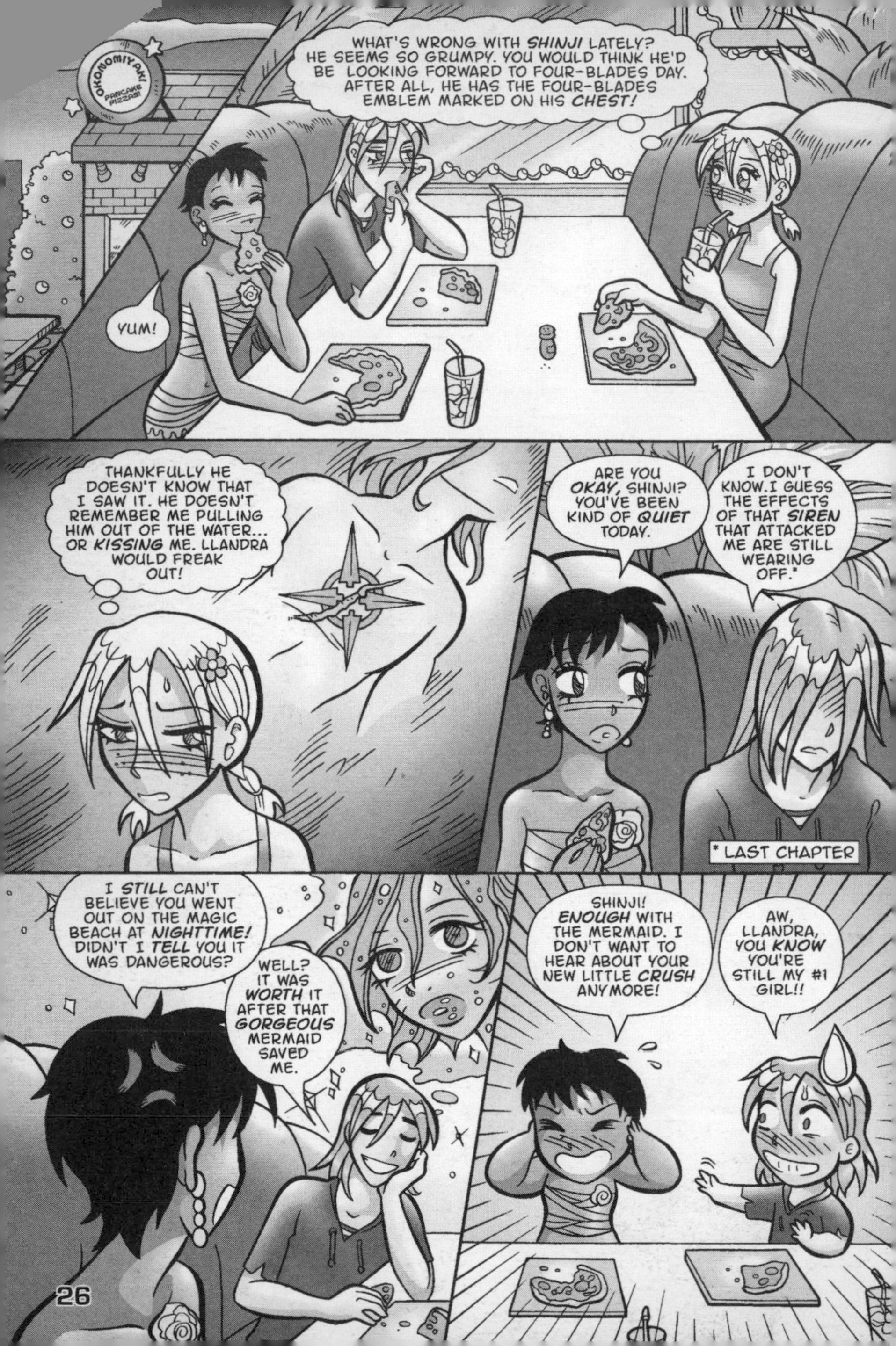
OKONOMIYAKI
PANCAKE PIZZAS!
WHAT'S WRONG WITH SHINJI LATELY? HE SEEMS SO GRUMPY. YOU WOULD THINK HE'D BE LOOKING FORWARD TO FOUR-BLADES DAY. AFTER ALL, HE HAS THE FOUR-BLADES EMBLEM MARKED ON HIS CHEST!
YUM!
THANKFULLY HE DOESN'T KNOW THAT I SAW IT. HE DOESN'T REMEMBER ME PULLING HIM OUT OF THE WATER... OR KISSING ME. LLANDRA WOULD FREAK OUT!
ARE YOU OKAY, SHINJI? YOU'VE BEEN KIND OF QUIET TODAY.
I DON'T KNOW. I GUESS THE EFFECTS OF THAT SIREN THAT ATTACKED ME ARE STILL WEARING OFF.*
* LAST CHAPTER
I STILL CAN'T BELIEVE YOU WENT OUT ON THE MAGIC BEACH AT NIGHTTIME! DIDN'T I TELL YOU IT WAS DANGEROUS?
WELL? IT WAS WORTH IT AFTER THAT GORGEOUS MERMAID SAVED ME.
SHINJI! ENOUGH WITH THE MERMAID. I DON'T WANT TO HEAR ABOUT YOUR NEW LITTLE CRUSH ANYMORE!
AW, LLANDRA, YOU KNOW YOU'RE STILL MY #1 GIRL!!

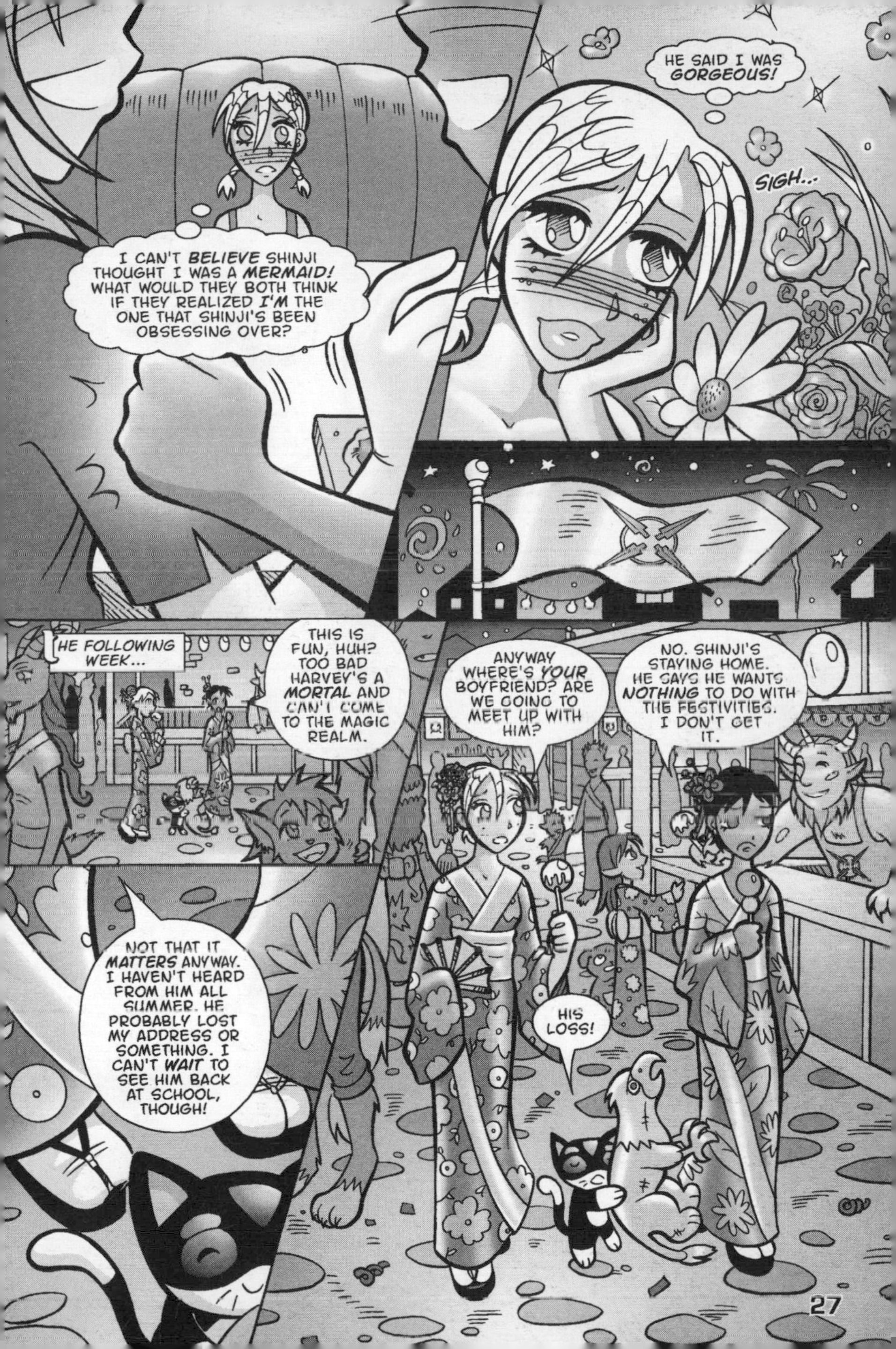
I CAN'T BELIEVE SHINJI THOUGHT I WAS A MERMAID! WHAT WOULD THEY BOTH THINK IF THEY REALIZED I'M THE ONE THAT SHINJI'S BEEN OBSESSING OVER?
HE SAID I WAS GORGEOUS!
SIGH...
THE FOLLOWING WEEK...
THIS IS FUN, HUH? TOO BAD HARVEY'S A MORTAL AND CAN'T COME TO THE MAGIC REALM.
ANYWAY WHERE'S YOUR BOYFRIEND? ARE WE GOING TO MEET UP WITH HIM?
NO. SHINJI'S STAYING HOME. HE SAYS HE WANTS NOTHING TO DO WITH THE FESTIVITIES. I DON'T GET IT.
NOT THAT IT MATTERS ANYWAY. I HAVEN'T HEARD FROM HIM ALL SUMMER. HE PROBABLY LOST MY ADDRESS OR SOMETHING. I CAN'T WAIT TO SEE HIM BACK AT SCHOOL, THOUGH!
HIS LOSS!

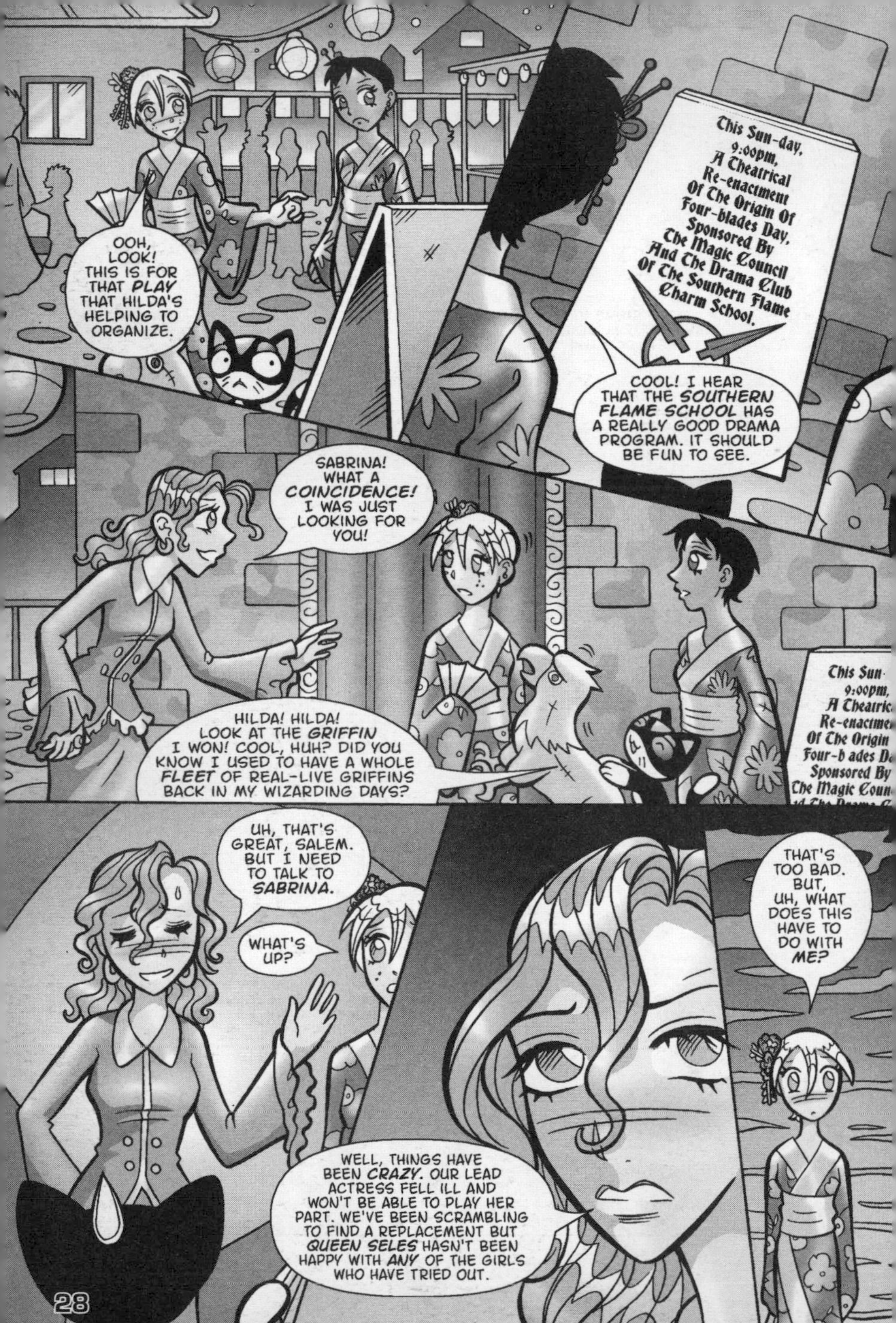
OOH, LOOK! THIS IS FOR THAT PLAY THAT HILDA'S HELPING TO ORGANIZE.
This Sun-day, 9:00pm, A Theatrical Re-enactment Of The Origin Of Four-blades Day, Sponsored By The Magic Council And The Drama Club Of The Southern Flame Charm School.
COOL! I HEAR THAT THE SOUTHERN FLAME SCHOOL HAS A REALLY GOOD DRAMA PROGRAM. IT SHOULD BE FUN TO SEE.
SABRINA! WHAT A COINCIDENCE! I WAS JUST LOOKING FOR YOU!
HILDA! HILDA! LOOK AT THE GRIFFIN I WON! COOL, HUH? DID YOU KNOW I USED TO HAVE A WHOLE FLEET OF REAL-LIVE GRIFFINS BACK IN MY WIZARDING DAYS?
UH, THAT'S GREAT, SALEM. BUT I NEED TO TALK TO SABRINA.
WHAT'S UP?
WELL, THINGS HAVE BEEN CRAZY. OUR LEAD ACTRESS FELL ILL AND WON'T BE ABLE TO PLAY HER PART. WE'VE BEEN SCRAMBLING TO FIND A REPLACEMENT BUT QUEEN SELES HASN'T BEEN HAPPY WITH ANY OF THE GIRLS WHO HAVE TRIED OUT.
THAT'S TOO BAD. BUT, UH, WHAT DOES THIS HAVE TO DO WITH ME?

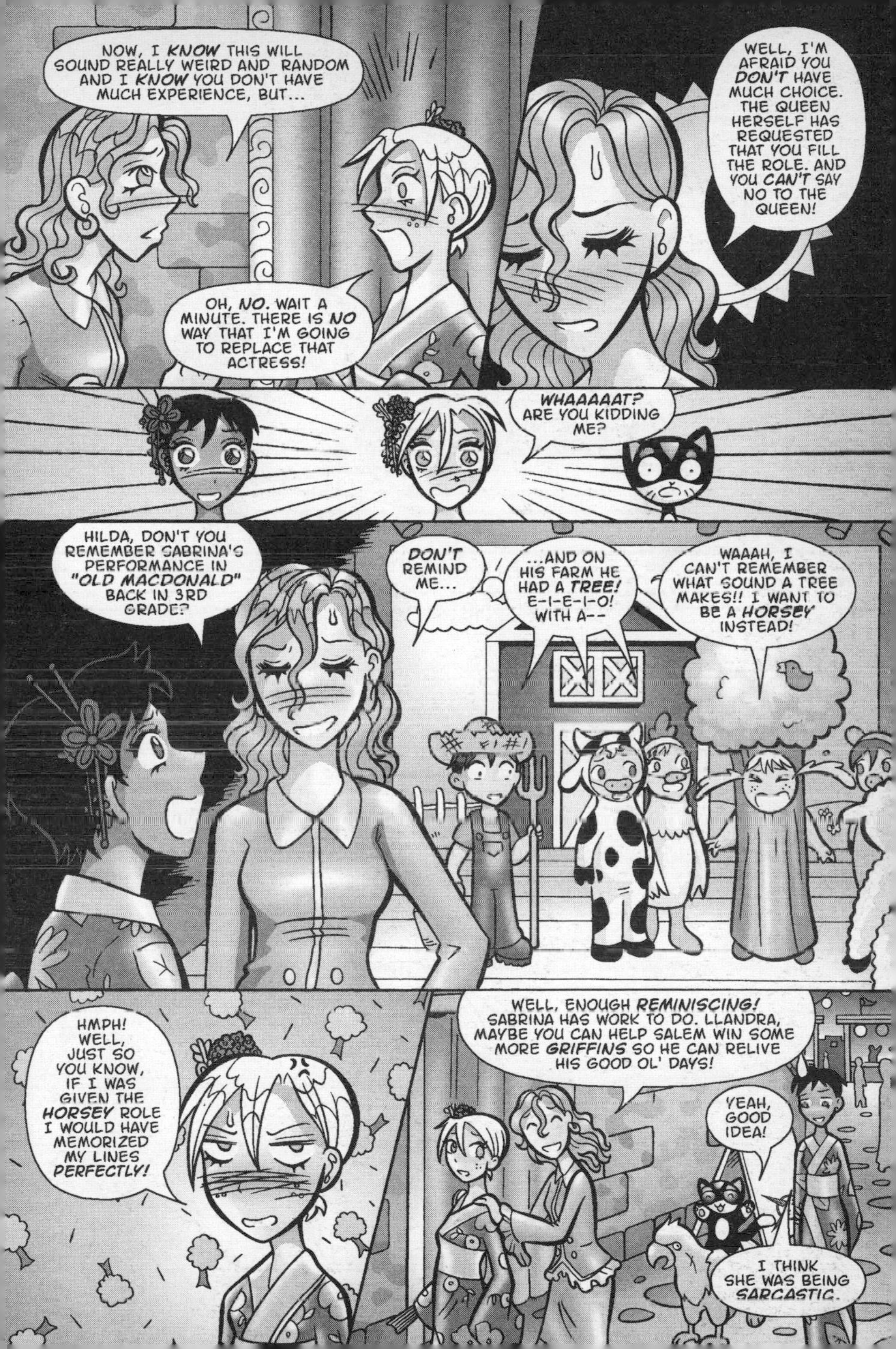
NOW, I KNOW THIS WILL SOUND REALLY WEIRD AND RANDOM AND I KNOW YOU DON'T HAVE MUCH EXPERIENCE, BUT...
OH, NO. WAIT A MINUTE. THERE IS NO WAY THAT I'M GOING TO REPLACE THAT ACTRESS!
WELL, I'M AFRAID YOU DON'T HAVE MUCH CHOICE. THE QUEEN HERSELF HAS REQUESTED THAT YOU FILL THE ROLE. AND YOU CAN'T SAY NO TO THE QUEEN!
WHAAAAAT? ARE YOU KIDDING ME?
HILDA, DON'T YOU REMEMBER SABRINA'S PERFORMANCE IN "OLD MACDONALD" BACK IN 3RD GRADE?
DON'T REMIND ME...
...AND ON HIS FARM HE HAD A TREE! E-I-E-I-O! WITH A--
WAAAH, I CAN'T REMEMBER WHAT SOUND A TREE MAKES!! I WANT TO BE A HORSEY INSTEAD!
HMPH! WELL, JUST SO YOU KNOW, IF I WAS GIVEN THE HORSEY ROLE I WOULD HAVE MEMORIZED MY LINES PERFECTLY!
WELL, ENOUGH REMINISCING! SABRINA HAS WORK TO DO. LLANDRA, MAYBE YOU CAN HELP SALEM WIN SOME MORE GRIFFINS SO HE CAN RELIVE HIS GOOD OL' DAYS!
YEAH, GOOD IDEA!
I THINK SHE WAS BEING SARCASTIC.

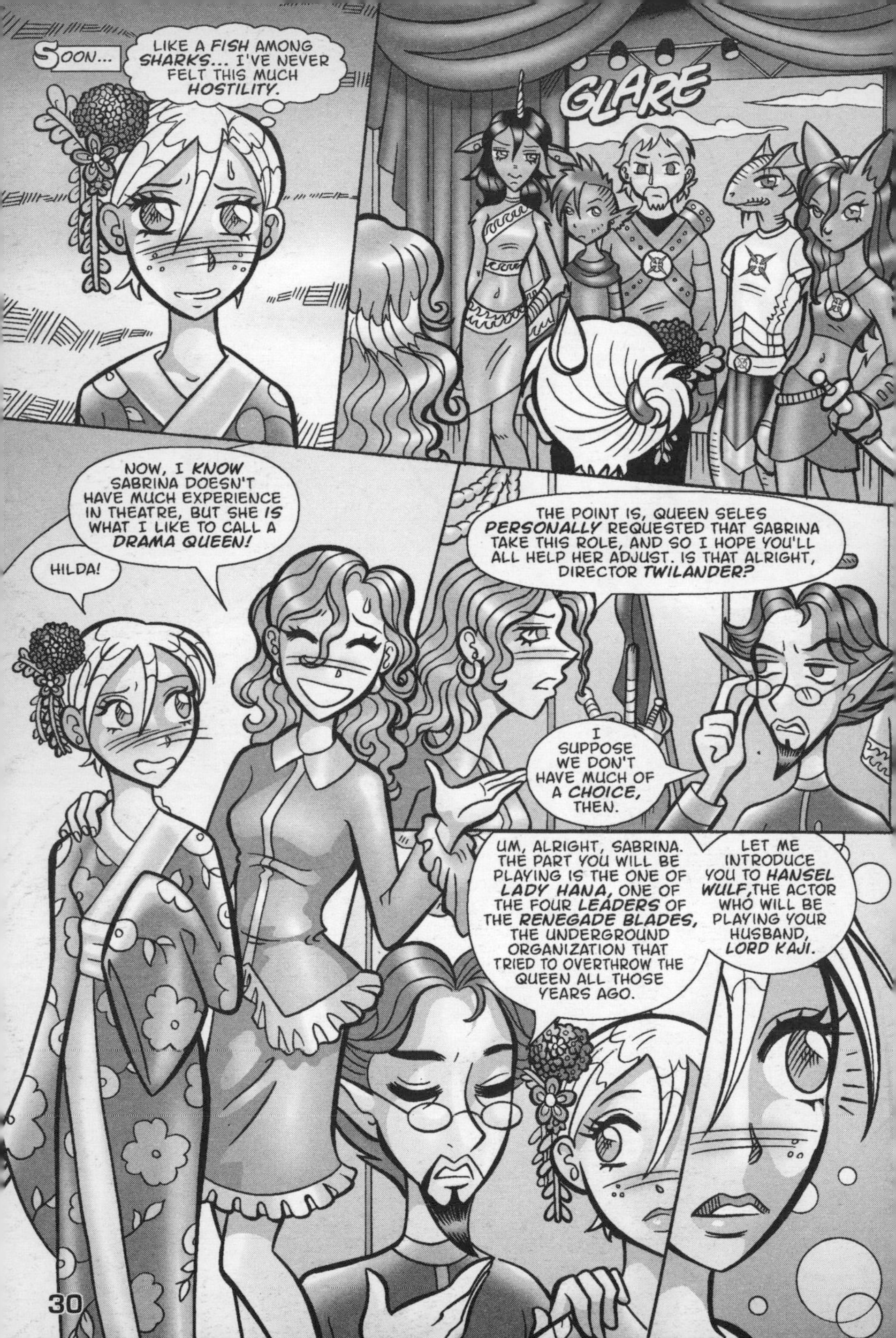
SOON...
LIKE A FISH AMONG SHARKS... I'VE NEVER FELT THIS MUCH HOSTILITY.
GLARE
NOW, I KNOW SABRINA DOESN'T HAVE MUCH EXPERIENCE IN THEATRE, BUT SHE IS WHAT I LIKE TO CALL A DRAMA QUEEN!
HILDA!
THE POINT IS, QUEEN SELES PERSONALLY REQUESTED THAT SABRINA TAKE THIS ROLE, AND SO I HOPE YOU'LL ALL HELP HER ADJUST. IS THAT ALRIGHT, DIRECTOR TWILANDER?
I SUPPOSE WE DON'T HAVE MUCH OF A CHOICE, THEN.
UM, ALRIGHT, SABRINA. THE PART YOU WILL BE PLAYING IS THE ONE OF LADY HANA, ONE OF THE FOUR LEADERS OF THE RENEGADE BLADES, THE UNDERGROUND ORGANIZATION THAT TRIED TO OVERTHROW THE QUEEN ALL THOSE YEARS AGO.
LET ME INTRODUCE YOU TO HANSEL WULF, THE ACTOR WHO WILL BE PLAYING YOUR HUSBAND, LORD KAJI.

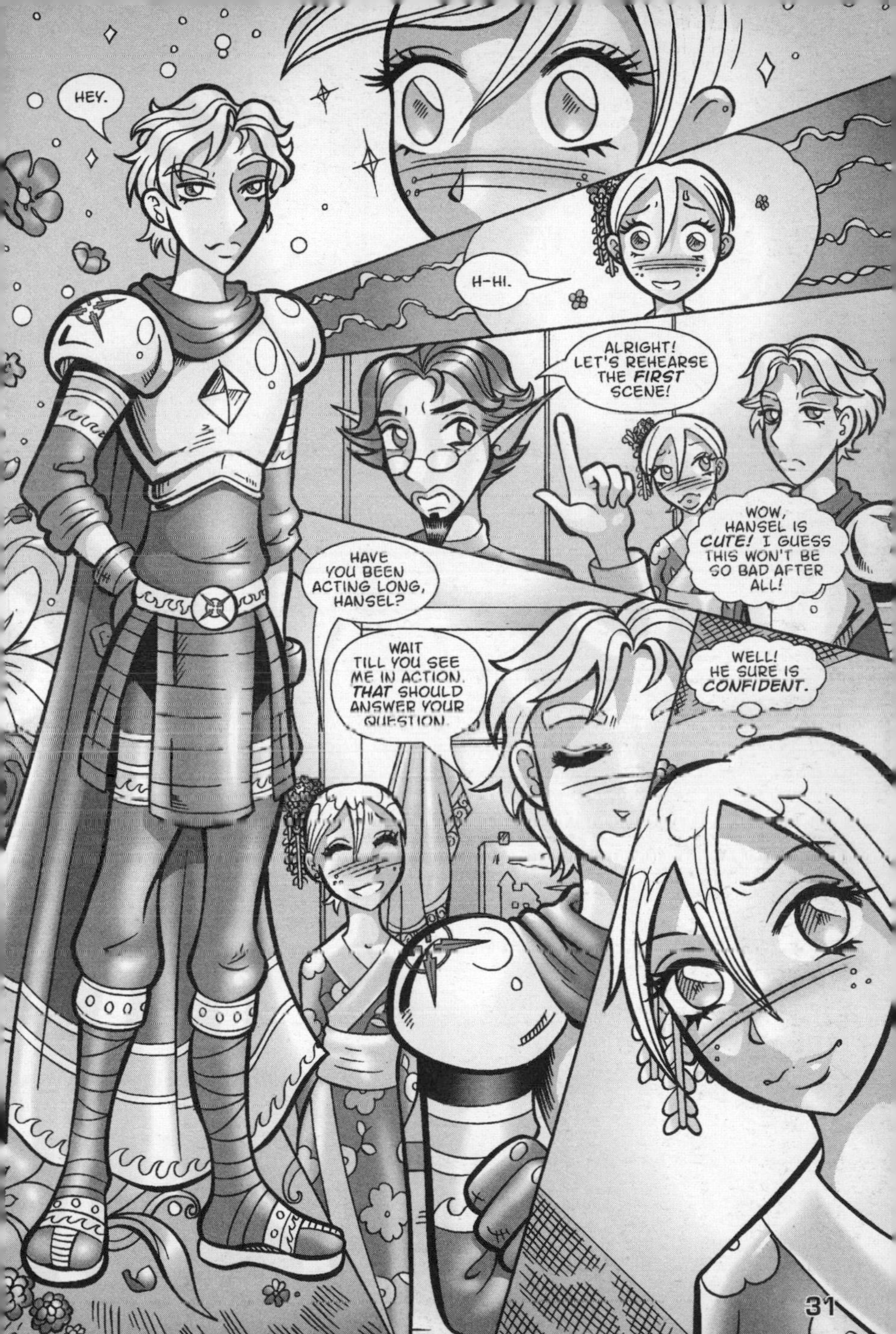
HEY.
H-HI.
ALRIGHT! LET'S REHEARSE THE *FIRST* SCENE!
WOW, HANSEL IS *CUTE!* I GUESS THIS WON'T BE SO BAD AFTER ALL!
HAVE YOU BEEN ACTING LONG, HANSEL?
WAIT TILL YOU SEE ME IN ACTION. *THAT* SHOULD ANSWER YOUR QUESTION.
WELL! HE SURE IS *CONFIDENT.*

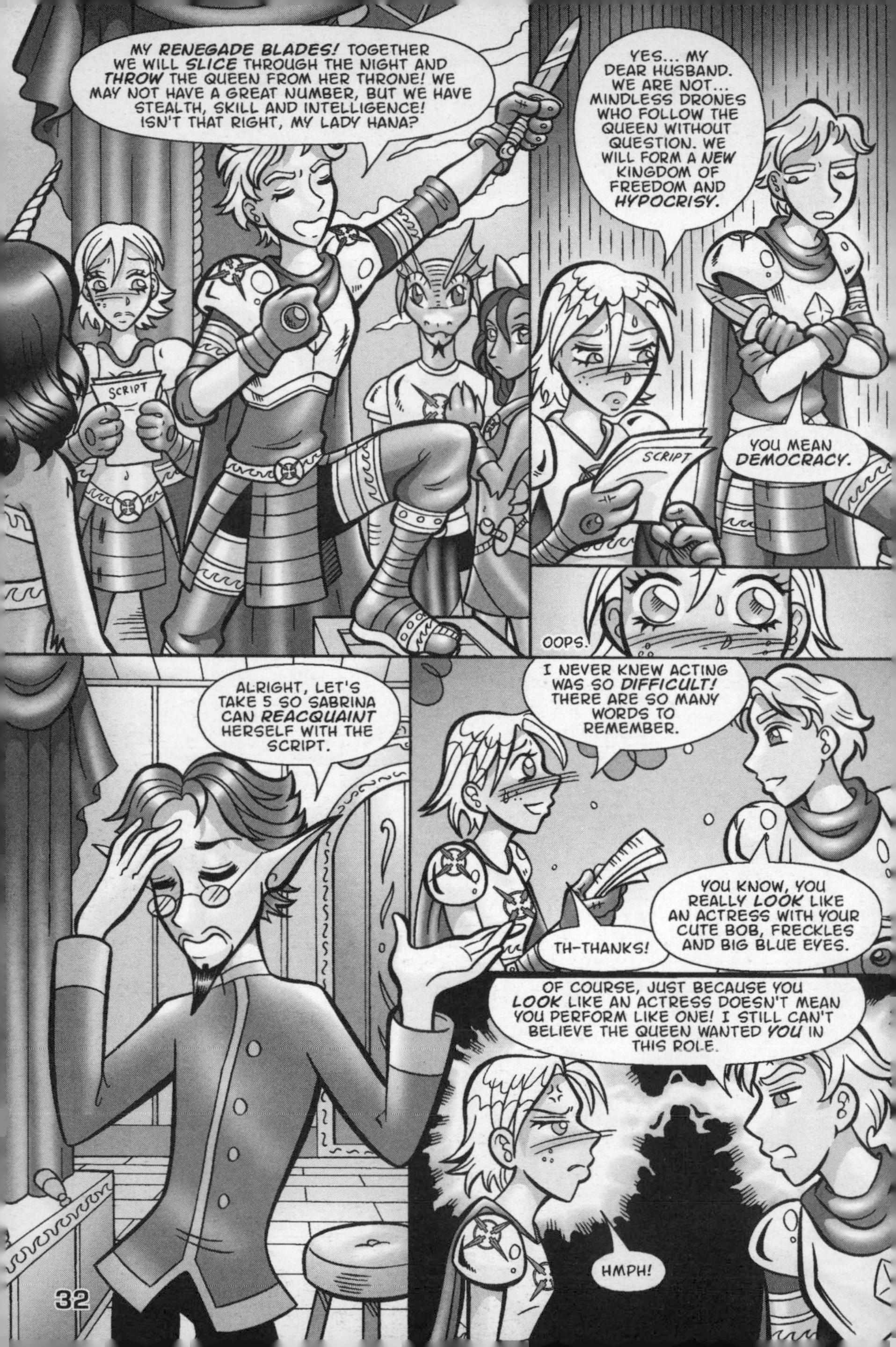
MY RENEGADE BLADES! TOGETHER WE WILL SLICE THROUGH THE NIGHT AND THROW THE QUEEN FROM HER THRONE! WE MAY NOT HAVE A GREAT NUMBER, BUT WE HAVE STEALTH, SKILL AND INTELLIGENCE! ISN'T THAT RIGHT, MY LADY HANA?
SCRIPT
YES... MY DEAR HUSBAND. WE ARE NOT... MINDLESS DRONES WHO FOLLOW THE QUEEN WITHOUT QUESTION. WE WILL FORM A NEW KINGDOM OF FREEDOM AND HYPOCRISY.
SCRIPT
YOU MEAN DEMOCRACY.
OOPS.
ALRIGHT, LET'S TAKE 5 SO SABRINA CAN REACQUAINT HERSELF WITH THE SCRIPT.
I NEVER KNEW ACTING WAS SO DIFFICULT! THERE ARE SO MANY WORDS TO REMEMBER.
YOU KNOW, YOU REALLY LOOK LIKE AN ACTRESS WITH YOUR CUTE BOB, FRECKLES AND BIG BLUE EYES.
TH-THANKS!
OF COURSE, JUST BECAUSE YOU LOOK LIKE AN ACTRESS DOESN'T MEAN YOU PERFORM LIKE ONE! I STILL CAN'T BELIEVE THE QUEEN WANTED YOU IN THIS ROLE.
HMPH!

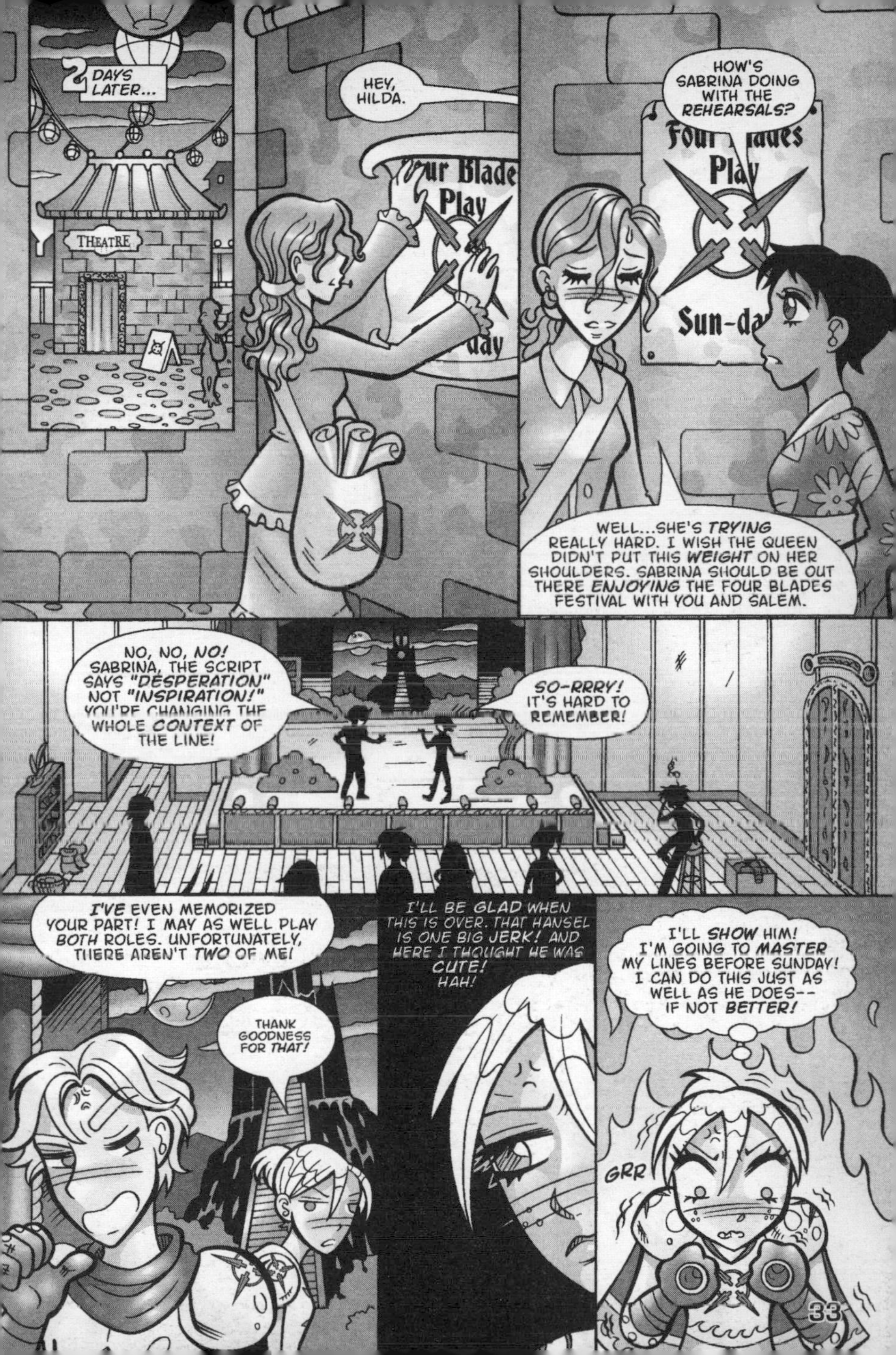

2 DAYS LATER...
THEATRE
HEY, HILDA.
Four Blades Play
HOW'S SABRINA DOING WITH THE REHEARSALS?
Four Blades Play Sun-da
WELL...SHE'S TRYING REALLY HARD. I WISH THE QUEEN DIDN'T PUT THIS WEIGHT ON HER SHOULDERS. SABRINA SHOULD BE OUT THERE ENJOYING THE FOUR BLADES FESTIVAL WITH YOU AND SALEM.
NO, NO, NO! SABRINA, THE SCRIPT SAYS "DESPERATION" NOT "INSPIRATION!" YOU'RE CHANGING THE WHOLE CONTEXT OF THE LINE!
SO-RRRY! IT'S HARD TO REMEMBER!
I'VE EVEN MEMORIZED YOUR PART! I MAY AS WELL PLAY BOTH ROLES. UNFORTUNATELY, THERE AREN'T TWO OF ME!
THANK GOODNESS FOR THAT!
I'LL BE GLAD WHEN THIS IS OVER. THAT HANSEL IS ONE BIG JERK! AND HERE I THOUGHT HE WAS CUTE! HAH!
I'LL SHOW HIM! I'M GOING TO MASTER MY LINES BEFORE SUNDAY! I CAN DO THIS JUST AS WELL AS HE DOES-- IF NOT BETTER!
GRR

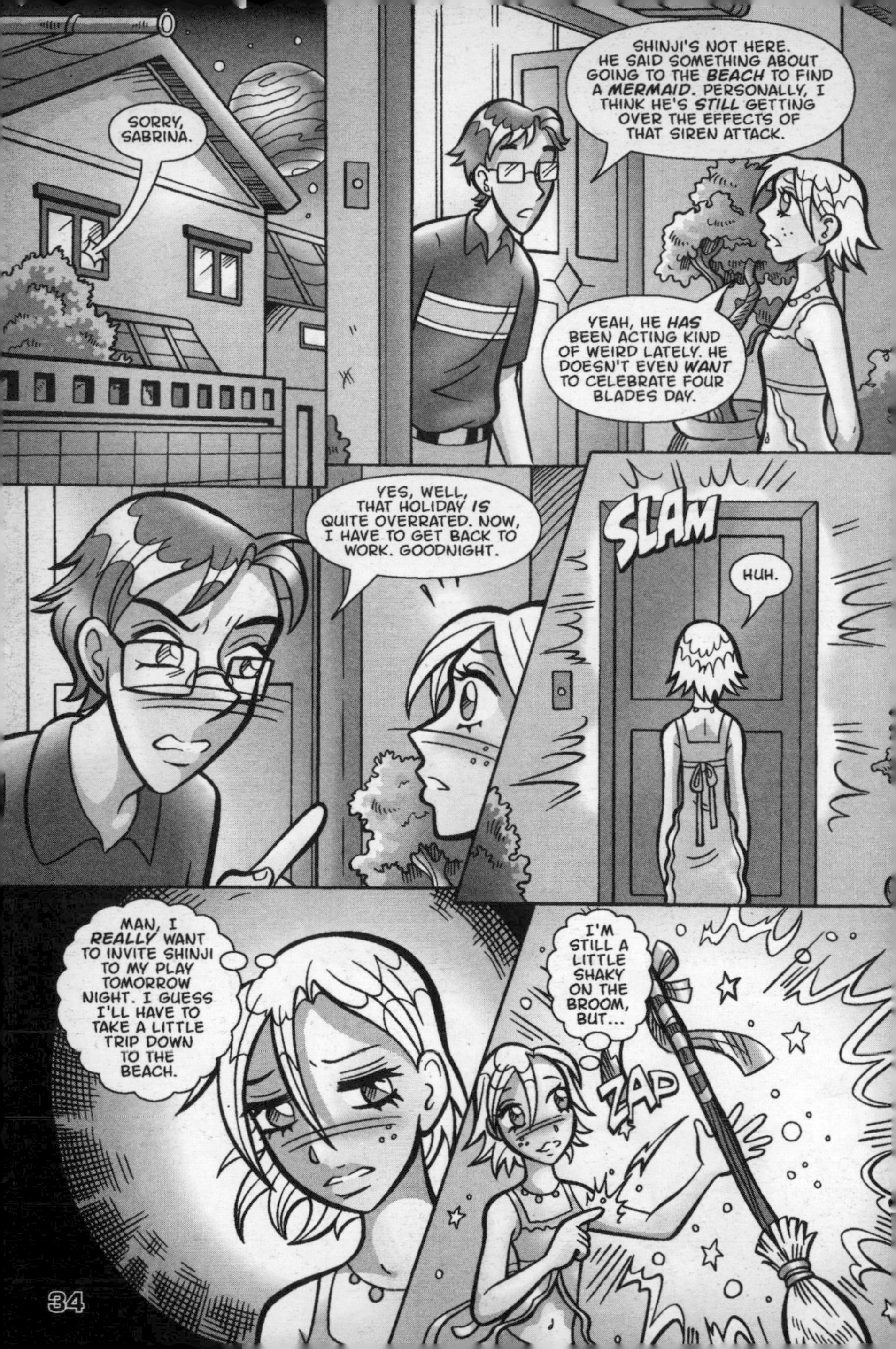

SORRY, SABRINA.
SHINJI'S NOT HERE. HE SAID SOMETHING ABOUT GOING TO THE BEACH TO FIND A MERMAID. PERSONALLY, I THINK HE'S STILL GETTING OVER THE EFFECTS OF THAT SIREN ATTACK.
YEAH, HE HAS BEEN ACTING KIND OF WEIRD LATELY. HE DOESN'T EVEN WANT TO CELEBRATE FOUR BLADES DAY.
YES, WELL, THAT HOLIDAY IS QUITE OVERRATED. NOW, I HAVE TO GET BACK TO WORK. GOODNIGHT.
SLAM
HUH.
MAN, I REALLY WANT TO INVITE SHINJI TO MY PLAY TOMORROW NIGHT. I GUESS I'LL HAVE TO TAKE A LITTLE TRIP DOWN TO THE BEACH.
I'M STILL A LITTLE SHAKY ON THE BROOM, BUT...
ZAP

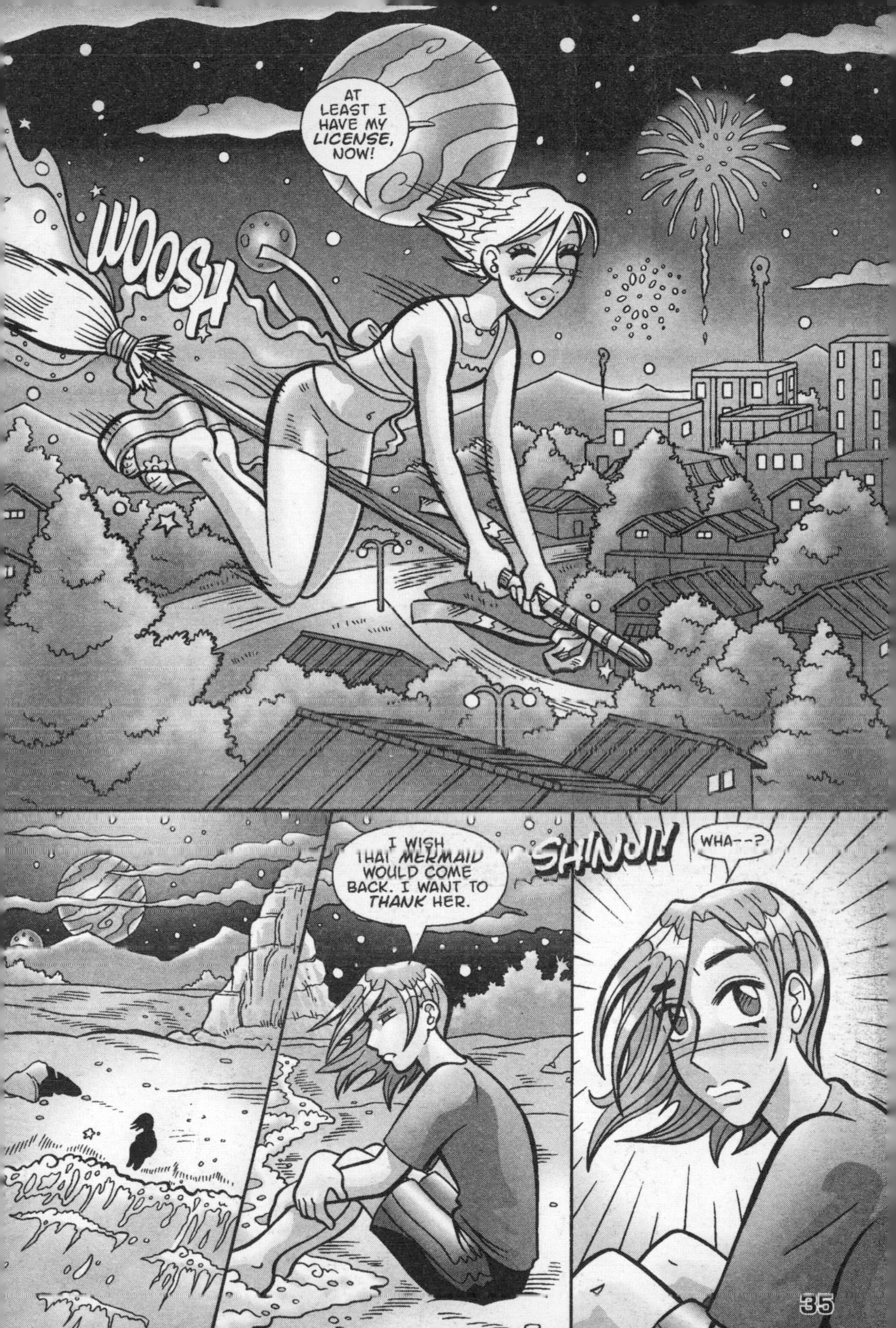
AT LEAST I HAVE MY LICENSE, NOW!
WOOSH
I WISH THAT MERMAID WOULD COME BACK. I WANT TO THANK HER.
SHINJI!
WHA--?

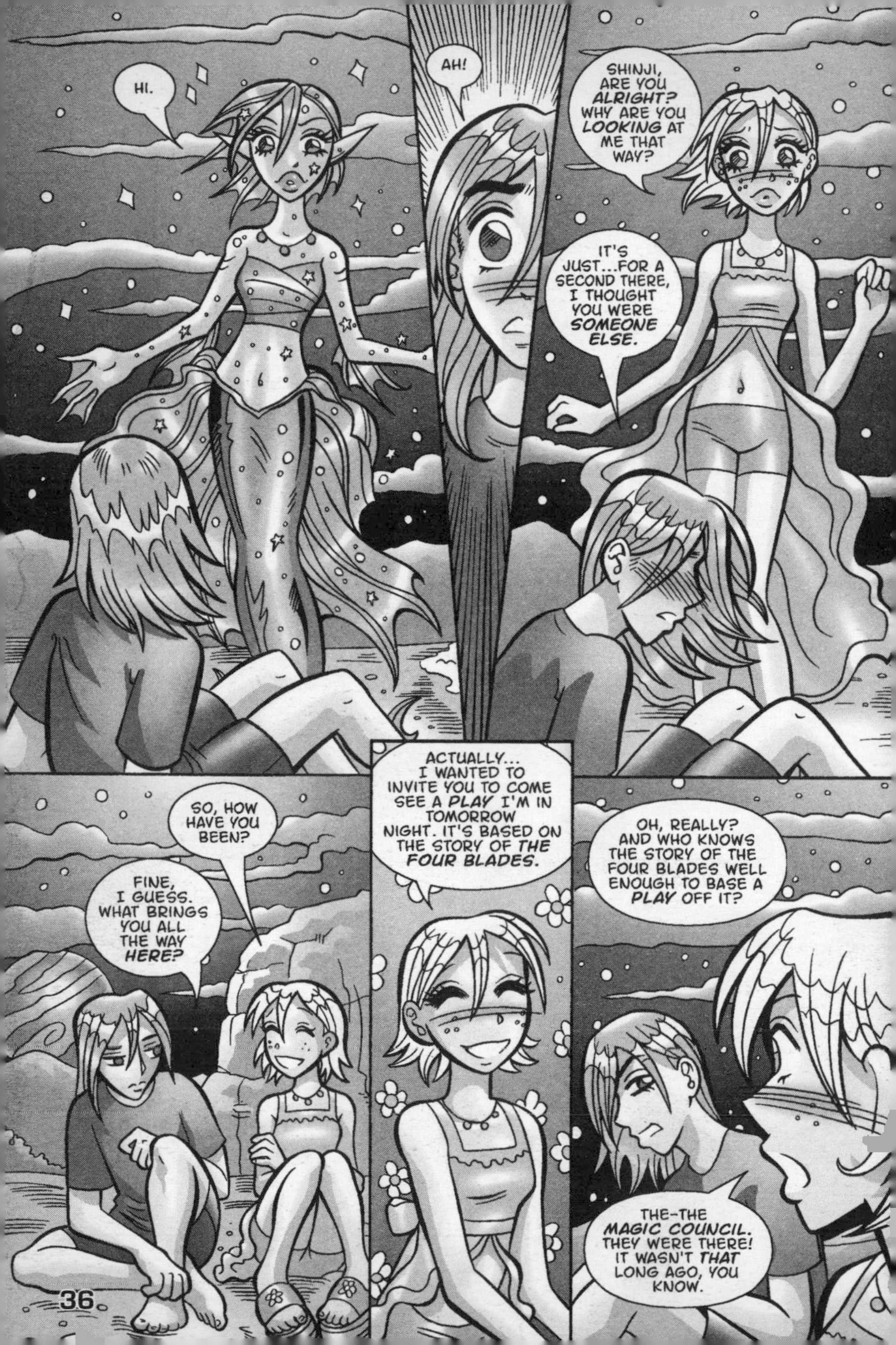
HI.
AH!
SHINJI, ARE YOU ALRIGHT? WHY ARE YOU LOOKING AT ME THAT WAY?
IT'S JUST...FOR A SECOND THERE, I THOUGHT YOU WERE SOMEONE ELSE.
SO, HOW HAVE YOU BEEN?
FINE, I GUESS. WHAT BRINGS YOU ALL THE WAY HERE?
ACTUALLY... I WANTED TO INVITE YOU TO COME SEE A PLAY I'M IN TOMORROW NIGHT. IT'S BASED ON THE STORY OF THE FOUR BLADES.
OH, REALLY? AND WHO KNOWS THE STORY OF THE FOUR BLADES WELL ENOUGH TO BASE A PLAY OFF IT?
THE-THE MAGIC COUNCIL. THEY WERE THERE! IT WASN'T THAT LONG AGO, YOU KNOW.

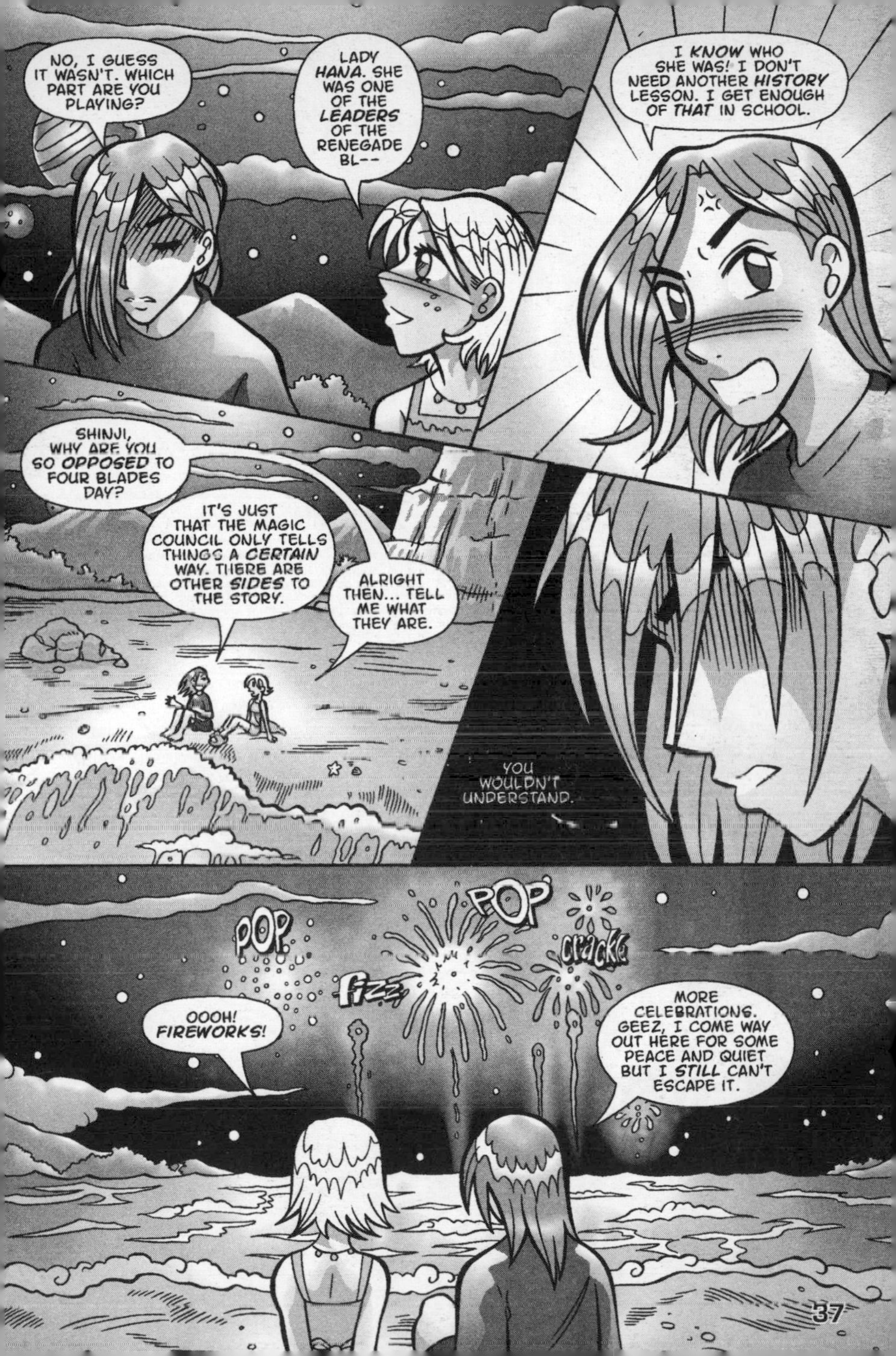

NO, I GUESS IT WASN'T. WHICH PART ARE YOU PLAYING?
LADY *HANA*. SHE WAS ONE OF THE *LEADERS* OF THE RENEGADE BL--
I *KNOW* WHO SHE WAS! I DON'T NEED ANOTHER *HISTORY* LESSON. I GET ENOUGH OF *THAT* IN SCHOOL.
SHINJI, WHY ARE YOU SO *OPPOSED* TO FOUR BLADES DAY?
IT'S JUST THAT THE MAGIC COUNCIL ONLY TELLS THINGS A *CERTAIN* WAY. THERE ARE OTHER *SIDES* TO THE STORY.
ALRIGHT THEN... TELL ME WHAT THEY ARE.
YOU WOULDN'T UNDERSTAND.
POP
POP
crackle
fizz
OOOH! *FIREWORKS*!
MORE CELEBRATIONS. GEEZ, I COME WAY OUT HERE FOR SOME PEACE AND QUIET BUT I *STILL* CAN'T ESCAPE IT.

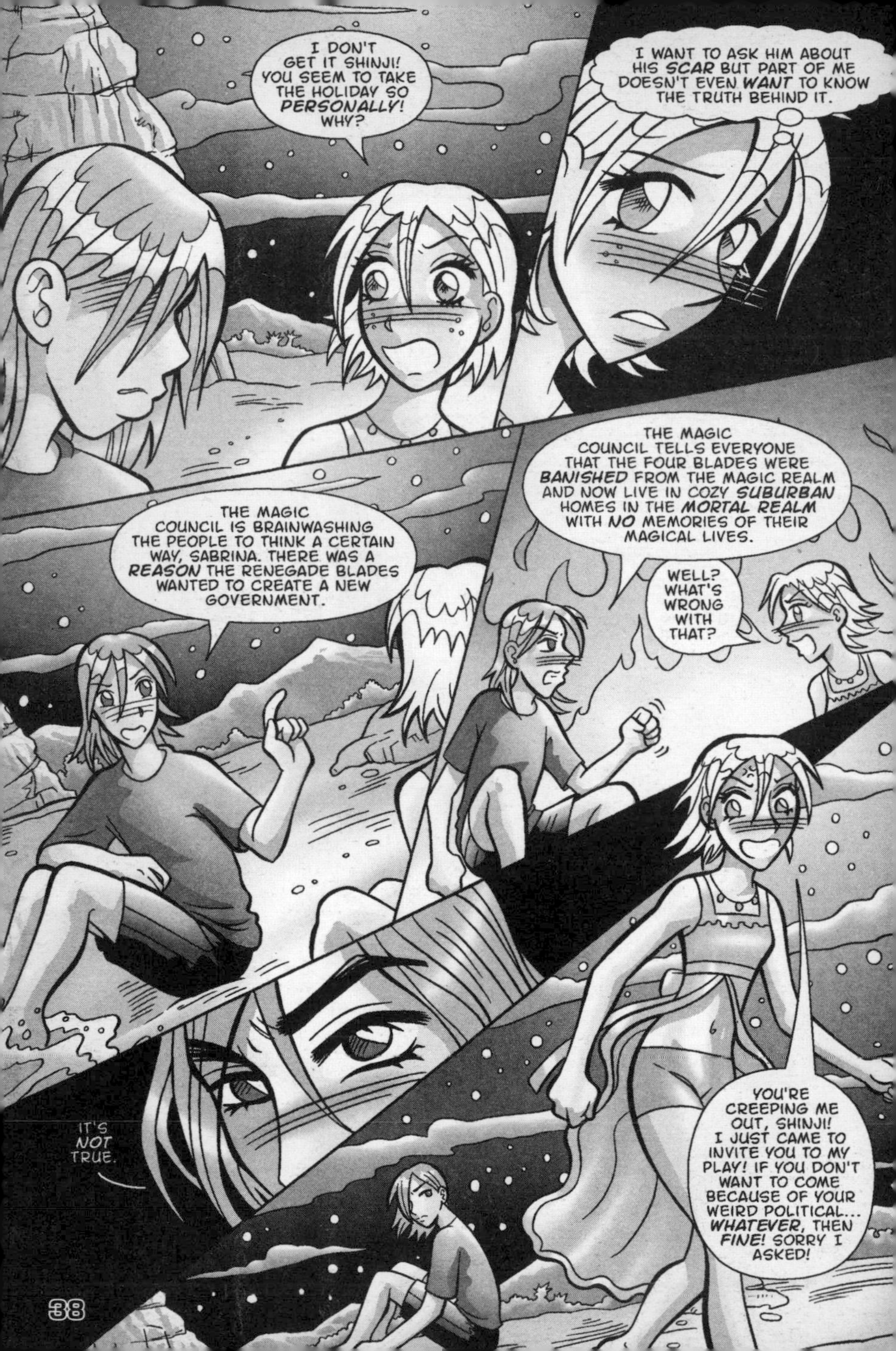
I DON'T GET IT SHINJI! YOU SEEM TO TAKE THE HOLIDAY SO *PERSONALLY*! WHY?
I WANT TO ASK HIM ABOUT HIS *SCAR* BUT PART OF ME DOESN'T EVEN *WANT* TO KNOW THE TRUTH BEHIND IT.
THE MAGIC COUNCIL IS BRAINWASHING THE PEOPLE TO THINK A CERTAIN WAY, SABRINA. THERE WAS A *REASON* THE RENEGADE BLADES WANTED TO CREATE A NEW GOVERNMENT.
THE MAGIC COUNCIL TELLS EVERYONE THAT THE FOUR BLADES WERE *BANISHED* FROM THE MAGIC REALM AND NOW LIVE IN COZY *SUBURBAN* HOMES IN THE *MORTAL REALM* WITH *NO* MEMORIES OF THEIR MAGICAL LIVES.
WELL? WHAT'S WRONG WITH THAT?
IT'S *NOT* TRUE.
YOU'RE CREEPING ME OUT, SHINJI! I JUST CAME TO INVITE YOU TO MY PLAY! IF YOU DON'T WANT TO COME BECAUSE OF YOUR WEIRD POLITICAL... *WHATEVER*, THEN *FINE*! SORRY I ASKED!

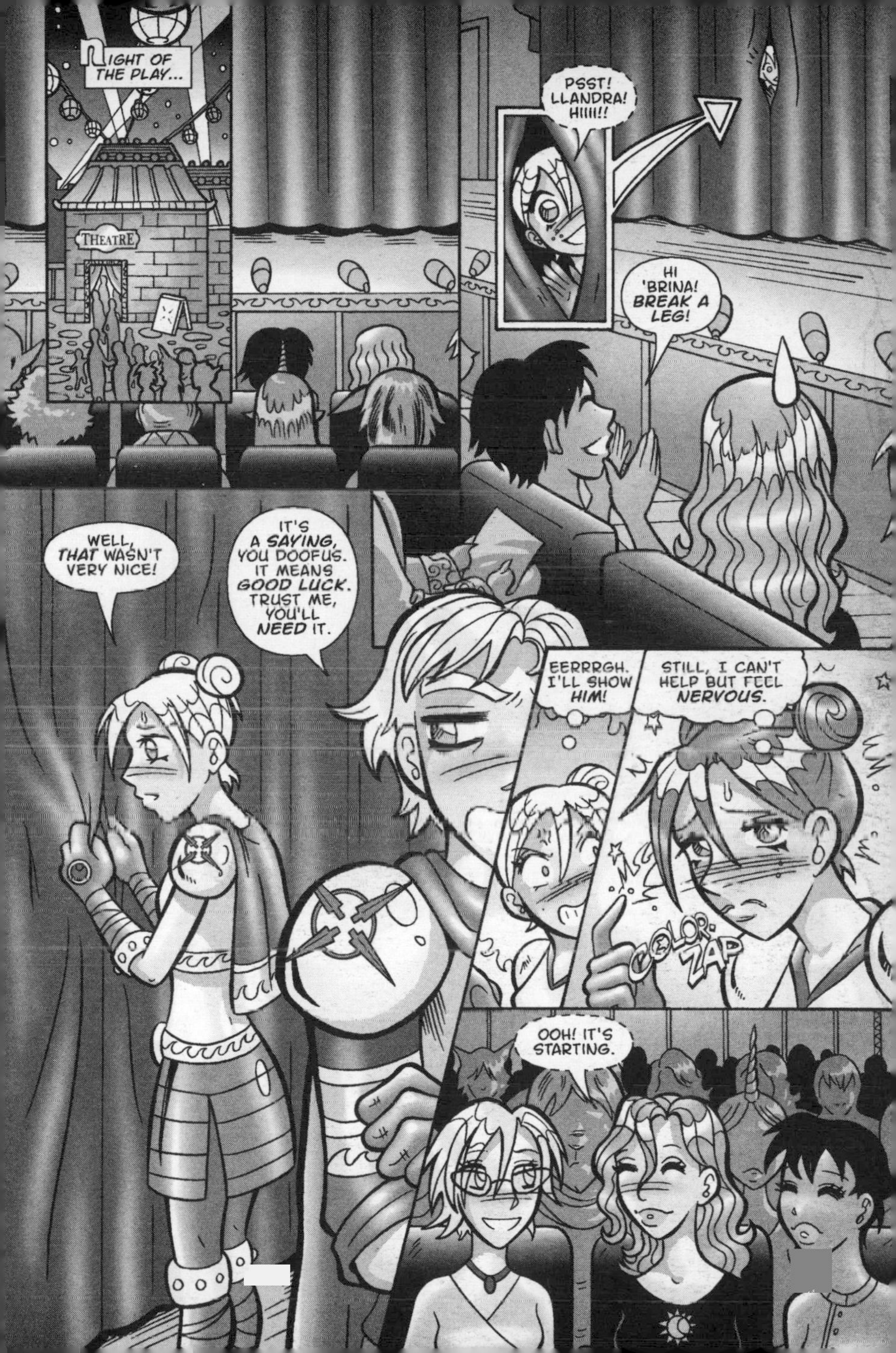
NIGHT OF THE PLAY...
THEATRE
PSST! LLANDRA! HIIII!!
HI 'BRINA! BREAK A LEG!
WELL, THAT WASN'T VERY NICE!
IT'S A SAYING, YOU DOOFUS. IT MEANS GOOD LUCK. TRUST ME, YOU'LL NEED IT.
EERRRGH. I'LL SHOW HIM!
STILL, I CAN'T HELP BUT FEEL NERVOUS.
COLOR ZAP
OOH! IT'S STARTING.

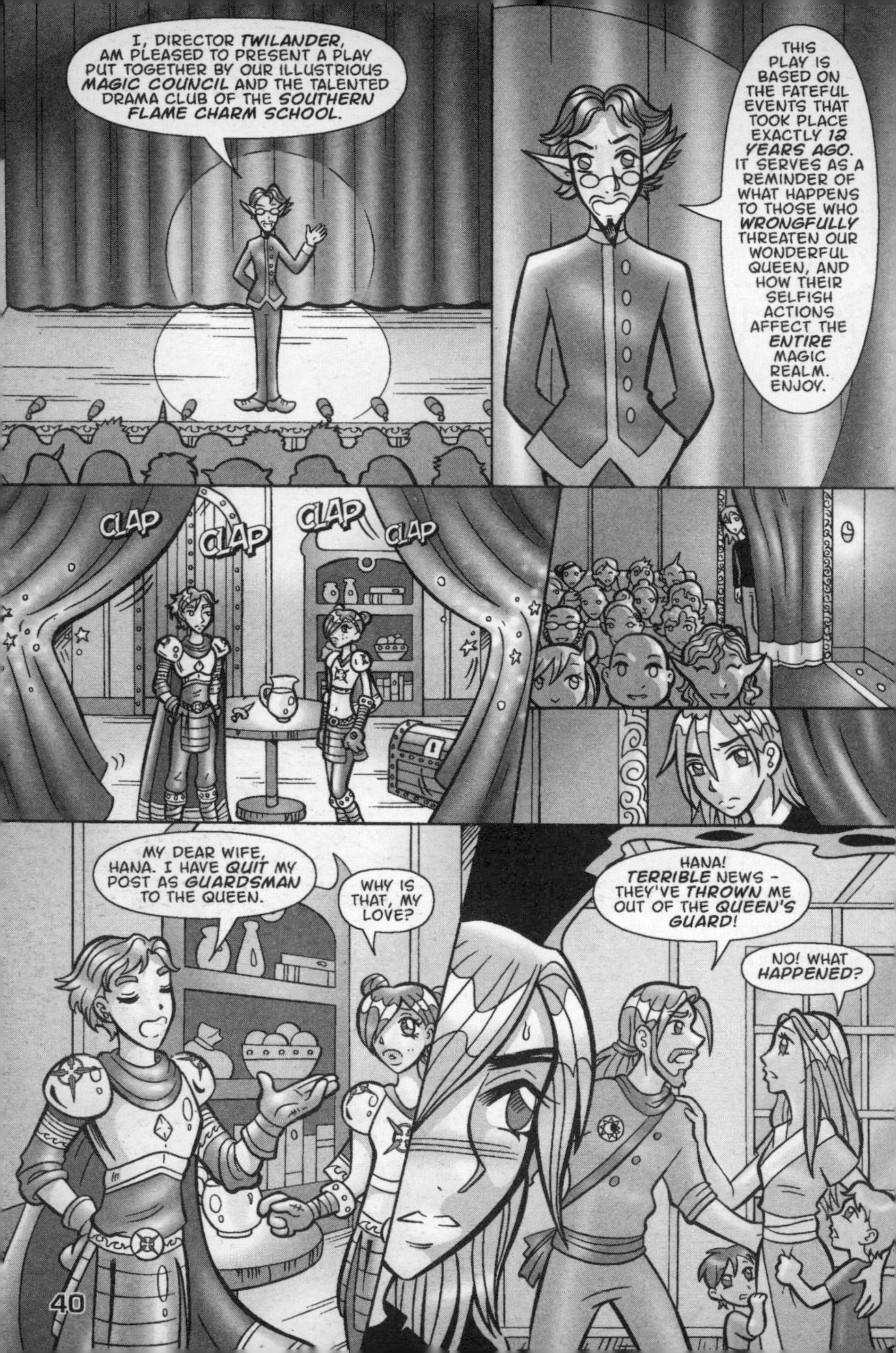

I, DIRECTOR TWILANDER, AM PLEASED TO PRESENT A PLAY PUT TOGETHER BY OUR ILLUSTRIOUS MAGIC COUNCIL AND THE TALENTED DRAMA CLUB OF THE SOUTHERN FLAME CHARM SCHOOL.
THIS PLAY IS BASED ON THE FATEFUL EVENTS THAT TOOK PLACE EXACTLY 12 YEARS AGO. IT SERVES AS A REMINDER OF WHAT HAPPENS TO THOSE WHO WRONGFULLY THREATEN OUR WONDERFUL QUEEN, AND HOW THEIR SELFISH ACTIONS AFFECT THE ENTIRE MAGIC REALM. ENJOY.
CLAP
CLAP
CLAP
CLAP
MY DEAR WIFE, HANA. I HAVE QUIT MY POST AS GUARDSMAN TO THE QUEEN.
WHY IS THAT, MY LOVE?
HANA! TERRIBLE NEWS - THEY'VE THROWN ME OUT OF THE QUEEN'S GUARD!
NO! WHAT HAPPENED?

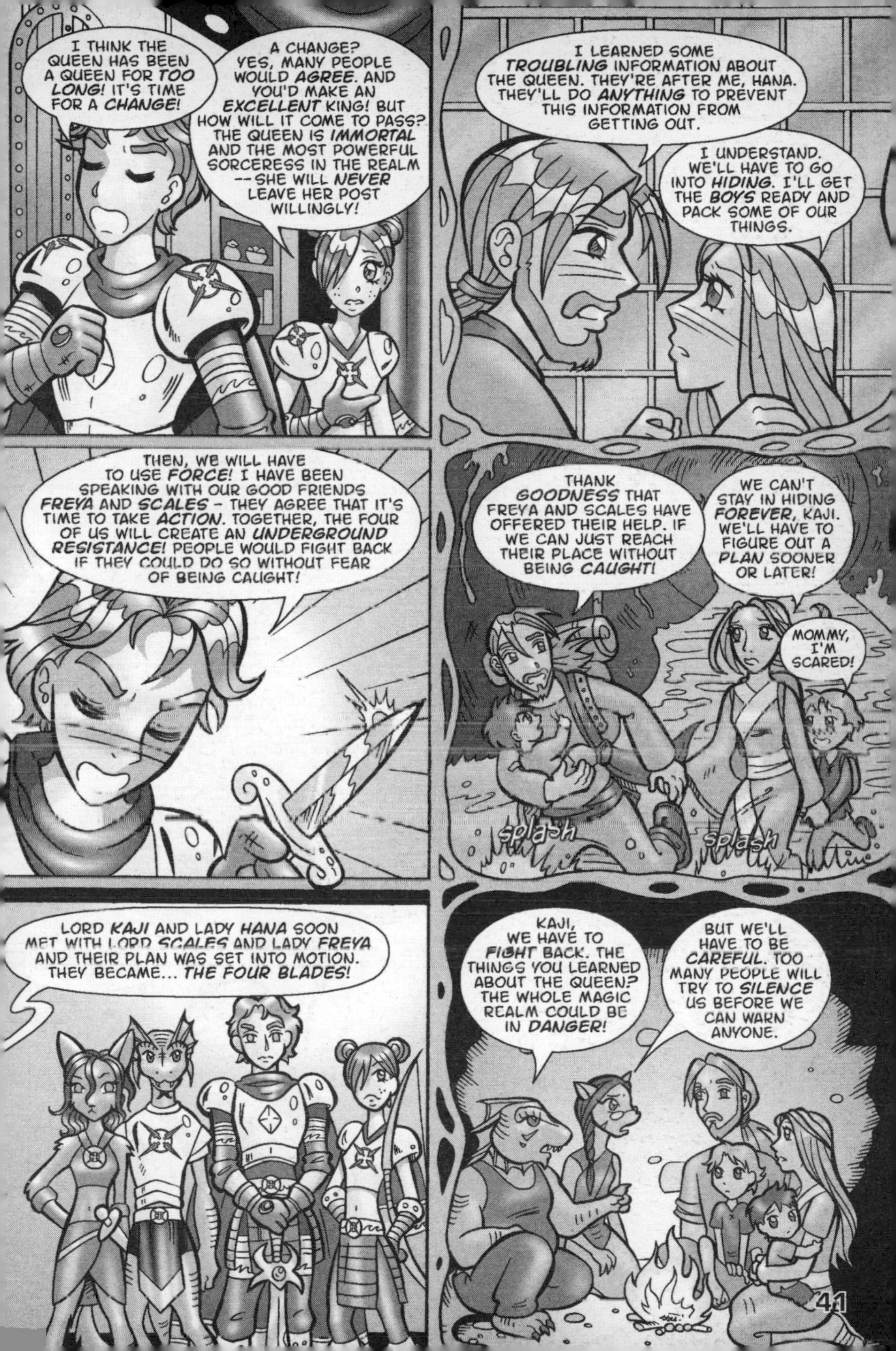
I THINK THE QUEEN HAS BEEN A QUEEN FOR TOO LONG! IT'S TIME FOR A CHANGE!
A CHANGE? YES, MANY PEOPLE WOULD AGREE. AND YOU'D MAKE AN EXCELLENT KING! BUT HOW WILL IT COME TO PASS? THE QUEEN IS IMMORTAL AND THE MOST POWERFUL SORCERESS IN THE REALM -- SHE WILL NEVER LEAVE HER POST WILLINGLY!
I LEARNED SOME TROUBLING INFORMATION ABOUT THE QUEEN. THEY'RE AFTER ME, HANA. THEY'LL DO ANYTHING TO PREVENT THIS INFORMATION FROM GETTING OUT.
I UNDERSTAND. WE'LL HAVE TO GO INTO HIDING. I'LL GET THE BOYS READY AND PACK SOME OF OUR THINGS.
THEN, WE WILL HAVE TO USE FORCE! I HAVE BEEN SPEAKING WITH OUR GOOD FRIENDS FREYA AND SCALES - THEY AGREE THAT IT'S TIME TO TAKE ACTION. TOGETHER, THE FOUR OF US WILL CREATE AN UNDERGROUND RESISTANCE! PEOPLE WOULD FIGHT BACK IF THEY COULD DO SO WITHOUT FEAR OF BEING CAUGHT!
THANK GOODNESS THAT FREYA AND SCALES HAVE OFFERED THEIR HELP. IF WE CAN JUST REACH THEIR PLACE WITHOUT BEING CAUGHT!
WE CAN'T STAY IN HIDING FOREVER, KAJI. WE'LL HAVE TO FIGURE OUT A PLAN SOONER OR LATER!
MOMMY, I'M SCARED!
splash
splash
LORD KAJI AND LADY HANA SOON MET WITH LORD SCALES AND LADY FREYA AND THEIR PLAN WAS SET INTO MOTION. THEY BECAME... THE FOUR BLADES!
KAJI, WE HAVE TO FIGHT BACK. THE THINGS YOU LEARNED ABOUT THE QUEEN? THE WHOLE MAGIC REALM COULD BE IN DANGER!
BUT WE'LL HAVE TO BE CAREFUL. TOO MANY PEOPLE WILL TRY TO SILENCE US BEFORE WE CAN WARN ANYONE.

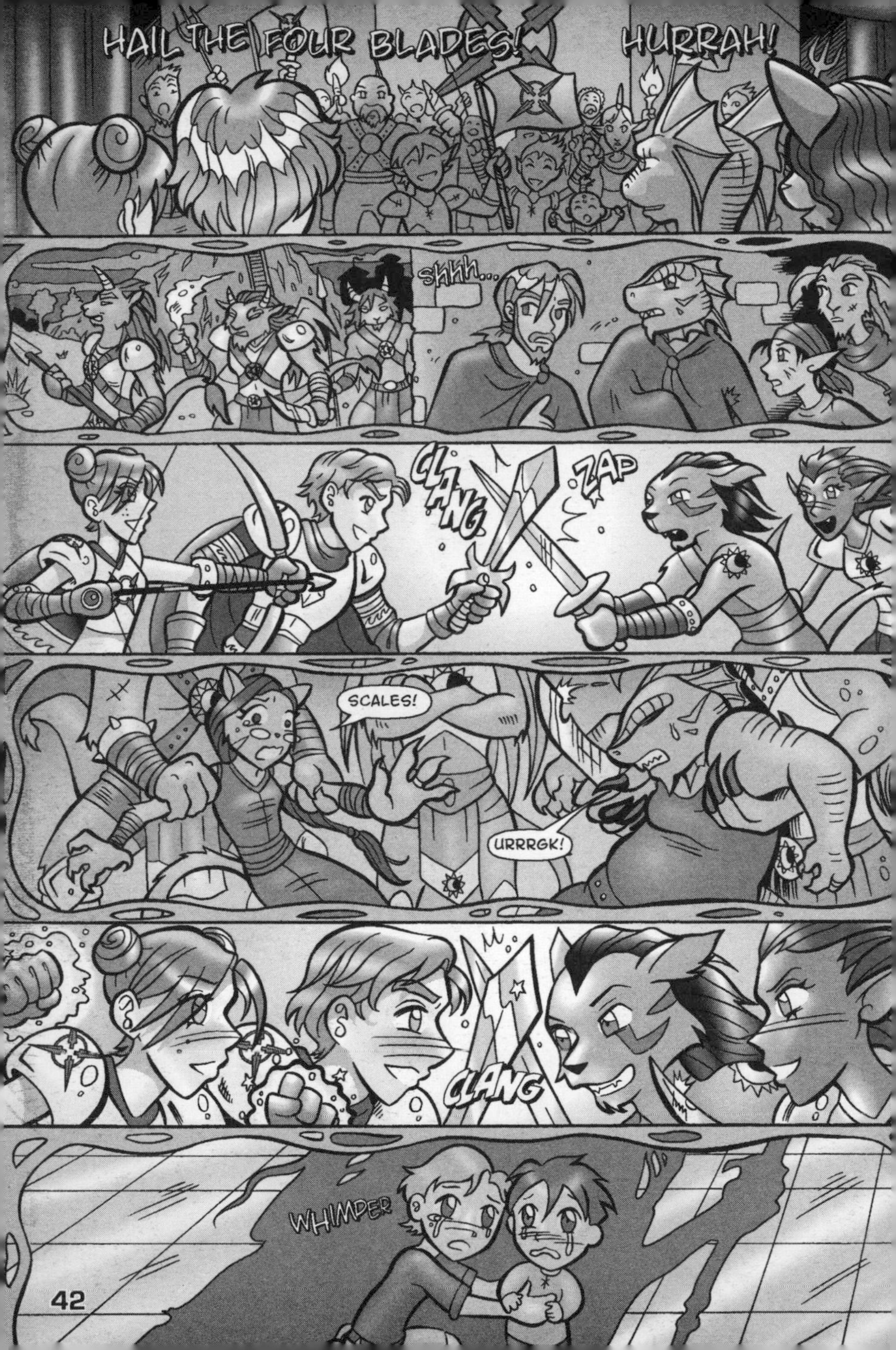
HAIL THE FOUR BLADES!
HURRAH!
shhh...
CLANG
ZAP
SCALES!
URRRGK!
CLANG
WHIMPER

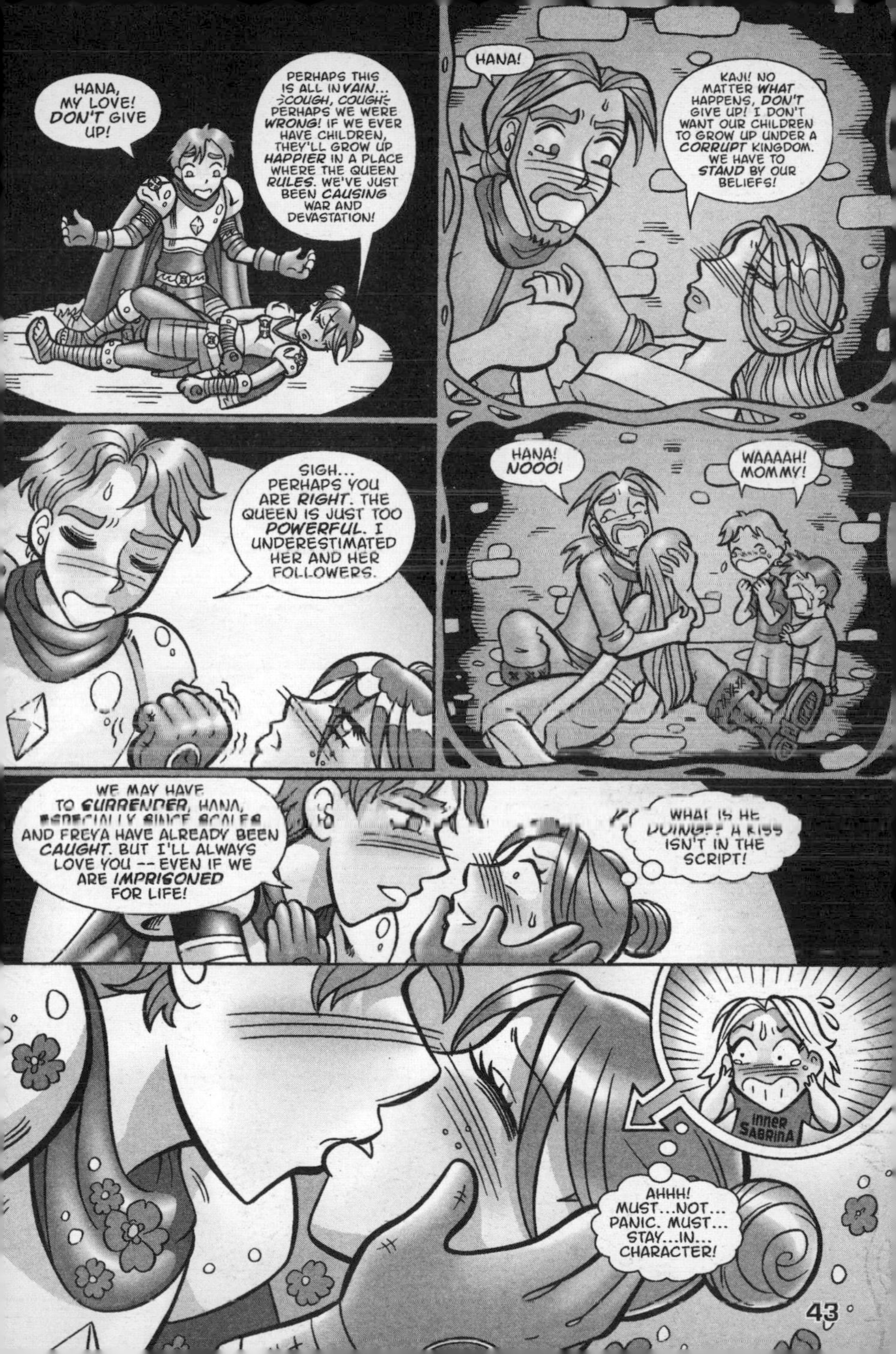
HANA, MY LOVE! DON'T GIVE UP!
PERHAPS THIS IS ALL IN VAIN... COUGH, COUGH PERHAPS WE WERE WRONG! IF WE EVER HAVE CHILDREN, THEY'LL GROW UP HAPPIER IN A PLACE WHERE THE QUEEN RULES. WE'VE JUST BEEN CAUSING WAR AND DEVASTATION!
HANA!
KAJI! NO MATTER WHAT HAPPENS, DON'T GIVE UP! I DON'T WANT OUR CHILDREN TO GROW UP UNDER A CORRUPT KINGDOM. WE HAVE TO STAND BY OUR BELIEFS!
SIGH... PERHAPS YOU ARE RIGHT. THE QUEEN IS JUST TOO POWERFUL. I UNDERESTIMATED HER AND HER FOLLOWERS.
HANA! NOOO!
WAAAAH! MOMMY!
WE MAY HAVE TO SURRENDER, HANA, ESPECIALLY SINCE SCALER AND FREYA HAVE ALREADY BEEN CAUGHT. BUT I'LL ALWAYS LOVE YOU -- EVEN IF WE ARE IMPRISONED FOR LIFE!
WHAT IS HE DOING!? A KISS ISN'T IN THE SCRIPT!
inner SABRINA
AHHH! MUST...NOT... PANIC. MUST... STAY...IN... CHARACTER!

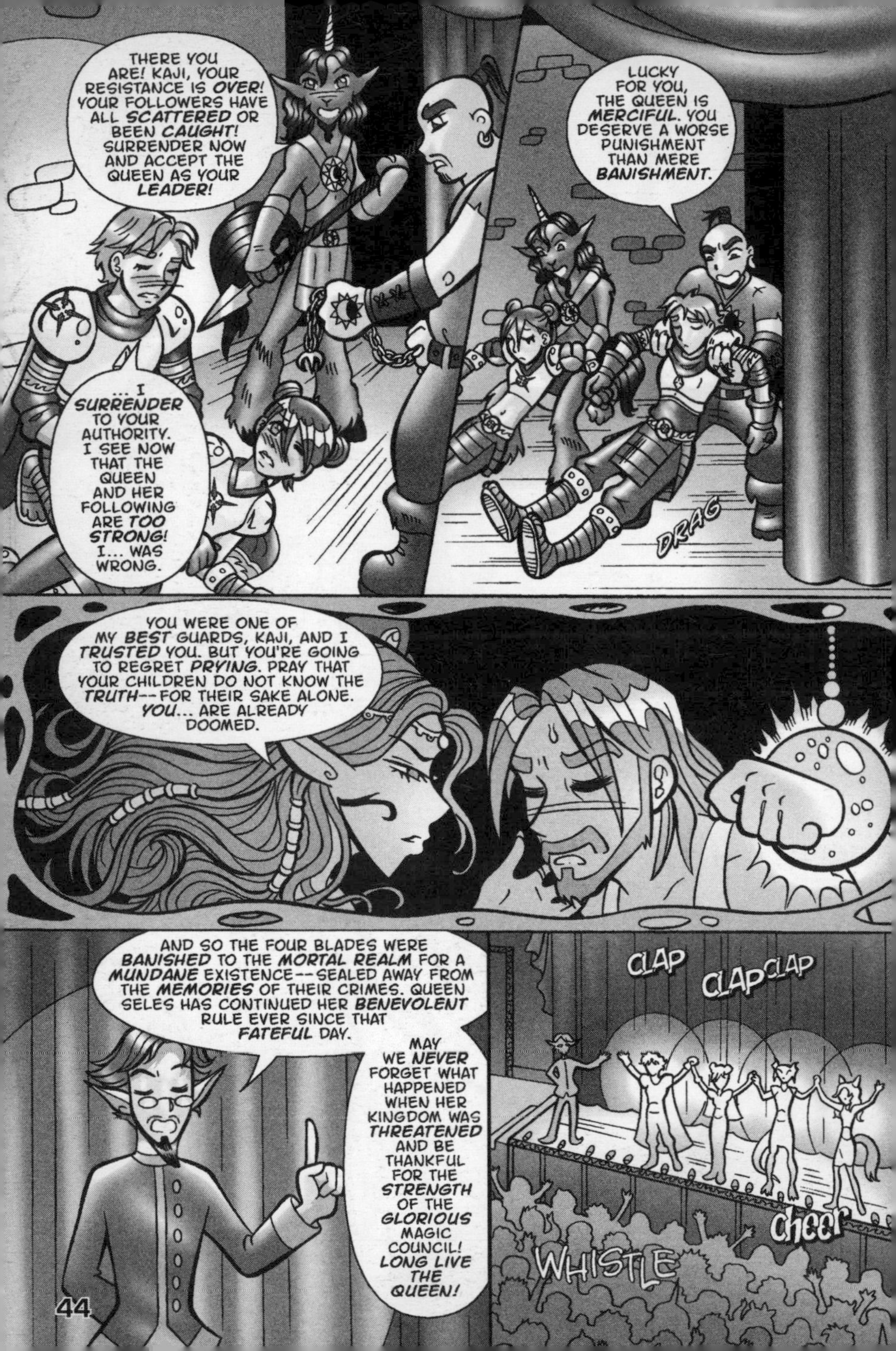
THERE YOU ARE! KAJI, YOUR RESISTANCE IS OVER! YOUR FOLLOWERS HAVE ALL SCATTERED OR BEEN CAUGHT! SURRENDER NOW AND ACCEPT THE QUEEN AS YOUR LEADER!
... I SURRENDER TO YOUR AUTHORITY. I SEE NOW THAT THE QUEEN AND HER FOLLOWING ARE TOO STRONG! I... WAS WRONG.
LUCKY FOR YOU, THE QUEEN IS MERCIFUL. YOU DESERVE A WORSE PUNISHMENT THAN MERE BANISHMENT.
DRAG
YOU WERE ONE OF MY BEST GUARDS, KAJI, AND I TRUSTED YOU. BUT YOU'RE GOING TO REGRET PRYING. PRAY THAT YOUR CHILDREN DO NOT KNOW THE TRUTH-- FOR THEIR SAKE ALONE. YOU... ARE ALREADY DOOMED.
AND SO THE FOUR BLADES WERE BANISHED TO THE MORTAL REALM FOR A MUNDANE EXISTENCE-- SEALED AWAY FROM THE MEMORIES OF THEIR CRIMES. QUEEN SELES HAS CONTINUED HER BENEVOLENT RULE EVER SINCE THAT FATEFUL DAY.
MAY WE NEVER FORGET WHAT HAPPENED WHEN HER KINGDOM WAS THREATENED AND BE THANKFUL FOR THE STRENGTH OF THE GLORIOUS MAGIC COUNCIL! LONG LIVE THE QUEEN!
CLAP
CLAP CLAP
CHEER
WHISTLE

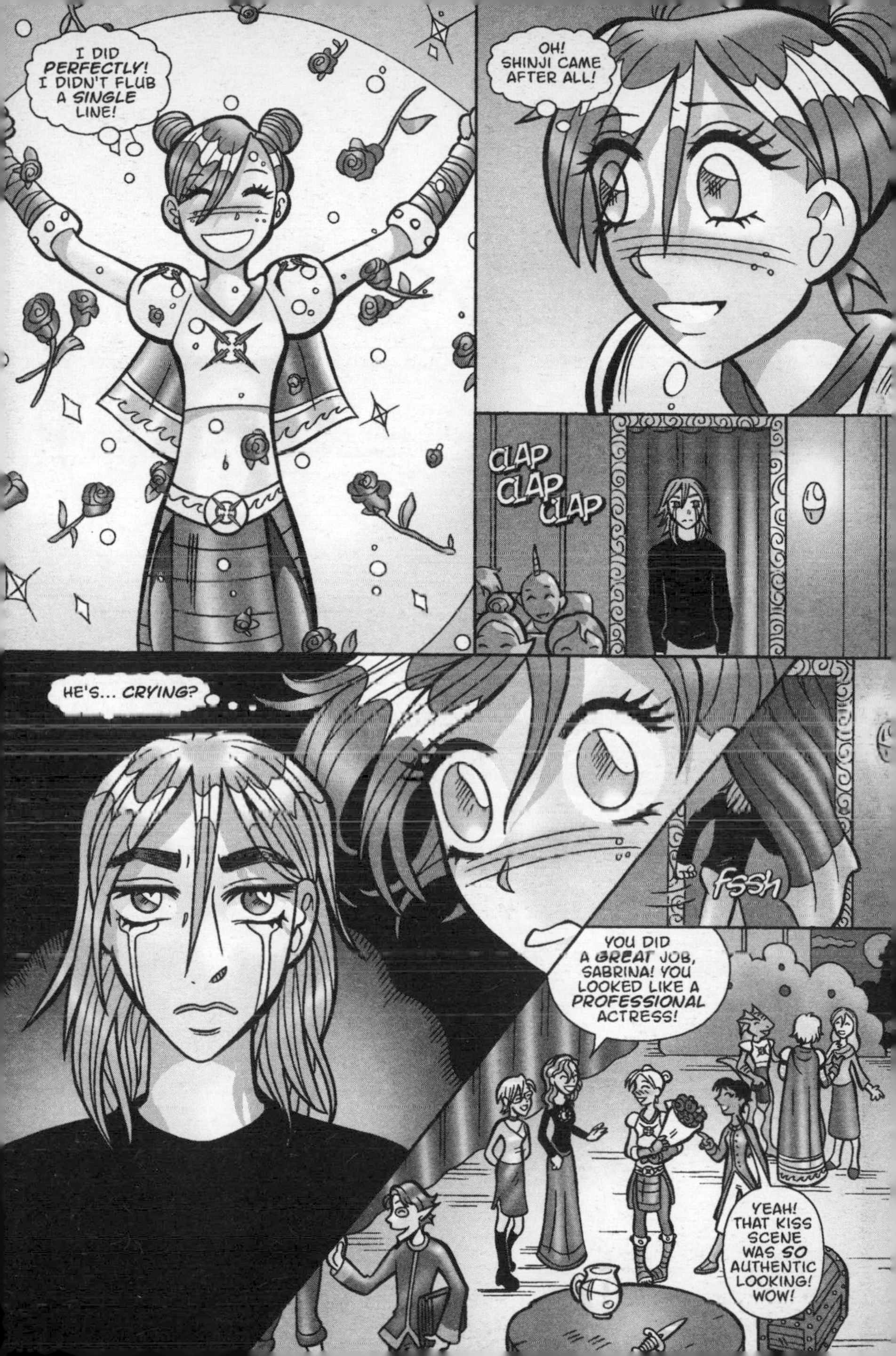
I DID PERFECTLY! I DIDN'T FLUB A SINGLE LINE!
OH! SHINJI CAME AFTER ALL!
CLAP CLAP CLAP
HE'S... CRYING?
fssh
YOU DID A GREAT JOB, SABRINA! YOU LOOKED LIKE A PROFESSIONAL ACTRESS!
YEAH! THAT KISS SCENE WAS SO AUTHENTIC LOOKING! WOW!

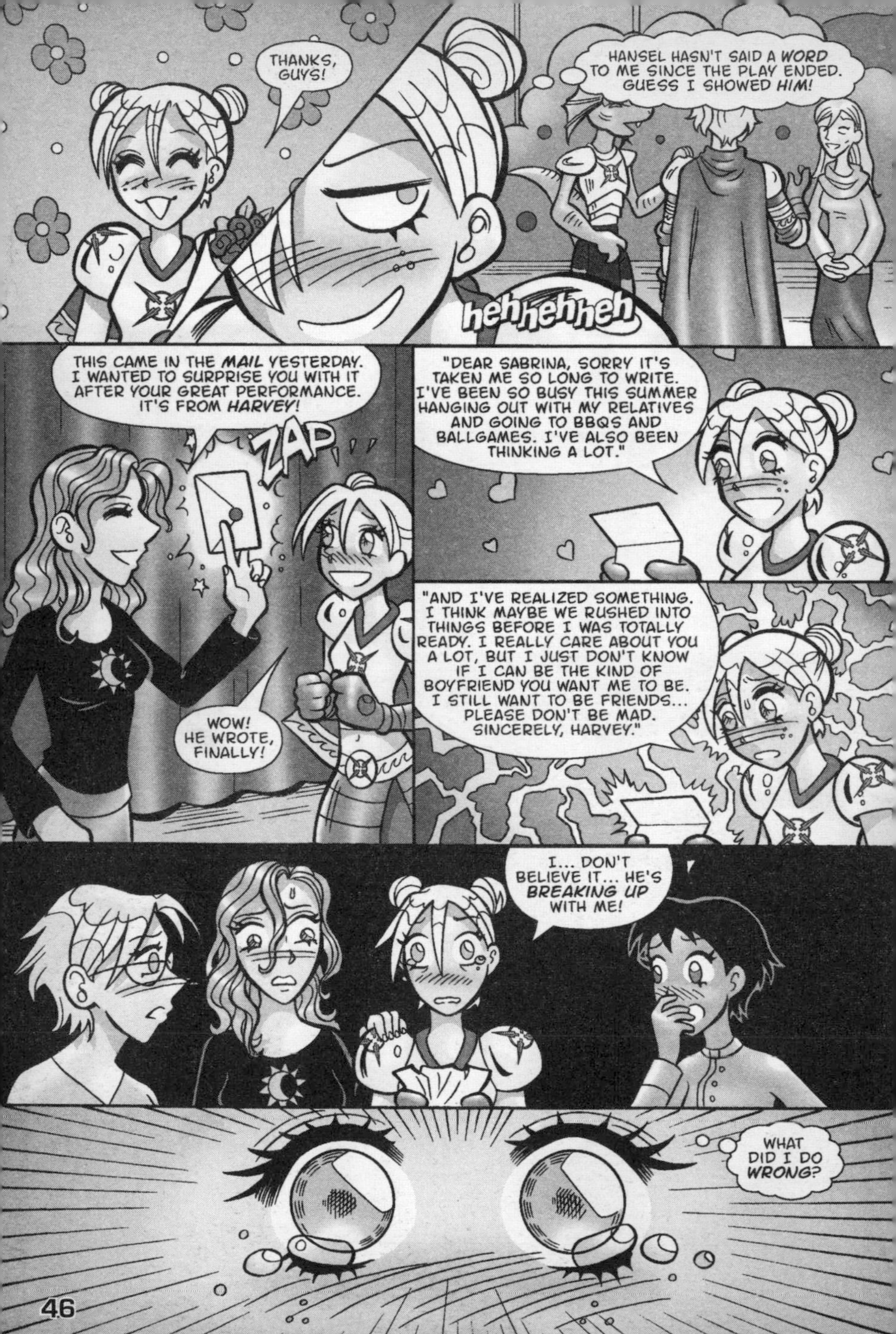
THANKS, GUYS!
HANSEL HASN'T SAID A WORD TO ME SINCE THE PLAY ENDED. GUESS I SHOWED HIM!
heh heh heh
THIS CAME IN THE MAIL YESTERDAY. I WANTED TO SURPRISE YOU WITH IT AFTER YOUR GREAT PERFORMANCE. IT'S FROM HARVEY!
ZAP
WOW! HE WROTE, FINALLY!
"DEAR SABRINA, SORRY IT'S TAKEN ME SO LONG TO WRITE. I'VE BEEN SO BUSY THIS SUMMER HANGING OUT WITH MY RELATIVES AND GOING TO BBQS AND BALLGAMES. I'VE ALSO BEEN THINKING A LOT."
"AND I'VE REALIZED SOMETHING. I THINK MAYBE WE RUSHED INTO THINGS BEFORE I WAS TOTALLY READY. I REALLY CARE ABOUT YOU A LOT, BUT I JUST DON'T KNOW IF I CAN BE THE KIND OF BOYFRIEND YOU WANT ME TO BE. I STILL WANT TO BE FRIENDS... PLEASE DON'T BE MAD. SINCERELY, HARVEY."
I... DON'T BELIEVE IT... HE'S BREAKING UP WITH ME!
WHAT DID I DO WRONG?

Chapter 3

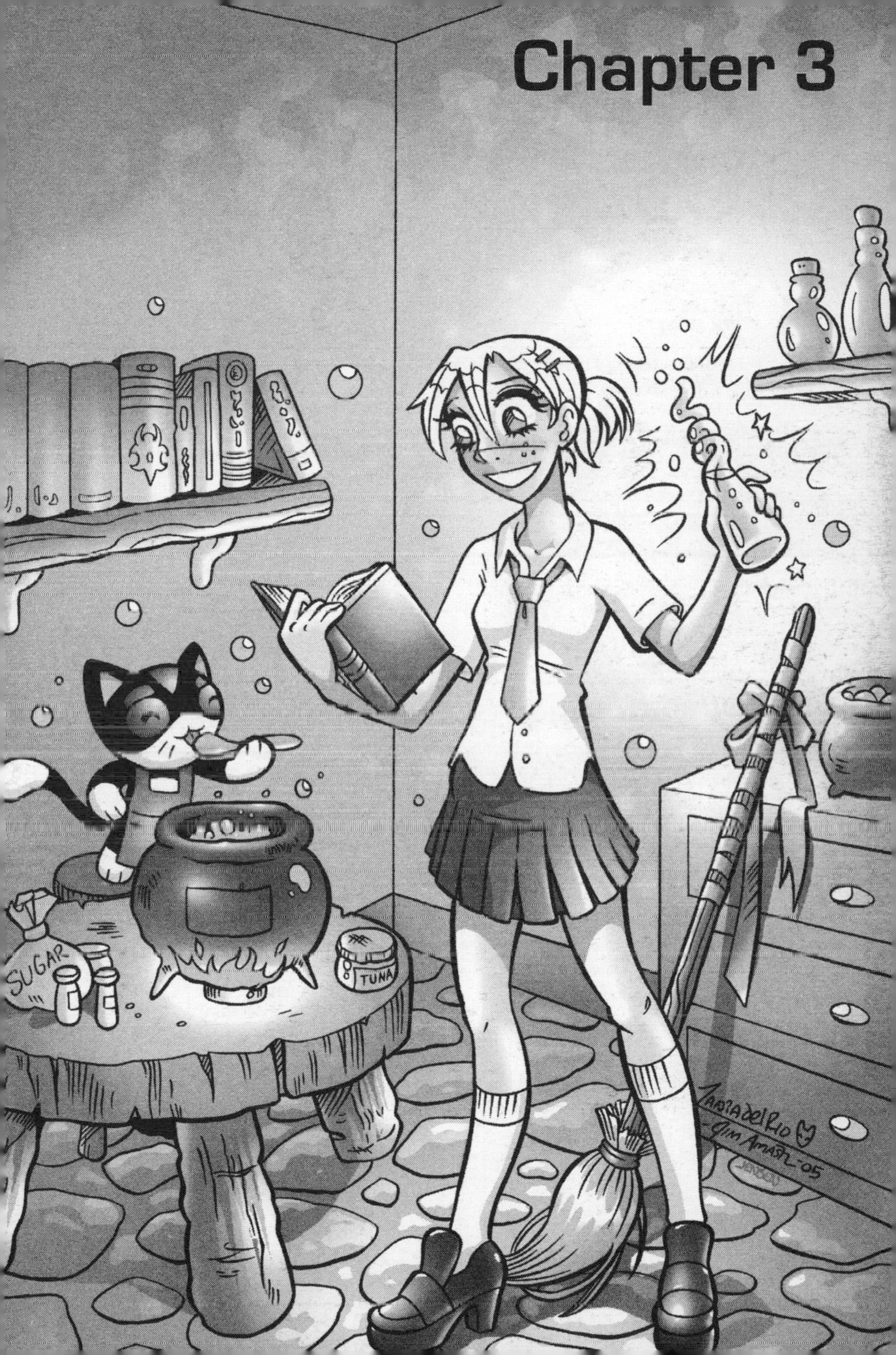
SUGAR
TUNA

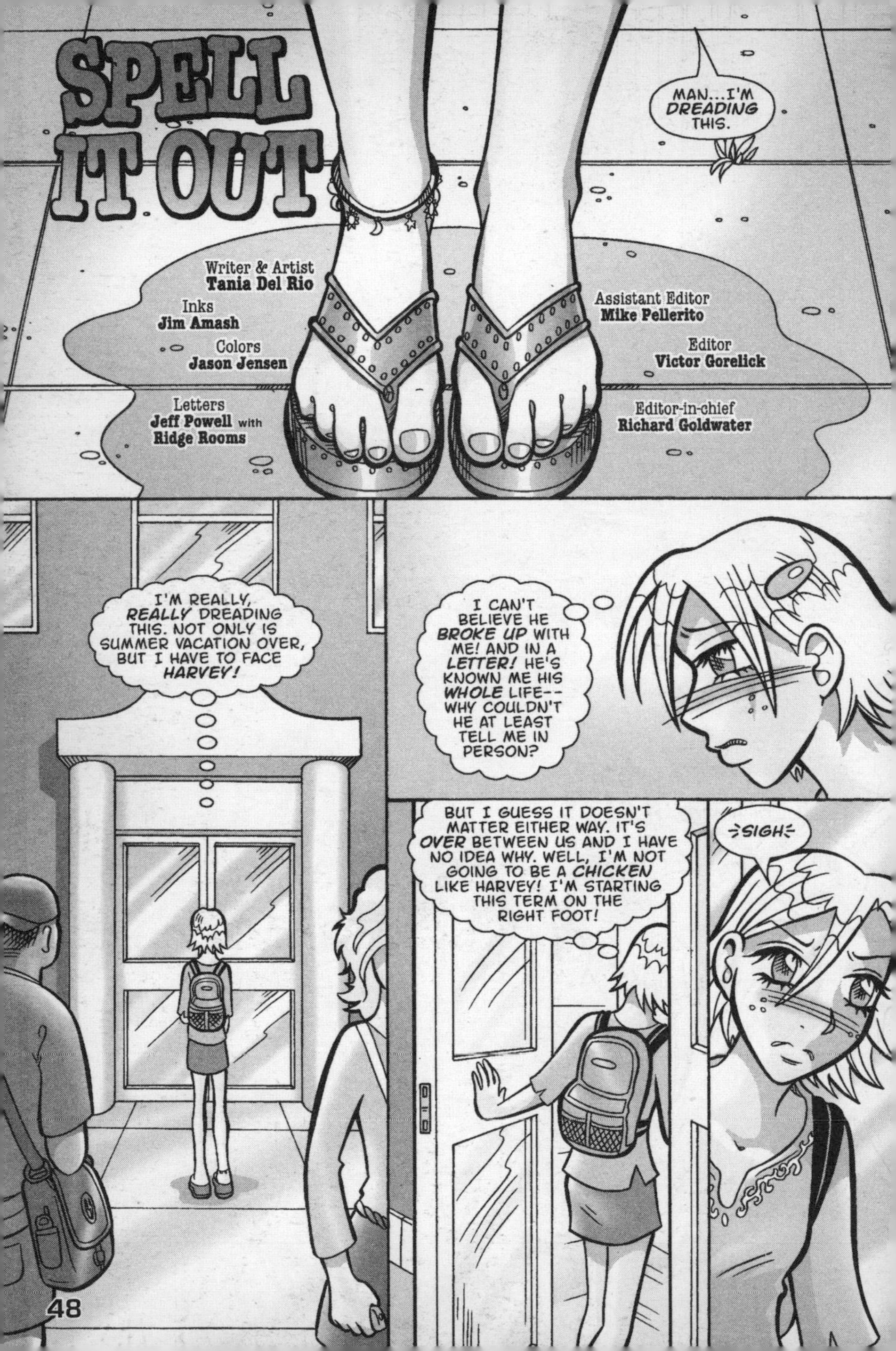
SPELL IT OUT
Writer & Artist Tania Del Rio
Inks Jim Amash
Colors Jason Jensen
Letters Jeff Powell with Ridge Rooms
Assistant Editor Mike Pellerito
Editor Victor Gorelick
Editor-in-chief Richard Goldwater
MAN...I'M DREADING THIS.
I'M REALLY, REALLY DREADING THIS. NOT ONLY IS SUMMER VACATION OVER, BUT I HAVE TO FACE HARVEY!
I CAN'T BELIEVE HE BROKE UP WITH ME! AND IN A LETTER! HE'S KNOWN ME HIS WHOLE LIFE--WHY COULDN'T HE AT LEAST TELL ME IN PERSON?
BUT I GUESS IT DOESN'T MATTER EITHER WAY. IT'S OVER BETWEEN US AND I HAVE NO IDEA WHY. WELL, I'M NOT GOING TO BE A CHICKEN LIKE HARVEY! I'M STARTING THIS TERM ON THE RIGHT FOOT!
SIGH

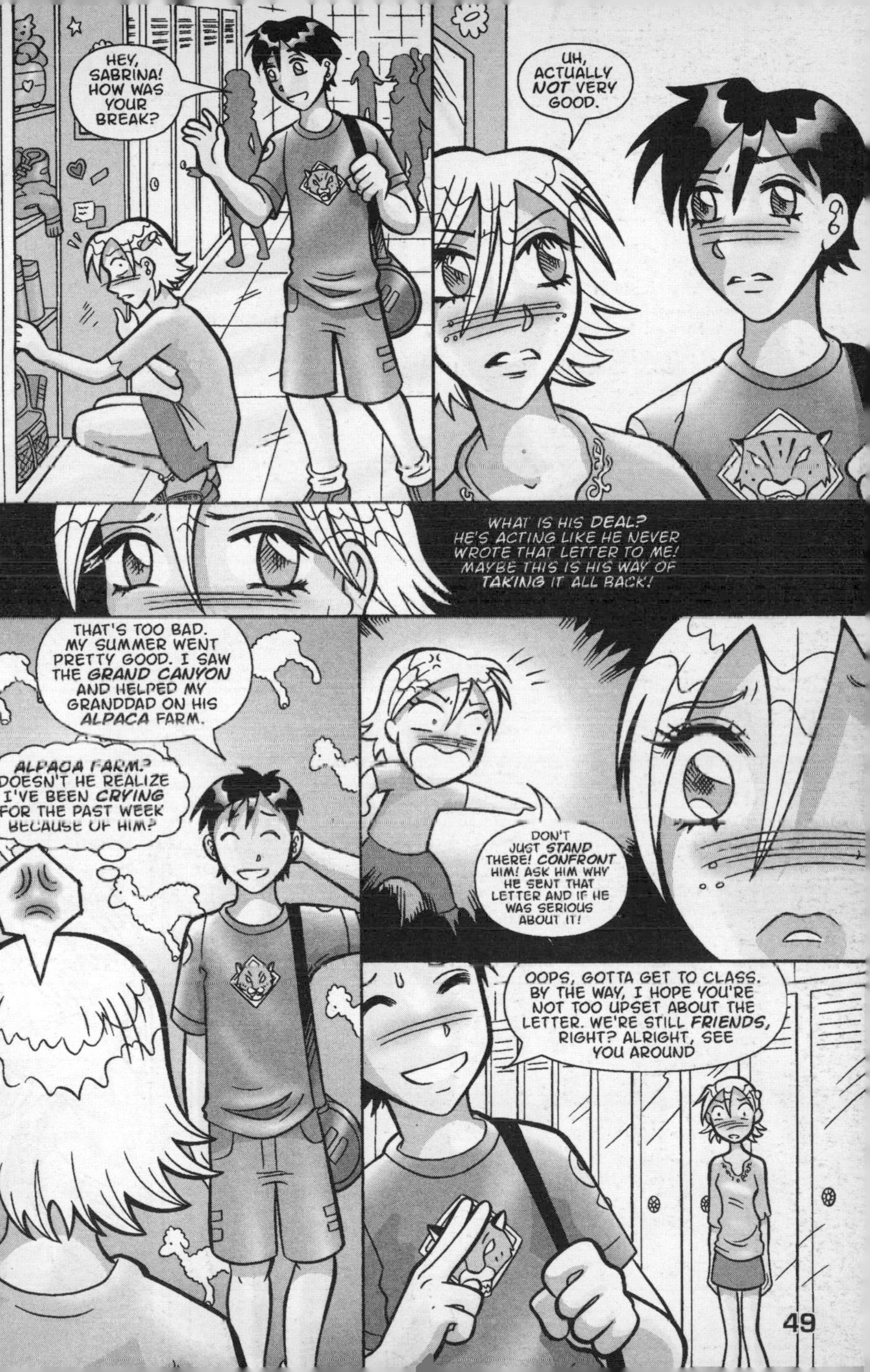
HEY, SABRINA! HOW WAS YOUR BREAK?
UH, ACTUALLY NOT VERY GOOD.
WHAT IS HIS DEAL? HE'S ACTING LIKE HE NEVER WROTE THAT LETTER TO ME! MAYBE THIS IS HIS WAY OF TAKING IT ALL BACK!
THAT'S TOO BAD. MY SUMMER WENT PRETTY GOOD. I SAW THE GRAND CANYON AND HELPED MY GRANDDAD ON HIS ALPACA FARM.
ALPACA FARM? DOESN'T HE REALIZE I'VE BEEN CRYING FOR THE PAST WEEK BECAUSE OF HIM?
DON'T JUST STAND THERE! CONFRONT HIM! ASK HIM WHY HE SENT THAT LETTER AND IF HE WAS SERIOUS ABOUT IT!
OOPS, GOTTA GET TO CLASS. BY THE WAY, I HOPE YOU'RE NOT TOO UPSET ABOUT THE LETTER. WE'RE STILL FRIENDS, RIGHT? ALRIGHT, SEE YOU AROUND

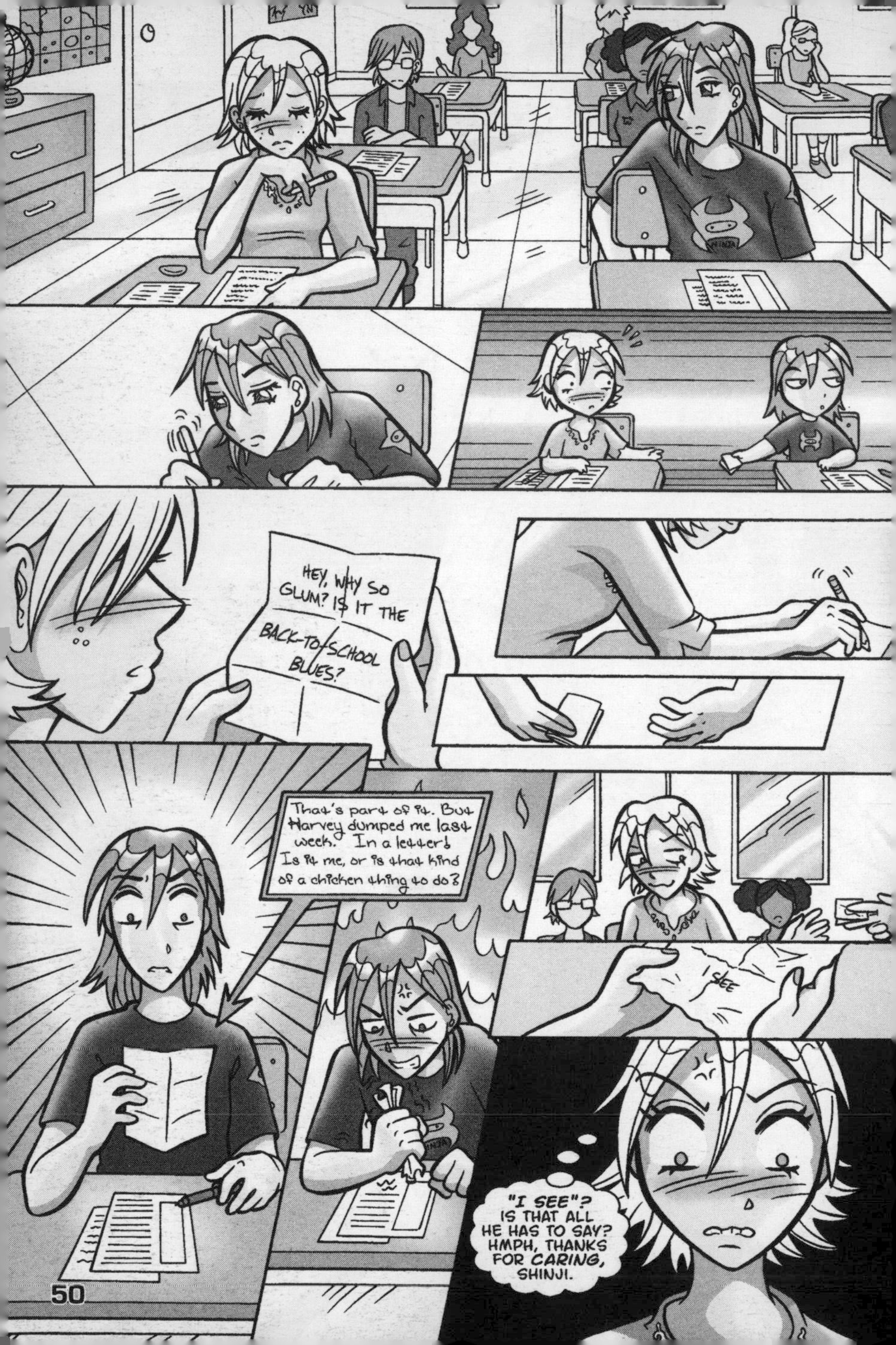
HEY, WHY SO GLUM? IS IT THE BACK-TO-SCHOOL BLUES?
That's part of it. But Harvey dumped me last week. In a letter! Is it me, or is that kind of a chicken thing to do?
SEE
"I SEE"? IS THAT ALL HE HAS TO SAY? HMPH, THANKS FOR CARING, SHINJI.

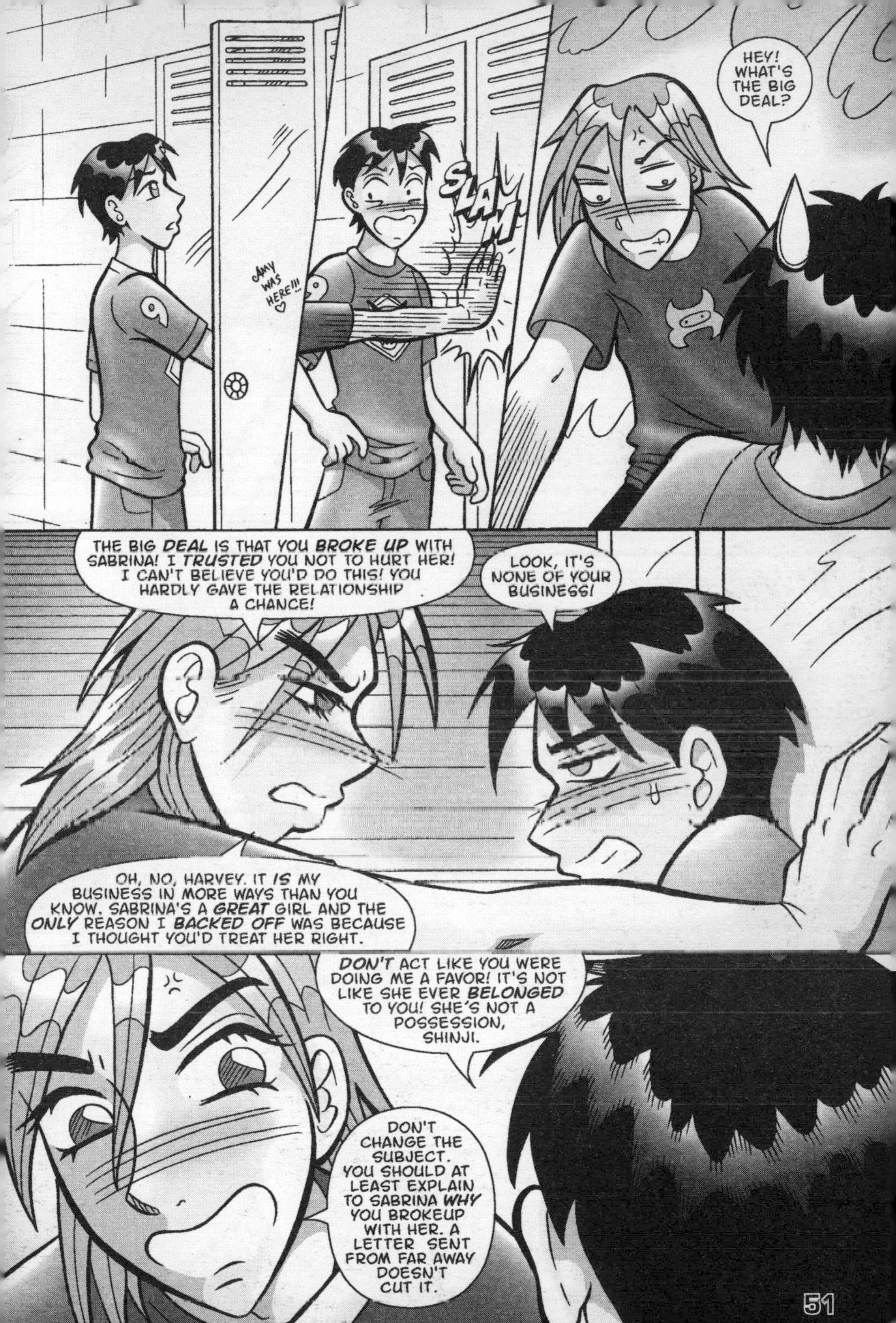
AMY WAS HERE!!! ♡
SLAM
HEY! WHAT'S THE BIG DEAL?
THE BIG *DEAL* IS THAT YOU *BROKE UP* WITH SABRINA! I *TRUSTED* YOU NOT TO HURT HER! I CAN'T BELIEVE YOU'D DO THIS! YOU HARDLY GAVE THE RELATIONSHIP A CHANCE!
LOOK, IT'S NONE OF YOUR BUSINESS!
OH, NO, HARVEY. IT *IS* MY BUSINESS IN MORE WAYS THAN YOU KNOW. SABRINA'S A *GREAT* GIRL AND THE *ONLY* REASON I *BACKED OFF* WAS BECAUSE I THOUGHT YOU'D TREAT HER RIGHT.
DON'T ACT LIKE YOU WERE DOING ME A FAVOR! IT'S NOT LIKE SHE EVER *BELONGED* TO YOU! SHE'S NOT A POSSESSION, SHINJI.
DON'T CHANGE THE SUBJECT. YOU SHOULD AT LEAST EXPLAIN TO SABRINA *WHY* YOU BROKEUP WITH HER. A LETTER SENT FROM FAR AWAY DOESN'T CUT IT.

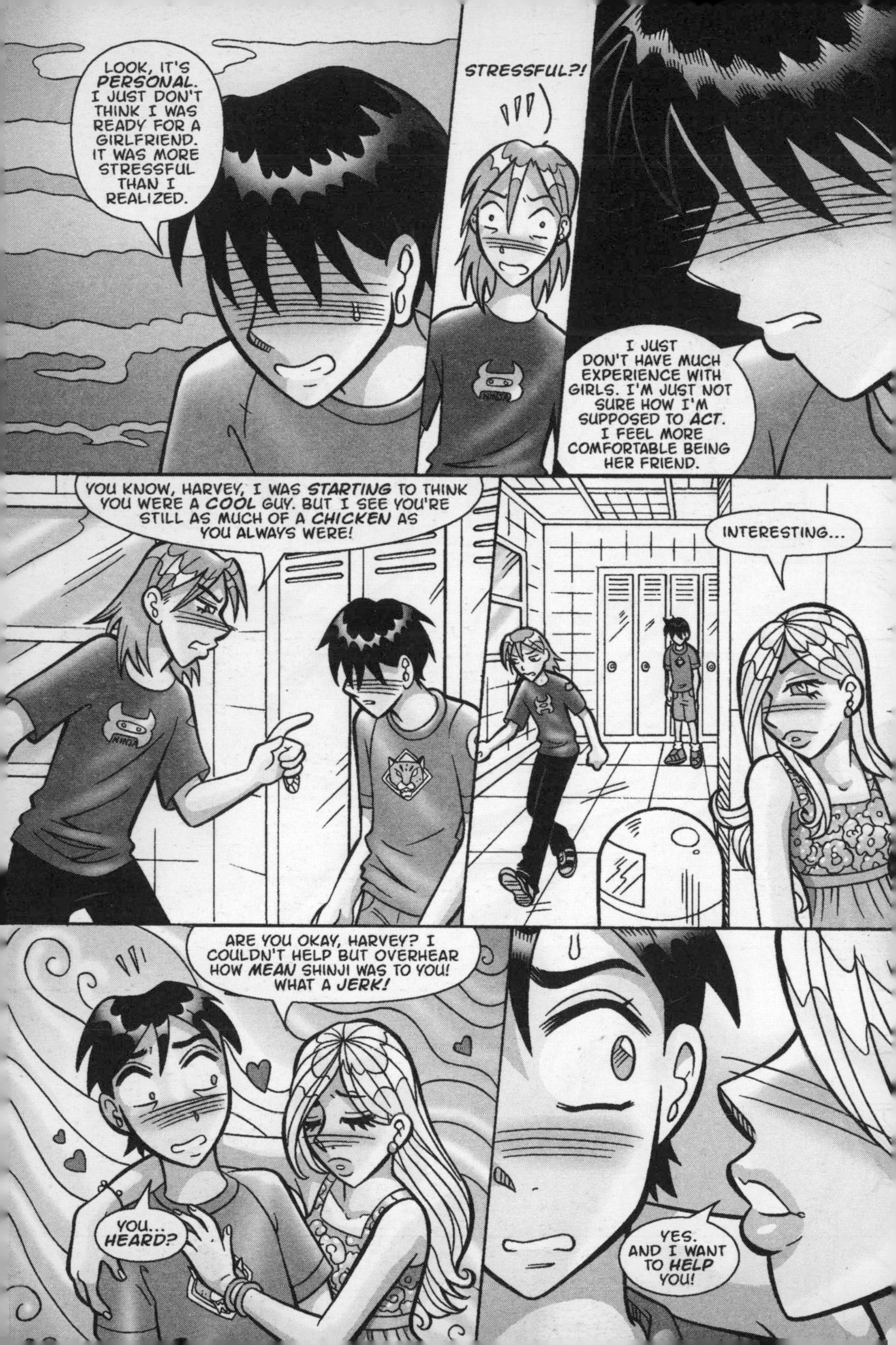
LOOK, IT'S PERSONAL. I JUST DON'T THINK I WAS READY FOR A GIRLFRIEND. IT WAS MORE STRESSFUL THAN I REALIZED.
STRESSFUL?!
I JUST DON'T HAVE MUCH EXPERIENCE WITH GIRLS. I'M JUST NOT SURE HOW I'M SUPPOSED TO ACT. I FEEL MORE COMFORTABLE BEING HER FRIEND.
YOU KNOW, HARVEY, I WAS STARTING TO THINK YOU WERE A COOL GUY. BUT I SEE YOU'RE STILL AS MUCH OF A CHICKEN AS YOU ALWAYS WERE!
INTERESTING...
ARE YOU OKAY, HARVEY? I COULDN'T HELP BUT OVERHEAR HOW MEAN SHINJI WAS TO YOU! WHAT A JERK!
YOU... HEARD?
YES. AND I WANT TO HELP YOU!

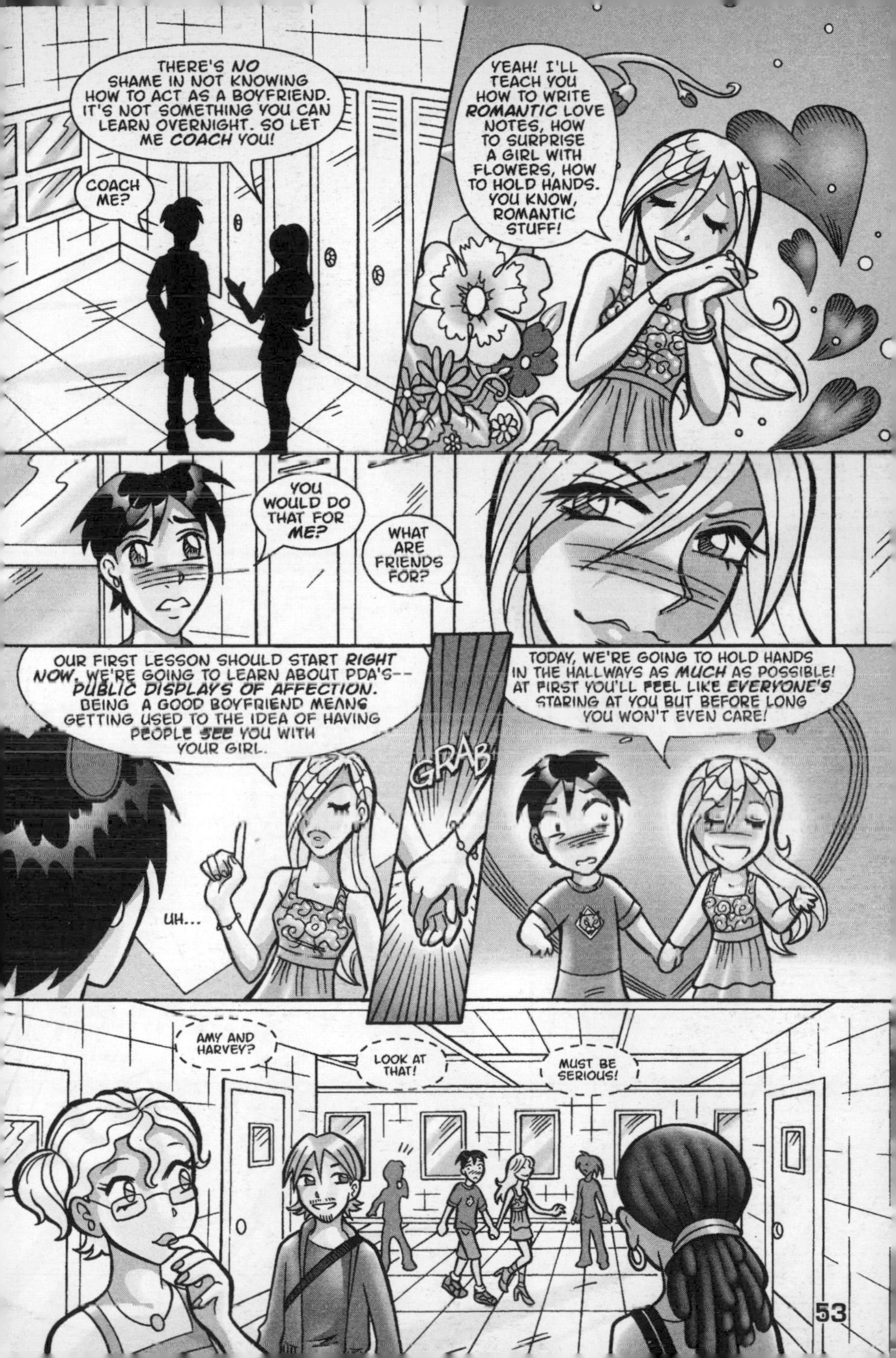
THERE'S NO SHAME IN NOT KNOWING HOW TO ACT AS A BOYFRIEND. IT'S NOT SOMETHING YOU CAN LEARN OVERNIGHT. SO LET ME COACH YOU!
COACH ME?
YEAH! I'LL TEACH YOU HOW TO WRITE ROMANTIC LOVE NOTES, HOW TO SURPRISE A GIRL WITH FLOWERS, HOW TO HOLD HANDS. YOU KNOW, ROMANTIC STUFF!
YOU WOULD DO THAT FOR ME?
WHAT ARE FRIENDS FOR?
OUR FIRST LESSON SHOULD START RIGHT NOW. WE'RE GOING TO LEARN ABOUT PDA'S-- PUBLIC DISPLAYS OF AFFECTION. BEING A GOOD BOYFRIEND MEANS GETTING USED TO THE IDEA OF HAVING PEOPLE SEE YOU WITH YOUR GIRL.
UH...
GRAB
TODAY, WE'RE GOING TO HOLD HANDS IN THE HALLWAYS AS MUCH AS POSSIBLE! AT FIRST YOU'LL FEEL LIKE EVERYONE'S STARING AT YOU BUT BEFORE LONG YOU WON'T EVEN CARE!
AMY AND HARVEY?
LOOK AT THAT!
MUST BE SERIOUS!

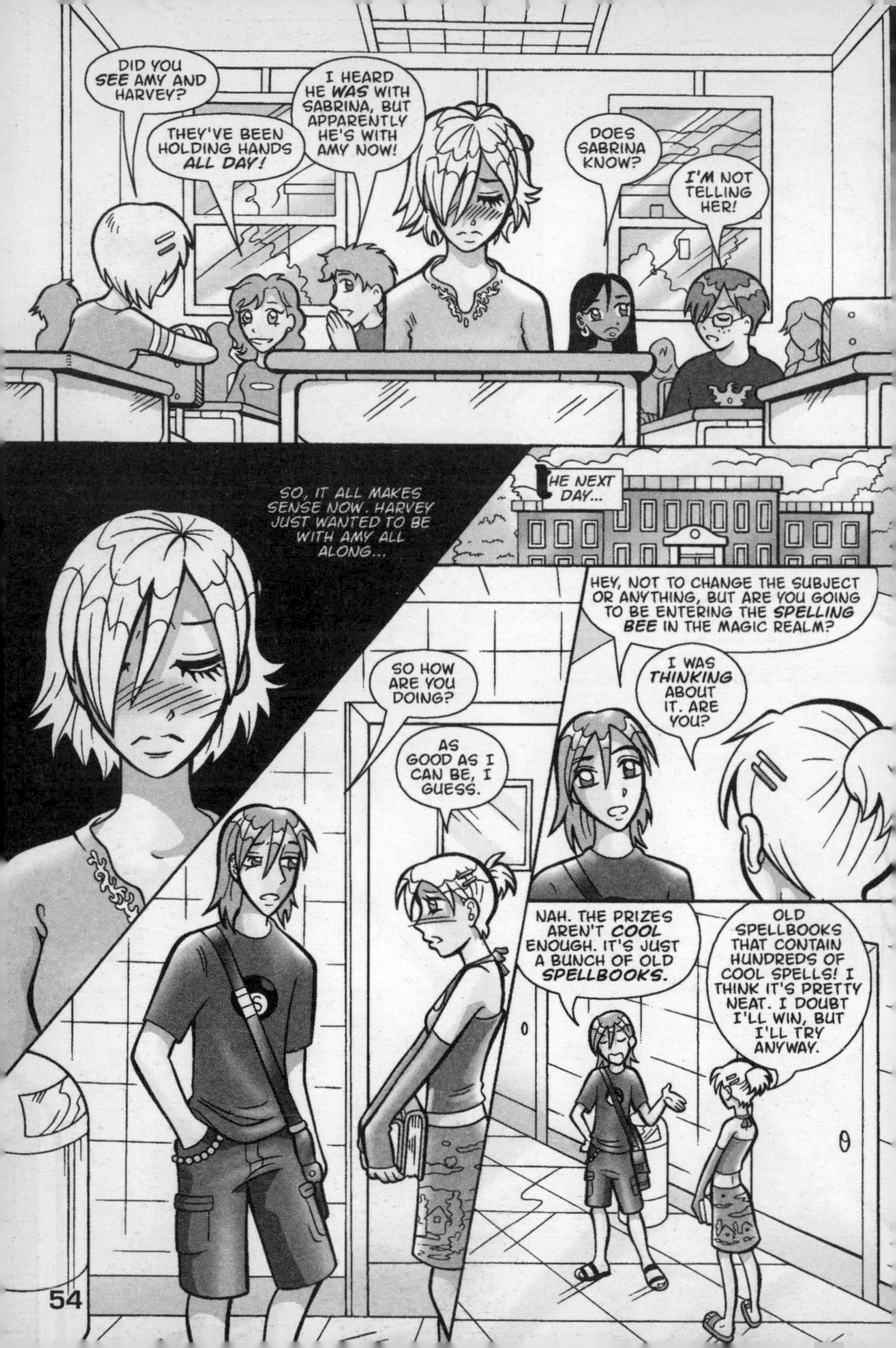
DID YOU SEE AMY AND HARVEY?
THEY'VE BEEN HOLDING HANDS ALL DAY!
I HEARD HE WAS WITH SABRINA, BUT APPARENTLY HE'S WITH AMY NOW!
DOES SABRINA KNOW?
I'M NOT TELLING HER!
SO, IT ALL MAKES SENSE NOW. HARVEY JUST WANTED TO BE WITH AMY ALL ALONG...
THE NEXT DAY...
SO HOW ARE YOU DOING?
AS GOOD AS I CAN BE, I GUESS.
HEY, NOT TO CHANGE THE SUBJECT OR ANYTHING, BUT ARE YOU GOING TO BE ENTERING THE SPELLING BEE IN THE MAGIC REALM?
I WAS THINKING ABOUT IT. ARE YOU?
NAH. THE PRIZES AREN'T COOL ENOUGH. IT'S JUST A BUNCH OF OLD SPELLBOOKS.
OLD SPELLBOOKS THAT CONTAIN HUNDREDS OF COOL SPELLS! I THINK IT'S PRETTY NEAT. I DOUBT I'LL WIN, BUT I'LL TRY ANYWAY.

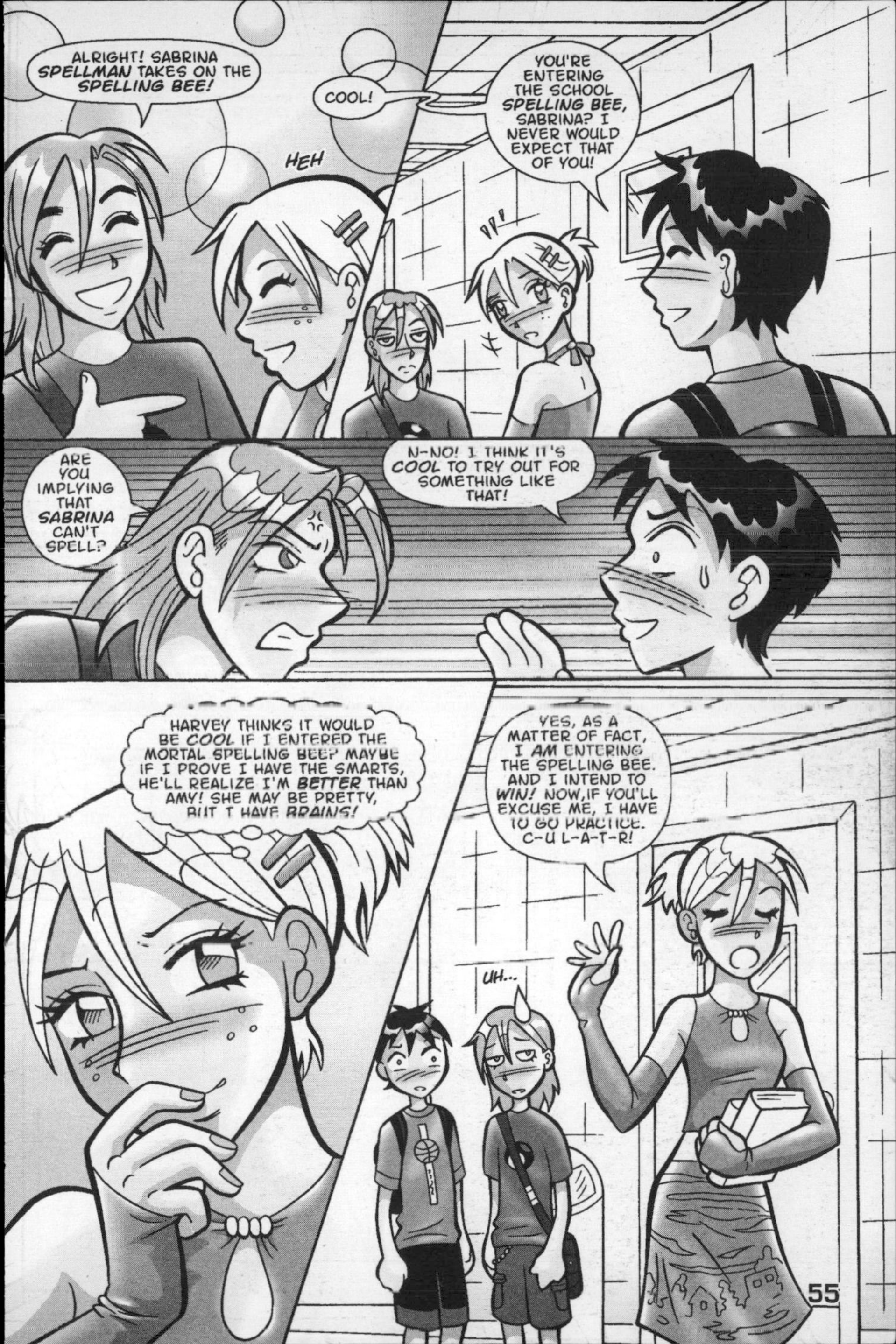
ALRIGHT! SABRINA SPELLMAN TAKES ON THE SPELLING BEE!
COOL!
HEH
YOU'RE ENTERING THE SCHOOL SPELLING BEE, SABRINA? I NEVER WOULD EXPECT THAT OF YOU!
ARE YOU IMPLYING THAT SABRINA CAN'T SPELL?
N-NO! I THINK IT'S COOL TO TRY OUT FOR SOMETHING LIKE THAT!
HARVEY THINKS IT WOULD BE COOL IF I ENTERED THE MORTAL SPELLING BEE? MAYBE IF I PROVE I HAVE THE SMARTS, HE'LL REALIZE I'M BETTER THAN AMY! SHE MAY BE PRETTY, BUT I HAVE BRAINS!
YES, AS A MATTER OF FACT, I AM ENTERING THE SPELLING BEE. AND I INTEND TO WIN! NOW, IF YOU'LL EXCUSE ME, I HAVE TO GO PRACTICE. C-U L-A-T-R!
UH...

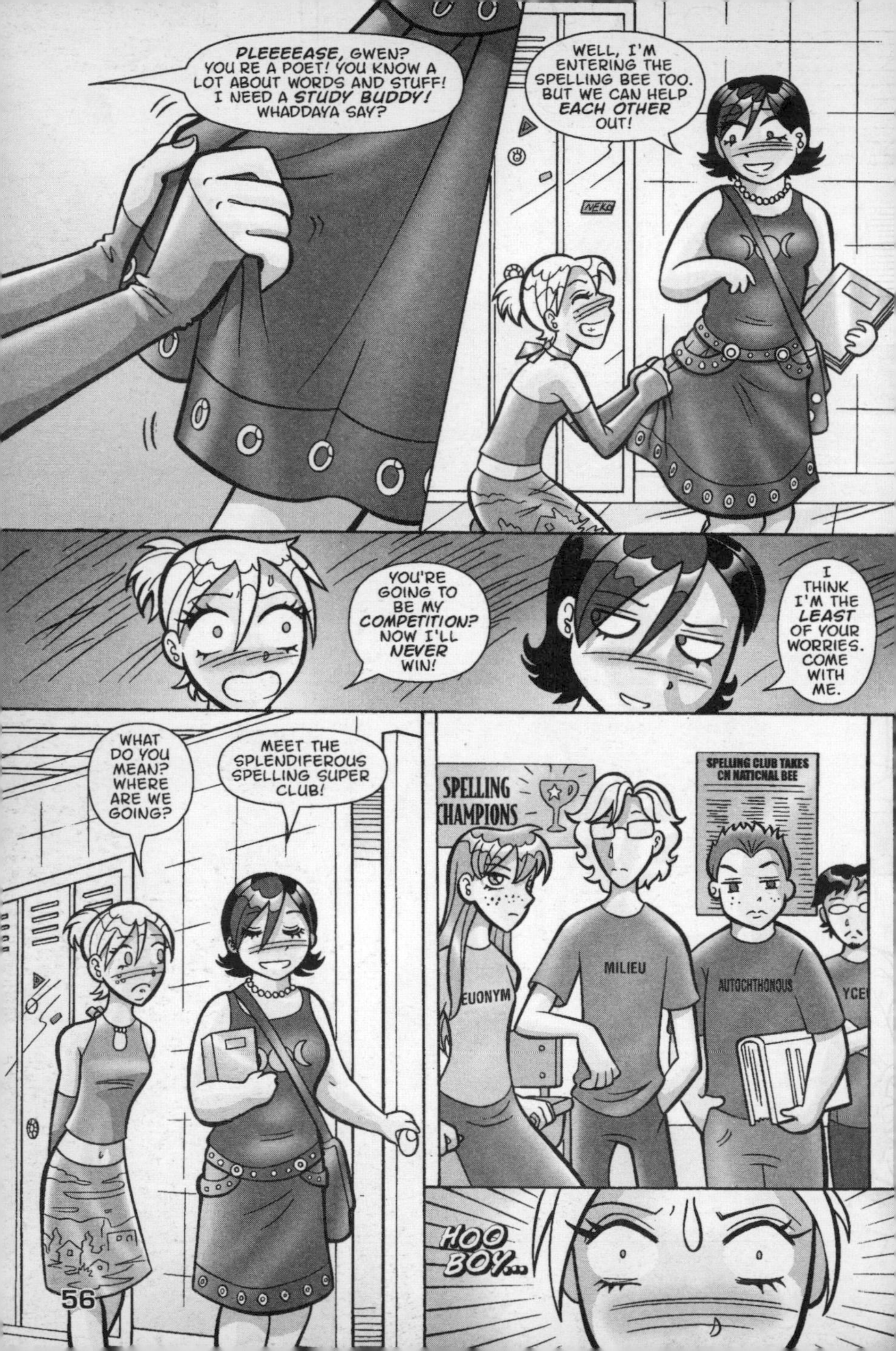
PLEEEEASE, GWEN? YOU'RE A POET! YOU KNOW A LOT ABOUT WORDS AND STUFF! I NEED A STUDY BUDDY! WHADDAYA SAY?
WELL, I'M ENTERING THE SPELLING BEE TOO. BUT WE CAN HELP EACH OTHER OUT!
NEKO
YOU'RE GOING TO BE MY COMPETITION? NOW I'LL NEVER WIN!
I THINK I'M THE LEAST OF YOUR WORRIES. COME WITH ME.
WHAT DO YOU MEAN? WHERE ARE WE GOING?
MEET THE SPLENDIFEROUS SPELLING SUPER CLUB!
SPELLING CHAMPIONS
SPELLING CLUB TAKES CN NATICNAL BEE
EUONYM
MILIEU
AUTOCHTHONOUS
HOO BOY...

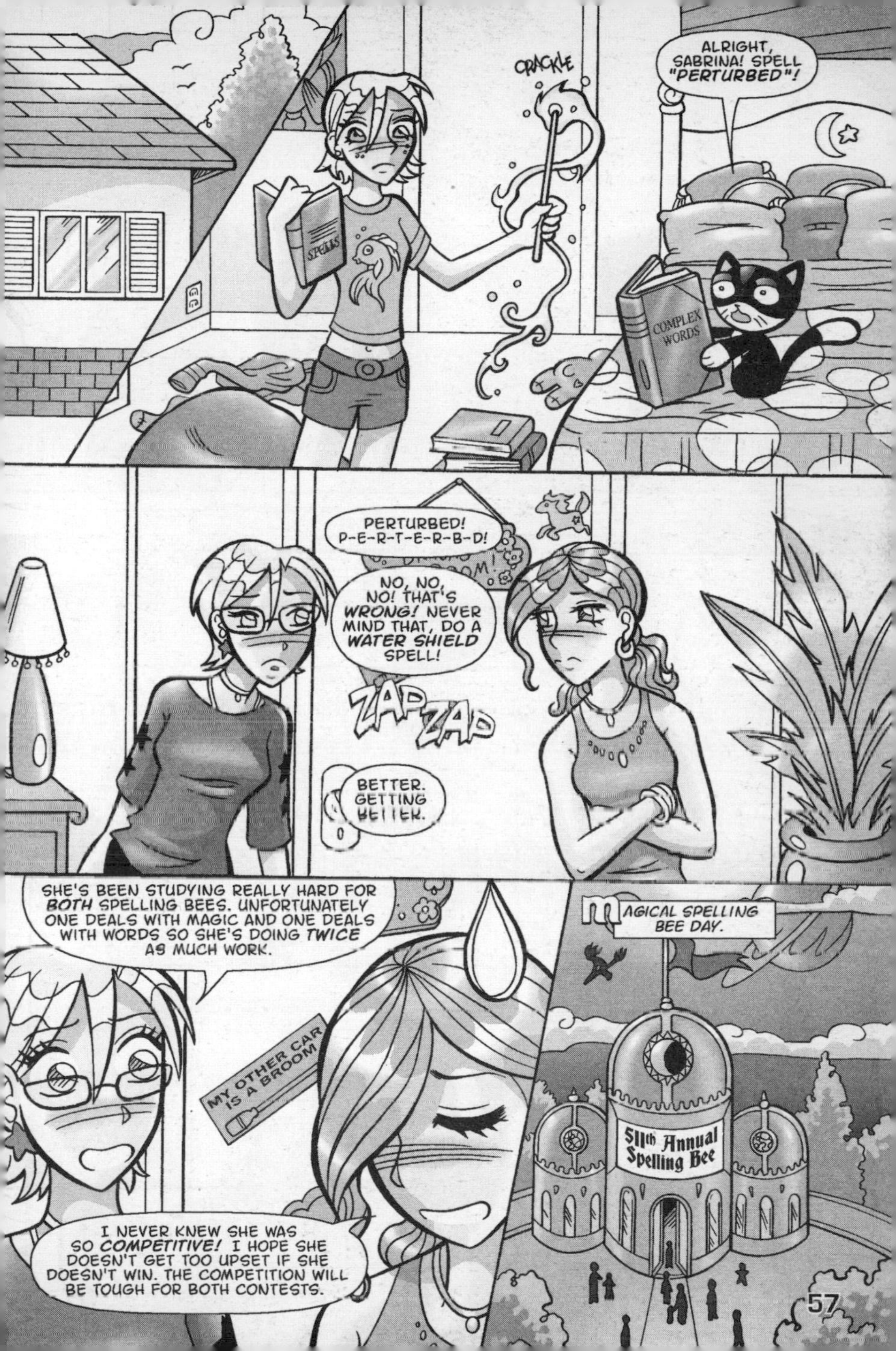

CRACKLE
SPELLS
ALRIGHT, SABRINA! SPELL "PERTURBED"!
COMPLEX WORDS
PERTURBED! P-E-R-T-E-R-B-D!
NO, NO, NO! THAT'S WRONG! NEVER MIND THAT, DO A WATER SHIELD SPELL!
ZAP ZAP
BETTER. GETTING BETTER.
SHE'S BEEN STUDYING REALLY HARD FOR BOTH SPELLING BEES. UNFORTUNATELY ONE DEALS WITH MAGIC AND ONE DEALS WITH WORDS SO SHE'S DOING TWICE AS MUCH WORK.
MY OTHER CAR IS A BROOM
I NEVER KNEW SHE WAS SO COMPETITIVE! I HOPE SHE DOESN'T GET TOO UPSET IF SHE DOESN'T WIN. THE COMPETITION WILL BE TOUGH FOR BOTH CONTESTS.
MAGICAL SPELLING BEE DAY.
511th Annual Spelling Bee

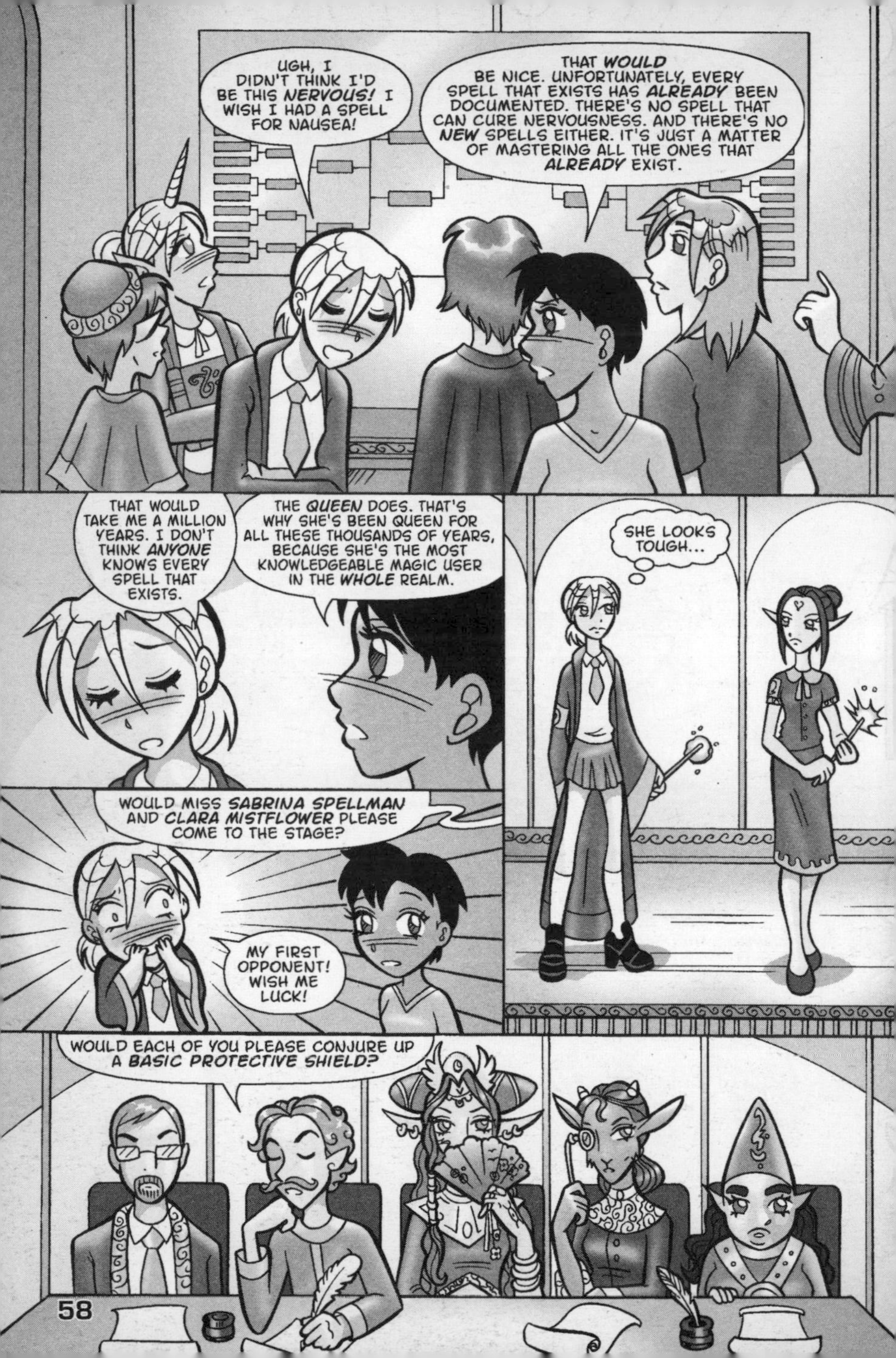
UGH, I DIDN'T THINK I'D BE THIS NERVOUS! I WISH I HAD A SPELL FOR NAUSEA!
THAT WOULD BE NICE. UNFORTUNATELY, EVERY SPELL THAT EXISTS HAS ALREADY BEEN DOCUMENTED. THERE'S NO SPELL THAT CAN CURE NERVOUSNESS. AND THERE'S NO NEW SPELLS EITHER. IT'S JUST A MATTER OF MASTERING ALL THE ONES THAT ALREADY EXIST.
THAT WOULD TAKE ME A MILLION YEARS. I DON'T THINK ANYONE KNOWS EVERY SPELL THAT EXISTS.
THE QUEEN DOES. THAT'S WHY SHE'S BEEN QUEEN FOR ALL THESE THOUSANDS OF YEARS, BECAUSE SHE'S THE MOST KNOWLEDGEABLE MAGIC USER IN THE WHOLE REALM.
WOULD MISS SABRINA SPELLMAN AND CLARA MISTFLOWER PLEASE COME TO THE STAGE?
MY FIRST OPPONENT! WISH ME LUCK!
SHE LOOKS TOUGH...
WOULD EACH OF YOU PLEASE CONJURE UP A BASIC PROTECTIVE SHIELD?

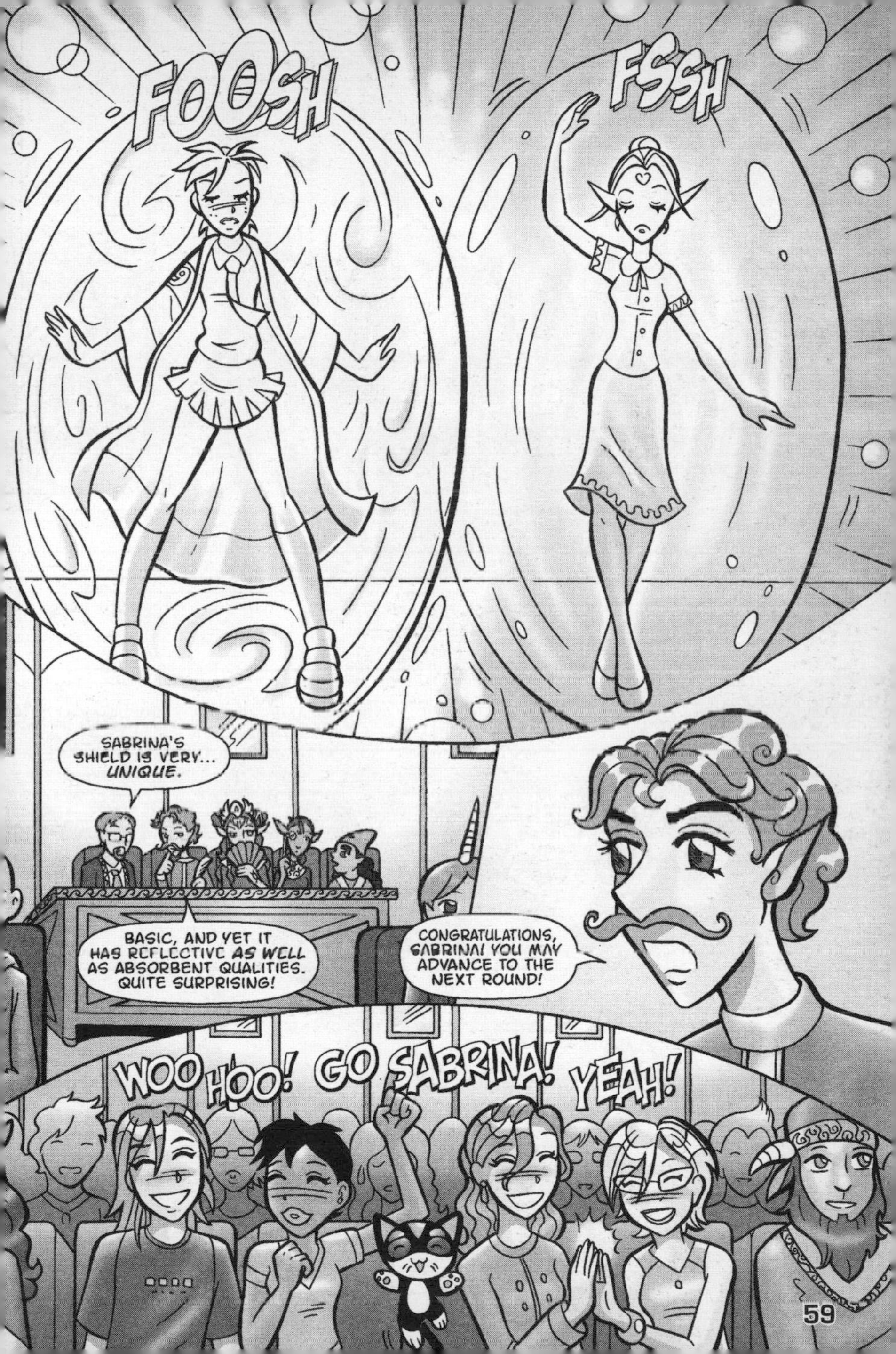
FOOSH
FSSH
SABRINA'S SHIELD IS VERY... UNIQUE.
BASIC, AND YET IT HAS REFLECTIVE AS WELL AS ABSORBENT QUALITIES. QUITE SURPRISING!
CONGRATULATIONS, SABRINA! YOU MAY ADVANCE TO THE NEXT ROUND!
WOO HOO! GO SABRINA! YEAH!

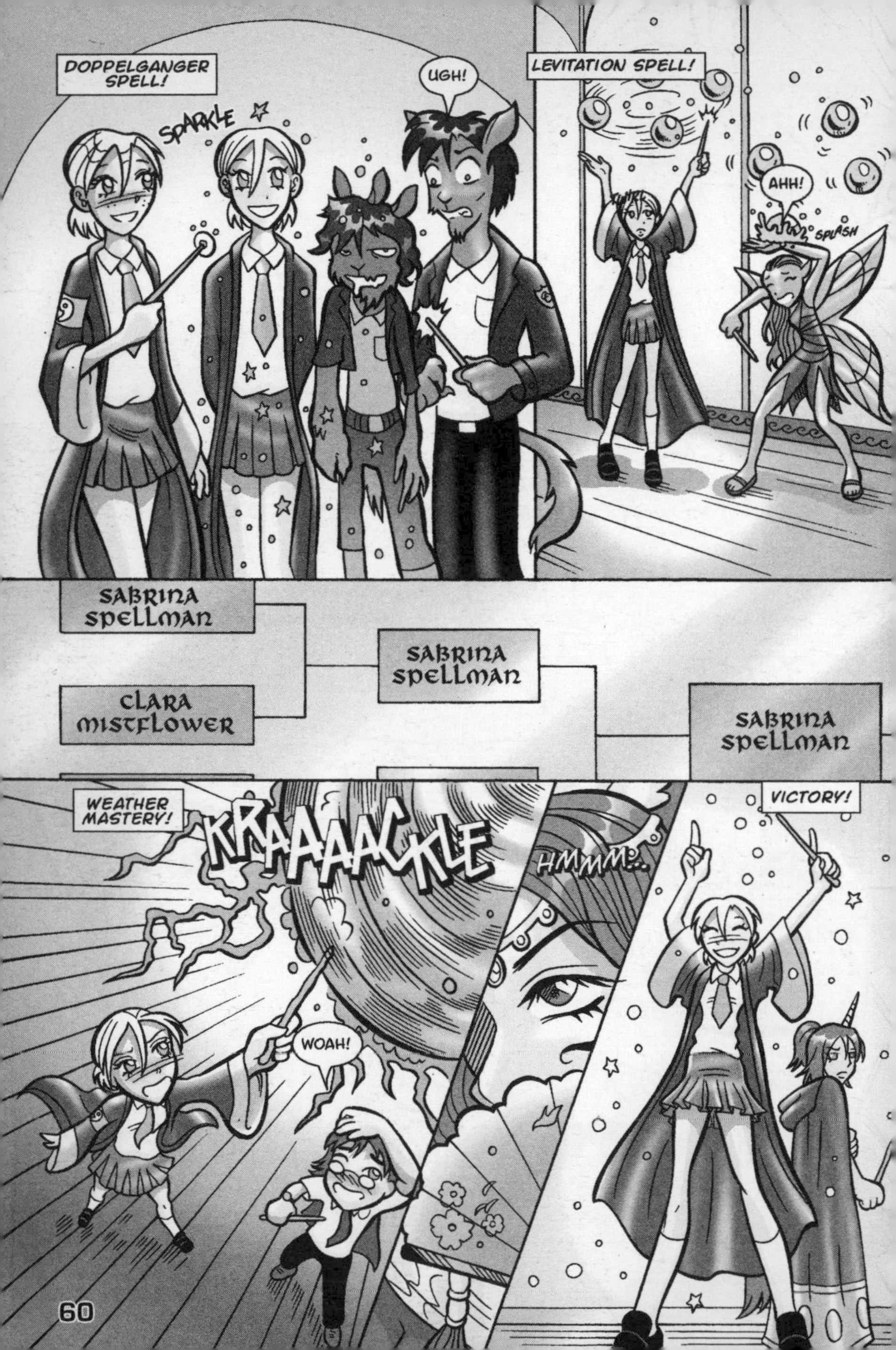
DOPPELGANGER SPELL!
SPARKLE
UGH!
LEVITATION SPELL!
AHH!
SPLASH
SABRINA SPELLMAN
CLARA MISTFLOWER
SABRINA SPELLMAN
SABRINA SPELLMAN
WEATHER MASTERY!
KRAAAAACKLE
WOAH!
HMMM...
VICTORY!

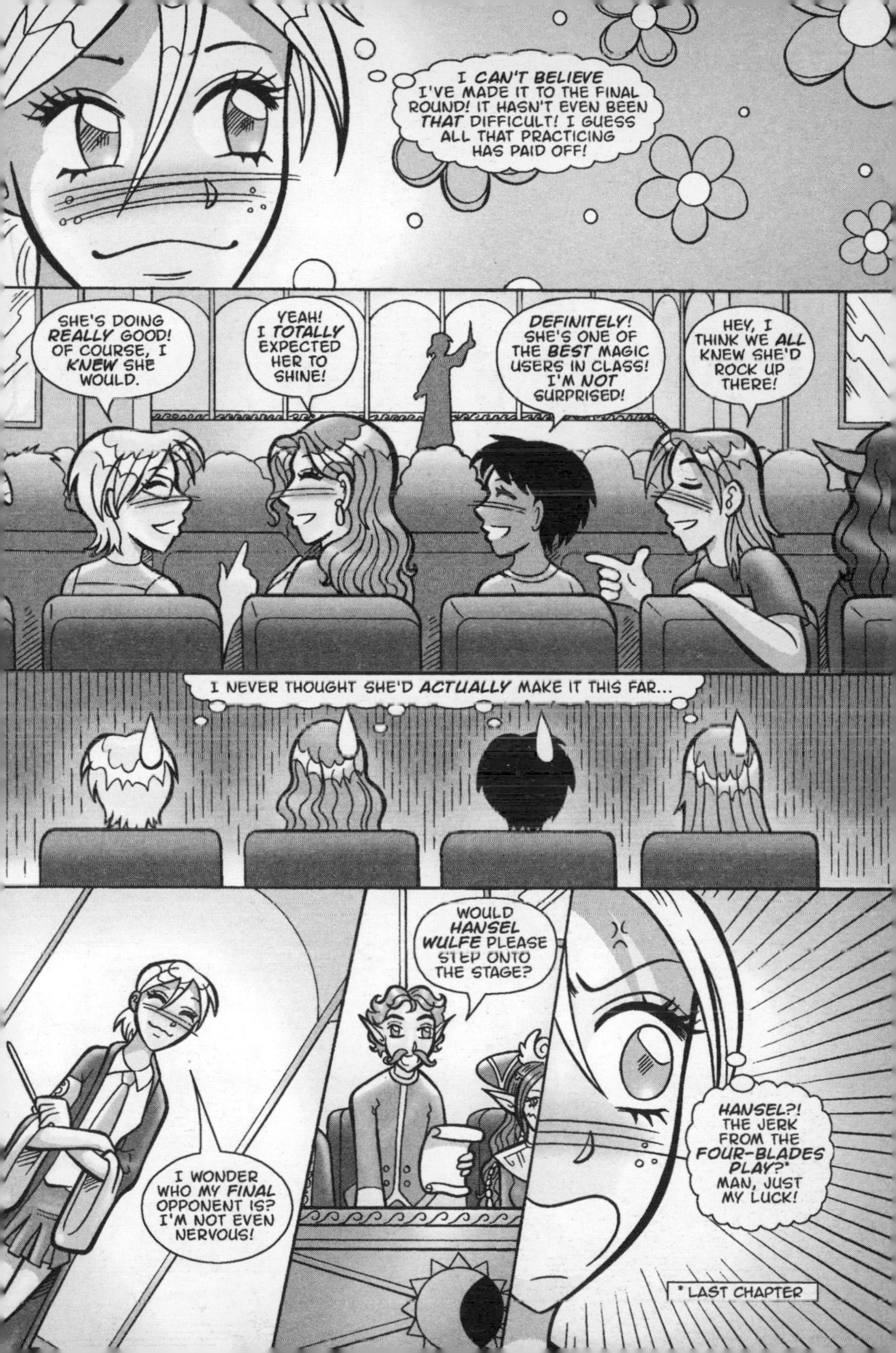
I CAN'T BELIEVE I'VE MADE IT TO THE FINAL ROUND! IT HASN'T EVEN BEEN THAT DIFFICULT! I GUESS ALL THAT PRACTICING HAS PAID OFF!
SHE'S DOING REALLY GOOD! OF COURSE, I KNEW SHE WOULD.
YEAH! I TOTALLY EXPECTED HER TO SHINE!
DEFINITELY! SHE'S ONE OF THE BEST MAGIC USERS IN CLASS! I'M NOT SURPRISED!
HEY, I THINK WE ALL KNEW SHE'D ROCK UP THERE!
I NEVER THOUGHT SHE'D ACTUALLY MAKE IT THIS FAR...
I WONDER WHO MY FINAL OPPONENT IS? I'M NOT EVEN NERVOUS!
WOULD HANSEL WULFE PLEASE STEP ONTO THE STAGE?
HANSEL?! THE JERK FROM THE FOUR-BLADES PLAY?* MAN, JUST MY LUCK!
* LAST CHAPTER

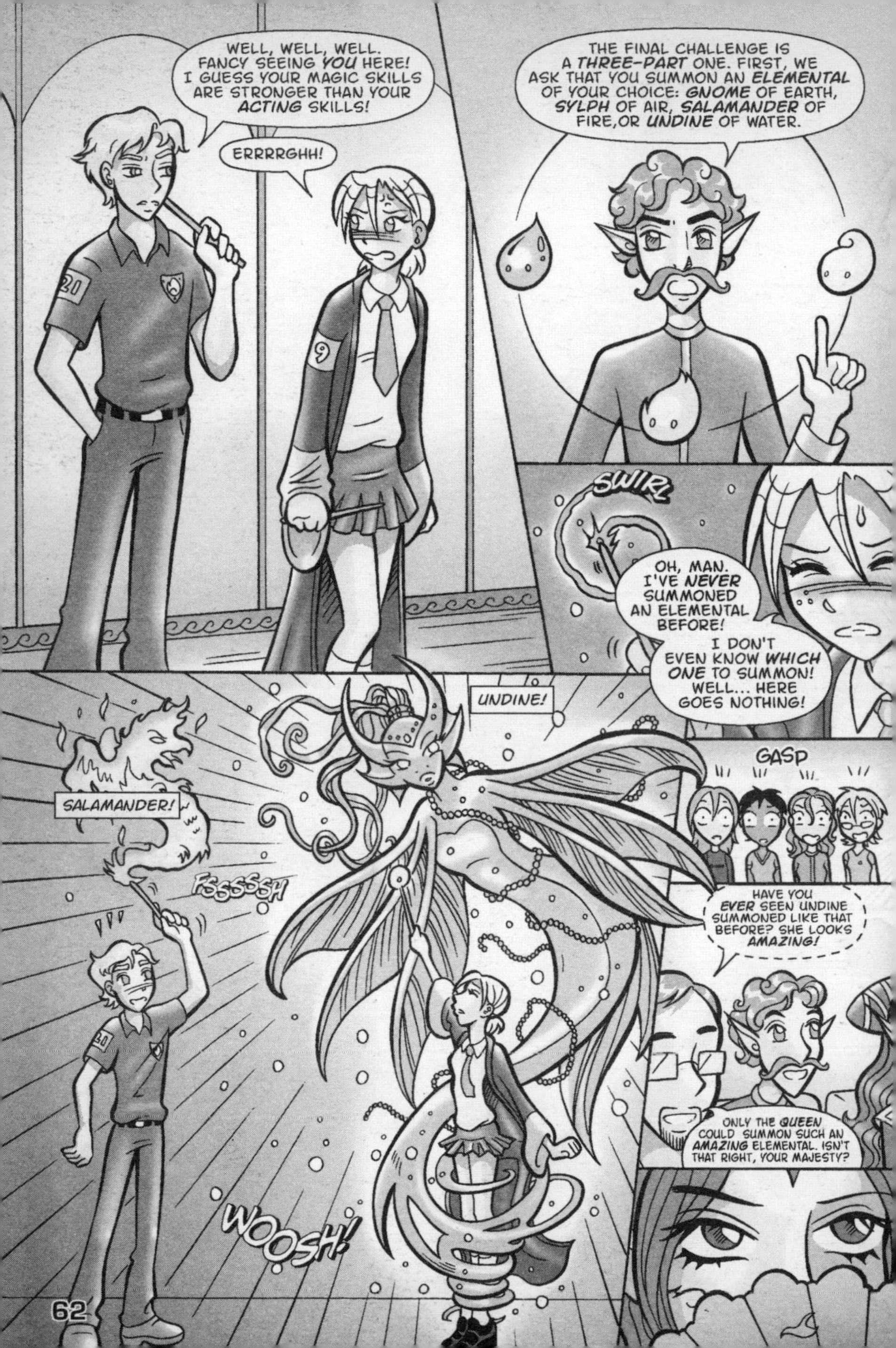

WELL, WELL, WELL. FANCY SEEING *YOU* HERE! I GUESS YOUR MAGIC SKILLS ARE STRONGER THAN YOUR *ACTING* SKILLS!
ERRRRGHH!
THE FINAL CHALLENGE IS A *THREE-PART* ONE. FIRST, WE ASK THAT YOU SUMMON AN *ELEMENTAL* OF YOUR CHOICE: *GNOME* OF EARTH, *SYLPH* OF AIR, *SALAMANDER* OF FIRE,OR *UNDINE* OF WATER.
SWIRL
OH, MAN. I'VE *NEVER* SUMMONED AN ELEMENTAL BEFORE!
I DON'T EVEN KNOW *WHICH ONE* TO SUMMON! WELL... HERE GOES NOTHING!
SALAMANDER!
FSSSSSH
UNDINE!
WOOSH!
GASP
HAVE YOU *EVER* SEEN UNDINE SUMMONED LIKE THAT BEFORE? SHE LOOKS *AMAZING!*
ONLY THE *QUEEN* COULD SUMMON SUCH AN *AMAZING* ELEMENTAL. ISN'T THAT RIGHT, YOUR MAJESTY?

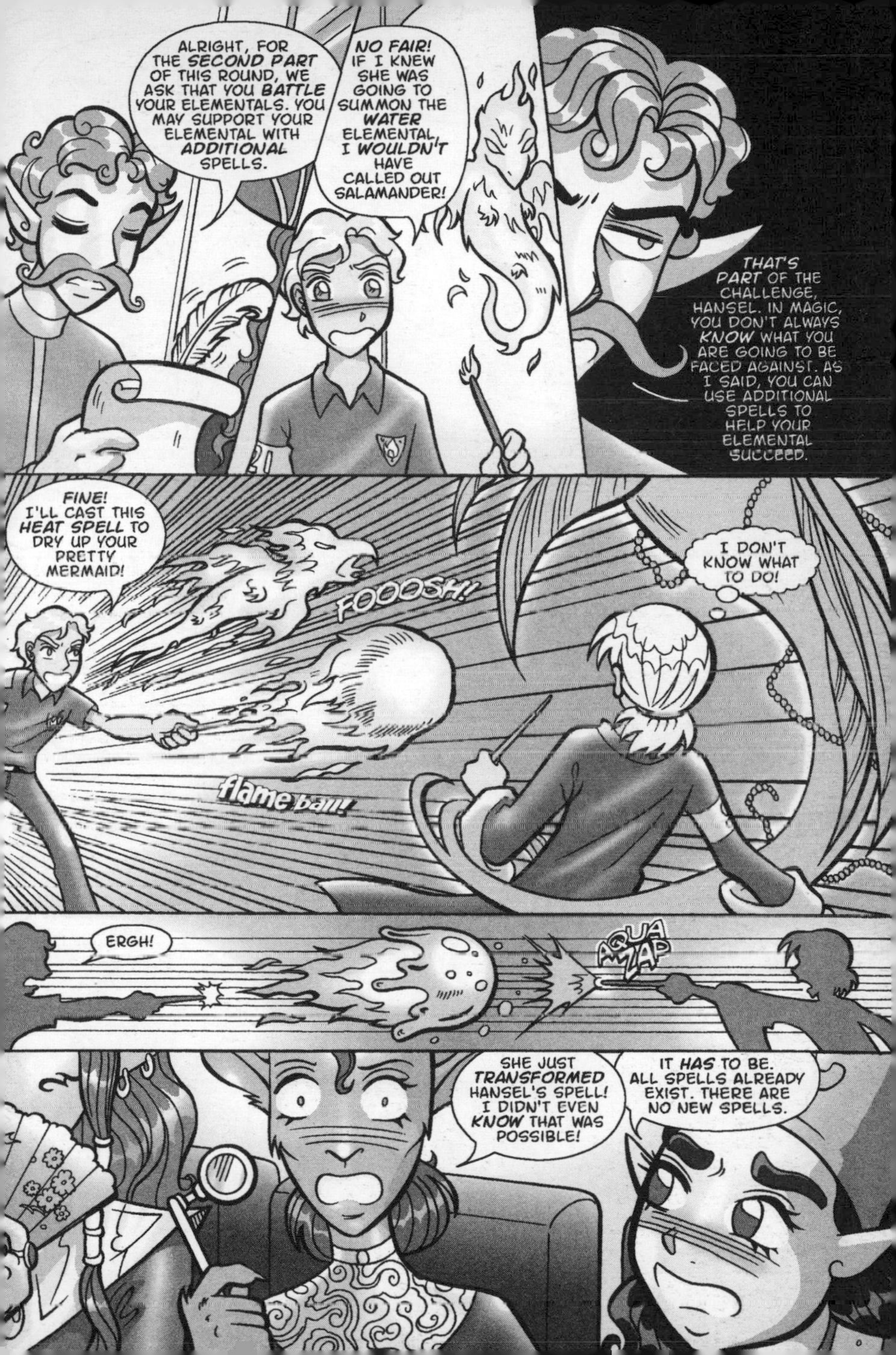
ALRIGHT, FOR THE SECOND PART OF THIS ROUND, WE ASK THAT YOU BATTLE YOUR ELEMENTALS. YOU MAY SUPPORT YOUR ELEMENTAL WITH ADDITIONAL SPELLS.
NO FAIR! IF I KNEW SHE WAS GOING TO SUMMON THE WATER ELEMENTAL, I WOULDN'T HAVE CALLED OUT SALAMANDER!
THAT'S PART OF THE CHALLENGE, HANSEL. IN MAGIC, YOU DON'T ALWAYS KNOW WHAT YOU ARE GOING TO BE FACED AGAINST. AS I SAID, YOU CAN USE ADDITIONAL SPELLS TO HELP YOUR ELEMENTAL SUCCEED.
FINE! I'LL CAST THIS HEAT SPELL TO DRY UP YOUR PRETTY MERMAID!
FOOOOSH!
I DON'T KNOW WHAT TO DO!
flame ball!
ERGH!
AQUA ZAP
SHE JUST TRANSFORMED HANSEL'S SPELL! I DIDN'T EVEN KNOW THAT WAS POSSIBLE!
IT HAS TO BE. ALL SPELLS ALREADY EXIST. THERE ARE NO NEW SPELLS.

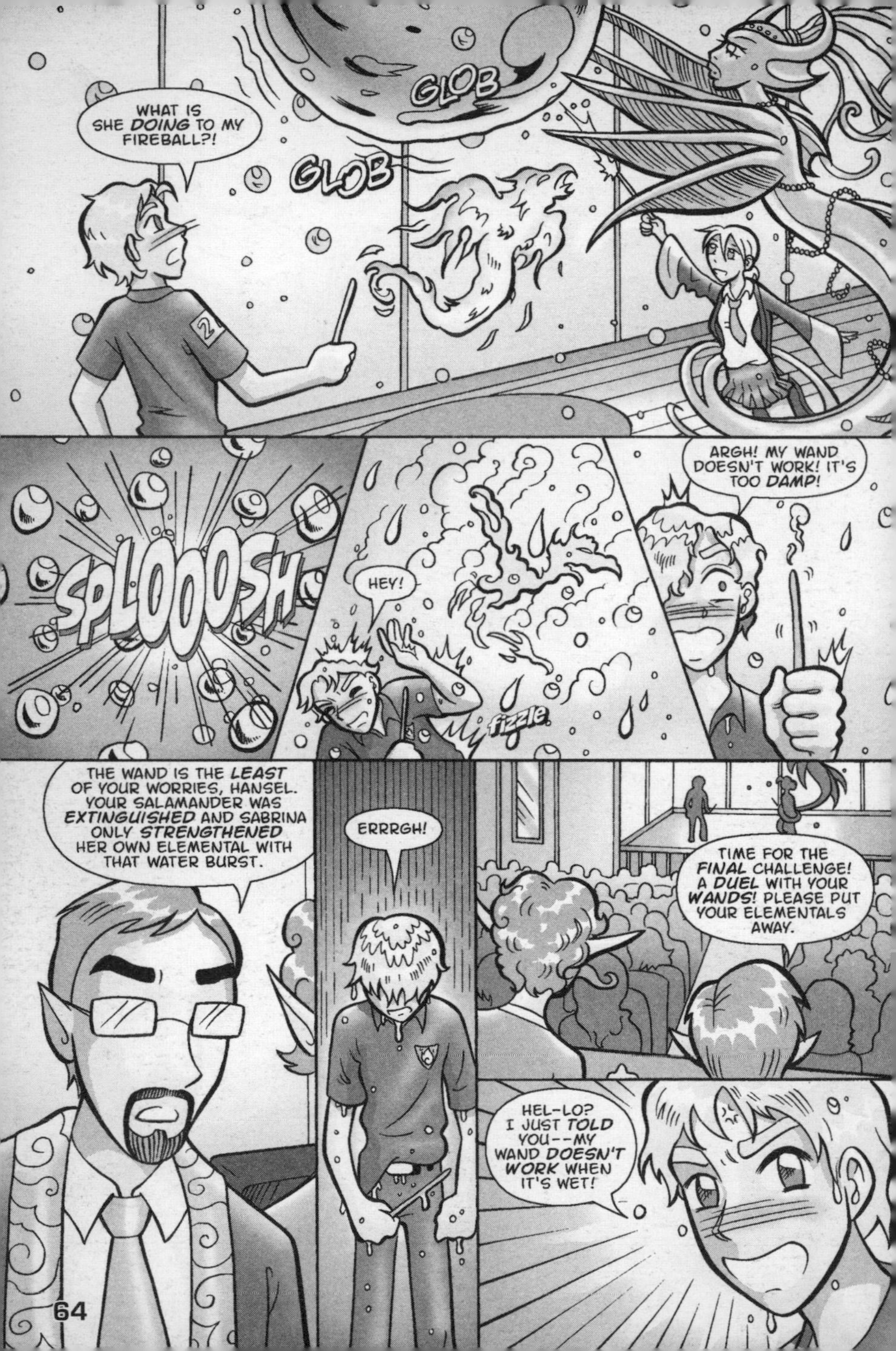
WHAT IS SHE DOING TO MY FIREBALL?!
GLOB
GLOB
SPLOOOSH
HEY!
fizzle
ARGH! MY WAND DOESN'T WORK! IT'S TOO DAMP!
THE WAND IS THE LEAST OF YOUR WORRIES, HANSEL. YOUR SALAMANDER WAS EXTINGUISHED AND SABRINA ONLY STRENGTHENED HER OWN ELEMENTAL WITH THAT WATER BURST.
ERRRGH!
TIME FOR THE FINAL CHALLENGE! A DUEL WITH YOUR WANDS! PLEASE PUT YOUR ELEMENTALS AWAY.
HEL-LO? I JUST TOLD YOU--MY WAND DOESN'T WORK WHEN IT'S WET!

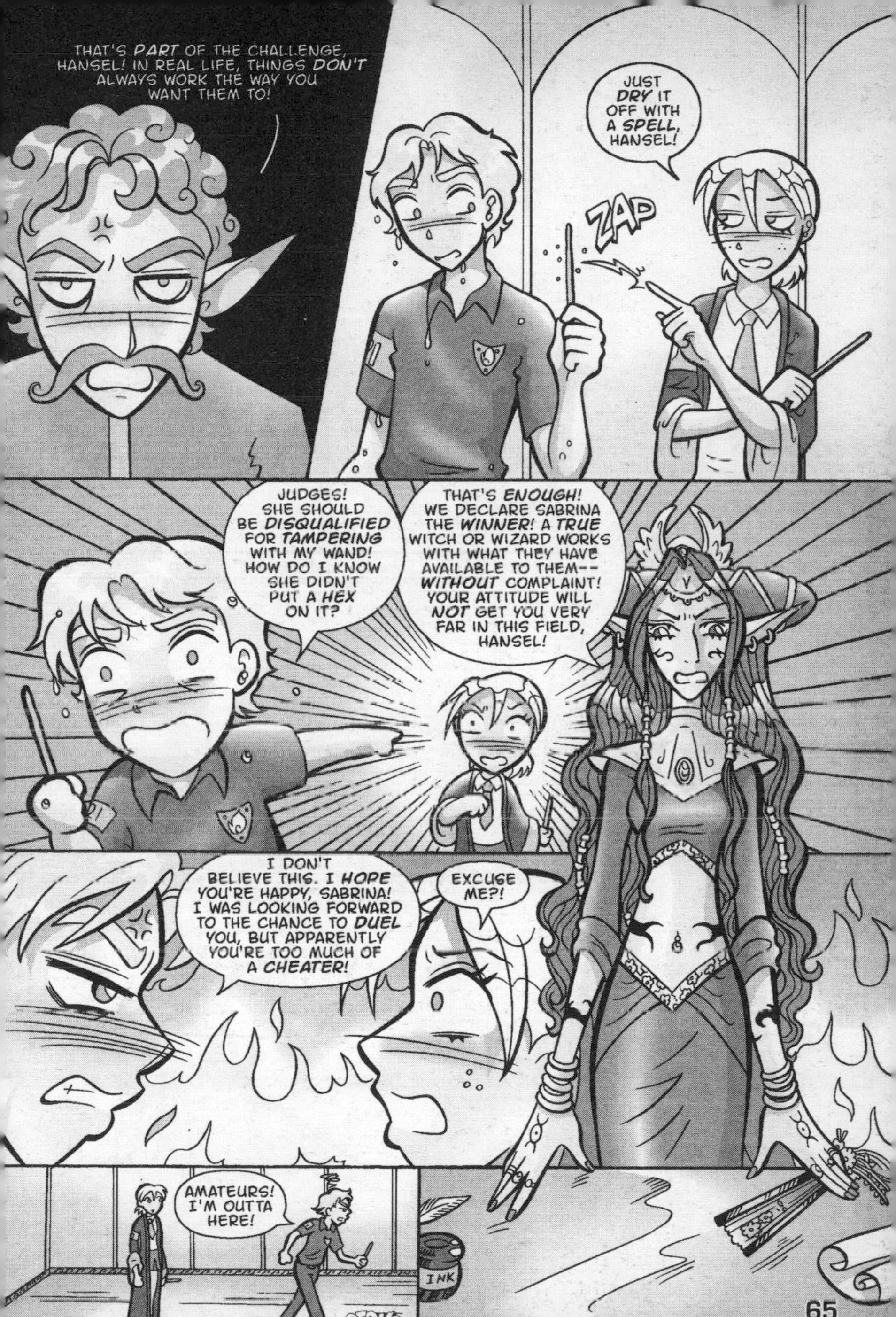
THAT'S PART OF THE CHALLENGE, HANSEL! IN REAL LIFE, THINGS DON'T ALWAYS WORK THE WAY YOU WANT THEM TO!
JUST DRY IT OFF WITH A SPELL, HANSEL!
ZAP
JUDGES! SHE SHOULD BE DISQUALIFIED FOR TAMPERING WITH MY WAND! HOW DO I KNOW SHE DIDN'T PUT A HEX ON IT?
THAT'S ENOUGH! WE DECLARE SABRINA THE WINNER! A TRUE WITCH OR WIZARD WORKS WITH WHAT THEY HAVE AVAILABLE TO THEM-- WITHOUT COMPLAINT! YOUR ATTITUDE WILL NOT GET YOU VERY FAR IN THIS FIELD, HANSEL!
I DON'T BELIEVE THIS. I HOPE YOU'RE HAPPY, SABRINA! I WAS LOOKING FORWARD TO THE CHANCE TO DUEL YOU, BUT APPARENTLY YOU'RE TOO MUCH OF A CHEATER!
EXCUSE ME?!
AMATEURS! I'M OUTTA HERE!
STOMP
STOMP
INK

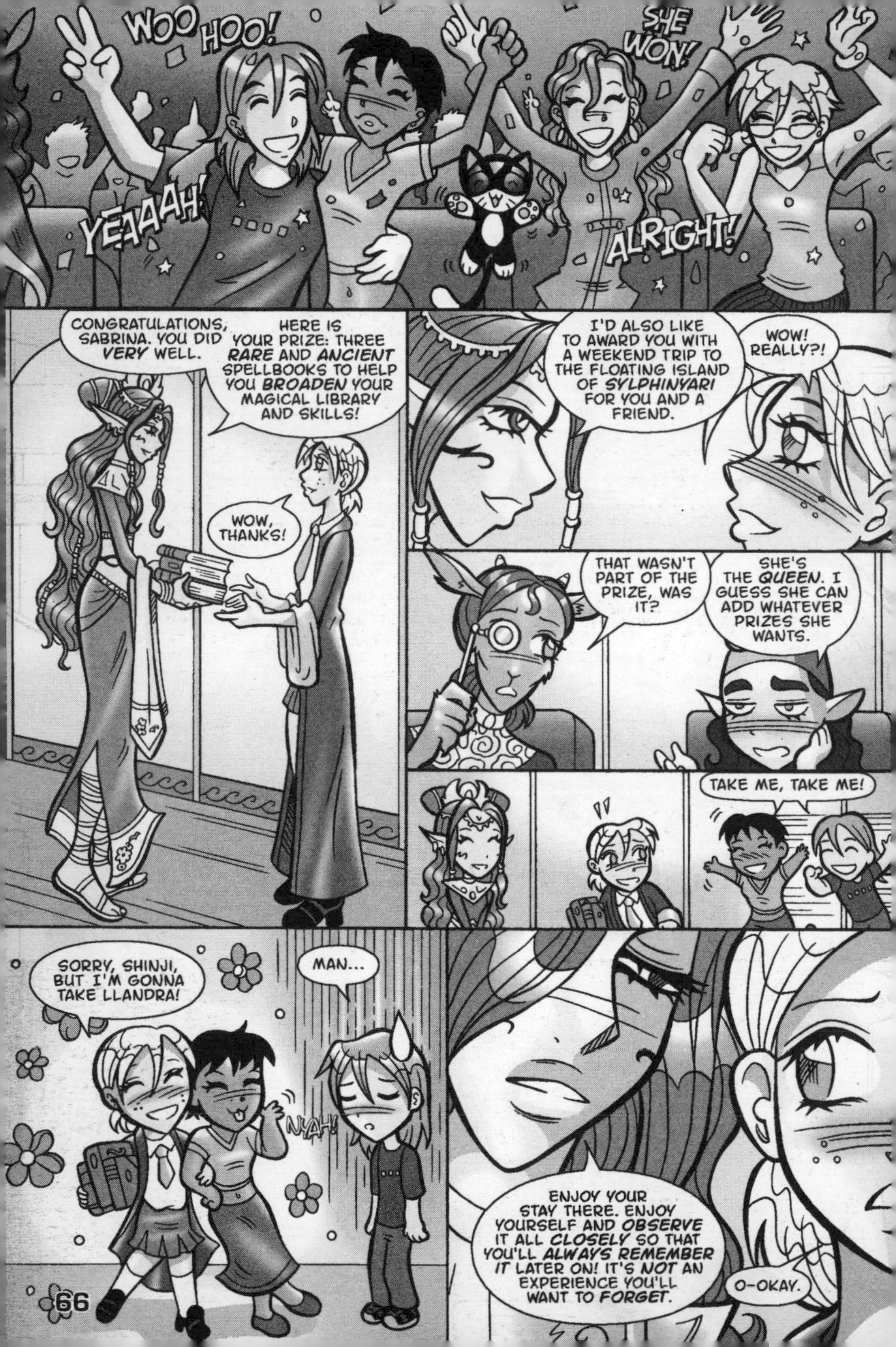
WOO HOO!
YEAAAH!
SHE WON!
ALRIGHT!
CONGRATULATIONS, SABRINA. YOU DID VERY WELL.
HERE IS YOUR PRIZE: THREE RARE AND ANCIENT SPELLBOOKS TO HELP YOU BROADEN YOUR MAGICAL LIBRARY AND SKILLS!
WOW, THANKS!
I'D ALSO LIKE TO AWARD YOU WITH A WEEKEND TRIP TO THE FLOATING ISLAND OF SYLPHINYARI FOR YOU AND A FRIEND.
WOW! REALLY?!
THAT WASN'T PART OF THE PRIZE, WAS IT?
SHE'S THE QUEEN. I GUESS SHE CAN ADD WHATEVER PRIZES SHE WANTS.
TAKE ME, TAKE ME!
SORRY, SHINJI, BUT I'M GONNA TAKE LLANDRA!
MAN...
NYAH!
ENJOY YOUR STAY THERE. ENJOY YOURSELF AND OBSERVE IT ALL CLOSELY SO THAT YOU'LL ALWAYS REMEMBER IT LATER ON! IT'S NOT AN EXPERIENCE YOU'LL WANT TO FORGET.
O-OKAY.

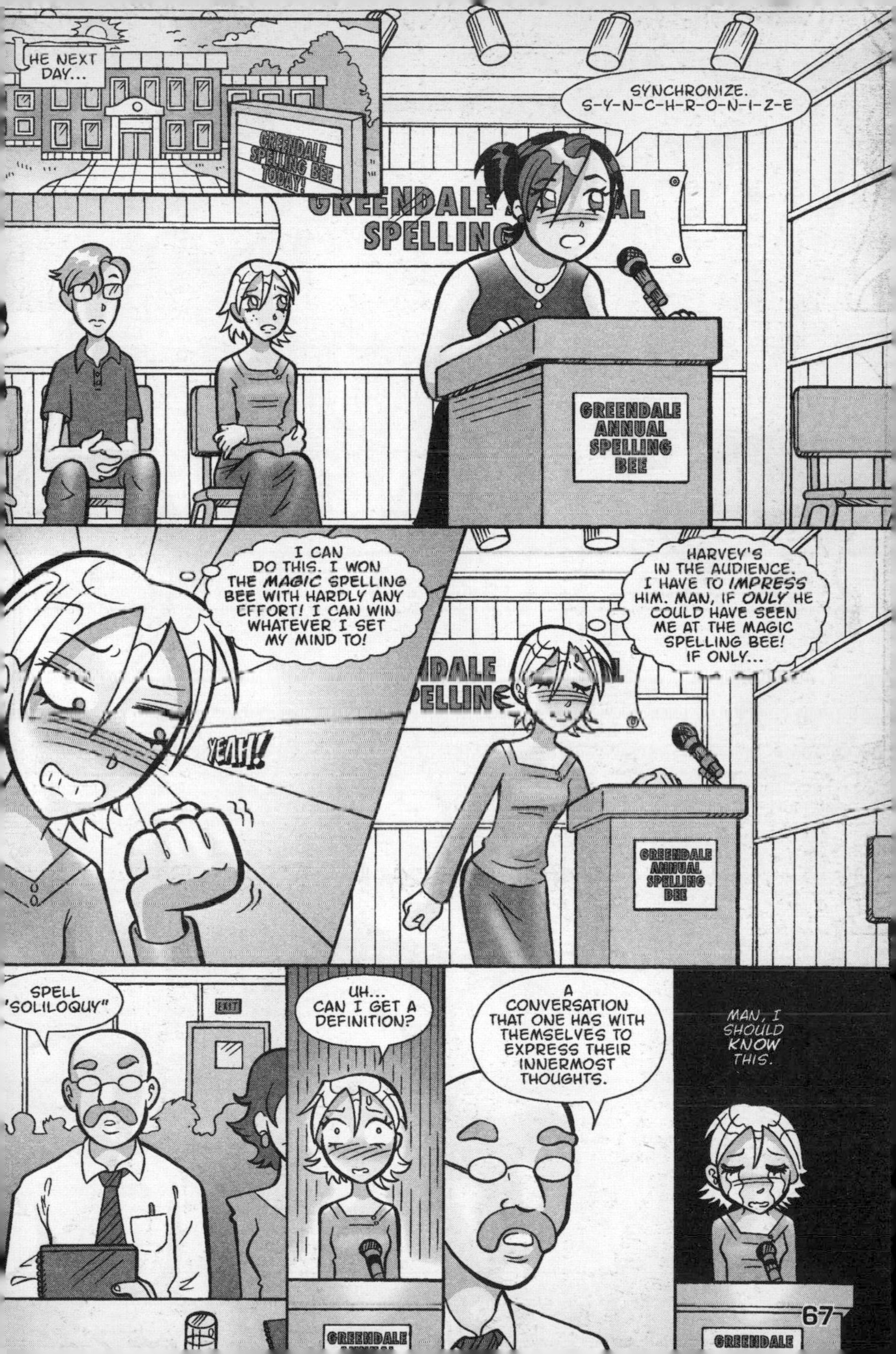

THE NEXT DAY...
GREENDALE SPELLING BEE TODAY!
SYNCHRONIZE. S-Y-N-C-H-R-O-N-I-Z-E
GREENDALE ANNUAL SPELLING BEE
I CAN DO THIS. I WON THE MAGIC SPELLING BEE WITH HARDLY ANY EFFORT! I CAN WIN WHATEVER I SET MY MIND TO!
YEAH!
HARVEY'S IN THE AUDIENCE. I HAVE TO IMPRESS HIM. MAN, IF ONLY HE COULD HAVE SEEN ME AT THE MAGIC SPELLING BEE! IF ONLY...
GREENDALE ANNUAL SPELLING BEE
SPELL "SOLILOQUY"
EXIT
UH... CAN I GET A DEFINITION?
A CONVERSATION THAT ONE HAS WITH THEMSELVES TO EXPRESS THEIR INNERMOST THOUGHTS.
MAN, I SHOULD KNOW THIS.
GREENDALE
GREENDALE

GREENDALE ANN SPELL... EE

S-O-L-O--

BZZZT!

DOH!

HEY SABRINA. YOU DID GOOD.

NO I DIDN'T. I DIDN'T EVEN GET PAST THE FIRST ROUND.

STILL, IT TAKES A LOT OF COURAGE TO GET UP ON STAGE LIKE THAT. I COULD NEVER DO THAT. I THINK IT'S COOL THAT YOU TRIED.

TH-THANKS.

RBOOK CLUB
ooking for writers and tograph

LET'S GO, HARVEY! WE HAVE A DATE, REMEMBER?

UHHH...

BOOK B ing rs

I GUESS I CAN'T BE NUMBER ONE AT EVERYTHING. NOT EVEN LOVE. MAYBE ONE DAY HARVEY WILL REALIZE WHAT HE'S MISSING. UNTIL THEN, I'LL BE WAITING. I'LL GIVE HIM WHATEVER TIME HE NEEDS.

HOW'S THAT FOR A SOLILOQUY?

END!

Chapter 4

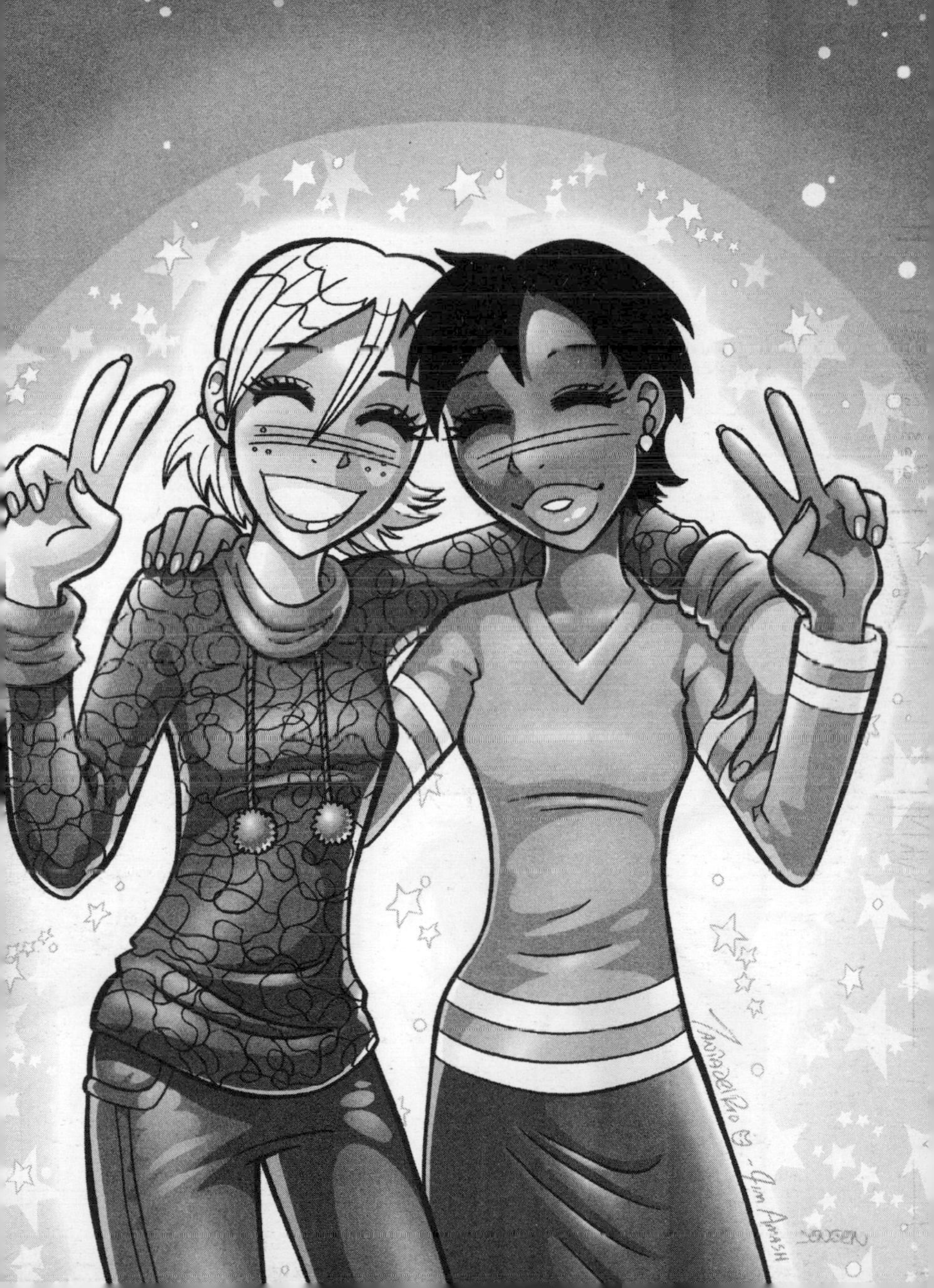

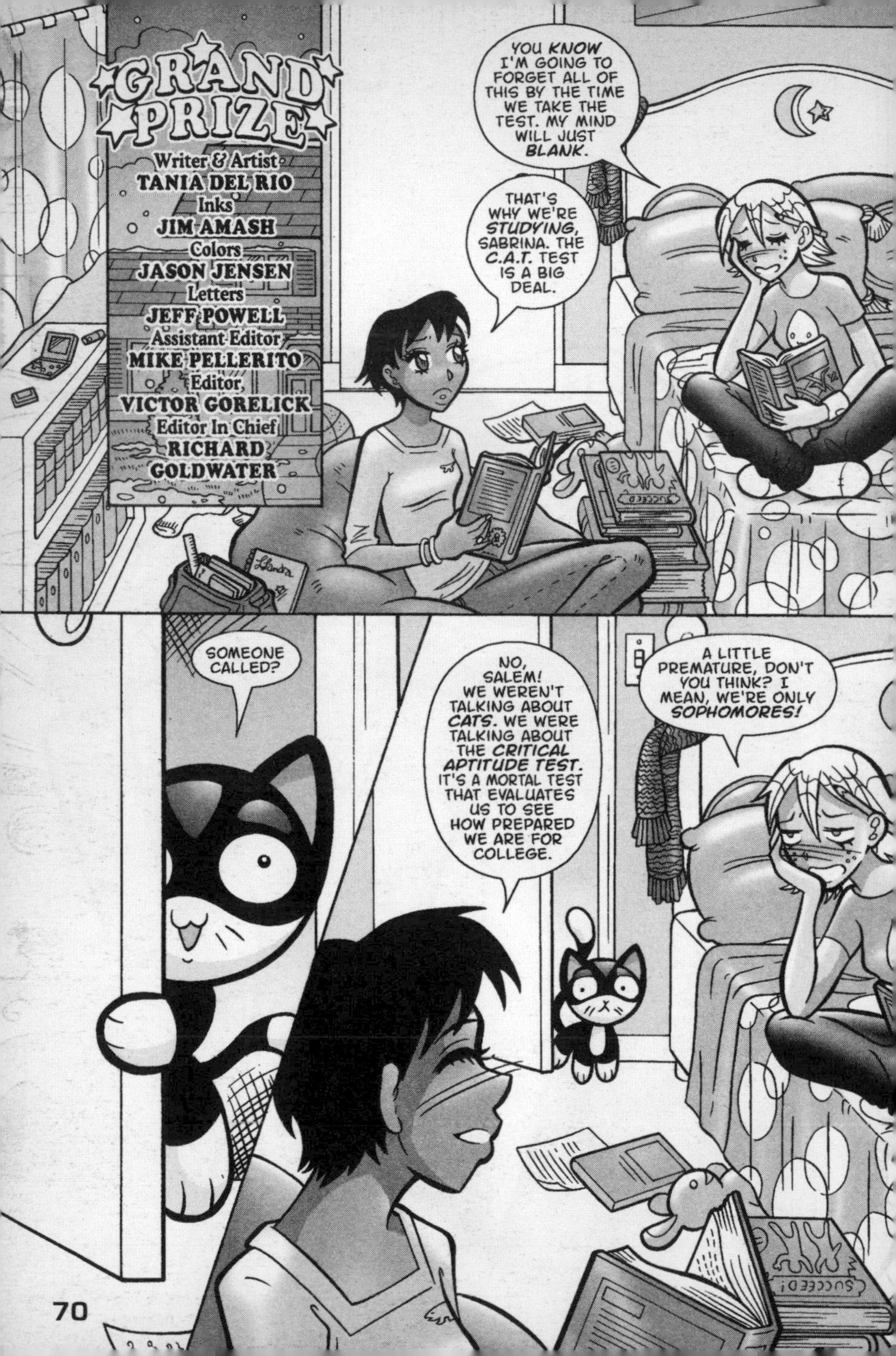
GRAND PRIZE
Writer & Artist TANIA DEL RIO
Inks JIM AMASH
Colors JASON JENSEN
Letters JEFF POWELL
Assistant Editor MIKE PELLERITO
Editor VICTOR GORELICK
Editor In Chief RICHARD GOLDWATER
YOU KNOW I'M GOING TO FORGET ALL OF THIS BY THE TIME WE TAKE THE TEST. MY MIND WILL JUST BLANK.
THAT'S WHY WE'RE STUDYING, SABRINA. THE C.A.T. TEST IS A BIG DEAL.
SOMEONE CALLED?
NO, SALEM! WE WEREN'T TALKING ABOUT CATS. WE WERE TALKING ABOUT THE CRITICAL APTITUDE TEST. IT'S A MORTAL TEST THAT EVALUATES US TO SEE HOW PREPARED WE ARE FOR COLLEGE.
A LITTLE PREMATURE, DON'T YOU THINK? I MEAN, WE'RE ONLY SOPHOMORES!

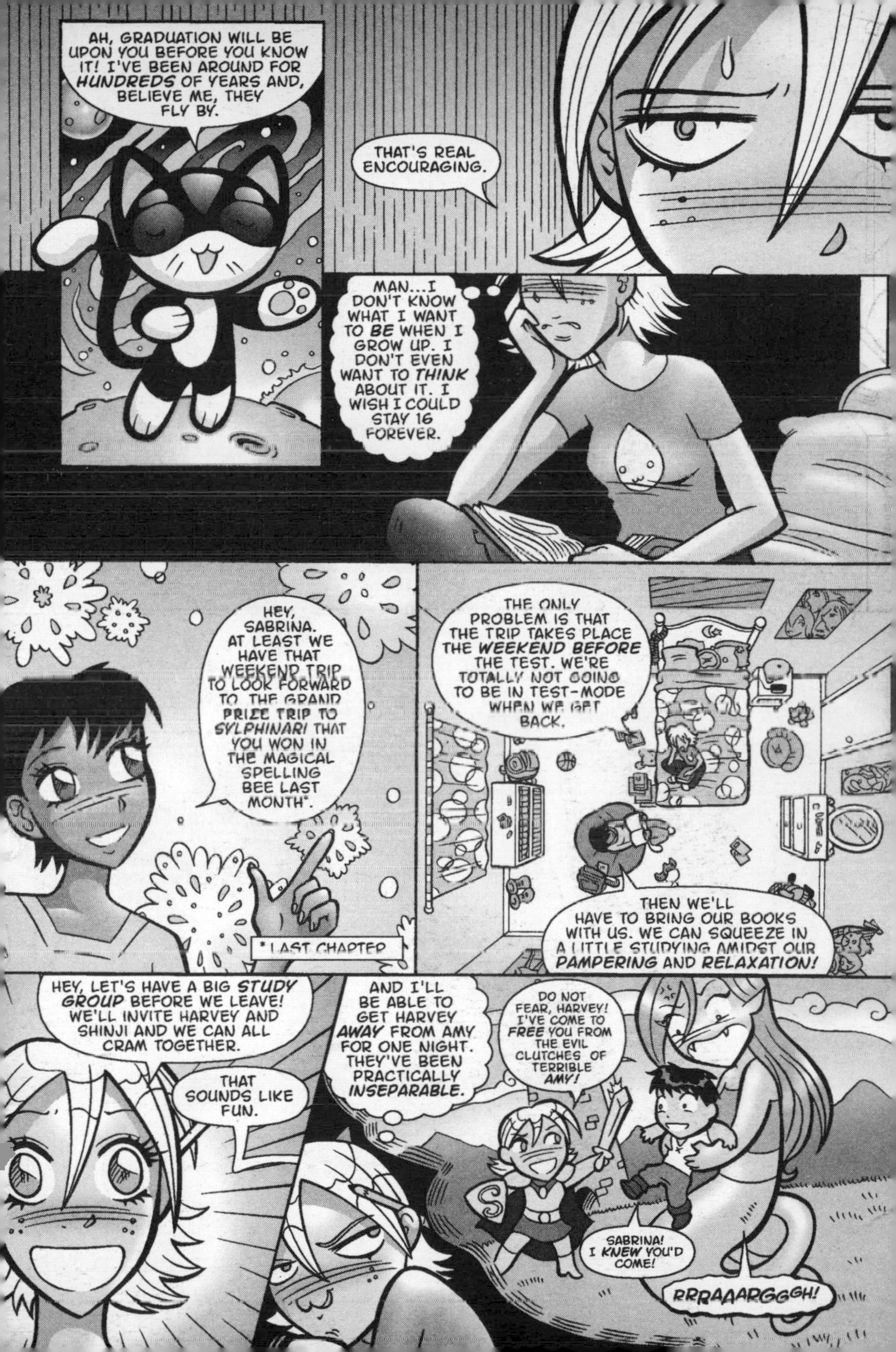

AH, GRADUATION WILL BE UPON YOU BEFORE YOU KNOW IT! I'VE BEEN AROUND FOR *HUNDREDS* OF YEARS AND, BELIEVE ME, THEY FLY BY.
THAT'S REAL ENCOURAGING.
MAN...I DON'T KNOW WHAT I WANT TO *BE* WHEN I GROW UP. I DON'T EVEN WANT TO *THINK* ABOUT IT. I WISH I COULD STAY 16 FOREVER.
HEY, SABRINA. AT LEAST WE HAVE THAT WEEKEND TRIP TO LOOK FORWARD TO. THE GRAND PRIZE TRIP TO *SYLPHINARI* THAT YOU WON IN THE MAGICAL SPELLING BEE LAST MONTH*.
*LAST CHAPTER
THE ONLY PROBLEM IS THAT THE TRIP TAKES PLACE THE *WEEKEND BEFORE* THE TEST. WE'RE TOTALLY NOT GOING TO BE IN TEST-MODE WHEN WE GET BACK.
THEN WE'LL HAVE TO BRING OUR BOOKS WITH US. WE CAN SQUEEZE IN A LITTLE STUDYING AMIDST OUR *PAMPERING* AND *RELAXATION!*
HEY, LET'S HAVE A BIG *STUDY GROUP* BEFORE WE LEAVE! WE'LL INVITE HARVEY AND SHINJI AND WE CAN ALL CRAM TOGETHER.
THAT SOUNDS LIKE FUN.
AND I'LL BE ABLE TO GET HARVEY *AWAY* FROM AMY FOR ONE NIGHT. THEY'VE BEEN PRACTICALLY *INSEPARABLE*.
DO NOT FEAR, HARVEY! I'VE COME TO *FREE* YOU FROM THE EVIL CLUTCHES OF TERRIBLE *AMY!*
SABRINA! I *KNEW* YOU'D COME!
RRRAAARGGGH!

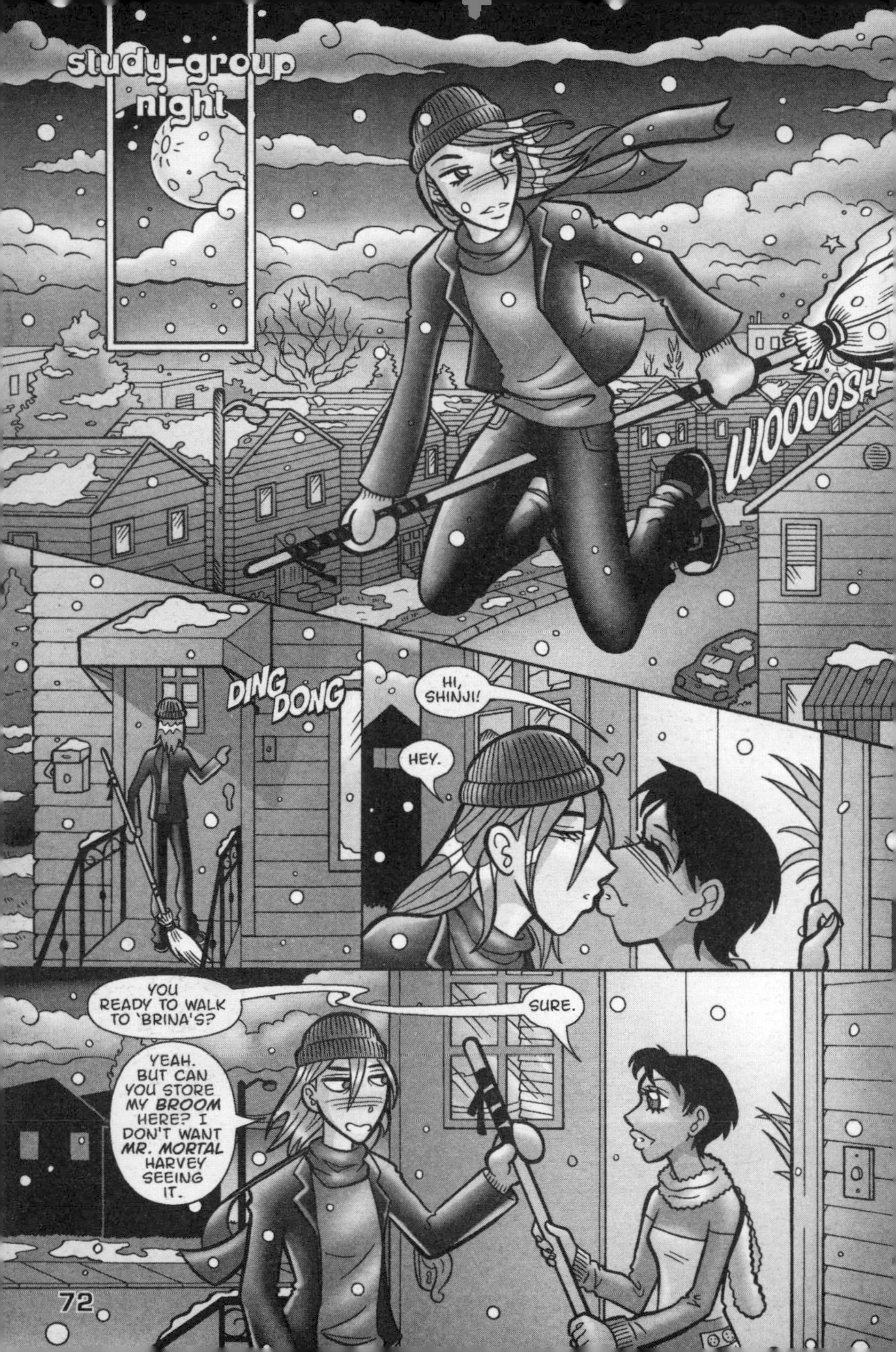
study-group night
WOOOOSH
DING DONG
HI, SHINJI!
HEY.
YOU READY TO WALK TO 'BRINA'S?
SURE.
YEAH. BUT CAN YOU STORE MY BROOM HERE? I DON'T WANT MR. MORTAL HARVEY SEEING IT.

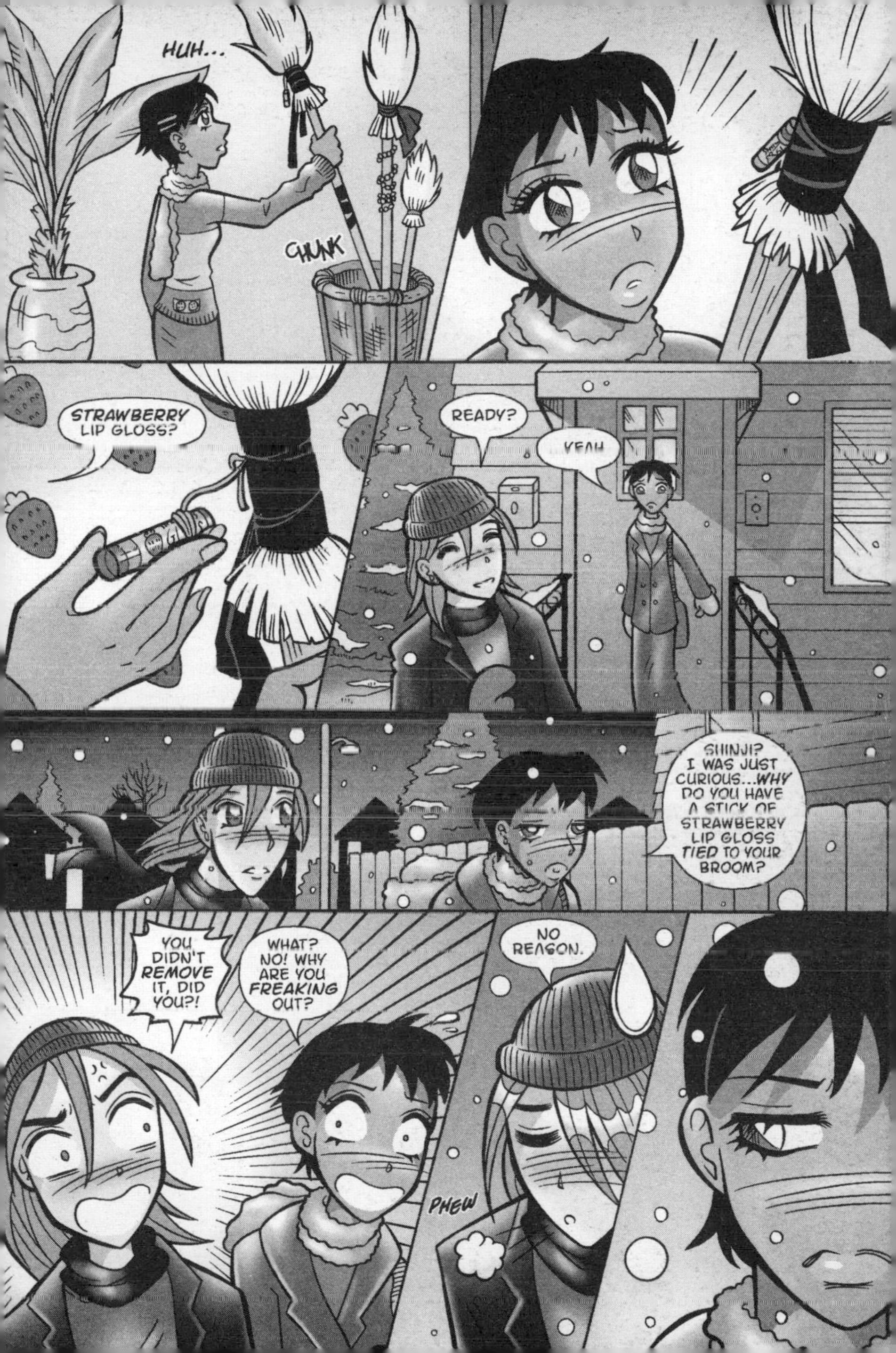
HUH...
CHUNK
STRAWBERRY LIP GLOSS?
READY?
YEAH
SHINJI? I WAS JUST CURIOUS...WHY DO YOU HAVE A STICK OF STRAWBERRY LIP GLOSS TIED TO YOUR BROOM?
YOU DIDN'T REMOVE IT, DID YOU?!
WHAT? NO! WHY ARE YOU FREAKING OUT?
PHEW
NO REASON.

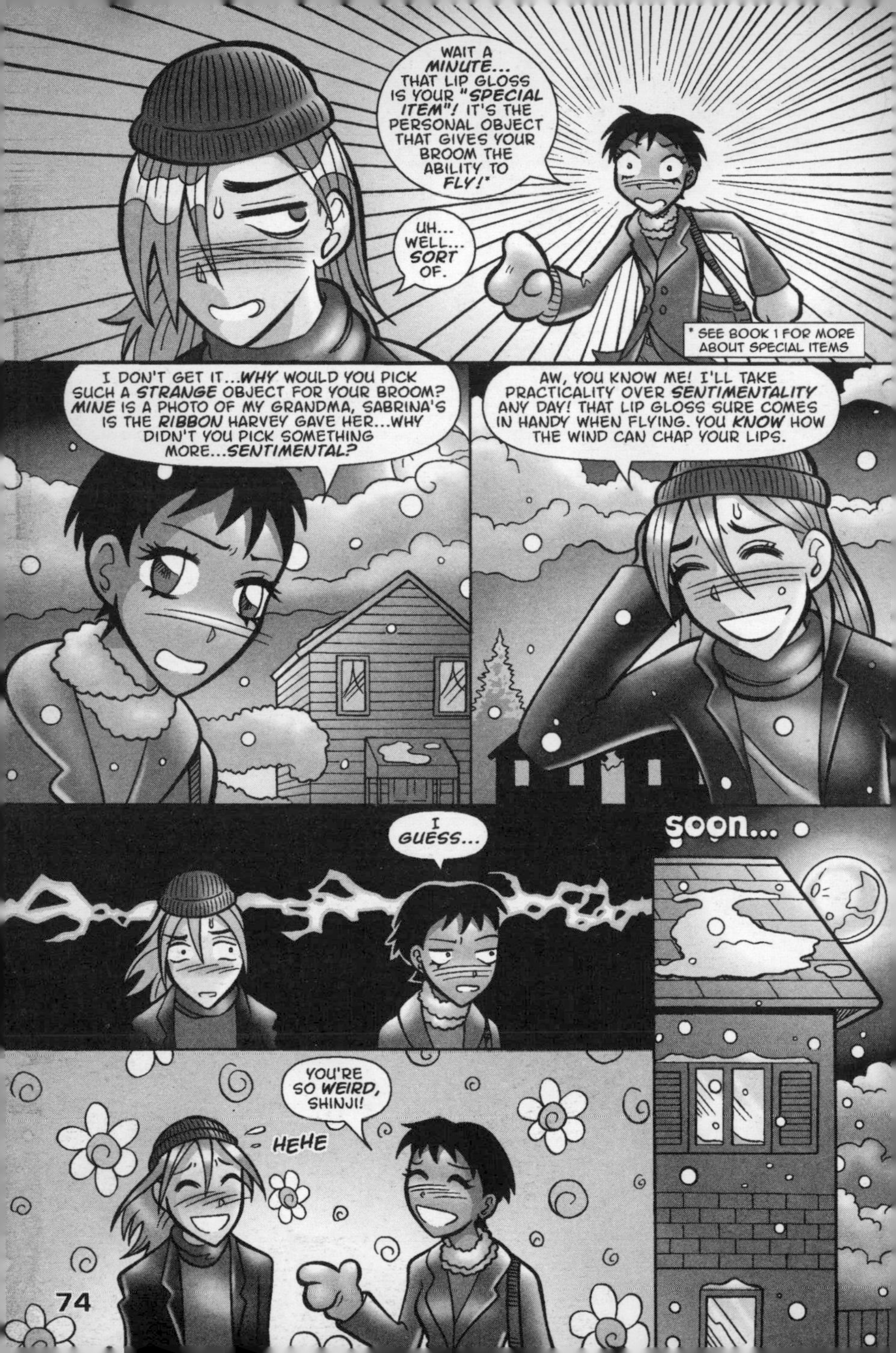
WAIT A MINUTE... THAT LIP GLOSS IS YOUR "SPECIAL ITEM"! IT'S THE PERSONAL OBJECT THAT GIVES YOUR BROOM THE ABILITY TO FLY!*
UH... WELL... SORT OF.
* SEE BOOK 1 FOR MORE ABOUT SPECIAL ITEMS
I DON'T GET IT...WHY WOULD YOU PICK SUCH A STRANGE OBJECT FOR YOUR BROOM? MINE IS A PHOTO OF MY GRANDMA, SABRINA'S IS THE RIBBON HARVEY GAVE HER...WHY DIDN'T YOU PICK SOMETHING MORE...SENTIMENTAL?
AW, YOU KNOW ME! I'LL TAKE PRACTICALITY OVER SENTIMENTALITY ANY DAY! THAT LIP GLOSS SURE COMES IN HANDY WHEN FLYING. YOU KNOW HOW THE WIND CAN CHAP YOUR LIPS.
I GUESS...
SOON...
YOU'RE SO WEIRD, SHINJI!
HEHE

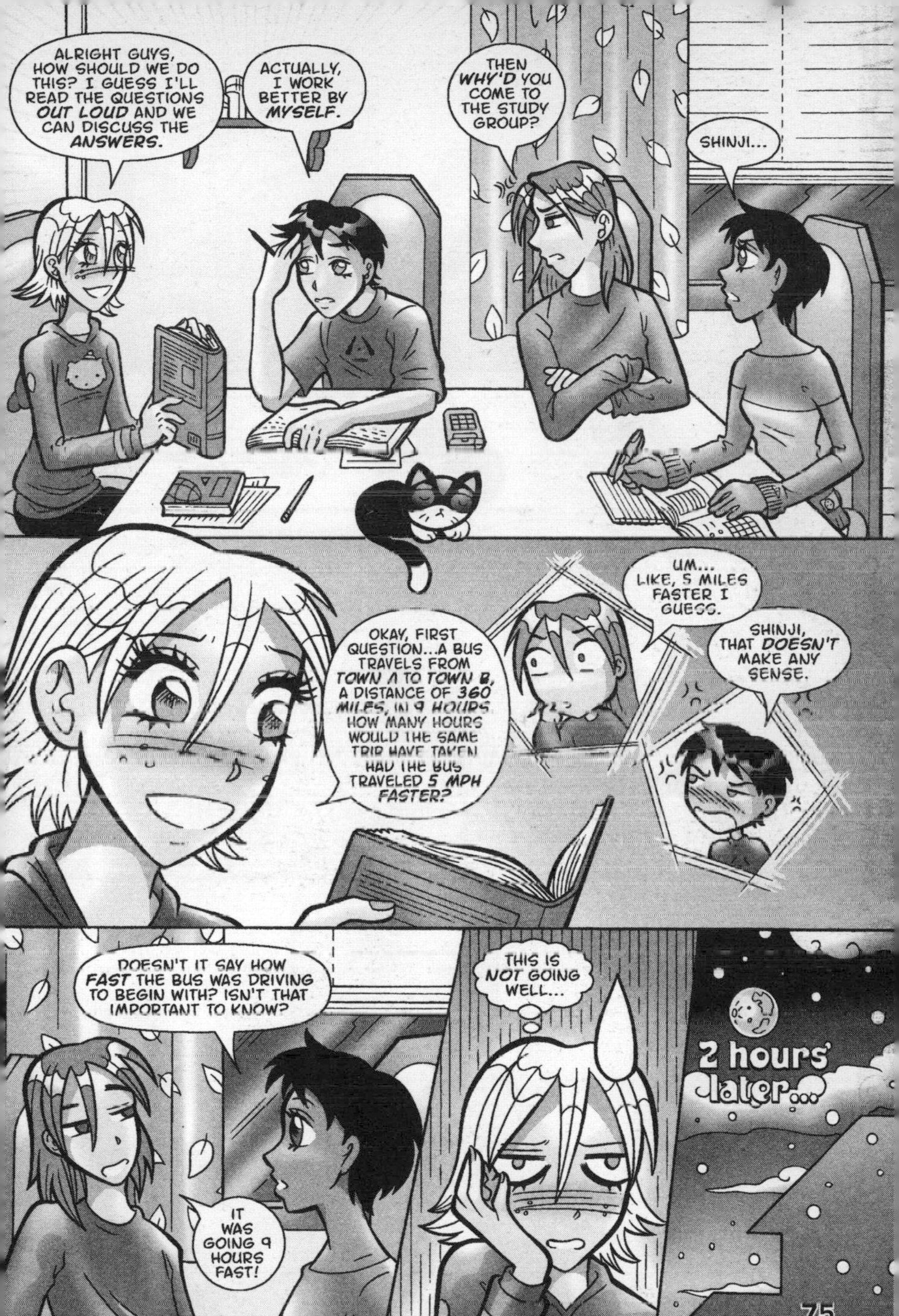

ALRIGHT GUYS, HOW SHOULD WE DO THIS? I GUESS I'LL READ THE QUESTIONS OUT LOUD AND WE CAN DISCUSS THE ANSWERS.
ACTUALLY, I WORK BETTER BY MYSELF.
THEN WHY'D YOU COME TO THE STUDY GROUP?
SHINJI...
OKAY, FIRST QUESTION...A BUS TRAVELS FROM TOWN A TO TOWN B, A DISTANCE OF 360 MILES, IN 9 HOURS. HOW MANY HOURS WOULD THE SAME TRIP HAVE TAKEN HAD THE BUS TRAVELED 5 MPH FASTER?
UM... LIKE, 5 MILES FASTER I GUESS.
SHINJI, THAT DOESN'T MAKE ANY SENSE.
DOESN'T IT SAY HOW FAST THE BUS WAS DRIVING TO BEGIN WITH? ISN'T THAT IMPORTANT TO KNOW?
IT WAS GOING 9 HOURS FAST!
THIS IS NOT GOING WELL...
2 hours' later...

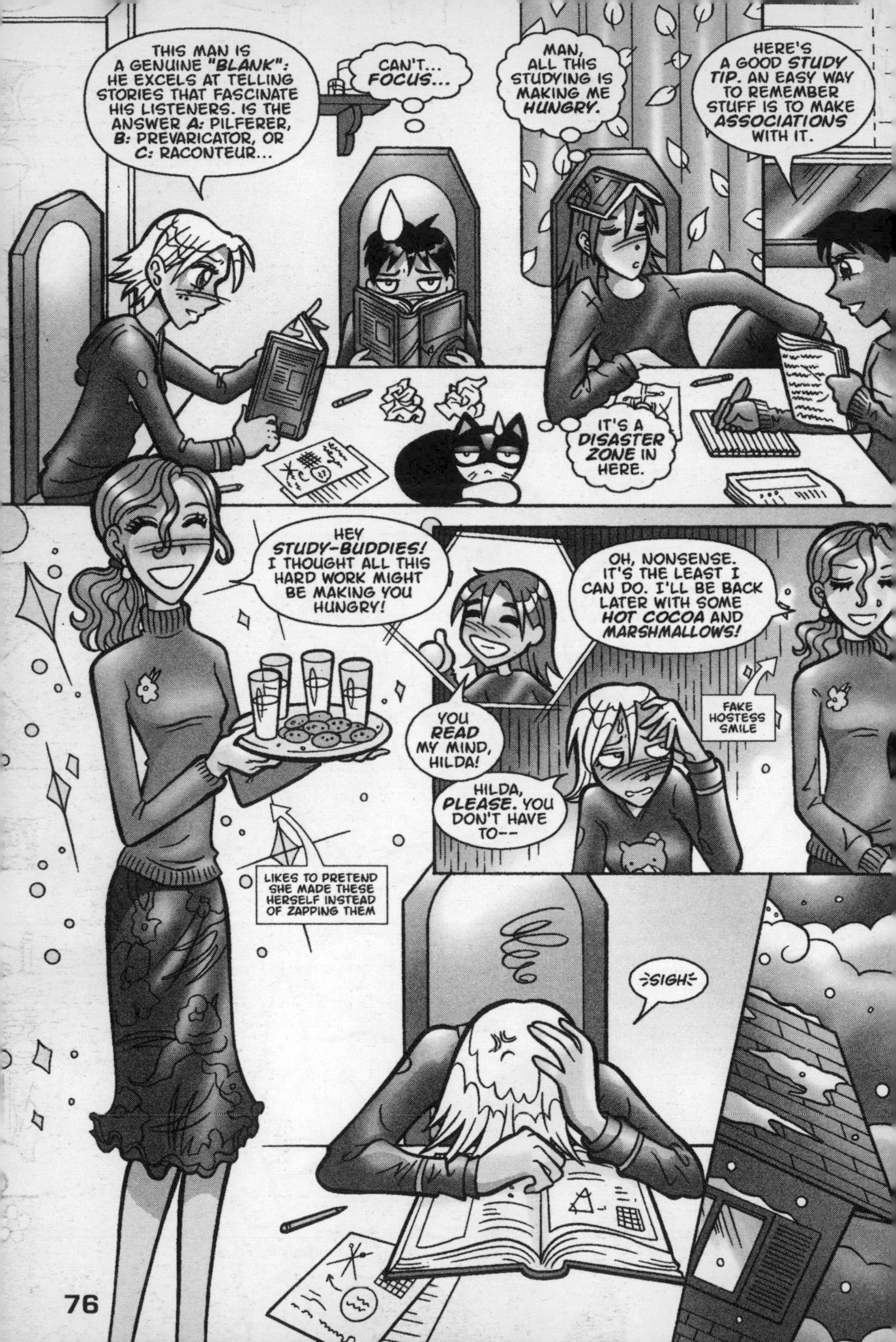

THIS MAN IS A GENUINE "BLANK": HE EXCELS AT TELLING STORIES THAT FASCINATE HIS LISTENERS. IS THE ANSWER A: PILFERER, B: PREVARICATOR, OR C: RACONTEUR...
CAN'T... FOCUS...
MAN, ALL THIS STUDYING IS MAKING ME HUNGRY.
HERE'S A GOOD STUDY TIP. AN EASY WAY TO REMEMBER STUFF IS TO MAKE ASSOCIATIONS WITH IT.
IT'S A DISASTER ZONE IN HERE.
HEY STUDY-BUDDIES! I THOUGHT ALL THIS HARD WORK MIGHT BE MAKING YOU HUNGRY!
LIKES TO PRETEND SHE MADE THESE HERSELF INSTEAD OF ZAPPING THEM
YOU READ MY MIND, HILDA!
HILDA, PLEASE. YOU DON'T HAVE TO--
OH, NONSENSE. IT'S THE LEAST I CAN DO. I'LL BE BACK LATER WITH SOME HOT COCOA AND MARSHMALLOWS!
FAKE HOSTESS SMILE
-SIGH-

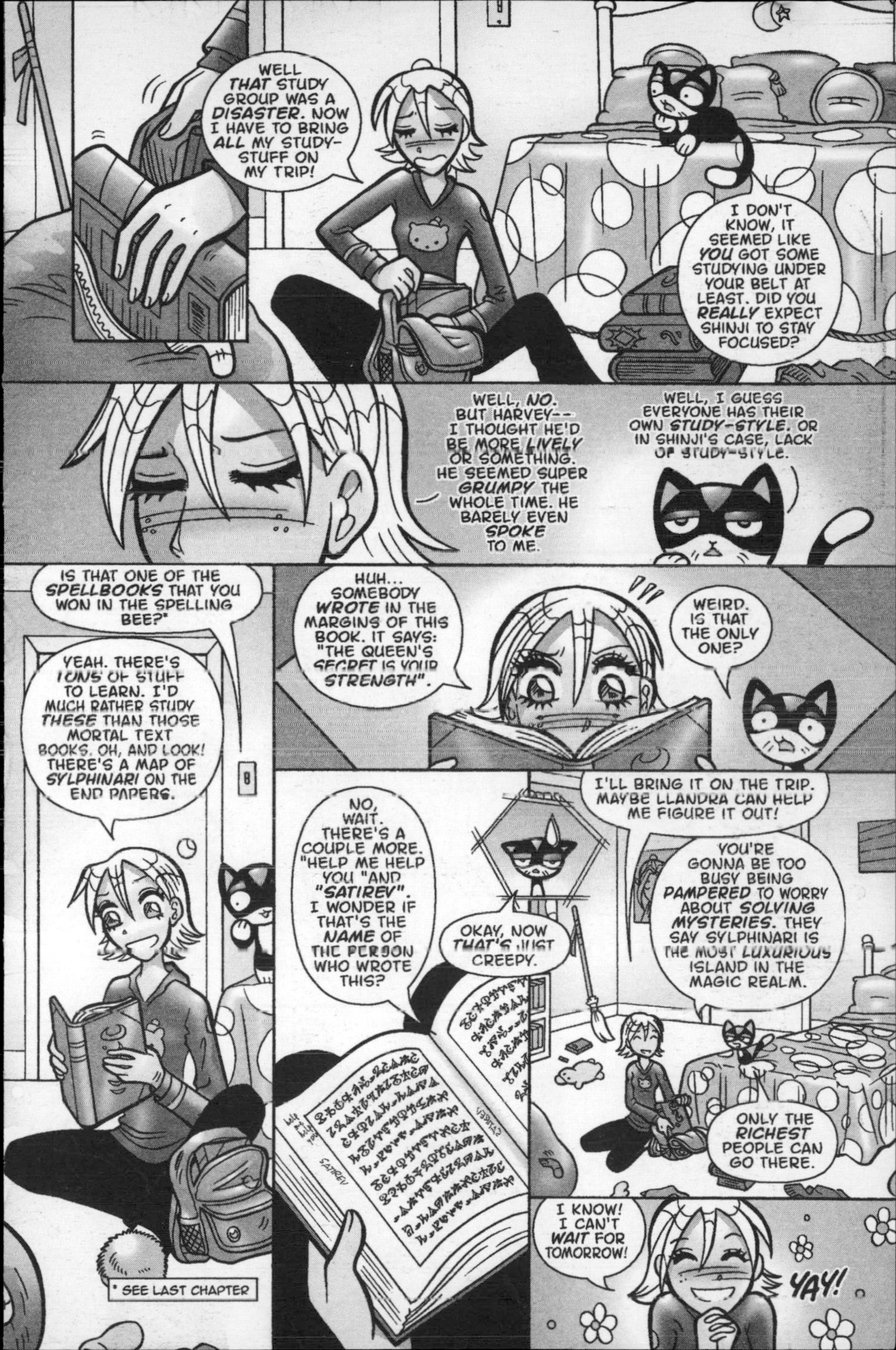
WELL THAT STUDY GROUP WAS A DISASTER. NOW I HAVE TO BRING ALL MY STUDY-STUFF ON MY TRIP!
I DON'T KNOW, IT SEEMED LIKE YOU GOT SOME STUDYING UNDER YOUR BELT AT LEAST. DID YOU REALLY EXPECT SHINJI TO STAY FOCUSED?
WELL, NO. BUT HARVEY-- I THOUGHT HE'D BE MORE LIVELY OR SOMETHING. HE SEEMED SUPER GRUMPY THE WHOLE TIME. HE BARELY EVEN SPOKE TO ME.
WELL, I GUESS EVERYONE HAS THEIR OWN STUDY-STYLE. OR IN SHINJI'S CASE, LACK OF STUDY-STYLE.
IS THAT ONE OF THE SPELLBOOKS THAT YOU WON IN THE SPELLING BEE?*
YEAH. THERE'S TONS OF STUFF TO LEARN. I'D MUCH RATHER STUDY THESE THAN THOSE MORTAL TEXT BOOKS. OH, AND LOOK! THERE'S A MAP OF SYLPHINARI ON THE END PAPERS.
* SEE LAST CHAPTER
HUH... SOMEBODY WROTE IN THE MARGINS OF THIS BOOK. IT SAYS: "THE QUEEN'S SECRET IS YOUR STRENGTH".
WEIRD. IS THAT THE ONLY ONE?
NO, WAIT. THERE'S A COUPLE MORE. "HELP ME HELP YOU" AND "SATIREV". I WONDER IF THAT'S THE NAME OF THE PERSON WHO WROTE THIS?
OKAY, NOW THAT'S JUST CREEPY.
SATIREV
I'LL BRING IT ON THE TRIP. MAYBE LLANDRA CAN HELP ME FIGURE IT OUT!
YOU'RE GONNA BE TOO BUSY BEING PAMPERED TO WORRY ABOUT SOLVING MYSTERIES. THEY SAY SYLPHINARI IS THE MOST LUXURIOUS ISLAND IN THE MAGIC REALM.
ONLY THE RICHEST PEOPLE CAN GO THERE.
I KNOW! I CAN'T WAIT FOR TOMORROW!
YAY!

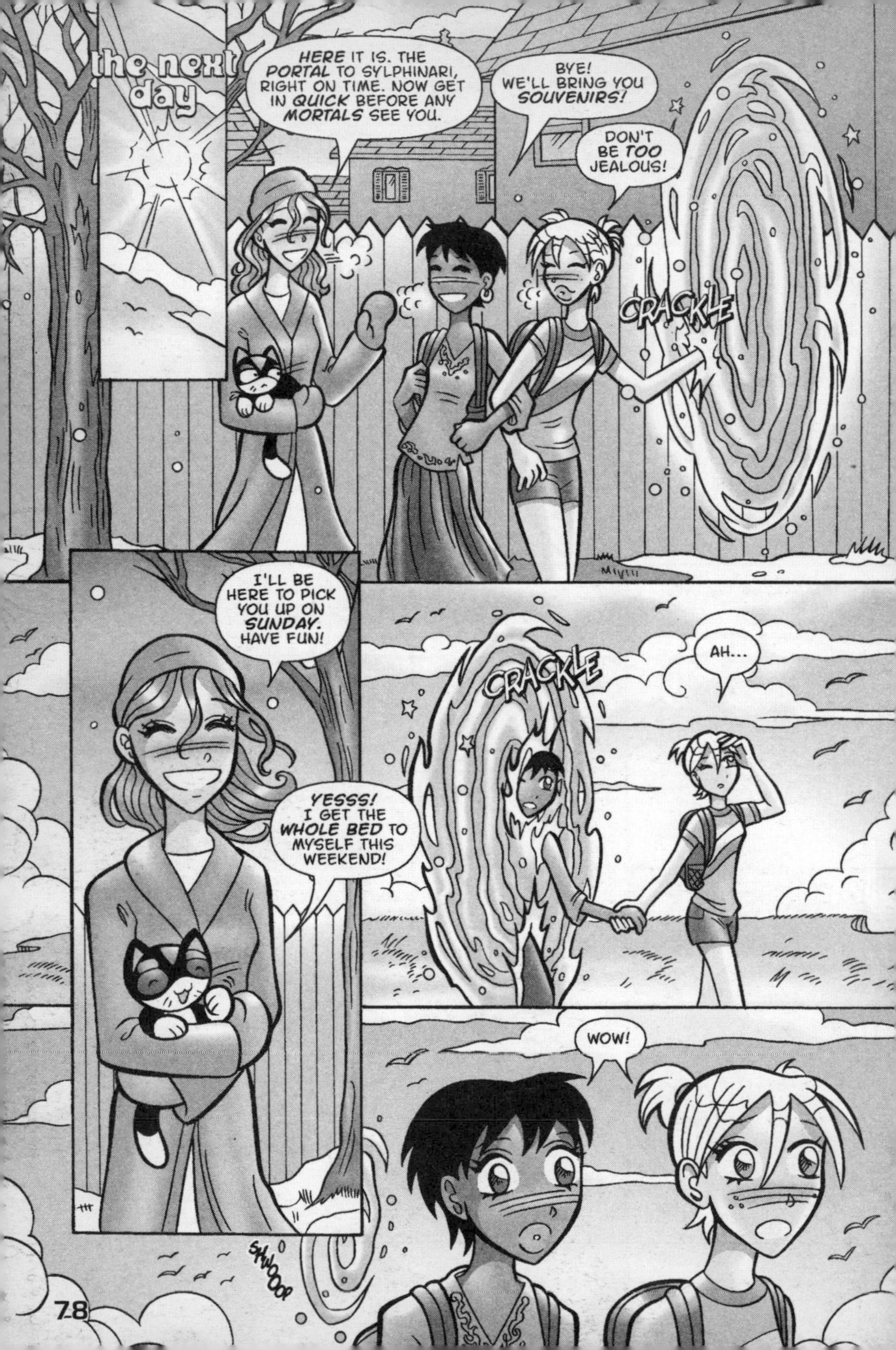
the next day
HERE IT IS. THE PORTAL TO SYLPHINARI, RIGHT ON TIME. NOW GET IN QUICK BEFORE ANY MORTALS SEE YOU.
BYE! WE'LL BRING YOU SOUVENIRS!
DON'T BE TOO JEALOUS!
CRACKLE
I'LL BE HERE TO PICK YOU UP ON SUNDAY. HAVE FUN!
YESSS! I GET THE WHOLE BED TO MYSELF THIS WEEKEND!
CRACKLE
AH...
WOW!
SHWOOOP

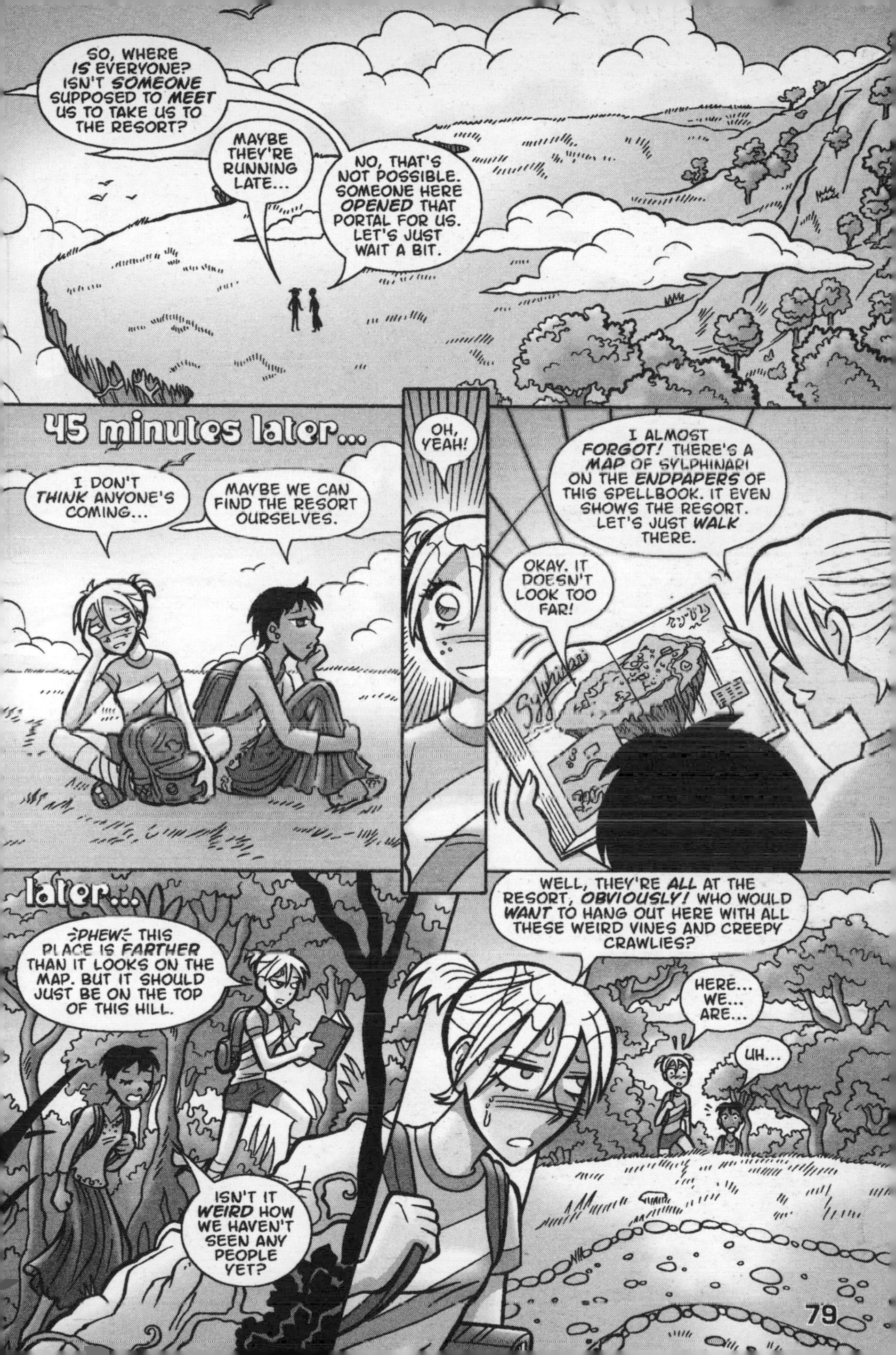
SO, WHERE *IS* EVERYONE? ISN'T *SOMEONE* SUPPOSED TO *MEET* US TO TAKE US TO THE RESORT?
MAYBE THEY'RE RUNNING LATE...
NO, THAT'S NOT POSSIBLE. SOMEONE HERE *OPENED* THAT PORTAL FOR US. LET'S JUST WAIT A BIT.
45 minutes later...
I DON'T *THINK* ANYONE'S COMING...
MAYBE WE CAN FIND THE RESORT OURSELVES.
OH, YEAH!
I ALMOST *FORGOT!* THERE'S A *MAP* OF SYLPHINARI ON THE *ENDPAPERS* OF THIS SPELLBOOK. IT EVEN SHOWS THE RESORT. LET'S JUST *WALK* THERE.
OKAY. IT DOESN'T LOOK TOO FAR!
later...
PHEW THIS PLACE IS *FARTHER* THAN IT LOOKS ON THE MAP. BUT IT SHOULD JUST BE ON THE TOP OF THIS HILL.
ISN'T IT *WEIRD* HOW WE HAVEN'T SEEN ANY PEOPLE YET?
WELL, THEY'RE *ALL* AT THE RESORT, *OBVIOUSLY!* WHO WOULD *WANT* TO HANG OUT HERE WITH ALL THESE WEIRD VINES AND CREEPY CRAWLIES?
HERE... WE... ARE...
UH...

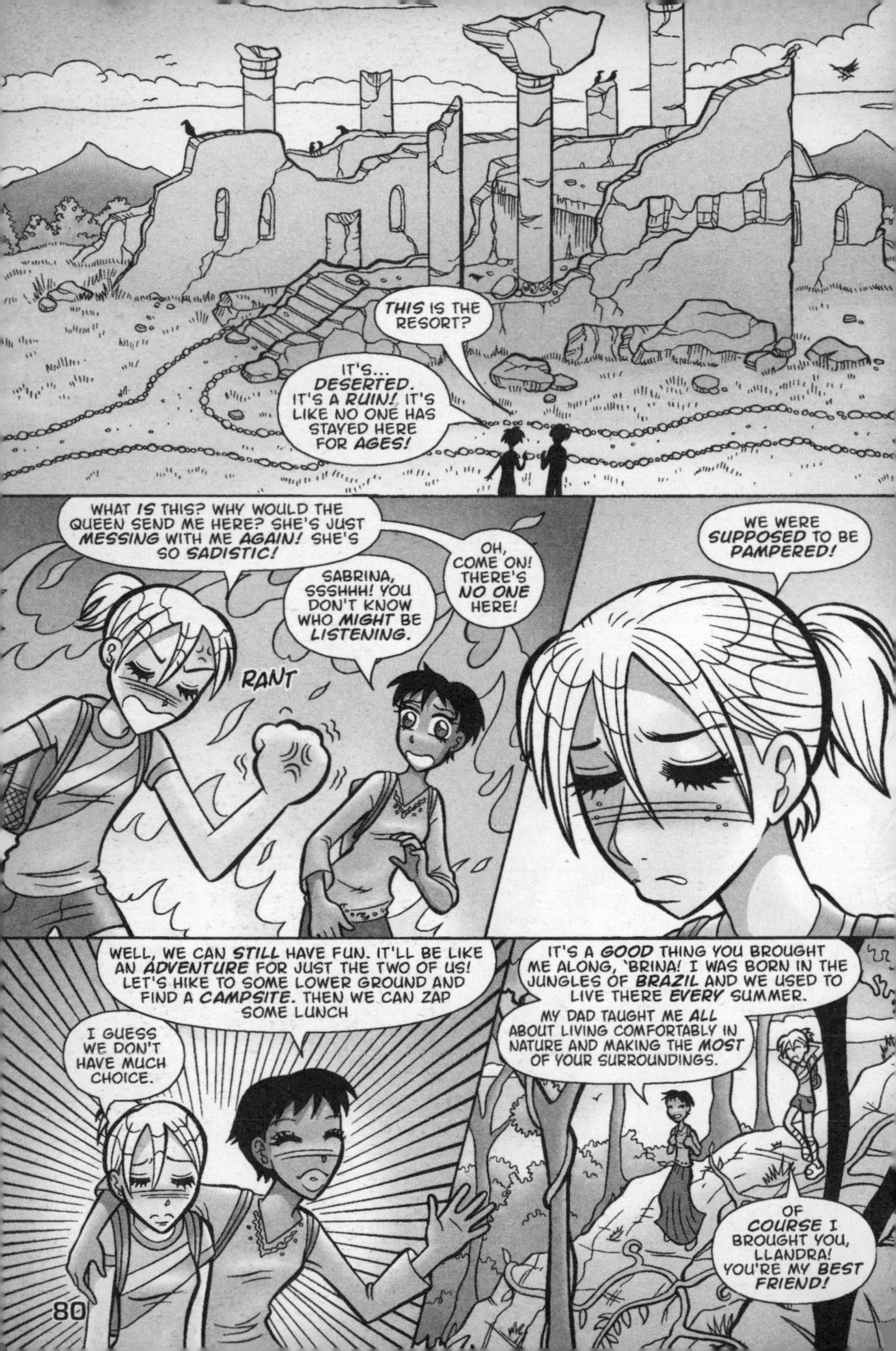
THIS IS THE RESORT?
IT'S... DESERTED. IT'S A RUIN! IT'S LIKE NO ONE HAS STAYED HERE FOR AGES!
WHAT IS THIS? WHY WOULD THE QUEEN SEND ME HERE? SHE'S JUST MESSING WITH ME AGAIN! SHE'S SO SADISTIC!
SABRINA, SSSHHH! YOU DON'T KNOW WHO MIGHT BE LISTENING.
OH, COME ON! THERE'S NO ONE HERE!
RANT
WE WERE SUPPOSED TO BE PAMPERED!
WELL, WE CAN STILL HAVE FUN. IT'LL BE LIKE AN ADVENTURE FOR JUST THE TWO OF US! LET'S HIKE TO SOME LOWER GROUND AND FIND A CAMPSITE. THEN WE CAN ZAP SOME LUNCH
I GUESS WE DON'T HAVE MUCH CHOICE.
IT'S A GOOD THING YOU BROUGHT ME ALONG, 'BRINA! I WAS BORN IN THE JUNGLES OF BRAZIL AND WE USED TO LIVE THERE EVERY SUMMER.
MY DAD TAUGHT ME ALL ABOUT LIVING COMFORTABLY IN NATURE AND MAKING THE MOST OF YOUR SURROUNDINGS.
OF COURSE I BROUGHT YOU, LLANDRA! YOU'RE MY BEST FRIEND!

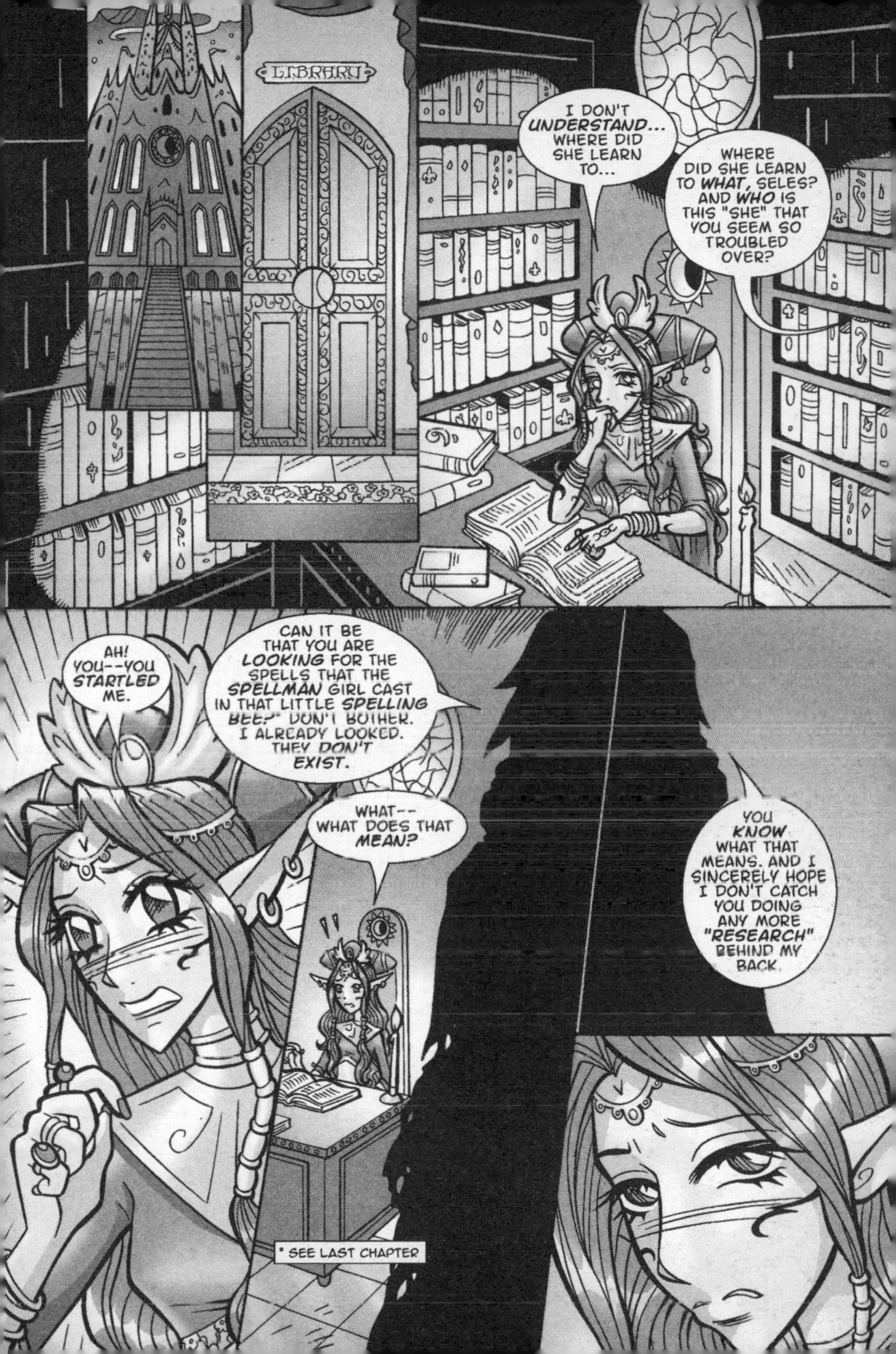
LIBRARY
I DON'T UNDERSTAND... WHERE DID SHE LEARN TO...
WHERE DID SHE LEARN TO WHAT, SELES? AND WHO IS THIS "SHE" THAT YOU SEEM SO TROUBLED OVER?
AH! YOU--YOU STARTLED ME.
CAN IT BE THAT YOU ARE LOOKING FOR THE SPELLS THAT THE SPELLMAN GIRL CAST IN THAT LITTLE SPELLING BEE?* DON'T BOTHER. I ALREADY LOOKED. THEY DON'T EXIST.
WHAT-- WHAT DOES THAT MEAN?
YOU KNOW WHAT THAT MEANS. AND I SINCERELY HOPE I DON'T CATCH YOU DOING ANY MORE "RESEARCH" BEHIND MY BACK.
* SEE LAST CHAPTER

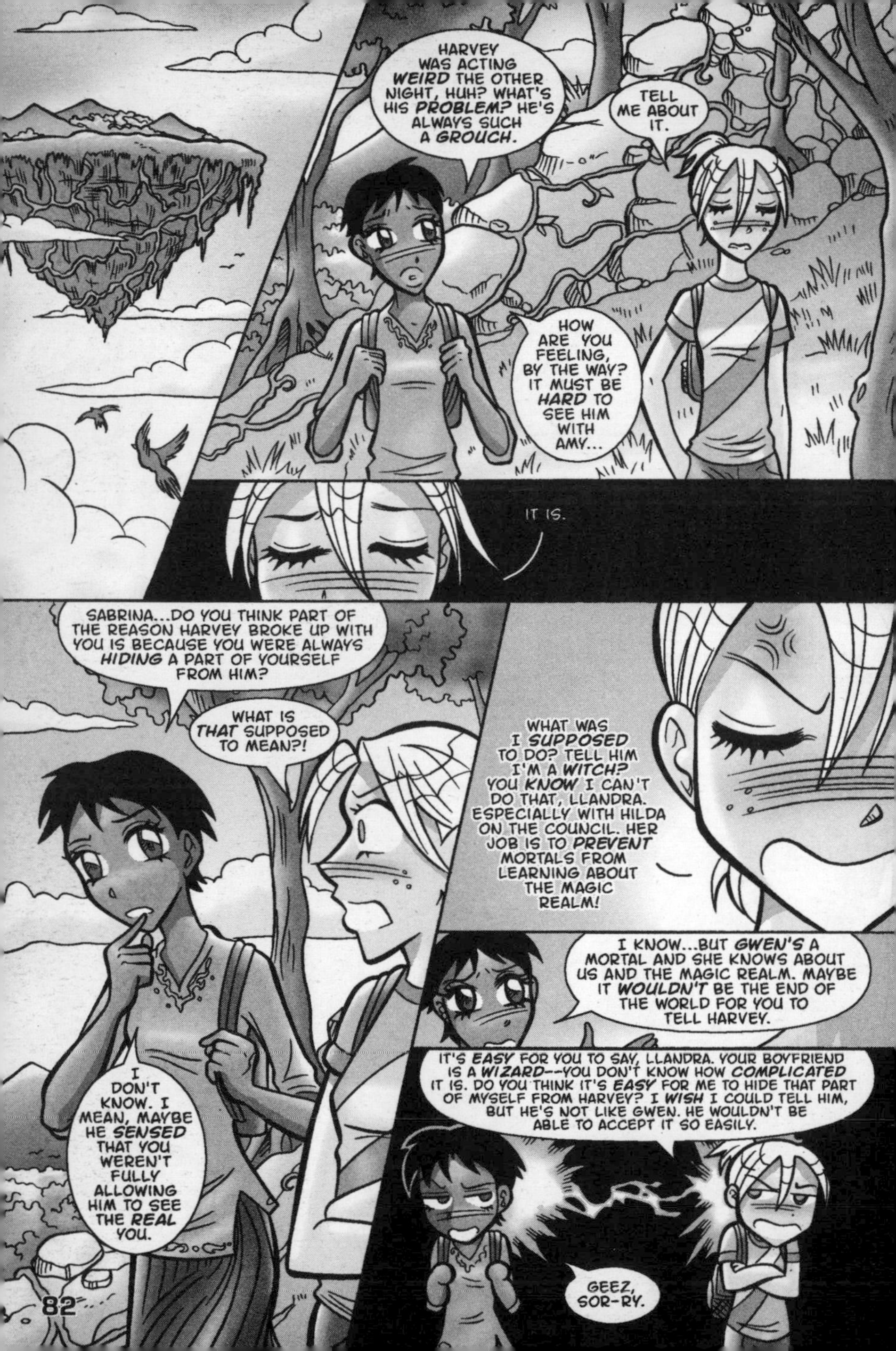
HARVEY WAS ACTING WEIRD THE OTHER NIGHT, HUH? WHAT'S HIS PROBLEM? HE'S ALWAYS SUCH A GROUCH.
TELL ME ABOUT IT.
HOW ARE YOU FEELING, BY THE WAY? IT MUST BE HARD TO SEE HIM WITH AMY...
IT IS.
SABRINA...DO YOU THINK PART OF THE REASON HARVEY BROKE UP WITH YOU IS BECAUSE YOU WERE ALWAYS HIDING A PART OF YOURSELF FROM HIM?
WHAT IS THAT SUPPOSED TO MEAN?!
I DON'T KNOW. I MEAN, MAYBE HE SENSED THAT YOU WEREN'T FULLY ALLOWING HIM TO SEE THE REAL YOU.
WHAT WAS I SUPPOSED TO DO? TELL HIM I'M A WITCH? YOU KNOW I CAN'T DO THAT, LLANDRA. ESPECIALLY WITH HILDA ON THE COUNCIL. HER JOB IS TO PREVENT MORTALS FROM LEARNING ABOUT THE MAGIC REALM!
I KNOW...BUT GWEN'S A MORTAL AND SHE KNOWS ABOUT US AND THE MAGIC REALM. MAYBE IT WOULDN'T BE THE END OF THE WORLD FOR YOU TO TELL HARVEY.
IT'S EASY FOR YOU TO SAY, LLANDRA. YOUR BOYFRIEND IS A WIZARD--YOU DON'T KNOW HOW COMPLICATED IT IS. DO YOU THINK IT'S EASY FOR ME TO HIDE THAT PART OF MYSELF FROM HARVEY? I WISH I COULD TELL HIM, BUT HE'S NOT LIKE GWEN. HE WOULDN'T BE ABLE TO ACCEPT IT SO EASILY.
GEEZ, SOR-RY.

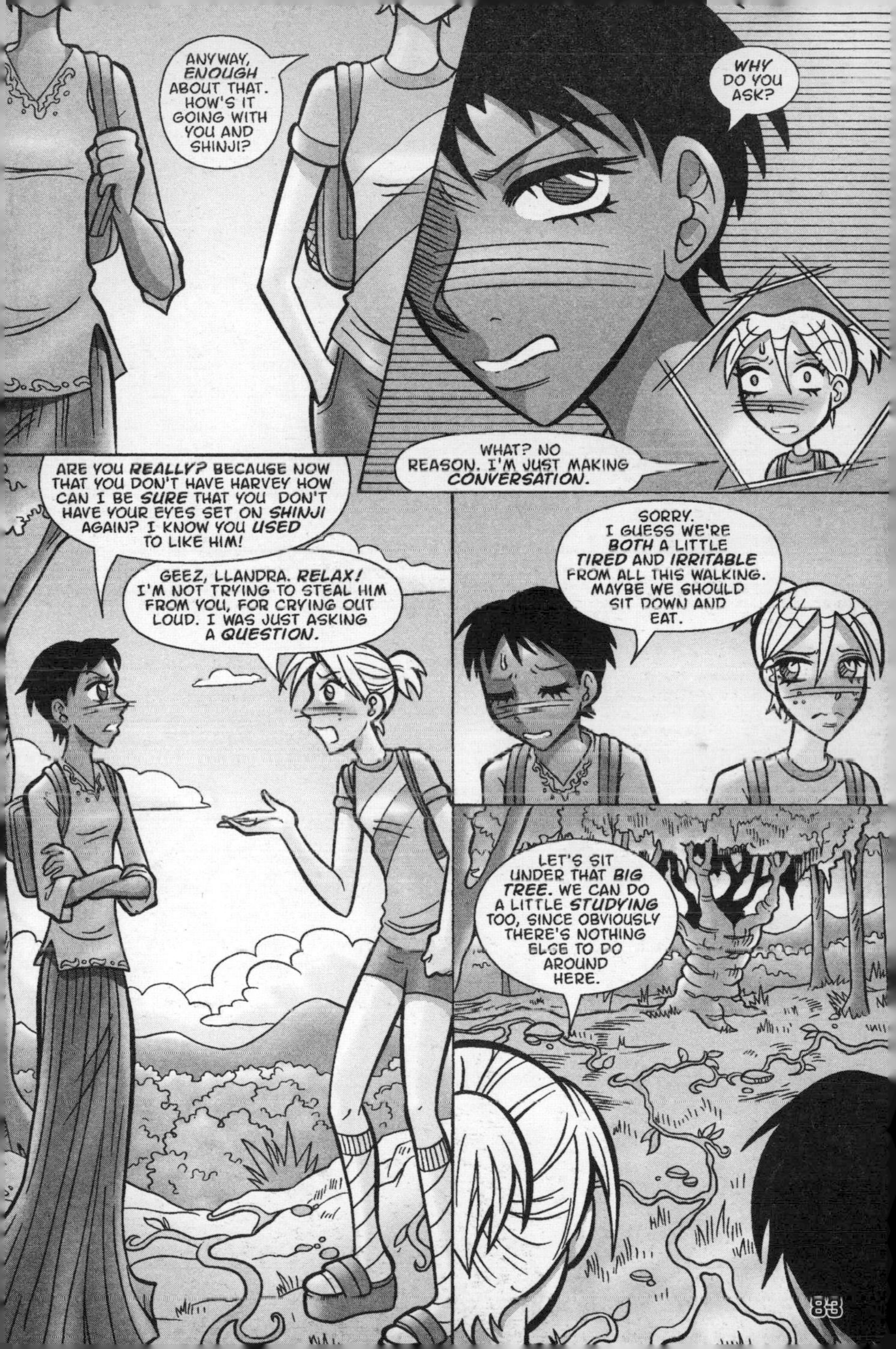
ANYWAY, ENOUGH ABOUT THAT. HOW'S IT GOING WITH YOU AND SHINJI?
WHY DO YOU ASK?
WHAT? NO REASON. I'M JUST MAKING CONVERSATION.
ARE YOU REALLY? BECAUSE NOW THAT YOU DON'T HAVE HARVEY HOW CAN I BE SURE THAT YOU DON'T HAVE YOUR EYES SET ON SHINJI AGAIN? I KNOW YOU USED TO LIKE HIM!
GEEZ, LLANDRA. RELAX! I'M NOT TRYING TO STEAL HIM FROM YOU, FOR CRYING OUT LOUD. I WAS JUST ASKING A QUESTION.
SORRY. I GUESS WE'RE BOTH A LITTLE TIRED AND IRRITABLE FROM ALL THIS WALKING. MAYBE WE SHOULD SIT DOWN AND EAT.
LET'S SIT UNDER THAT BIG TREE. WE CAN DO A LITTLE STUDYING TOO, SINCE OBVIOUSLY THERE'S NOTHING ELSE TO DO AROUND HERE.

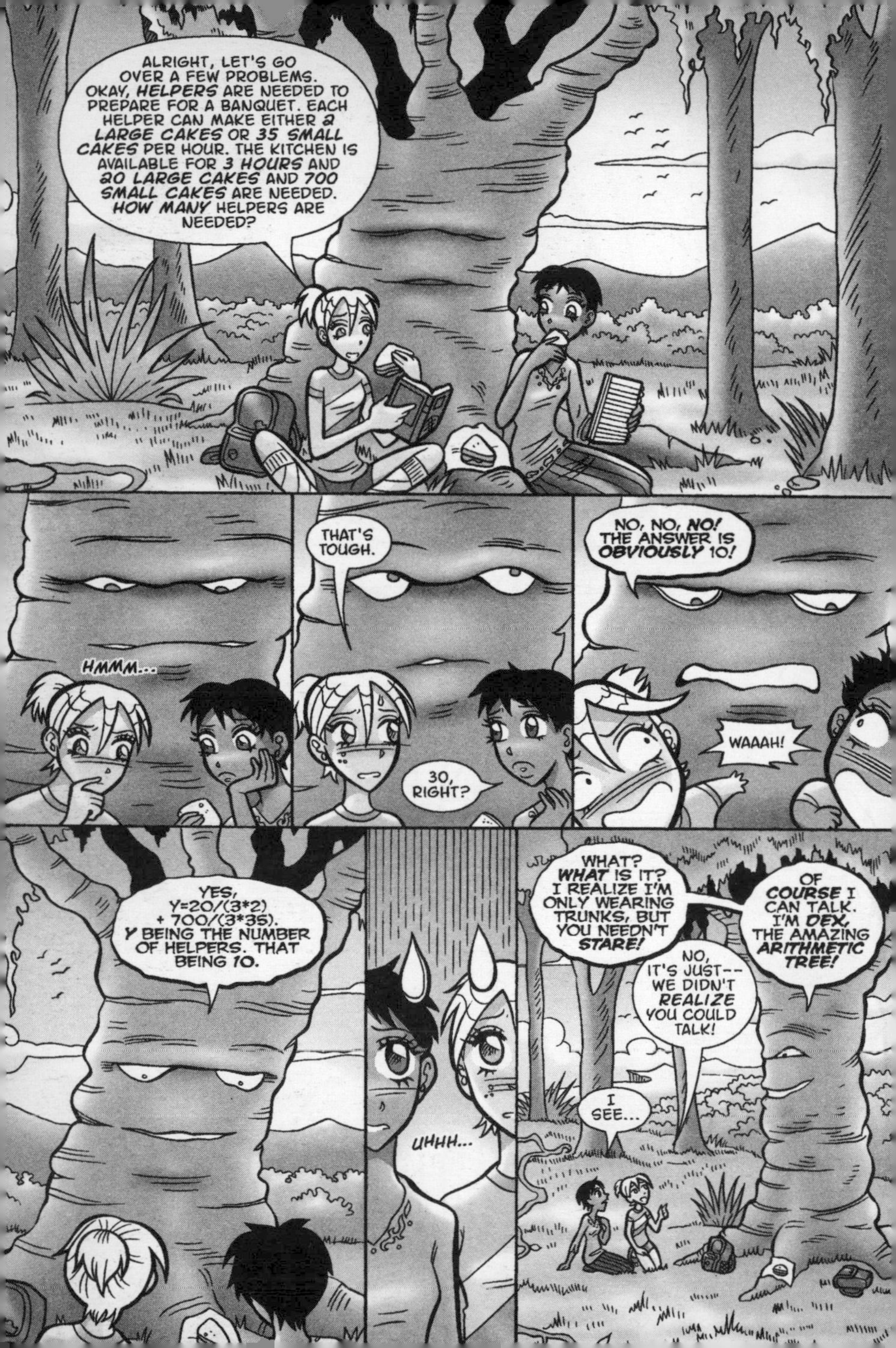
ALRIGHT, LET'S GO OVER A FEW PROBLEMS. OKAY, HELPERS ARE NEEDED TO PREPARE FOR A BANQUET. EACH HELPER CAN MAKE EITHER 2 LARGE CAKES OR 35 SMALL CAKES PER HOUR. THE KITCHEN IS AVAILABLE FOR 3 HOURS AND 20 LARGE CAKES AND 700 SMALL CAKES ARE NEEDED. HOW MANY HELPERS ARE NEEDED?
HMMM...
THAT'S TOUGH.
30, RIGHT?
NO, NO, NO! THE ANSWER IS OBVIOUSLY 10!
WAAAH!
YES, Y=20/(3*2) + 700/(3*35). Y BEING THE NUMBER OF HELPERS. THAT BEING 10.
UHHH...
WHAT? WHAT IS IT? I REALIZE I'M ONLY WEARING TRUNKS, BUT YOU NEEDN'T STARE!
NO, IT'S JUST-- WE DIDN'T REALIZE YOU COULD TALK!
OF COURSE I CAN TALK. I'M DEX, THE AMAZING ARITHMETIC TREE!
I SEE...

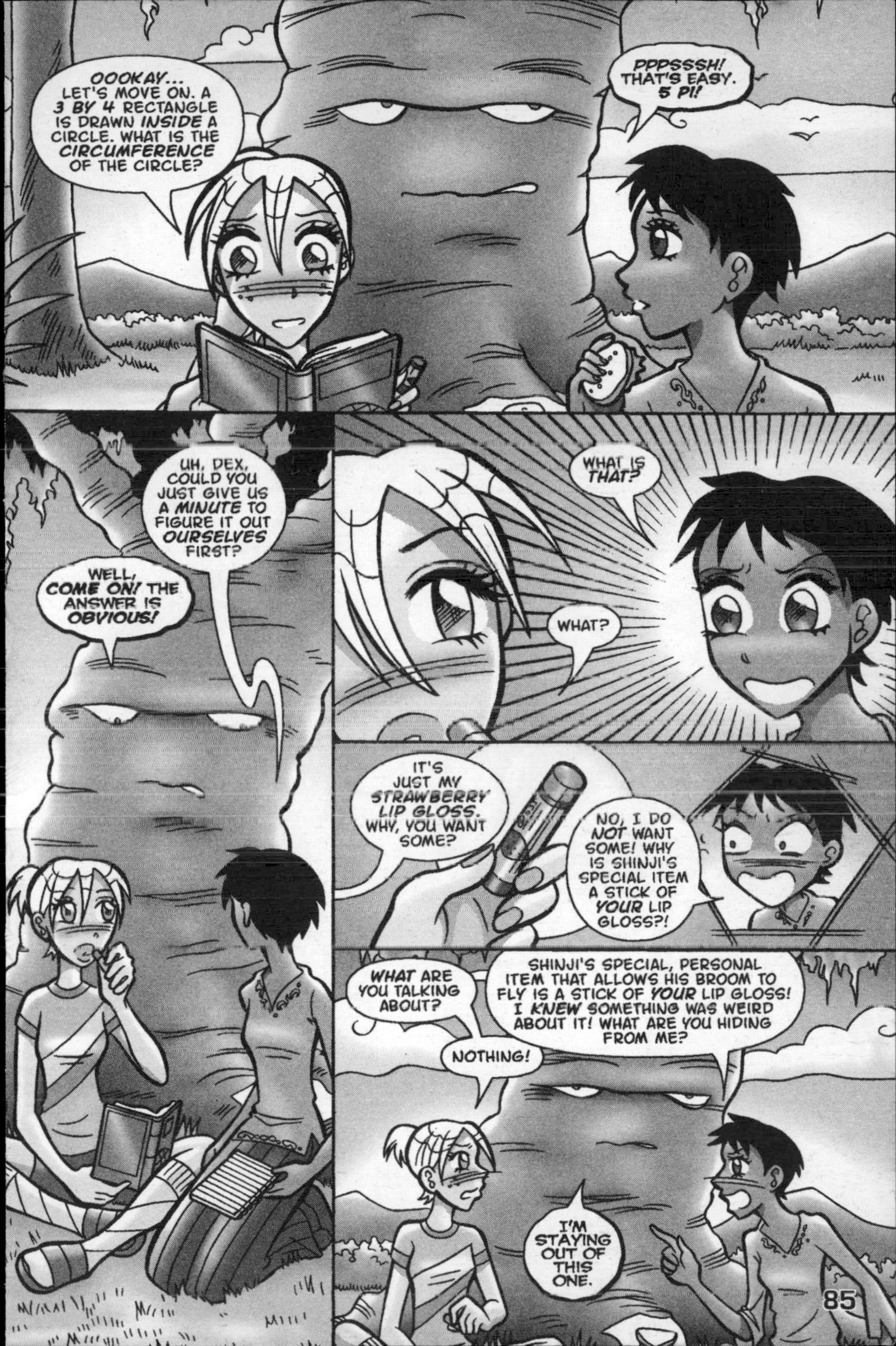
OOOKAY... LET'S MOVE ON. A 3 BY 4 RECTANGLE IS DRAWN INSIDE A CIRCLE. WHAT IS THE CIRCUMFERENCE OF THE CIRCLE?
PPPSSSH! THAT'S EASY. 5 PI!
UH, DEX, COULD YOU JUST GIVE US A MINUTE TO FIGURE IT OUT OURSELVES FIRST?
WELL, COME ON! THE ANSWER IS OBVIOUS!
WHAT IS THAT?
WHAT?
IT'S JUST MY STRAWBERRY LIP GLOSS. WHY, YOU WANT SOME?
NO, I DO NOT WANT SOME! WHY IS SHINJI'S SPECIAL ITEM A STICK OF YOUR LIP GLOSS?!
WHAT ARE YOU TALKING ABOUT?
SHINJI'S SPECIAL, PERSONAL ITEM THAT ALLOWS HIS BROOM TO FLY IS A STICK OF YOUR LIP GLOSS! I KNEW SOMETHING WAS WEIRD ABOUT IT! WHAT ARE YOU HIDING FROM ME?
NOTHING!
I'M STAYING OUT OF THIS ONE.

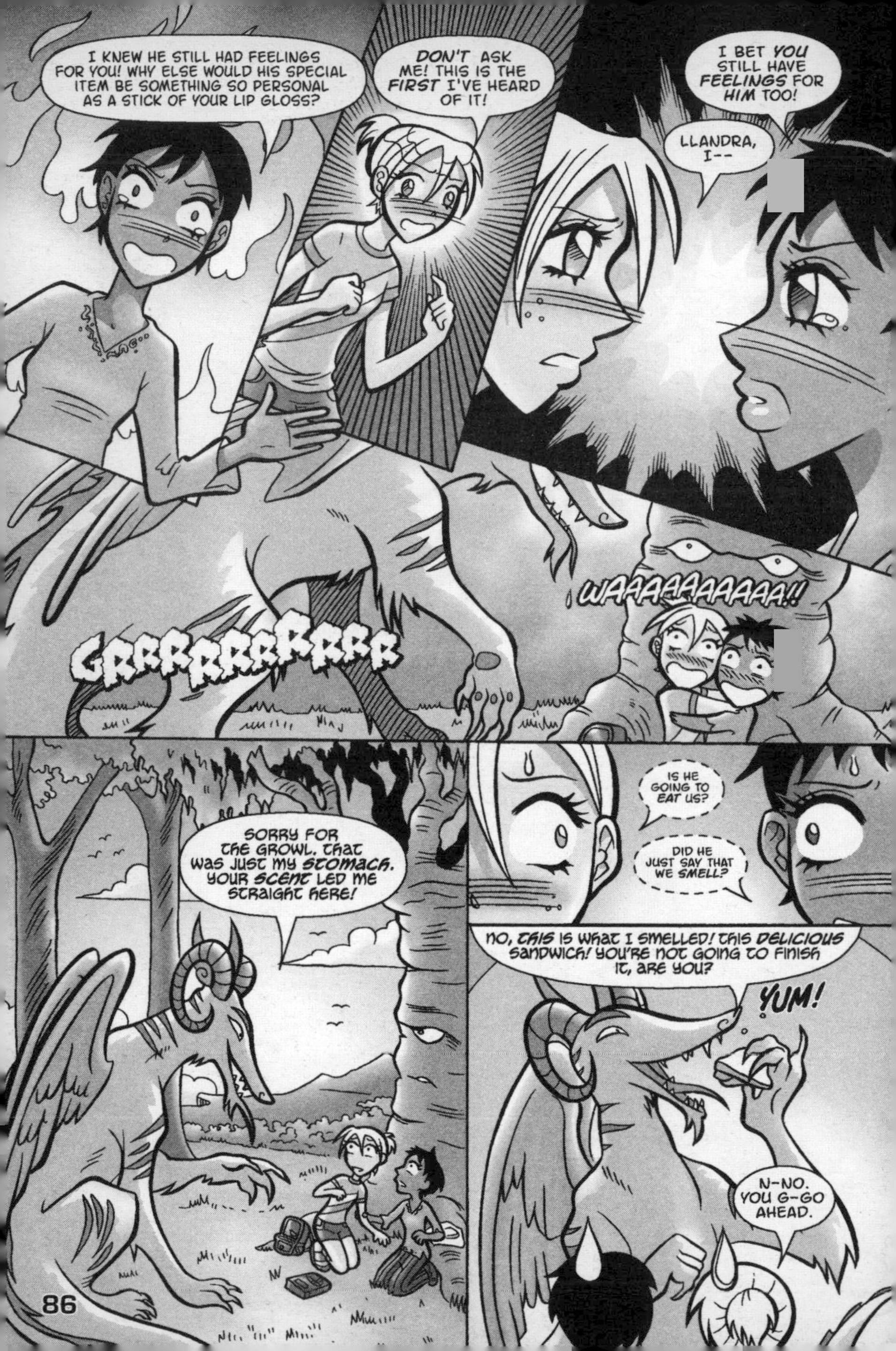
I KNEW HE STILL HAD FEELINGS FOR YOU! WHY ELSE WOULD HIS SPECIAL ITEM BE SOMETHING SO PERSONAL AS A STICK OF YOUR LIP GLOSS?
DON'T ASK ME! THIS IS THE FIRST I'VE HEARD OF IT!
I BET YOU STILL HAVE FEELINGS FOR HIM TOO!
LLANDRA, I--
GRRRRRRRRRR
WAAAAAAAAAA!!
SORRY FOR THE GROWL. THAT WAS JUST MY STOMACH. YOUR SCENT LED ME STRAIGHT HERE!
IS HE GOING TO EAT US?
DID HE JUST SAY THAT WE SMELL?
NO, THIS IS WHAT I SMELLED! THIS DELICIOUS SANDWICH! YOU'RE NOT GOING TO FINISH IT, ARE YOU?
YUM!
N-NO. YOU G-GO AHEAD.

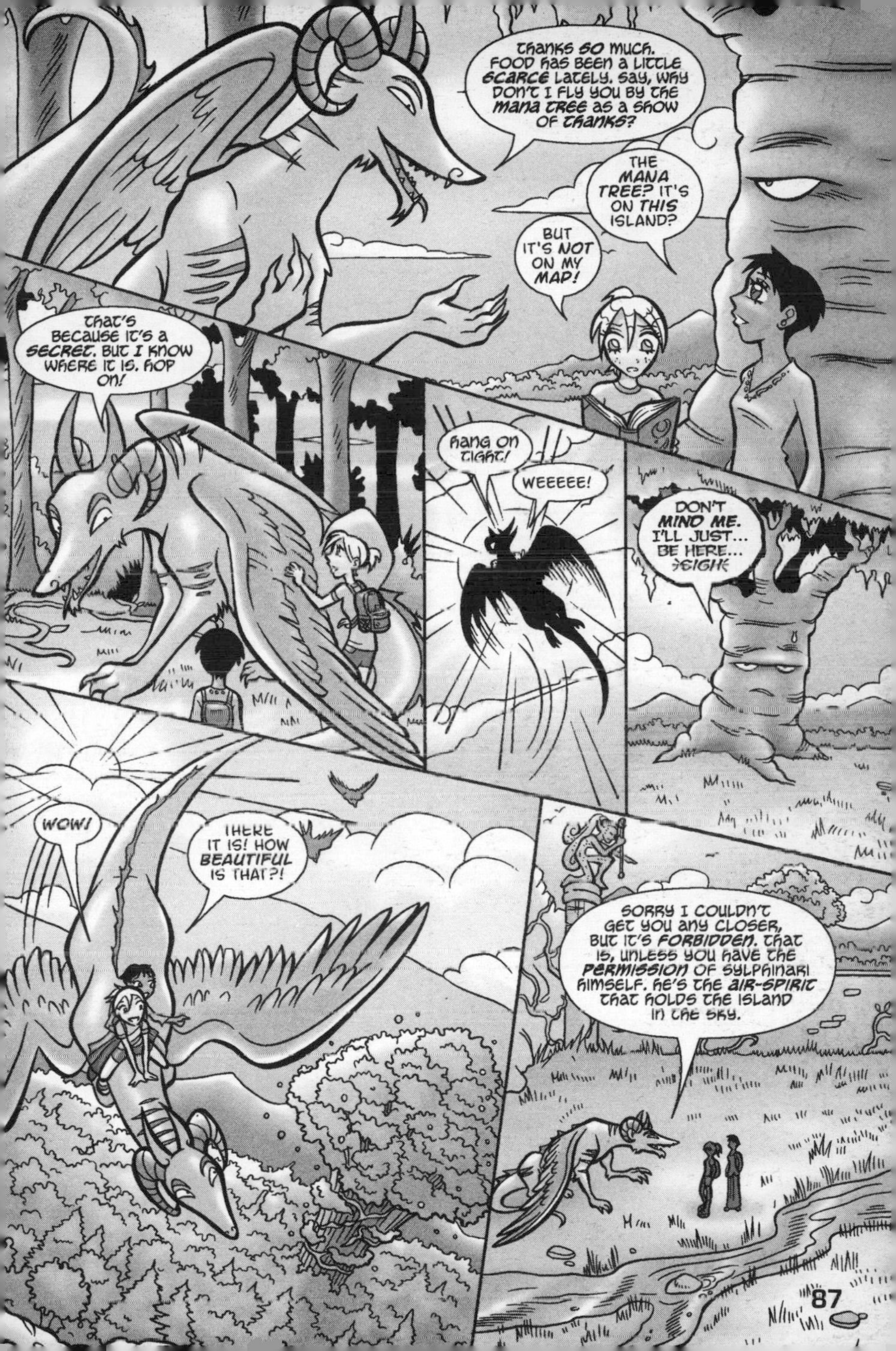
THANKS SO MUCH. FOOD HAS BEEN A LITTLE SCARCE LATELY. SAY, WHY DON'T I FLY YOU BY THE MANA TREE AS A SHOW OF THANKS?
THE MANA TREE? IT'S ON THIS ISLAND?
BUT IT'S NOT ON MY MAP!
THAT'S BECAUSE IT'S A SECRET. BUT I KNOW WHERE IT IS. HOP ON!
HANG ON TIGHT!
WEEEEE!
DON'T MIND ME. I'LL JUST... BE HERE... SIGH
WOW!
THERE IT IS! HOW BEAUTIFUL IS THAT?!
SORRY I COULDN'T GET YOU ANY CLOSER, BUT IT'S FORBIDDEN. THAT IS, UNLESS YOU HAVE THE PERMISSION OF SYLPHINARI HIMSELF. HE'S THE AIR-SPIRIT THAT HOLDS THE ISLAND IN THE SKY.

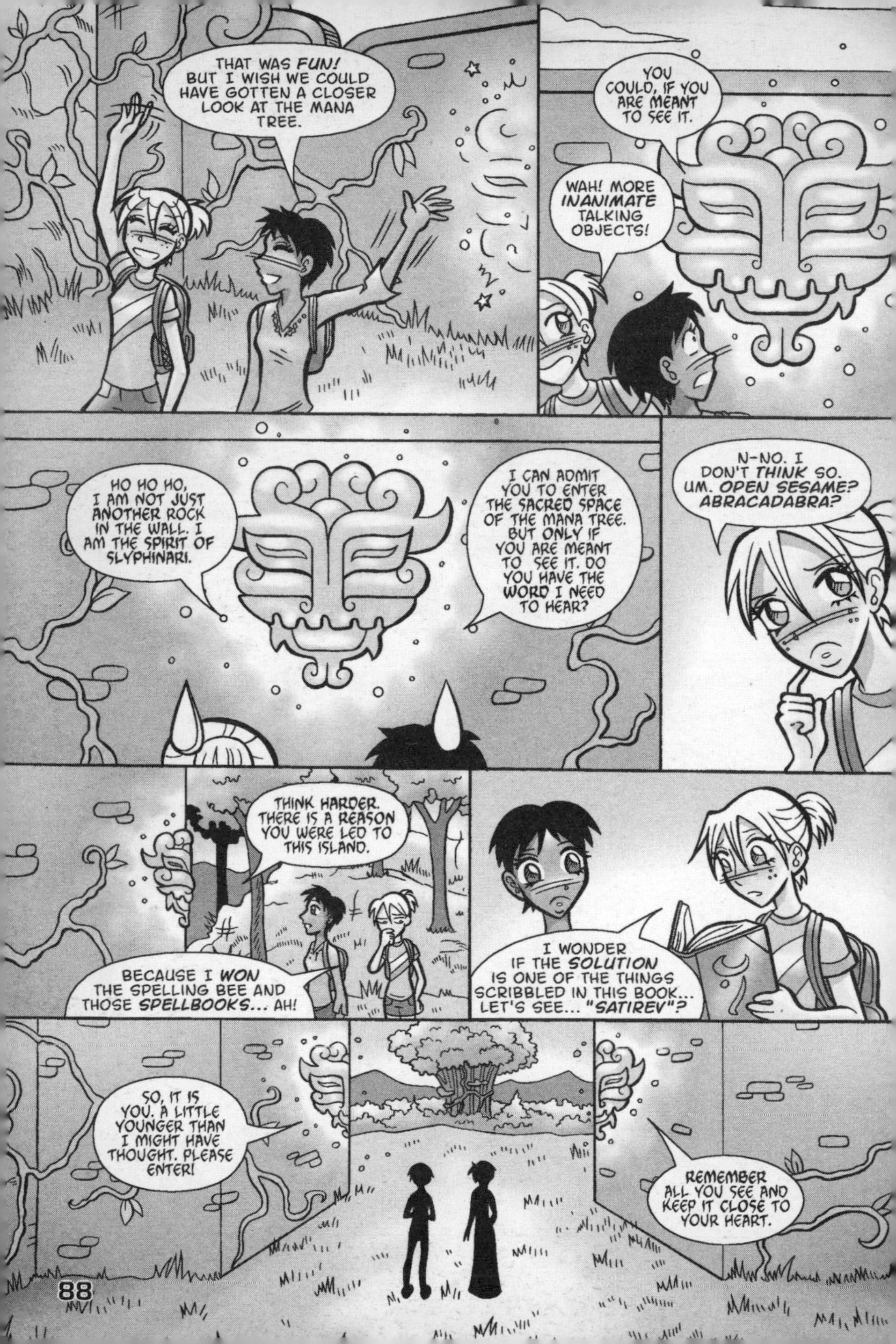
THAT WAS FUN! BUT I WISH WE COULD HAVE GOTTEN A CLOSER LOOK AT THE MANA TREE.
YOU COULD, IF YOU ARE MEANT TO SEE IT.
WAH! MORE INANIMATE TALKING OBJECTS!
HO HO HO, I AM NOT JUST ANOTHER ROCK IN THE WALL. I AM THE SPIRIT OF SLYPHINARI.
I CAN ADMIT YOU TO ENTER THE SACRED SPACE OF THE MANA TREE. BUT ONLY IF YOU ARE MEANT TO SEE IT. DO YOU HAVE THE WORD I NEED TO HEAR?
N-NO. I DON'T THINK SO. UM. OPEN SESAME? ABRACADABRA?
THINK HARDER. THERE IS A REASON YOU WERE LED TO THIS ISLAND.
BECAUSE I WON THE SPELLING BEE AND THOSE SPELLBOOKS... AH!
I WONDER IF THE SOLUTION IS ONE OF THE THINGS SCRIBBLED IN THIS BOOK... LET'S SEE... "SATIREV"?
SO, IT IS YOU. A LITTLE YOUNGER THAN I MIGHT HAVE THOUGHT. PLEASE ENTER!
REMEMBER ALL YOU SEE AND KEEP IT CLOSE TO YOUR HEART.

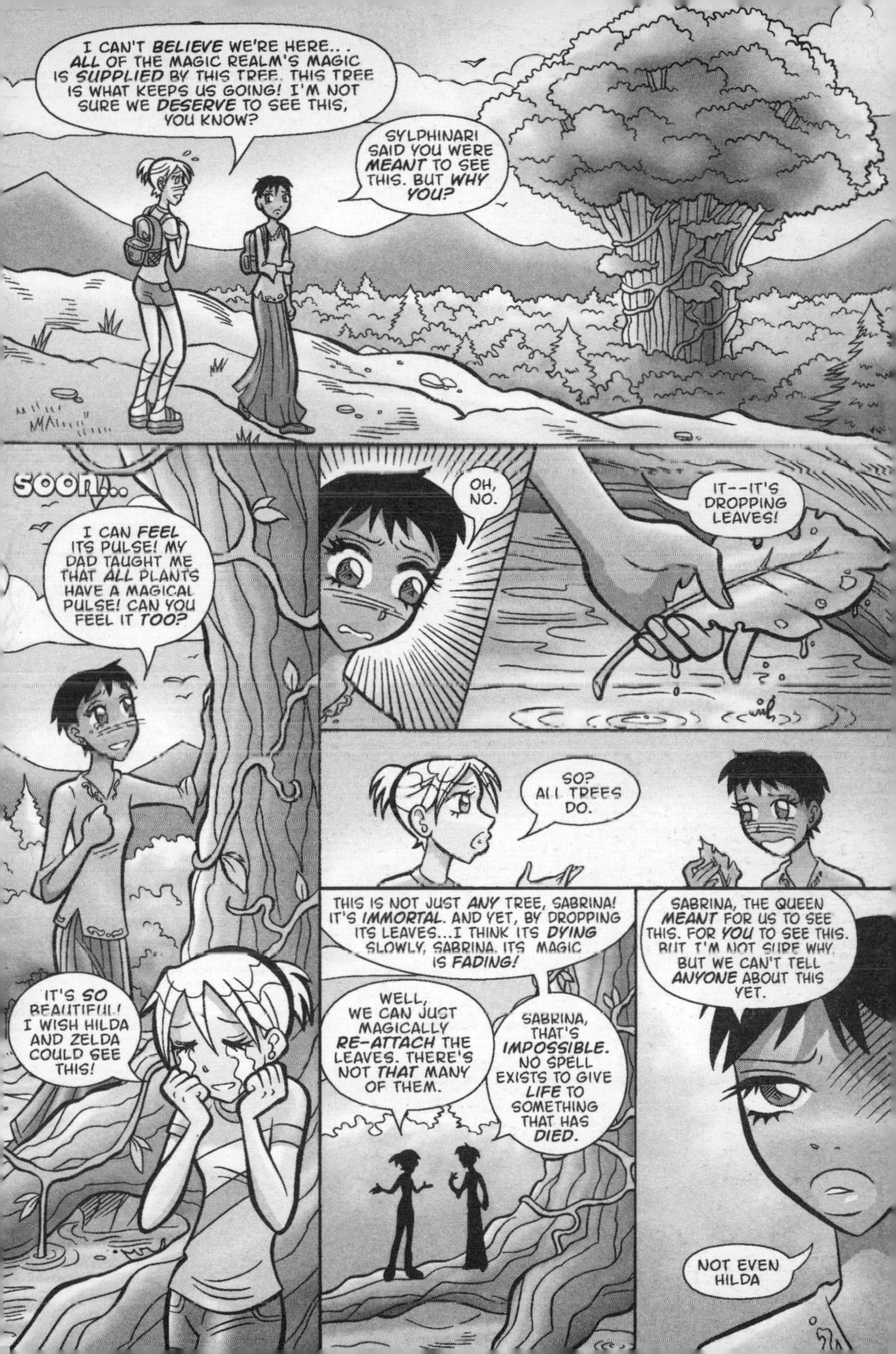
I CAN'T BELIEVE WE'RE HERE... ALL OF THE MAGIC REALM'S MAGIC IS SUPPLIED BY THIS TREE. THIS TREE IS WHAT KEEPS US GOING! I'M NOT SURE WE DESERVE TO SEE THIS, YOU KNOW?
SYLPHINARI SAID YOU WERE MEANT TO SEE THIS. BUT WHY YOU?
SOON...
I CAN FEEL ITS PULSE! MY DAD TAUGHT ME THAT ALL PLANTS HAVE A MAGICAL PULSE! CAN YOU FEEL IT TOO?
IT'S SO BEAUTIFUL! I WISH HILDA AND ZELDA COULD SEE THIS!
OH, NO.
IT--IT'S DROPPING LEAVES!
SO? ALL TREES DO.
THIS IS NOT JUST ANY TREE, SABRINA! IT'S IMMORTAL. AND YET, BY DROPPING ITS LEAVES...I THINK ITS DYING SLOWLY, SABRINA. ITS MAGIC IS FADING!
WELL, WE CAN JUST MAGICALLY RE-ATTACH THE LEAVES. THERE'S NOT THAT MANY OF THEM.
SABRINA, THAT'S IMPOSSIBLE. NO SPELL EXISTS TO GIVE LIFE TO SOMETHING THAT HAS DIED.
SABRINA, THE QUEEN MEANT FOR US TO SEE THIS. FOR YOU TO SEE THIS. BUT I'M NOT SURE WHY. BUT WE CAN'T TELL ANYONE ABOUT THIS YET.
NOT EVEN HILDA

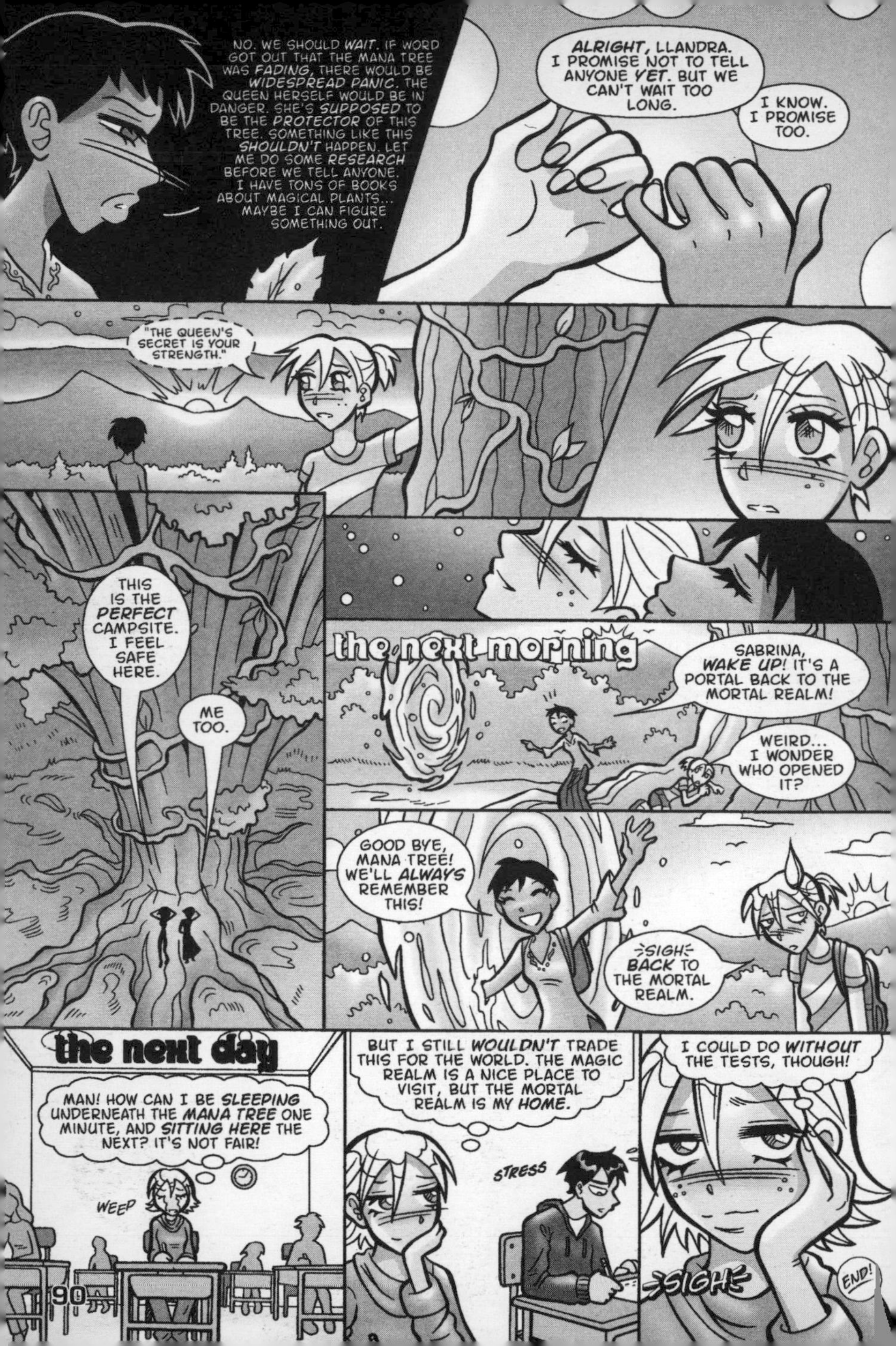

NO. WE SHOULD WAIT. IF WORD GOT OUT THAT THE MANA TREE WAS FADING, THERE WOULD BE WIDESPREAD PANIC. THE QUEEN HERSELF WOULD BE IN DANGER. SHE'S SUPPOSED TO BE THE PROTECTOR OF THIS TREE. SOMETHING LIKE THIS SHOULDN'T HAPPEN. LET ME DO SOME RESEARCH BEFORE WE TELL ANYONE. I HAVE TONS OF BOOKS ABOUT MAGICAL PLANTS... MAYBE I CAN FIGURE SOMETHING OUT.
ALRIGHT, LLANDRA. I PROMISE NOT TO TELL ANYONE YET. BUT WE CAN'T WAIT TOO LONG.
I KNOW. I PROMISE TOO.
"THE QUEEN'S SECRET IS YOUR STRENGTH."
THIS IS THE PERFECT CAMPSITE. I FEEL SAFE HERE.
ME TOO.
the next morning
SABRINA, WAKE UP! IT'S A PORTAL BACK TO THE MORTAL REALM!
WEIRD... I WONDER WHO OPENED IT?
GOOD BYE, MANA TREE! WE'LL ALWAYS REMEMBER THIS!
SIGH BACK TO THE MORTAL REALM.
the next day
MAN! HOW CAN I BE SLEEPING UNDERNEATH THE MANA TREE ONE MINUTE, AND SITTING HERE THE NEXT? IT'S NOT FAIR!
WEEP
BUT I STILL WOULDN'T TRADE THIS FOR THE WORLD. THE MAGIC REALM IS A NICE PLACE TO VISIT, BUT THE MORTAL REALM IS MY HOME.
STRESS
I COULD DO WITHOUT THE TESTS, THOUGH!
SIGH
END!

Chapter 5

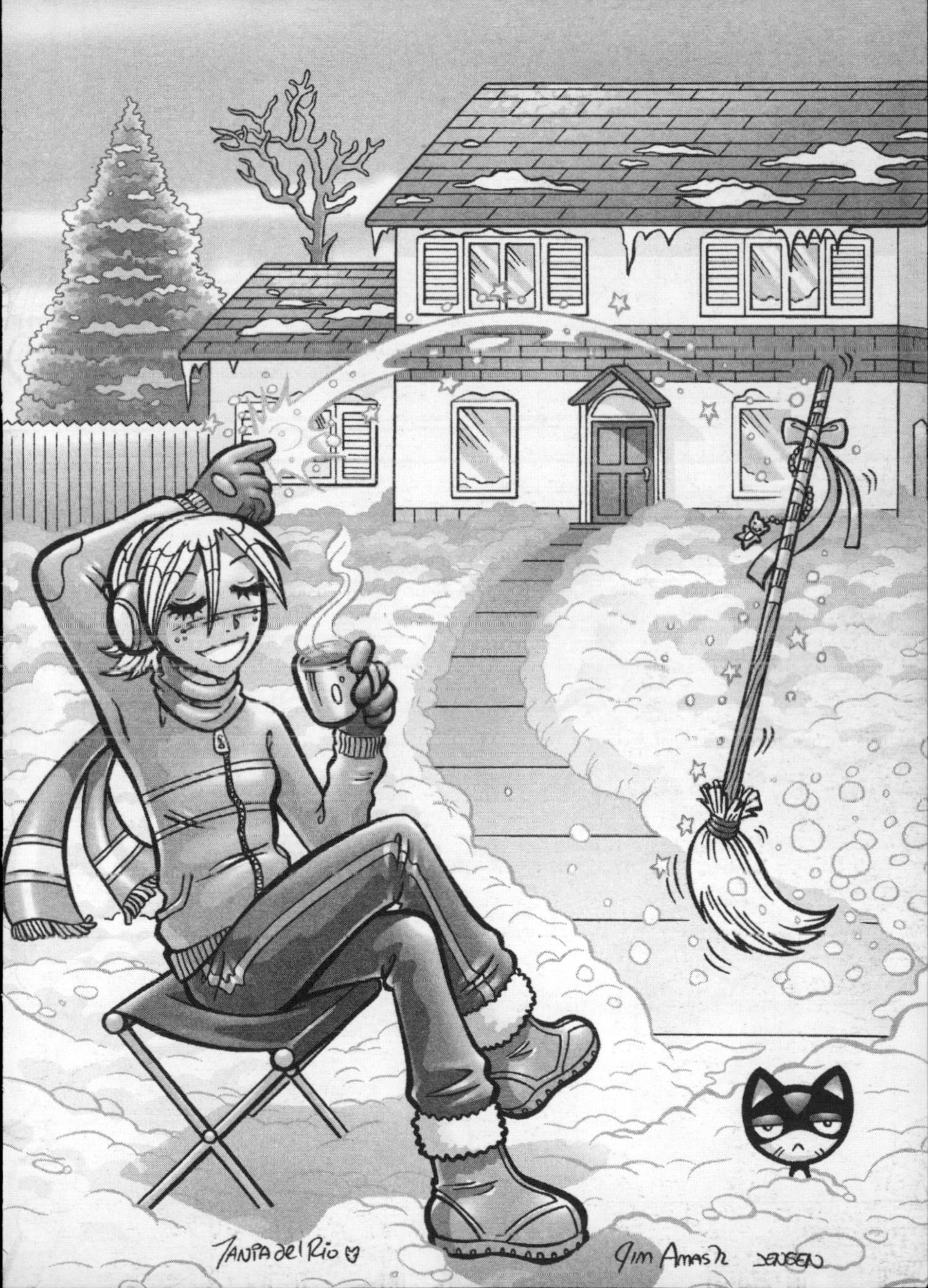
Tania del Rio
Jim Amash
Jensen

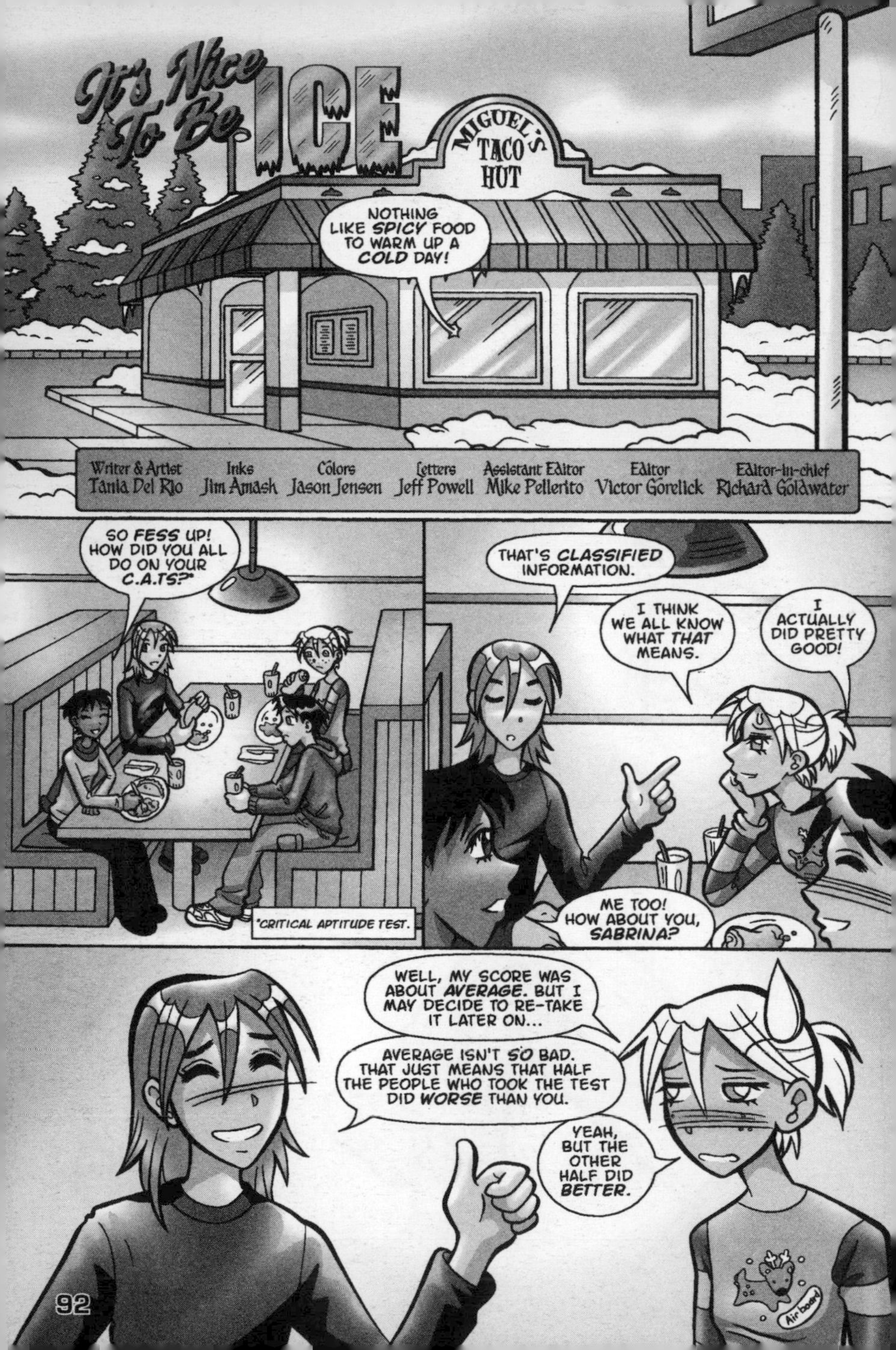

It's Nice To Be ICE
MIGUEL'S TACO HUT
NOTHING LIKE SPICY FOOD TO WARM UP A COLD DAY!
Writer & Artist Tania Del Rio
Inks Jim Amash
Colors Jason Jensen
Letters Jeff Powell
Assistant Editor Mike Pellerito
Editor Victor Gorelick
Editor-in-chief Richard Goldwater
SO FESS UP! HOW DID YOU ALL DO ON YOUR C.A.TS?*
*CRITICAL APTITUDE TEST.
THAT'S CLASSIFIED INFORMATION.
I THINK WE ALL KNOW WHAT THAT MEANS.
I ACTUALLY DID PRETTY GOOD!
ME TOO! HOW ABOUT YOU, SABRINA?
WELL, MY SCORE WAS ABOUT AVERAGE. BUT I MAY DECIDE TO RE-TAKE IT LATER ON...
AVERAGE ISN'T SO BAD. THAT JUST MEANS THAT HALF THE PEOPLE WHO TOOK THE TEST DID WORSE THAN YOU.
YEAH, BUT THE OTHER HALF DID BETTER.
Air board

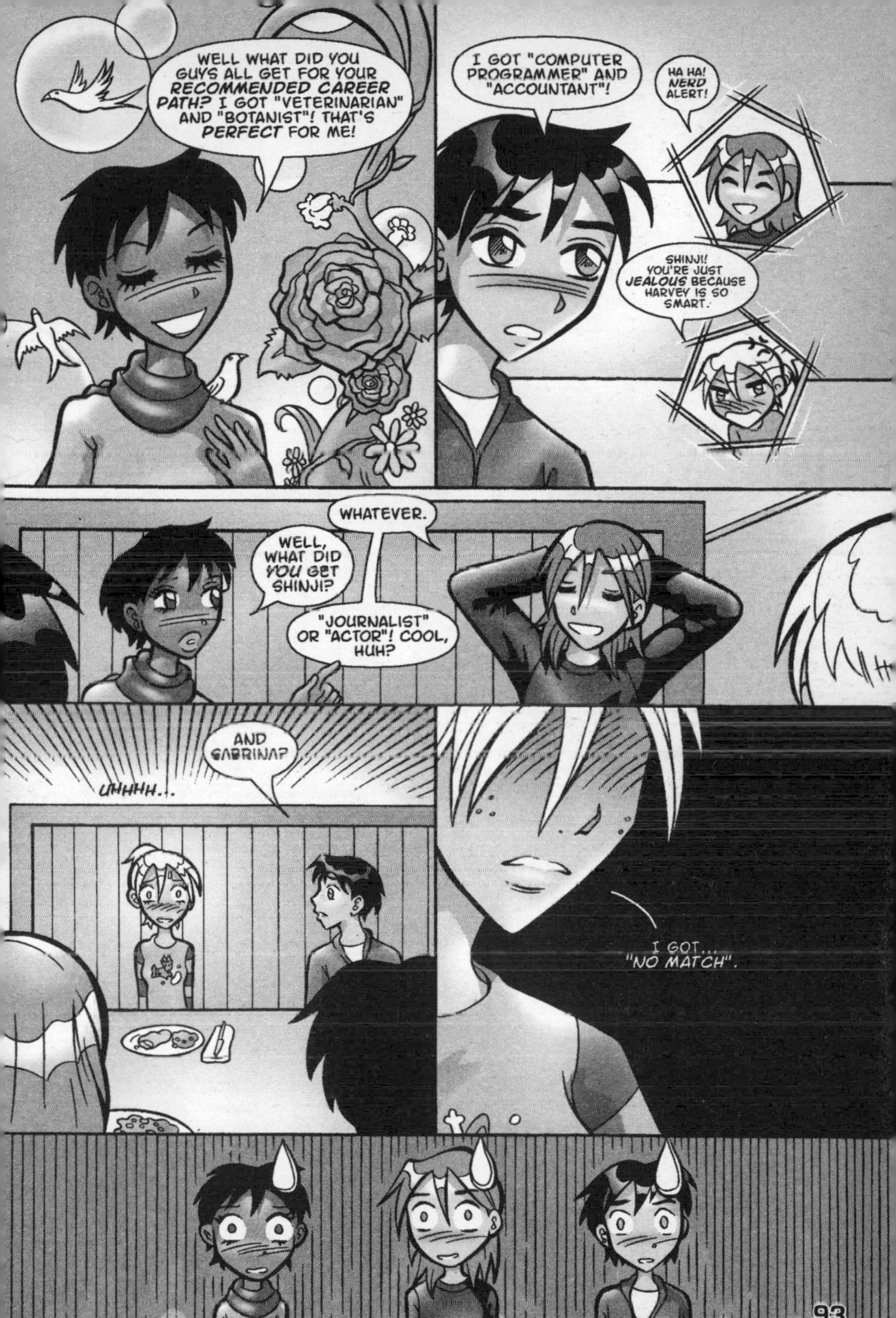

WELL WHAT DID YOU GUYS ALL GET FOR YOUR RECOMMENDED CAREER PATH? I GOT "VETERINARIAN" AND "BOTANIST"! THAT'S PERFECT FOR ME!
I GOT "COMPUTER PROGRAMMER" AND "ACCOUNTANT"!
HA HA! NERD ALERT!
SHINJI! YOU'RE JUST JEALOUS BECAUSE HARVEY IS SO SMART.
WELL, WHAT DID YOU GET SHINJI?
WHATEVER.
"JOURNALIST" OR "ACTOR"! COOL, HUH?
AND SABRINA?
UHHHH...
I GOT... "NO MATCH".

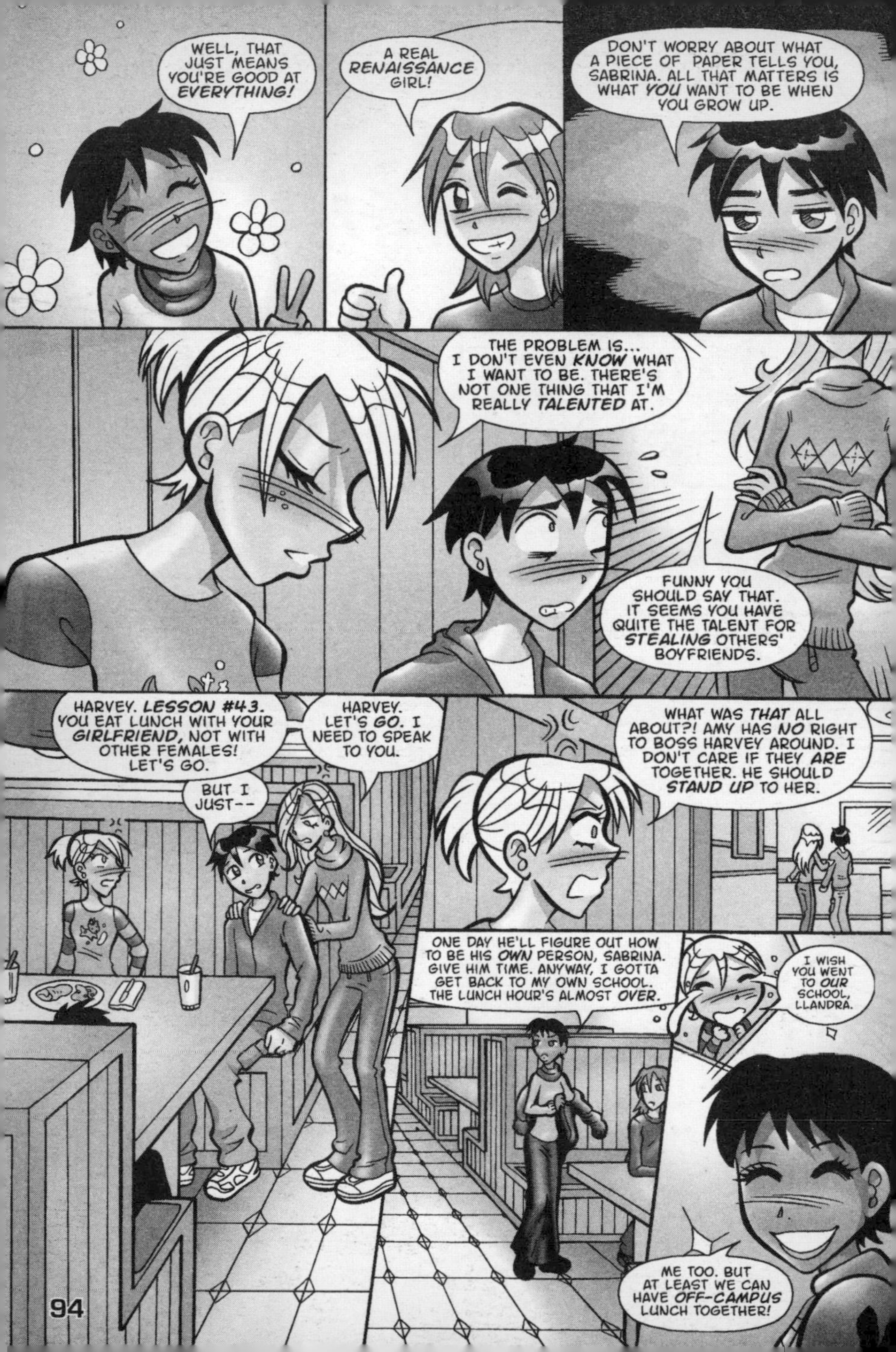
WELL, THAT JUST MEANS YOU'RE GOOD AT EVERYTHING!
A REAL RENAISSANCE GIRL!
DON'T WORRY ABOUT WHAT A PIECE OF PAPER TELLS YOU, SABRINA. ALL THAT MATTERS IS WHAT YOU WANT TO BE WHEN YOU GROW UP.
THE PROBLEM IS... I DON'T EVEN KNOW WHAT I WANT TO BE. THERE'S NOT ONE THING THAT I'M REALLY TALENTED AT.
FUNNY YOU SHOULD SAY THAT. IT SEEMS YOU HAVE QUITE THE TALENT FOR STEALING OTHERS' BOYFRIENDS.
HARVEY. LESSON #43. YOU EAT LUNCH WITH YOUR GIRLFRIEND, NOT WITH OTHER FEMALES! LET'S GO.
HARVEY. LET'S GO. I NEED TO SPEAK TO YOU.
BUT I JUST--
WHAT WAS THAT ALL ABOUT?! AMY HAS NO RIGHT TO BOSS HARVEY AROUND. I DON'T CARE IF THEY ARE TOGETHER. HE SHOULD STAND UP TO HER.
ONE DAY HE'LL FIGURE OUT HOW TO BE HIS OWN PERSON, SABRINA. GIVE HIM TIME. ANYWAY, I GOTTA GET BACK TO MY OWN SCHOOL. THE LUNCH HOUR'S ALMOST OVER.
I WISH YOU WENT TO OUR SCHOOL, LLANDRA.
ME TOO. BUT AT LEAST WE CAN HAVE OFF-CAMPUS LUNCH TOGETHER!

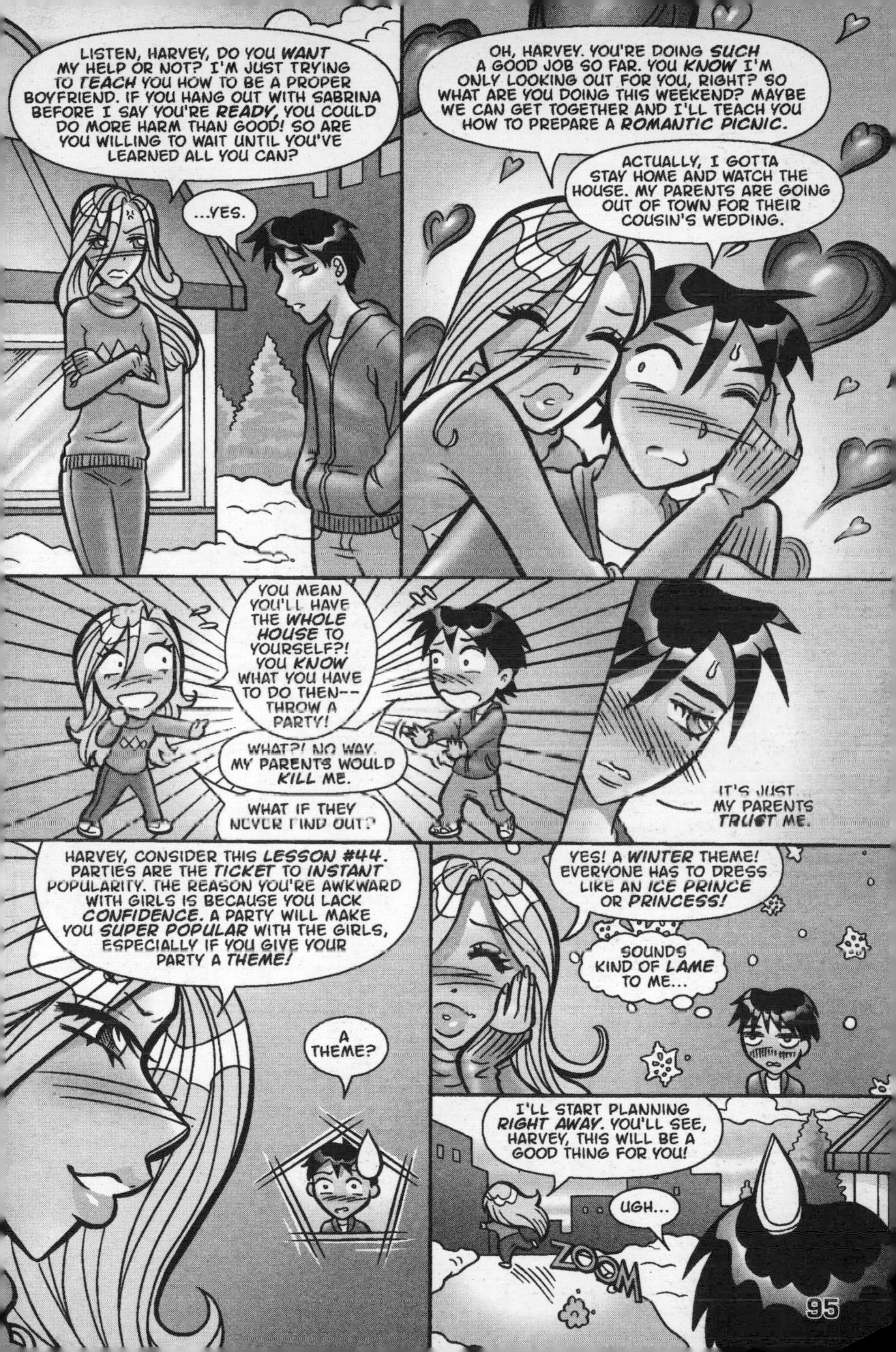

LISTEN, HARVEY, DO YOU WANT MY HELP OR NOT? I'M JUST TRYING TO TEACH YOU HOW TO BE A PROPER BOYFRIEND. IF YOU HANG OUT WITH SABRINA BEFORE I SAY YOU'RE READY, YOU COULD DO MORE HARM THAN GOOD! SO ARE YOU WILLING TO WAIT UNTIL YOU'VE LEARNED ALL YOU CAN?
...YES.
OH, HARVEY. YOU'RE DOING SUCH A GOOD JOB SO FAR. YOU KNOW I'M ONLY LOOKING OUT FOR YOU, RIGHT? SO WHAT ARE YOU DOING THIS WEEKEND? MAYBE WE CAN GET TOGETHER AND I'LL TEACH YOU HOW TO PREPARE A ROMANTIC PICNIC.
ACTUALLY, I GOTTA STAY HOME AND WATCH THE HOUSE. MY PARENTS ARE GOING OUT OF TOWN FOR THEIR COUSIN'S WEDDING.
YOU MEAN YOU'LL HAVE THE WHOLE HOUSE TO YOURSELF?! YOU KNOW WHAT YOU HAVE TO DO THEN-- THROW A PARTY!
WHAT?! NO WAY. MY PARENTS WOULD KILL ME.
WHAT IF THEY NEVER FIND OUT?
IT'S JUST... MY PARENTS TRUST ME.
HARVEY, CONSIDER THIS LESSON #44. PARTIES ARE THE TICKET TO INSTANT POPULARITY. THE REASON YOU'RE AWKWARD WITH GIRLS IS BECAUSE YOU LACK CONFIDENCE. A PARTY WILL MAKE YOU SUPER POPULAR WITH THE GIRLS, ESPECIALLY IF YOU GIVE YOUR PARTY A THEME!
A THEME?
YES! A WINTER THEME! EVERYONE HAS TO DRESS LIKE AN ICE PRINCE OR PRINCESS!
SOUNDS KIND OF LAME TO ME...
I'LL START PLANNING RIGHT AWAY. YOU'LL SEE, HARVEY, THIS WILL BE A GOOD THING FOR YOU!
UGH...
ZOOM

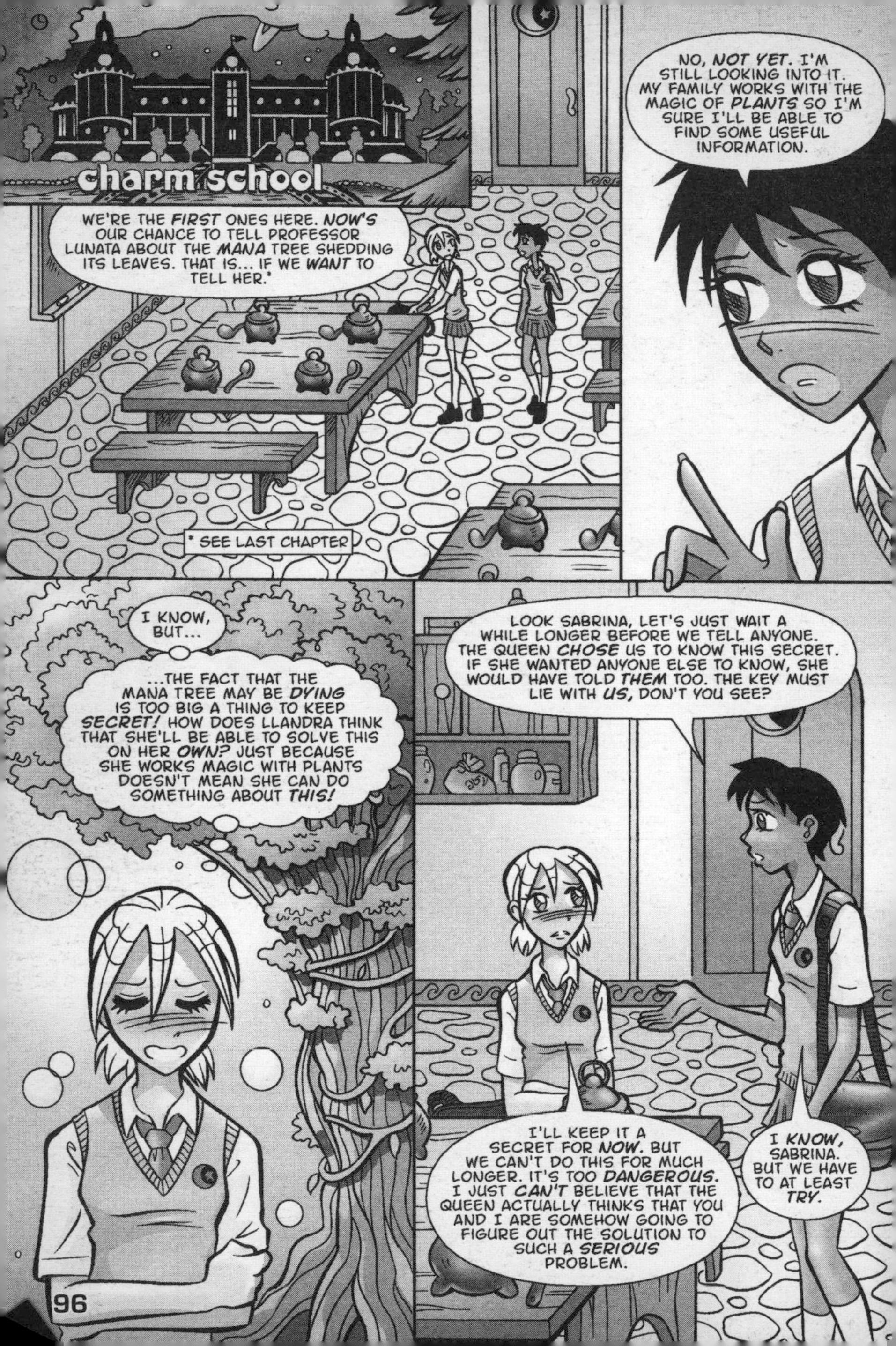
charm school
WE'RE THE *FIRST* ONES HERE. *NOW'S* OUR CHANCE TO TELL PROFESSOR LUNATA ABOUT THE *MANA* TREE SHEDDING ITS LEAVES. THAT IS... IF WE *WANT* TO TELL HER.*
* SEE LAST CHAPTER
NO, *NOT YET*. I'M STILL LOOKING INTO IT. MY FAMILY WORKS WITH THE MAGIC OF *PLANTS* SO I'M SURE I'LL BE ABLE TO FIND SOME USEFUL INFORMATION.
I KNOW, BUT...
...THE FACT THAT THE MANA TREE MAY BE *DYING* IS TOO BIG A THING TO KEEP *SECRET!* HOW DOES LLANDRA THINK THAT SHE'LL BE ABLE TO SOLVE THIS ON HER *OWN?* JUST BECAUSE SHE WORKS MAGIC WITH PLANTS DOESN'T MEAN SHE CAN DO SOMETHING ABOUT *THIS!*
LOOK SABRINA, LET'S JUST WAIT A WHILE LONGER BEFORE WE TELL ANYONE. THE QUEEN *CHOSE* US TO KNOW THIS SECRET. IF SHE WANTED ANYONE ELSE TO KNOW, SHE WOULD HAVE TOLD *THEM* TOO. THE KEY MUST LIE WITH *US,* DON'T YOU SEE?
I'LL KEEP IT A SECRET FOR *NOW*. BUT WE CAN'T DO THIS FOR MUCH LONGER. IT'S TOO *DANGEROUS*. I JUST *CAN'T* BELIEVE THAT THE QUEEN ACTUALLY THINKS THAT YOU AND I ARE SOMEHOW GOING TO FIGURE OUT THE SOLUTION TO SUCH A *SERIOUS* PROBLEM.
I *KNOW,* SABRINA. BUT WE HAVE TO AT LEAST *TRY*.

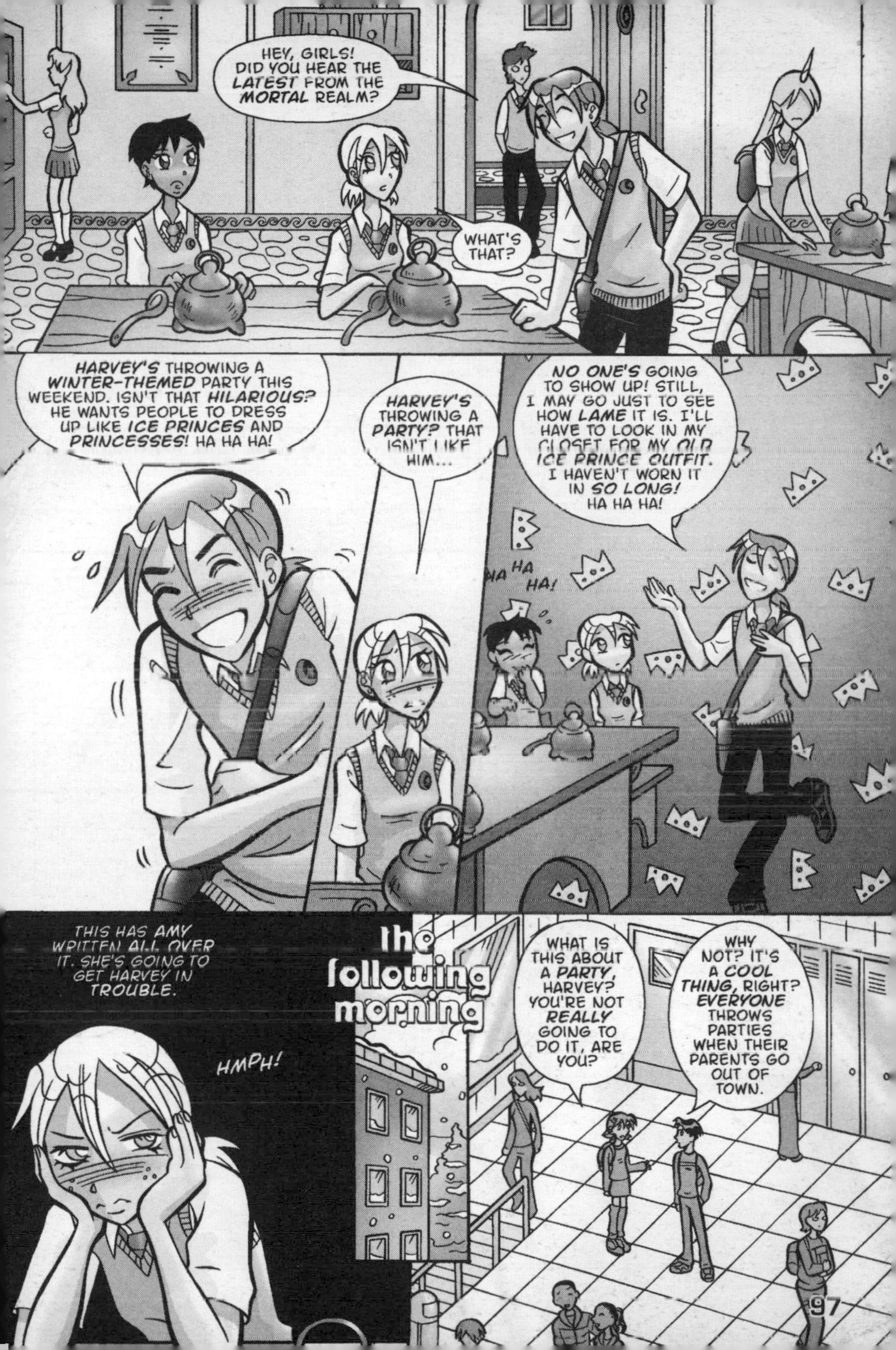

HEY, GIRLS! DID YOU HEAR THE LATEST FROM THE MORTAL REALM?
WHAT'S THAT?
HARVEY'S THROWING A WINTER-THEMED PARTY THIS WEEKEND. ISN'T THAT HILARIOUS? HE WANTS PEOPLE TO DRESS UP LIKE ICE PRINCES AND PRINCESSES! HA HA HA!
HARVEY'S THROWING A PARTY? THAT ISN'T LIKE HIM...
NO ONE'S GOING TO SHOW UP! STILL, I MAY GO JUST TO SEE HOW LAME IT IS. I'LL HAVE TO LOOK IN MY CLOSET FOR MY OLD ICE PRINCE OUTFIT. I HAVEN'T WORN IT IN SO LONG! HA HA HA!
HA HA HA!
THIS HAS AMY WRITTEN ALL OVER IT. SHE'S GOING TO GET HARVEY IN TROUBLE.
HMPH!
the following morning
WHAT IS THIS ABOUT A PARTY, HARVEY? YOU'RE NOT REALLY GOING TO DO IT, ARE YOU?
WHY NOT? IT'S A COOL THING, RIGHT? EVERYONE THROWS PARTIES WHEN THEIR PARENTS GO OUT OF TOWN.

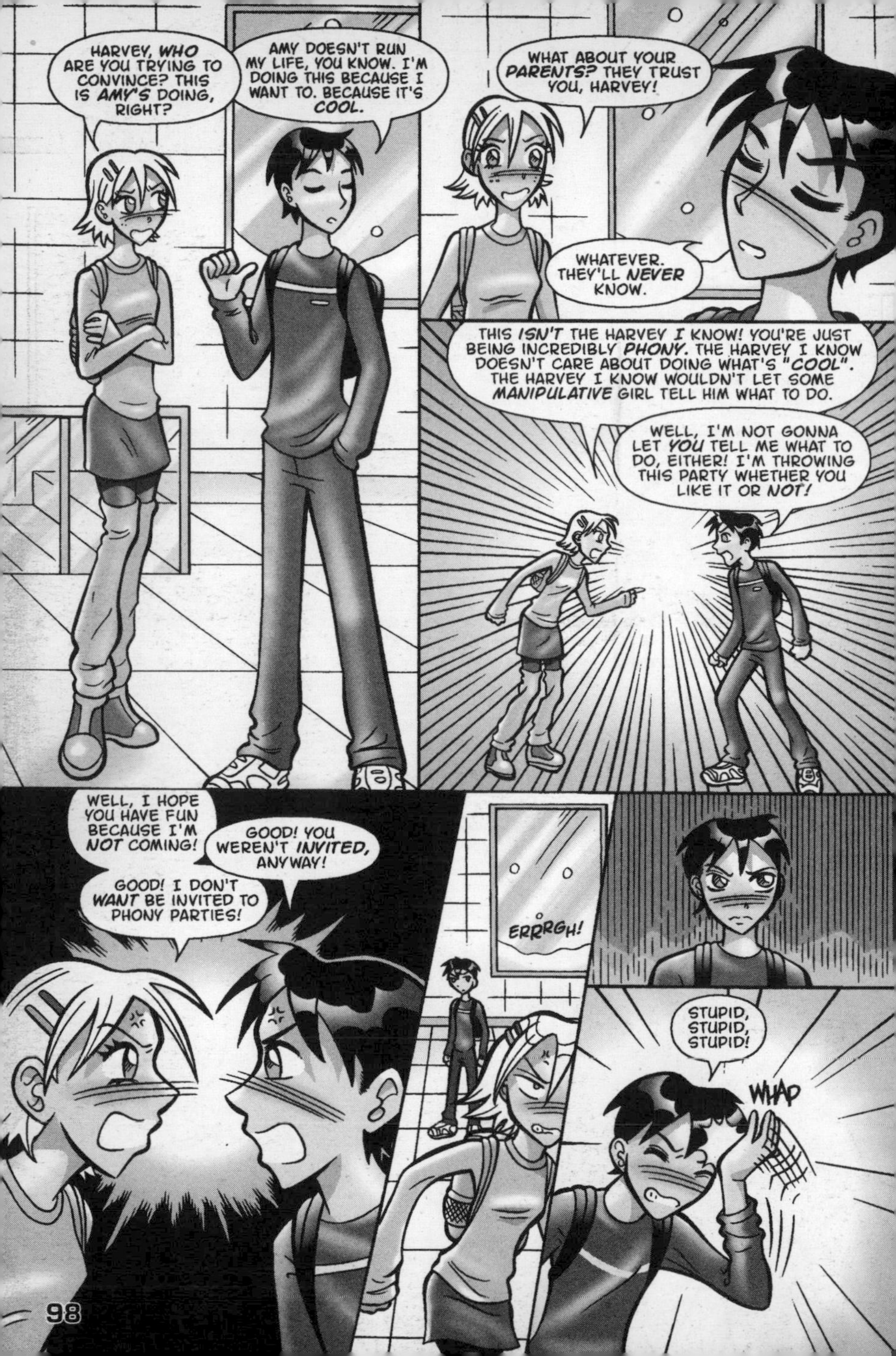
HARVEY, WHO ARE YOU TRYING TO CONVINCE? THIS IS AMY'S DOING, RIGHT?
AMY DOESN'T RUN MY LIFE, YOU KNOW. I'M DOING THIS BECAUSE I WANT TO. BECAUSE IT'S COOL.
WHAT ABOUT YOUR PARENTS? THEY TRUST YOU, HARVEY!
WHATEVER. THEY'LL NEVER KNOW.
THIS ISN'T THE HARVEY I KNOW! YOU'RE JUST BEING INCREDIBLY PHONY. THE HARVEY I KNOW DOESN'T CARE ABOUT DOING WHAT'S "COOL". THE HARVEY I KNOW WOULDN'T LET SOME MANIPULATIVE GIRL TELL HIM WHAT TO DO.
WELL, I'M NOT GONNA LET YOU TELL ME WHAT TO DO, EITHER! I'M THROWING THIS PARTY WHETHER YOU LIKE IT OR NOT!
WELL, I HOPE YOU HAVE FUN BECAUSE I'M NOT COMING!
GOOD! YOU WEREN'T INVITED, ANYWAY!
GOOD! I DON'T WANT BE INVITED TO PHONY PARTIES!
ERRRGH!
STUPID, STUPID, STUPID!
WHAP

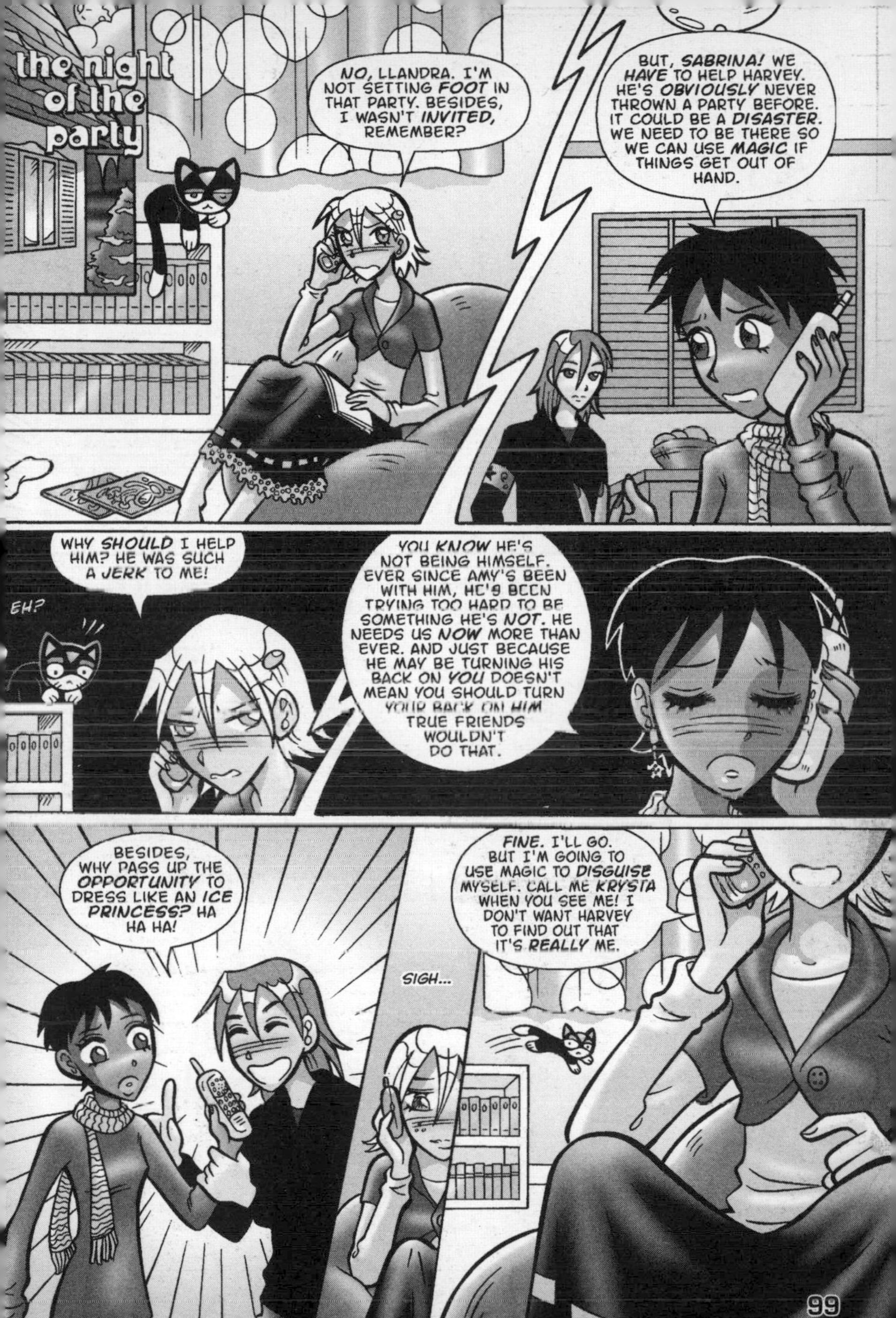
the night of the party
NO, LLANDRA. I'M NOT SETTING FOOT IN THAT PARTY. BESIDES, I WASN'T INVITED, REMEMBER?
BUT, SABRINA! WE HAVE TO HELP HARVEY. HE'S OBVIOUSLY NEVER THROWN A PARTY BEFORE. IT COULD BE A DISASTER. WE NEED TO BE THERE SO WE CAN USE MAGIC IF THINGS GET OUT OF HAND.
EH?
WHY SHOULD I HELP HIM? HE WAS SUCH A JERK TO ME!
YOU KNOW HE'S NOT BEING HIMSELF. EVER SINCE AMY'S BEEN WITH HIM, HE'S BEEN TRYING TOO HARD TO BE SOMETHING HE'S NOT. HE NEEDS US NOW MORE THAN EVER. AND JUST BECAUSE HE MAY BE TURNING HIS BACK ON YOU DOESN'T MEAN YOU SHOULD TURN YOUR BACK ON HIM. TRUE FRIENDS WOULDN'T DO THAT.
BESIDES, WHY PASS UP THE OPPORTUNITY TO DRESS LIKE AN ICE PRINCESS? HA HA HA!
SIGH...
FINE. I'LL GO. BUT I'M GOING TO USE MAGIC TO DISGUISE MYSELF. CALL ME KRYSTA WHEN YOU SEE ME! I DON'T WANT HARVEY TO FIND OUT THAT IT'S REALLY ME.

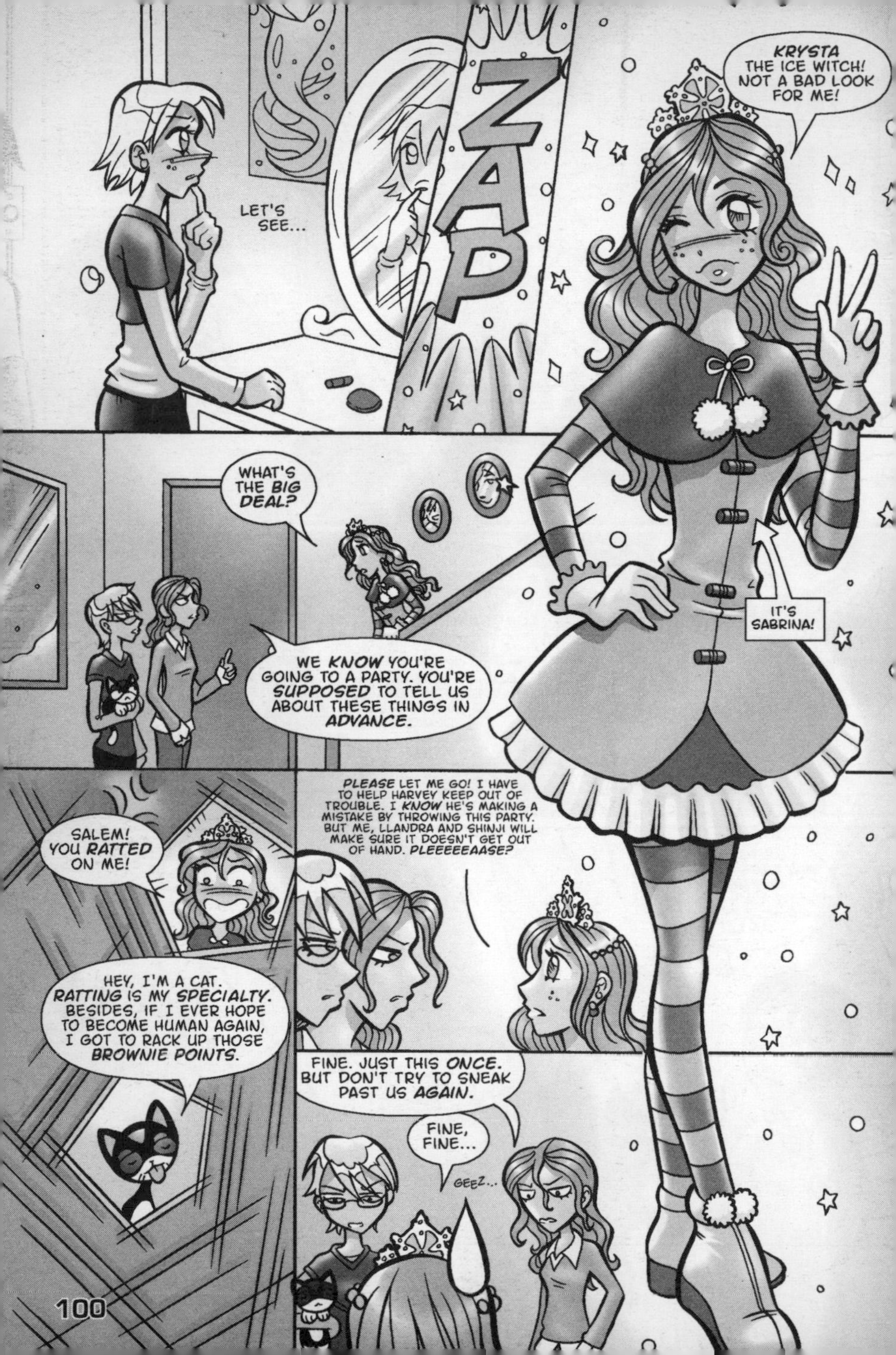
LET'S SEE...
ZAP
KRYSTA THE ICE WITCH! NOT A BAD LOOK FOR ME!
IT'S SABRINA!
WHAT'S THE BIG DEAL?
WE KNOW YOU'RE GOING TO A PARTY. YOU'RE SUPPOSED TO TELL US ABOUT THESE THINGS IN ADVANCE.
SALEM! YOU RATTED ON ME!
HEY, I'M A CAT. RATTING IS MY SPECIALTY. BESIDES, IF I EVER HOPE TO BECOME HUMAN AGAIN, I GOT TO RACK UP THOSE BROWNIE POINTS.
PLEASE LET ME GO! I HAVE TO HELP HARVEY KEEP OUT OF TROUBLE. I KNOW HE'S MAKING A MISTAKE BY THROWING THIS PARTY. BUT ME, LLANDRA AND SHINJI WILL MAKE SURE IT DOESN'T GET OUT OF HAND. PLEEEEEAASE?
FINE. JUST THIS ONCE. BUT DON'T TRY TO SNEAK PAST US AGAIN.
FINE, FINE...
GEEZ...

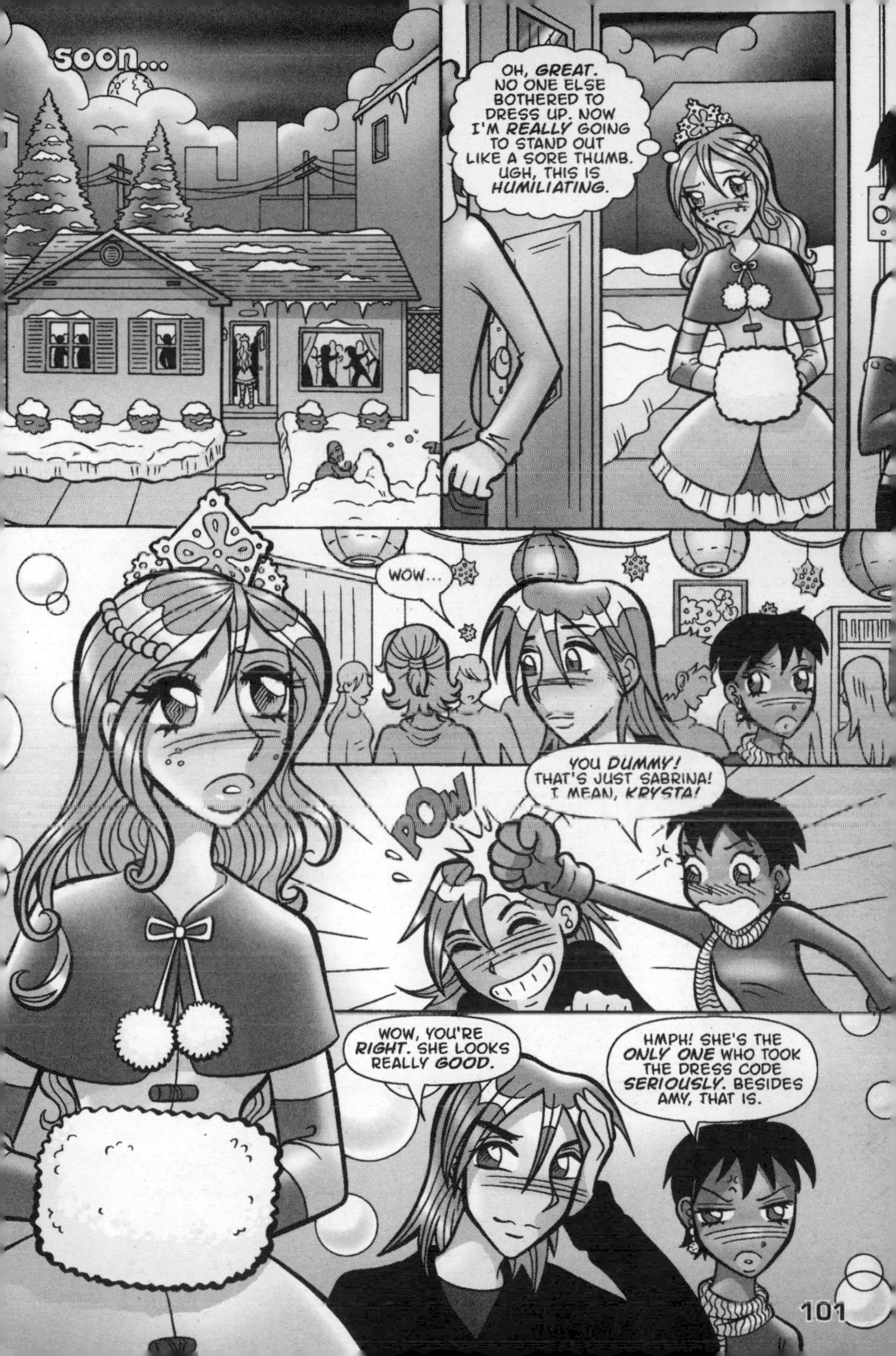
SOON...
OH, GREAT. NO ONE ELSE BOTHERED TO DRESS UP. NOW I'M REALLY GOING TO STAND OUT LIKE A SORE THUMB. UGH, THIS IS HUMILIATING.
WOW...
YOU DUMMY! THAT'S JUST SABRINA! I MEAN, KRYSTA!
POW
WOW, YOU'RE RIGHT. SHE LOOKS REALLY GOOD.
HMPH! SHE'S THE ONLY ONE WHO TOOK THE DRESS CODE SERIOUSLY. BESIDES AMY, THAT IS.

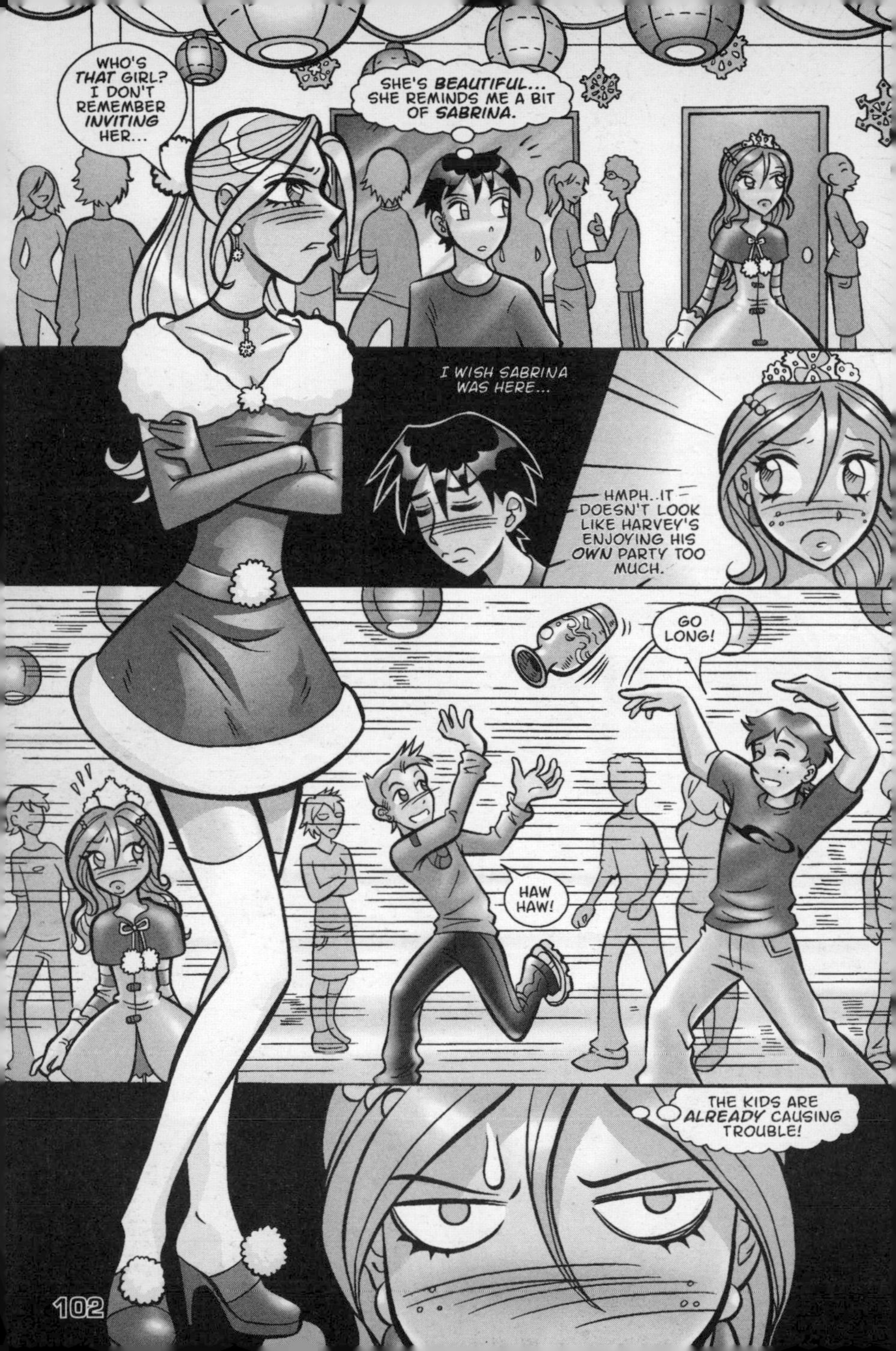
WHO'S *THAT* GIRL? I DON'T REMEMBER *INVITING* HER...
SHE'S ***BEAUTIFUL...*** SHE REMINDS ME A BIT OF **SABRINA**.
I WISH SABRINA WAS HERE...
HMPH..IT DOESN'T LOOK LIKE HARVEY'S ENJOYING HIS *OWN* PARTY TOO MUCH.
GO LONG!
HAW HAW!
THE KIDS ARE ***ALREADY*** CAUSING TROUBLE!

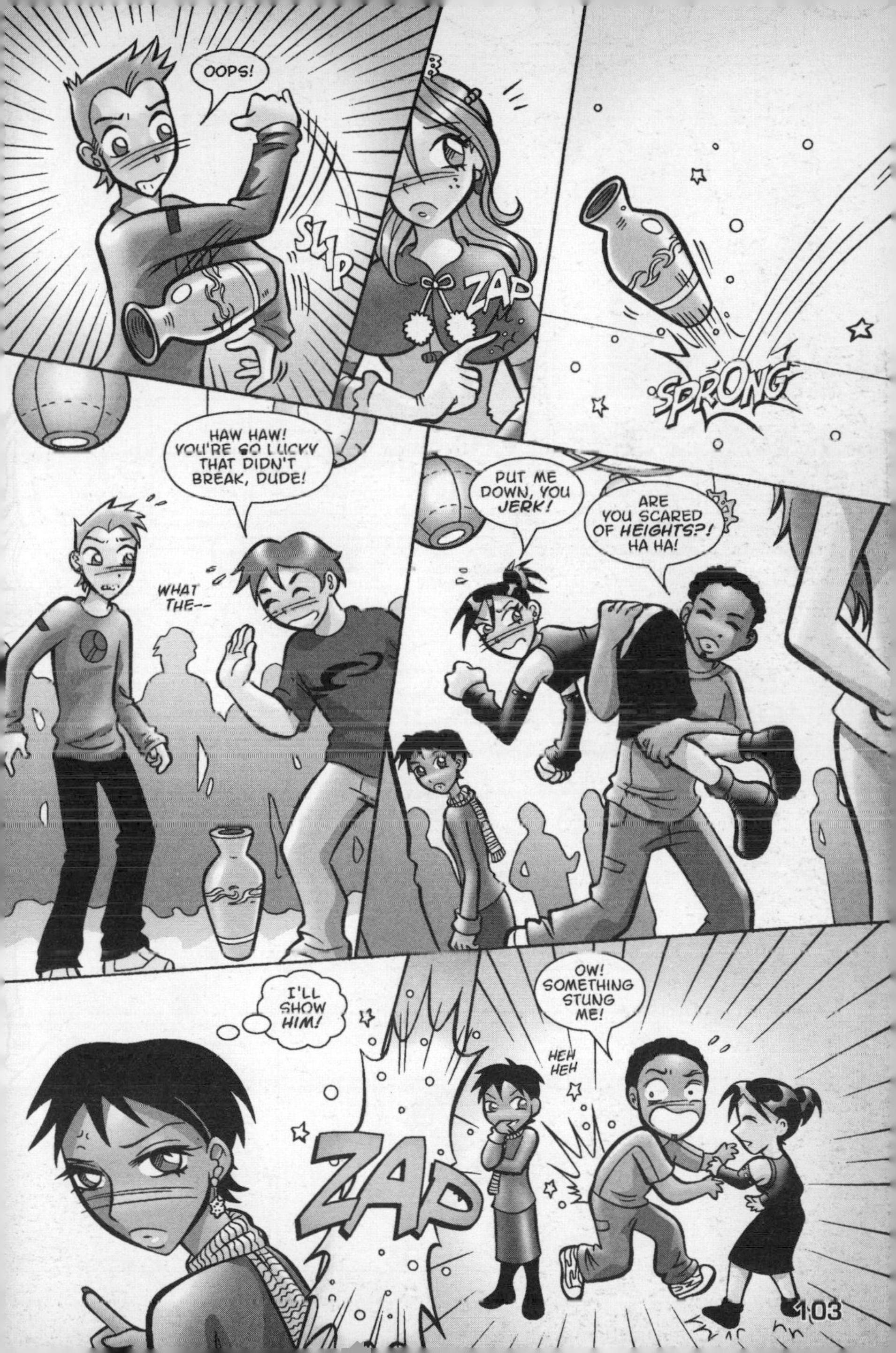

OOPS!
SLIP
ZAP
SPRONG
HAW HAW! YOU'RE SO LUCKY THAT DIDN'T BREAK, DUDE!
WHAT THE--
PUT ME DOWN, YOU JERK!
ARE YOU SCARED OF HEIGHTS?! HA HA!
I'LL SHOW HIM!
ZAP
HEH HEH
OW! SOMETHING STUNG ME!

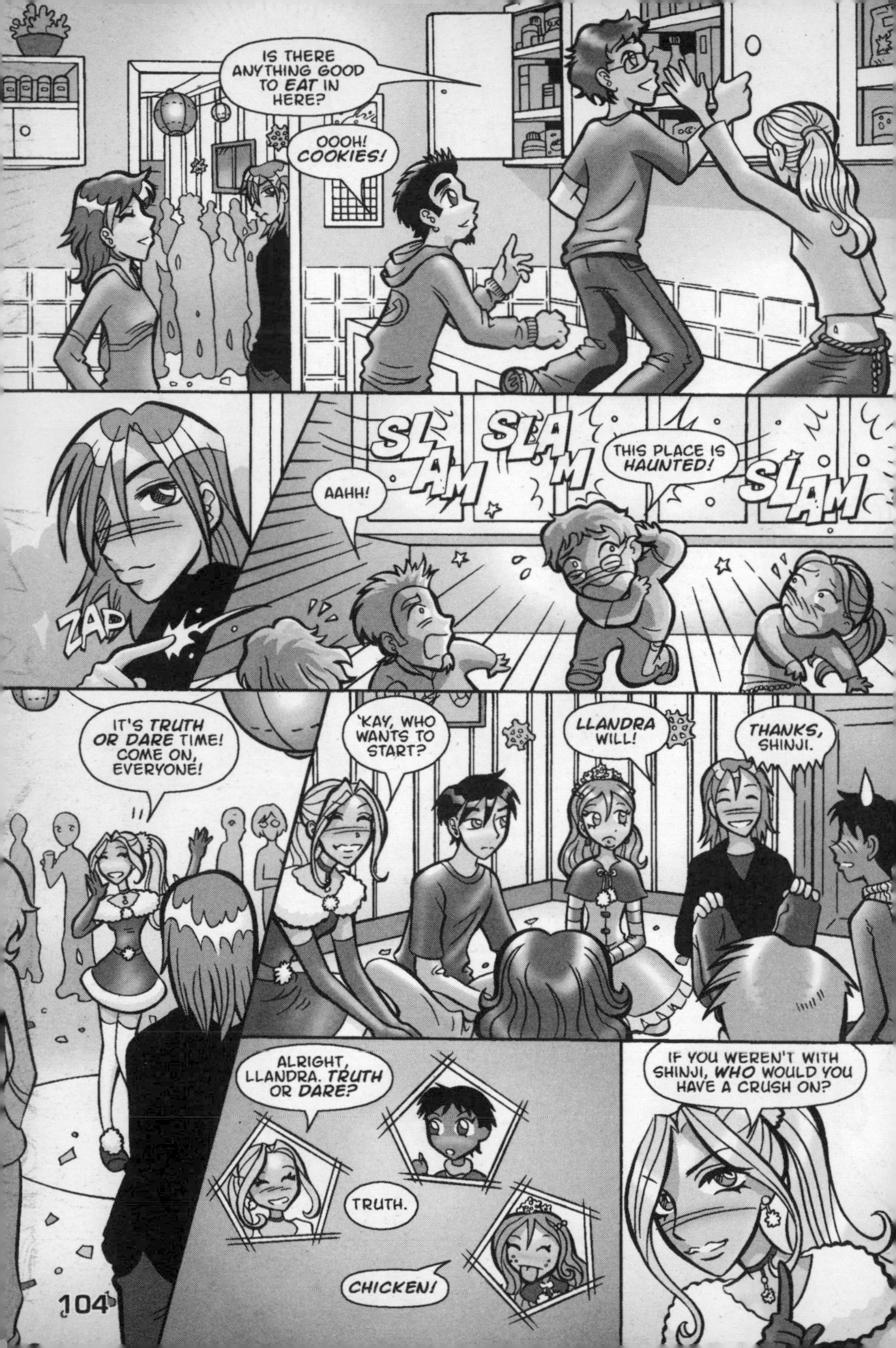
IS THERE ANYTHING GOOD TO *EAT* IN HERE?
OOOH! *COOKIES!*
SLAM
SLAM
THIS PLACE IS *HAUNTED!*
AAHH!
SLAM
ZAP
IT'S *TRUTH OR DARE* TIME! COME ON, EVERYONE!
'KAY, WHO WANTS TO START?
LLANDRA WILL!
THANKS, SHINJI.
ALRIGHT, LLANDRA. *TRUTH* OR *DARE?*
TRUTH.
CHICKEN!
IF YOU WEREN'T WITH SHINJI, *WHO* WOULD YOU HAVE A CRUSH ON?

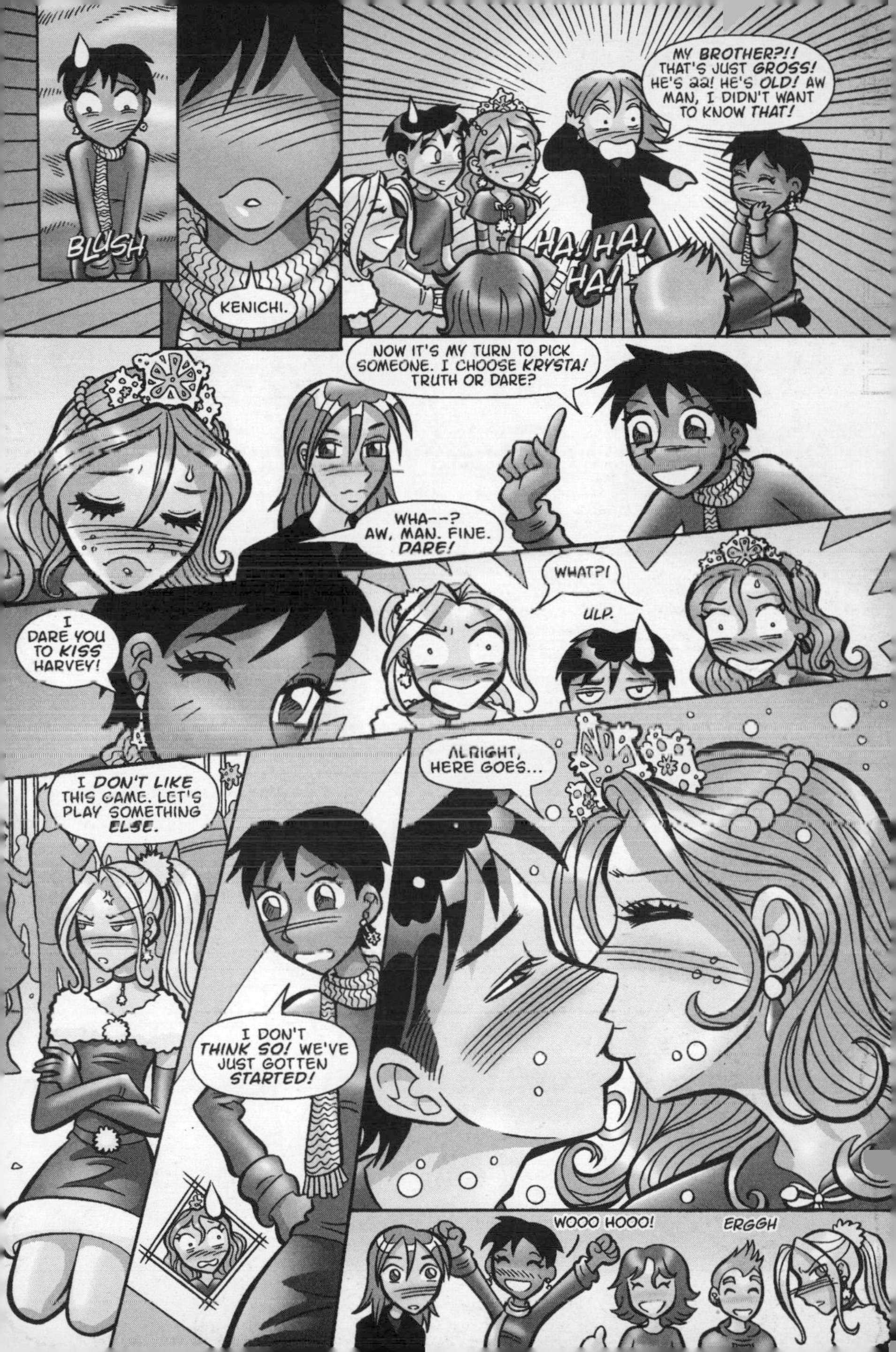
BLUSH
KENICHI.
MY BROTHER?!! THAT'S JUST GROSS! HE'S 22! HE'S OLD! AW MAN, I DIDN'T WANT TO KNOW THAT!
HA! HA! HA!
NOW IT'S MY TURN TO PICK SOMEONE. I CHOOSE KRYSTA! TRUTH OR DARE?
WHA--? AW, MAN. FINE. DARE!
I DARE YOU TO KISS HARVEY!
WHAT?!
ULP.
I DON'T LIKE THIS GAME. LET'S PLAY SOMETHING ELSE.
I DON'T THINK SO! WE'VE JUST GOTTEN STARTED!
ALRIGHT, HERE GOES...
WOOO HOOO!
ERGGH

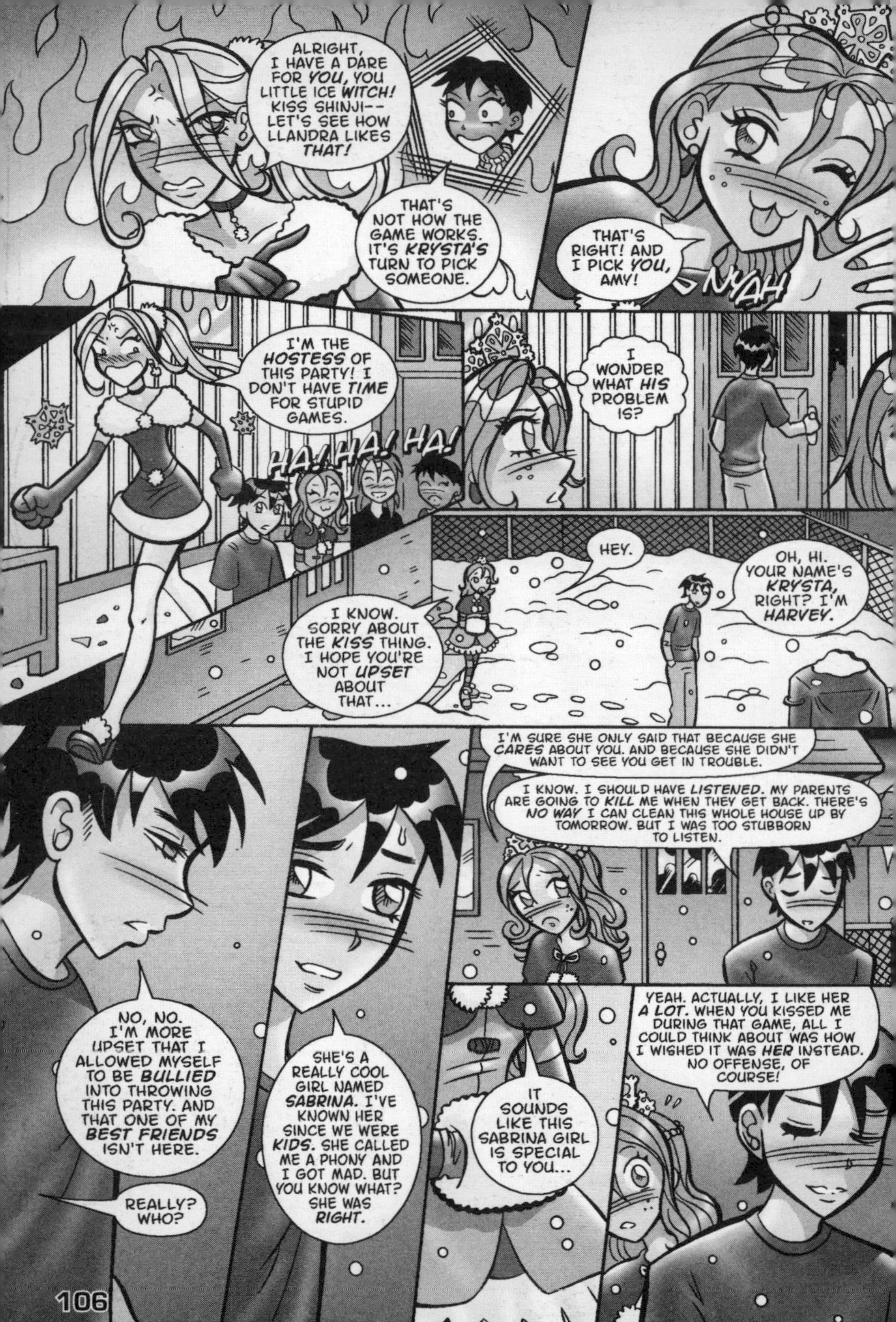
ALRIGHT, I HAVE A DARE FOR *YOU*, YOU LITTLE ICE *WITCH!* KISS SHINJI-- LET'S SEE HOW LLANDRA LIKES *THAT!*
THAT'S NOT HOW THE GAME WORKS. IT'S *KRYSTA'S* TURN TO PICK SOMEONE.
THAT'S RIGHT! AND I PICK *YOU*, AMY!
NYAH
I'M THE *HOSTESS* OF THIS PARTY! I DON'T HAVE *TIME* FOR STUPID GAMES.
HA! HA! HA!
I WONDER WHAT *HIS* PROBLEM IS?
HEY.
OH, HI. YOUR NAME'S *KRYSTA*, RIGHT? I'M *HARVEY*.
I KNOW. SORRY ABOUT THE *KISS* THING. I HOPE YOU'RE NOT *UPSET* ABOUT THAT...
NO, NO. I'M MORE UPSET THAT I ALLOWED MYSELF TO BE *BULLIED* INTO THROWING THIS PARTY. AND THAT ONE OF MY *BEST FRIENDS* ISN'T HERE.
REALLY? WHO?
SHE'S A REALLY COOL GIRL NAMED *SABRINA*. I'VE KNOWN HER SINCE WE WERE *KIDS*. SHE CALLED ME A PHONY AND I GOT MAD. BUT YOU KNOW WHAT? SHE WAS *RIGHT*.
I'M SURE SHE ONLY SAID THAT BECAUSE SHE *CARES* ABOUT YOU. AND BECAUSE SHE DIDN'T WANT TO SEE YOU GET IN TROUBLE.
I KNOW. I SHOULD HAVE *LISTENED*. MY PARENTS ARE GOING TO *KILL ME* WHEN THEY GET BACK. THERE'S *NO WAY* I CAN CLEAN THIS WHOLE HOUSE UP BY TOMORROW. BUT I WAS TOO STUBBORN TO LISTEN.
IT SOUNDS LIKE THIS SABRINA GIRL IS SPECIAL TO YOU...
YEAH. ACTUALLY, I LIKE HER *A LOT*. WHEN YOU KISSED ME DURING THAT GAME, ALL I COULD THINK ABOUT WAS HOW I WISHED IT WAS *HER* INSTEAD. NO OFFENSE, OF COURSE!

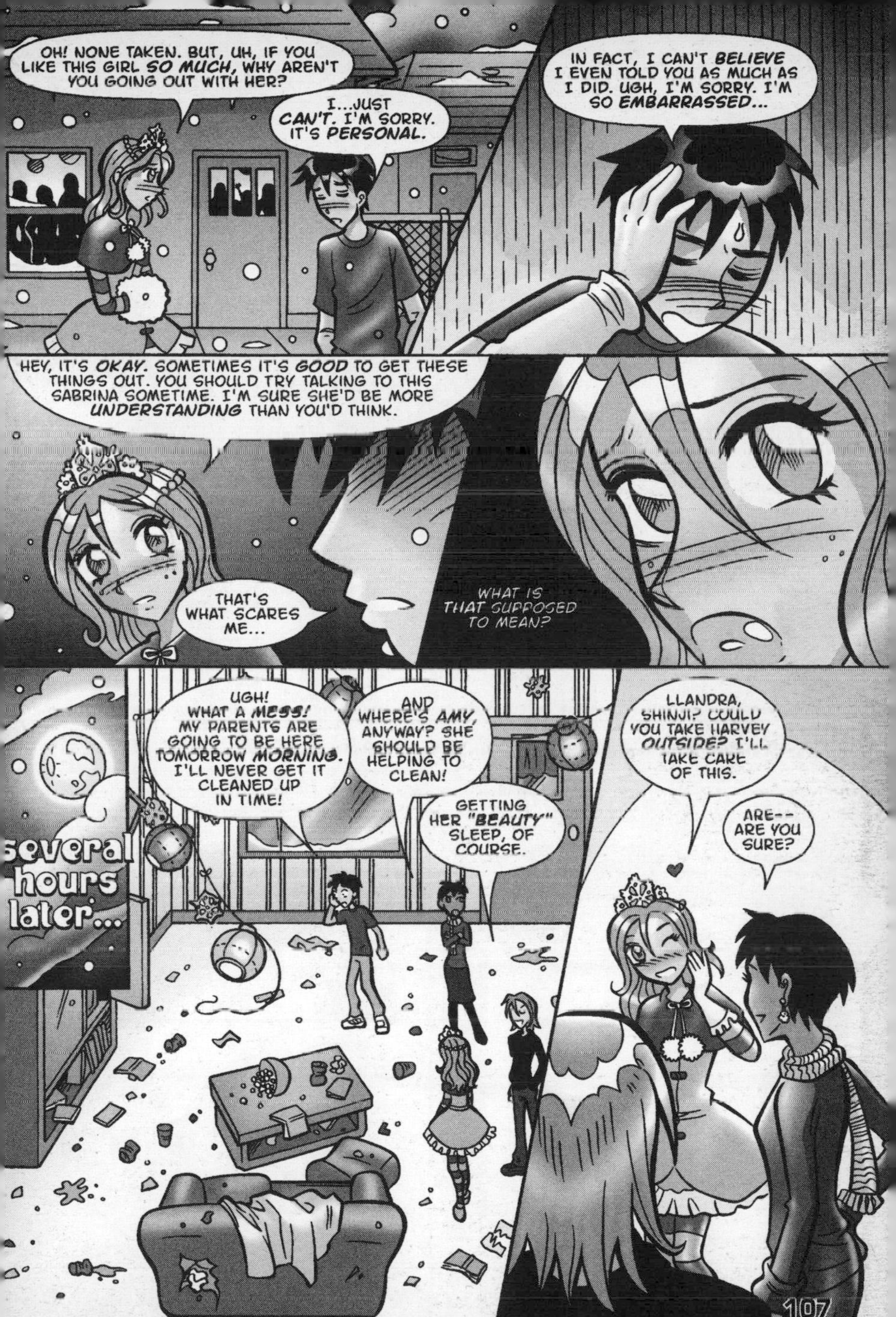
OH! NONE TAKEN. BUT, UH, IF YOU LIKE THIS GIRL SO MUCH, WHY AREN'T YOU GOING OUT WITH HER?
I...JUST CAN'T. I'M SORRY. IT'S PERSONAL.
IN FACT, I CAN'T BELIEVE I EVEN TOLD YOU AS MUCH AS I DID. UGH, I'M SORRY. I'M SO EMBARRASSED...
HEY, IT'S OKAY. SOMETIMES IT'S GOOD TO GET THESE THINGS OUT. YOU SHOULD TRY TALKING TO THIS SABRINA SOMETIME. I'M SURE SHE'D BE MORE UNDERSTANDING THAN YOU'D THINK.
THAT'S WHAT SCARES ME...
WHAT IS THAT SUPPOSED TO MEAN?
several hours later...
UGH! WHAT A MESS! MY PARENTS ARE GOING TO BE HERE TOMORROW MORNING. I'LL NEVER GET IT CLEANED UP IN TIME!
AND WHERE'S AMY, ANYWAY? SHE SHOULD BE HELPING TO CLEAN!
GETTING HER "BEAUTY" SLEEP, OF COURSE.
LLANDRA, SHINJI? COULD YOU TAKE HARVEY OUTSIDE? I'LL TAKE CARE OF THIS.
ARE-- ARE YOU SURE?

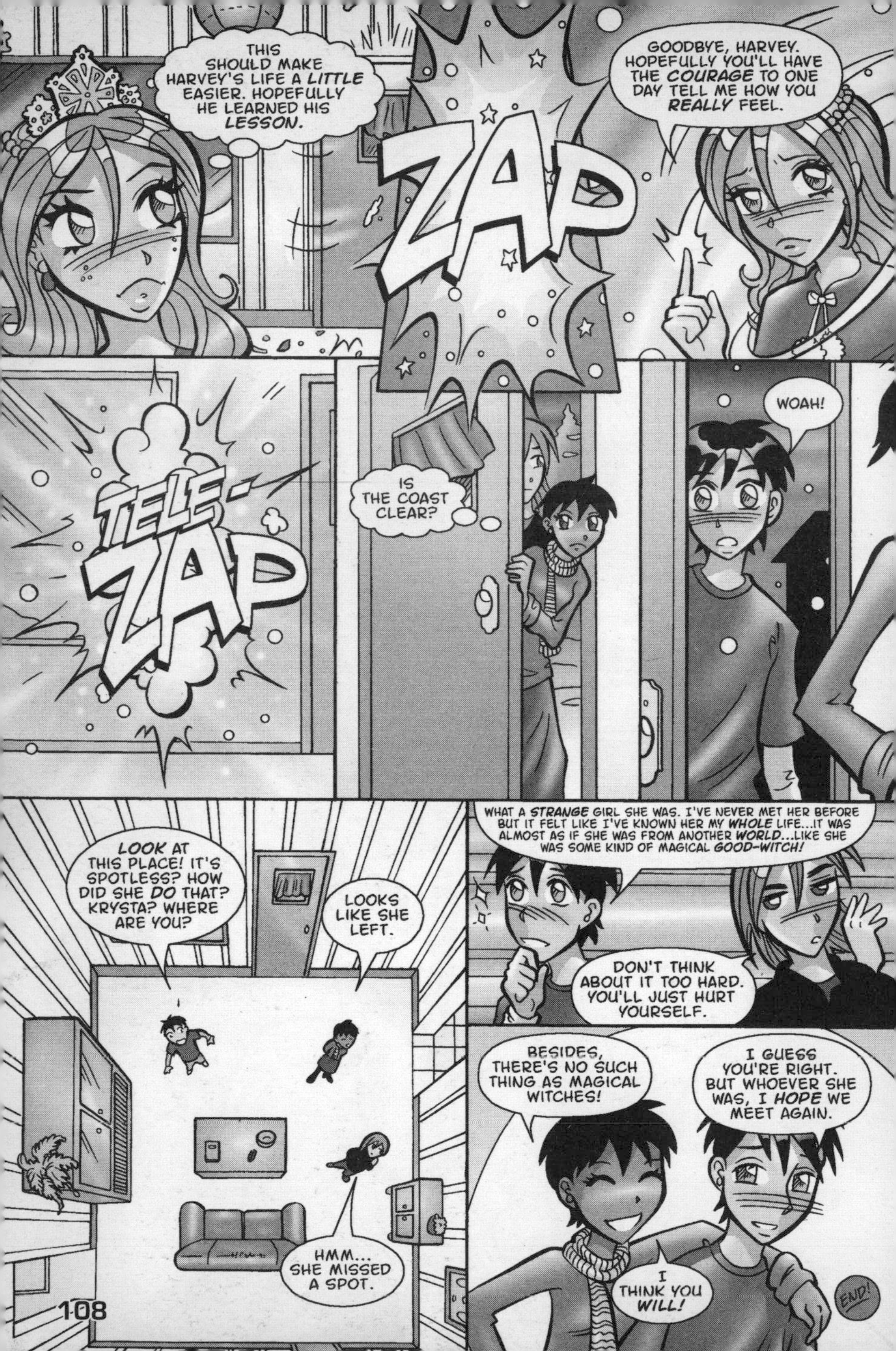

THIS SHOULD MAKE HARVEY'S LIFE A LITTLE EASIER. HOPEFULLY HE LEARNED HIS LESSON.
ZAP
GOODBYE, HARVEY. HOPEFULLY YOU'LL HAVE THE COURAGE TO ONE DAY TELL ME HOW YOU REALLY FEEL.
TELE-ZAP
IS THE COAST CLEAR?
WOAH!
LOOK AT THIS PLACE! IT'S SPOTLESS? HOW DID SHE DO THAT? KRYSTA? WHERE ARE YOU?
LOOKS LIKE SHE LEFT.
HMM... SHE MISSED A SPOT.
WHAT A STRANGE GIRL SHE WAS. I'VE NEVER MET HER BEFORE BUT IT FELT LIKE I'VE KNOWN HER MY WHOLE LIFE...IT WAS ALMOST AS IF SHE WAS FROM ANOTHER WORLD...LIKE SHE WAS SOME KIND OF MAGICAL GOOD-WITCH!
DON'T THINK ABOUT IT TOO HARD. YOU'LL JUST HURT YOURSELF.
BESIDES, THERE'S NO SUCH THING AS MAGICAL WITCHES!
I GUESS YOU'RE RIGHT. BUT WHOEVER SHE WAS, I HOPE WE MEET AGAIN.
I THINK YOU WILL!
END!

Chapter 6

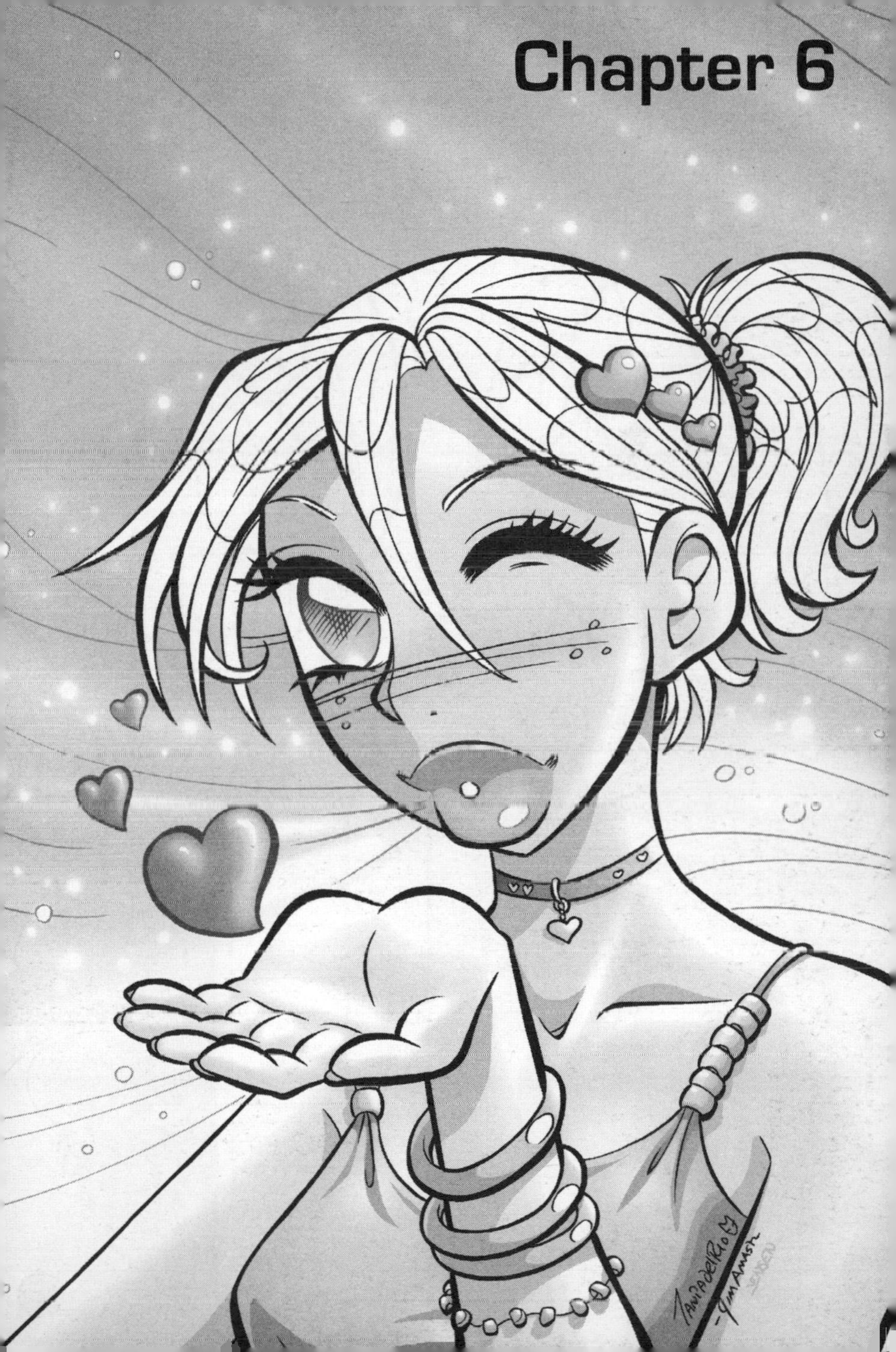

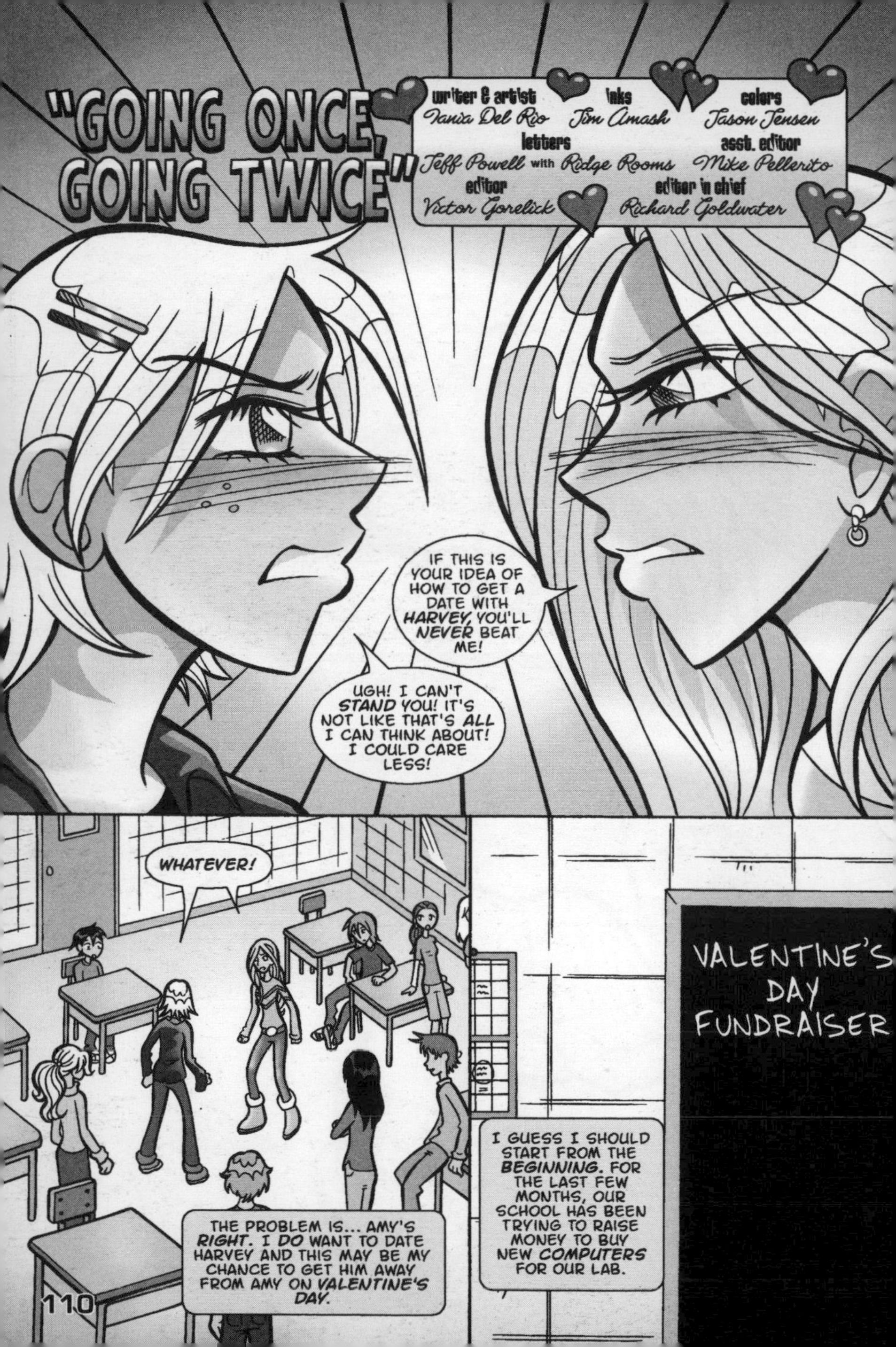
"GOING ONCE, GOING TWICE"
writer & artist Tania Del Rio
inks Jim Amash
colors Jason Jensen
letters Jeff Powell with Ridge Rooms
asst. editor Mike Pellerito
editor Victor Gorelick
editor in chief Richard Goldwater
IF THIS IS YOUR IDEA OF HOW TO GET A DATE WITH HARVEY, YOU'LL NEVER BEAT ME!
UGH! I CAN'T STAND YOU! IT'S NOT LIKE THAT'S ALL I CAN THINK ABOUT! I COULD CARE LESS!
WHATEVER!
THE PROBLEM IS... AMY'S RIGHT. I DO WANT TO DATE HARVEY AND THIS MAY BE MY CHANCE TO GET HIM AWAY FROM AMY ON VALENTINE'S DAY.
I GUESS I SHOULD START FROM THE BEGINNING. FOR THE LAST FEW MONTHS, OUR SCHOOL HAS BEEN TRYING TO RAISE MONEY TO BUY NEW COMPUTERS FOR OUR LAB.
VALENTINE'S DAY FUNDRAISER

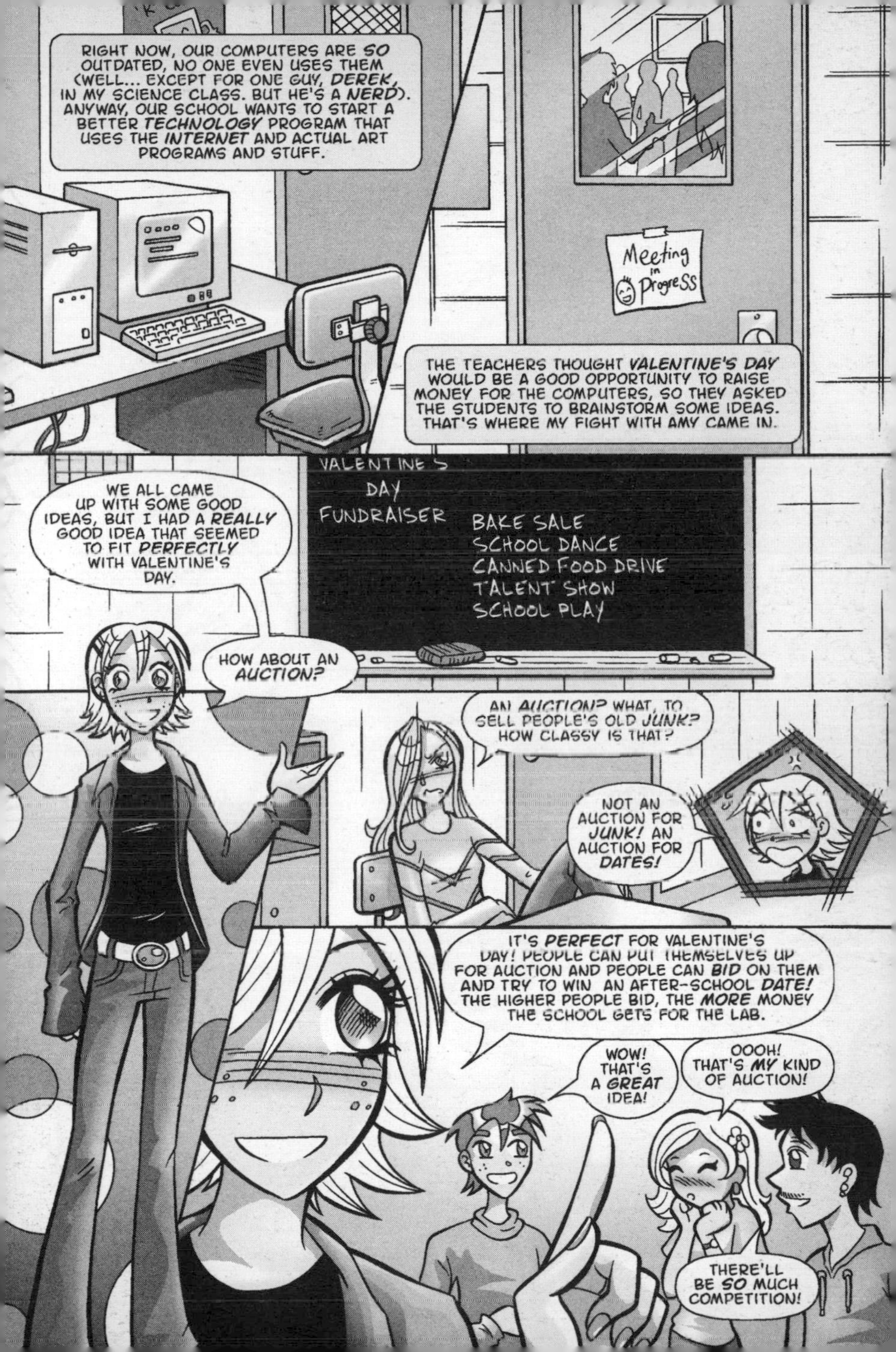

RIGHT NOW, OUR COMPUTERS ARE *SO* OUTDATED, NO ONE EVEN USES THEM (WELL... EXCEPT FOR ONE GUY, *DEREK*, IN MY SCIENCE CLASS. BUT HE'S A *NERD*). ANYWAY, OUR SCHOOL WANTS TO START A BETTER *TECHNOLOGY* PROGRAM THAT USES THE *INTERNET* AND ACTUAL ART PROGRAMS AND STUFF.
Meeting in Progress
THE TEACHERS THOUGHT *VALENTINE'S DAY* WOULD BE A GOOD OPPORTUNITY TO RAISE MONEY FOR THE COMPUTERS, SO THEY ASKED THE STUDENTS TO BRAINSTORM SOME IDEAS. THAT'S WHERE MY FIGHT WITH AMY CAME IN.
WE ALL CAME UP WITH SOME GOOD IDEAS, BUT I HAD A *REALLY* GOOD IDEA THAT SEEMED TO FIT *PERFECTLY* WITH VALENTINE'S DAY.
VALENTINE'S DAY FUNDRAISER
BAKE SALE
SCHOOL DANCE
CANNED FOOD DRIVE
TALENT SHOW
SCHOOL PLAY
HOW ABOUT AN *AUCTION?*
AN *AUCTION?* WHAT, TO SELL PEOPLE'S OLD *JUNK?* HOW CLASSY IS THAT?
NOT AN AUCTION FOR *JUNK!* AN AUCTION FOR *DATES!*
IT'S *PERFECT* FOR VALENTINE'S DAY! PEOPLE CAN PUT THEMSELVES UP FOR AUCTION AND PEOPLE CAN *BID* ON THEM AND TRY TO WIN AN AFTER-SCHOOL *DATE!* THE HIGHER PEOPLE BID, THE *MORE* MONEY THE SCHOOL GETS FOR THE LAB.
WOW! THAT'S A *GREAT* IDEA!
OOOH! THAT'S *MY* KIND OF AUCTION!
THERE'LL BE *SO* MUCH COMPETITION!

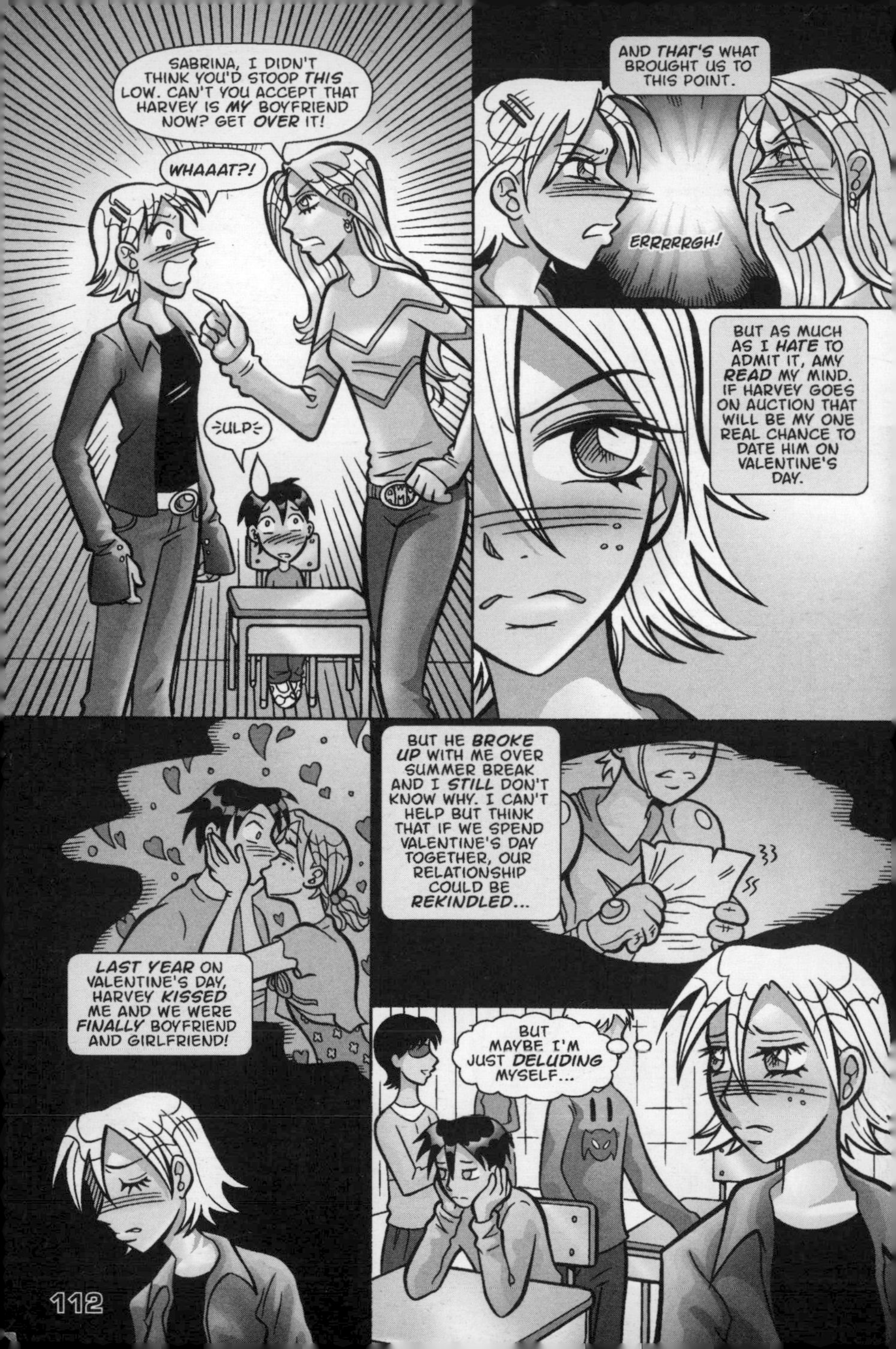
SABRINA, I DIDN'T THINK YOU'D STOOP THIS LOW. CAN'T YOU ACCEPT THAT HARVEY IS MY BOYFRIEND NOW? GET OVER IT!
WHAAAT?!
ULP
AND THAT'S WHAT BROUGHT US TO THIS POINT.
ERRRRRGH!
BUT AS MUCH AS I HATE TO ADMIT IT, AMY READ MY MIND. IF HARVEY GOES ON AUCTION THAT WILL BE MY ONE REAL CHANCE TO DATE HIM ON VALENTINE'S DAY.
LAST YEAR ON VALENTINE'S DAY, HARVEY KISSED ME AND WE WERE FINALLY BOYFRIEND AND GIRLFRIEND!
BUT HE BROKE UP WITH ME OVER SUMMER BREAK AND I STILL DON'T KNOW WHY. I CAN'T HELP BUT THINK THAT IF WE SPEND VALENTINE'S DAY TOGETHER, OUR RELATIONSHIP COULD BE REKINDLED...
BUT MAYBE I'M JUST DELUDING MYSELF...

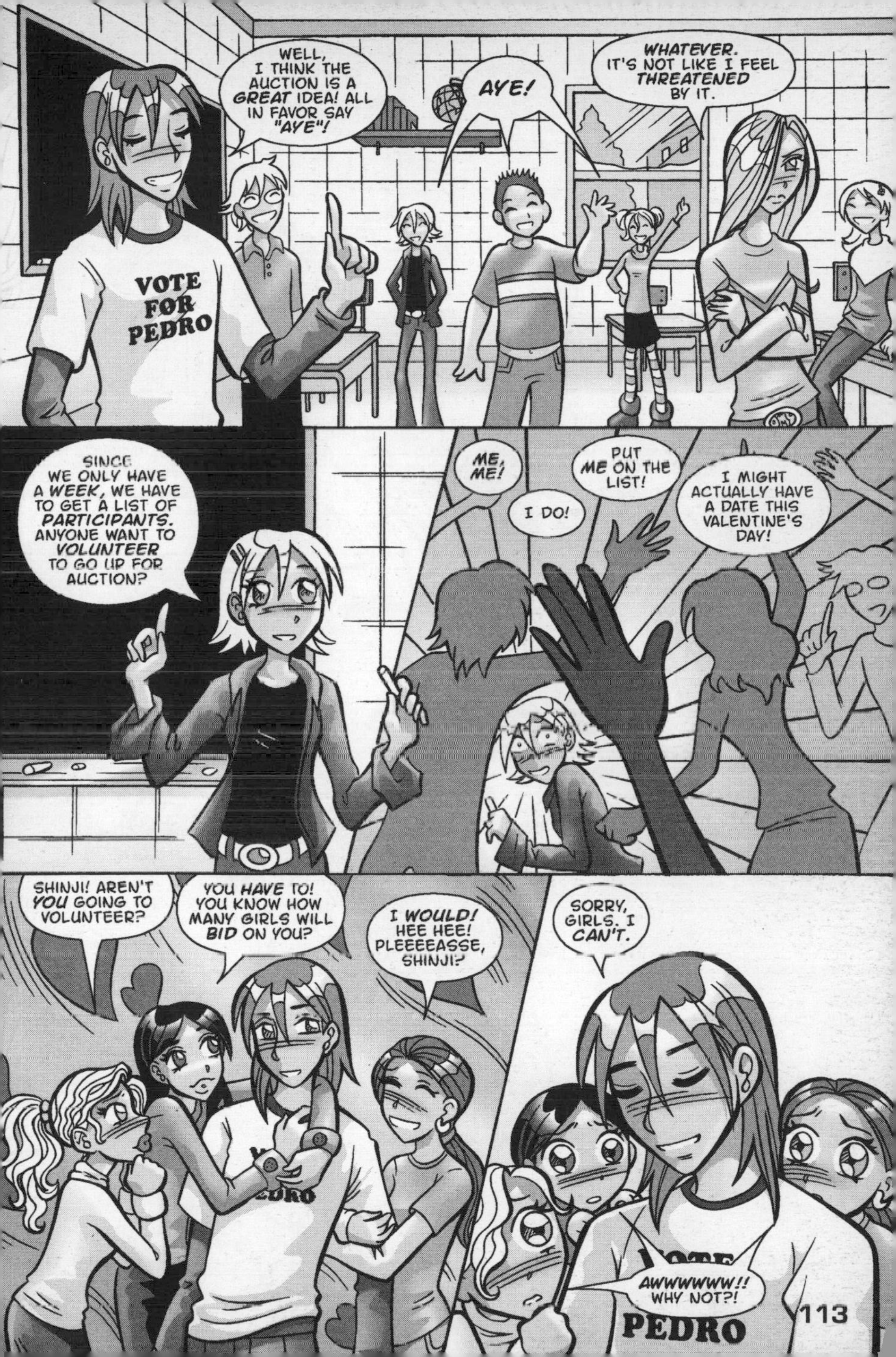

WELL, I THINK THE AUCTION IS A GREAT IDEA! ALL IN FAVOR SAY "AYE"!
AYE!
WHATEVER. IT'S NOT LIKE I FEEL THREATENED BY IT.
VOTE FOR PEDRO
SINCE WE ONLY HAVE A WEEK, WE HAVE TO GET A LIST OF PARTICIPANTS. ANYONE WANT TO VOLUNTEER TO GO UP FOR AUCTION?
ME, ME!
I DO!
PUT ME ON THE LIST!
I MIGHT ACTUALLY HAVE A DATE THIS VALENTINE'S DAY!
SHINJI! AREN'T YOU GOING TO VOLUNTEER?
YOU HAVE TO! YOU KNOW HOW MANY GIRLS WILL BID ON YOU?
I WOULD! HEE HEE! PLEEEEASSE, SHINJI?
SORRY, GIRLS. I CAN'T.
AWWWWWW!! WHY NOT?!
PEDRO

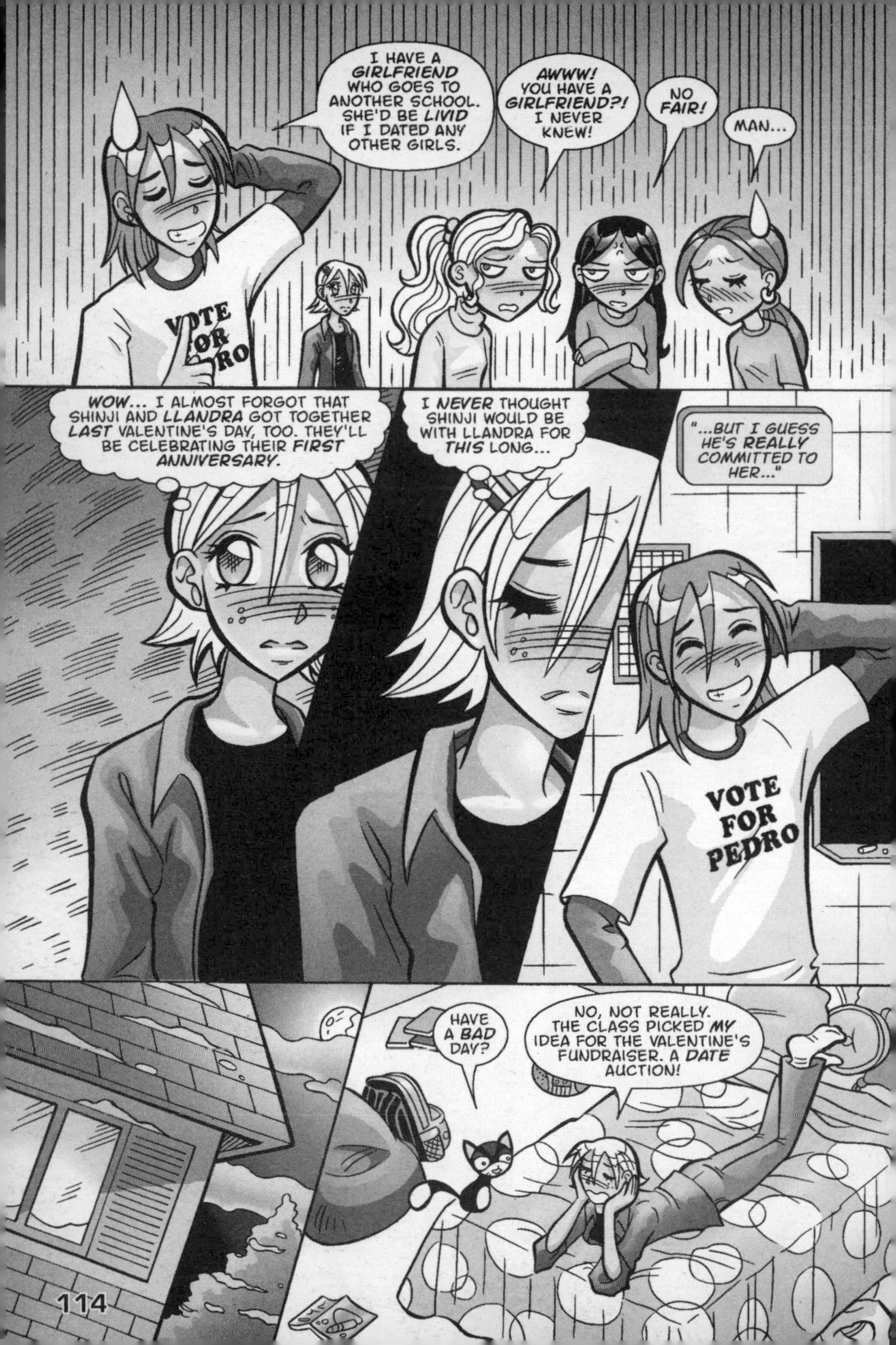

I HAVE A GIRLFRIEND WHO GOES TO ANOTHER SCHOOL. SHE'D BE LIVID IF I DATED ANY OTHER GIRLS.
AWWW! YOU HAVE A GIRLFRIEND?! I NEVER KNEW!
NO FAIR!
MAN...
VOTE FOR PEDRO
WOW... I ALMOST FORGOT THAT SHINJI AND LLANDRA GOT TOGETHER LAST VALENTINE'S DAY, TOO. THEY'LL BE CELEBRATING THEIR FIRST ANNIVERSARY.
I NEVER THOUGHT SHINJI WOULD BE WITH LLANDRA FOR THIS LONG...
"...BUT I GUESS HE'S REALLY COMMITTED TO HER..."
VOTE FOR PEDRO
HAVE A BAD DAY?
NO, NOT REALLY. THE CLASS PICKED MY IDEA FOR THE VALENTINE'S FUNDRAISER. A DATE AUCTION!

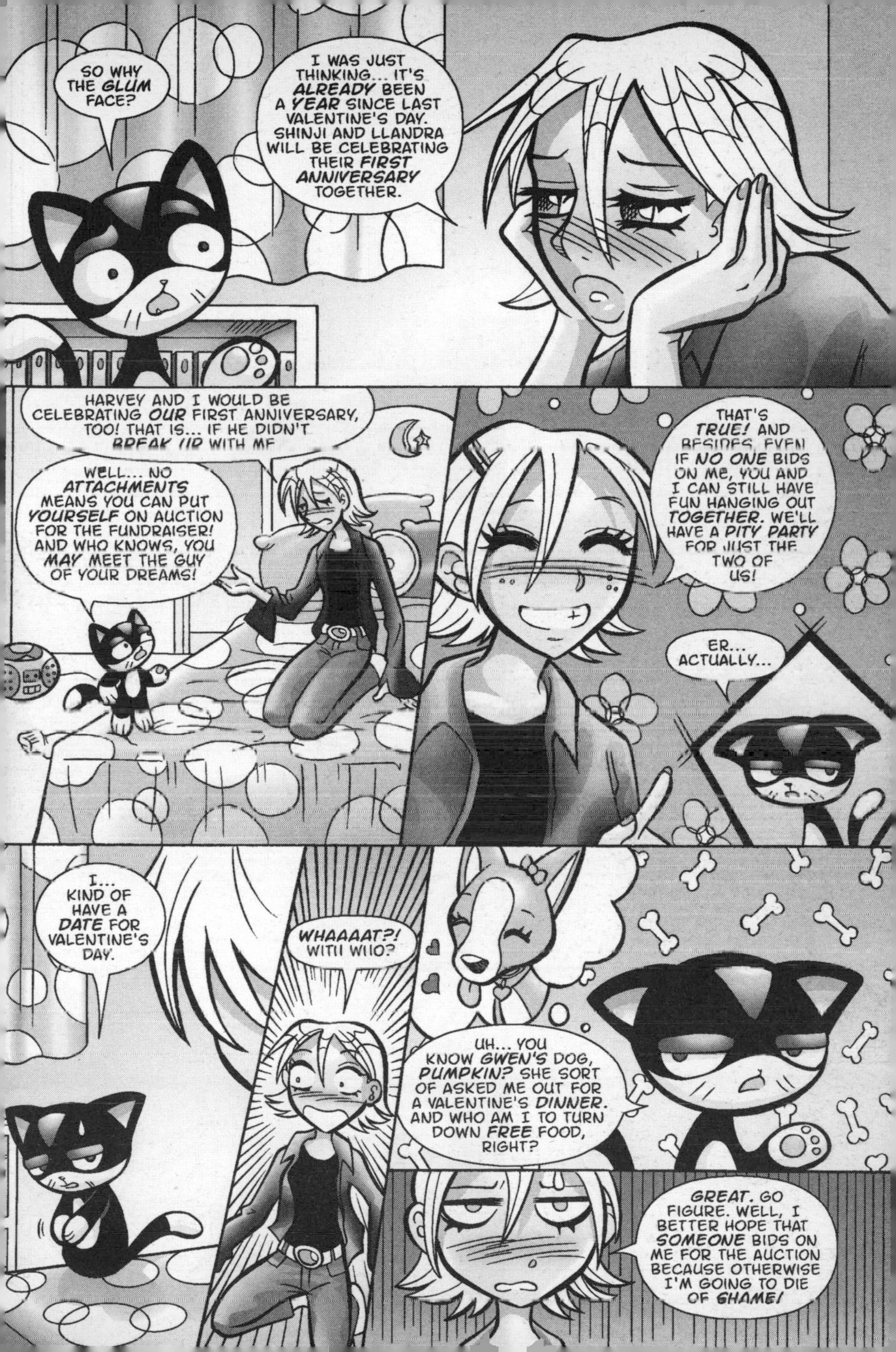
SO WHY THE GLUM FACE?
I WAS JUST THINKING... IT'S ALREADY BEEN A YEAR SINCE LAST VALENTINE'S DAY. SHINJI AND LLANDRA WILL BE CELEBRATING THEIR FIRST ANNIVERSARY TOGETHER.
HARVEY AND I WOULD BE CELEBRATING OUR FIRST ANNIVERSARY, TOO! THAT IS... IF HE DIDN'T BREAK UP WITH ME.
WELL... NO ATTACHMENTS MEANS YOU CAN PUT YOURSELF ON AUCTION FOR THE FUNDRAISER! AND WHO KNOWS, YOU MAY MEET THE GUY OF YOUR DREAMS!
THAT'S TRUE! AND BESIDES, EVEN IF NO ONE BIDS ON ME, YOU AND I CAN STILL HAVE FUN HANGING OUT TOGETHER. WE'LL HAVE A PITY PARTY FOR JUST THE TWO OF US!
ER... ACTUALLY...
I... KIND OF HAVE A DATE FOR VALENTINE'S DAY.
WHAAAAT?! WITH WHO?
UH... YOU KNOW GWEN'S DOG, PUMPKIN? SHE SORT OF ASKED ME OUT FOR A VALENTINE'S DINNER. AND WHO AM I TO TURN DOWN FREE FOOD, RIGHT?
GREAT. GO FIGURE. WELL, I BETTER HOPE THAT SOMEONE BIDS ON ME FOR THE AUCTION BECAUSE OTHERWISE I'M GOING TO DIE OF SHAME!

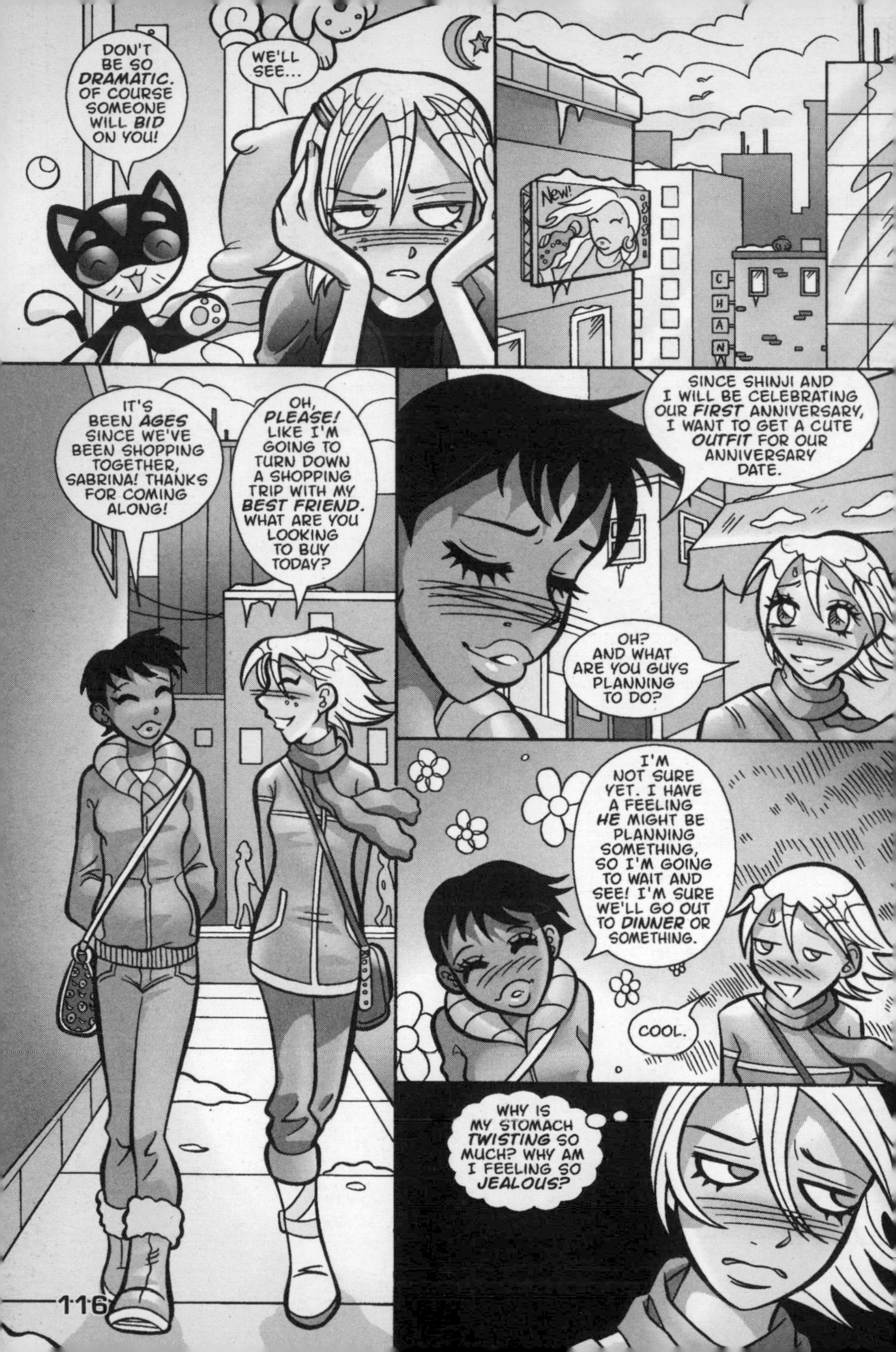
DON'T BE SO *DRAMATIC*. OF COURSE SOMEONE WILL *BID* ON YOU!
WE'LL SEE...
New!
CHAN
IT'S BEEN *AGES* SINCE WE'VE BEEN SHOPPING TOGETHER, SABRINA! THANKS FOR COMING ALONG!
OH, *PLEASE!* LIKE I'M GOING TO TURN DOWN A SHOPPING TRIP WITH MY *BEST FRIEND*. WHAT ARE YOU LOOKING TO BUY TODAY?
SINCE SHINJI AND I WILL BE CELEBRATING OUR *FIRST* ANNIVERSARY, I WANT TO GET A CUTE *OUTFIT* FOR OUR ANNIVERSARY DATE.
OH? AND WHAT ARE YOU GUYS PLANNING TO DO?
I'M NOT SURE YET. I HAVE A FEELING *HE* MIGHT BE PLANNING SOMETHING, SO I'M GOING TO WAIT AND SEE! I'M SURE WE'LL GO OUT TO *DINNER* OR SOMETHING.
COOL.
WHY IS MY STOMACH *TWISTING* SO MUCH? WHY AM I FEELING SO *JEALOUS?*

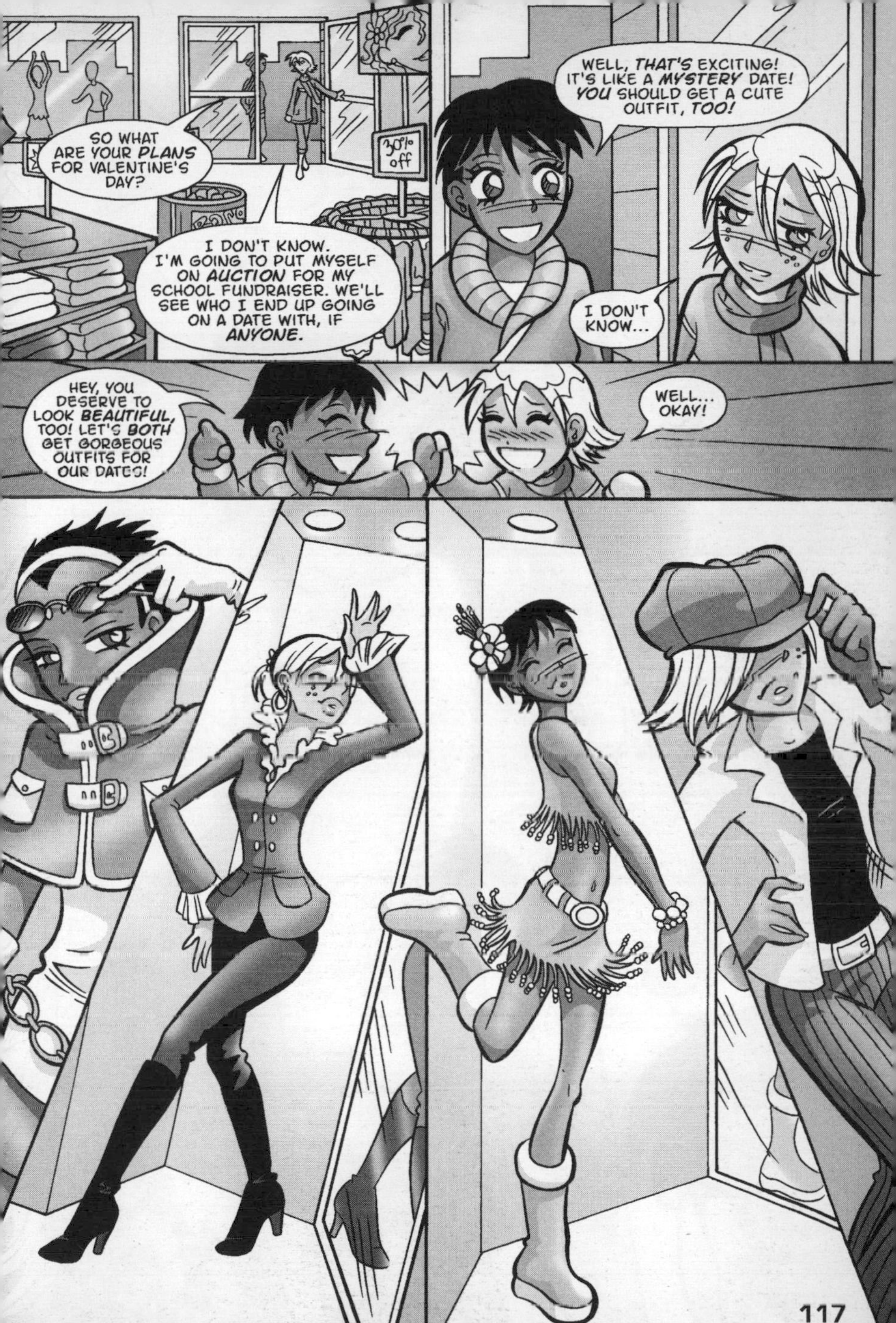
SO WHAT ARE YOUR PLANS FOR VALENTINE'S DAY?
30% off
I DON'T KNOW. I'M GOING TO PUT MYSELF ON AUCTION FOR MY SCHOOL FUNDRAISER. WE'LL SEE WHO I END UP GOING ON A DATE WITH, IF ANYONE.
WELL, THAT'S EXCITING! IT'S LIKE A MYSTERY DATE! YOU SHOULD GET A CUTE OUTFIT, TOO!
I DON'T KNOW...
HEY, YOU DESERVE TO LOOK BEAUTIFUL, TOO! LET'S BOTH GET GORGEOUS OUTFITS FOR OUR DATES!
WELL... OKAY!

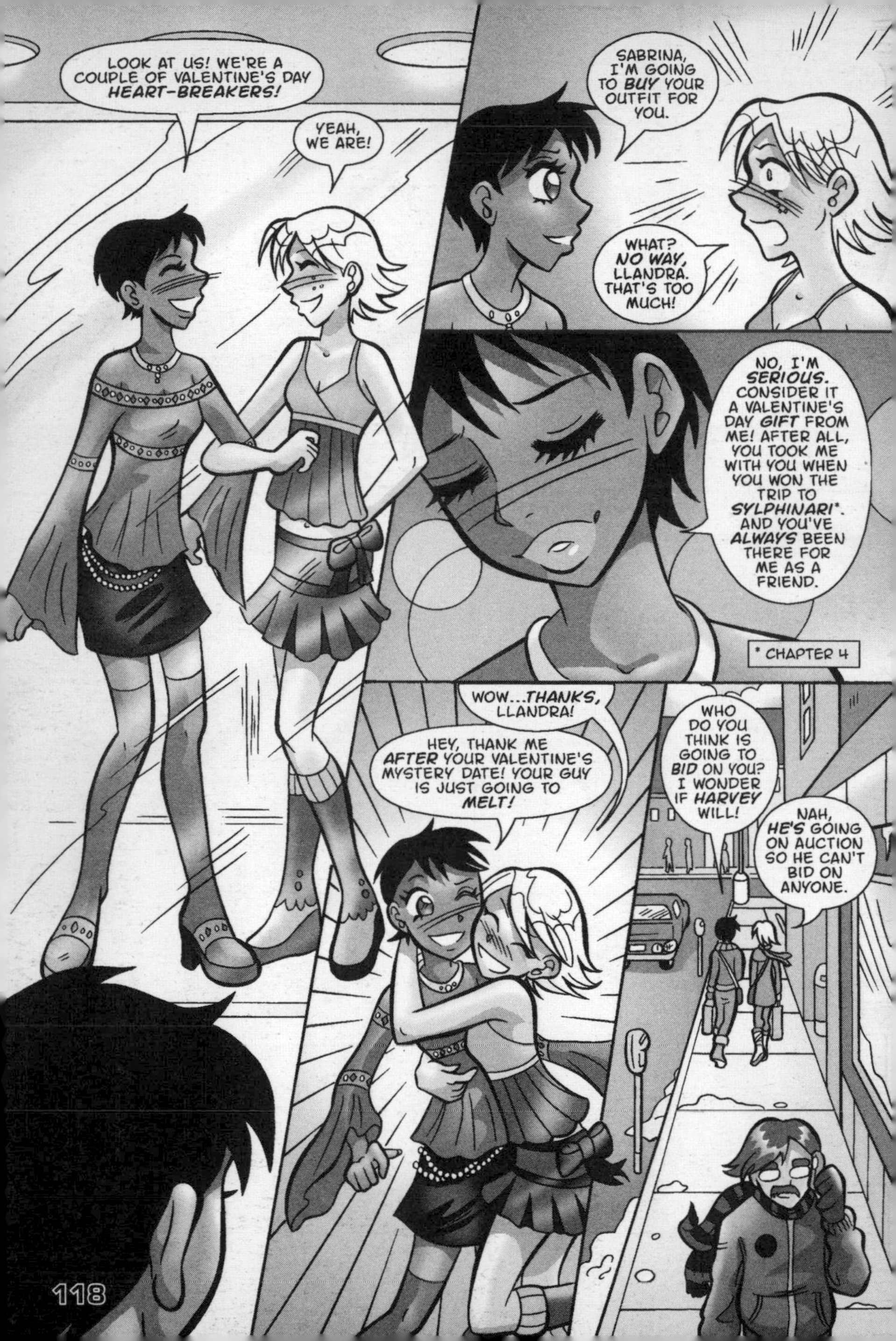
LOOK AT US! WE'RE A COUPLE OF VALENTINE'S DAY *HEART-BREAKERS!*
YEAH, WE ARE!
SABRINA, I'M GOING TO *BUY* YOUR OUTFIT FOR YOU.
WHAT? *NO WAY,* LLANDRA. THAT'S TOO MUCH!
NO, I'M *SERIOUS.* CONSIDER IT A VALENTINE'S DAY *GIFT* FROM ME! AFTER ALL, YOU TOOK ME WITH YOU WHEN YOU WON THE TRIP TO *SYLPHINARI**. AND YOU'VE *ALWAYS* BEEN THERE FOR ME AS A FRIEND.
* CHAPTER 4
WOW...*THANKS,* LLANDRA!
HEY, THANK ME *AFTER* YOUR VALENTINE'S MYSTERY DATE! YOUR GUY IS JUST GOING TO *MELT!*
WHO DO YOU THINK IS GOING TO *BID* ON YOU? I WONDER IF *HARVEY* WILL!
NAH, *HE'S* GOING ON AUCTION SO HE CAN'T BID ON ANYONE.

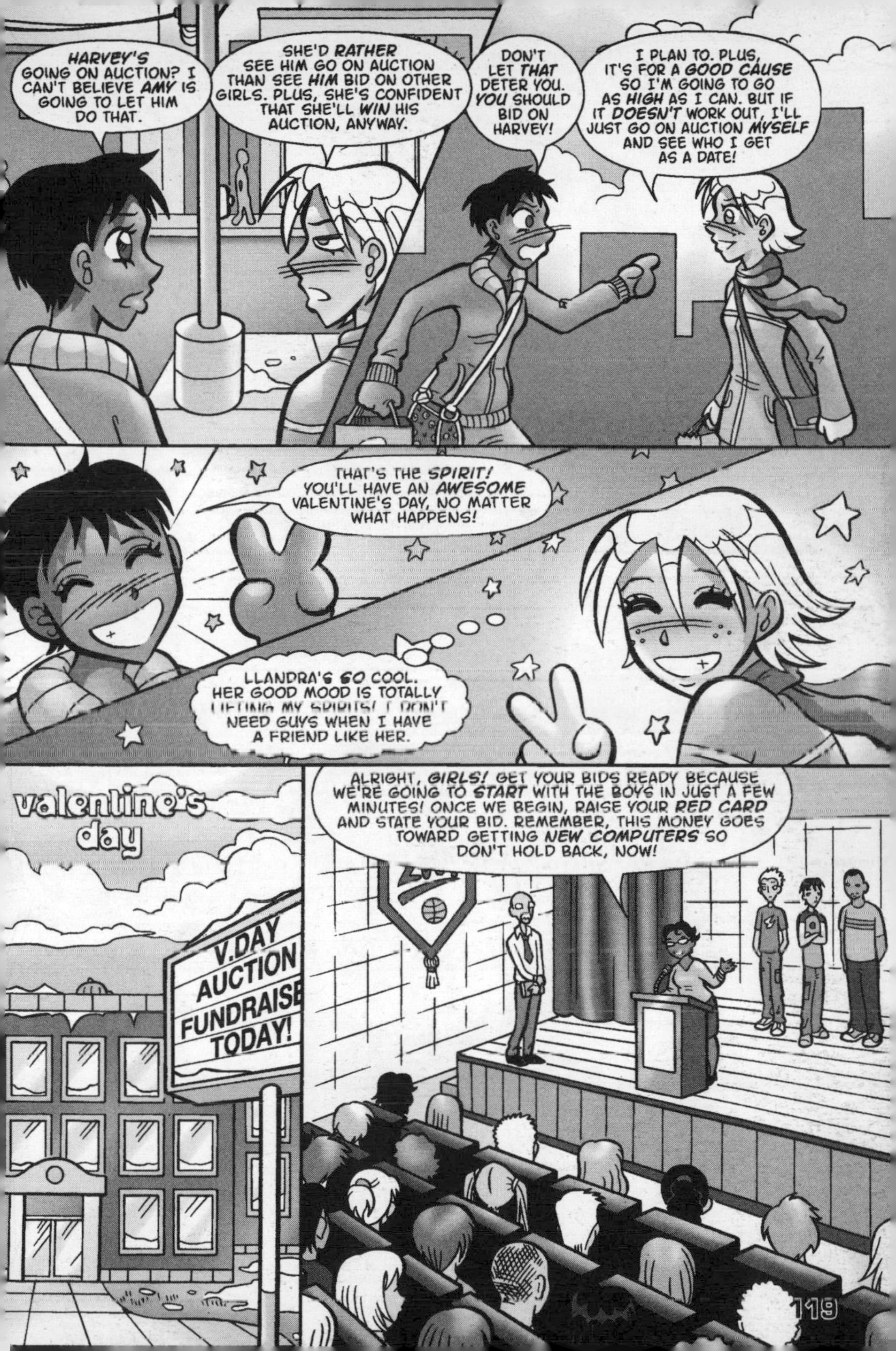
HARVEY'S GOING ON AUCTION? I CAN'T BELIEVE AMY IS GOING TO LET HIM DO THAT.
SHE'D RATHER SEE HIM GO ON AUCTION THAN SEE HIM BID ON OTHER GIRLS. PLUS, SHE'S CONFIDENT THAT SHE'LL WIN HIS AUCTION, ANYWAY.
DON'T LET THAT DETER YOU. YOU SHOULD BID ON HARVEY!
I PLAN TO. PLUS, IT'S FOR A GOOD CAUSE SO I'M GOING TO GO AS HIGH AS I CAN. BUT IF IT DOESN'T WORK OUT, I'LL JUST GO ON AUCTION MYSELF AND SEE WHO I GET AS A DATE!
THAT'S THE SPIRIT! YOU'LL HAVE AN AWESOME VALENTINE'S DAY, NO MATTER WHAT HAPPENS!
LLANDRA'S SO COOL. HER GOOD MOOD IS TOTALLY LIFTING MY SPIRITS! I DON'T NEED GUYS WHEN I HAVE A FRIEND LIKE HER.
valentine's day
V.DAY AUCTION FUNDRAISE TODAY!
ALRIGHT, GIRLS! GET YOUR BIDS READY BECAUSE WE'RE GOING TO START WITH THE BOYS IN JUST A FEW MINUTES! ONCE WE BEGIN, RAISE YOUR RED CARD AND STATE YOUR BID. REMEMBER, THIS MONEY GOES TOWARD GETTING NEW COMPUTERS SO DON'T HOLD BACK, NOW!

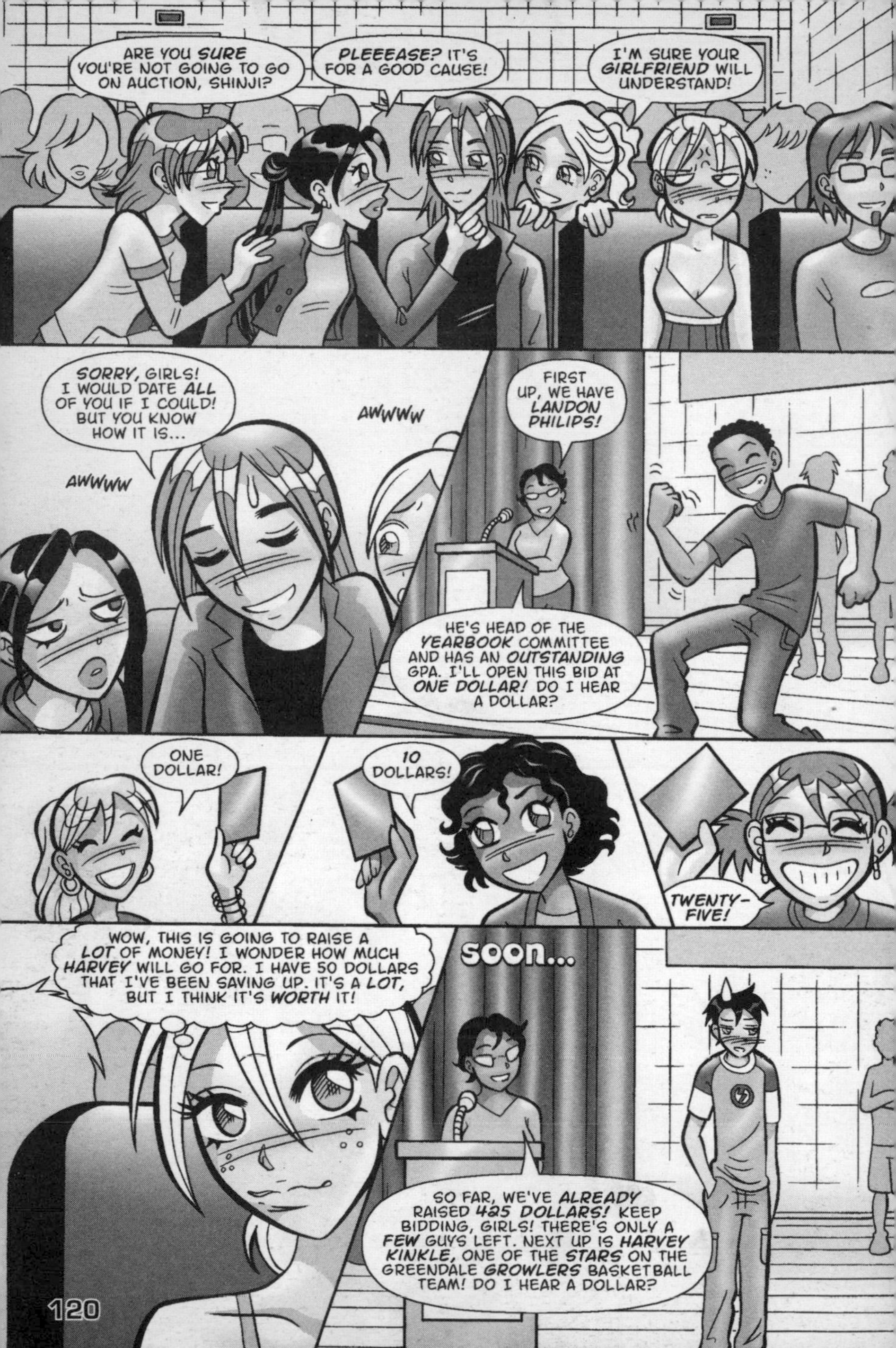

ARE YOU SURE YOU'RE NOT GOING TO GO ON AUCTION, SHINJI?
PLEEEASE? IT'S FOR A GOOD CAUSE!
I'M SURE YOUR GIRLFRIEND WILL UNDERSTAND!
SORRY, GIRLS! I WOULD DATE ALL OF YOU IF I COULD! BUT YOU KNOW HOW IT IS...
AWWWW
AWWWW
FIRST UP, WE HAVE LANDON PHILIPS!
HE'S HEAD OF THE YEARBOOK COMMITTEE AND HAS AN OUTSTANDING GPA. I'LL OPEN THIS BID AT ONE DOLLAR! DO I HEAR A DOLLAR?
ONE DOLLAR!
10 DOLLARS!
TWENTY-FIVE!
WOW, THIS IS GOING TO RAISE A LOT OF MONEY! I WONDER HOW MUCH HARVEY WILL GO FOR. I HAVE 50 DOLLARS THAT I'VE BEEN SAVING UP. IT'S A LOT, BUT I THINK IT'S WORTH IT!
soon...
SO FAR, WE'VE ALREADY RAISED 425 DOLLARS! KEEP BIDDING, GIRLS! THERE'S ONLY A FEW GUYS LEFT. NEXT UP IS HARVEY KINKLE, ONE OF THE STARS ON THE GREENDALE GROWLERS BASKETBALL TEAM! DO I HEAR A DOLLAR?

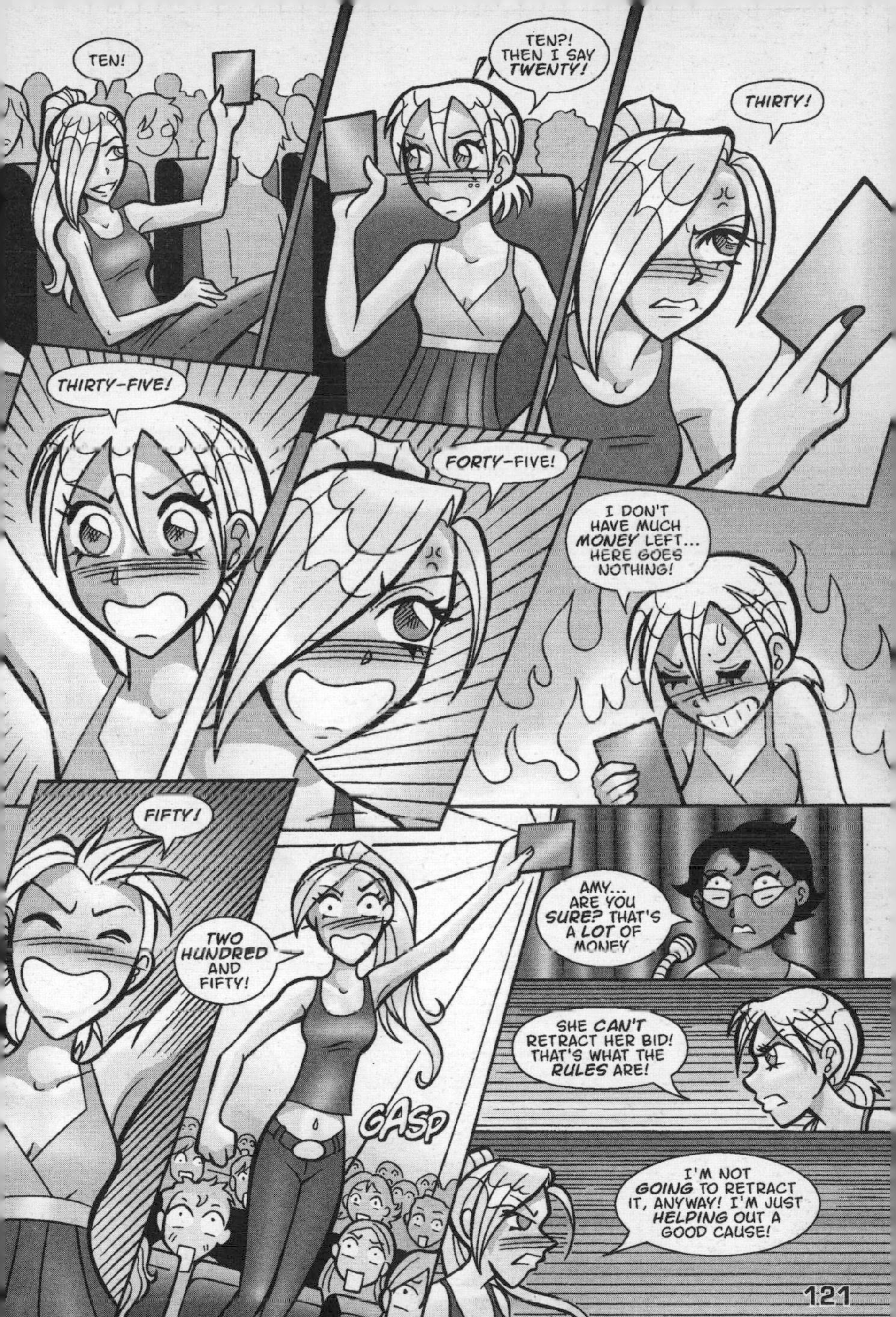
TEN!
TEN?! THEN I SAY TWENTY!
THIRTY!
THIRTY-FIVE!
FORTY-FIVE!
I DON'T HAVE MUCH MONEY LEFT... HERE GOES NOTHING!
FIFTY!
TWO HUNDRED AND FIFTY!
GASP
AMY... ARE YOU SURE? THAT'S A LOT OF MONEY
SHE CAN'T RETRACT HER BID! THAT'S WHAT THE RULES ARE!
I'M NOT GOING TO RETRACT IT, ANYWAY! I'M JUST HELPING OUT A GOOD CAUSE!

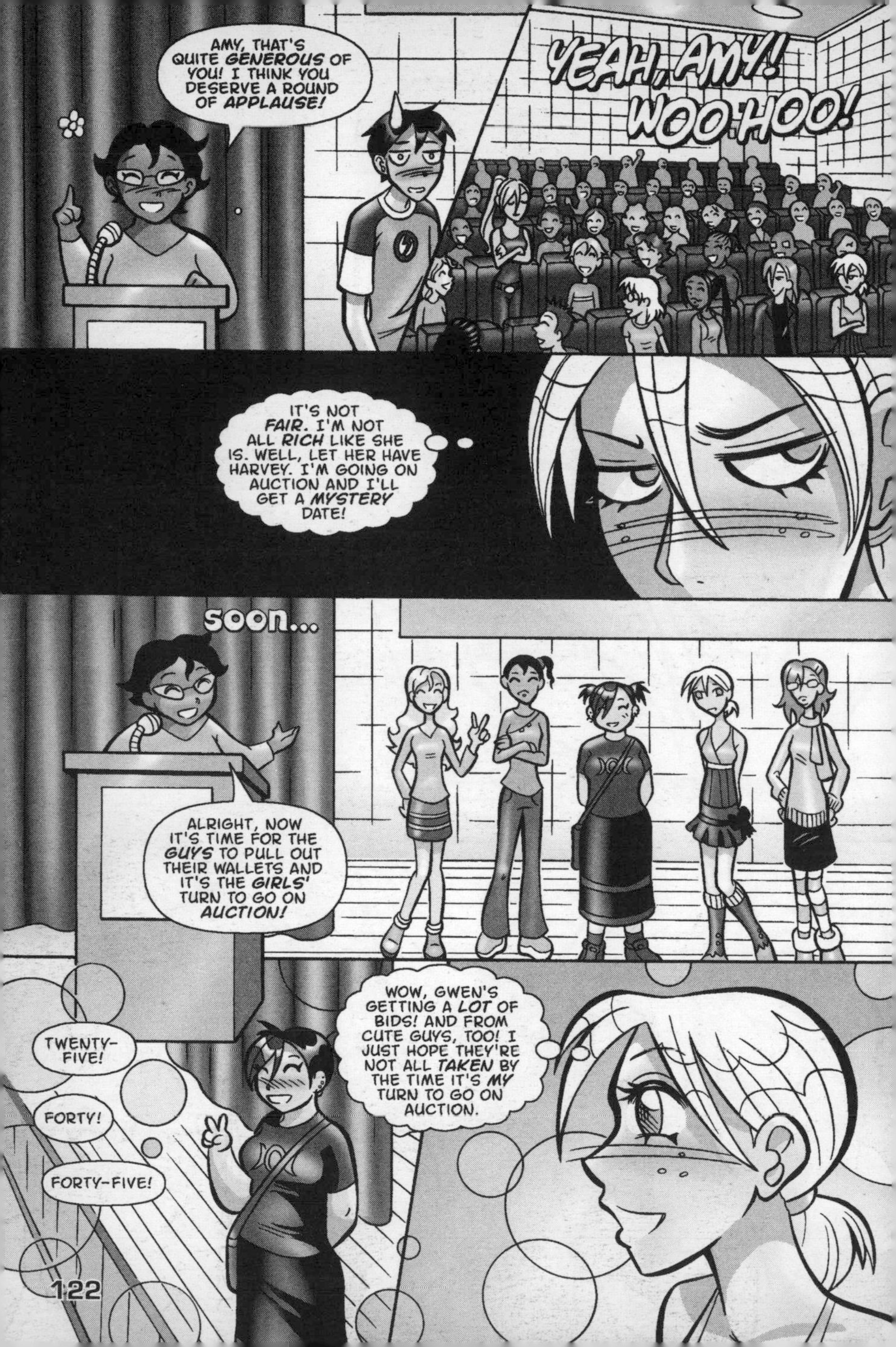
AMY, THAT'S QUITE GENEROUS OF YOU! I THINK YOU DESERVE A ROUND OF APPLAUSE!
YEAH, AMY! WOO HOO!
IT'S NOT FAIR. I'M NOT ALL RICH LIKE SHE IS. WELL, LET HER HAVE HARVEY. I'M GOING ON AUCTION AND I'LL GET A MYSTERY DATE!
soon...
ALRIGHT, NOW IT'S TIME FOR THE GUYS TO PULL OUT THEIR WALLETS AND IT'S THE GIRLS' TURN TO GO ON AUCTION!
TWENTY-FIVE!
FORTY!
FORTY-FIVE!
WOW, GWEN'S GETTING A LOT OF BIDS! AND FROM CUTE GUYS, TOO! I JUST HOPE THEY'RE NOT ALL TAKEN BY THE TIME IT'S MY TURN TO GO ON AUCTION.

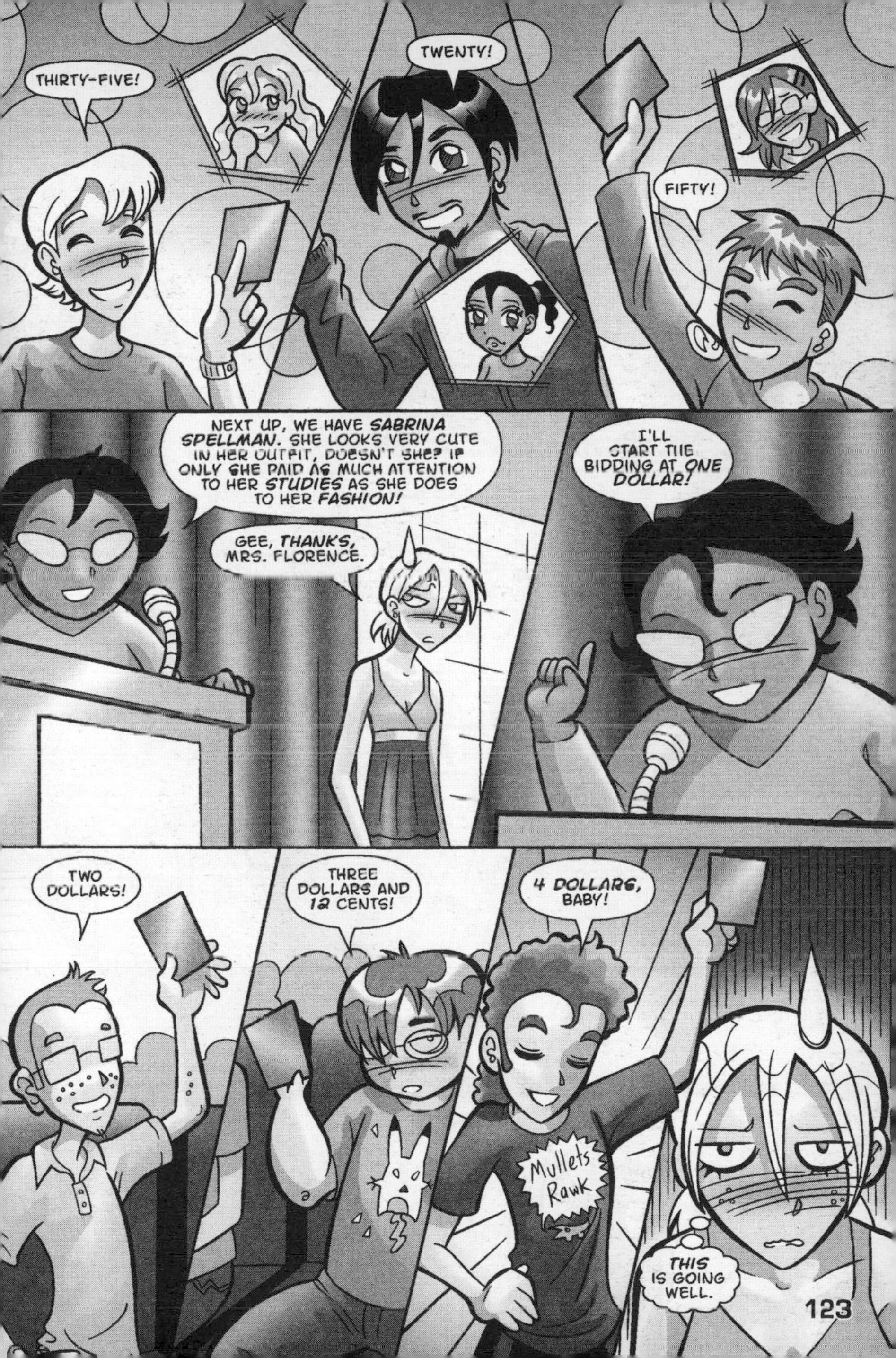
THIRTY-FIVE!
TWENTY!
FIFTY!
NEXT UP, WE HAVE SABRINA SPELLMAN. SHE LOOKS VERY CUTE IN HER OUTFIT, DOESN'T SHE? IF ONLY SHE PAID AS MUCH ATTENTION TO HER STUDIES AS SHE DOES TO HER FASHION!
GEE, THANKS, MRS. FLORENCE.
I'LL START THE BIDDING AT ONE DOLLAR!
TWO DOLLARS!
THREE DOLLARS AND 12 CENTS!
4 DOLLARS, BABY!
Mullets Rawk
THIS IS GOING WELL.

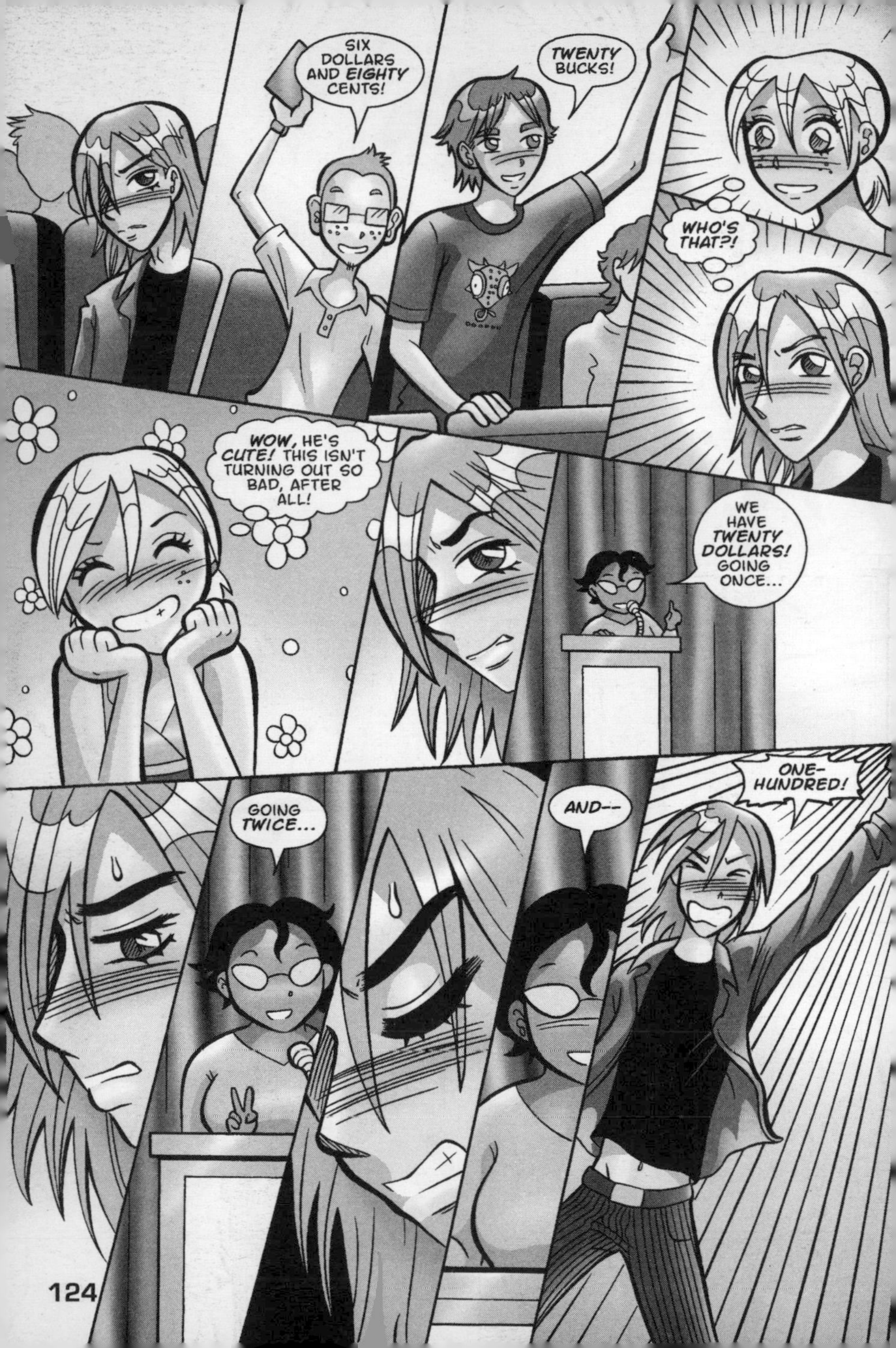
SIX DOLLARS AND EIGHTY CENTS!
TWENTY BUCKS!
WHO'S THAT?!
WOW, HE'S CUTE! THIS ISN'T TURNING OUT SO BAD, AFTER ALL!
WE HAVE TWENTY DOLLARS! GOING ONCE...
GOING TWICE...
AND--
ONE-HUNDRED!

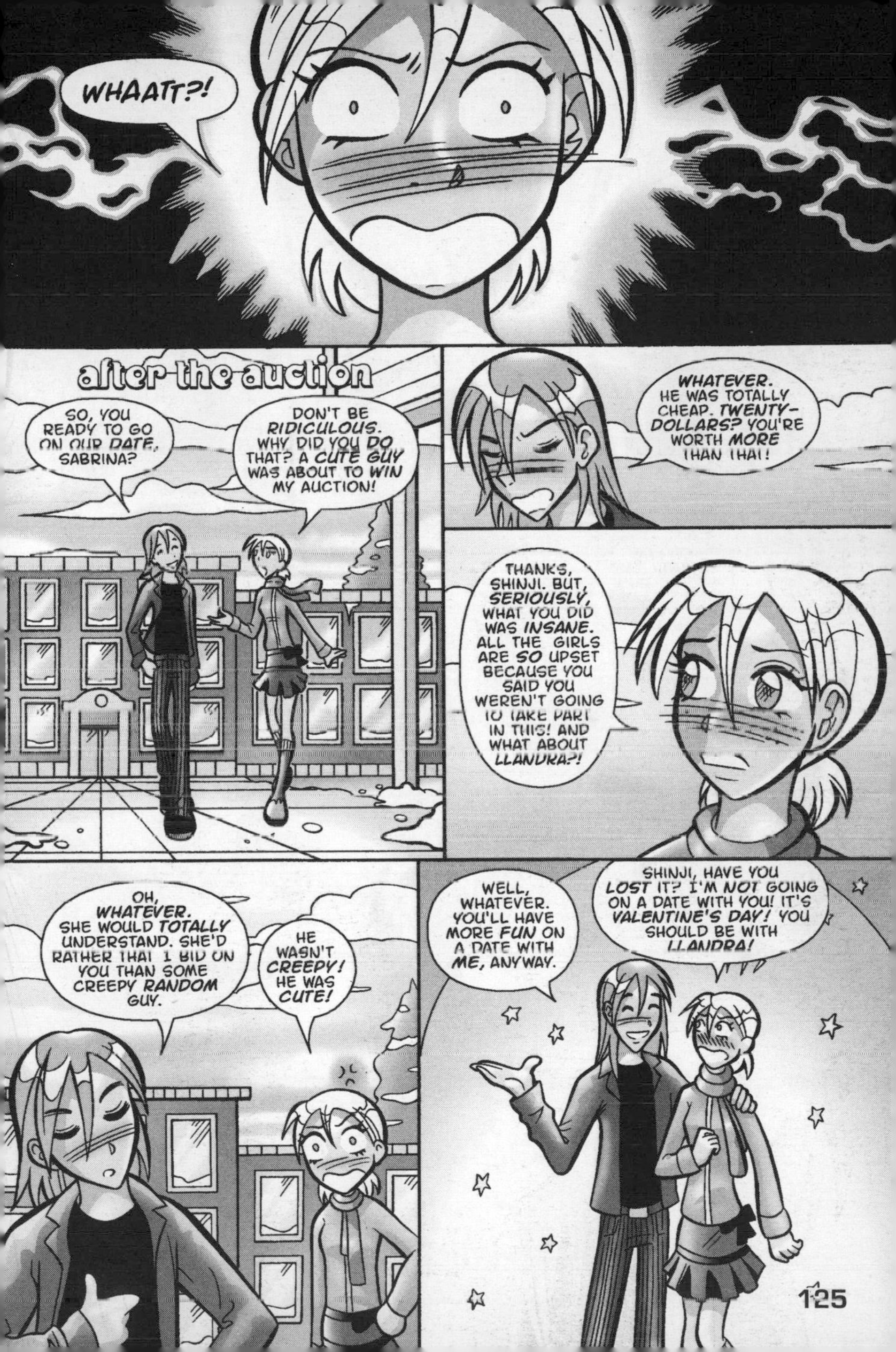
WHAATT?!
after the auction
SO, YOU READY TO GO ON OUR DATE, SABRINA?
DON'T BE RIDICULOUS. WHY DID YOU DO THAT? A CUTE GUY WAS ABOUT TO WIN MY AUCTION!
WHATEVER. HE WAS TOTALLY CHEAP. TWENTY-DOLLARS? YOU'RE WORTH MORE THAN THAT!
THANKS, SHINJI. BUT, SERIOUSLY, WHAT YOU DID WAS INSANE. ALL THE GIRLS ARE SO UPSET BECAUSE YOU SAID YOU WEREN'T GOING TO TAKE PART IN THIS! AND WHAT ABOUT LLANDRA?!
OH, WHATEVER. SHE WOULD TOTALLY UNDERSTAND. SHE'D RATHER THAT I BID ON YOU THAN SOME CREEPY RANDOM GUY.
HE WASN'T CREEPY! HE WAS CUTE!
WELL, WHATEVER. YOU'LL HAVE MORE FUN ON A DATE WITH ME, ANYWAY.
SHINJI, HAVE YOU LOST IT? I'M NOT GOING ON A DATE WITH YOU! IT'S VALENTINE'S DAY! YOU SHOULD BE WITH LLANDRA!

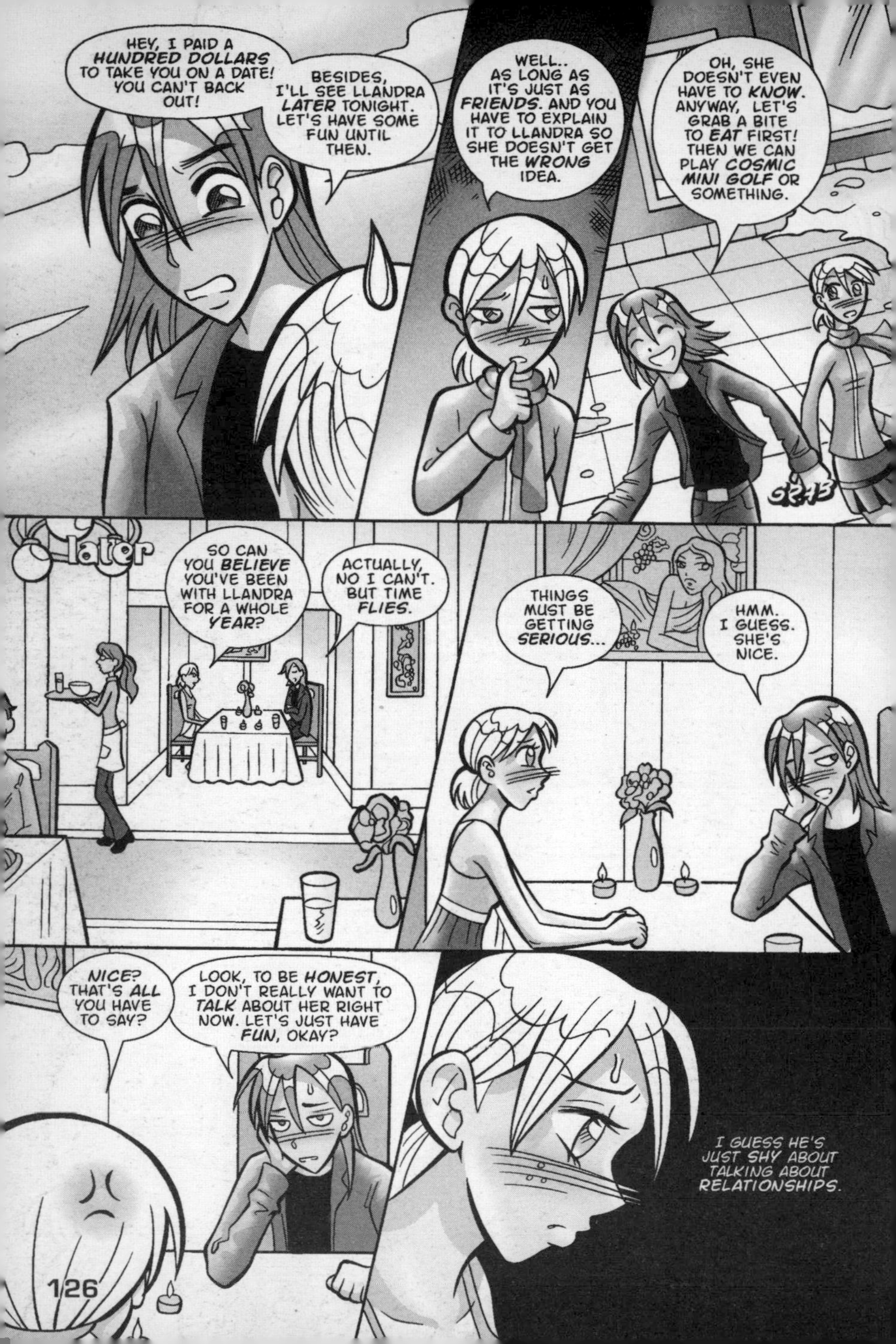
HEY, I PAID A HUNDRED DOLLARS TO TAKE YOU ON A DATE! YOU CAN'T BACK OUT!
BESIDES, I'LL SEE LLANDRA LATER TONIGHT. LET'S HAVE SOME FUN UNTIL THEN.
WELL.. AS LONG AS IT'S JUST AS FRIENDS. AND YOU HAVE TO EXPLAIN IT TO LLANDRA SO SHE DOESN'T GET THE WRONG IDEA.
OH, SHE DOESN'T EVEN HAVE TO KNOW. ANYWAY, LET'S GRAB A BITE TO EAT FIRST! THEN WE CAN PLAY COSMIC MINI GOLF OR SOMETHING.
later
SO CAN YOU BELIEVE YOU'VE BEEN WITH LLANDRA FOR A WHOLE YEAR?
ACTUALLY, NO I CAN'T. BUT TIME FLIES.
THINGS MUST BE GETTING SERIOUS...
HMM. I GUESS. SHE'S NICE.
NICE? THAT'S ALL YOU HAVE TO SAY?
LOOK, TO BE HONEST, I DON'T REALLY WANT TO TALK ABOUT HER RIGHT NOW. LET'S JUST HAVE FUN, OKAY?
I GUESS HE'S JUST SHY ABOUT TALKING ABOUT RELATIONSHIPS.

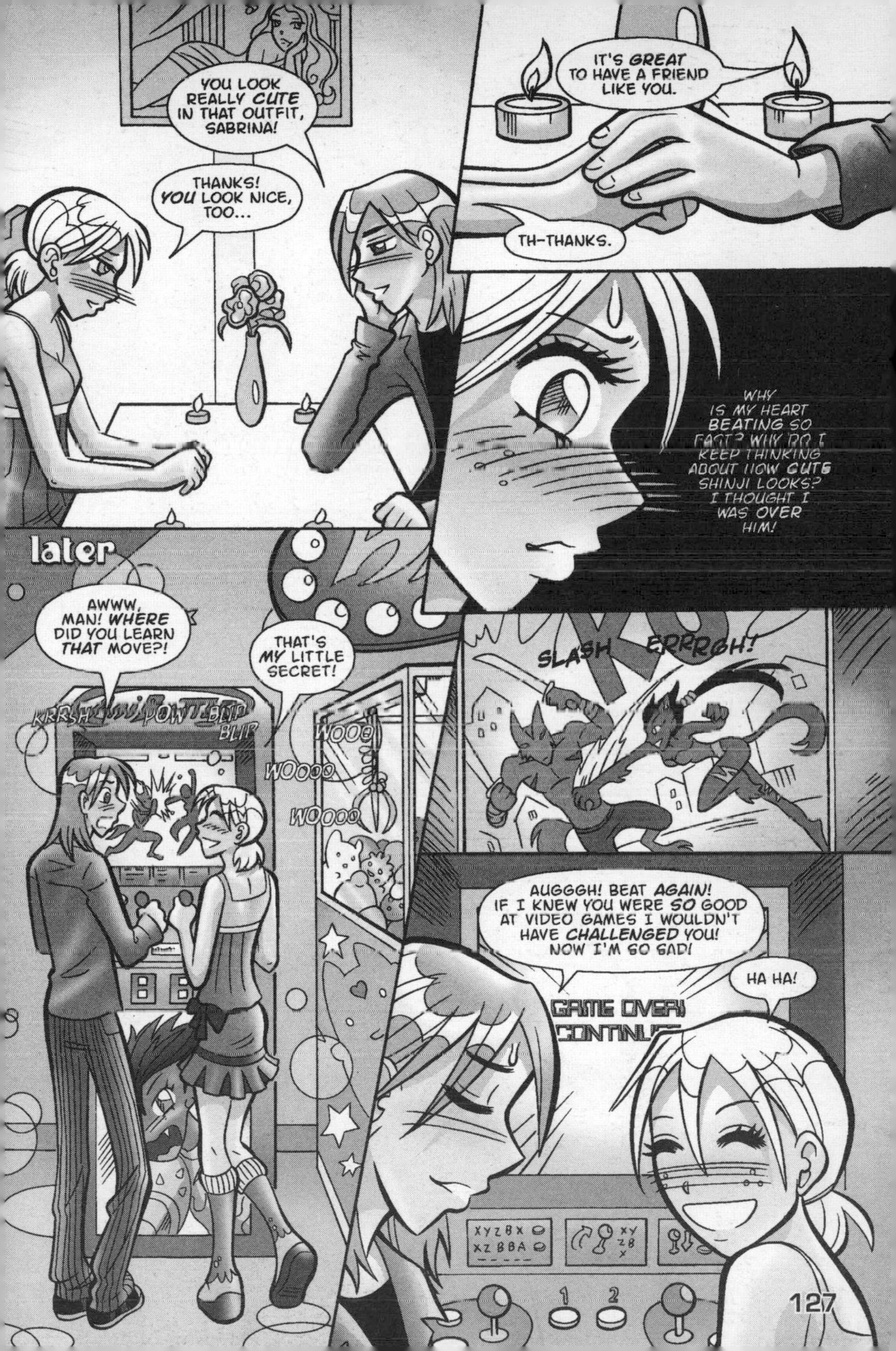
YOU LOOK REALLY CUTE IN THAT OUTFIT, SABRINA!
THANKS! YOU LOOK NICE, TOO...
IT'S GREAT TO HAVE A FRIEND LIKE YOU.
TH-THANKS.
WHY IS MY HEART BEATING SO FAST? WHY DO I KEEP THINKING ABOUT HOW CUTE SHINJI LOOKS? I THOUGHT I WAS OVER HIM!
later
AWWW, MAN! WHERE DID YOU LEARN THAT MOVE?!
THAT'S MY LITTLE SECRET!
KRRSH
BLIP
WOOO
WOOOO
WOOOO
SLASH
ERRRGH!
AUGGGH! BEAT AGAIN! IF I KNEW YOU WERE SO GOOD AT VIDEO GAMES I WOULDN'T HAVE CHALLENGED YOU! NOW I'M SO SAD!
HA HA!
GAME OVER!
1
2

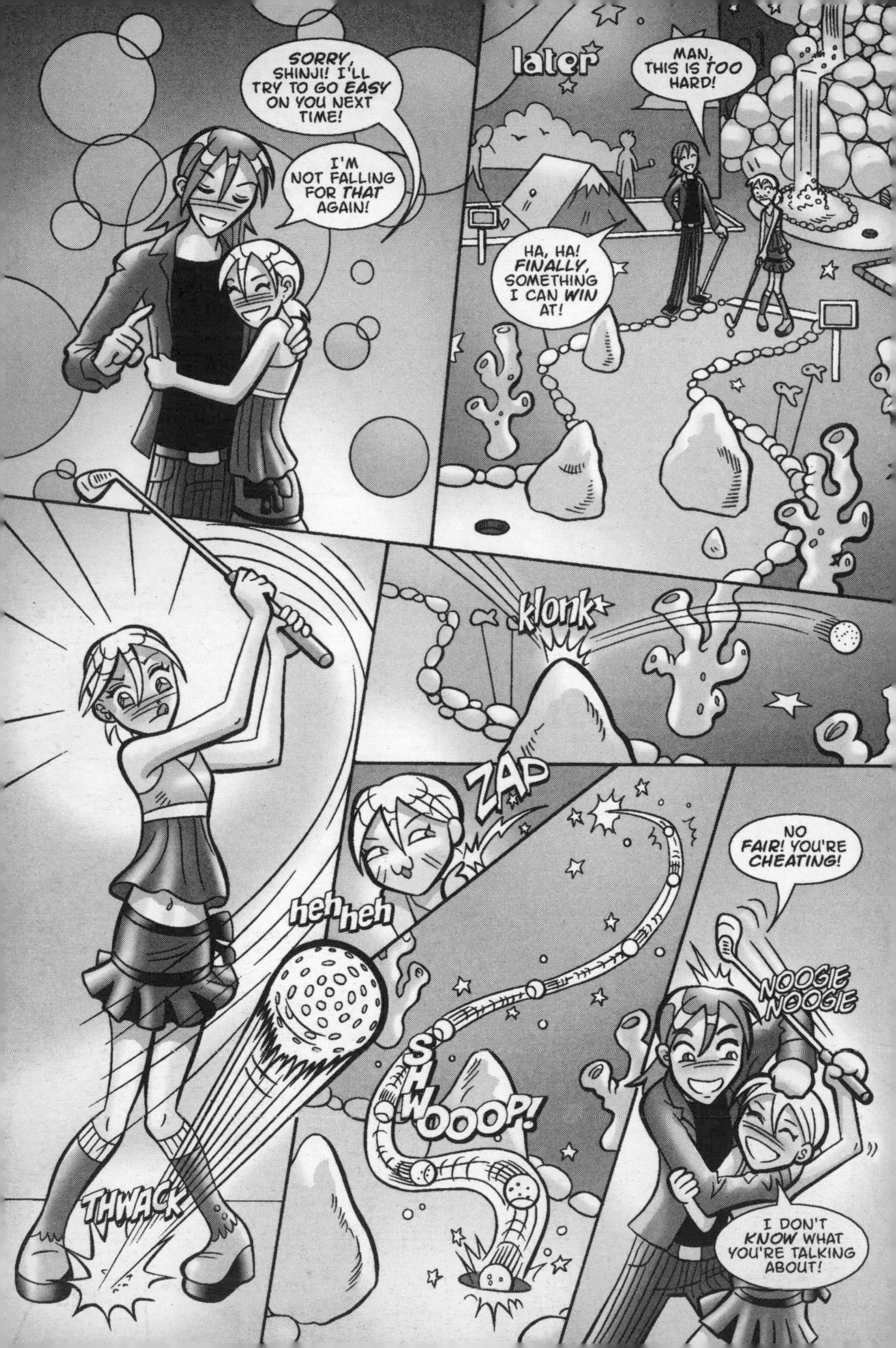
SORRY, SHINJI! I'LL TRY TO GO EASY ON YOU NEXT TIME!
I'M NOT FALLING FOR THAT AGAIN!
later
MAN, THIS IS TOO HARD!
HA, HA! FINALLY, SOMETHING I CAN WIN AT!
THWACK
klonk
ZAP
heh heh
SHWOOOP!
NO FAIR! YOU'RE CHEATING!
NOOGIE NOOGIE
I DON'T KNOW WHAT YOU'RE TALKING ABOUT!

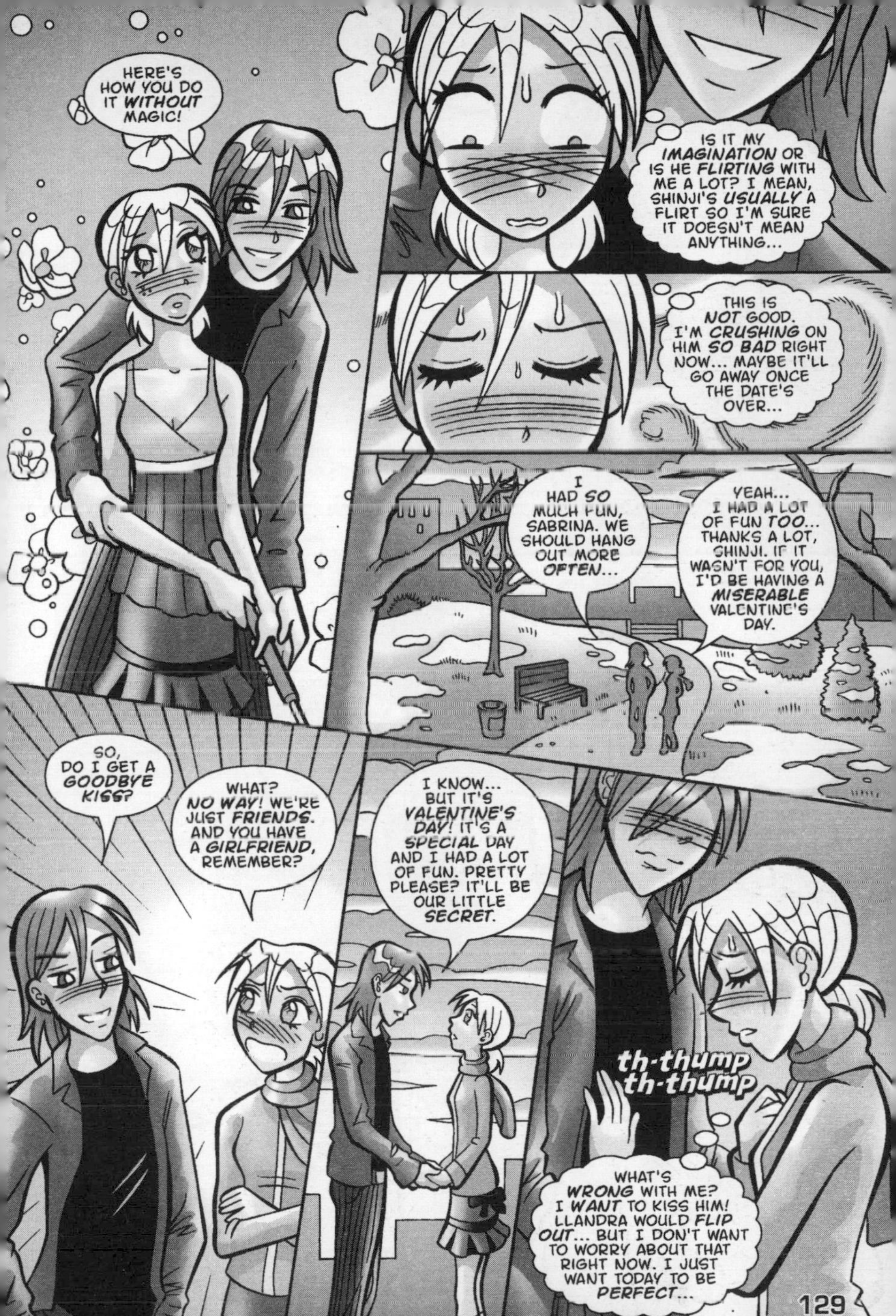

HERE'S HOW YOU DO IT WITHOUT MAGIC!
IS IT MY IMAGINATION OR IS HE FLIRTING WITH ME A LOT? I MEAN, SHINJI'S USUALLY A FLIRT SO I'M SURE IT DOESN'T MEAN ANYTHING...
THIS IS NOT GOOD. I'M CRUSHING ON HIM SO BAD RIGHT NOW... MAYBE IT'LL GO AWAY ONCE THE DATE'S OVER...
I HAD SO MUCH FUN, SABRINA. WE SHOULD HANG OUT MORE OFTEN...
YEAH... I HAD A LOT OF FUN TOO... THANKS A LOT, SHINJI. IF IT WASN'T FOR YOU, I'D BE HAVING A MISERABLE VALENTINE'S DAY.
SO, DO I GET A GOODBYE KISS?
WHAT? NO WAY! WE'RE JUST FRIENDS. AND YOU HAVE A GIRLFRIEND, REMEMBER?
I KNOW... BUT IT'S VALENTINE'S DAY! IT'S A SPECIAL DAY AND I HAD A LOT OF FUN. PRETTY PLEASE? IT'LL BE OUR LITTLE SECRET.
th-thump th-thump
WHAT'S WRONG WITH ME? I WANT TO KISS HIM! LLANDRA WOULD FLIP OUT... BUT I DON'T WANT TO WORRY ABOUT THAT RIGHT NOW. I JUST WANT TODAY TO BE PERFECT...

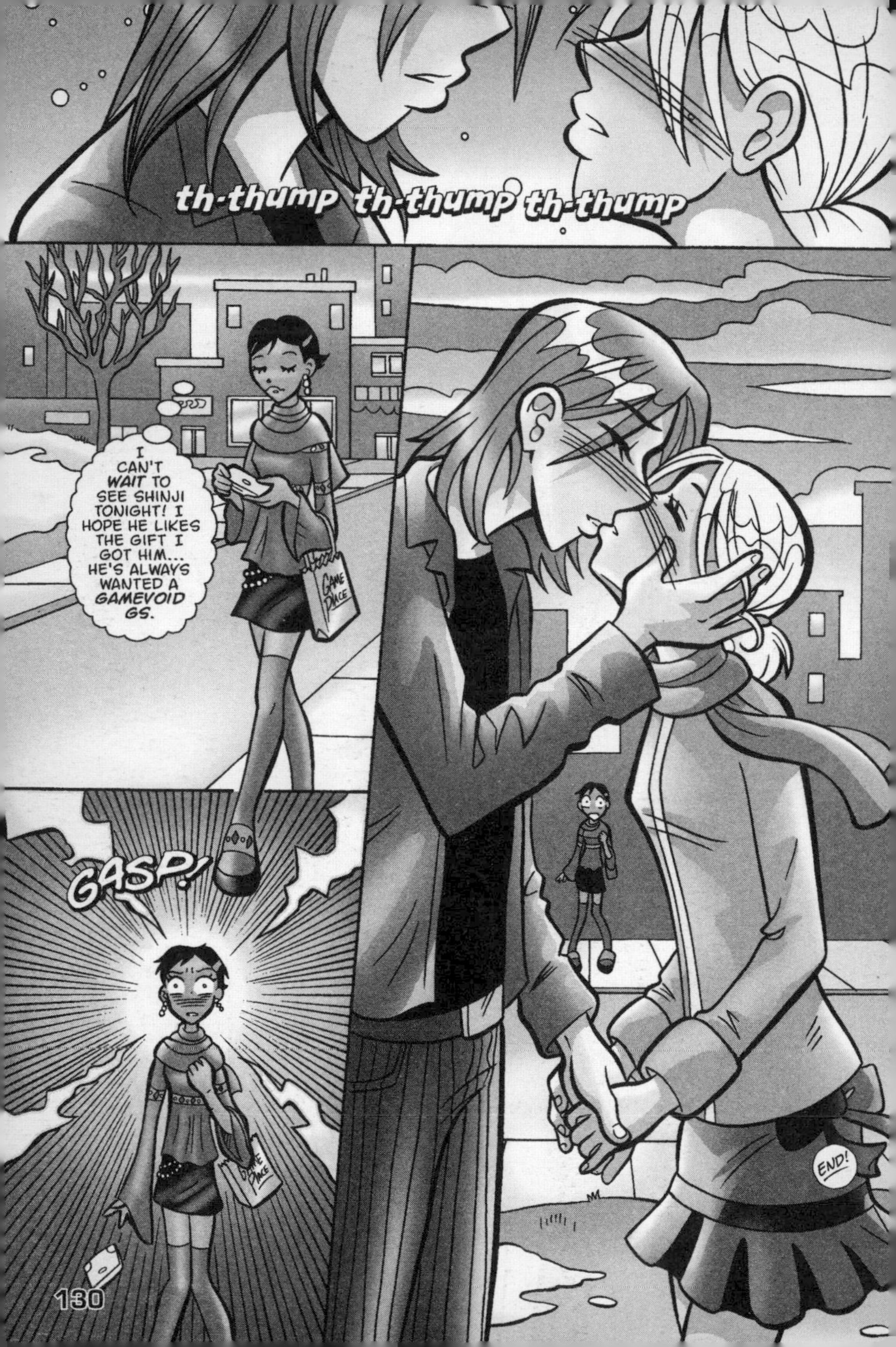
th-thump th-thump th-thump
I CAN'T WAIT TO SEE SHINJI TONIGHT! I HOPE HE LIKES THE GIFT I GOT HIM... HE'S ALWAYS WANTED A GAMEVOID GS.
GAME PLACE
GASP!
GAME PLACE
END!

Chapter 7

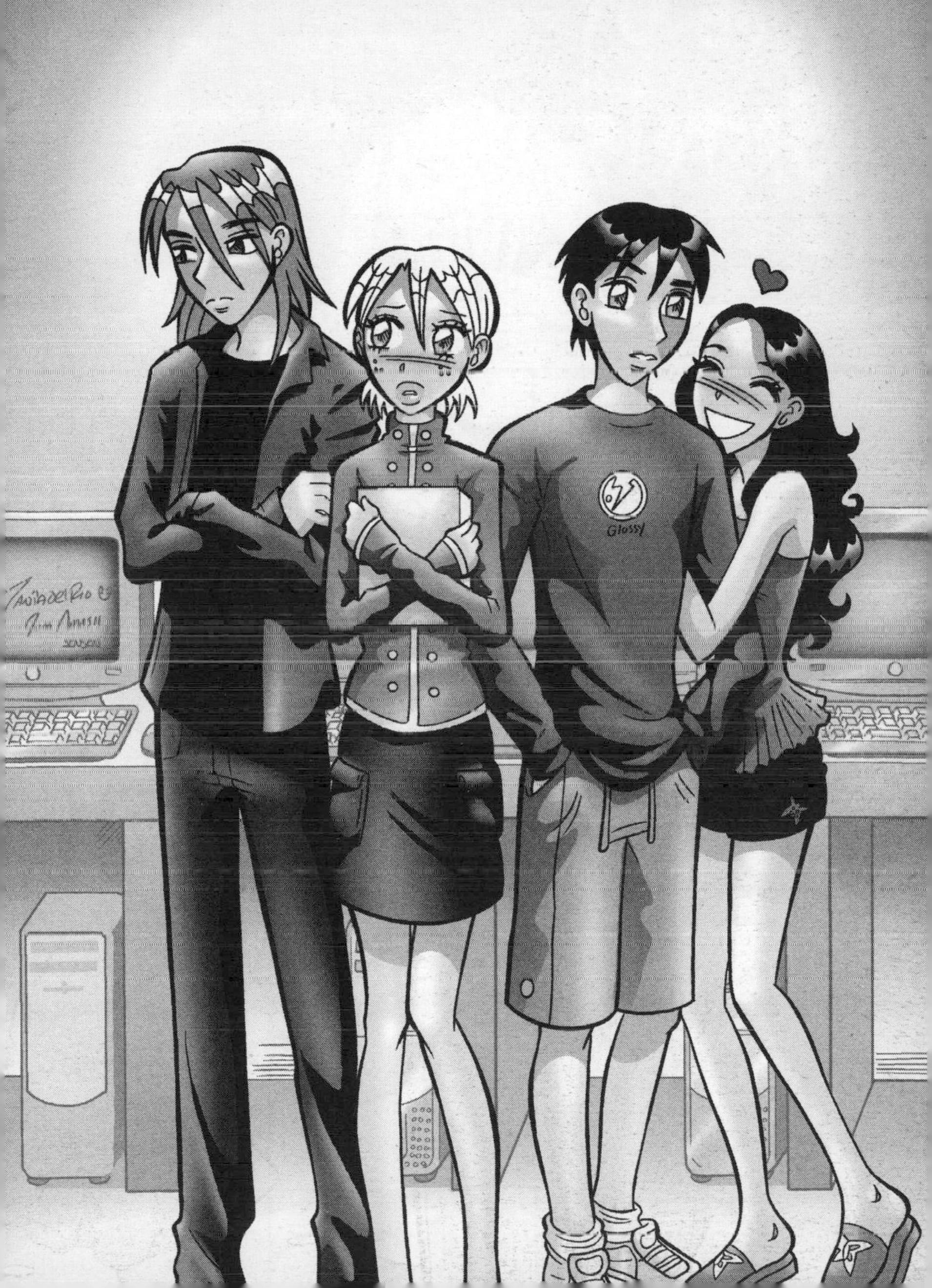
Glossy

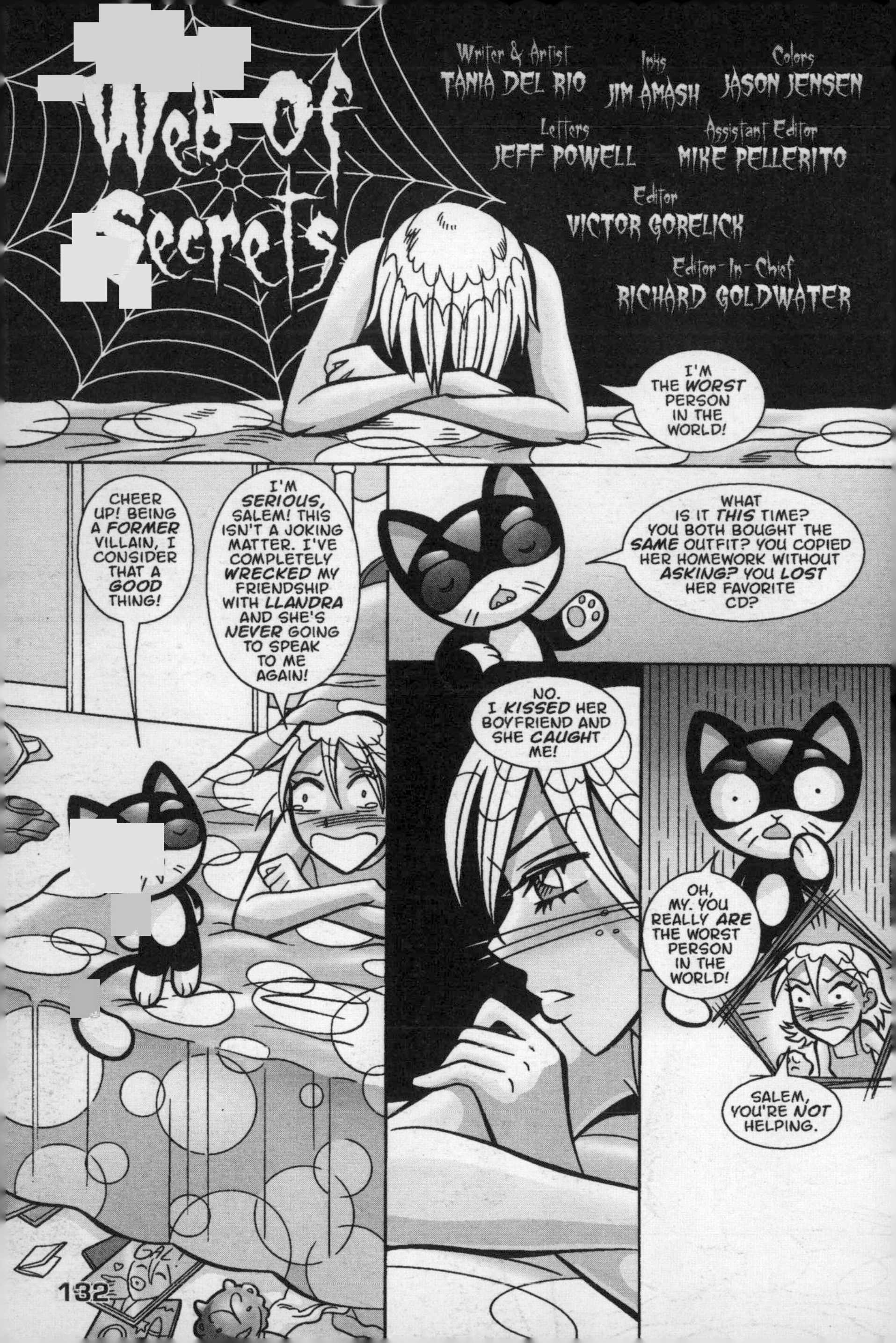
Web of Secrets
Writer & Artist TANIA DEL RIO
Inks JIM AMASH
Colors JASON JENSEN
Letters JEFF POWELL
Assistant Editor MIKE PELLERITO
Editor VICTOR GORELICK
Editor-In-Chief RICHARD GOLDWATER
I'M THE WORST PERSON IN THE WORLD!
CHEER UP! BEING A FORMER VILLAIN, I CONSIDER THAT A GOOD THING!
I'M SERIOUS, SALEM! THIS ISN'T A JOKING MATTER. I'VE COMPLETELY WRECKED MY FRIENDSHIP WITH LLANDRA AND SHE'S NEVER GOING TO SPEAK TO ME AGAIN!
GAL!
WHAT IS IT THIS TIME? YOU BOTH BOUGHT THE SAME OUTFIT? YOU COPIED HER HOMEWORK WITHOUT ASKING? YOU LOST HER FAVORITE CD?
NO. I KISSED HER BOYFRIEND AND SHE CAUGHT ME!
OH, MY. YOU REALLY ARE THE WORST PERSON IN THE WORLD!
SALEM, YOU'RE NOT HELPING.

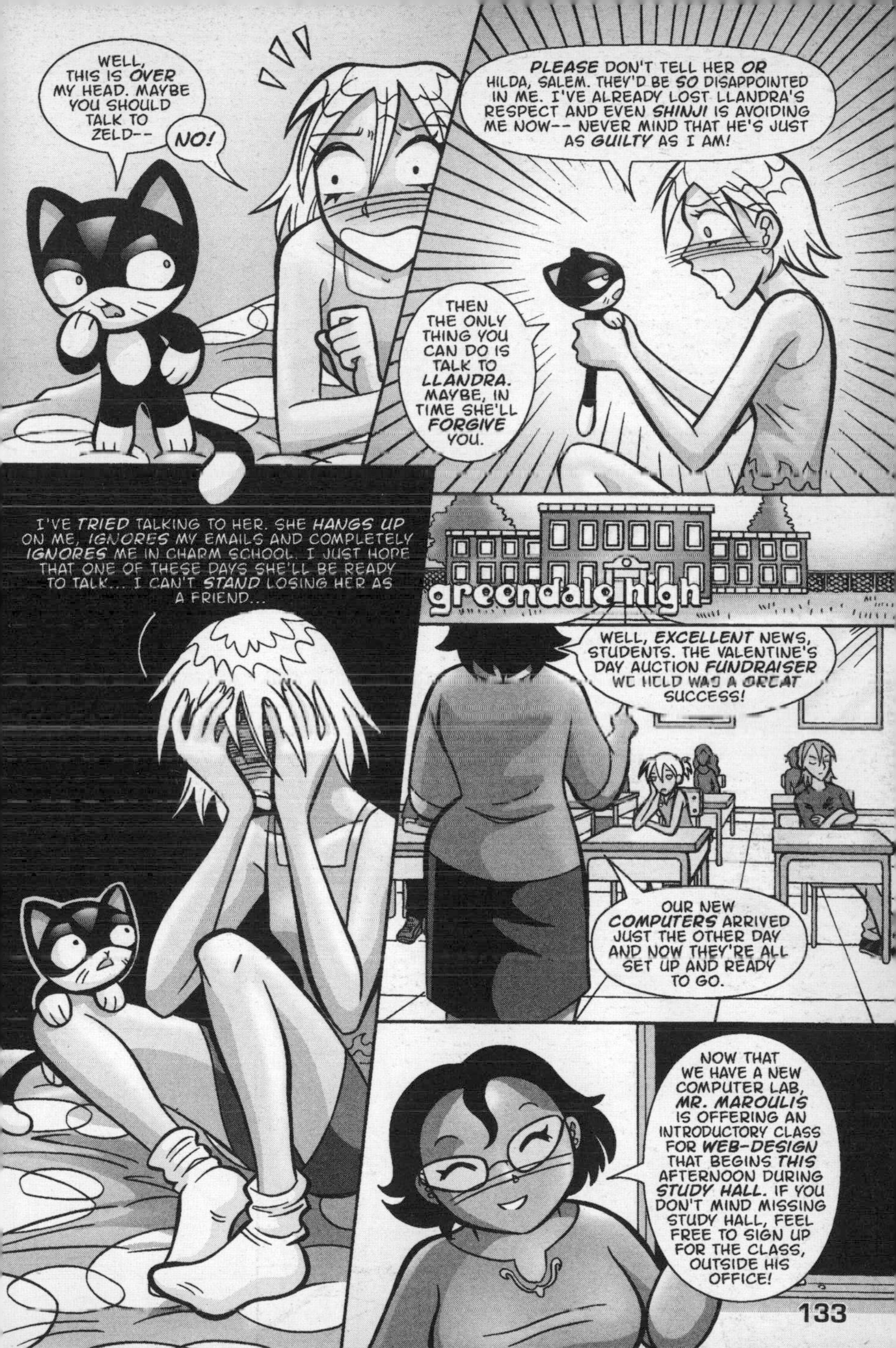
WELL, THIS IS OVER MY HEAD. MAYBE YOU SHOULD TALK TO ZELD--
NO!
PLEASE DON'T TELL HER OR HILDA, SALEM. THEY'D BE SO DISAPPOINTED IN ME. I'VE ALREADY LOST LLANDRA'S RESPECT AND EVEN SHINJI IS AVOIDING ME NOW-- NEVER MIND THAT HE'S JUST AS GUILTY AS I AM!
THEN THE ONLY THING YOU CAN DO IS TALK TO LLANDRA. MAYBE, IN TIME SHE'LL FORGIVE YOU.
I'VE TRIED TALKING TO HER. SHE HANGS UP ON ME, IGNORES MY EMAILS AND COMPLETELY IGNORES ME IN CHARM SCHOOL. I JUST HOPE THAT ONE OF THESE DAYS SHE'LL BE READY TO TALK... I CAN'T STAND LOSING HER AS A FRIEND...
greendale high
WELL, EXCELLENT NEWS, STUDENTS. THE VALENTINE'S DAY AUCTION FUNDRAISER WE HELD WAS A GREAT SUCCESS!
OUR NEW COMPUTERS ARRIVED JUST THE OTHER DAY AND NOW THEY'RE ALL SET UP AND READY TO GO.
NOW THAT WE HAVE A NEW COMPUTER LAB, MR. MAROULIS IS OFFERING AN INTRODUCTORY CLASS FOR WEB-DESIGN THAT BEGINS THIS AFTERNOON DURING STUDY HALL. IF YOU DON'T MIND MISSING STUDY HALL, FEEL FREE TO SIGN UP FOR THE CLASS, OUTSIDE HIS OFFICE!

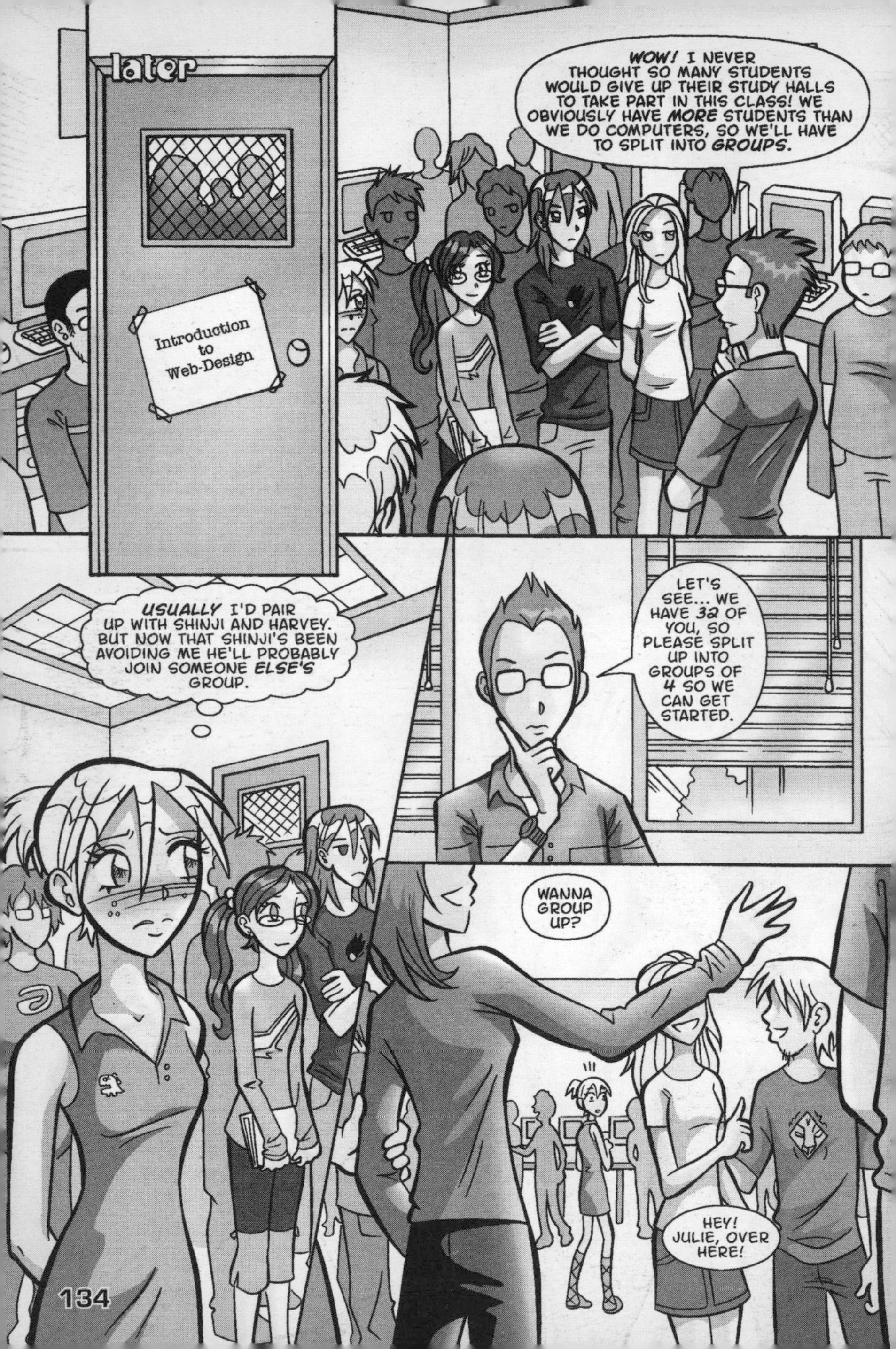
later
Introduction to Web-Design
WOW! I NEVER THOUGHT SO MANY STUDENTS WOULD GIVE UP THEIR STUDY HALLS TO TAKE PART IN THIS CLASS! WE OBVIOUSLY HAVE MORE STUDENTS THAN WE DO COMPUTERS, SO WE'LL HAVE TO SPLIT INTO GROUPS.
USUALLY I'D PAIR UP WITH SHINJI AND HARVEY. BUT NOW THAT SHINJI'S BEEN AVOIDING ME HE'LL PROBABLY JOIN SOMEONE ELSE'S GROUP.
LET'S SEE... WE HAVE 32 OF YOU, SO PLEASE SPLIT UP INTO GROUPS OF 4 SO WE CAN GET STARTED.
WANNA GROUP UP?
HEY! JULIE, OVER HERE!

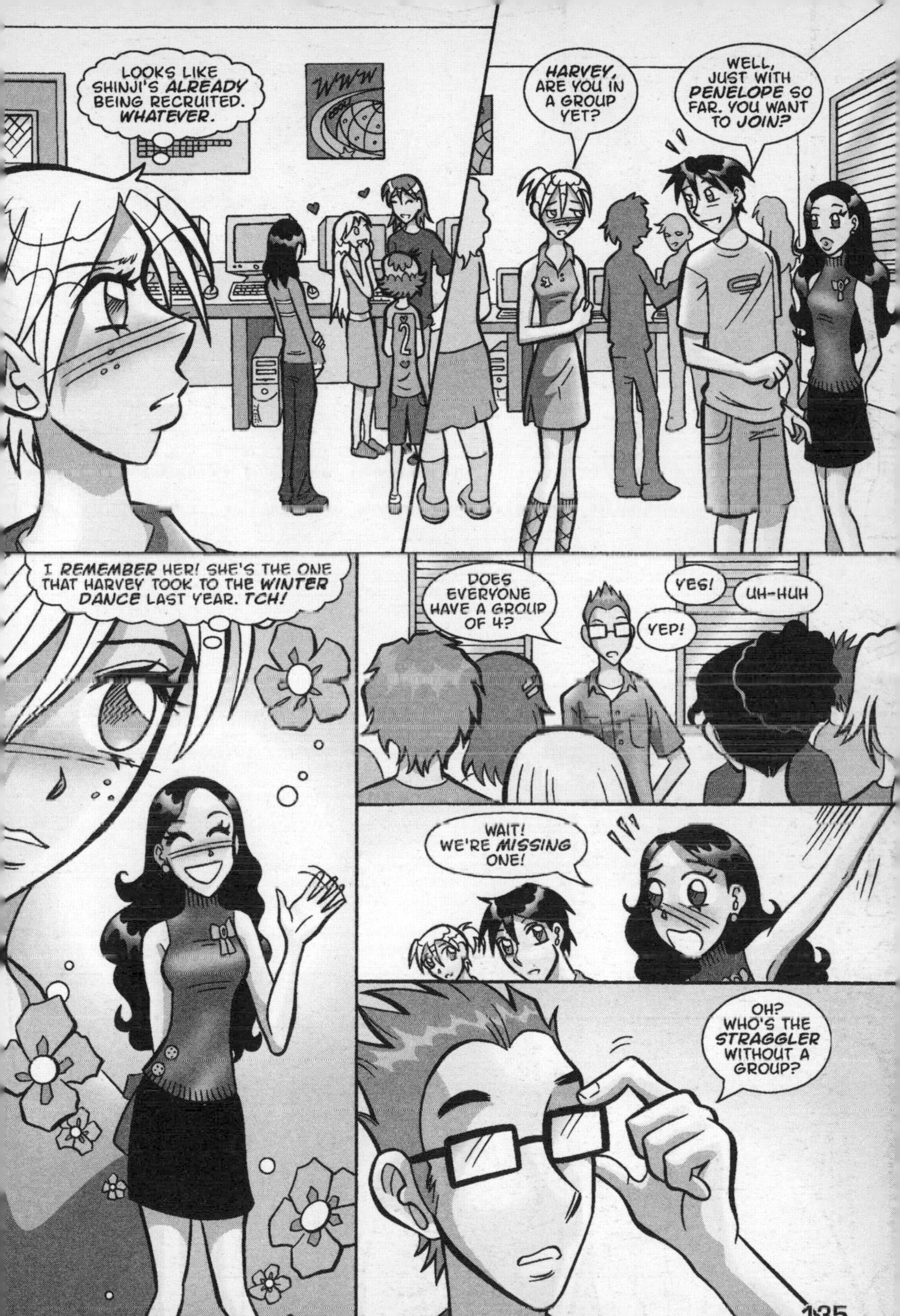
LOOKS LIKE SHINJI'S *ALREADY* BEING RECRUITED. *WHATEVER.*
HARVEY, ARE YOU IN A GROUP YET?
WELL, JUST WITH *PENELOPE* SO FAR. YOU WANT TO *JOIN?*
I *REMEMBER* HER! SHE'S THE ONE THAT HARVEY TOOK TO THE *WINTER DANCE* LAST YEAR. *TCH!*
DOES EVERYONE HAVE A GROUP OF 4?
YES!
UH-HUH
YEP!
WAIT! WE'RE *MISSING* ONE!
OH? WHO'S THE *STRAGGLER* WITHOUT A GROUP?

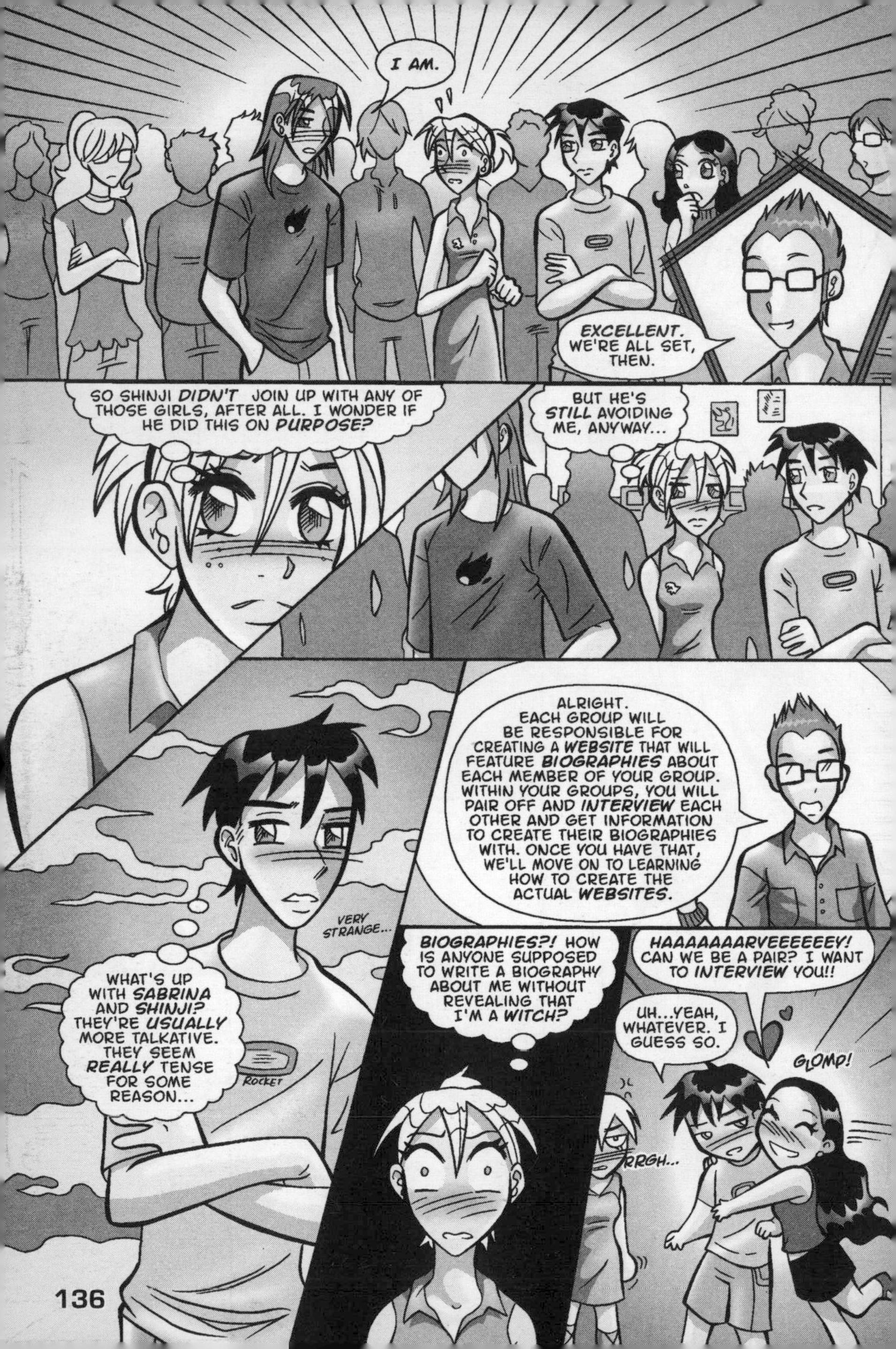
I AM.
EXCELLENT. WE'RE ALL SET, THEN.
SO SHINJI DIDN'T JOIN UP WITH ANY OF THOSE GIRLS, AFTER ALL. I WONDER IF HE DID THIS ON PURPOSE?
BUT HE'S STILL AVOIDING ME, ANYWAY...
ALRIGHT. EACH GROUP WILL BE RESPONSIBLE FOR CREATING A WEBSITE THAT WILL FEATURE BIOGRAPHIES ABOUT EACH MEMBER OF YOUR GROUP. WITHIN YOUR GROUPS, YOU WILL PAIR OFF AND INTERVIEW EACH OTHER AND GET INFORMATION TO CREATE THEIR BIOGRAPHIES WITH. ONCE YOU HAVE THAT, WE'LL MOVE ON TO LEARNING HOW TO CREATE THE ACTUAL WEBSITES.
VERY STRANGE...
WHAT'S UP WITH SABRINA AND SHINJI? THEY'RE USUALLY MORE TALKATIVE. THEY SEEM REALLY TENSE FOR SOME REASON...
ROCKET
BIOGRAPHIES?! HOW IS ANYONE SUPPOSED TO WRITE A BIOGRAPHY ABOUT ME WITHOUT REVEALING THAT I'M A WITCH?
HAAAAAAARVEEEEEEY! CAN WE BE A PAIR? I WANT TO INTERVIEW YOU!!
UH...YEAH, WHATEVER. I GUESS SO.
GLOMP!
RRGH...

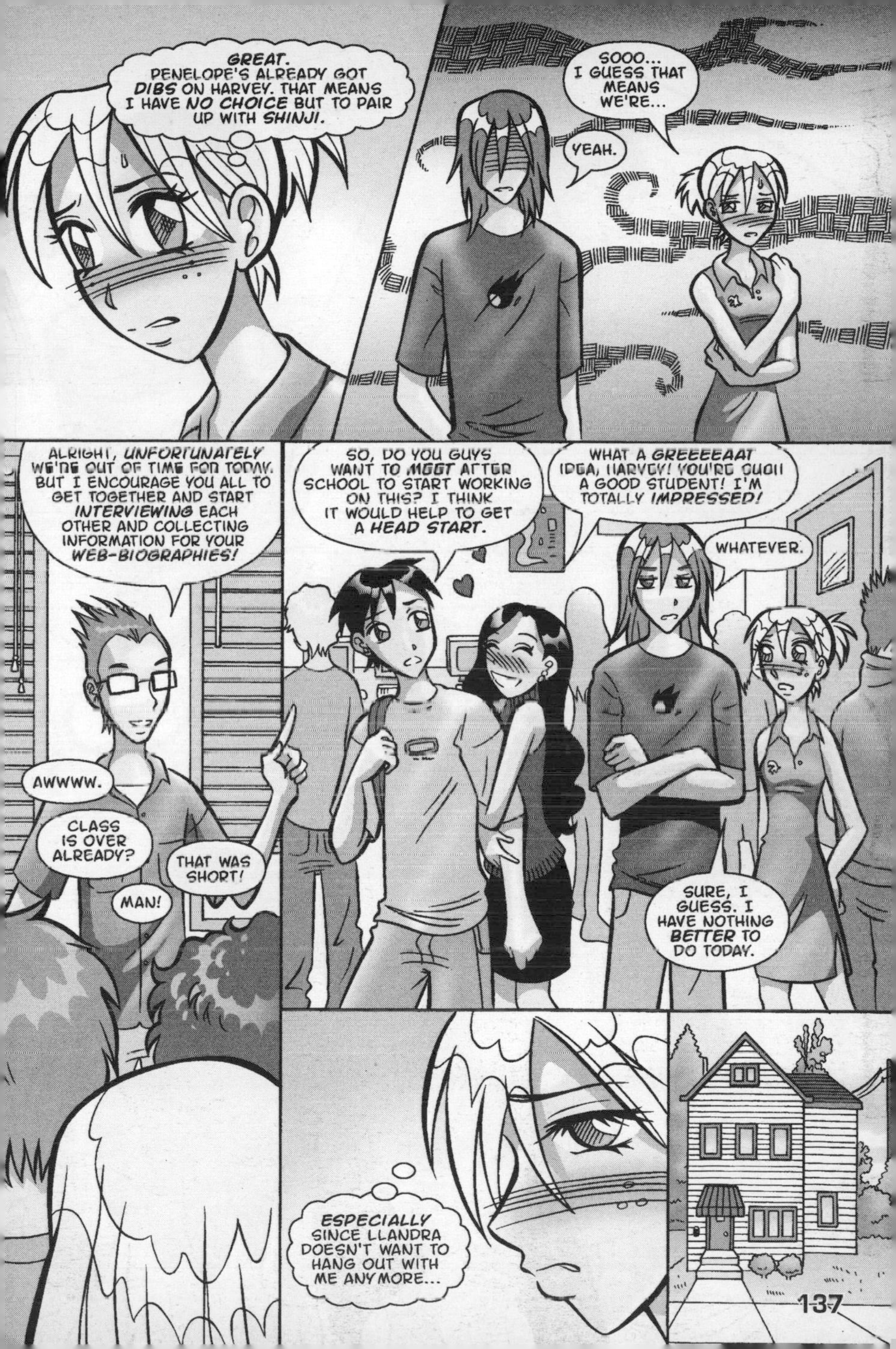
GREAT. PENELOPE'S ALREADY GOT DIBS ON HARVEY. THAT MEANS I HAVE NO CHOICE BUT TO PAIR UP WITH SHINJI.
SOOO... I GUESS THAT MEANS WE'RE...
YEAH.
ALRIGHT, UNFORTUNATELY WE'RE OUT OF TIME FOR TODAY. BUT I ENCOURAGE YOU ALL TO GET TOGETHER AND START INTERVIEWING EACH OTHER AND COLLECTING INFORMATION FOR YOUR WEB-BIOGRAPHIES!
AWWWW.
CLASS IS OVER ALREADY?
THAT WAS SHORT!
MAN!
SO, DO YOU GUYS WANT TO MEET AFTER SCHOOL TO START WORKING ON THIS? I THINK IT WOULD HELP TO GET A HEAD START.
WHAT A GREEEEAAT IDEA, HARVEY! YOU'RE SUCH A GOOD STUDENT! I'M TOTALLY IMPRESSED!
WHATEVER.
SURE, I GUESS. I HAVE NOTHING BETTER TO DO TODAY.
ESPECIALLY SINCE LLANDRA DOESN'T WANT TO HANG OUT WITH ME ANYMORE...

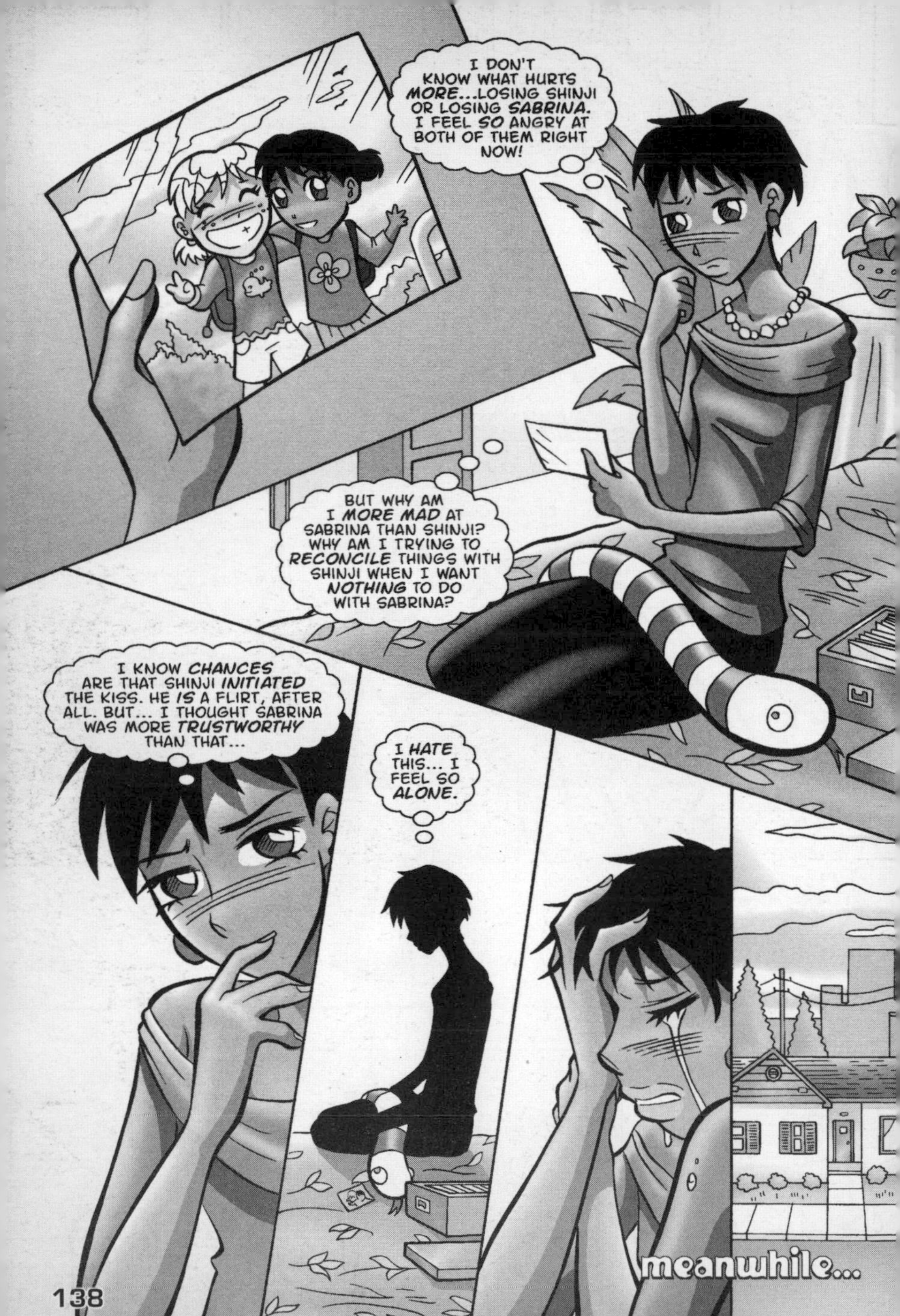

I DON'T KNOW WHAT HURTS *MORE*... LOSING SHINJI OR LOSING *SABRINA.* I FEEL *SO* ANGRY AT BOTH OF THEM RIGHT NOW!
BUT WHY AM I *MORE MAD* AT SABRINA THAN SHINJI? WHY AM I TRYING TO *RECONCILE* THINGS WITH SHINJI WHEN I WANT *NOTHING* TO DO WITH SABRINA?
I KNOW *CHANCES* ARE THAT SHINJI *INITIATED* THE KISS. HE *IS* A FLIRT, AFTER ALL. BUT... I THOUGHT SABRINA WAS MORE *TRUSTWORTHY* THAN THAT...
I *HATE* THIS... I FEEL SO *ALONE.*
meanwhile...

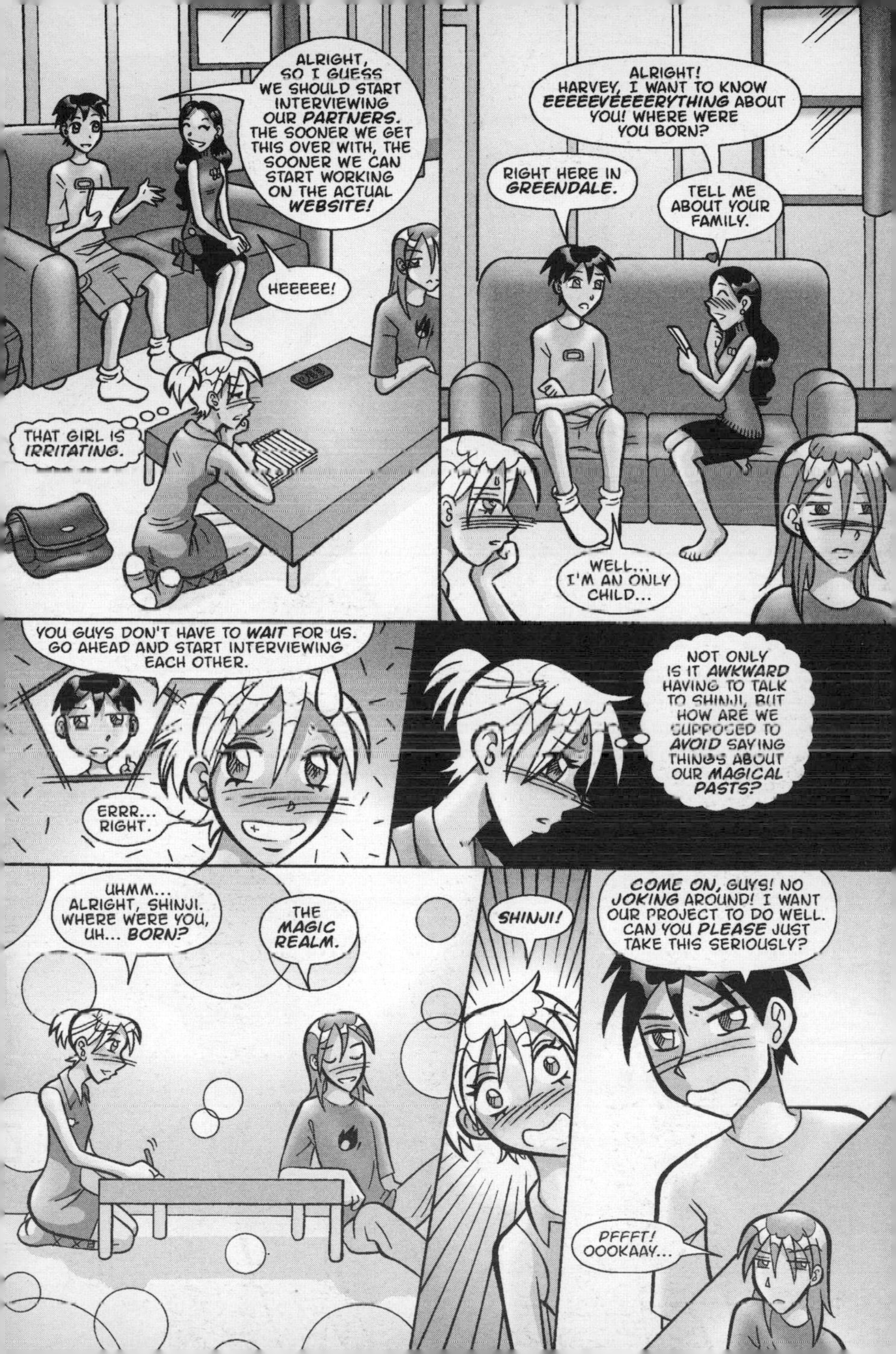
ALRIGHT, SO I GUESS WE SHOULD START INTERVIEWING OUR PARTNERS. THE SOONER WE GET THIS OVER WITH, THE SOONER WE CAN START WORKING ON THE ACTUAL WEBSITE!
HEEEEE!
THAT GIRL IS IRRITATING.
ALRIGHT! HARVEY, I WANT TO KNOW EEEEEVEEEERYTHING ABOUT YOU! WHERE WERE YOU BORN?
RIGHT HERE IN GREENDALE.
TELL ME ABOUT YOUR FAMILY.
WELL... I'M AN ONLY CHILD...
YOU GUYS DON'T HAVE TO WAIT FOR US. GO AHEAD AND START INTERVIEWING EACH OTHER.
ERRR... RIGHT.
NOT ONLY IS IT AWKWARD HAVING TO TALK TO SHINJI, BUT HOW ARE WE SUPPOSED TO AVOID SAYING THINGS ABOUT OUR MAGICAL PASTS?
UHMM... ALRIGHT, SHINJI. WHERE WERE YOU, UH... BORN?
THE MAGIC REALM.
SHINJI!
COME ON, GUYS! NO JOKING AROUND! I WANT OUR PROJECT TO DO WELL. CAN YOU PLEASE JUST TAKE THIS SERIOUSLY?
PFFFT! OOOKAAY...

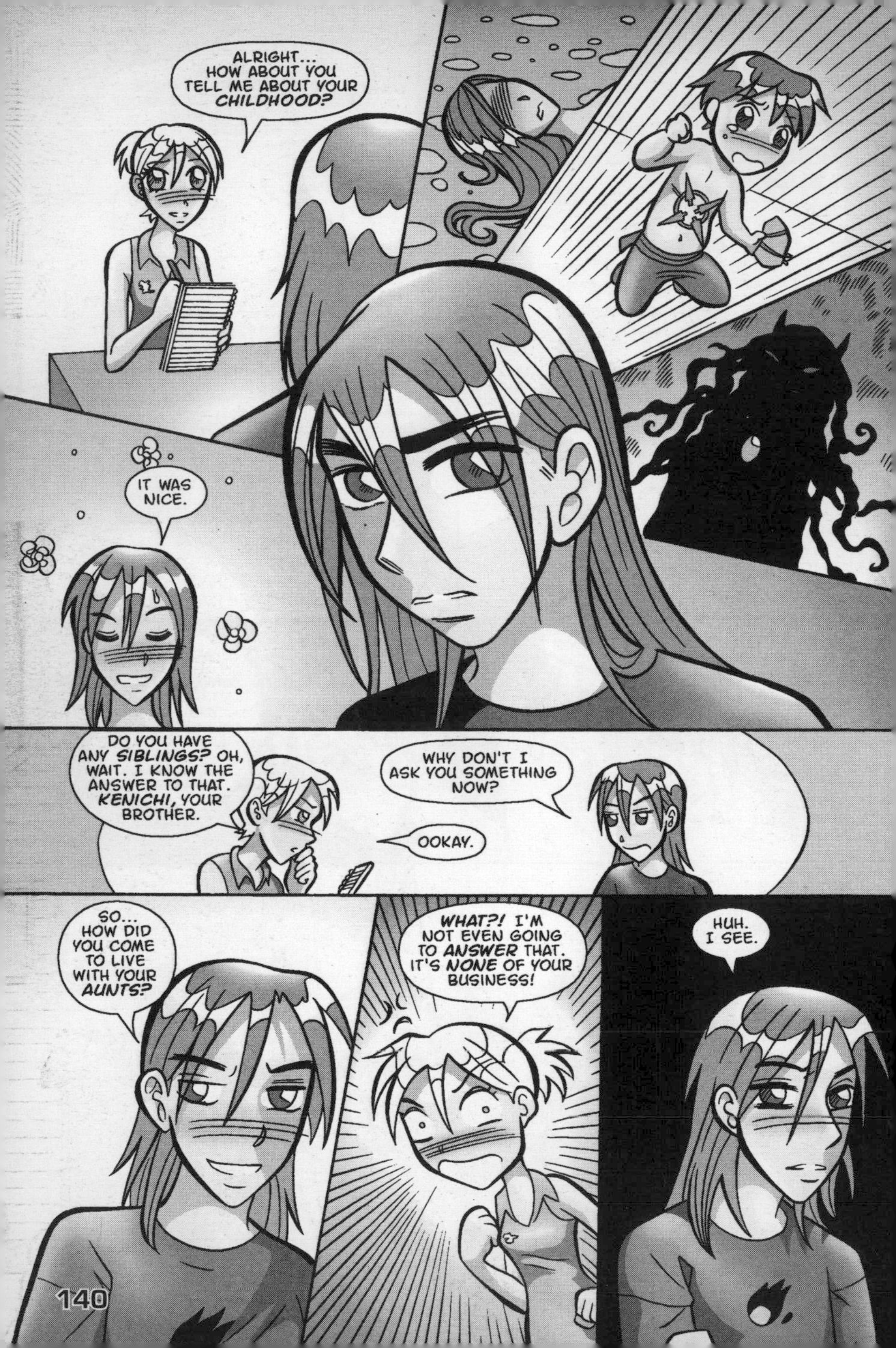

ALRIGHT... HOW ABOUT YOU TELL ME ABOUT YOUR CHILDHOOD?
IT WAS NICE.
DO YOU HAVE ANY SIBLINGS? OH, WAIT. I KNOW THE ANSWER TO THAT. KENICHI, YOUR BROTHER.
OOKAY.
WHY DON'T I ASK YOU SOMETHING NOW?
SO... HOW DID YOU COME TO LIVE WITH YOUR AUNTS?
WHAT?! I'M NOT EVEN GOING TO ANSWER THAT. IT'S NONE OF YOUR BUSINESS!
HUH. I SEE.

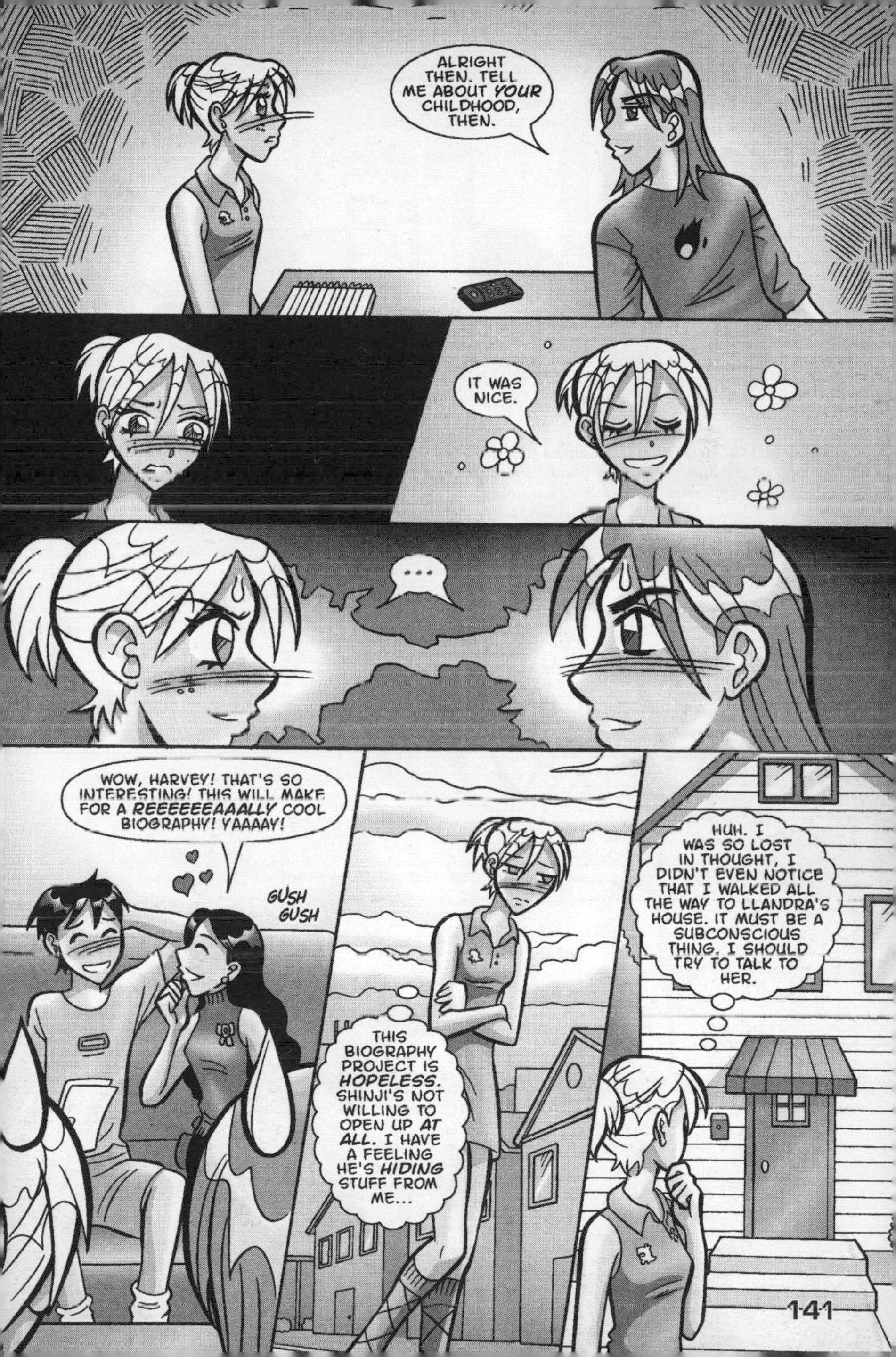

ALRIGHT THEN. TELL ME ABOUT *YOUR* CHILDHOOD, THEN.
IT WAS NICE.
...
WOW, HARVEY! THAT'S SO INTERESTING! THIS WILL MAKE FOR A *REEEEEEAAAALLY* COOL BIOGRAPHY! YAAAAY!
GUSH GUSH
THIS BIOGRAPHY PROJECT IS *HOPELESS*. SHINJI'S NOT WILLING TO OPEN UP *AT ALL*. I HAVE A FEELING HE'S *HIDING* STUFF FROM ME...
HUH. I WAS SO LOST IN THOUGHT, I DIDN'T EVEN NOTICE THAT I WALKED ALL THE WAY TO LLANDRA'S HOUSE. IT MUST BE A SUBCONSCIOUS THING. I SHOULD TRY TO TALK TO HER.

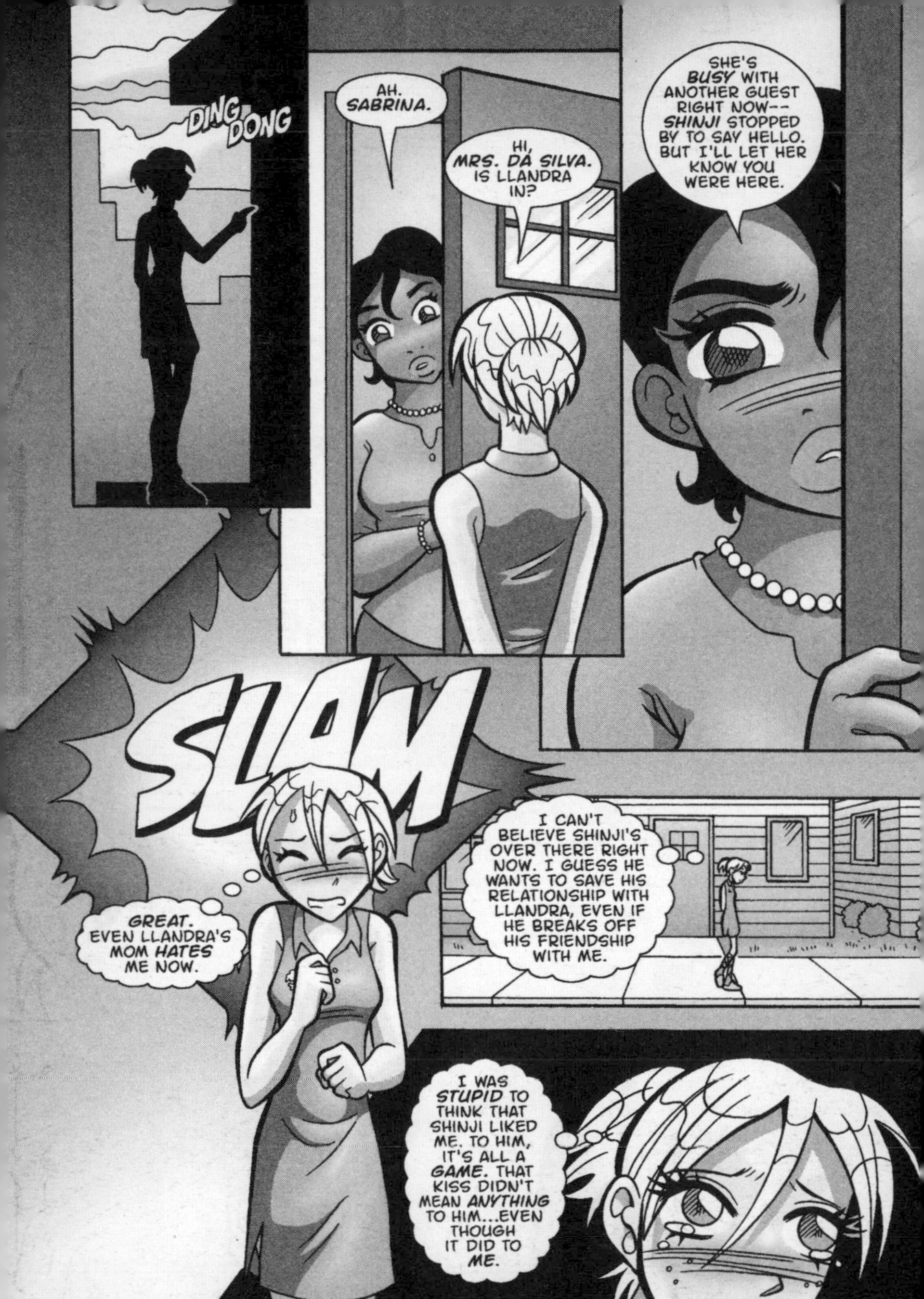

DING DONG
AH. SABRINA.
HI, MRS. DA SILVA. IS LLANDRA IN?
SHE'S BUSY WITH ANOTHER GUEST RIGHT NOW-- SHINJI STOPPED BY TO SAY HELLO. BUT I'LL LET HER KNOW YOU WERE HERE.
SLAM
GREAT. EVEN LLANDRA'S MOM HATES ME NOW.
I CAN'T BELIEVE SHINJI'S OVER THERE RIGHT NOW. I GUESS HE WANTS TO SAVE HIS RELATIONSHIP WITH LLANDRA, EVEN IF HE BREAKS OFF HIS FRIENDSHIP WITH ME.
I WAS STUPID TO THINK THAT SHINJI LIKED ME. TO HIM, IT'S ALL A GAME. THAT KISS DIDN'T MEAN ANYTHING TO HIM...EVEN THOUGH IT DID TO ME.

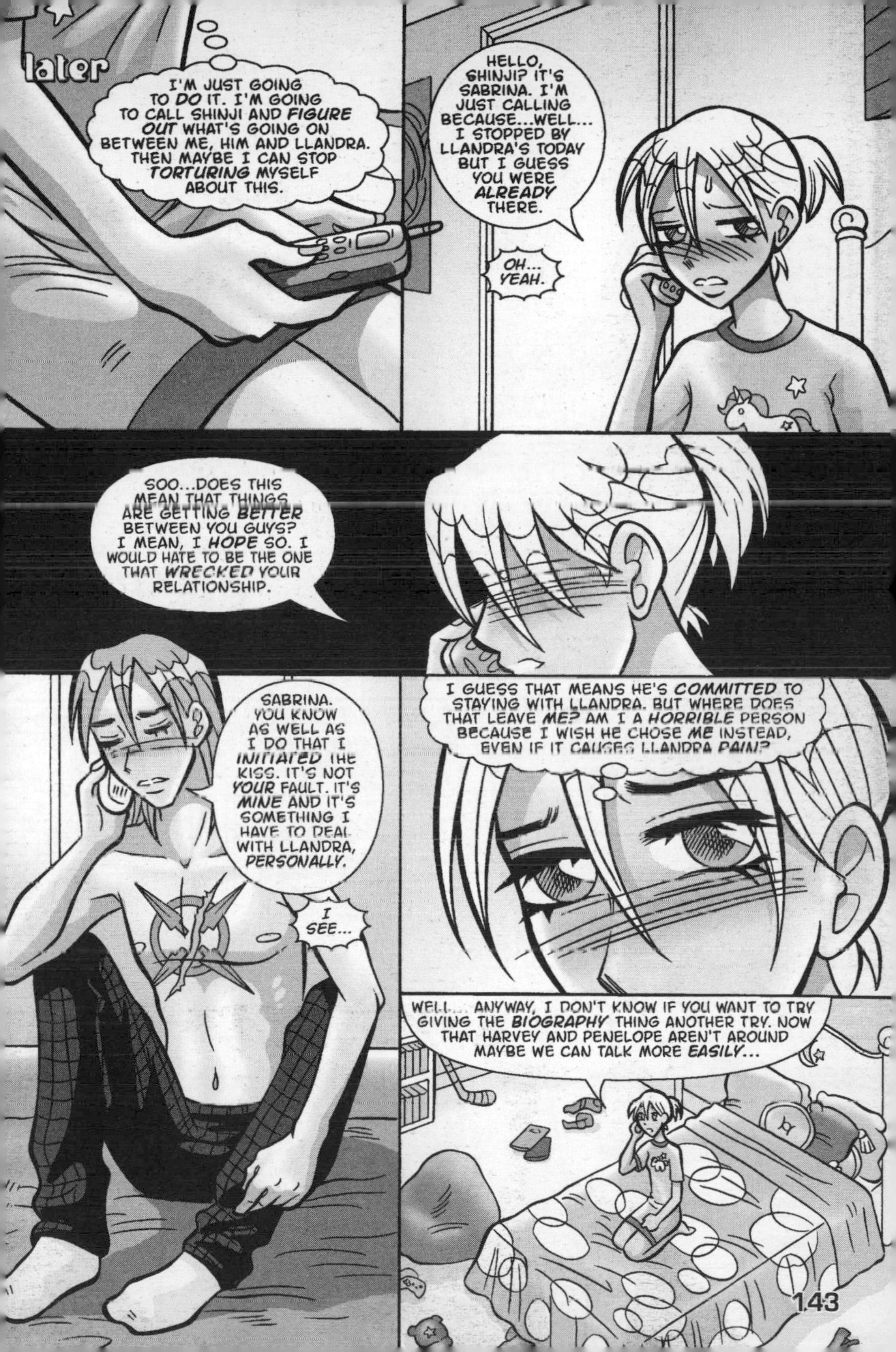
later
I'M JUST GOING TO *DO* IT. I'M GOING TO CALL SHINJI AND *FIGURE OUT* WHAT'S GOING ON BETWEEN ME, HIM AND LLANDRA. THEN MAYBE I CAN STOP *TORTURING* MYSELF ABOUT THIS.
HELLO, SHINJI? IT'S SABRINA. I'M JUST CALLING BECAUSE...WELL... I STOPPED BY LLANDRA'S TODAY BUT I GUESS YOU WERE *ALREADY* THERE.
OH... YEAH.
SOO...DOES THIS MEAN THAT THINGS ARE GETTING *BETTER* BETWEEN YOU GUYS? I MEAN, I *HOPE* SO. I WOULD HATE TO BE THE ONE THAT *WRECKED* YOUR RELATIONSHIP.
SABRINA. YOU KNOW AS WELL AS I DO THAT I *INITIATED* THE KISS. IT'S NOT *YOUR* FAULT. IT'S *MINE* AND IT'S SOMETHING I HAVE TO DEAL WITH LLANDRA, *PERSONALLY.*
I SEE...
I GUESS THAT MEANS HE'S *COMMITTED* TO STAYING WITH LLANDRA. BUT WHERE DOES THAT LEAVE *ME?* AM I A *HORRIBLE* PERSON BECAUSE I WISH HE CHOSE *ME* INSTEAD, EVEN IF IT CAUSES LLANDRA *PAIN?*
WELL... ANYWAY, I DON'T KNOW IF YOU WANT TO TRY GIVING THE *BIOGRAPHY* THING ANOTHER TRY. NOW THAT HARVEY AND PENELOPE AREN'T AROUND MAYBE WE CAN TALK MORE *EASILY...*

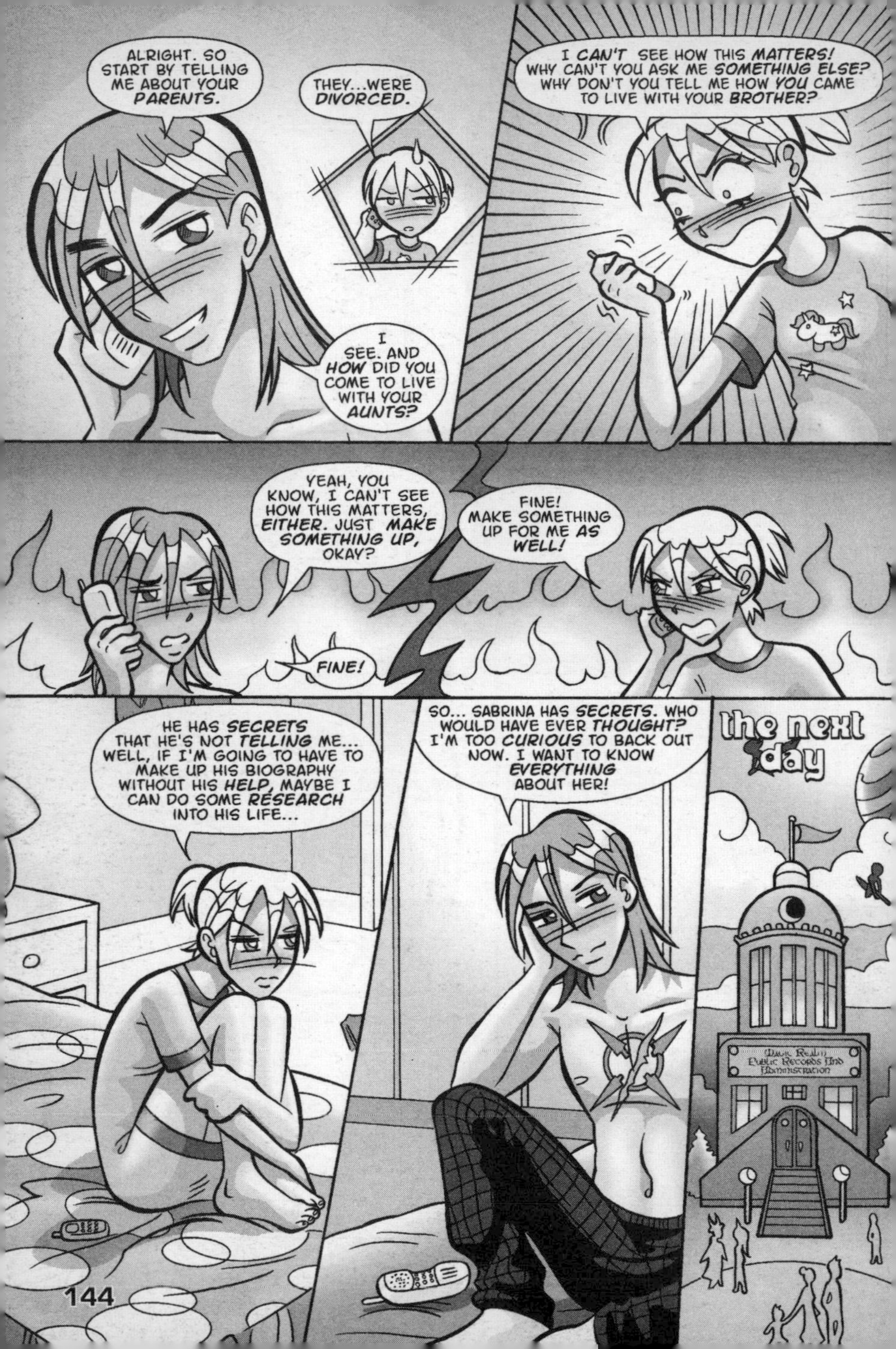
ALRIGHT. SO START BY TELLING ME ABOUT YOUR *PARENTS.*
THEY...WERE *DIVORCED.*
I SEE. AND *HOW* DID YOU COME TO LIVE WITH YOUR *AUNTS?*
I *CAN'T* SEE HOW THIS *MATTERS!* WHY CAN'T YOU ASK ME *SOMETHING ELSE?* WHY DON'T YOU TELL ME HOW *YOU* CAME TO LIVE WITH YOUR *BROTHER?*
YEAH, YOU KNOW, I CAN'T SEE HOW THIS MATTERS, *EITHER.* JUST *MAKE SOMETHING UP,* OKAY?
FINE! MAKE SOMETHING UP FOR ME *AS WELL!*
FINE!
HE HAS *SECRETS* THAT HE'S NOT *TELLING* ME... WELL, IF I'M GOING TO HAVE TO MAKE UP HIS BIOGRAPHY WITHOUT HIS *HELP,* MAYBE I CAN DO SOME *RESEARCH* INTO HIS LIFE...
SO... SABRINA HAS *SECRETS.* WHO WOULD HAVE EVER *THOUGHT?* I'M TOO *CURIOUS* TO BACK OUT NOW. I WANT TO KNOW *EVERYTHING* ABOUT HER!
the next day
Public Records And Administration

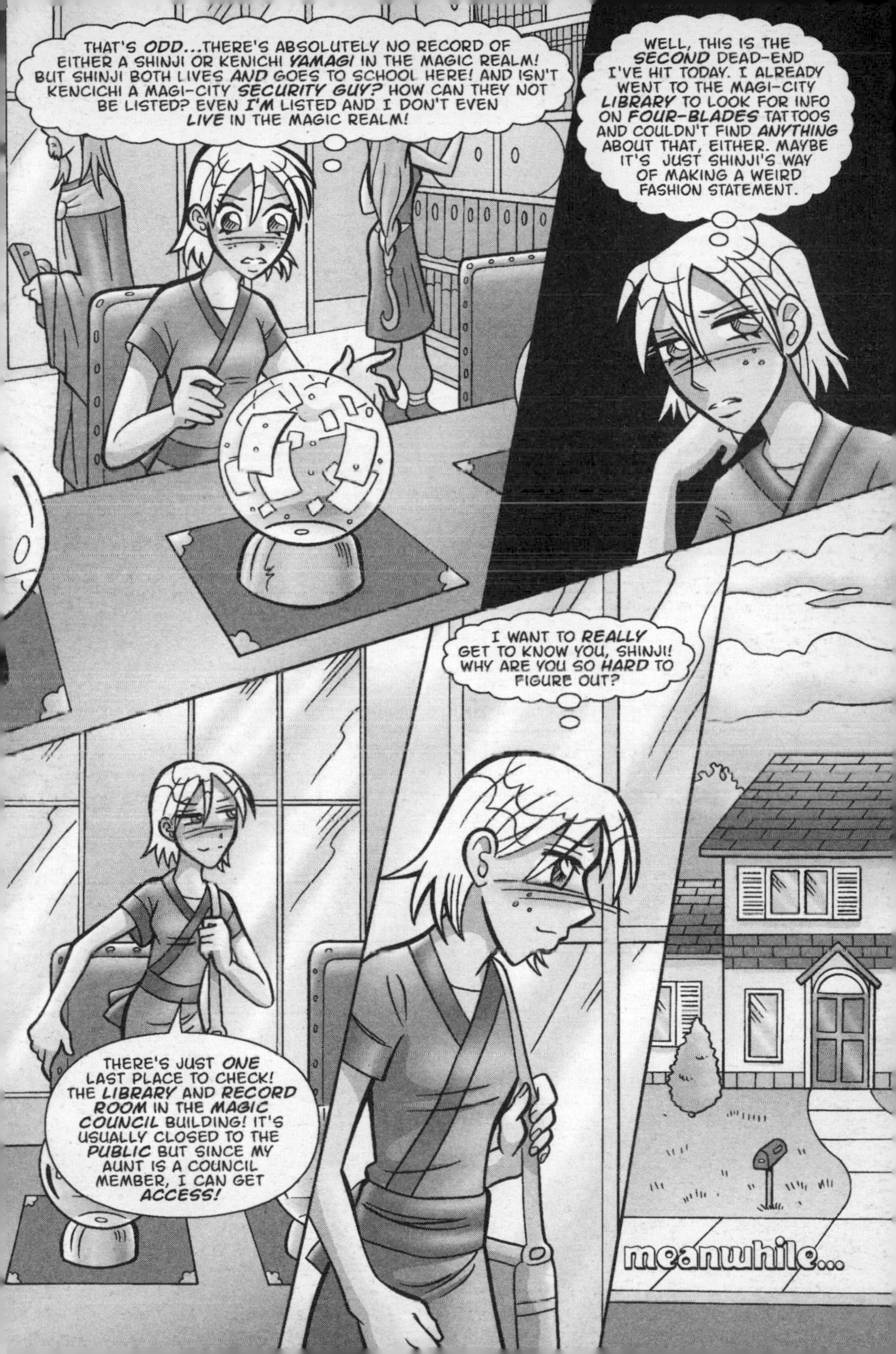
THAT'S ODD...THERE'S ABSOLUTELY NO RECORD OF EITHER A SHINJI OR KENICHI YAMAGI IN THE MAGIC REALM! BUT SHINJI BOTH LIVES AND GOES TO SCHOOL HERE! AND ISN'T KENCICHI A MAGI-CITY SECURITY GUY? HOW CAN THEY NOT BE LISTED? EVEN I'M LISTED AND I DON'T EVEN LIVE IN THE MAGIC REALM!
WELL, THIS IS THE SECOND DEAD-END I'VE HIT TODAY. I ALREADY WENT TO THE MAGI-CITY LIBRARY TO LOOK FOR INFO ON FOUR-BLADES TATTOOS AND COULDN'T FIND ANYTHING ABOUT THAT, EITHER. MAYBE IT'S JUST SHINJI'S WAY OF MAKING A WEIRD FASHION STATEMENT.
THERE'S JUST ONE LAST PLACE TO CHECK! THE LIBRARY AND RECORD ROOM IN THE MAGIC COUNCIL BUILDING! IT'S USUALLY CLOSED TO THE PUBLIC BUT SINCE MY AUNT IS A COUNCIL MEMBER, I CAN GET ACCESS!
I WANT TO REALLY GET TO KNOW YOU, SHINJI! WHY ARE YOU SO HARD TO FIGURE OUT?
meanwhile...

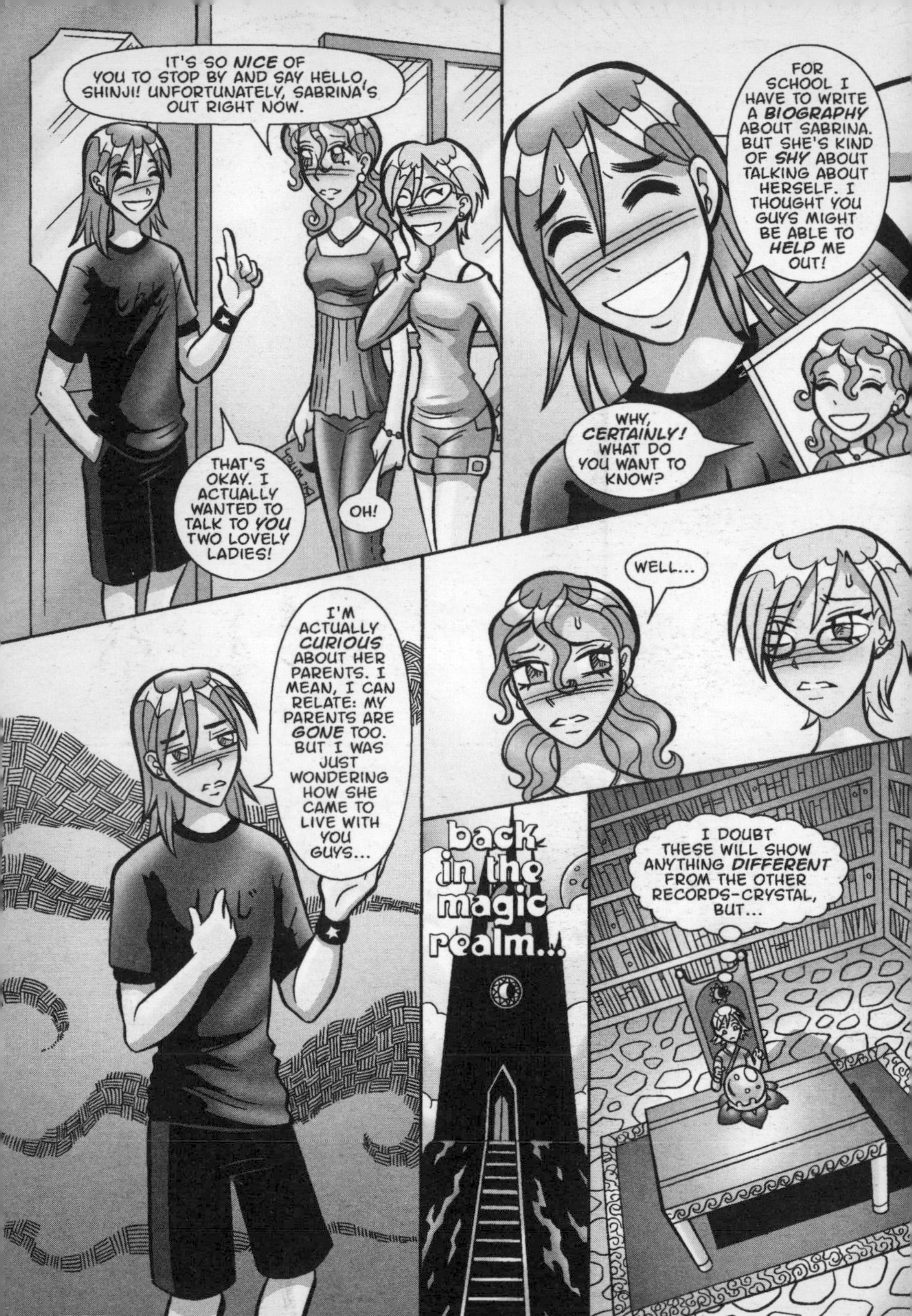
IT'S SO NICE OF YOU TO STOP BY AND SAY HELLO, SHINJI! UNFORTUNATELY, SABRINA'S OUT RIGHT NOW.
THAT'S OKAY. I ACTUALLY WANTED TO TALK TO YOU TWO LOVELY LADIES!
OH!
FOR SCHOOL I HAVE TO WRITE A BIOGRAPHY ABOUT SABRINA. BUT SHE'S KIND OF SHY ABOUT TALKING ABOUT HERSELF. I THOUGHT YOU GUYS MIGHT BE ABLE TO HELP ME OUT!
WHY, CERTAINLY! WHAT DO YOU WANT TO KNOW?
I'M ACTUALLY CURIOUS ABOUT HER PARENTS. I MEAN, I CAN RELATE: MY PARENTS ARE GONE TOO. BUT I WAS JUST WONDERING HOW SHE CAME TO LIVE WITH YOU GUYS...
WELL...
back in the magic realm...
I DOUBT THESE WILL SHOW ANYTHING DIFFERENT FROM THE OTHER RECORDS-CRYSTAL, BUT...

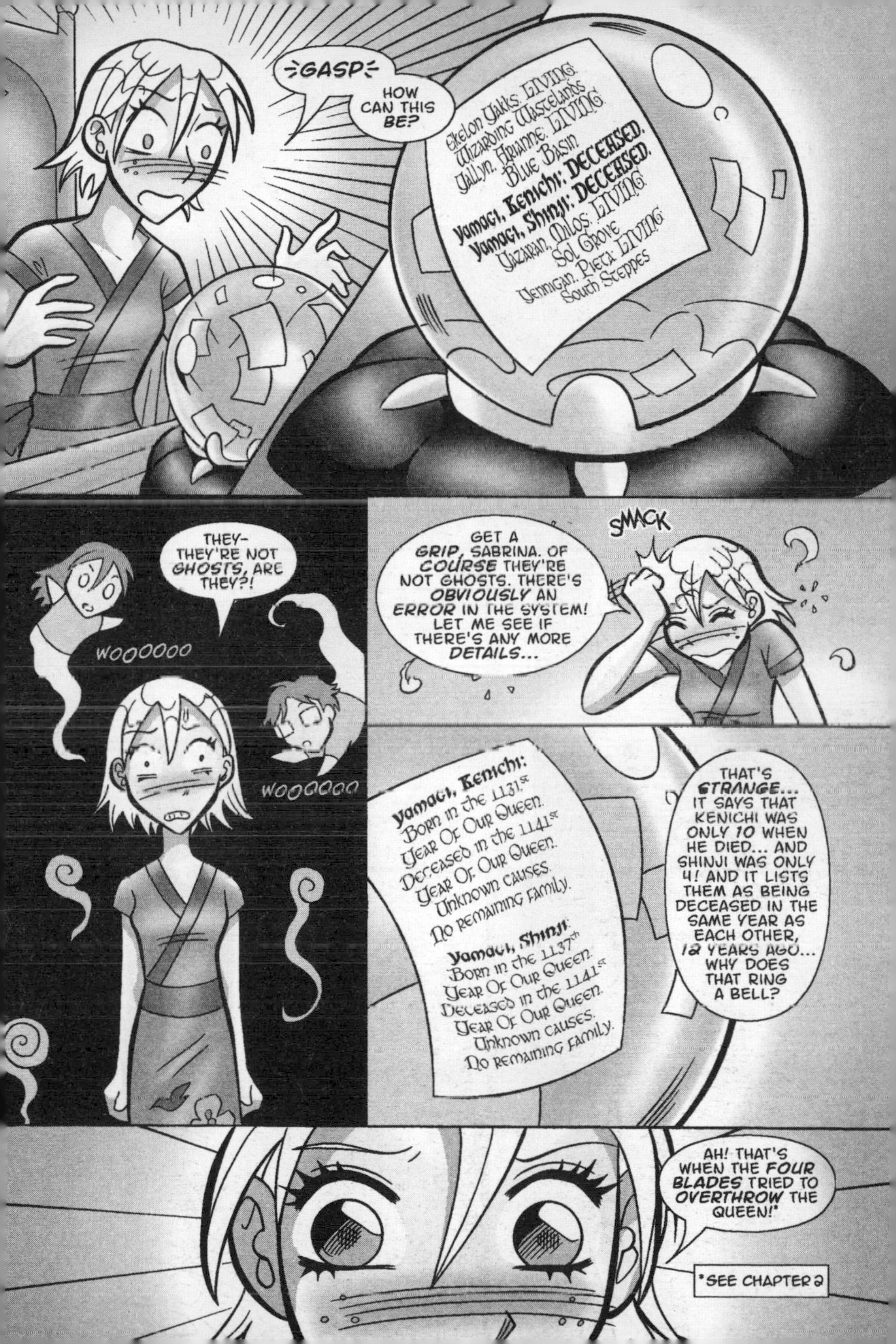
GASP
HOW CAN THIS BE?
Ekelon, Yakks: LIVING
Wizarding Wastelands
Gallyn, Arianne: LIVING
Blue Basin
Yamagi, Kenichi: DECEASED
Yamagi, Shinji: DECEASED
Yazaran, Milos: LIVING
Sol Grove
Yennigan, Pieta: LIVING
South Steppes
THEY- THEY'RE NOT GHOSTS, ARE THEY?!
WOOOOOO
WOOOOOO
SMACK
GET A GRIP, SABRINA. OF COURSE THEY'RE NOT GHOSTS. THERE'S OBVIOUSLY AN ERROR IN THE SYSTEM! LET ME SEE IF THERE'S ANY MORE DETAILS...
Yamagi, Kenichi: Born in the 1131st Year Of Our Queen. Deceased in the 1141st Year Of Our Queen. Unknown causes. No remaining family.
Yamagi, Shinji: Born in the 1137th Year Of Our Queen. Deceased in the 1141st Year Of Our Queen. Unknown causes. No remaining family.
THAT'S STRANGE... IT SAYS THAT KENICHI WAS ONLY 10 WHEN HE DIED... AND SHINJI WAS ONLY 4! AND IT LISTS THEM AS BEING DECEASED IN THE SAME YEAR AS EACH OTHER, 12 YEARS AGO... WHY DOES THAT RING A BELL?
AH! THAT'S WHEN THE FOUR BLADES TRIED TO OVERTHROW THE QUEEN!*
*SEE CHAPTER 2

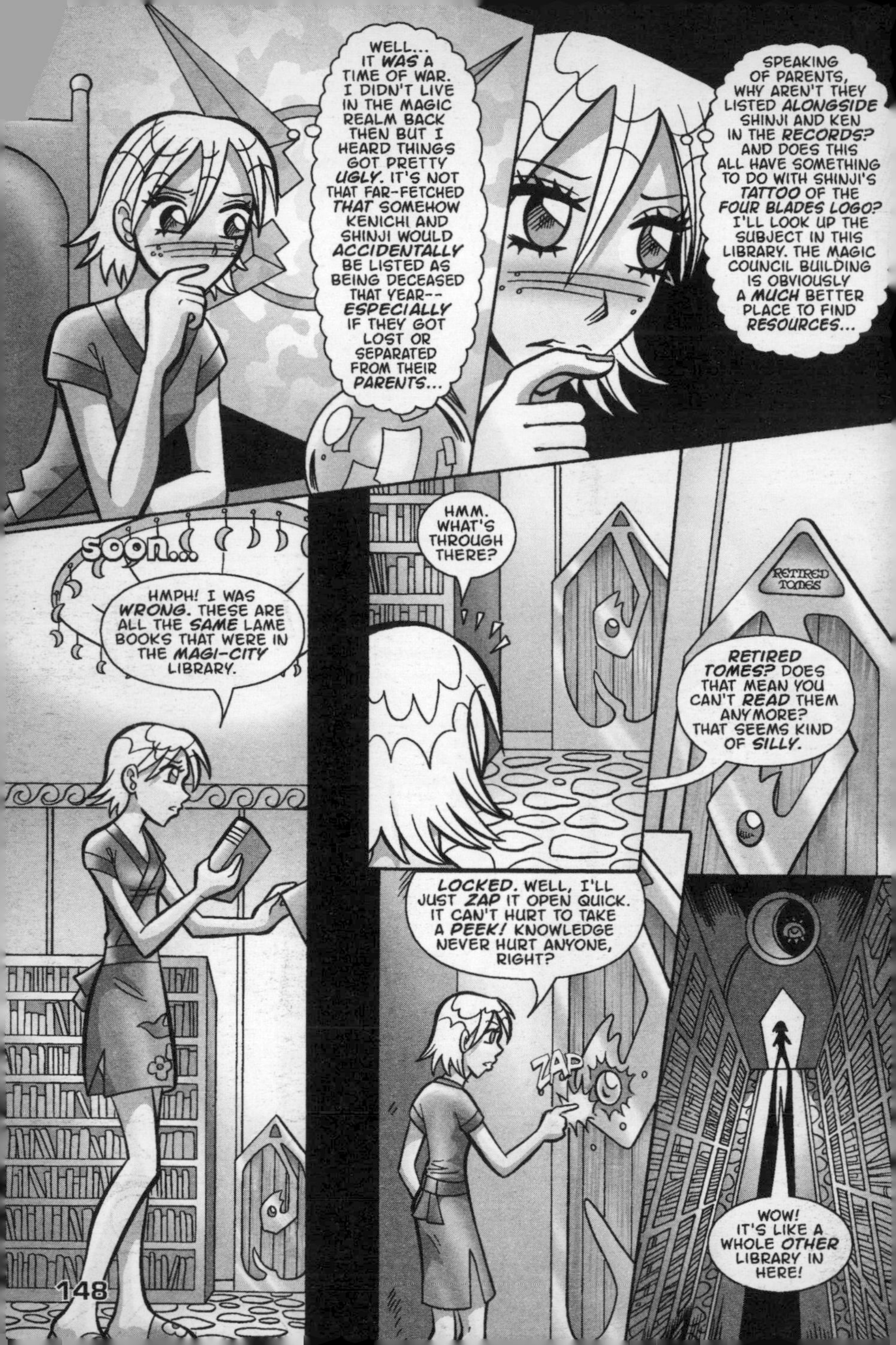

WELL... IT WAS A TIME OF WAR. I DIDN'T LIVE IN THE MAGIC REALM BACK THEN BUT I HEARD THINGS GOT PRETTY UGLY. IT'S NOT THAT FAR-FETCHED THAT SOMEHOW KENICHI AND SHINJI WOULD ACCIDENTALLY BE LISTED AS BEING DECEASED THAT YEAR-- ESPECIALLY IF THEY GOT LOST OR SEPARATED FROM THEIR PARENTS...
SPEAKING OF PARENTS, WHY AREN'T THEY LISTED ALONGSIDE SHINJI AND KEN IN THE RECORDS? AND DOES THIS ALL HAVE SOMETHING TO DO WITH SHINJI'S TATTOO OF THE FOUR BLADES LOGO? I'LL LOOK UP THE SUBJECT IN THIS LIBRARY. THE MAGIC COUNCIL BUILDING IS OBVIOUSLY A MUCH BETTER PLACE TO FIND RESOURCES...
SOON...
HMPH! I WAS WRONG. THESE ARE ALL THE SAME LAME BOOKS THAT WERE IN THE MAGI-CITY LIBRARY.
HMM. WHAT'S THROUGH THERE?
RETIRED TOMES
RETIRED TOMES? DOES THAT MEAN YOU CAN'T READ THEM ANYMORE? THAT SEEMS KIND OF SILLY.
LOCKED. WELL, I'LL JUST ZAP IT OPEN QUICK. IT CAN'T HURT TO TAKE A PEEK! KNOWLEDGE NEVER HURT ANYONE, RIGHT?
ZAP
WOW! IT'S LIKE A WHOLE OTHER LIBRARY IN HERE!

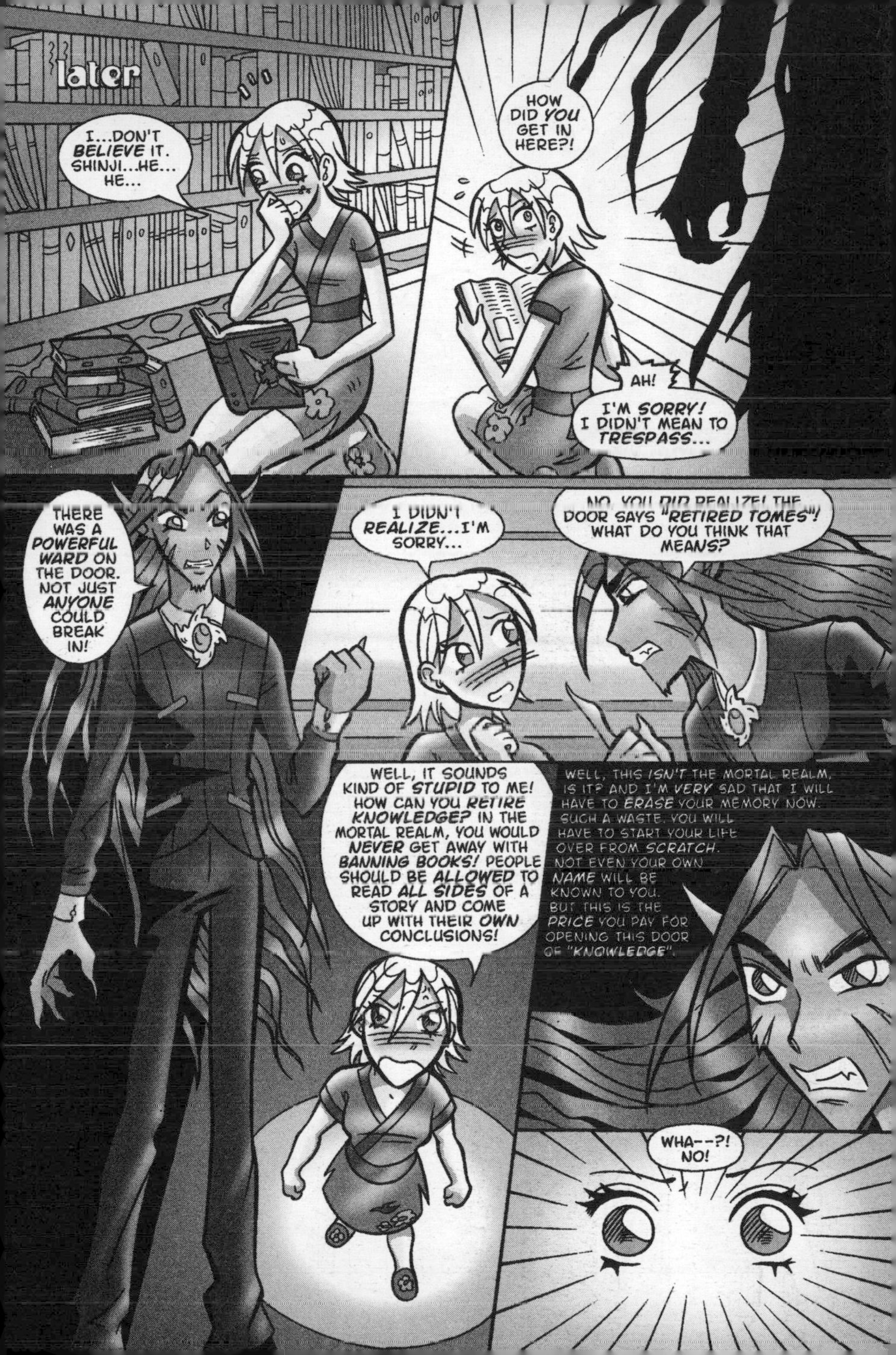
later
I...DON'T BELIEVE IT. SHINJI...HE... HE...
HOW DID YOU GET IN HERE?!
AH!
I'M SORRY! I DIDN'T MEAN TO TRESPASS...
THERE WAS A POWERFUL WARD ON THE DOOR. NOT JUST ANYONE COULD BREAK IN!
I DIDN'T REALIZE...I'M SORRY...
NO, YOU DID REALIZE! THE DOOR SAYS "RETIRED TOMES"! WHAT DO YOU THINK THAT MEANS?
WELL, IT SOUNDS KIND OF STUPID TO ME! HOW CAN YOU RETIRE KNOWLEDGE? IN THE MORTAL REALM, YOU WOULD NEVER GET AWAY WITH BANNING BOOKS! PEOPLE SHOULD BE ALLOWED TO READ ALL SIDES OF A STORY AND COME UP WITH THEIR OWN CONCLUSIONS!
WELL, THIS ISN'T THE MORTAL REALM, IS IT? AND I'M VERY SAD THAT I WILL HAVE TO ERASE YOUR MEMORY NOW. SUCH A WASTE. YOU WILL HAVE TO START YOUR LIFE OVER FROM SCRATCH. NOT EVEN YOUR OWN NAME WILL BE KNOWN TO YOU. BUT THIS IS THE PRICE YOU PAY FOR OPENING THIS DOOR OF "KNOWLEDGE".
WHA--?! NO!

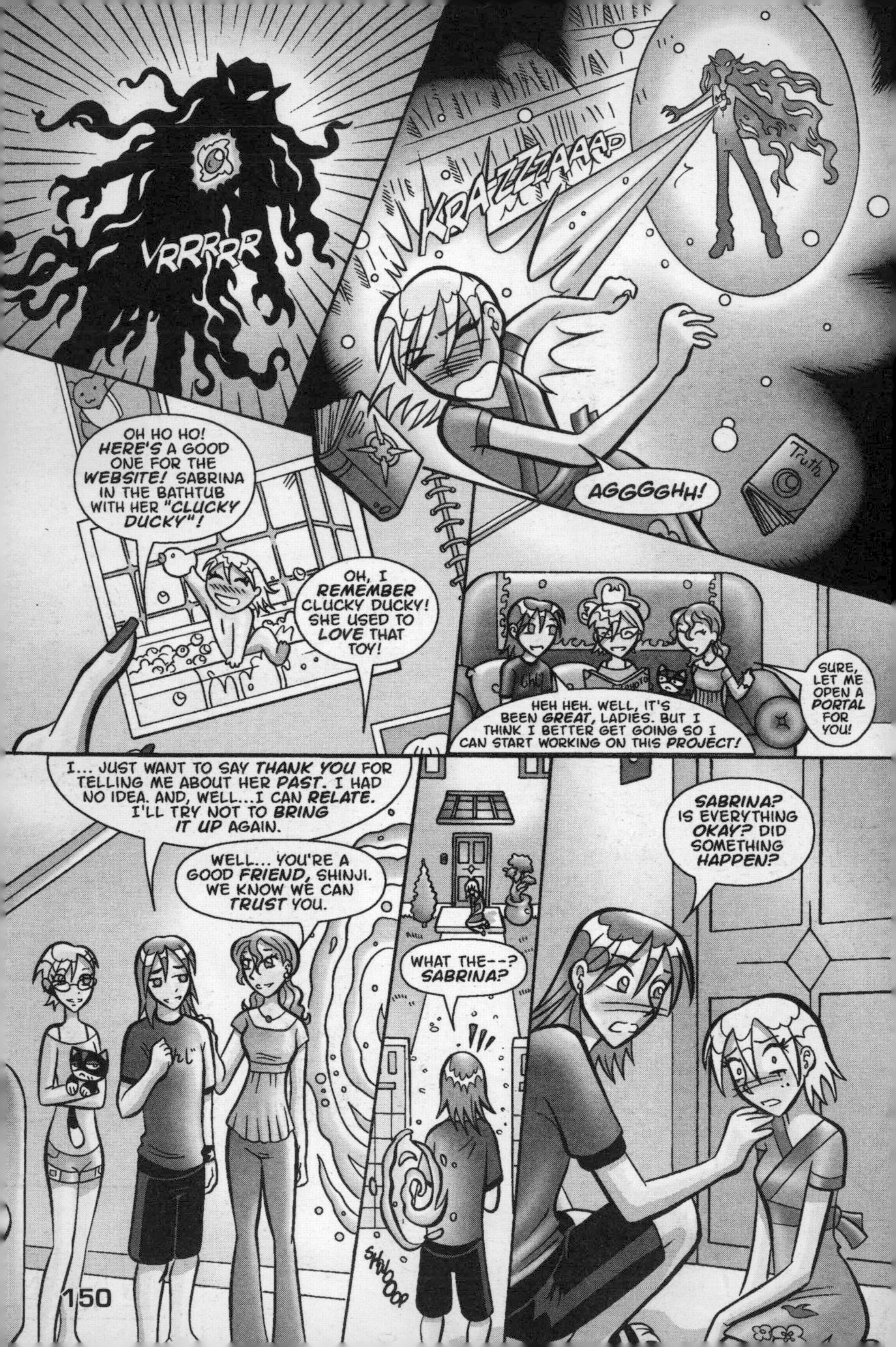
VRRRRR
KRAZZZAAAP
AGGGGHH!
Truth
OH HO HO! HERE'S A GOOD ONE FOR THE WEBSITE! SABRINA IN THE BATHTUB WITH HER "CLUCKY DUCKY"!
OH, I REMEMBER CLUCKY DUCKY! SHE USED TO LOVE THAT TOY!
HEH HEH. WELL, IT'S BEEN GREAT, LADIES. BUT I THINK I BETTER GET GOING SO I CAN START WORKING ON THIS PROJECT!
SURE, LET ME OPEN A PORTAL FOR YOU!
I... JUST WANT TO SAY THANK YOU FOR TELLING ME ABOUT HER PAST. I HAD NO IDEA. AND, WELL...I CAN RELATE. I'LL TRY NOT TO BRING IT UP AGAIN.
WELL... YOU'RE A GOOD FRIEND, SHINJI. WE KNOW WE CAN TRUST YOU.
SHLOOOP
WHAT THE--? SABRINA?
SABRINA? IS EVERYTHING OKAY? DID SOMETHING HAPPEN?

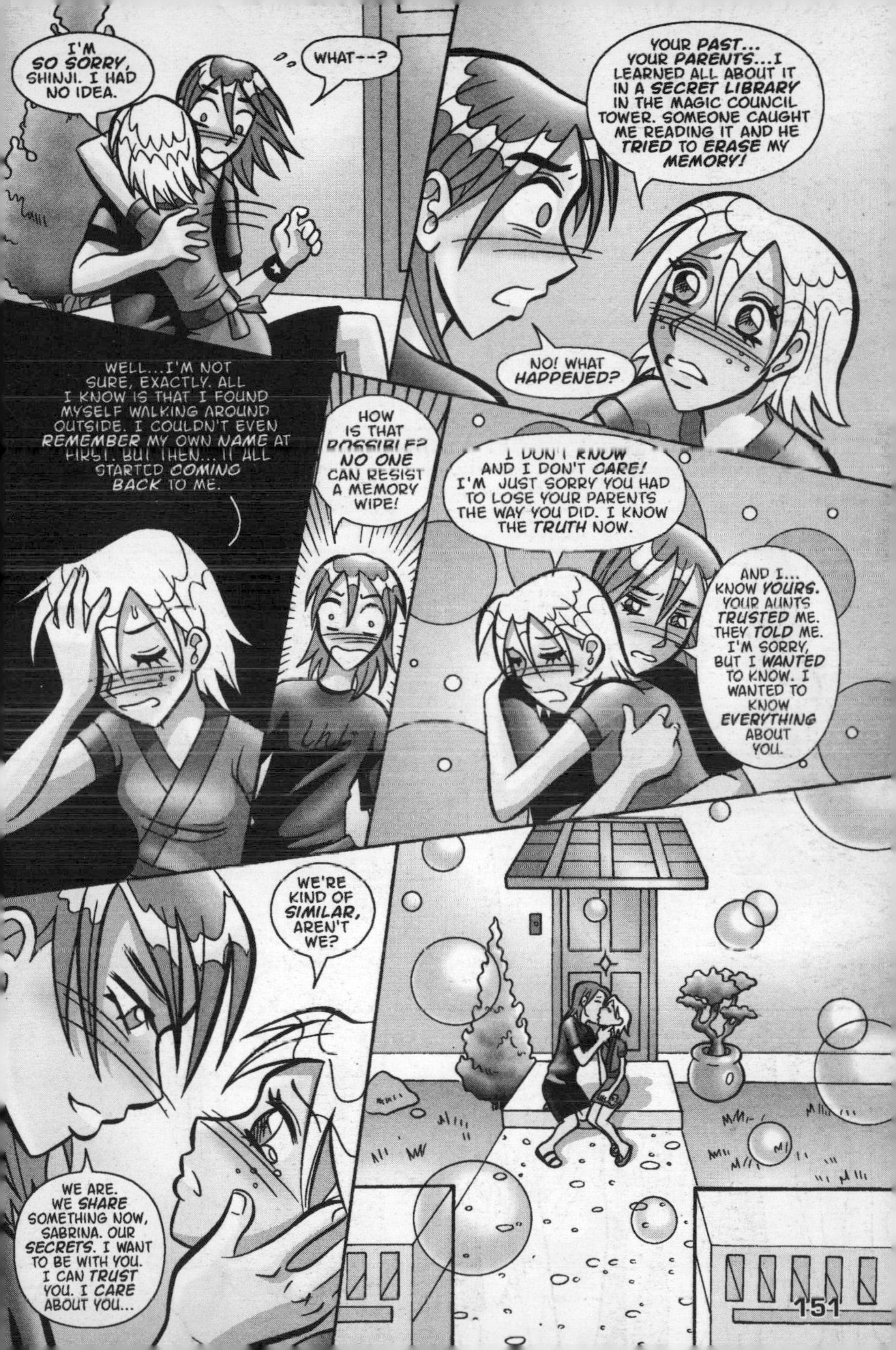
I'M SO SORRY, SHINJI. I HAD NO IDEA.
WHAT--?
YOUR PAST... YOUR PARENTS...I LEARNED ALL ABOUT IT IN A SECRET LIBRARY IN THE MAGIC COUNCIL TOWER. SOMEONE CAUGHT ME READING IT AND HE TRIED TO ERASE MY MEMORY!
NO! WHAT HAPPENED?
WELL...I'M NOT SURE, EXACTLY. ALL I KNOW IS THAT I FOUND MYSELF WALKING AROUND OUTSIDE. I COULDN'T EVEN REMEMBER MY OWN NAME AT FIRST. BUT THEN... IT ALL STARTED COMING BACK TO ME.
HOW IS THAT POSSIBLE? NO ONE CAN RESIST A MEMORY WIPE!
I DON'T KNOW AND I DON'T CARE! I'M JUST SORRY YOU HAD TO LOSE YOUR PARENTS THE WAY YOU DID. I KNOW THE TRUTH NOW.
AND I... KNOW YOURS. YOUR AUNTS TRUSTED ME. THEY TOLD ME. I'M SORRY, BUT I WANTED TO KNOW. I WANTED TO KNOW EVERYTHING ABOUT YOU.
WE'RE KIND OF SIMILAR, AREN'T WE?
WE ARE. WE SHARE SOMETHING NOW, SABRINA. OUR SECRETS. I WANT TO BE WITH YOU. I CAN TRUST YOU. I CARE ABOUT YOU...

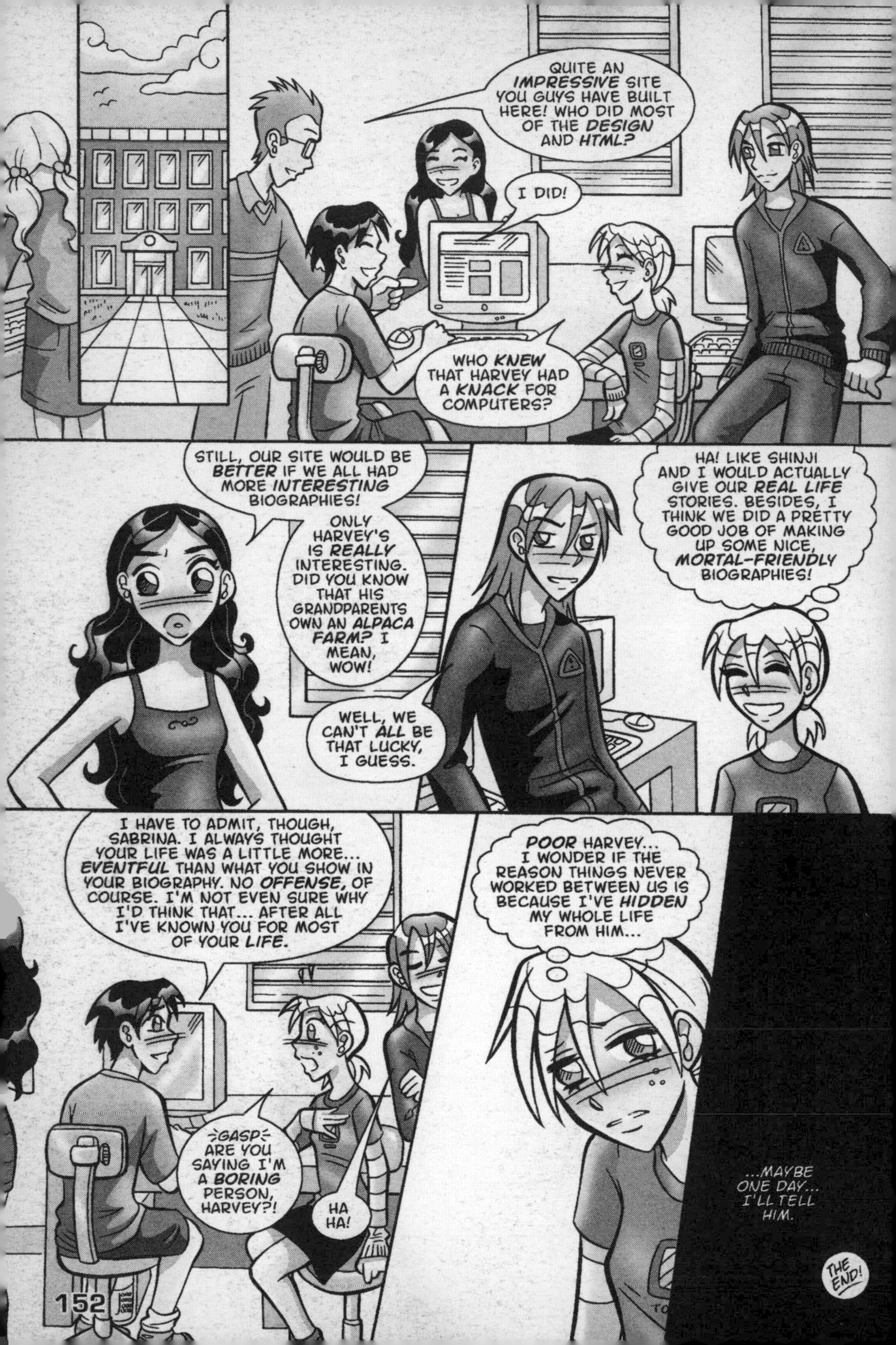
QUITE AN IMPRESSIVE SITE YOU GUYS HAVE BUILT HERE! WHO DID MOST OF THE DESIGN AND HTML?
I DID!
WHO KNEW THAT HARVEY HAD A KNACK FOR COMPUTERS?
STILL, OUR SITE WOULD BE BETTER IF WE ALL HAD MORE INTERESTING BIOGRAPHIES!
ONLY HARVEY'S IS REALLY INTERESTING. DID YOU KNOW THAT HIS GRANDPARENTS OWN AN ALPACA FARM? I MEAN, WOW!
WELL, WE CAN'T ALL BE THAT LUCKY, I GUESS.
HA! LIKE SHINJI AND I WOULD ACTUALLY GIVE OUR REAL LIFE STORIES. BESIDES, I THINK WE DID A PRETTY GOOD JOB OF MAKING UP SOME NICE, MORTAL-FRIENDLY BIOGRAPHIES!
I HAVE TO ADMIT, THOUGH, SABRINA. I ALWAYS THOUGHT YOUR LIFE WAS A LITTLE MORE... EVENTFUL THAN WHAT YOU SHOW IN YOUR BIOGRAPHY. NO OFFENSE, OF COURSE. I'M NOT EVEN SURE WHY I'D THINK THAT... AFTER ALL I'VE KNOWN YOU FOR MOST OF YOUR LIFE.
GASP ARE YOU SAYING I'M A BORING PERSON, HARVEY?!
HA HA!
POOR HARVEY... I WONDER IF THE REASON THINGS NEVER WORKED BETWEEN US IS BECAUSE I'VE HIDDEN MY WHOLE LIFE FROM HIM...
...MAYBE ONE DAY... I'LL TELL HIM.
THE END!

Chapter 8

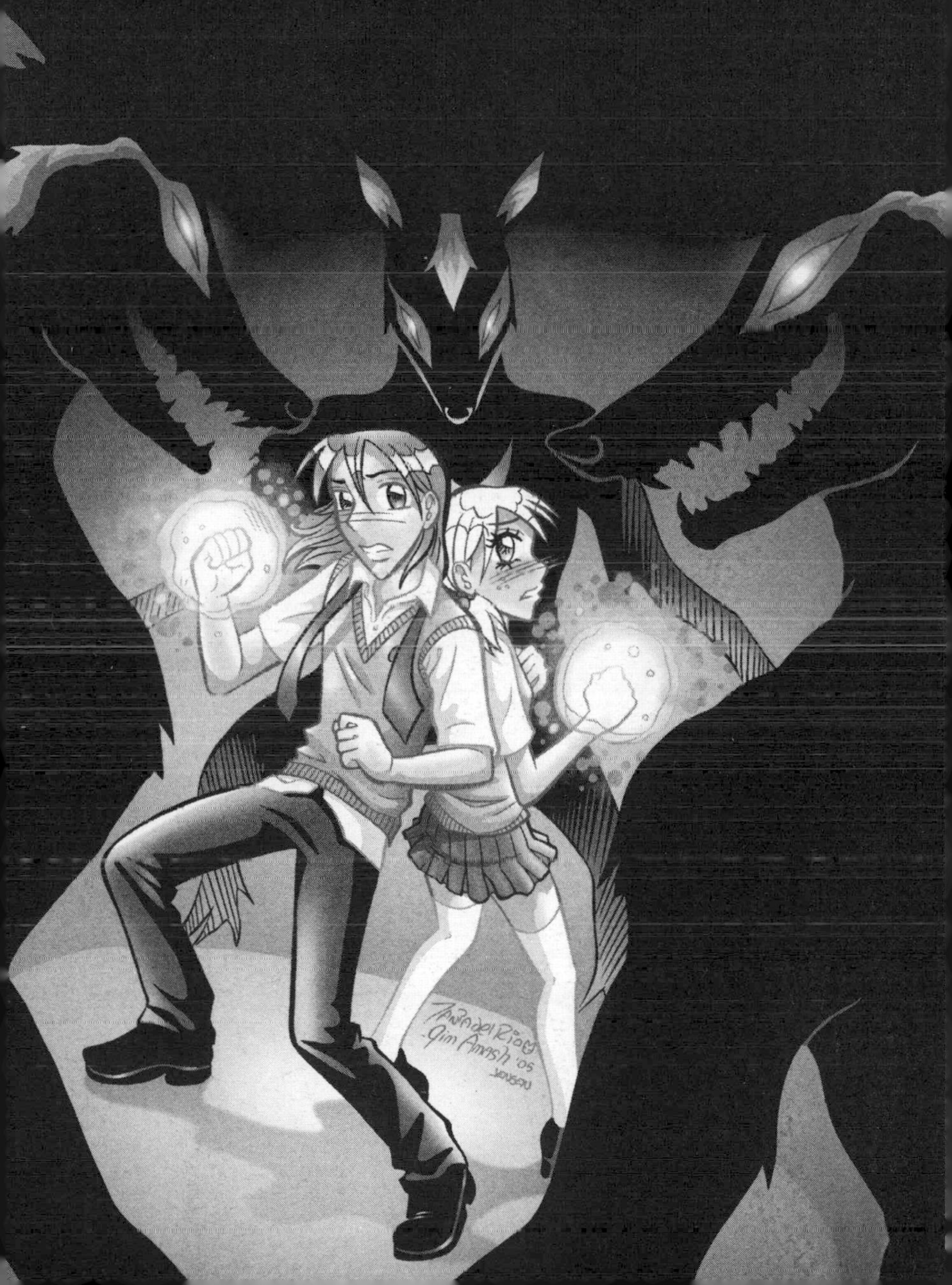

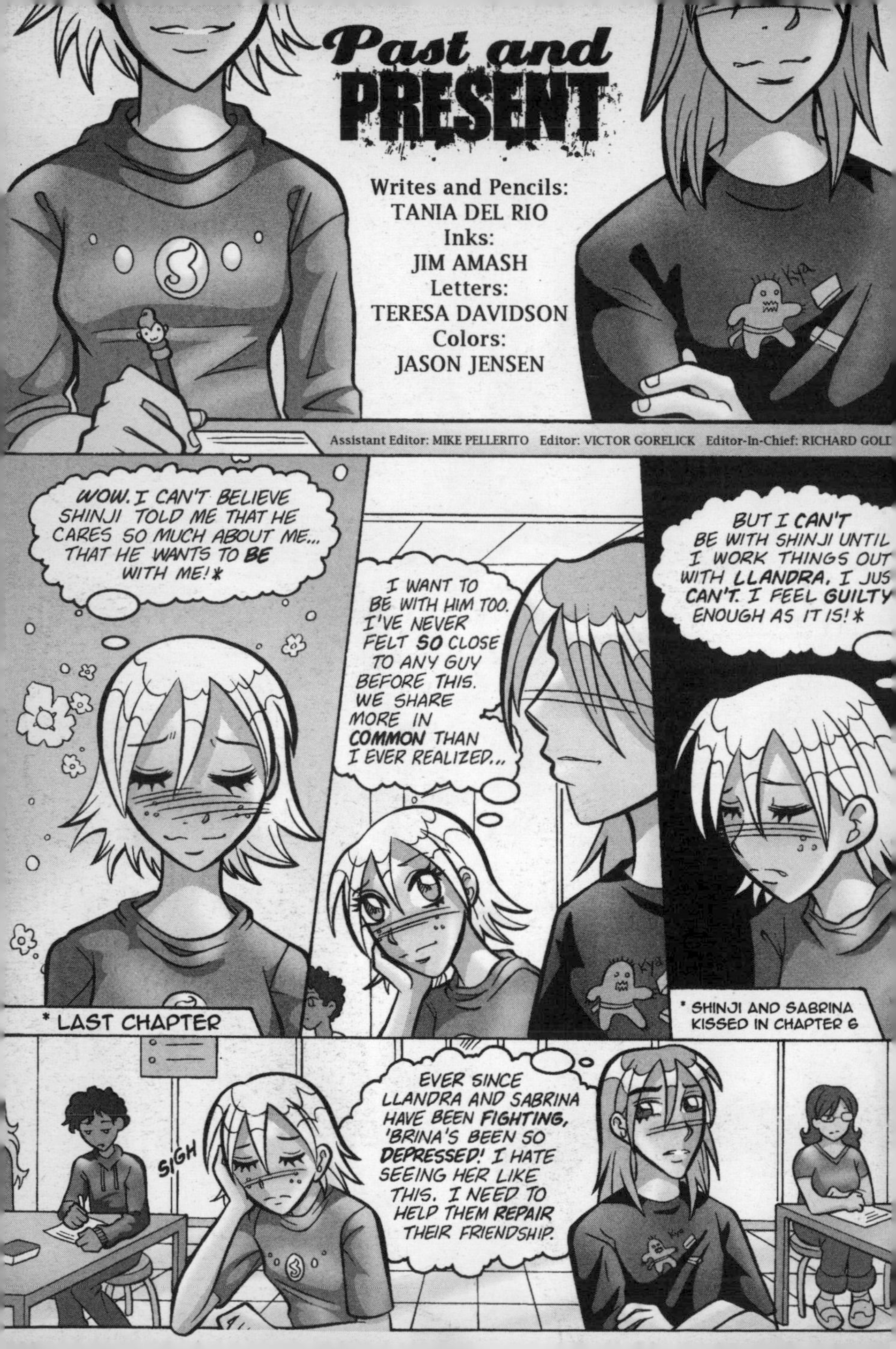
Past and PRESENT
Writes and Pencils: TANIA DEL RIO
Inks: JIM AMASH
Letters: TERESA DAVIDSON
Colors: JASON JENSEN
Assistant Editor: MIKE PELLERITO Editor: VICTOR GORELICK Editor-In-Chief: RICHARD GOLD
WOW. I CAN'T BELIEVE SHINJI TOLD ME THAT HE CARES SO MUCH ABOUT ME... THAT HE WANTS TO BE WITH ME!*
* LAST CHAPTER
I WANT TO BE WITH HIM TOO. I'VE NEVER FELT SO CLOSE TO ANY GUY BEFORE THIS. WE SHARE MORE IN COMMON THAN I EVER REALIZED...
BUT I CAN'T BE WITH SHINJI UNTIL I WORK THINGS OUT WITH LLANDRA. I JUS CAN'T. I FEEL GUILTY ENOUGH AS IT IS!*
* SHINJI AND SABRINA KISSED IN CHAPTER 6
SIGH
EVER SINCE LLANDRA AND SABRINA HAVE BEEN FIGHTING, 'BRINA'S BEEN SO DEPRESSED! I HATE SEEING HER LIKE THIS. I NEED TO HELP THEM REPAIR THEIR FRIENDSHIP.

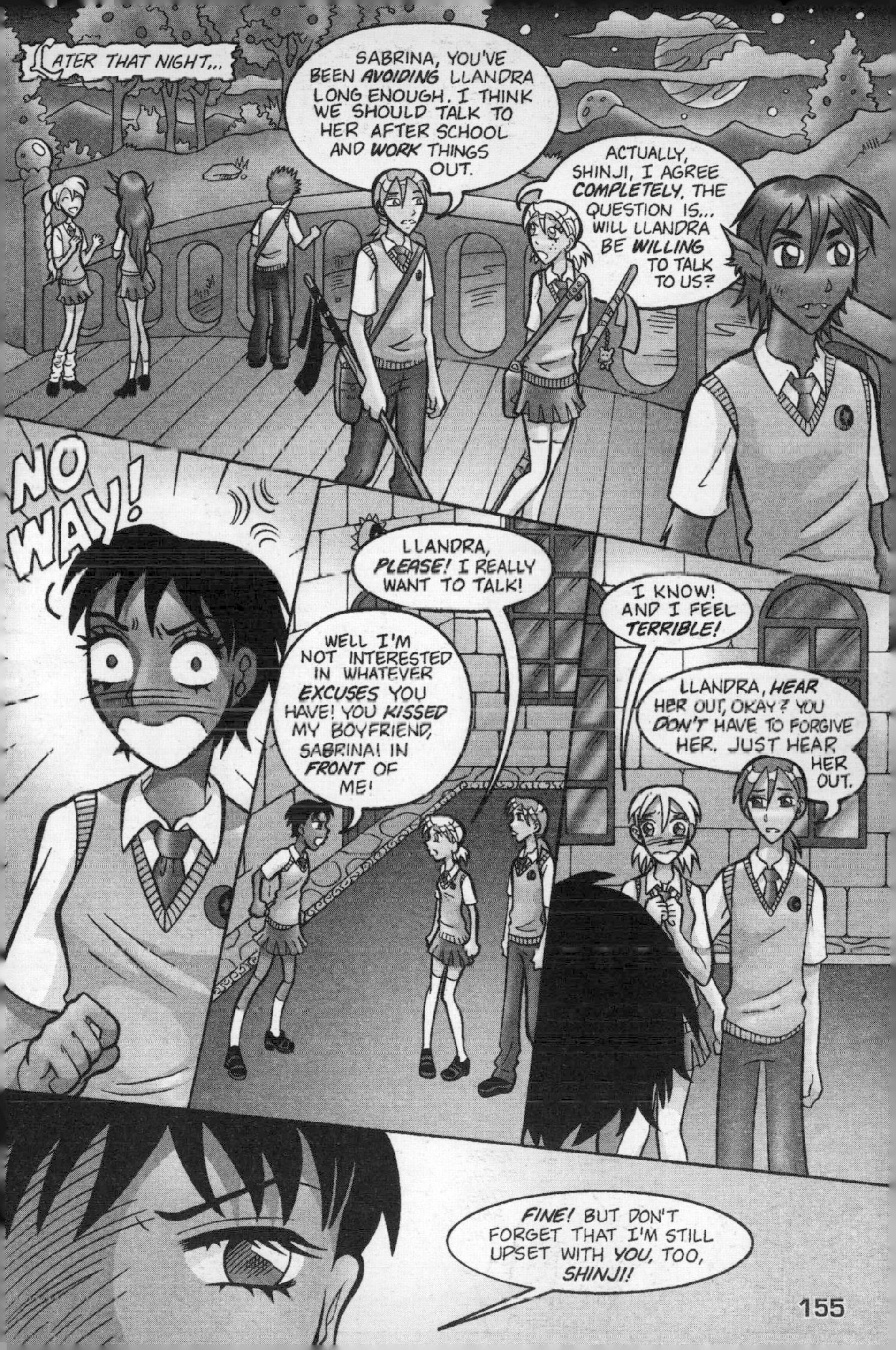
LATER THAT NIGHT...
SABRINA, YOU'VE BEEN AVOIDING LLANDRA LONG ENOUGH. I THINK WE SHOULD TALK TO HER AFTER SCHOOL AND WORK THINGS OUT.
ACTUALLY, SHINJI, I AGREE COMPLETELY. THE QUESTION IS... WILL LLANDRA BE WILLING TO TALK TO US?
NO WAY!
LLANDRA, PLEASE! I REALLY WANT TO TALK!
WELL I'M NOT INTERESTED IN WHATEVER EXCUSES YOU HAVE! YOU KISSED MY BOYFRIEND, SABRINA! IN FRONT OF ME!
I KNOW! AND I FEEL TERRIBLE!
LLANDRA, HEAR HER OUT, OKAY? YOU DON'T HAVE TO FORGIVE HER. JUST HEAR HER OUT.
FINE! BUT DON'T FORGET THAT I'M STILL UPSET WITH YOU, TOO, SHINJI!

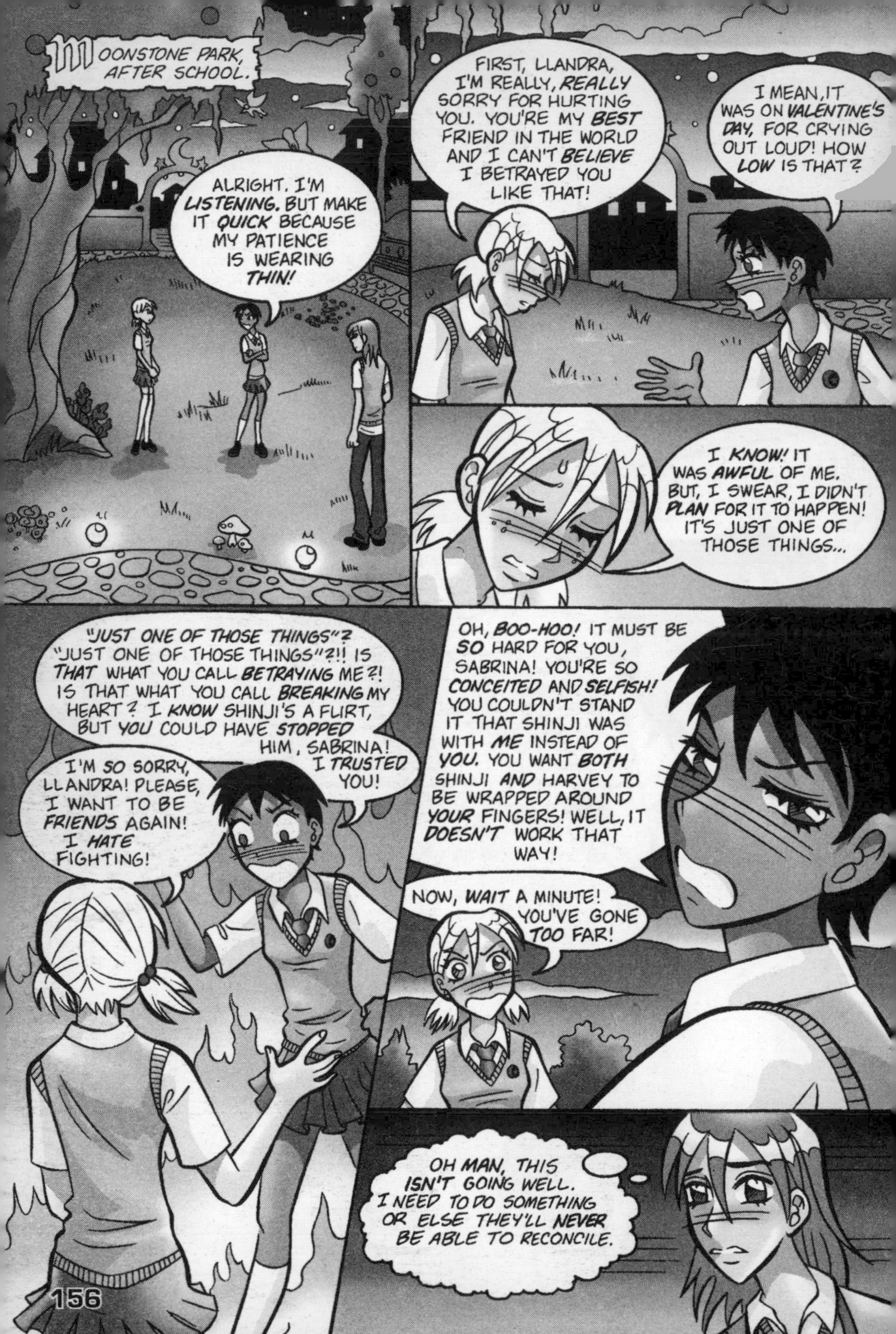
MOONSTONE PARK, AFTER SCHOOL.
ALRIGHT. I'M LISTENING. BUT MAKE IT QUICK BECAUSE MY PATIENCE IS WEARING THIN!
FIRST, LLANDRA, I'M REALLY, REALLY SORRY FOR HURTING YOU. YOU'RE MY BEST FRIEND IN THE WORLD AND I CAN'T BELIEVE I BETRAYED YOU LIKE THAT!
I MEAN, IT WAS ON VALENTINE'S DAY, FOR CRYING OUT LOUD! HOW LOW IS THAT?
I KNOW! IT WAS AWFUL OF ME. BUT, I SWEAR, I DIDN'T PLAN FOR IT TO HAPPEN! IT'S JUST ONE OF THOSE THINGS...
"JUST ONE OF THOSE THINGS"? "JUST ONE OF THOSE THINGS"?!! IS THAT WHAT YOU CALL BETRAYING ME?! IS THAT WHAT YOU CALL BREAKING MY HEART? I KNOW SHINJI'S A FLIRT, BUT YOU COULD HAVE STOPPED HIM, SABRINA! I TRUSTED YOU!
I'M SO SORRY, LLANDRA! PLEASE, I WANT TO BE FRIENDS AGAIN! I HATE FIGHTING!
OH, BOO-HOO! IT MUST BE SO HARD FOR YOU, SABRINA! YOU'RE SO CONCEITED AND SELFISH! YOU COULDN'T STAND IT THAT SHINJI WAS WITH ME INSTEAD OF YOU. YOU WANT BOTH SHINJI AND HARVEY TO BE WRAPPED AROUND YOUR FINGERS! WELL, IT DOESN'T WORK THAT WAY!
NOW, WAIT A MINUTE! YOU'VE GONE TOO FAR!
OH MAN, THIS ISN'T GOING WELL. I NEED TO DO SOMETHING OR ELSE THEY'LL NEVER BE ABLE TO RECONCILE.

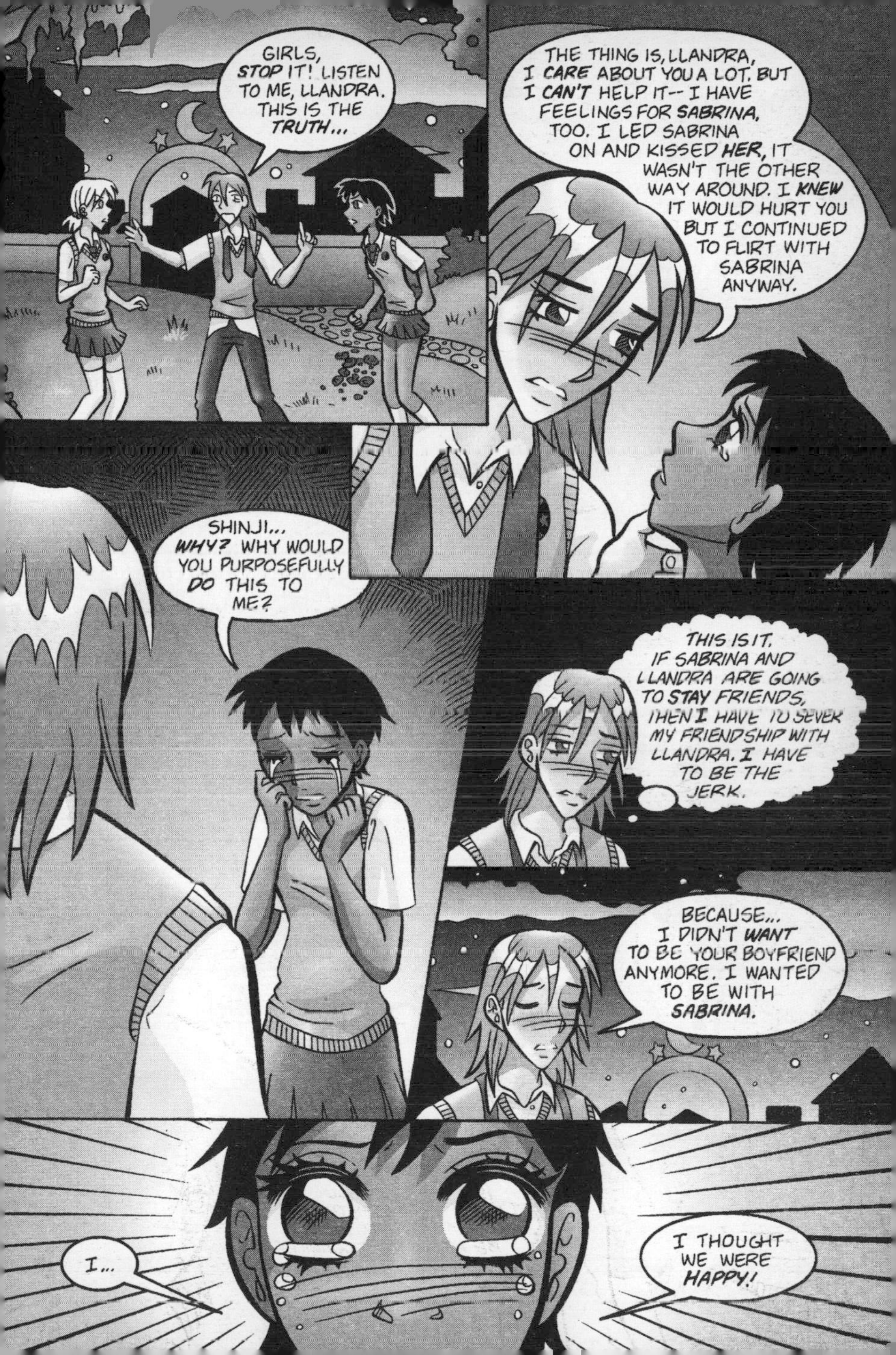
GIRLS, STOP IT! LISTEN TO ME, LLANDRA. THIS IS THE TRUTH...
THE THING IS, LLANDRA, I CARE ABOUT YOU A LOT. BUT I CAN'T HELP IT-- I HAVE FEELINGS FOR SABRINA, TOO. I LED SABRINA ON AND KISSED HER, IT WASN'T THE OTHER WAY AROUND. I KNEW IT WOULD HURT YOU BUT I CONTINUED TO FLIRT WITH SABRINA ANYWAY.
SHINJI... WHY? WHY WOULD YOU PURPOSEFULLY DO THIS TO ME?
THIS IS IT. IF SABRINA AND LLANDRA ARE GOING TO STAY FRIENDS, THEN I HAVE TO SEVER MY FRIENDSHIP WITH LLANDRA. I HAVE TO BE THE JERK.
BECAUSE... I DIDN'T WANT TO BE YOUR BOYFRIEND ANYMORE. I WANTED TO BE WITH SABRINA.
I...
I THOUGHT WE WERE HAPPY!

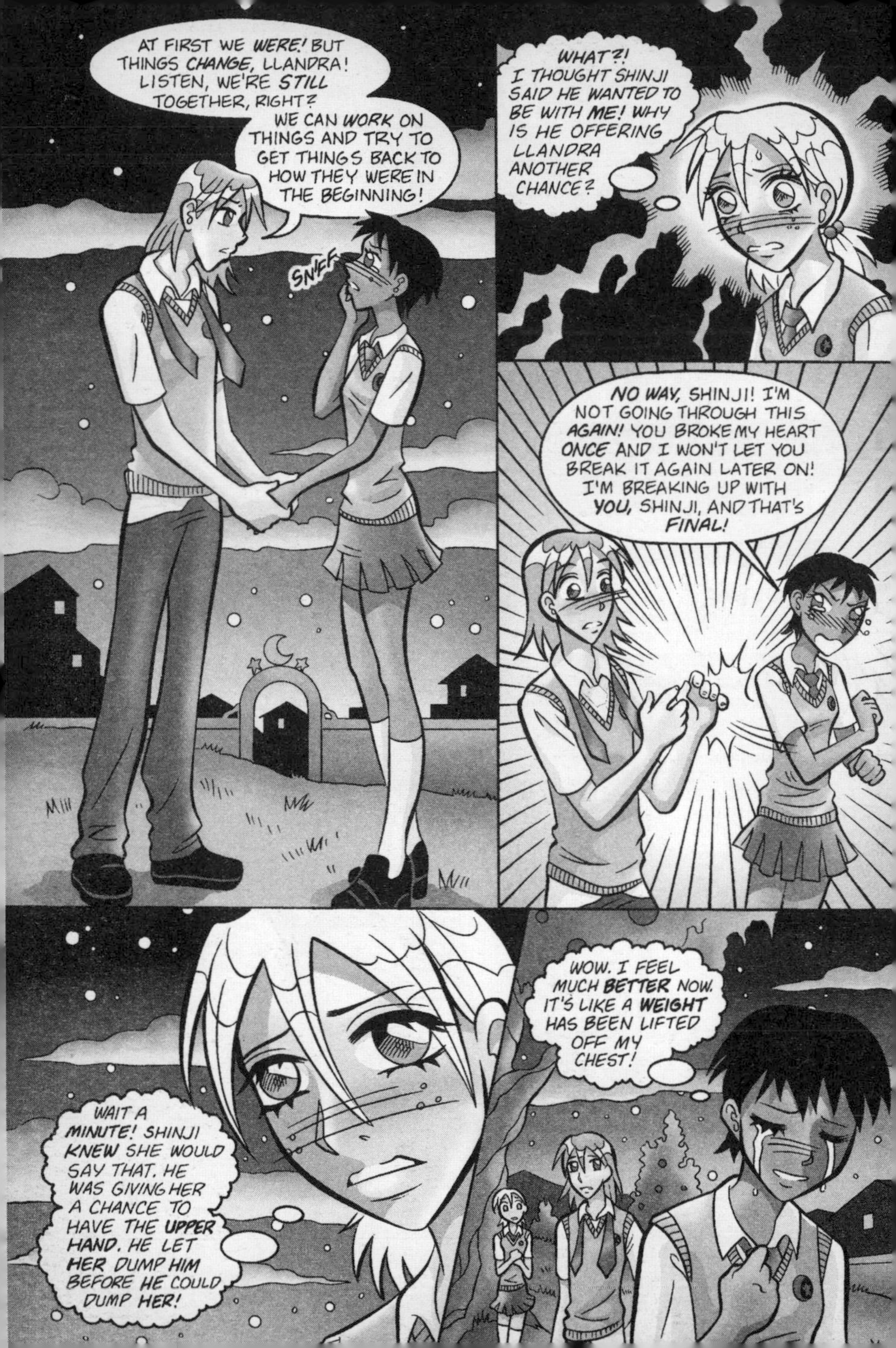
AT FIRST WE WERE! BUT THINGS CHANGE, LLANDRA! LISTEN, WE'RE STILL TOGETHER, RIGHT?
WE CAN WORK ON THINGS AND TRY TO GET THINGS BACK TO HOW THEY WERE IN THE BEGINNING!
SNIFF
WHAT?! I THOUGHT SHINJI SAID HE WANTED TO BE WITH ME! WHY IS HE OFFERING LLANDRA ANOTHER CHANCE?
NO WAY, SHINJI! I'M NOT GOING THROUGH THIS AGAIN! YOU BROKE MY HEART ONCE AND I WON'T LET YOU BREAK IT AGAIN LATER ON! I'M BREAKING UP WITH YOU, SHINJI, AND THAT'S FINAL!
WAIT A MINUTE! SHINJI KNEW SHE WOULD SAY THAT. HE WAS GIVING HER A CHANCE TO HAVE THE UPPER HAND. HE LET HER DUMP HIM BEFORE HE COULD DUMP HER!
WOW. I FEEL MUCH BETTER NOW. IT'S LIKE A WEIGHT HAS BEEN LIFTED OFF MY CHEST!

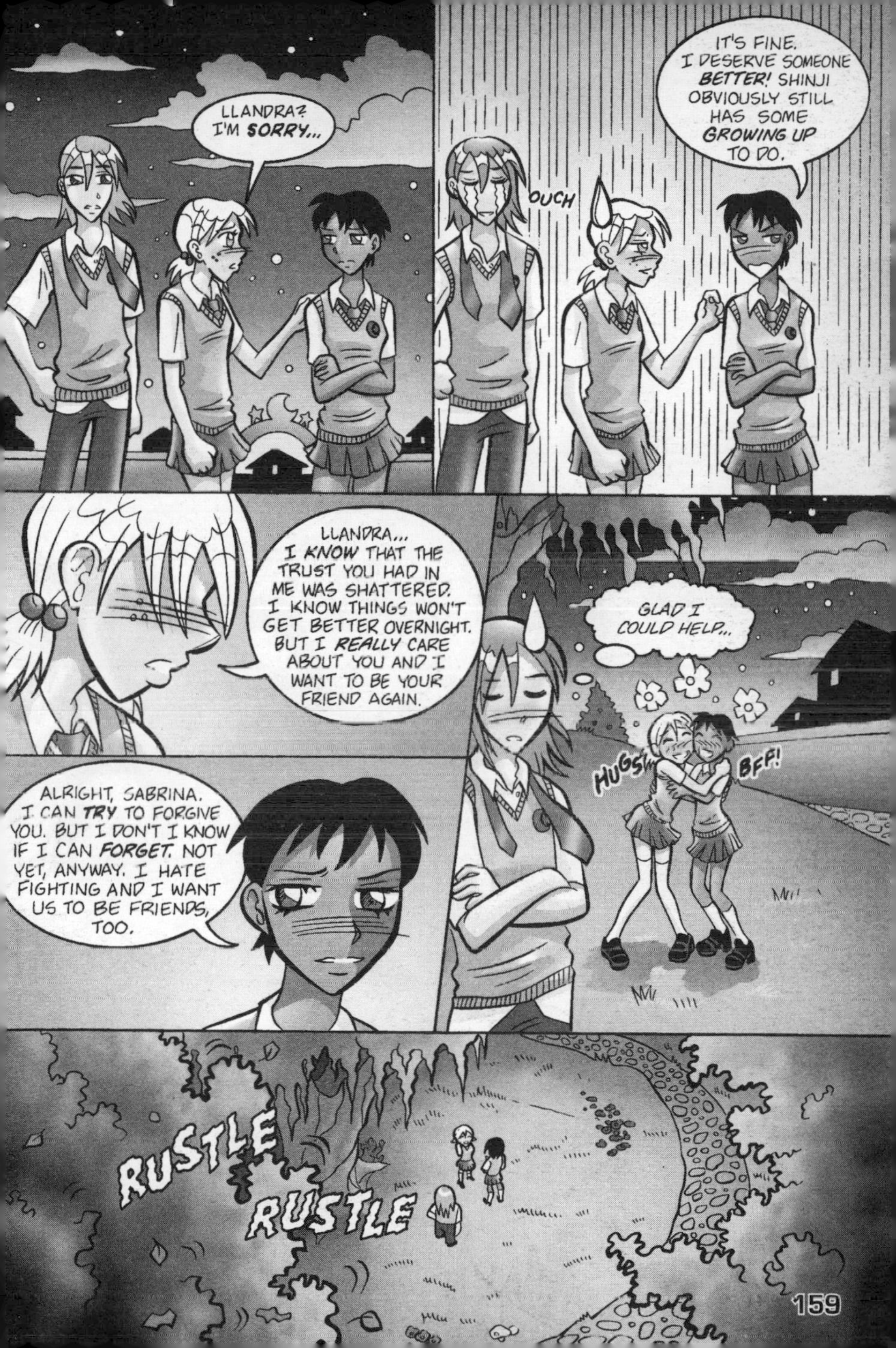
LLANDRA? I'M SORRY...
IT'S FINE. I DESERVE SOMEONE BETTER! SHINJI OBVIOUSLY STILL HAS SOME GROWING UP TO DO.
OUCH
LLANDRA... I KNOW THAT THE TRUST YOU HAD IN ME WAS SHATTERED. I KNOW THINGS WON'T GET BETTER OVERNIGHT. BUT I REALLY CARE ABOUT YOU AND I WANT TO BE YOUR FRIEND AGAIN.
ALRIGHT, SABRINA. I CAN TRY TO FORGIVE YOU. BUT I DON'T I KNOW IF I CAN FORGET. NOT YET, ANYWAY. I HATE FIGHTING AND I WANT US TO BE FRIENDS, TOO.
GLAD I COULD HELP...
HUGS!
BFF!
RUSTLE
RUSTLE

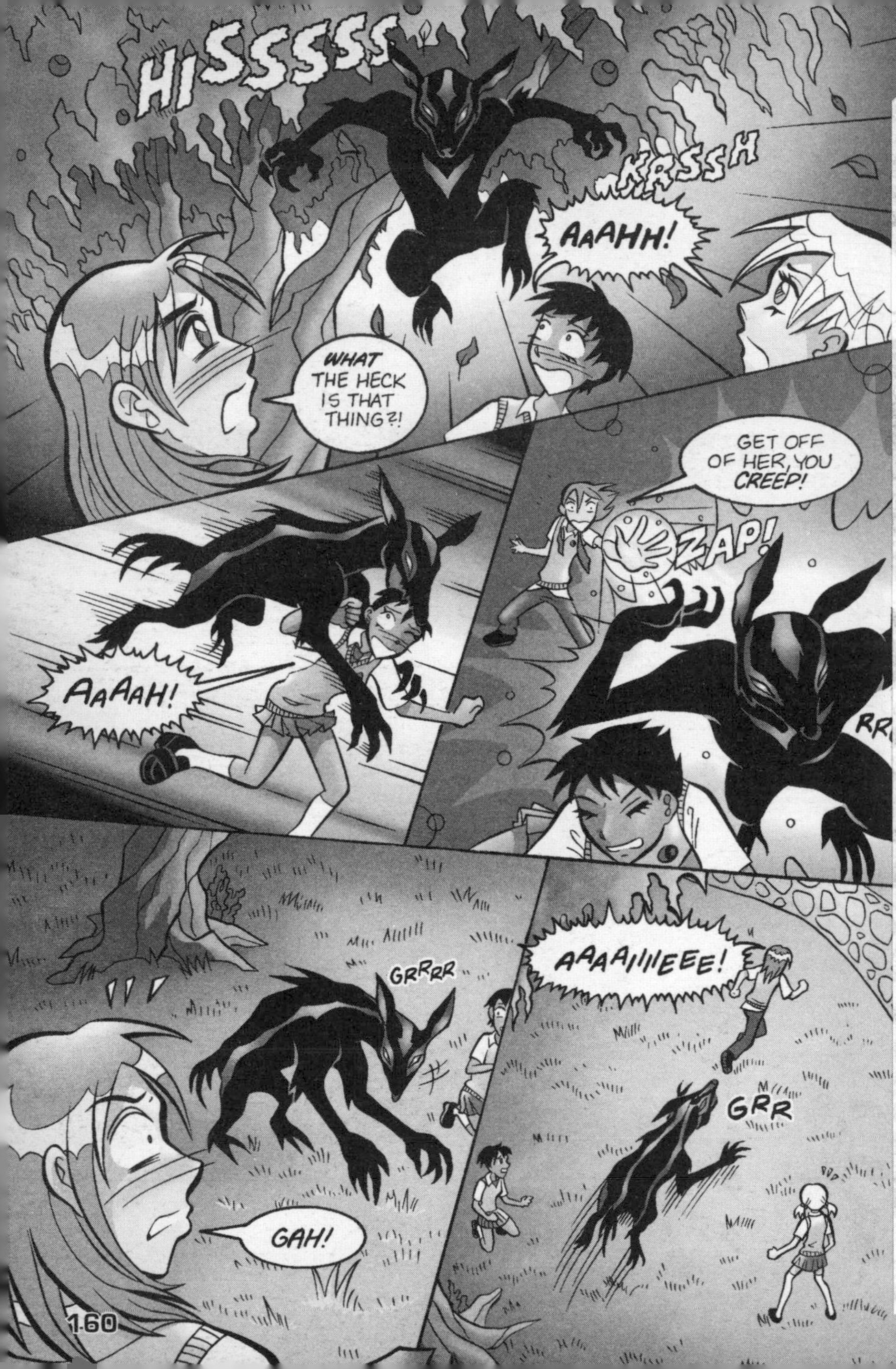
HISSSSS
KRSSH
AAAHH!
WHAT THE HECK IS THAT THING?!
AAAAH!
GET OFF OF HER, YOU CREEP!
ZAP!
RR
GRRRR
GAH!
AAAAIIIIEEEE!
GRR

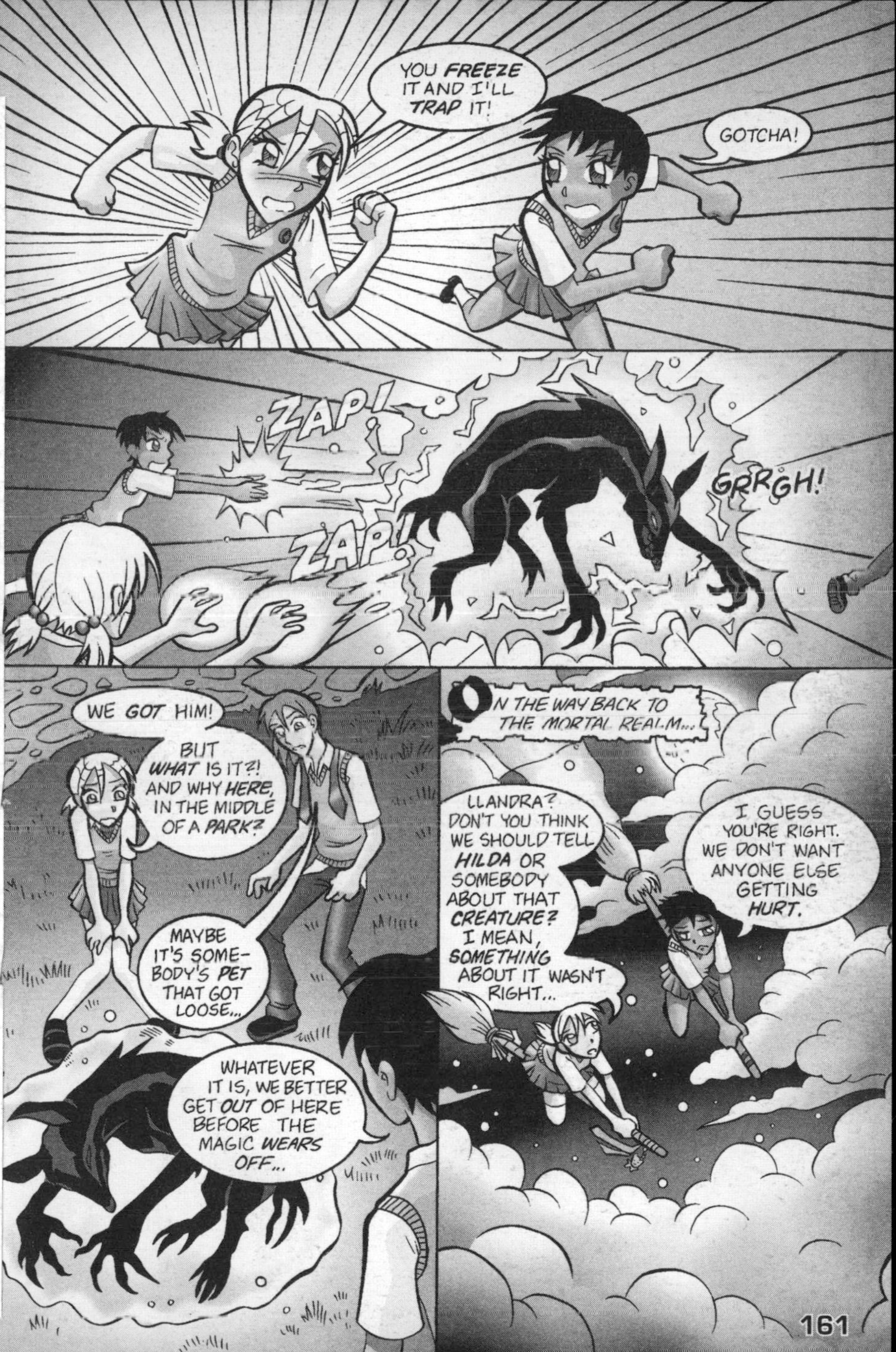
YOU FREEZE IT AND I'LL TRAP IT!
GOTCHA!
ZAP!
GRRGH!
ZAP!
WE GOT HIM!
BUT WHAT IS IT?! AND WHY HERE, IN THE MIDDLE OF A PARK?
MAYBE IT'S SOMEBODY'S PET THAT GOT LOOSE...
WHATEVER IT IS, WE BETTER GET OUT OF HERE BEFORE THE MAGIC WEARS OFF...
ON THE WAY BACK TO THE MORTAL REALM...
LLANDRA? DON'T YOU THINK WE SHOULD TELL HILDA OR SOMEBODY ABOUT THAT CREATURE? I MEAN, SOMETHING ABOUT IT WASN'T RIGHT...
I GUESS YOU'RE RIGHT. WE DON'T WANT ANYONE ELSE GETTING HURT.

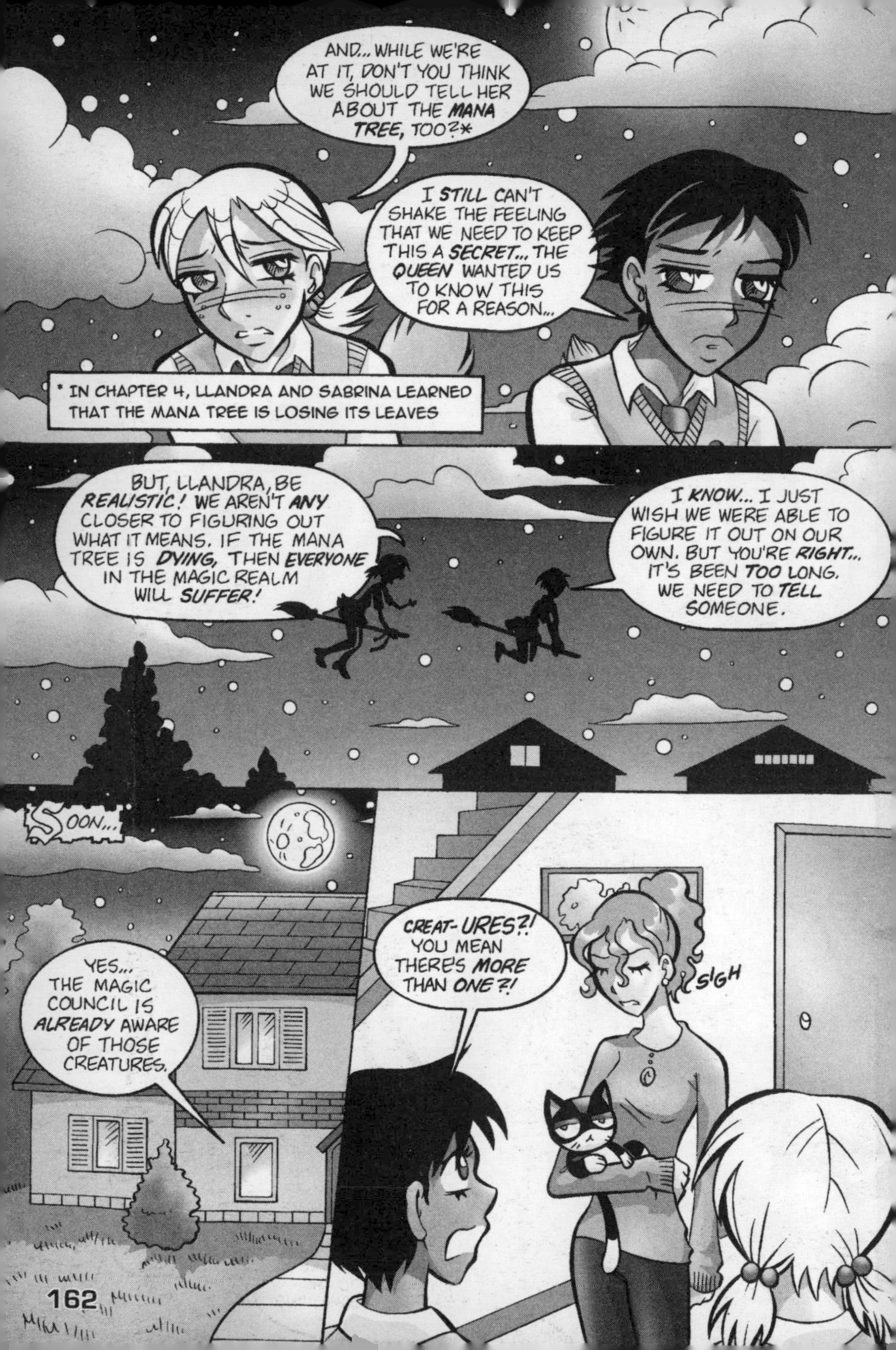
AND... WHILE WE'RE AT IT, DON'T YOU THINK WE SHOULD TELL HER ABOUT THE MANA TREE, TOO?*
I STILL CAN'T SHAKE THE FEELING THAT WE NEED TO KEEP THIS A SECRET... THE QUEEN WANTED US TO KNOW THIS FOR A REASON...
* IN CHAPTER 4, LLANDRA AND SABRINA LEARNED THAT THE MANA TREE IS LOSING ITS LEAVES
BUT, LLANDRA, BE REALISTIC! WE AREN'T ANY CLOSER TO FIGURING OUT WHAT IT MEANS. IF THE MANA TREE IS DYING, THEN EVERYONE IN THE MAGIC REALM WILL SUFFER!
I KNOW... I JUST WISH WE WERE ABLE TO FIGURE IT OUT ON OUR OWN. BUT YOU'RE RIGHT... IT'S BEEN TOO LONG. WE NEED TO TELL SOMEONE.
SOON...
YES... THE MAGIC COUNCIL IS ALREADY AWARE OF THOSE CREATURES.
CREAT-URES?! YOU MEAN THERE'S MORE THAN ONE?!
SIGH

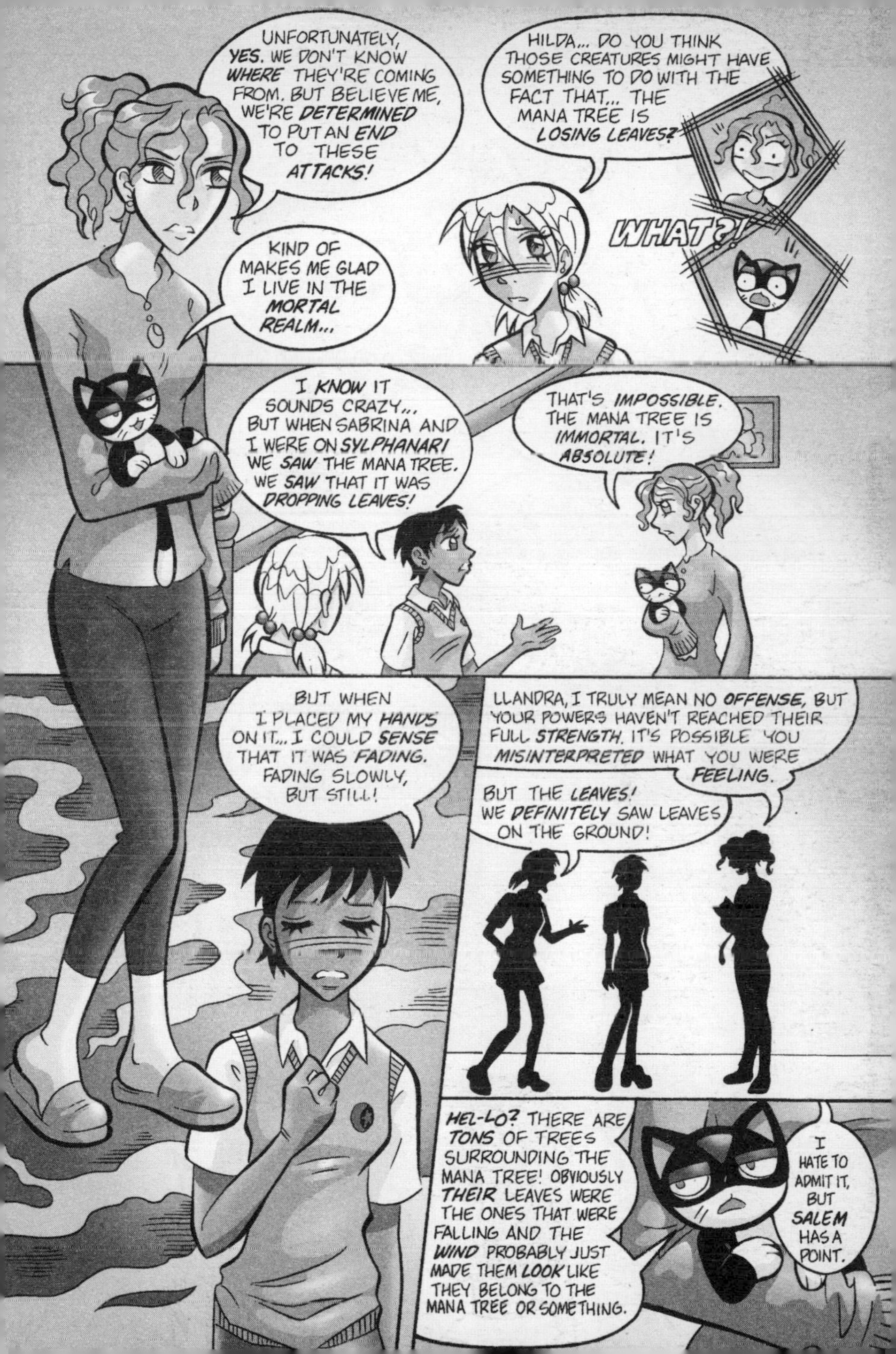
UNFORTUNATELY, YES. WE DON'T KNOW WHERE THEY'RE COMING FROM. BUT BELIEVE ME, WE'RE DETERMINED TO PUT AN END TO THESE ATTACKS!
KIND OF MAKES ME GLAD I LIVE IN THE MORTAL REALM...
HILDA... DO YOU THINK THOSE CREATURES MIGHT HAVE SOMETHING TO DO WITH THE FACT THAT... THE MANA TREE IS LOSING LEAVES?
WHAT?!
I KNOW IT SOUNDS CRAZY... BUT WHEN SABRINA AND I WERE ON SYLPHANARI WE SAW THE MANA TREE. WE SAW THAT IT WAS DROPPING LEAVES!
THAT'S IMPOSSIBLE. THE MANA TREE IS IMMORTAL. IT'S ABSOLUTE!
BUT WHEN I PLACED MY HANDS ON IT... I COULD SENSE THAT IT WAS FADING. FADING SLOWLY, BUT STILL!
LLANDRA, I TRULY MEAN NO OFFENSE, BUT YOUR POWERS HAVEN'T REACHED THEIR FULL STRENGTH. IT'S POSSIBLE YOU MISINTERPRETED WHAT YOU WERE FEELING.
BUT THE LEAVES! WE DEFINITELY SAW LEAVES ON THE GROUND!
HEL-LO? THERE ARE TONS OF TREES SURROUNDING THE MANA TREE! OBVIOUSLY THEIR LEAVES WERE THE ONES THAT WERE FALLING AND THE WIND PROBABLY JUST MADE THEM LOOK LIKE THEY BELONG TO THE MANA TREE OR SOMETHING.
I HATE TO ADMIT IT, BUT SALEM HAS A POINT.

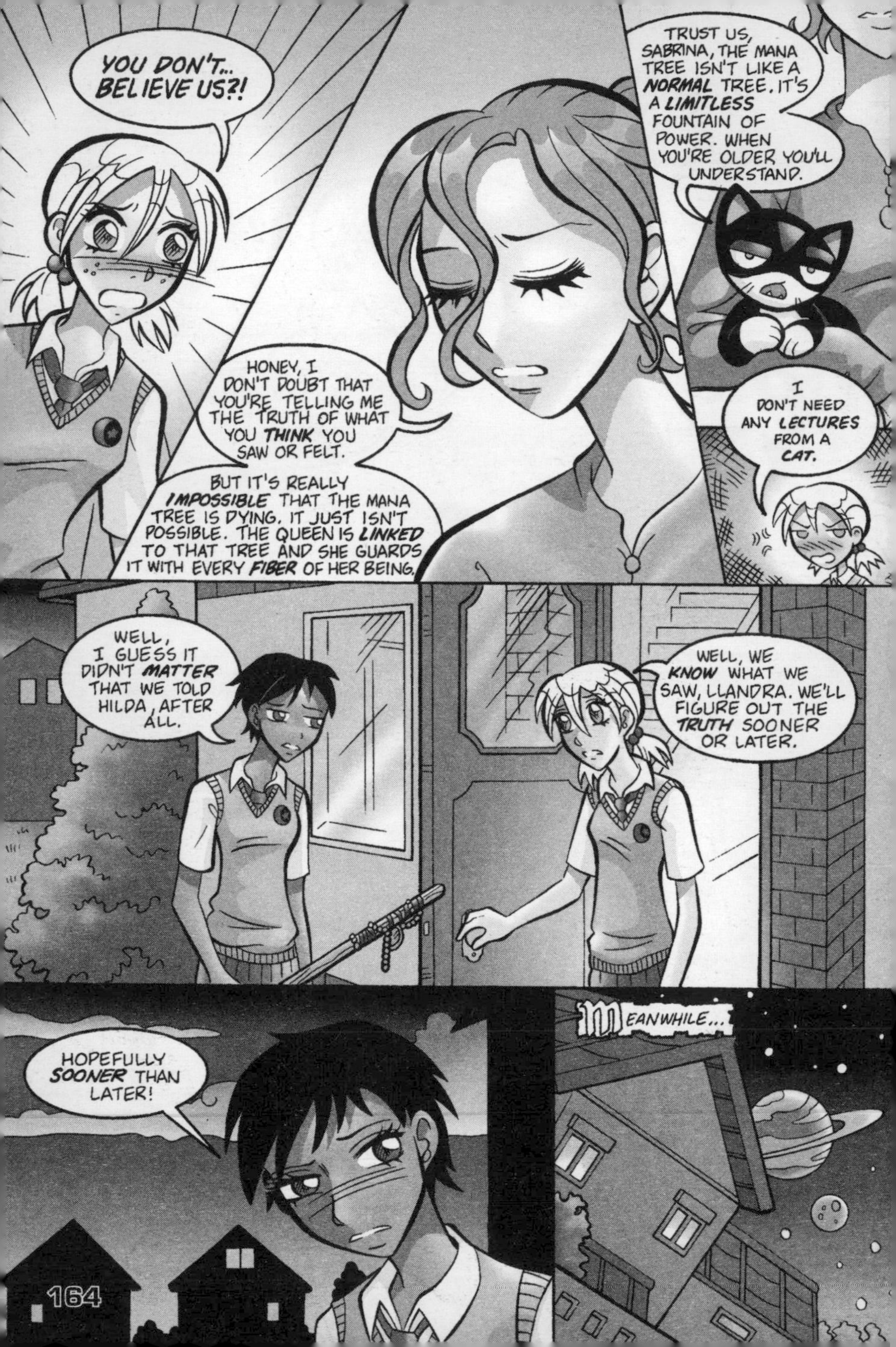
YOU DON'T... BELIEVE US?!
HONEY, I DON'T DOUBT THAT YOU'RE TELLING ME THE TRUTH OF WHAT YOU THINK YOU SAW OR FELT.
BUT IT'S REALLY IMPOSSIBLE THAT THE MANA TREE IS DYING. IT JUST ISN'T POSSIBLE. THE QUEEN IS LINKED TO THAT TREE AND SHE GUARDS IT WITH EVERY FIBER OF HER BEING.
TRUST US, SABRINA, THE MANA TREE ISN'T LIKE A NORMAL TREE. IT'S A LIMITLESS FOUNTAIN OF POWER. WHEN YOU'RE OLDER YOU'LL UNDERSTAND.
I DON'T NEED ANY LECTURES FROM A CAT.
WELL, I GUESS IT DIDN'T MATTER THAT WE TOLD HILDA, AFTER ALL.
WELL, WE KNOW WHAT WE SAW, LLANDRA. WE'LL FIGURE OUT THE TRUTH SOONER OR LATER.
HOPEFULLY SOONER THAN LATER!
MEANWHILE...

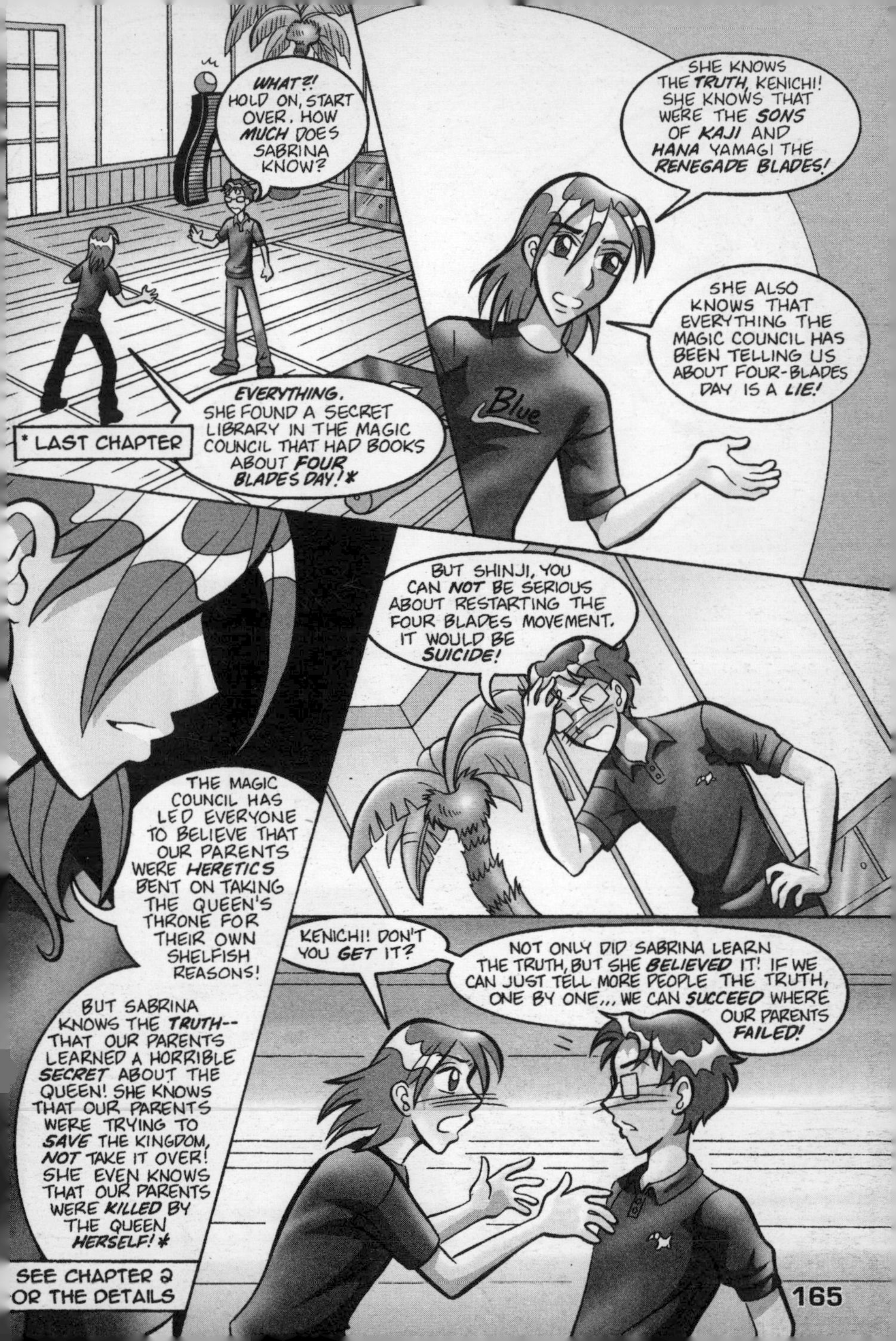
WHAT?! HOLD ON, START OVER. HOW MUCH DOES SABRINA KNOW?
EVERYTHING. SHE FOUND A SECRET LIBRARY IN THE MAGIC COUNCIL THAT HAD BOOKS ABOUT FOUR BLADES DAY! *
* LAST CHAPTER
SHE KNOWS THE TRUTH, KENICHI! SHE KNOWS THAT WERE THE SONS OF KAJI AND HANA YAMAGI THE RENEGADE BLADES!
SHE ALSO KNOWS THAT EVERYTHING THE MAGIC COUNCIL HAS BEEN TELLING US ABOUT FOUR-BLADES DAY IS A LIE!
THE MAGIC COUNCIL HAS LED EVERYONE TO BELIEVE THAT OUR PARENTS WERE HERETICS BENT ON TAKING THE QUEEN'S THRONE FOR THEIR OWN SHELFISH REASONS!
BUT SABRINA KNOWS THE TRUTH-- THAT OUR PARENTS LEARNED A HORRIBLE SECRET ABOUT THE QUEEN! SHE KNOWS THAT OUR PARENTS WERE TRYING TO SAVE THE KINGDOM, NOT TAKE IT OVER! SHE EVEN KNOWS THAT OUR PARENTS WERE KILLED BY THE QUEEN HERSELF! *
SEE CHAPTER 2 OR THE DETAILS
BUT SHINJI, YOU CAN NOT BE SERIOUS ABOUT RESTARTING THE FOUR BLADES MOVEMENT. IT WOULD BE SUICIDE!
KENICHI! DON'T YOU GET IT?
NOT ONLY DID SABRINA LEARN THE TRUTH, BUT SHE BELIEVED IT! IF WE CAN JUST TELL MORE PEOPLE THE TRUTH, ONE BY ONE... WE CAN SUCCEED WHERE OUR PARENTS FAILED!
Blue

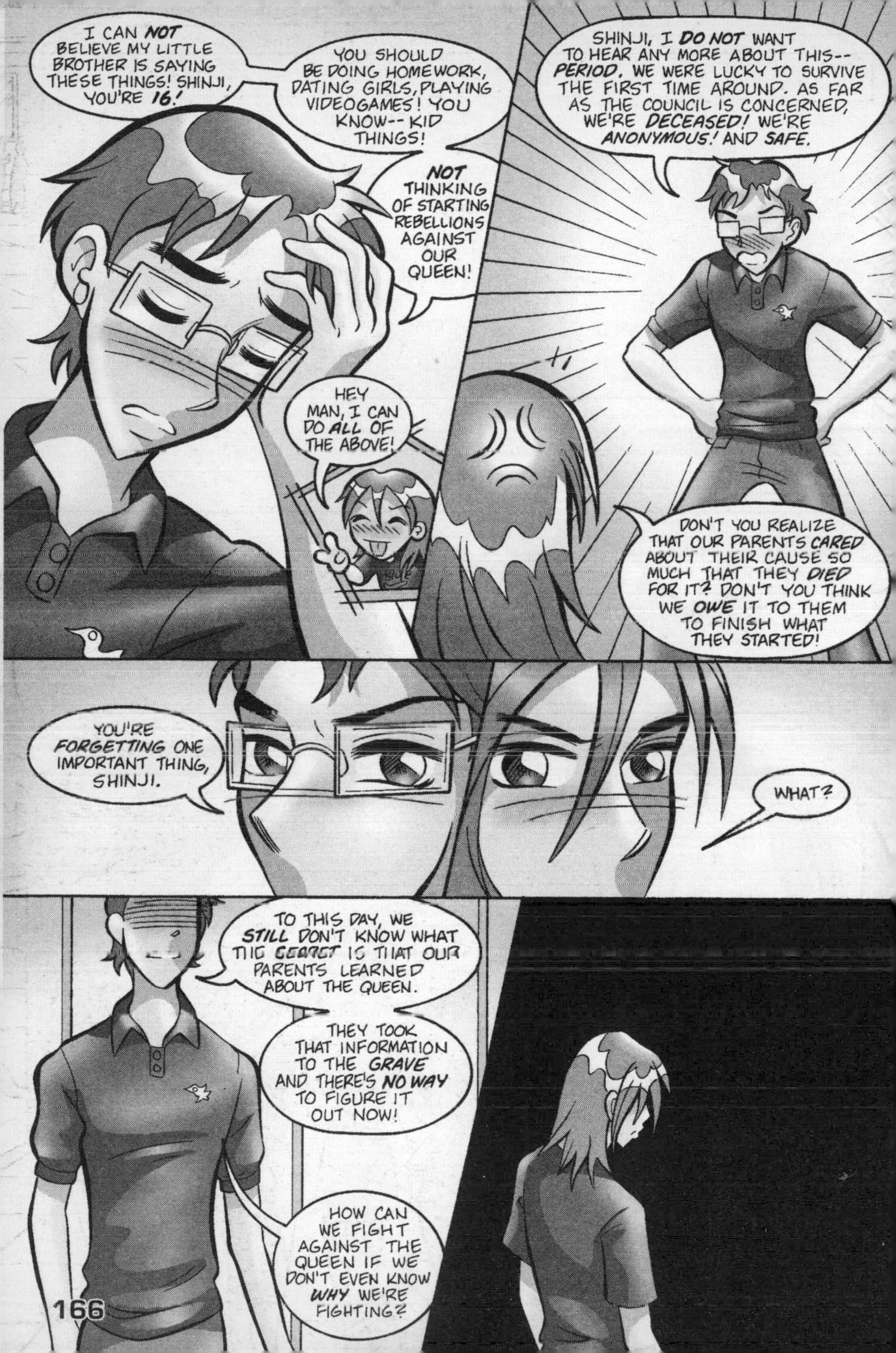
I CAN NOT BELIEVE MY LITTLE BROTHER IS SAYING THESE THINGS! SHINJI, YOU'RE 16!
YOU SHOULD BE DOING HOMEWORK, DATING GIRLS, PLAYING VIDEOGAMES! YOU KNOW-- KID THINGS!
NOT THINKING OF STARTING REBELLIONS AGAINST OUR QUEEN!
HEY MAN, I CAN DO ALL OF THE ABOVE!
SHINJI, I DO NOT WANT TO HEAR ANY MORE ABOUT THIS-- PERIOD. WE WERE LUCKY TO SURVIVE THE FIRST TIME AROUND. AS FAR AS THE COUNCIL IS CONCERNED, WE'RE DECEASED! WE'RE ANONYMOUS! AND SAFE.
DON'T YOU REALIZE THAT OUR PARENTS CARED ABOUT THEIR CAUSE SO MUCH THAT THEY DIED FOR IT? DON'T YOU THINK WE OWE IT TO THEM TO FINISH WHAT THEY STARTED!
YOU'RE FORGETTING ONE IMPORTANT THING, SHINJI.
WHAT?
TO THIS DAY, WE STILL DON'T KNOW WHAT THE SECRET IS THAT OUR PARENTS LEARNED ABOUT THE QUEEN.
THEY TOOK THAT INFORMATION TO THE GRAVE AND THERE'S NO WAY TO FIGURE IT OUT NOW!
HOW CAN WE FIGHT AGAINST THE QUEEN IF WE DON'T EVEN KNOW WHY WE'RE FIGHTING?

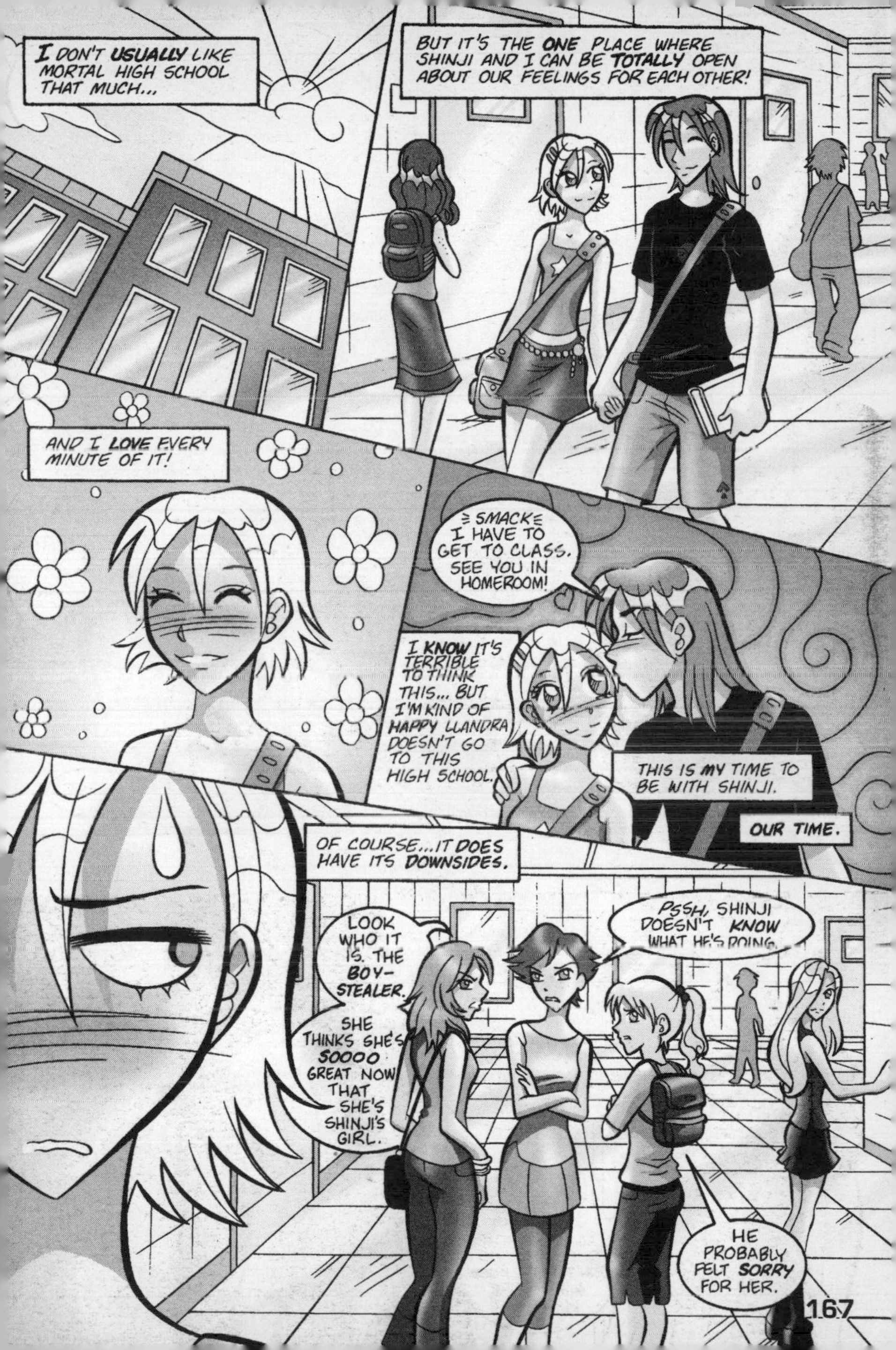
I DON'T USUALLY LIKE MORTAL HIGH SCHOOL THAT MUCH...
BUT IT'S THE ONE PLACE WHERE SHINJI AND I CAN BE TOTALLY OPEN ABOUT OUR FEELINGS FOR EACH OTHER!
AND I LOVE EVERY MINUTE OF IT!
SMACK
I HAVE TO GET TO CLASS. SEE YOU IN HOMEROOM!
I KNOW IT'S TERRIBLE TO THINK THIS... BUT I'M KIND OF HAPPY LLANDRA DOESN'T GO TO THIS HIGH SCHOOL.
THIS IS MY TIME TO BE WITH SHINJI.
OUR TIME.
OF COURSE...IT DOES HAVE ITS DOWNSIDES.
LOOK WHO IT IS. THE BOY-STEALER.
PSSH, SHINJI DOESN'T KNOW WHAT HE'S DOING.
SHE THINKS SHE'S SOOOO GREAT NOW THAT SHE'S SHINJI'S GIRL.
HE PROBABLY FELT SORRY FOR HER.

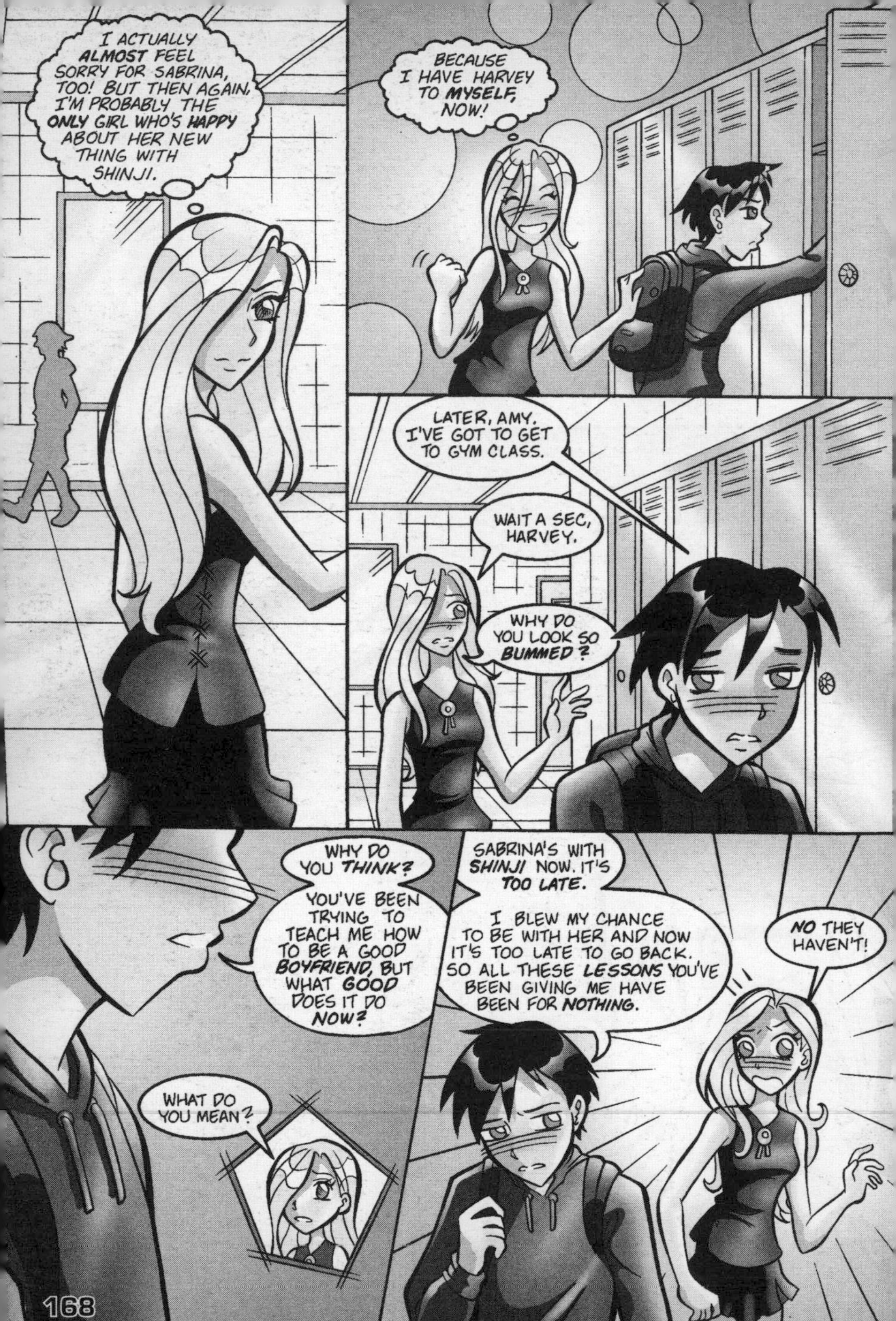
I ACTUALLY ALMOST FEEL SORRY FOR SABRINA, TOO! BUT THEN AGAIN, I'M PROBABLY THE ONLY GIRL WHO'S HAPPY ABOUT HER NEW THING WITH SHINJI.
BECAUSE I HAVE HARVEY TO MYSELF, NOW!
LATER, AMY. I'VE GOT TO GET TO GYM CLASS.
WAIT A SEC, HARVEY.
WHY DO YOU LOOK SO BUMMED?
WHY DO YOU THINK?
YOU'VE BEEN TRYING TO TEACH ME HOW TO BE A GOOD BOYFRIEND, BUT WHAT GOOD DOES IT DO NOW?
WHAT DO YOU MEAN?
SABRINA'S WITH SHINJI NOW. IT'S TOO LATE.
I BLEW MY CHANCE TO BE WITH HER AND NOW IT'S TOO LATE TO GO BACK. SO ALL THESE LESSONS YOU'VE BEEN GIVING ME HAVE BEEN FOR NOTHING.
NO THEY HAVEN'T!

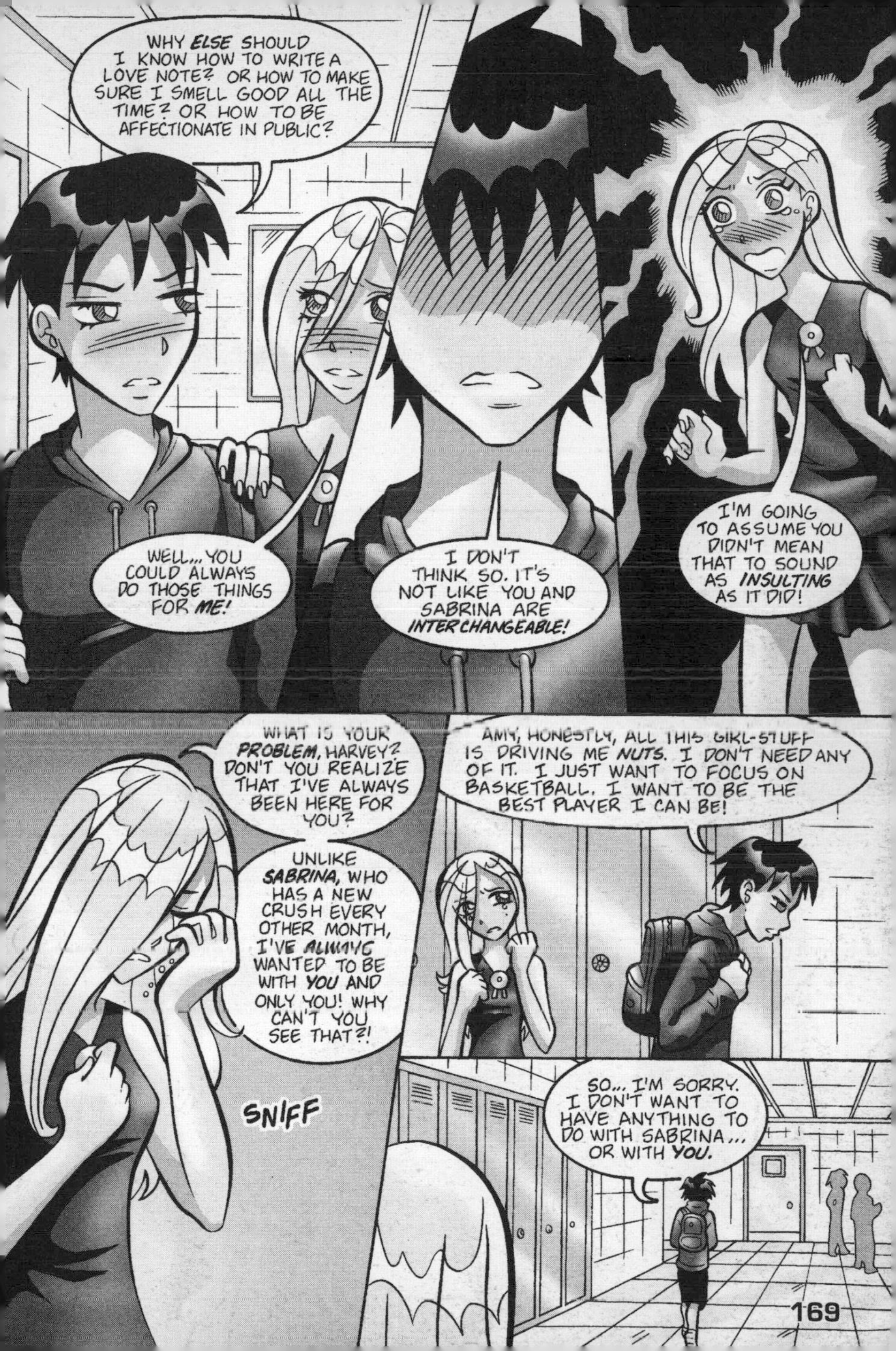
WHY ELSE SHOULD I KNOW HOW TO WRITE A LOVE NOTE? OR HOW TO MAKE SURE I SMELL GOOD ALL THE TIME? OR HOW TO BE AFFECTIONATE IN PUBLIC?
WELL... YOU COULD ALWAYS DO THOSE THINGS FOR ME!
I DON'T THINK SO. IT'S NOT LIKE YOU AND SABRINA ARE INTERCHANGEABLE!
I'M GOING TO ASSUME YOU DIDN'T MEAN THAT TO SOUND AS INSULTING AS IT DID!
WHAT IS YOUR PROBLEM, HARVEY? DON'T YOU REALIZE THAT I'VE ALWAYS BEEN HERE FOR YOU?
UNLIKE SABRINA, WHO HAS A NEW CRUSH EVERY OTHER MONTH, I'VE ALWAYS WANTED TO BE WITH YOU AND ONLY YOU! WHY CAN'T YOU SEE THAT?!
SNIFF
AMY, HONESTLY, ALL THIS GIRL-STUFF IS DRIVING ME NUTS. I DON'T NEED ANY OF IT. I JUST WANT TO FOCUS ON BASKETBALL. I WANT TO BE THE BEST PLAYER I CAN BE!
SO... I'M SORRY. I DON'T WANT TO HAVE ANYTHING TO DO WITH SABRINA... OR WITH YOU.

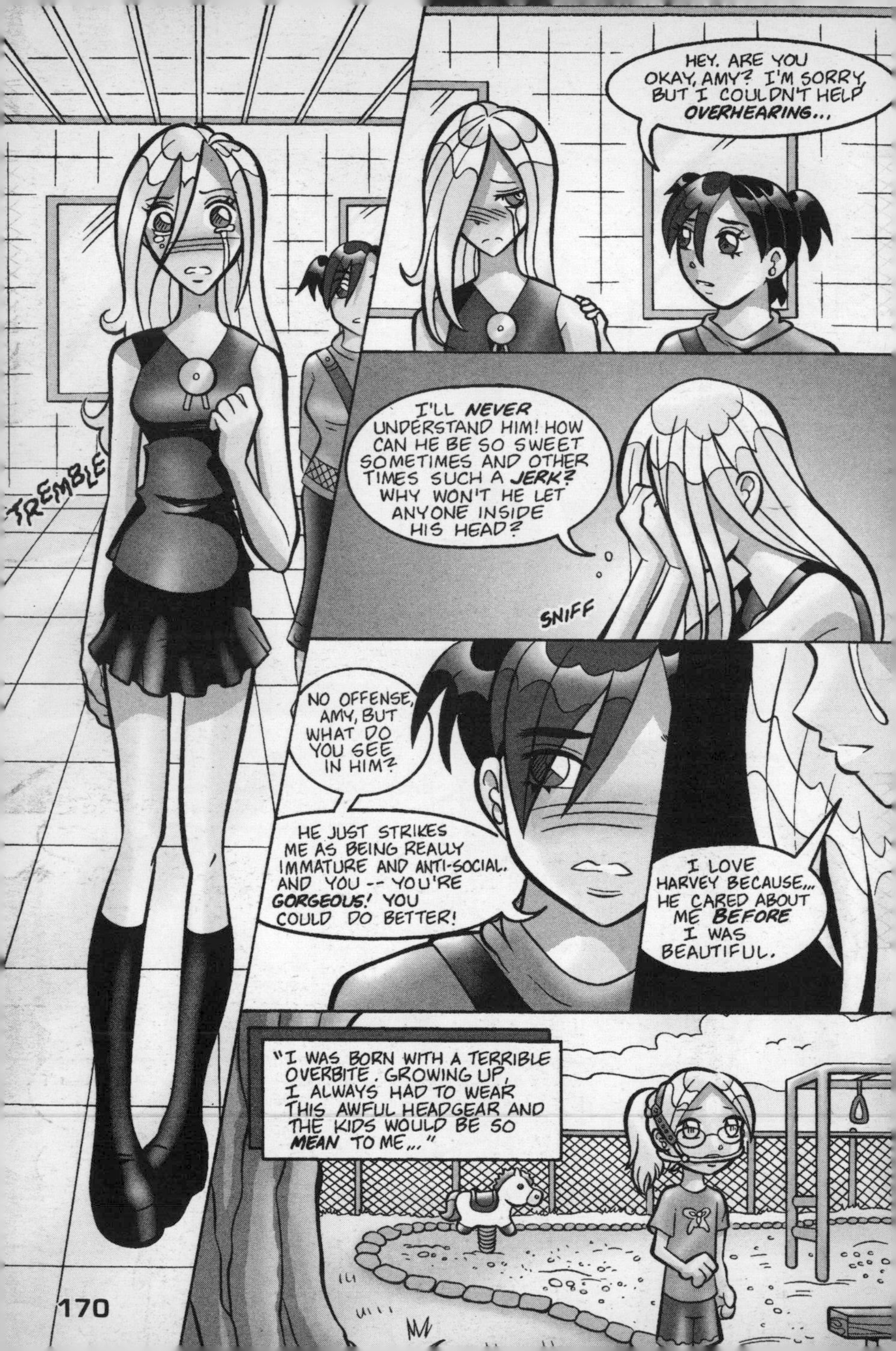
TREMBLE
HEY. ARE YOU OKAY, AMY? I'M SORRY, BUT I COULDN'T HELP **OVERHEARING...**
I'LL **NEVER** UNDERSTAND HIM! HOW CAN HE BE SO SWEET SOMETIMES AND OTHER TIMES SUCH A **JERK?** WHY WON'T HE LET ANYONE INSIDE HIS HEAD?
SNIFF
NO OFFENSE, AMY, BUT WHAT DO YOU SEE IN HIM?
HE JUST STRIKES ME AS BEING REALLY IMMATURE AND ANTI-SOCIAL. AND YOU -- YOU'RE **GORGEOUS!** YOU COULD DO BETTER!
I LOVE HARVEY BECAUSE... HE CARED ABOUT ME **BEFORE** I WAS BEAUTIFUL.
"I WAS BORN WITH A TERRIBLE OVERBITE. GROWING UP, I ALWAYS HAD TO WEAR THIS AWFUL HEADGEAR AND THE KIDS WOULD BE SO **MEAN** TO ME..."

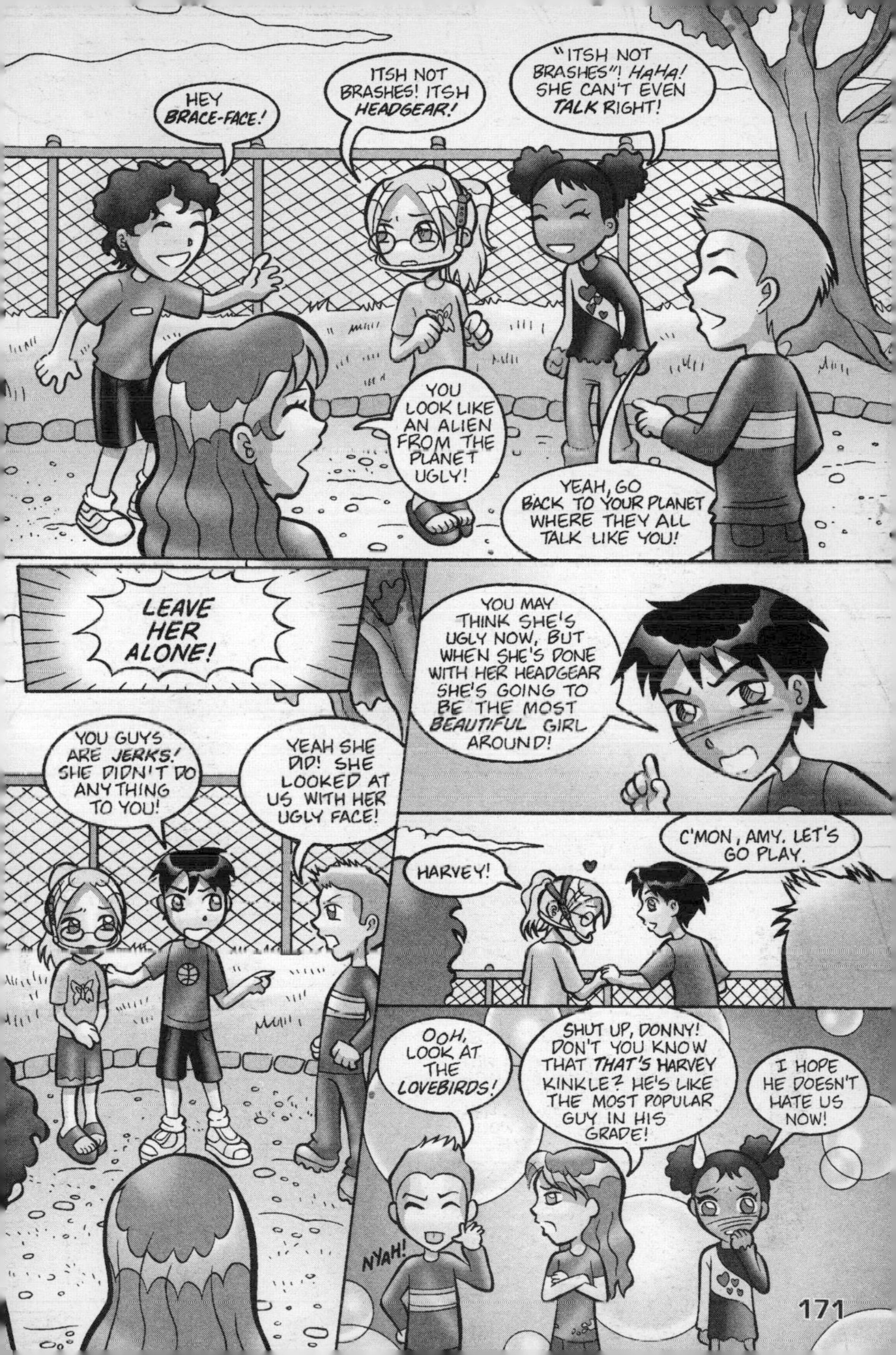
HEY BRACE-FACE!
ITSH NOT BRASHES! ITSH HEADGEAR!
"ITSH NOT BRASHES"! HaHa! SHE CAN'T EVEN TALK RIGHT!
YOU LOOK LIKE AN ALIEN FROM THE PLANET UGLY!
YEAH, GO BACK TO YOUR PLANET WHERE THEY ALL TALK LIKE YOU!
LEAVE HER ALONE!
YOU GUYS ARE JERKS! SHE DIDN'T DO ANYTHING TO YOU!
YEAH SHE DID! SHE LOOKED AT US WITH HER UGLY FACE!
YOU MAY THINK SHE'S UGLY NOW, BUT WHEN SHE'S DONE WITH HER HEADGEAR SHE'S GOING TO BE THE MOST BEAUTIFUL GIRL AROUND!
HARVEY!
C'MON, AMY. LET'S GO PLAY.
OOH, LOOK AT THE LOVEBIRDS!
NYAH!
SHUT UP, DONNY! DON'T YOU KNOW THAT THAT'S HARVEY KINKLE? HE'S LIKE THE MOST POPULAR GUY IN HIS GRADE!
I HOPE HE DOESN'T HATE US NOW!

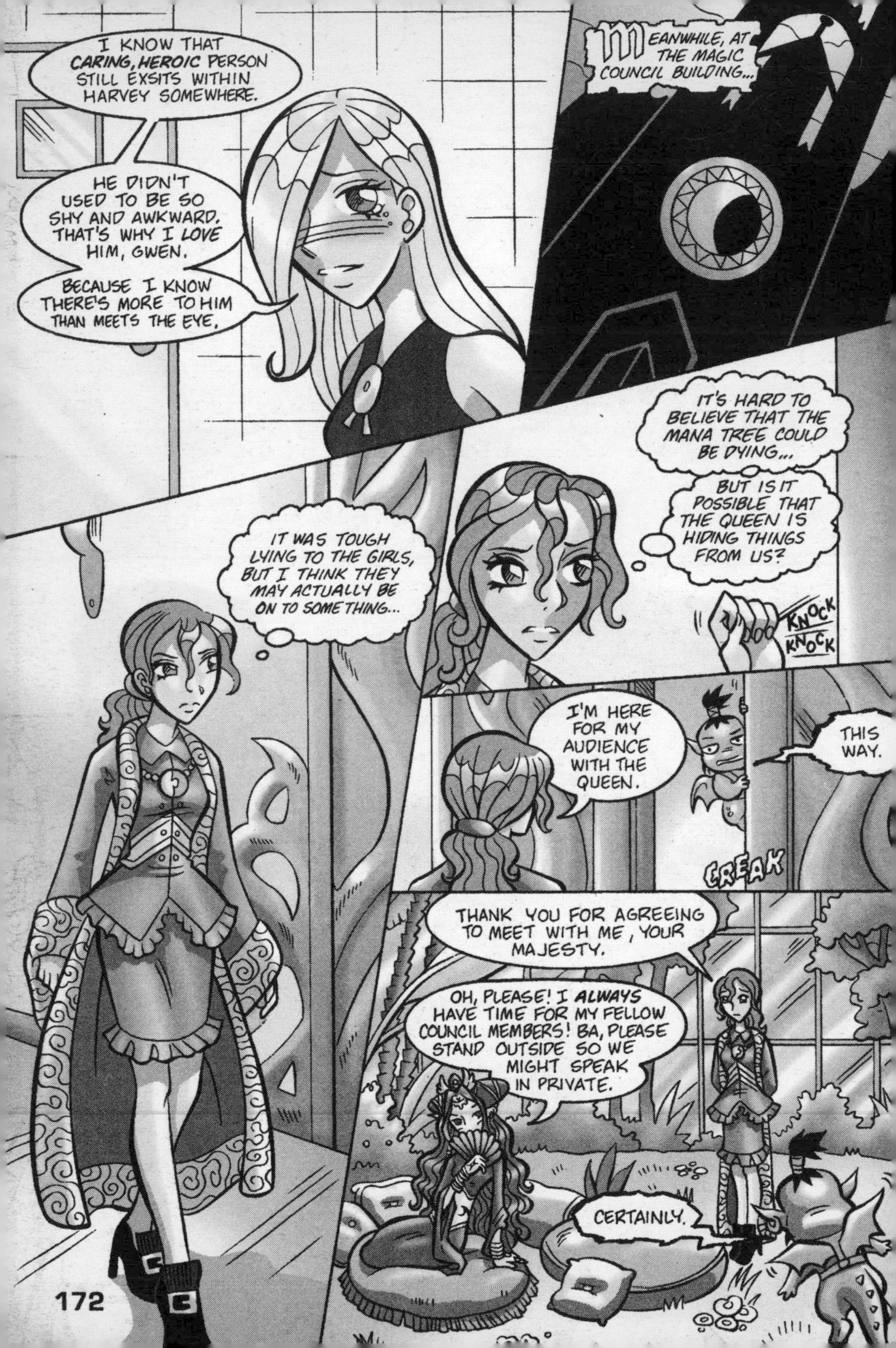
I KNOW THAT CARING, HEROIC PERSON STILL EXSITS WITHIN HARVEY SOMEWHERE.
HE DIDN'T USED TO BE SO SHY AND AWKWARD. THAT'S WHY I LOVE HIM, GWEN.
BECAUSE I KNOW THERE'S MORE TO HIM THAN MEETS THE EYE.
MEANWHILE, AT THE MAGIC COUNCIL BUILDING...
IT WAS TOUGH LYING TO THE GIRLS, BUT I THINK THEY MAY ACTUALLY BE ON TO SOMETHING...
IT'S HARD TO BELIEVE THAT THE MANA TREE COULD BE DYING...
BUT IS IT POSSIBLE THAT THE QUEEN IS HIDING THINGS FROM US?
KNOCK KNOCK
I'M HERE FOR MY AUDIENCE WITH THE QUEEN.
THIS WAY.
CREAK
THANK YOU FOR AGREEING TO MEET WITH ME, YOUR MAJESTY.
OH, PLEASE! I ALWAYS HAVE TIME FOR MY FELLOW COUNCIL MEMBERS! BA, PLEASE STAND OUTSIDE SO WE MIGHT SPEAK IN PRIVATE.
CERTAINLY.

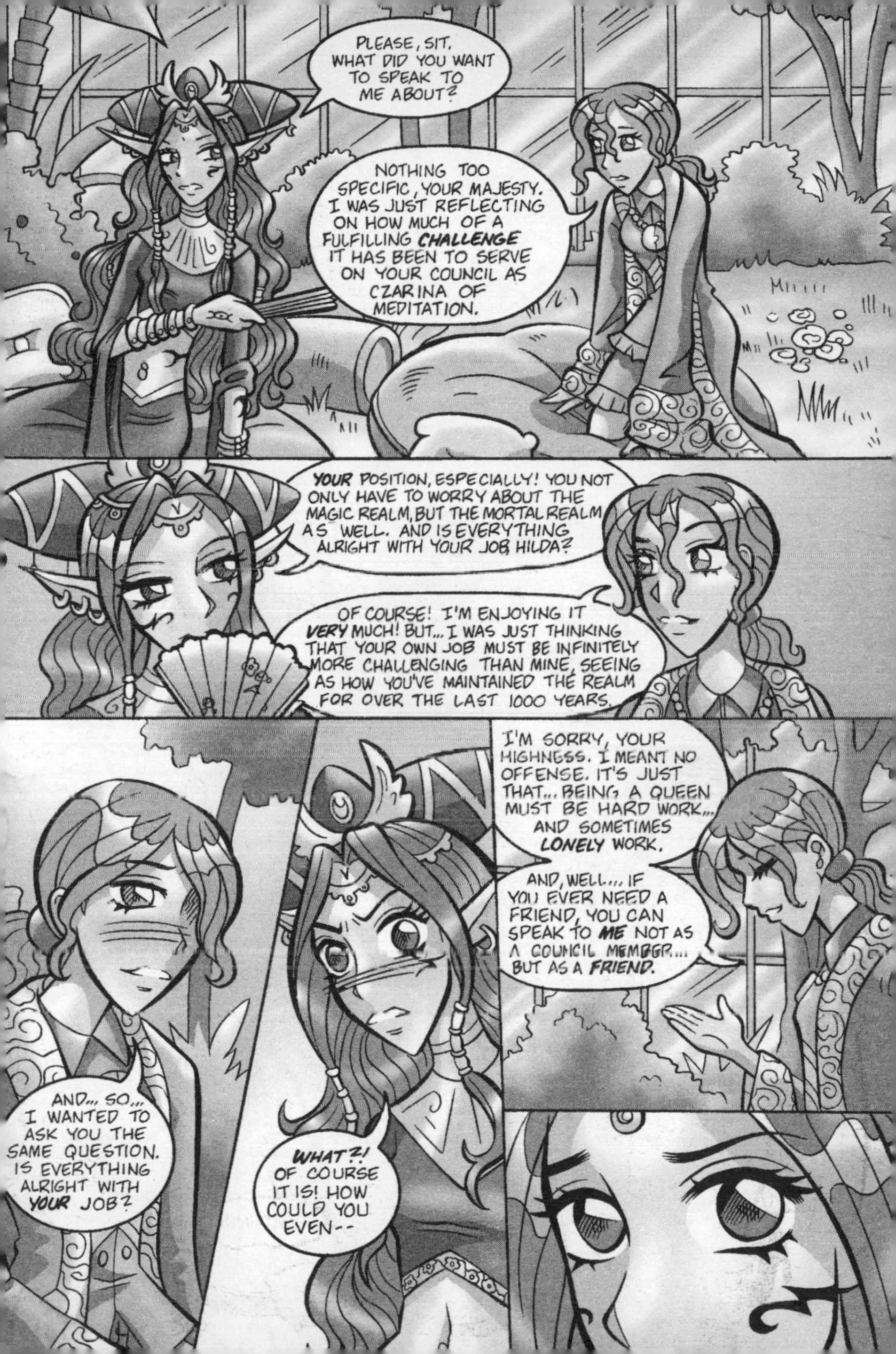
PLEASE, SIT. WHAT DID YOU WANT TO SPEAK TO ME ABOUT?
NOTHING TOO SPECIFIC, YOUR MAJESTY. I WAS JUST REFLECTING ON HOW MUCH OF A FULFILLING **CHALLENGE** IT HAS BEEN TO SERVE ON YOUR COUNCIL AS CZARINA OF MEDITATION.
YOUR POSITION, ESPECIALLY! YOU NOT ONLY HAVE TO WORRY ABOUT THE MAGIC REALM, BUT THE MORTAL REALM AS WELL. AND IS EVERYTHING ALRIGHT WITH YOUR JOB, HILDA?
OF COURSE! I'M ENJOYING IT **VERY** MUCH! BUT... I WAS JUST THINKING THAT YOUR OWN JOB MUST BE INFINITELY MORE CHALLENGING THAN MINE, SEEING AS HOW YOU'VE MAINTAINED THE REALM FOR OVER THE LAST 1000 YEARS.
AND... SO... I WANTED TO ASK YOU THE SAME QUESTION. IS EVERYTHING ALRIGHT WITH **YOUR** JOB?
WHAT?! OF COURSE IT IS! HOW COULD YOU EVEN--
I'M SORRY, YOUR HIGHNESS. I MEANT NO OFFENSE. IT'S JUST THAT... BEING A QUEEN MUST BE HARD WORK... AND SOMETIMES **LONELY** WORK.
AND, WELL... IF YOU EVER NEED A FRIEND, YOU CAN SPEAK TO **ME** NOT AS A COUNCIL MEMBER... BUT AS A **FRIEND**.

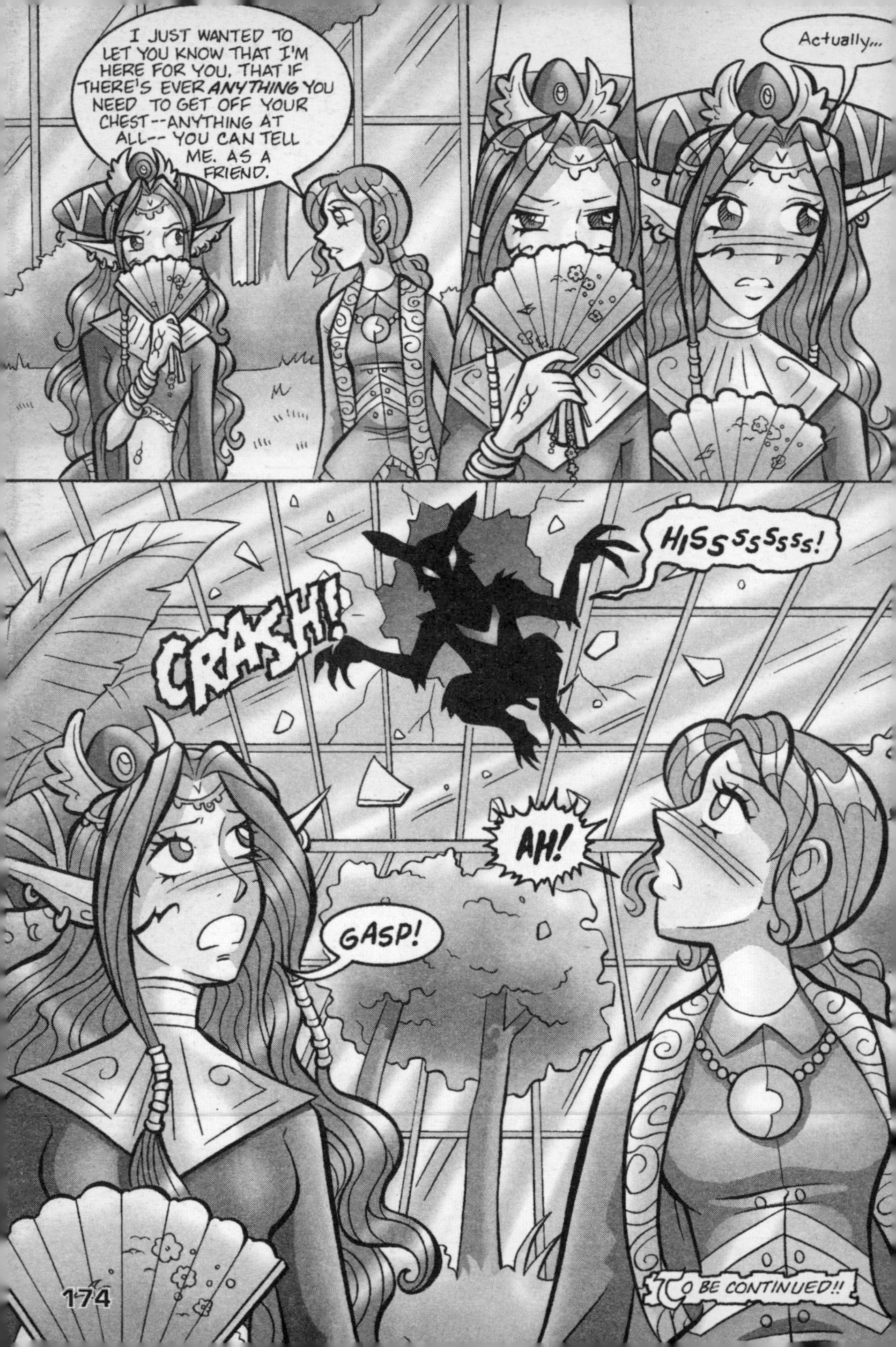
I JUST WANTED TO LET YOU KNOW THAT I'M HERE FOR YOU. THAT IF THERE'S EVER *ANYTHING* YOU NEED TO GET OFF YOUR CHEST--ANYTHING AT ALL-- YOU CAN TELL ME. AS A FRIEND.
Actually...
CRASH!
HISSSSSSSS!
AH!
GASP!
TO BE CONTINUED!!

Chapter 9

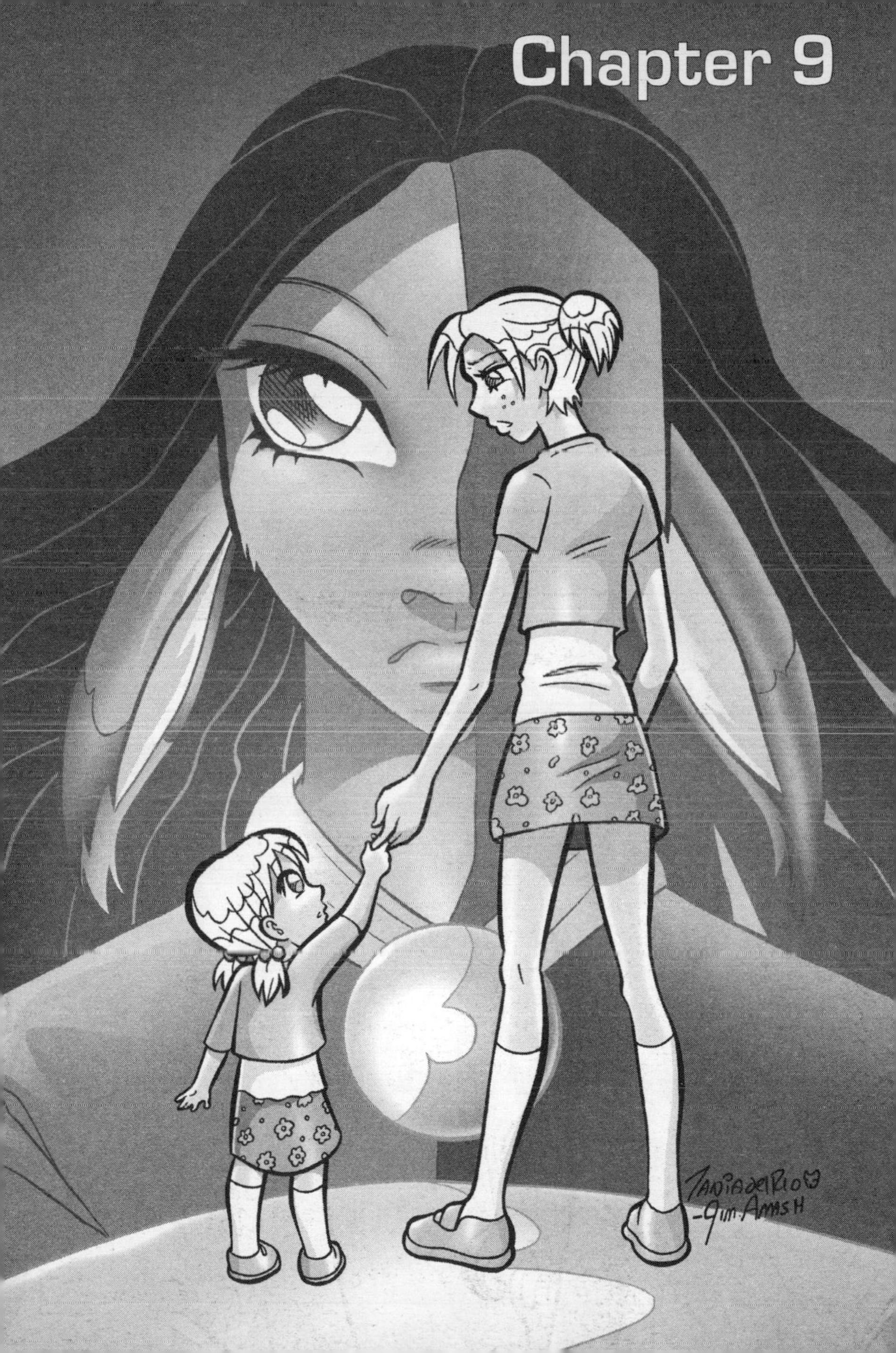

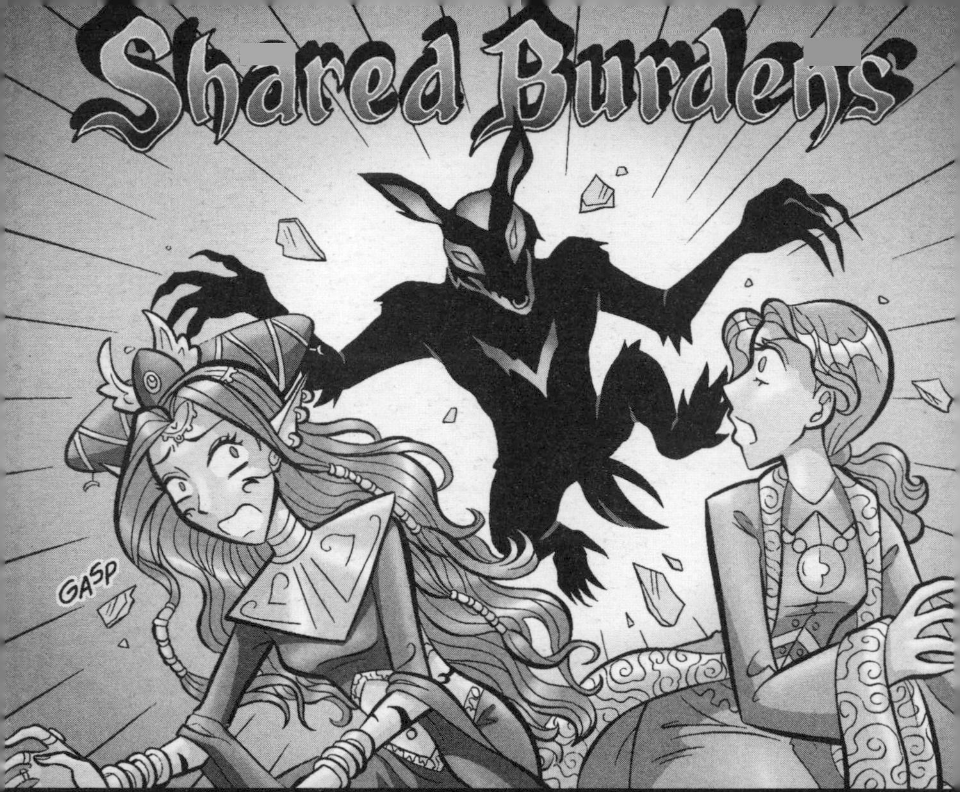
Shared Burdens
GASP

Writes and Pencils: Tania Del Rio Inks: Jim Amash Letters: Teresa Davidson Colors: Jason Jensen
Assistant Editor: Mike Pellerito Editor: Victor Gorelick Editor-In-Chief: Richard Goldwater

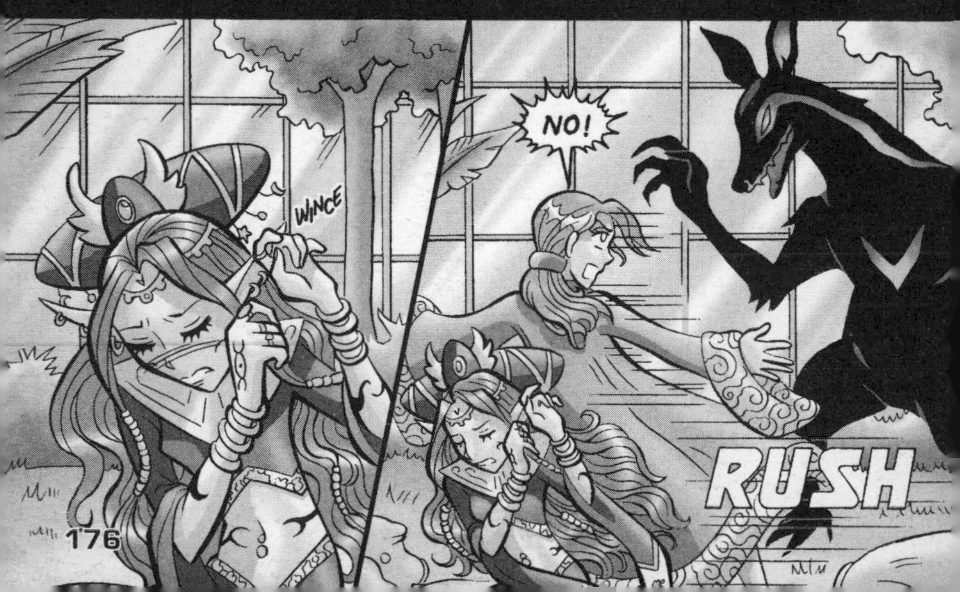
WINCE
NO!
RUSH

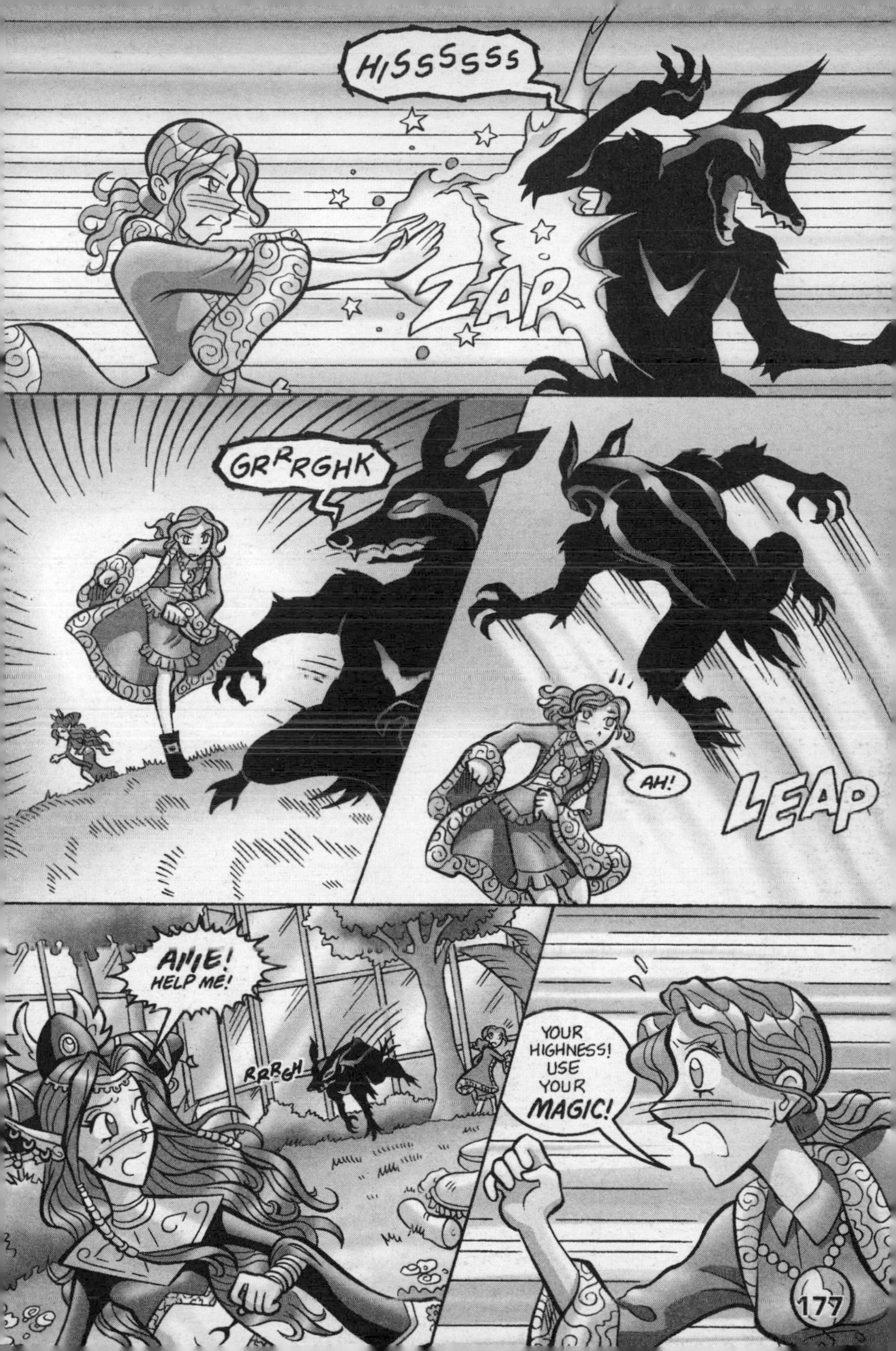
HISSSSSS
ZAP
GRRRGHK
AH!
LEAP
AIIIE! HELP ME!
RRRGH
YOUR HIGHNESS! USE YOUR MAGIC!

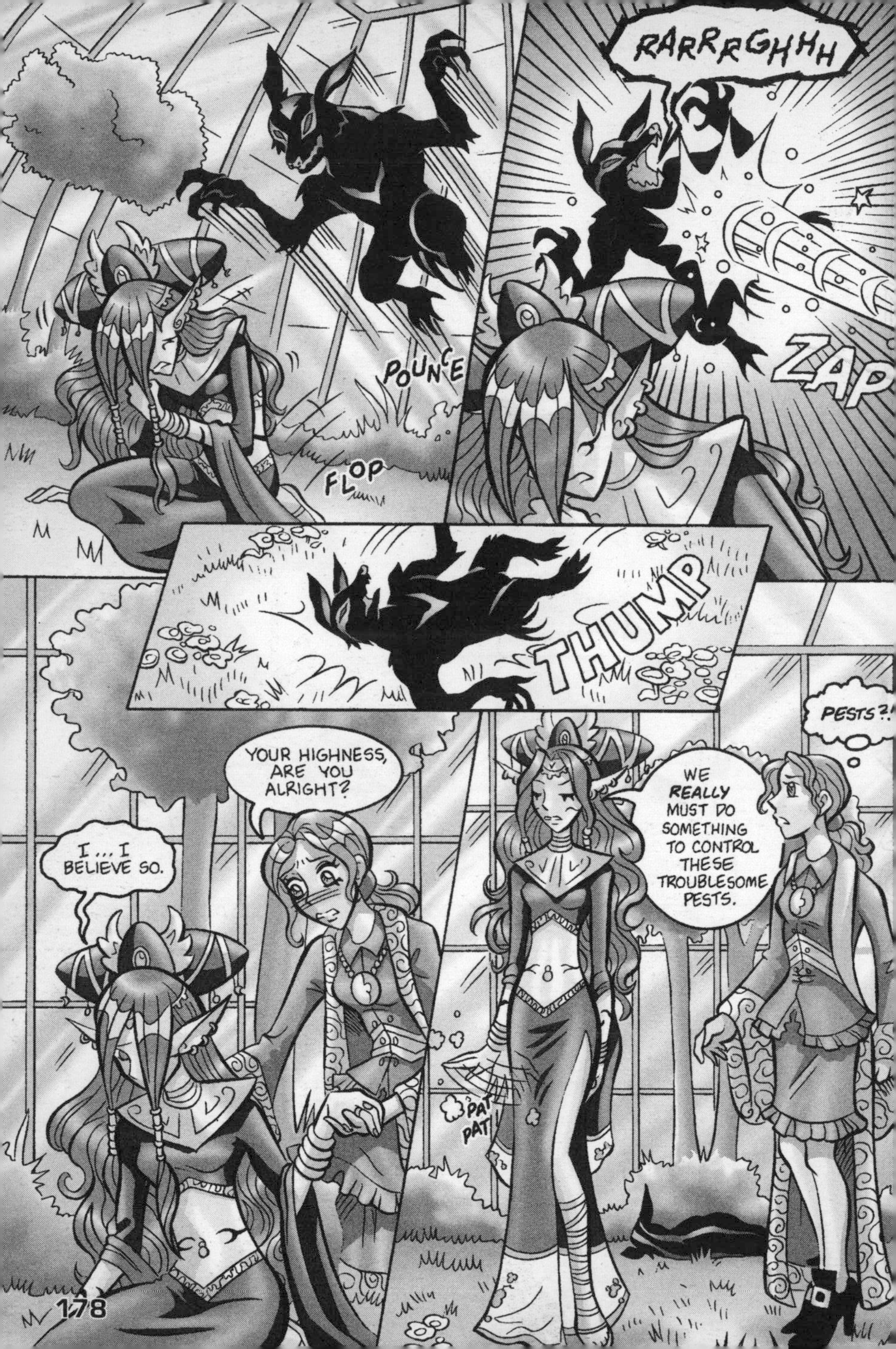

POUNCE
FLOP
RARRRRGHHHH
ZAP
THUMP
I... I BELIEVE SO.
YOUR HIGHNESS, ARE YOU ALRIGHT?
PAT PAT
WE REALLY MUST DO SOMETHING TO CONTROL THESE TROUBLESOME PESTS.
PESTS?!

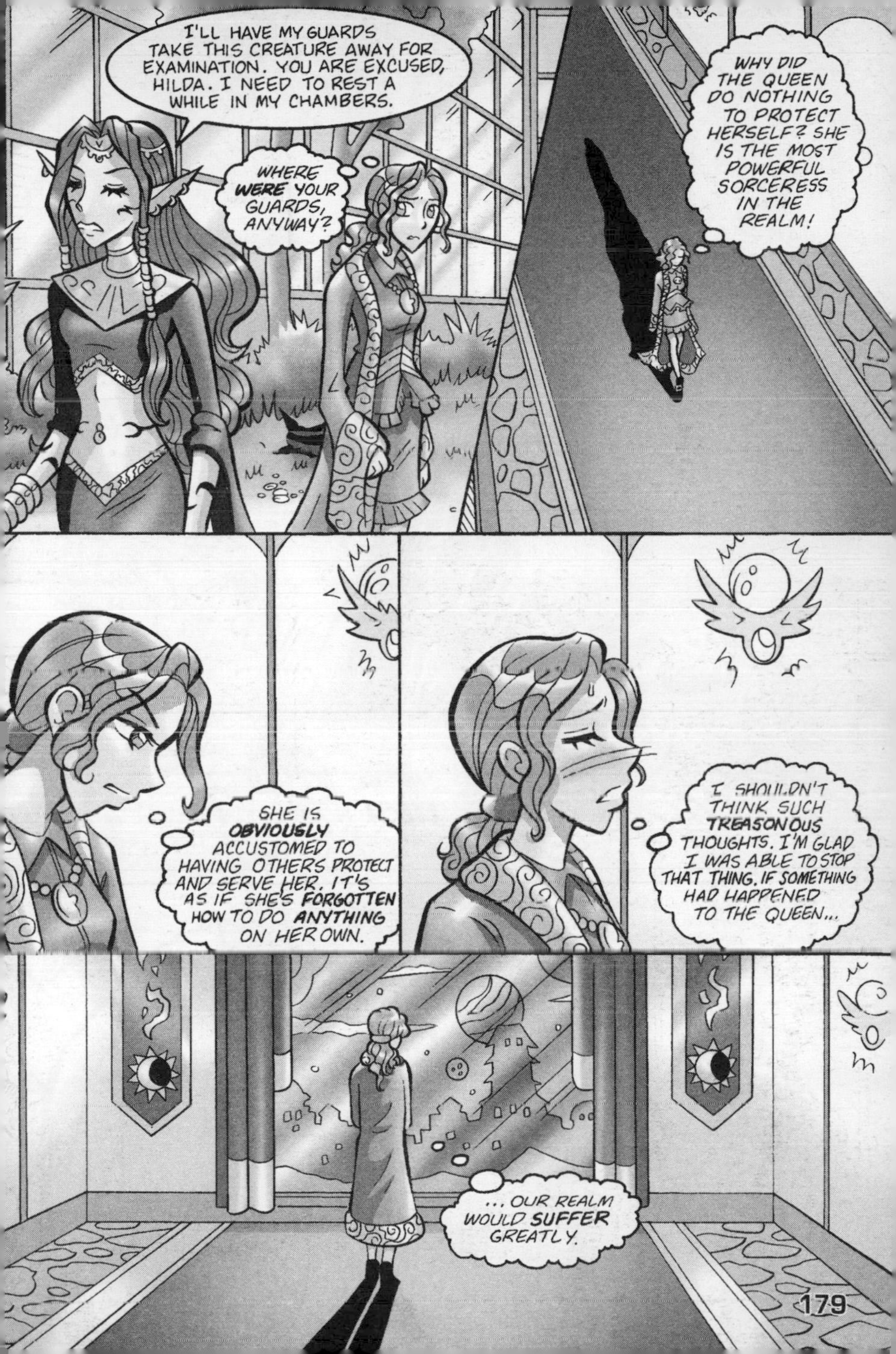
I'LL HAVE MY GUARDS TAKE THIS CREATURE AWAY FOR EXAMINATION. YOU ARE EXCUSED, HILDA. I NEED TO REST A WHILE IN MY CHAMBERS.
WHERE **WERE** YOUR GUARDS, ANYWAY?
WHY DID THE QUEEN DO NOTHING TO PROTECT HERSELF? SHE IS THE MOST POWERFUL SORCERESS IN THE REALM!
SHE IS **OBVIOUSLY** ACCUSTOMED TO HAVING OTHERS PROTECT AND SERVE HER. IT'S AS IF SHE'S **FORGOTTEN** HOW TO DO **ANYTHING** ON HER OWN.
I SHOULDN'T THINK SUCH **TREASONOUS** THOUGHTS. I'M GLAD I WAS ABLE TO STOP THAT THING. IF SOMETHING HAD HAPPENED TO THE QUEEN...
...OUR REALM WOULD **SUFFER** GREATLY.

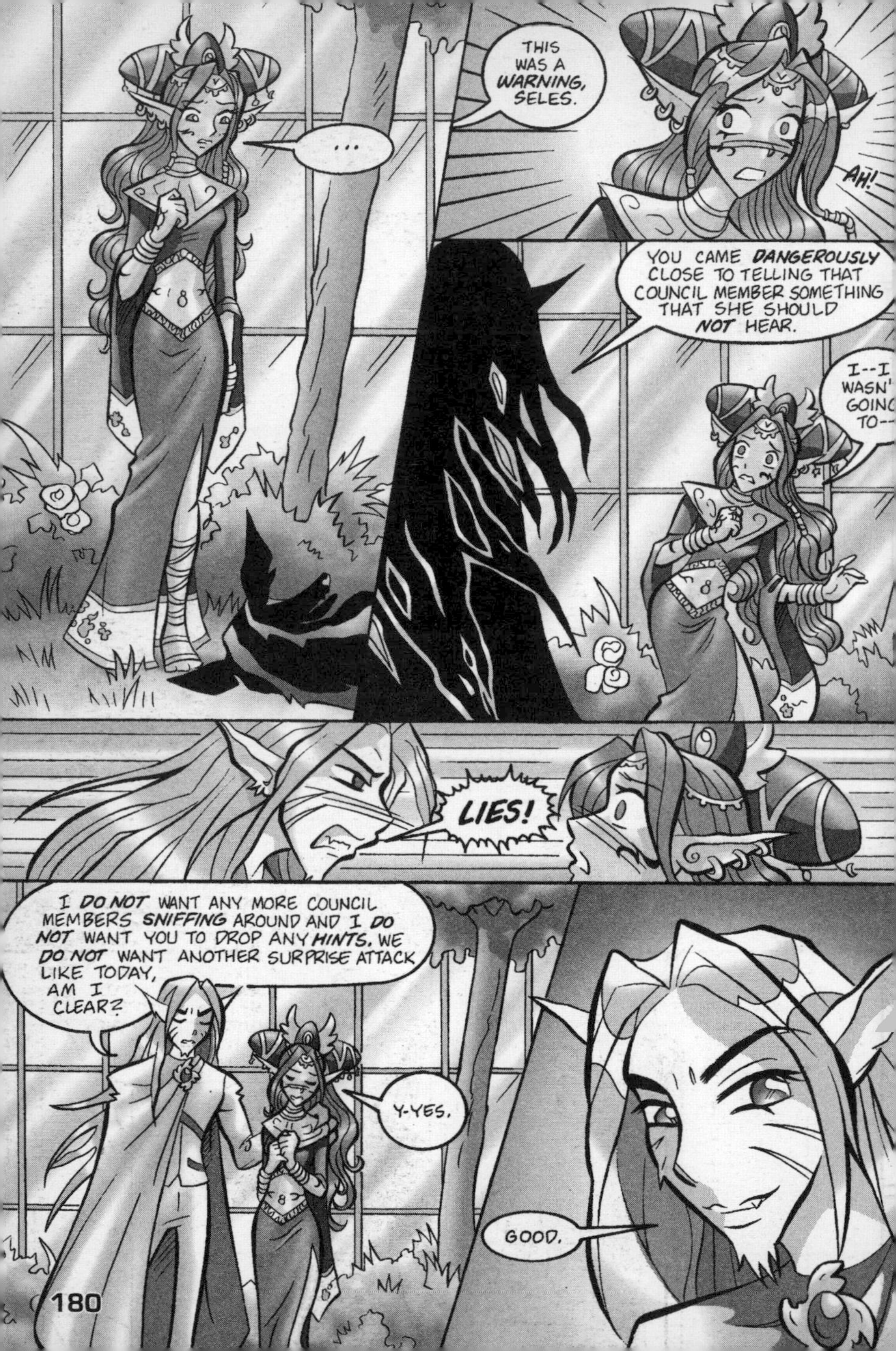

...
THIS WAS A WARNING, SELES.
AH!
YOU CAME DANGEROUSLY CLOSE TO TELLING THAT COUNCIL MEMBER SOMETHING THAT SHE SHOULD NOT HEAR.
I--I WASN'T GOING TO--
LIES!
I DO NOT WANT ANY MORE COUNCIL MEMBERS SNIFFING AROUND AND I DO NOT WANT YOU TO DROP ANY HINTS. WE DO NOT WANT ANOTHER SURPRISE ATTACK LIKE TODAY, AM I CLEAR?
Y-YES.
GOOD.

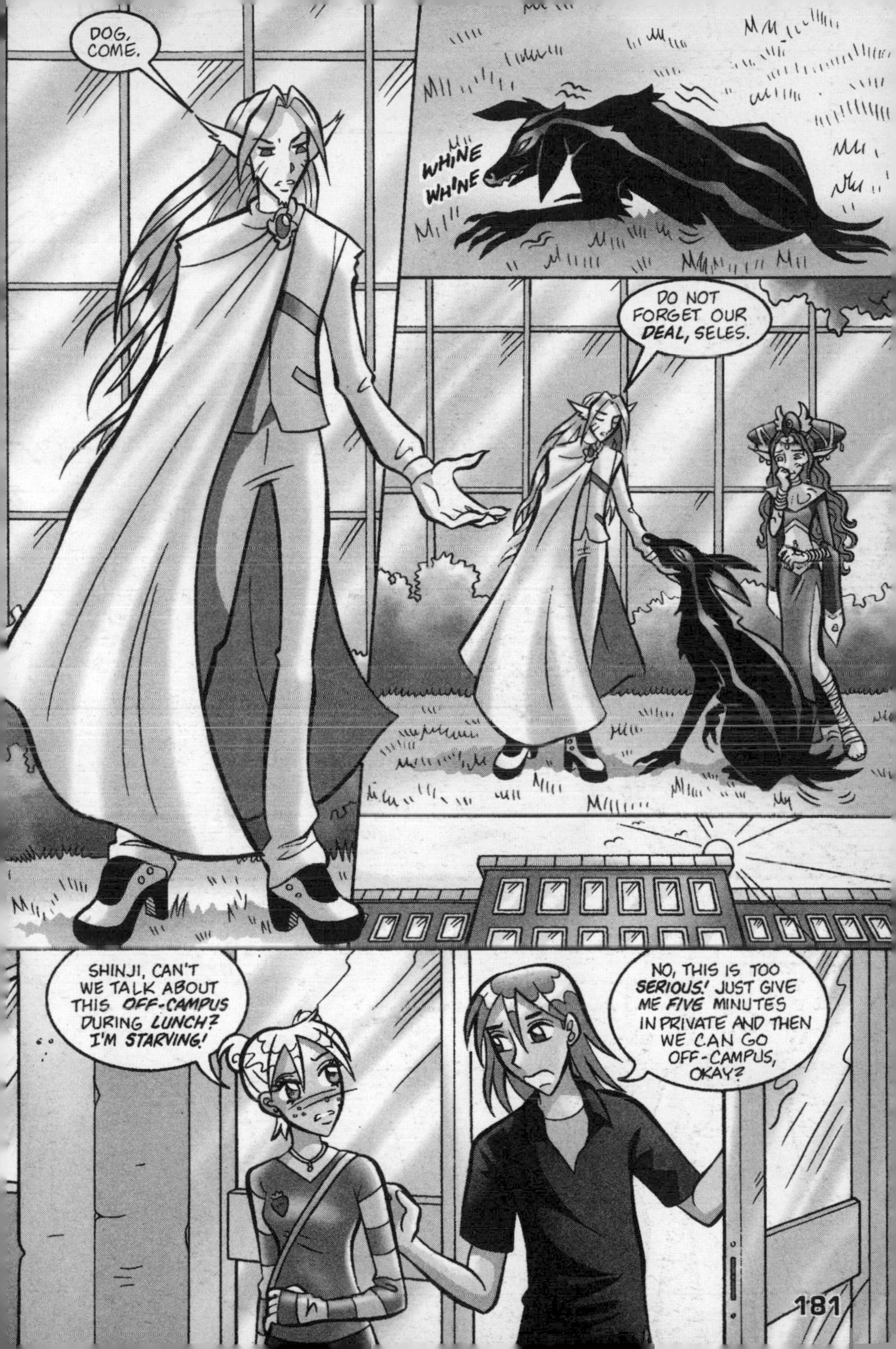
DOG, COME.
WHINE WHINE
DO NOT FORGET OUR DEAL, SELES.
SHINJI, CAN'T WE TALK ABOUT THIS OFF-CAMPUS DURING LUNCH? I'M STARVING!
NO, THIS IS TOO SERIOUS! JUST GIVE ME FIVE MINUTES IN PRIVATE AND THEN WE CAN GO OFF-CAMPUS, OKAY?

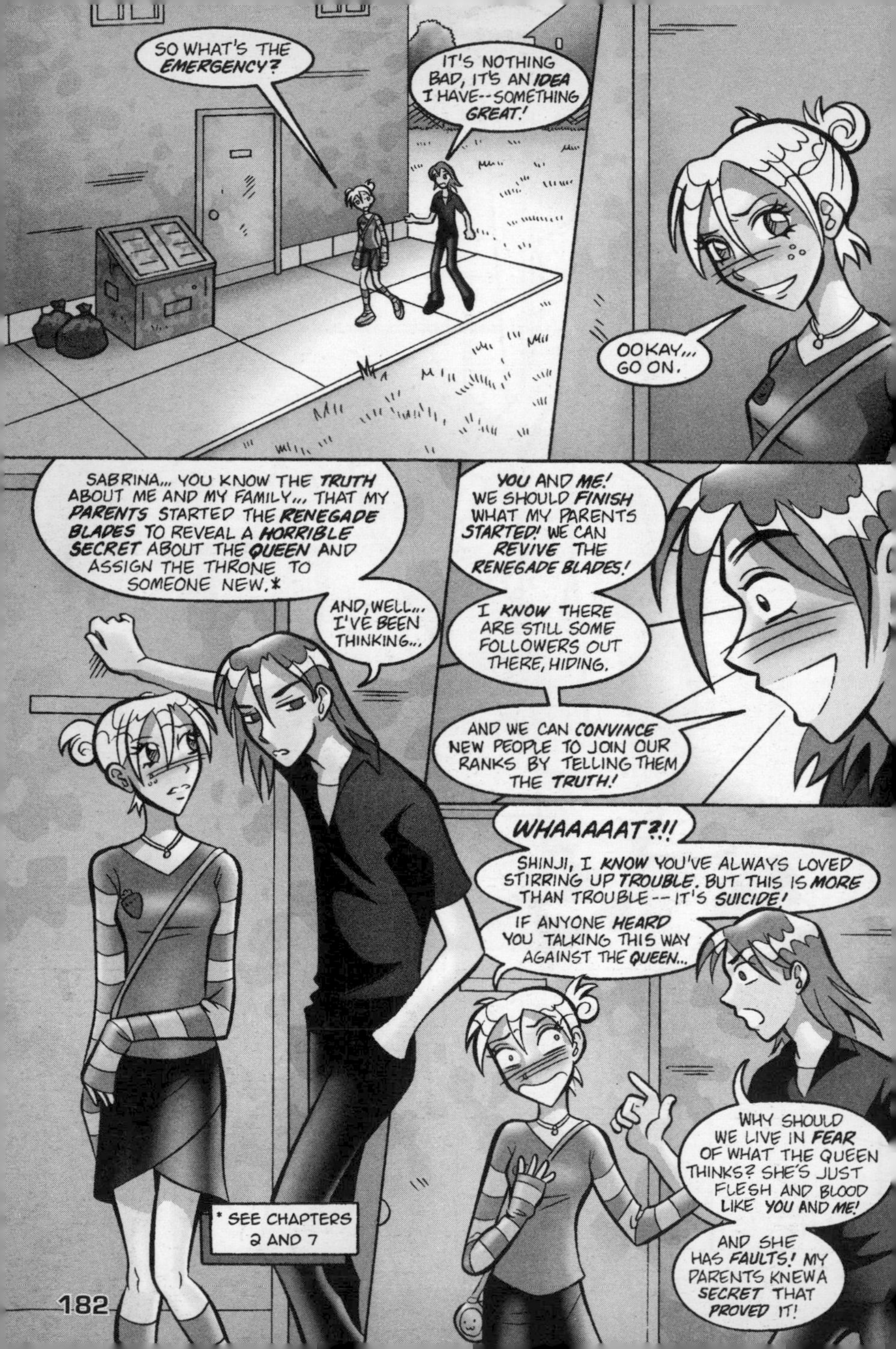

SO WHAT'S THE EMERGENCY?
IT'S NOTHING BAD, IT'S AN IDEA I HAVE--SOMETHING GREAT!
OOKAY... GO ON.
SABRINA... YOU KNOW THE TRUTH ABOUT ME AND MY FAMILY... THAT MY PARENTS STARTED THE RENEGADE BLADES TO REVEAL A HORRIBLE SECRET ABOUT THE QUEEN AND ASSIGN THE THRONE TO SOMEONE NEW.*
AND, WELL... I'VE BEEN THINKING...
* SEE CHAPTERS 2 AND 7
YOU AND ME! WE SHOULD FINISH WHAT MY PARENTS STARTED! WE CAN REVIVE THE RENEGADE BLADES!
I KNOW THERE ARE STILL SOME FOLLOWERS OUT THERE, HIDING.
AND WE CAN CONVINCE NEW PEOPLE TO JOIN OUR RANKS BY TELLING THEM THE TRUTH!
WHAAAAAT?!!
SHINJI, I KNOW YOU'VE ALWAYS LOVED STIRRING UP TROUBLE. BUT THIS IS MORE THAN TROUBLE -- IT'S SUICIDE!
IF ANYONE HEARD YOU TALKING THIS WAY AGAINST THE QUEEN...
WHY SHOULD WE LIVE IN FEAR OF WHAT THE QUEEN THINKS? SHE'S JUST FLESH AND BLOOD LIKE YOU AND ME!
AND SHE HAS FAULTS! MY PARENTS KNEW A SECRET THAT PROVED IT!

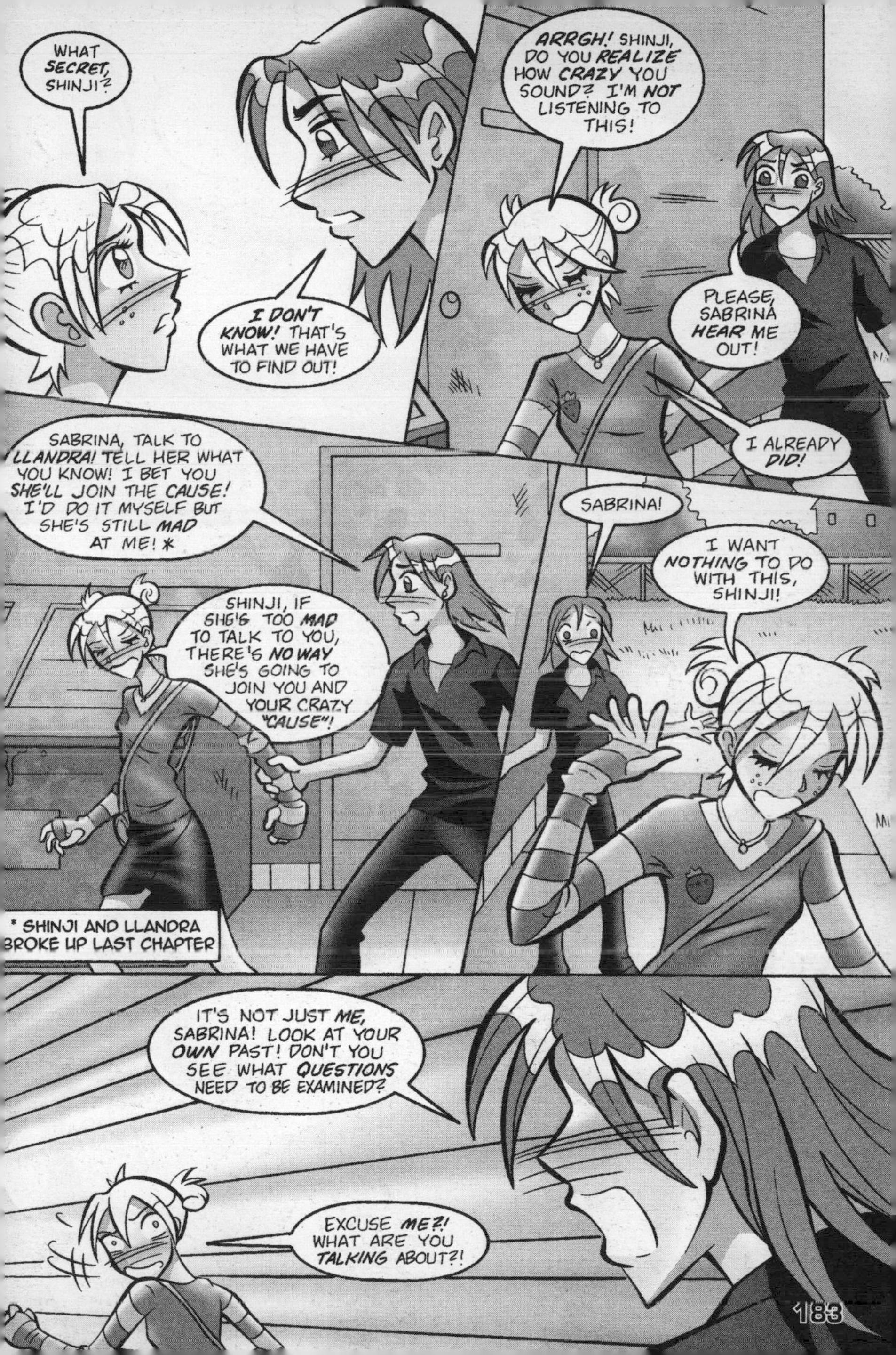

WHAT SECRET, SHINJI?
I DON'T KNOW! THAT'S WHAT WE HAVE TO FIND OUT!
ARRGH! SHINJI, DO YOU REALIZE HOW CRAZY YOU SOUND? I'M NOT LISTENING TO THIS!
PLEASE, SABRINA HEAR ME OUT!
I ALREADY DID!
SABRINA, TALK TO LLANDRA! TELL HER WHAT YOU KNOW! I BET YOU SHE'LL JOIN THE CAUSE! I'D DO IT MYSELF BUT SHE'S STILL MAD AT ME! *
SHINJI, IF SHE'S TOO MAD TO TALK TO YOU, THERE'S NO WAY SHE'S GOING TO JOIN YOU AND YOUR CRAZY "CAUSE"!
* SHINJI AND LLANDRA BROKE UP LAST CHAPTER
SABRINA!
I WANT NOTHING TO DO WITH THIS, SHINJI!
IT'S NOT JUST ME, SABRINA! LOOK AT YOUR OWN PAST! DON'T YOU SEE WHAT QUESTIONS NEED TO BE EXAMINED?
EXCUSE ME?! WHAT ARE YOU TALKING ABOUT?!

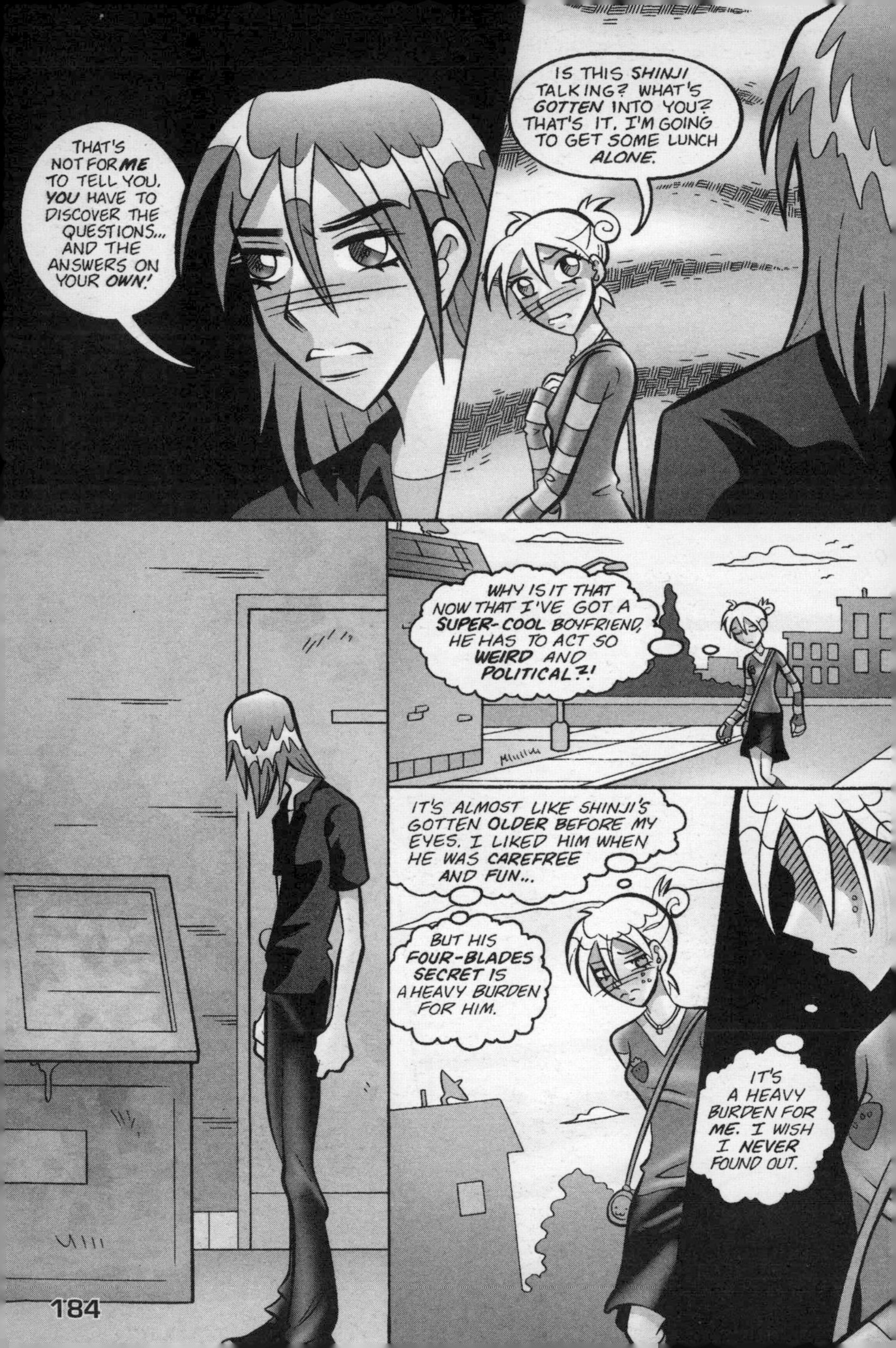
THAT'S NOT FOR ME TO TELL YOU. YOU HAVE TO DISCOVER THE QUESTIONS... AND THE ANSWERS ON YOUR OWN!
IS THIS SHINJI TALKING? WHAT'S GOTTEN INTO YOU? THAT'S IT. I'M GOING TO GET SOME LUNCH ALONE.
WHY IS IT THAT NOW THAT I'VE GOT A SUPER-COOL BOYFRIEND, HE HAS TO ACT SO WEIRD AND POLITICAL?!
IT'S ALMOST LIKE SHINJI'S GOTTEN OLDER BEFORE MY EYES. I LIKED HIM WHEN HE WAS CAREFREE AND FUN...
BUT HIS FOUR-BLADES SECRET IS A HEAVY BURDEN FOR HIM.
IT'S A HEAVY BURDEN FOR ME. I WISH I NEVER FOUND OUT.

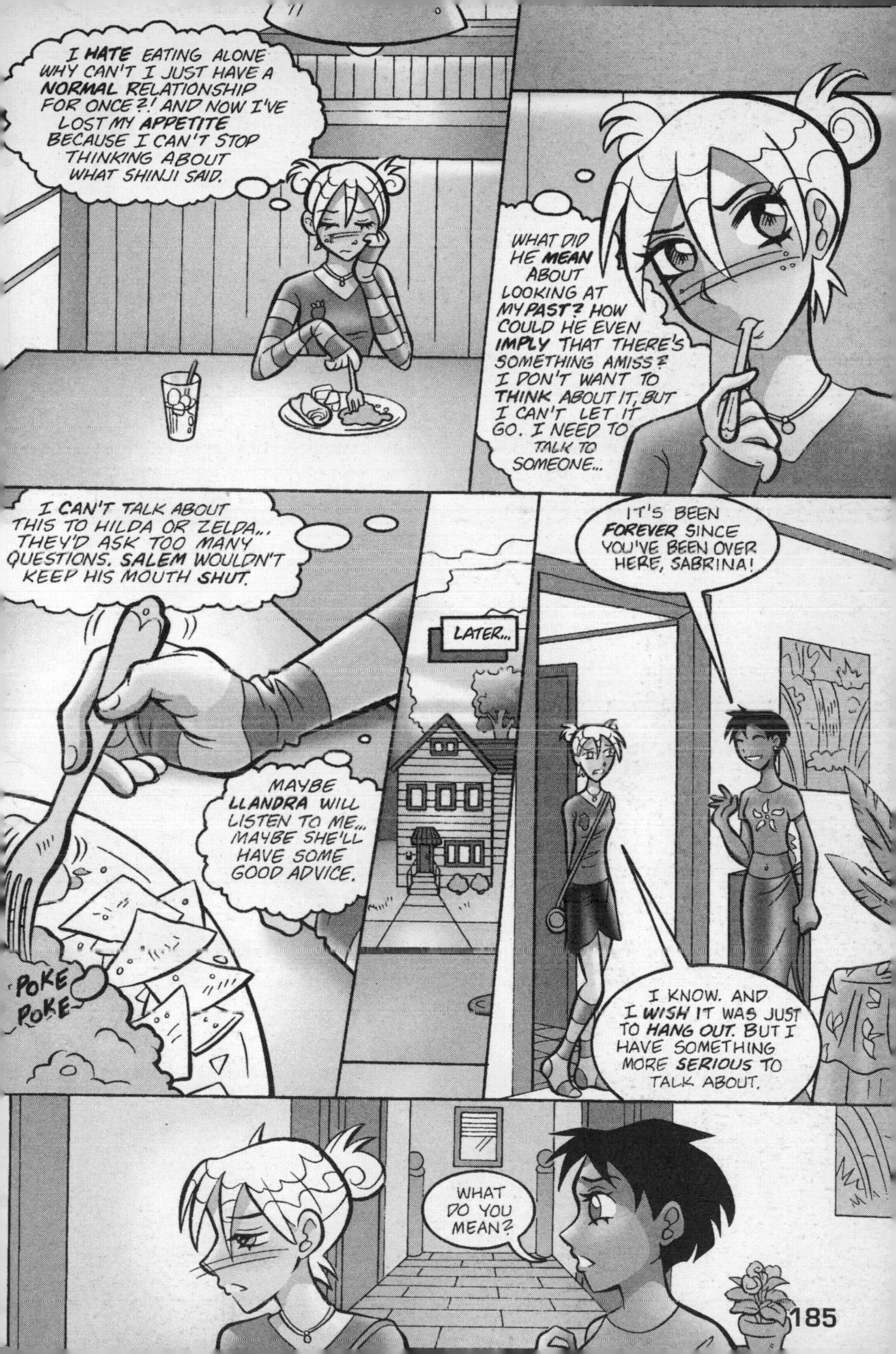
I HATE EATING ALONE WHY CAN'T I JUST HAVE A NORMAL RELATIONSHIP FOR ONCE?! AND NOW I'VE LOST MY APPETITE BECAUSE I CAN'T STOP THINKING ABOUT WHAT SHINJI SAID.
WHAT DID HE MEAN ABOUT LOOKING AT MY PAST? HOW COULD HE EVEN IMPLY THAT THERE'S SOMETHING AMISS? I DON'T WANT TO THINK ABOUT IT, BUT I CAN'T LET IT GO. I NEED TO TALK TO SOMEONE...
I CAN'T TALK ABOUT THIS TO HILDA OR ZELDA... THEY'D ASK TOO MANY QUESTIONS. SALEM WOULDN'T KEEP HIS MOUTH SHUT.
MAYBE LLANDRA WILL LISTEN TO ME... MAYBE SHE'LL HAVE SOME GOOD ADVICE.
POKE POKE
LATER...
IT'S BEEN FOREVER SINCE YOU'VE BEEN OVER HERE, SABRINA!
I KNOW. AND I WISH IT WAS JUST TO HANG OUT. BUT I HAVE SOMETHING MORE SERIOUS TO TALK ABOUT.
WHAT DO YOU MEAN?

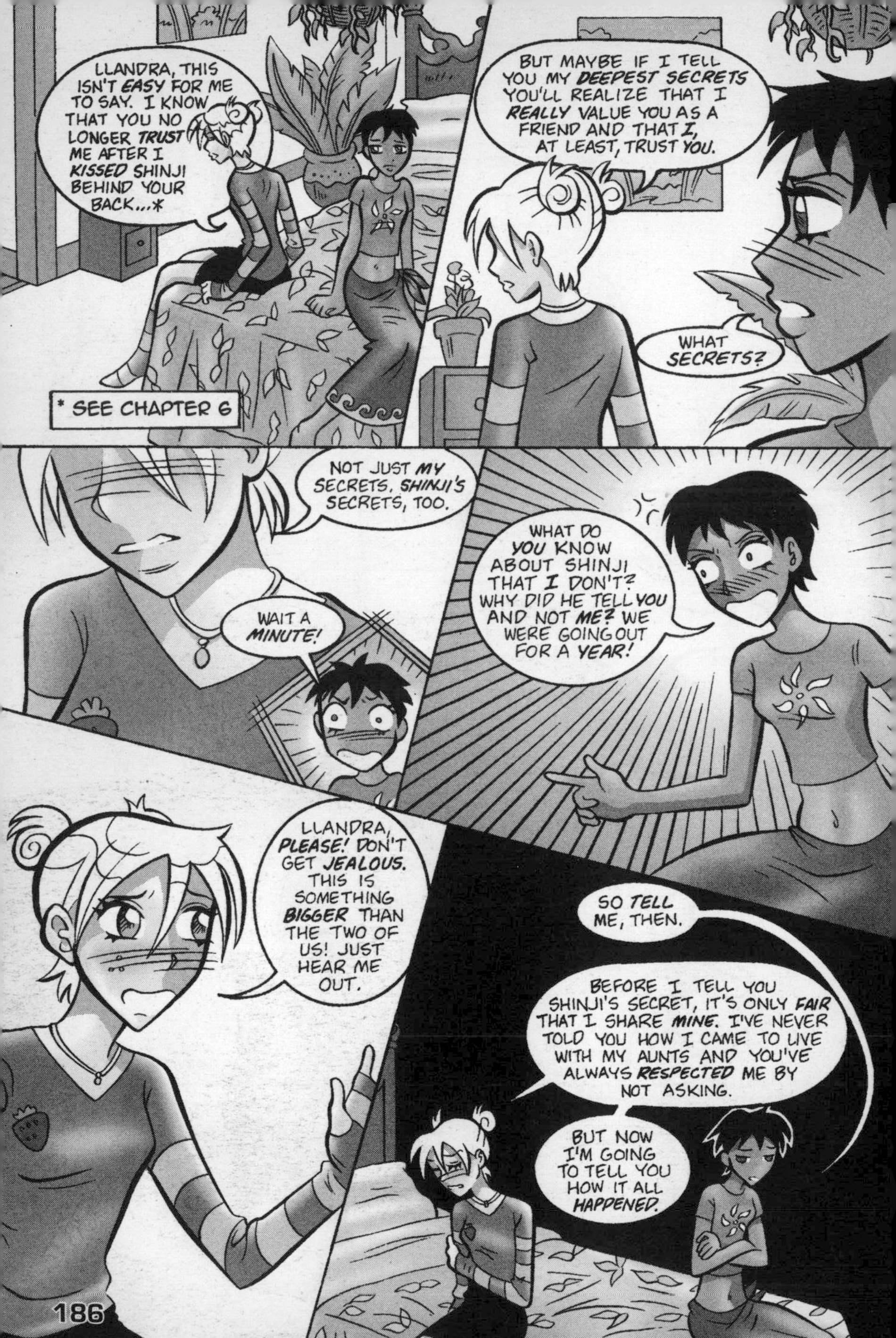
LLANDRA, THIS ISN'T EASY FOR ME TO SAY. I KNOW THAT YOU NO LONGER TRUST ME AFTER I KISSED SHINJI BEHIND YOUR BACK...*
* SEE CHAPTER 6
BUT MAYBE IF I TELL YOU MY DEEPEST SECRETS YOU'LL REALIZE THAT I REALLY VALUE YOU AS A FRIEND AND THAT I, AT LEAST, TRUST YOU.
WHAT SECRETS?
NOT JUST MY SECRETS. SHINJI'S SECRETS, TOO.
WAIT A MINUTE!
WHAT DO YOU KNOW ABOUT SHINJI THAT I DON'T? WHY DID HE TELL YOU AND NOT ME? WE WERE GOING OUT FOR A YEAR!
LLANDRA, PLEASE! DON'T GET JEALOUS. THIS IS SOMETHING BIGGER THAN THE TWO OF US! JUST HEAR ME OUT.
SO TELL ME, THEN.
BEFORE I TELL YOU SHINJI'S SECRET, IT'S ONLY FAIR THAT I SHARE MINE. I'VE NEVER TOLD YOU HOW I CAME TO LIVE WITH MY AUNTS AND YOU'VE ALWAYS RESPECTED ME BY NOT ASKING.
BUT NOW I'M GOING TO TELL YOU HOW IT ALL HAPPENED.

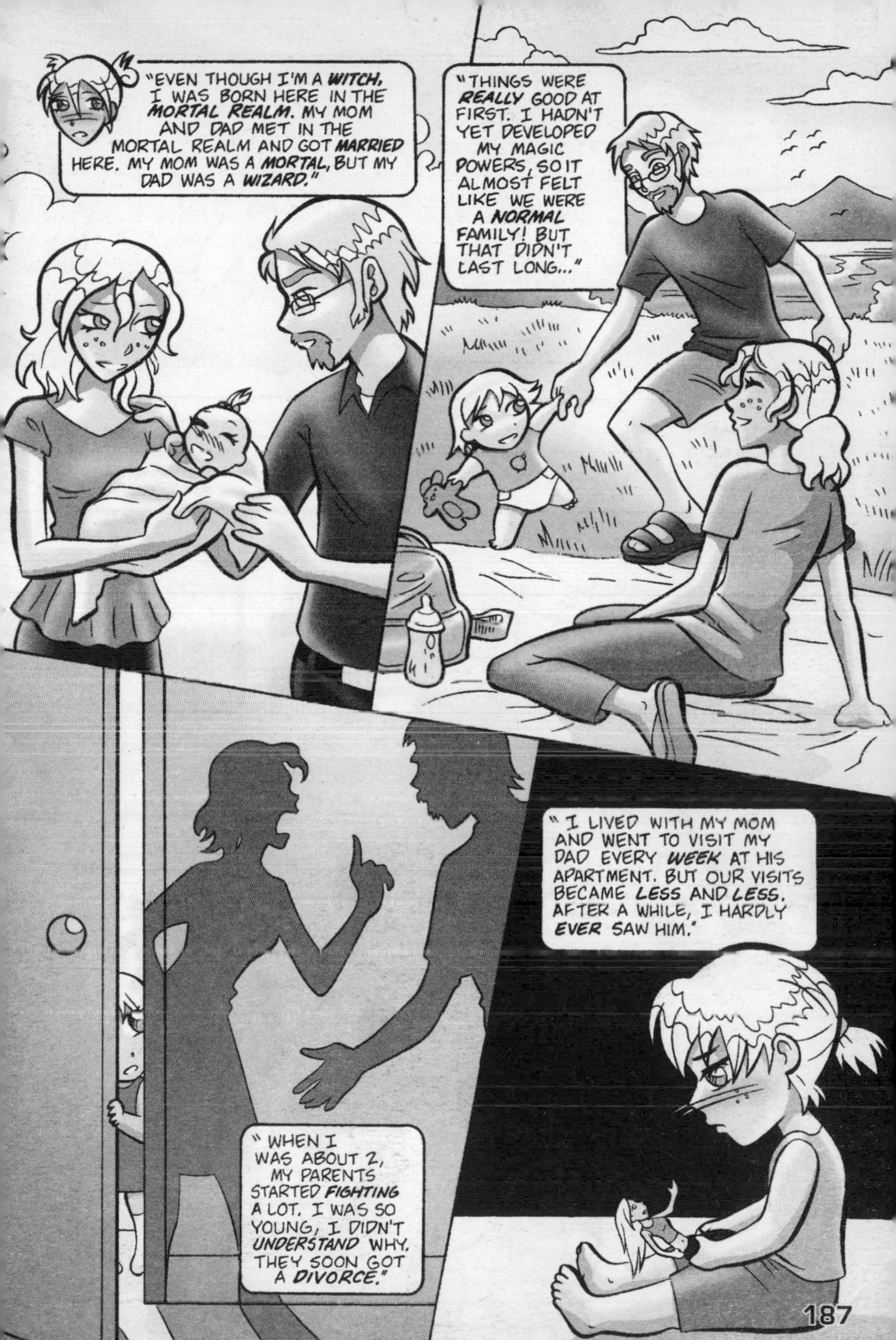

"EVEN THOUGH I'M A WITCH, I WAS BORN HERE IN THE MORTAL REALM. MY MOM AND DAD MET IN THE MORTAL REALM AND GOT MARRIED HERE. MY MOM WAS A MORTAL, BUT MY DAD WAS A WIZARD."
"THINGS WERE REALLY GOOD AT FIRST. I HADN'T YET DEVELOPED MY MAGIC POWERS, SO IT ALMOST FELT LIKE WE WERE A NORMAL FAMILY! BUT THAT DIDN'T LAST LONG..."
"WHEN I WAS ABOUT 2, MY PARENTS STARTED FIGHTING A LOT. I WAS SO YOUNG, I DIDN'T UNDERSTAND WHY. THEY SOON GOT A DIVORCE."
"I LIVED WITH MY MOM AND WENT TO VISIT MY DAD EVERY WEEK AT HIS APARTMENT. BUT OUR VISITS BECAME LESS AND LESS. AFTER A WHILE, I HARDLY EVER SAW HIM."

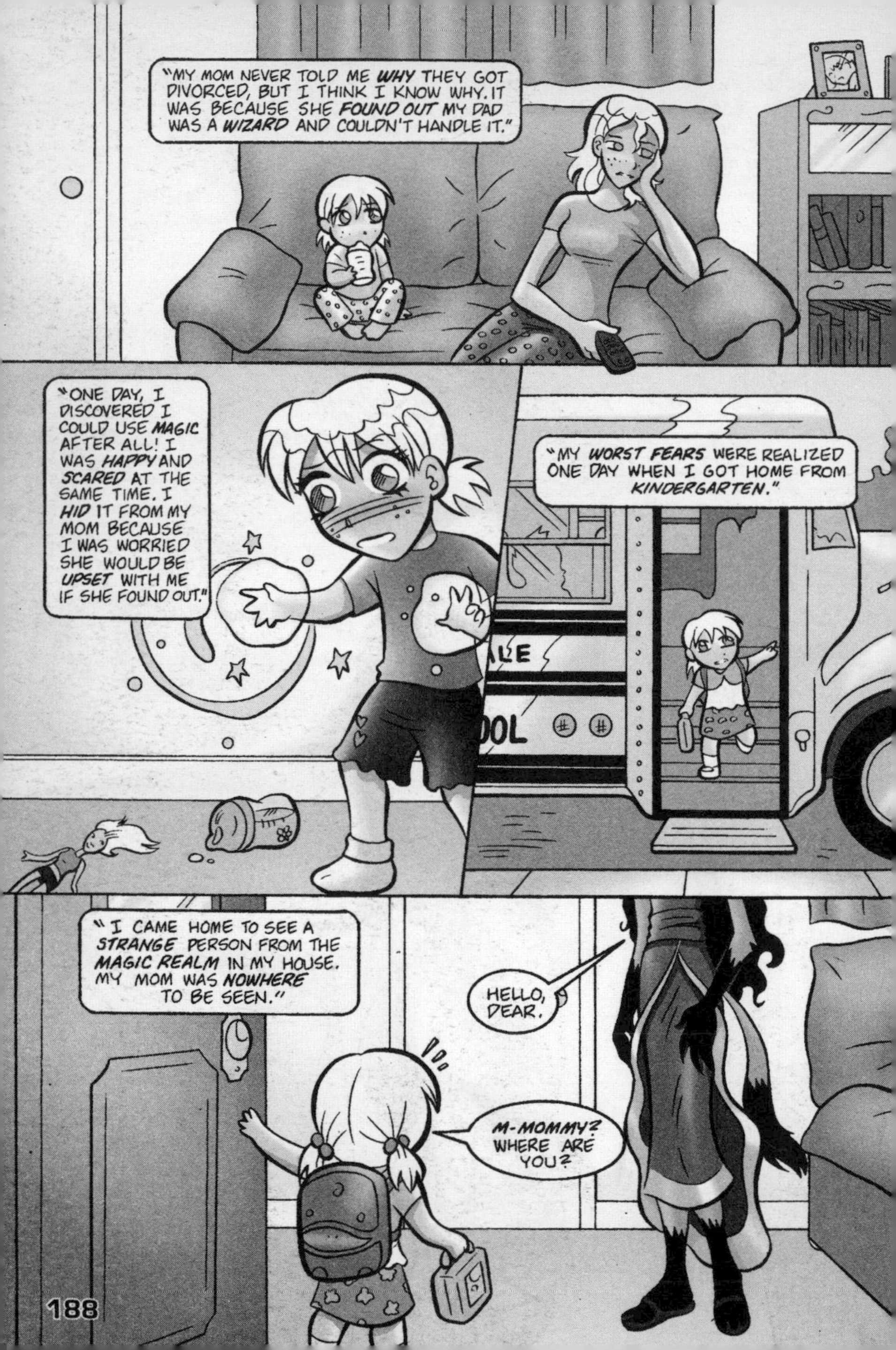
"MY MOM NEVER TOLD ME WHY THEY GOT DIVORCED, BUT I THINK I KNOW WHY. IT WAS BECAUSE SHE FOUND OUT MY DAD WAS A WIZARD AND COULDN'T HANDLE IT."
"ONE DAY, I DISCOVERED I COULD USE MAGIC AFTER ALL! I WAS HAPPY AND SCARED AT THE SAME TIME. I HID IT FROM MY MOM BECAUSE I WAS WORRIED SHE WOULD BE UPSET WITH ME IF SHE FOUND OUT."
"MY WORST FEARS WERE REALIZED ONE DAY WHEN I GOT HOME FROM KINDERGARTEN."
"I CAME HOME TO SEE A STRANGE PERSON FROM THE MAGIC REALM IN MY HOUSE. MY MOM WAS NOWHERE TO BE SEEN."
HELLO, DEAR.
M-MOMMY? WHERE ARE YOU?

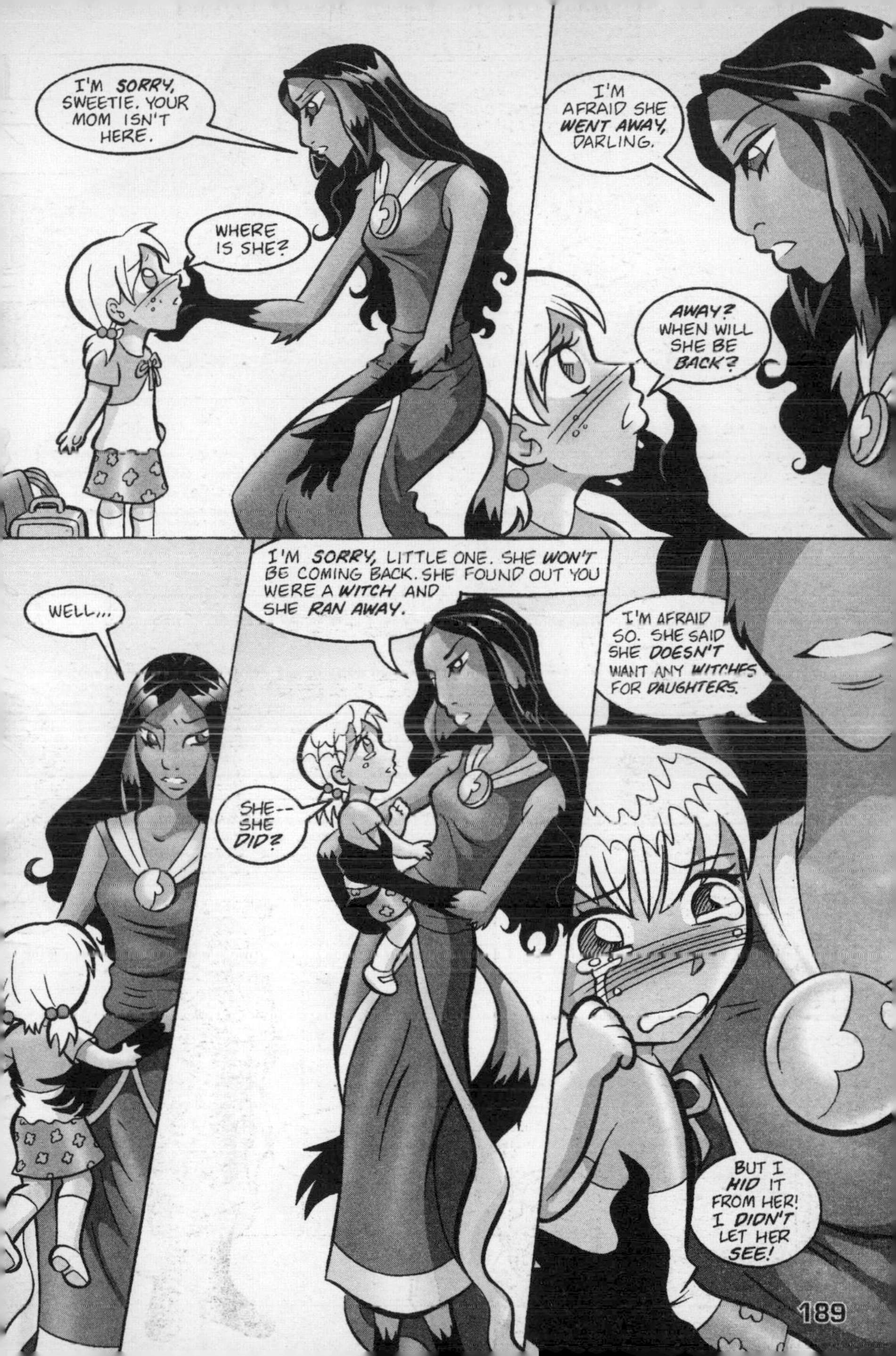
I'M SORRY, SWEETIE. YOUR MOM ISN'T HERE.
WHERE IS SHE?
I'M AFRAID SHE WENT AWAY, DARLING.
AWAY? WHEN WILL SHE BE BACK?
WELL...
I'M SORRY, LITTLE ONE. SHE WON'T BE COMING BACK. SHE FOUND OUT YOU WERE A WITCH AND SHE RAN AWAY.
SHE--SHE DID?
I'M AFRAID SO. SHE SAID SHE DOESN'T WANT ANY WITCHES FOR DAUGHTERS.
BUT I HID IT FROM HER! I DIDN'T LET HER SEE!

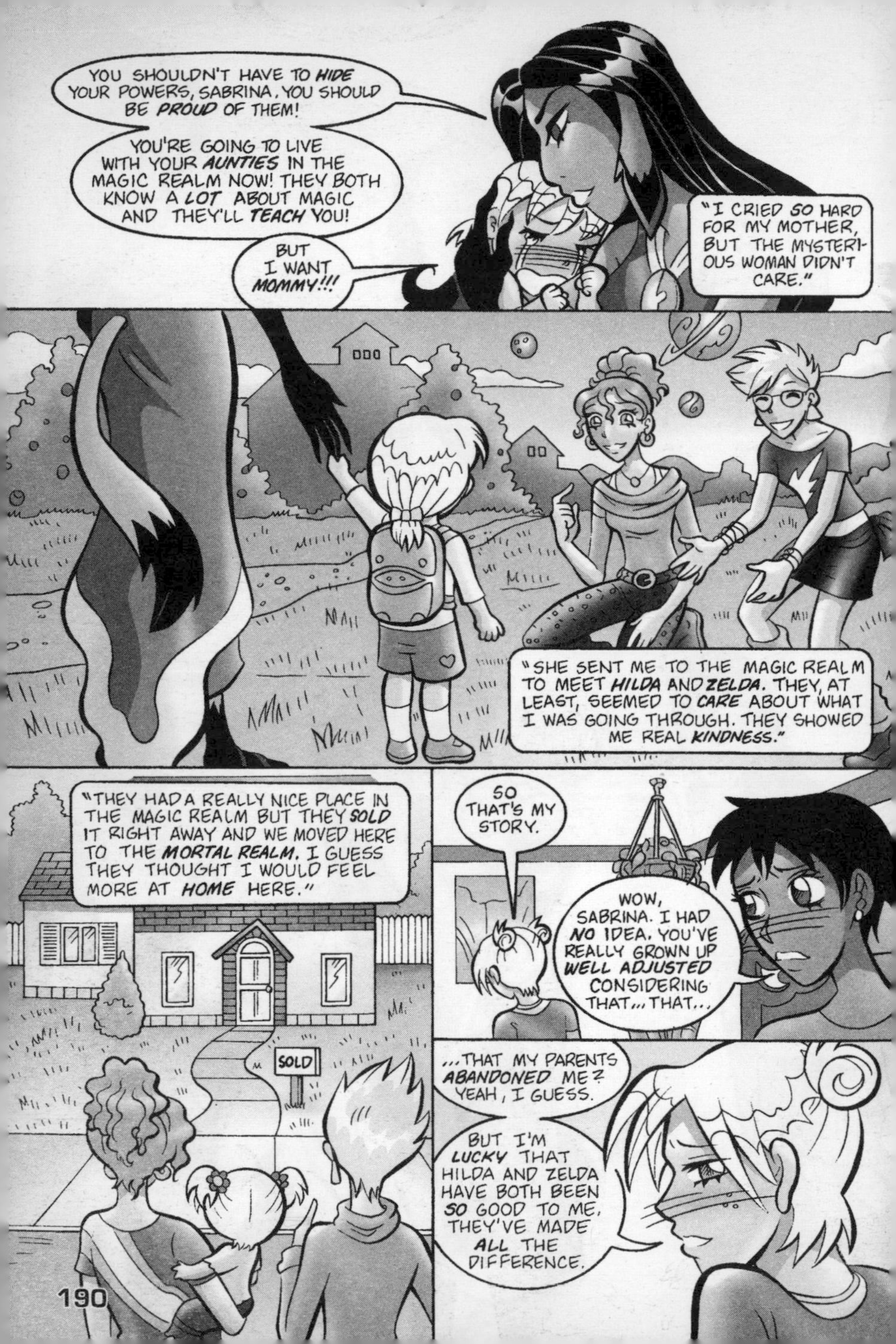

YOU SHOULDN'T HAVE TO HIDE YOUR POWERS, SABRINA, YOU SHOULD BE PROUD OF THEM!
YOU'RE GOING TO LIVE WITH YOUR AUNTIES IN THE MAGIC REALM NOW! THEY BOTH KNOW A LOT ABOUT MAGIC AND THEY'LL TEACH YOU!
BUT I WANT MOMMY!!!
"I CRIED SO HARD FOR MY MOTHER, BUT THE MYSTERIOUS WOMAN DIDN'T CARE."
"SHE SENT ME TO THE MAGIC REALM TO MEET HILDA AND ZELDA. THEY, AT LEAST, SEEMED TO CARE ABOUT WHAT I WAS GOING THROUGH. THEY SHOWED ME REAL KINDNESS."
"THEY HAD A REALLY NICE PLACE IN THE MAGIC REALM BUT THEY SOLD IT RIGHT AWAY AND WE MOVED HERE TO THE MORTAL REALM. I GUESS THEY THOUGHT I WOULD FEEL MORE AT HOME HERE."
SOLD
SO THAT'S MY STORY.
WOW, SABRINA. I HAD NO IDEA. YOU'VE REALLY GROWN UP WELL ADJUSTED CONSIDERING THAT... THAT...
...THAT MY PARENTS ABANDONED ME? YEAH, I GUESS.
BUT I'M LUCKY THAT HILDA AND ZELDA HAVE BOTH BEEN SO GOOD TO ME. THEY'VE MADE ALL THE DIFFERENCE.

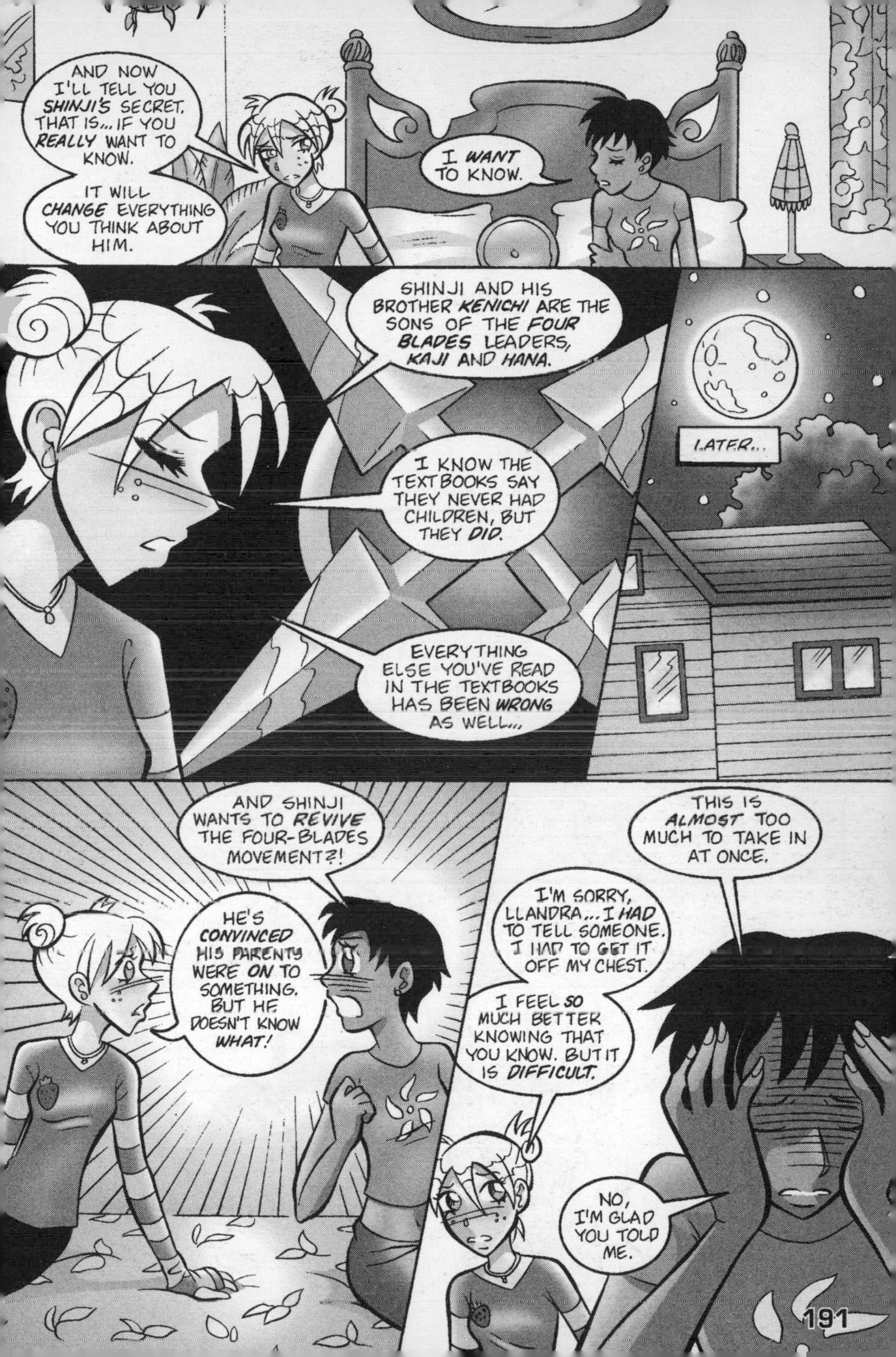
AND NOW I'LL TELL YOU SHINJI'S SECRET. THAT IS... IF YOU REALLY WANT TO KNOW.
IT WILL CHANGE EVERYTHING YOU THINK ABOUT HIM.
I WANT TO KNOW.
SHINJI AND HIS BROTHER KENICHI ARE THE SONS OF THE FOUR BLADES LEADERS, KAJI AND HANA.
I KNOW THE TEXTBOOKS SAY THEY NEVER HAD CHILDREN, BUT THEY DID.
EVERYTHING ELSE YOU'VE READ IN THE TEXTBOOKS HAS BEEN WRONG AS WELL...
LATER...
AND SHINJI WANTS TO REVIVE THE FOUR-BLADES MOVEMENT?!
HE'S CONVINCED HIS PARENTS WERE ON TO SOMETHING. BUT HE DOESN'T KNOW WHAT!
THIS IS ALMOST TOO MUCH TO TAKE IN AT ONCE.
I'M SORRY, LLANDRA... I HAD TO TELL SOMEONE. I HAD TO GET IT OFF MY CHEST.
I FEEL SO MUCH BETTER KNOWING THAT YOU KNOW. BUT IT IS DIFFICULT.
NO, I'M GLAD YOU TOLD ME.

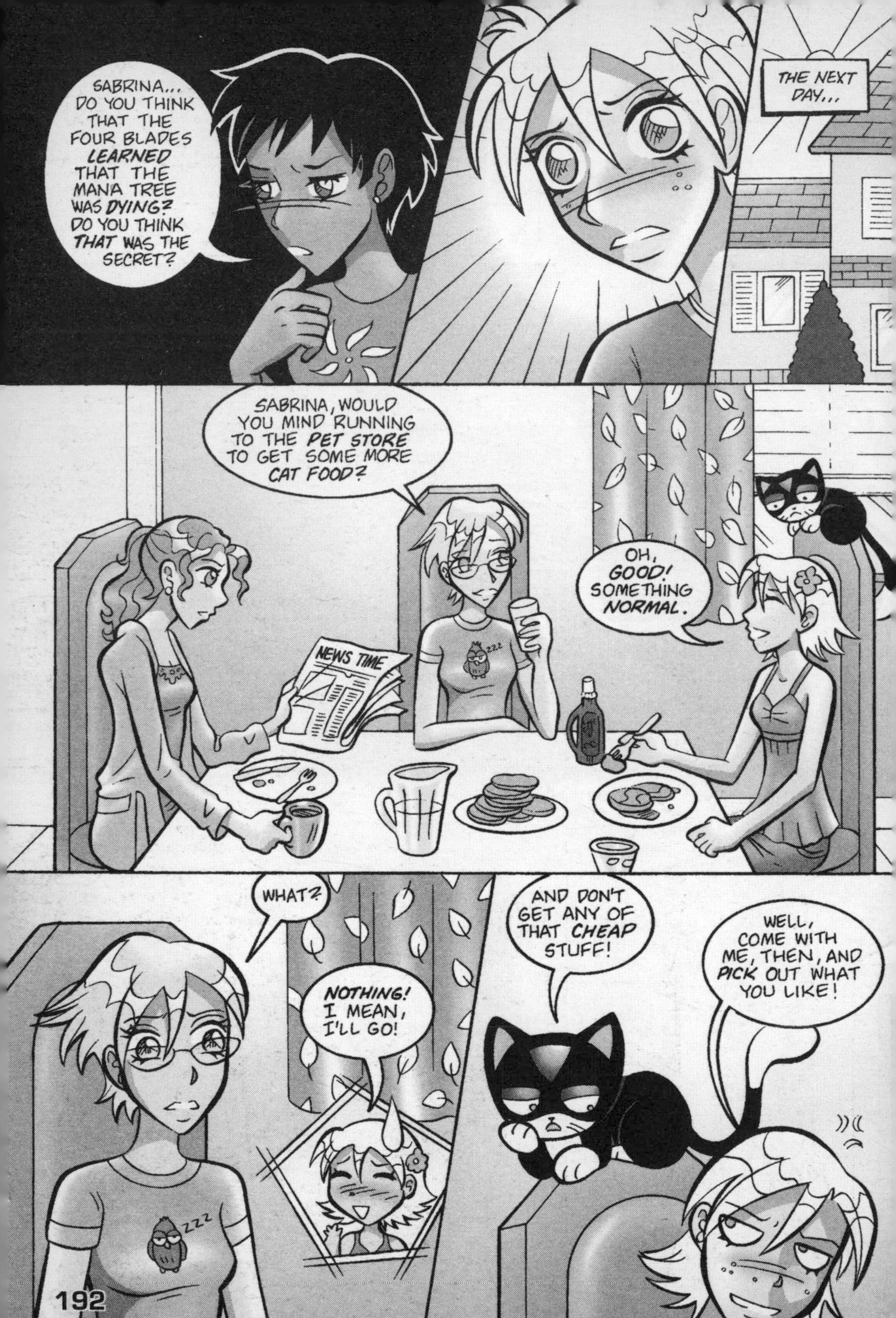
SABRINA... DO YOU THINK THAT THE FOUR BLADES LEARNED THAT THE MANA TREE WAS DYING? DO YOU THINK THAT WAS THE SECRET?
THE NEXT DAY...
SABRINA, WOULD YOU MIND RUNNING TO THE PET STORE TO GET SOME MORE CAT FOOD?
NEWS TIME
OH, GOOD! SOMETHING NORMAL.
WHAT?
NOTHING! I MEAN, I'LL GO!
AND DON'T GET ANY OF THAT CHEAP STUFF!
WELL, COME WITH ME, THEN, AND PICK OUT WHAT YOU LIKE!

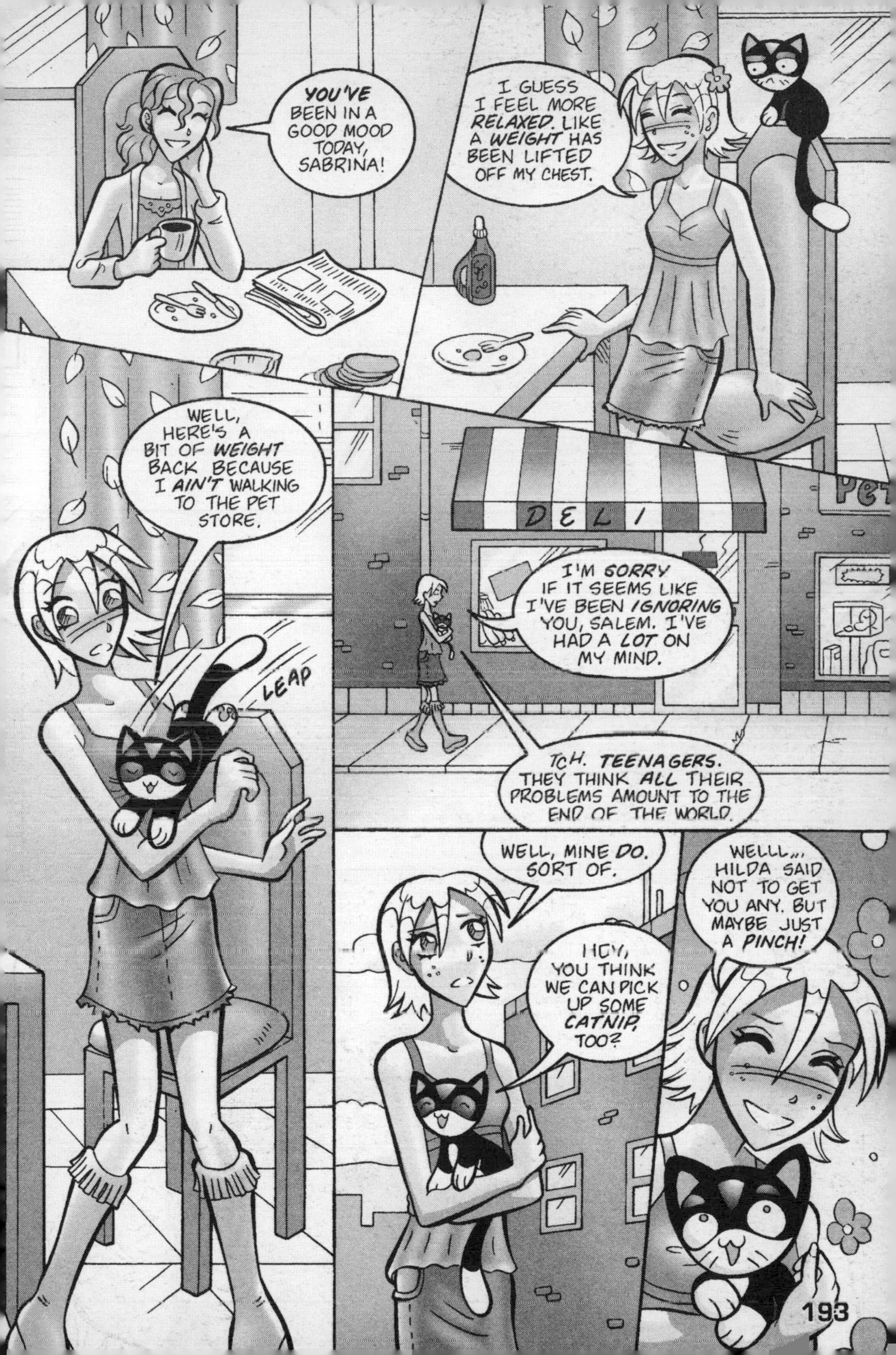

YOU'VE BEEN IN A GOOD MOOD TODAY, SABRINA!
I GUESS I FEEL MORE RELAXED. LIKE A WEIGHT HAS BEEN LIFTED OFF MY CHEST.
WELL, HERE'S A BIT OF WEIGHT BACK BECAUSE I AIN'T WALKING TO THE PET STORE.
LEAP
DELI
I'M SORRY IF IT SEEMS LIKE I'VE BEEN IGNORING YOU, SALEM. I'VE HAD A LOT ON MY MIND.
TCH. TEENAGERS. THEY THINK ALL THEIR PROBLEMS AMOUNT TO THE END OF THE WORLD.
WELL, MINE DO. SORT OF.
HEY, YOU THINK WE CAN PICK UP SOME CATNIP, TOO?
WELLL... HILDA SAID NOT TO GET YOU ANY. BUT MAYBE JUST A PINCH!

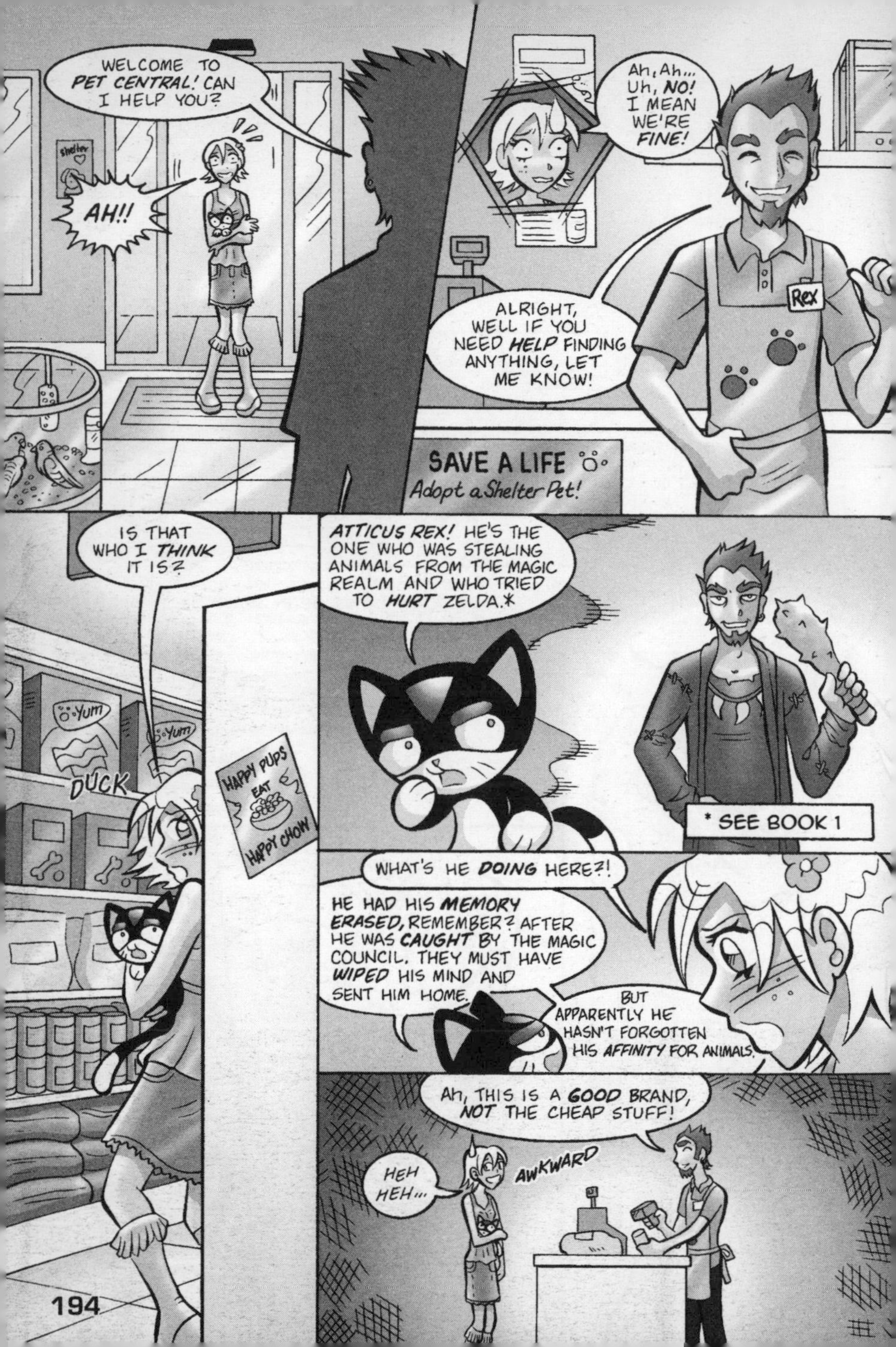

WELCOME TO PET CENTRAL! CAN I HELP YOU?
shelter
AH!!
Ah, Ah... Uh, NO! I MEAN WE'RE FINE!
Rex
ALRIGHT, WELL IF YOU NEED HELP FINDING ANYTHING, LET ME KNOW!
SAVE A LIFE
Adopt a Shelter Pet!
IS THAT WHO I THINK IT IS?
Yum
Yum
DUCK
HAPPY PUPS EAT HAPPY CHOW
ATTICUS REX! HE'S THE ONE WHO WAS STEALING ANIMALS FROM THE MAGIC REALM AND WHO TRIED TO HURT ZELDA.*
* SEE BOOK 1
WHAT'S HE DOING HERE?!
HE HAD HIS MEMORY ERASED, REMEMBER? AFTER HE WAS CAUGHT BY THE MAGIC COUNCIL. THEY MUST HAVE WIPED HIS MIND AND SENT HIM HOME.
BUT APPARENTLY HE HASN'T FORGOTTEN HIS AFFINITY FOR ANIMALS.
Ah, THIS IS A GOOD BRAND, NOT THE CHEAP STUFF!
HEH HEH...
AWKWARD

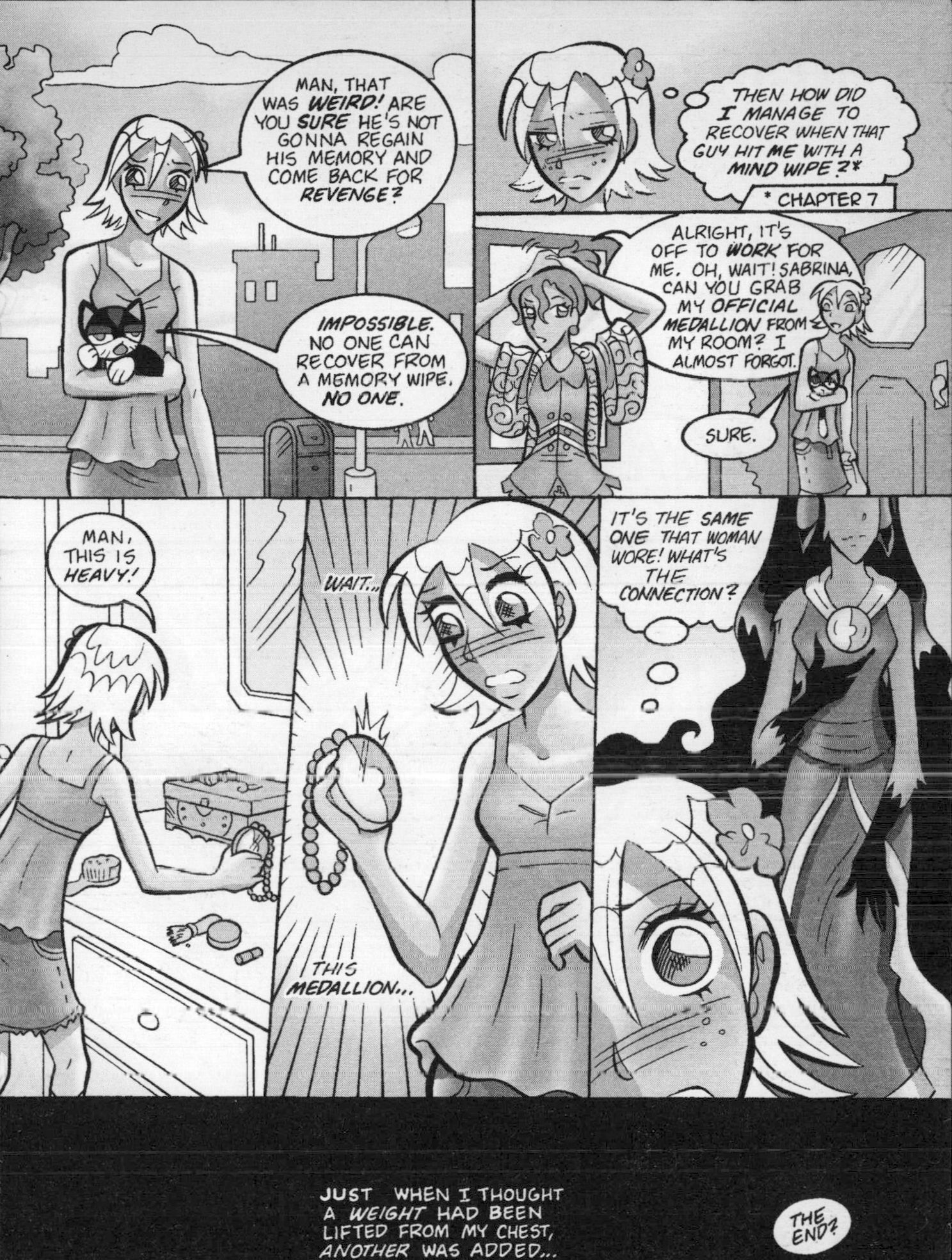
MAN, THAT WAS WEIRD! ARE YOU SURE HE'S NOT GONNA REGAIN HIS MEMORY AND COME BACK FOR REVENGE?
IMPOSSIBLE. NO ONE CAN RECOVER FROM A MEMORY WIPE. NO ONE.
THEN HOW DID I MANAGE TO RECOVER WHEN THAT GUY HIT ME WITH A MIND WIPE?*
* CHAPTER 7
ALRIGHT, IT'S OFF TO WORK FOR ME. OH, WAIT! SABRINA, CAN YOU GRAB MY OFFICIAL MEDALLION FROM MY ROOM? I ALMOST FORGOT.
SURE.
MAN, THIS IS HEAVY!
WAIT...
THIS MEDALLION...
IT'S THE SAME ONE THAT WOMAN WORE! WHAT'S THE CONNECTION?
JUST WHEN I THOUGHT A WEIGHT HAD BEEN LIFTED FROM MY CHEST, ANOTHER WAS ADDED...
THE END?

Chapter 10

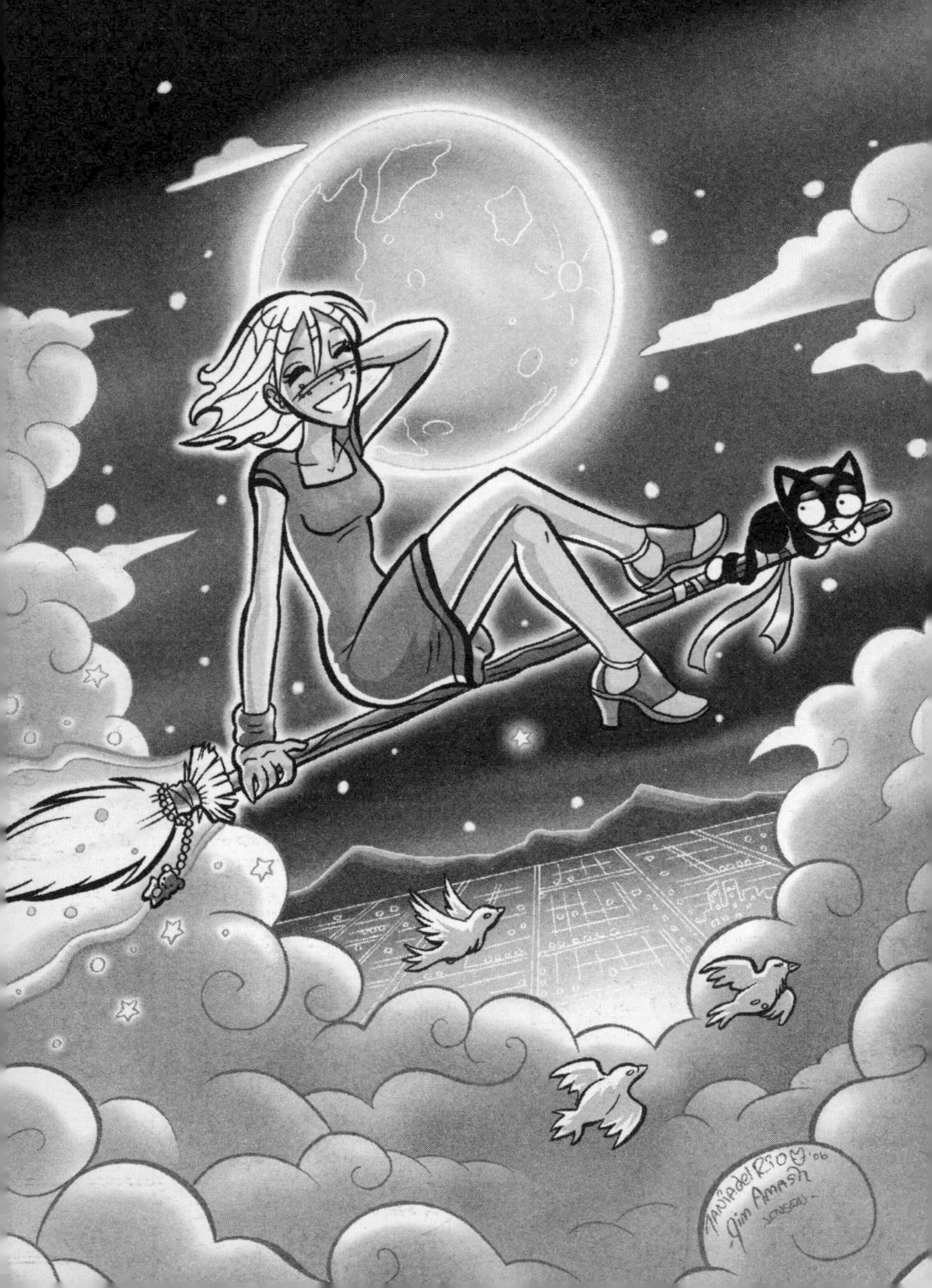

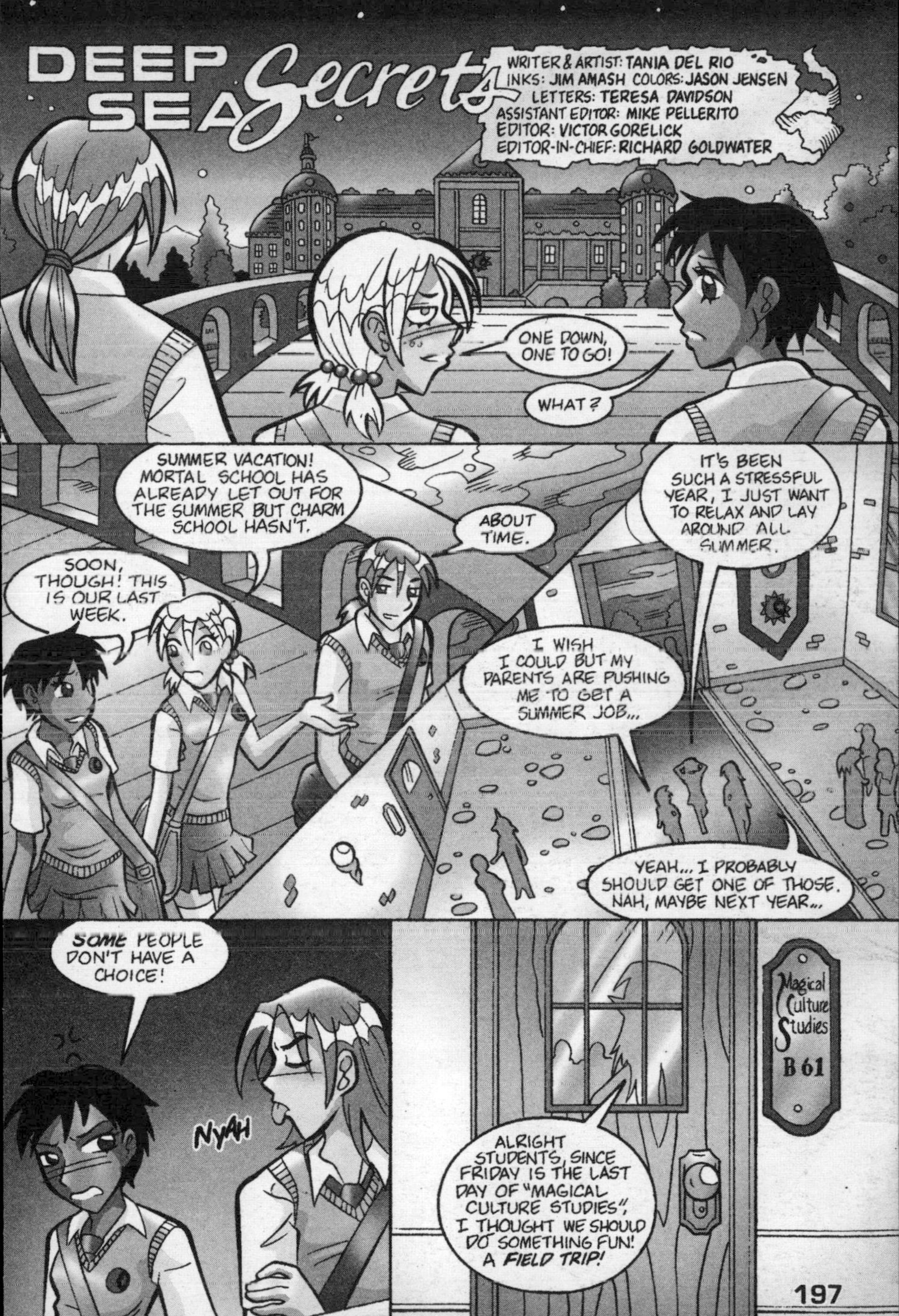

DEEP SEA Secrets
WRITER & ARTIST: TANIA DEL RIO
INKS: JIM AMASH COLORS: JASON JENSEN
LETTERS: TERESA DAVIDSON
ASSISTANT EDITOR: MIKE PELLERITO
EDITOR: VICTOR GORELICK
EDITOR-IN-CHIEF: RICHARD GOLDWATER
ONE DOWN, ONE TO GO!
WHAT?
SUMMER VACATION! MORTAL SCHOOL HAS ALREADY LET OUT FOR THE SUMMER BUT CHARM SCHOOL HASN'T.
ABOUT TIME.
SOON, THOUGH! THIS IS OUR LAST WEEK.
IT'S BEEN SUCH A STRESSFUL YEAR, I JUST WANT TO RELAX AND LAY AROUND ALL SUMMER.
I WISH I COULD BUT MY PARENTS ARE PUSHING ME TO GET A SUMMER JOB...
YEAH... I PROBABLY SHOULD GET ONE OF THOSE. NAH, MAYBE NEXT YEAR...
SOME PEOPLE DON'T HAVE A CHOICE!
NYAH
Magical Culture Studies
B 61
ALRIGHT STUDENTS, SINCE FRIDAY IS THE LAST DAY OF "MAGICAL CULTURE STUDIES", I THOUGHT WE SHOULD DO SOMETHING FUN! A FIELD TRIP!

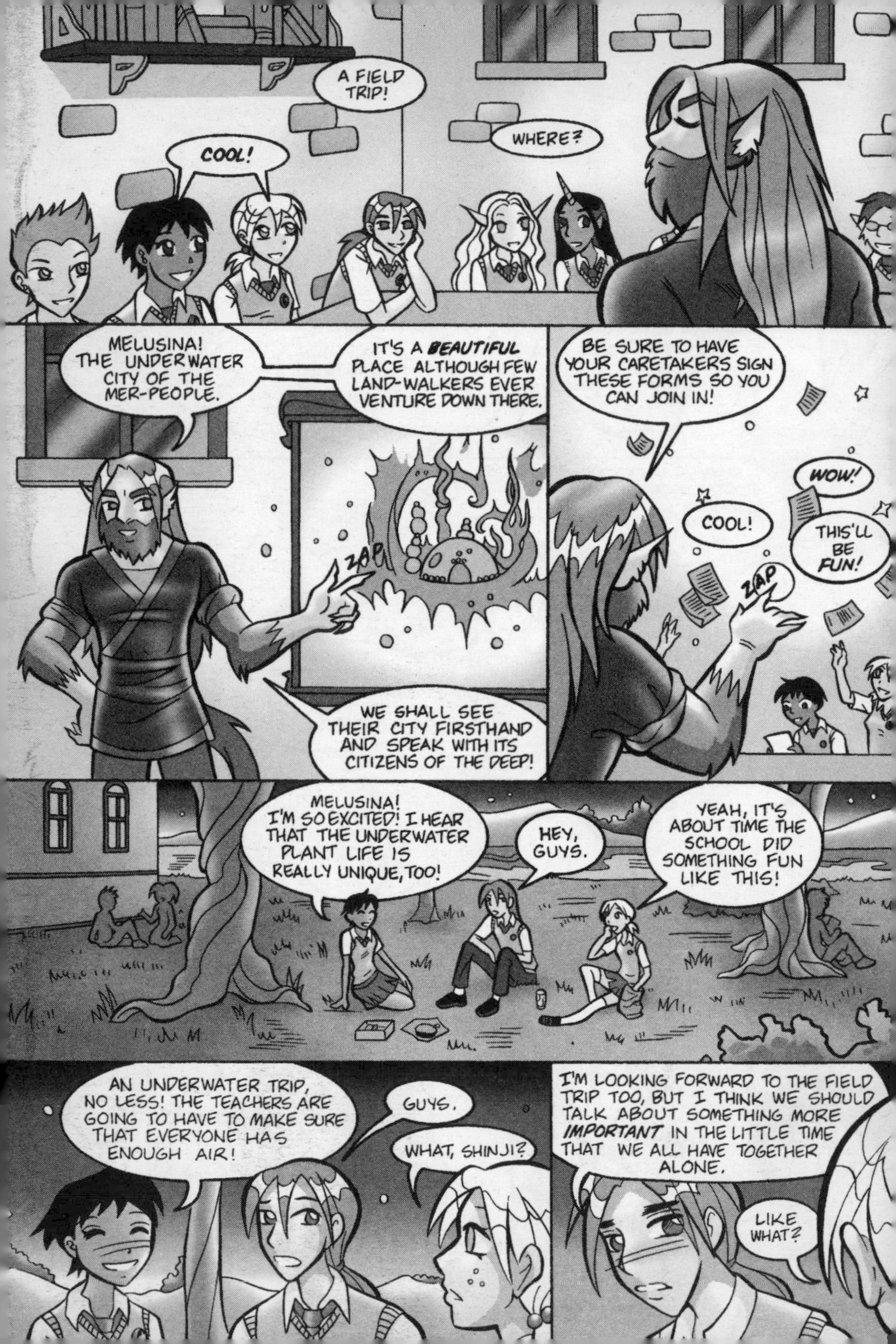
COOL!
A FIELD TRIP!
WHERE?
MELUSINA! THE UNDERWATER CITY OF THE MER-PEOPLE.
IT'S A **BEAUTIFUL** PLACE ALTHOUGH FEW LAND-WALKERS EVER VENTURE DOWN THERE.
ZAP
WE SHALL SEE THEIR CITY FIRSTHAND AND SPEAK WITH ITS CITIZENS OF THE DEEP!
BE SURE TO HAVE YOUR CARETAKERS SIGN THESE FORMS SO YOU CAN JOIN IN!
ZAP
WOW!
COOL!
THIS'LL BE *FUN!*
MELUSINA! I'M SO EXCITED! I HEAR THAT THE UNDERWATER PLANT LIFE IS REALLY UNIQUE, TOO!
HEY, GUYS.
YEAH, IT'S ABOUT TIME THE SCHOOL DID SOMETHING FUN LIKE THIS!
AN UNDERWATER TRIP, NO LESS! THE TEACHERS ARE GOING TO HAVE TO MAKE SURE THAT EVERYONE HAS ENOUGH AIR!
GUYS.
WHAT, SHINJI?
I'M LOOKING FORWARD TO THE FIELD TRIP TOO, BUT I THINK WE SHOULD TALK ABOUT SOMETHING MORE *IMPORTANT* IN THE LITTLE TIME THAT WE ALL HAVE TOGETHER ALONE.
LIKE WHAT?

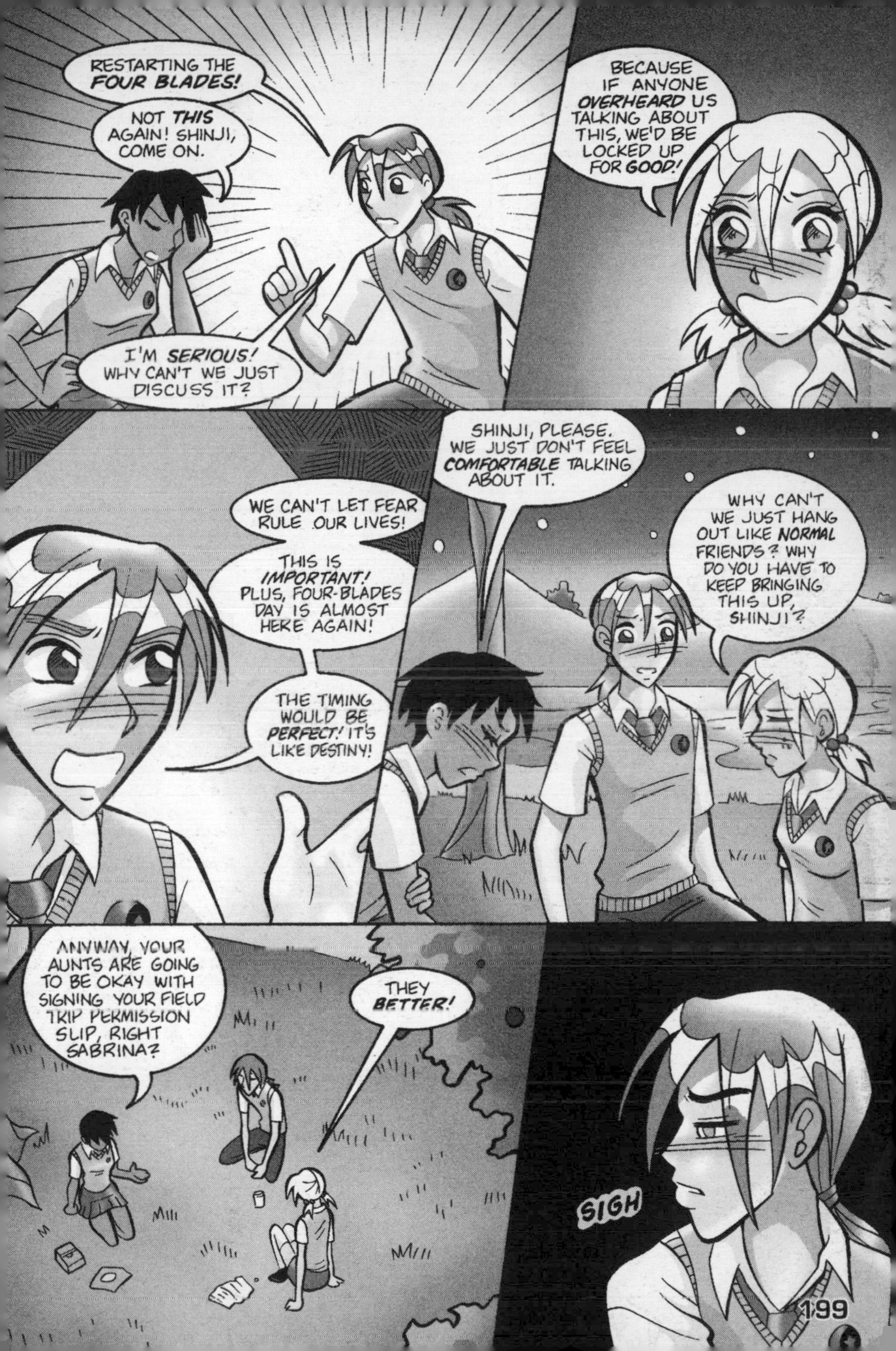
RESTARTING THE FOUR BLADES!
NOT THIS AGAIN! SHINJI, COME ON.
I'M SERIOUS! WHY CAN'T WE JUST DISCUSS IT?
BECAUSE IF ANYONE OVERHEARD US TALKING ABOUT THIS, WE'D BE LOCKED UP FOR GOOD!
WE CAN'T LET FEAR RULE OUR LIVES!
THIS IS IMPORTANT! PLUS, FOUR-BLADES DAY IS ALMOST HERE AGAIN!
THE TIMING WOULD BE PERFECT! IT'S LIKE DESTINY!
SHINJI, PLEASE. WE JUST DON'T FEEL COMFORTABLE TALKING ABOUT IT.
WHY CAN'T WE JUST HANG OUT LIKE NORMAL FRIENDS? WHY DO YOU HAVE TO KEEP BRINGING THIS UP, SHINJI?
ANYWAY, YOUR AUNTS ARE GOING TO BE OKAY WITH SIGNING YOUR FIELD TRIP PERMISSION SLIP, RIGHT SABRINA?
THEY BETTER!
SIGH

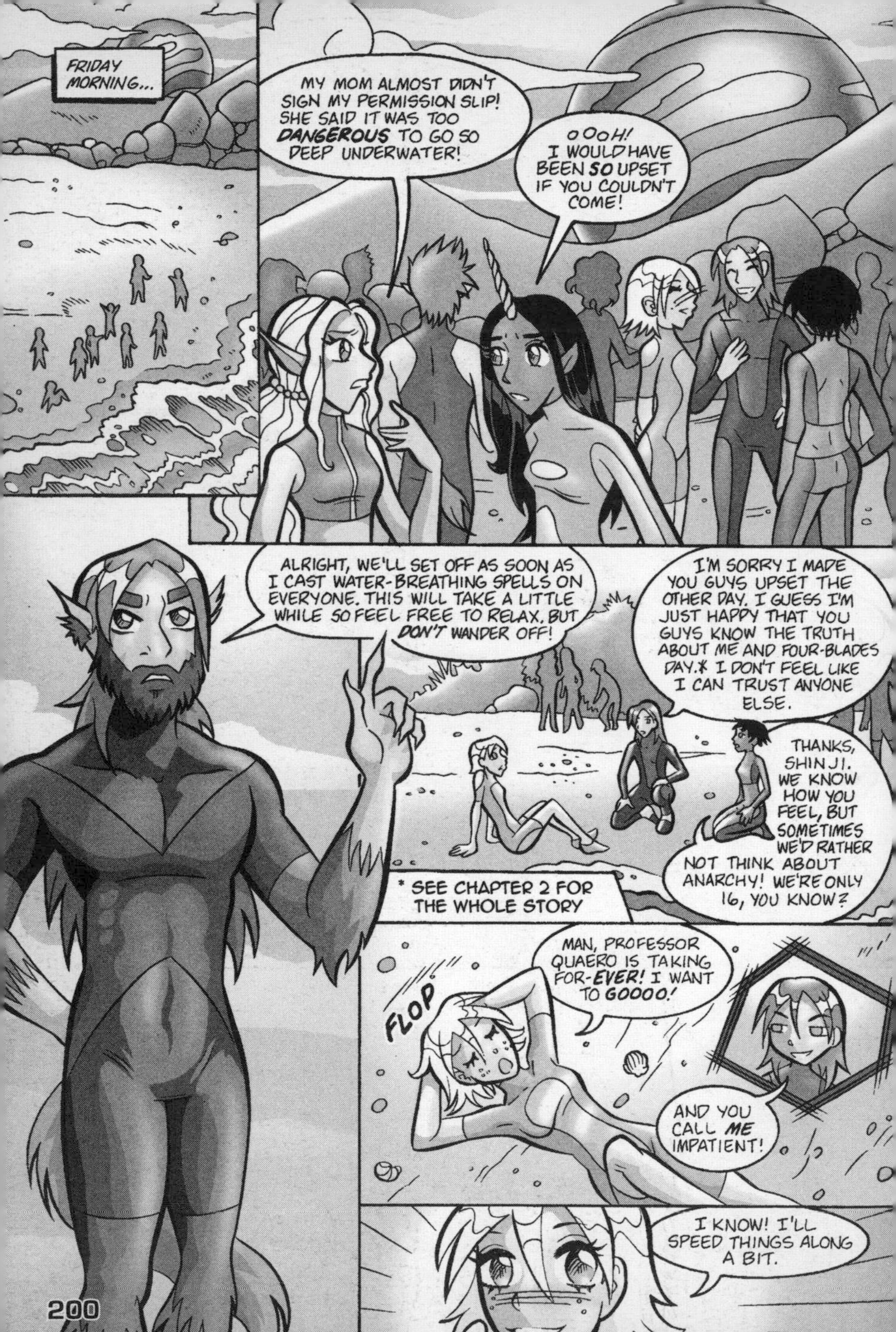
FRIDAY MORNING...
MY MOM ALMOST DIDN'T SIGN MY PERMISSION SLIP! SHE SAID IT WAS TOO DANGEROUS TO GO SO DEEP UNDERWATER!
OOOH! I WOULD HAVE BEEN SO UPSET IF YOU COULDN'T COME!
ALRIGHT, WE'LL SET OFF AS SOON AS I CAST WATER-BREATHING SPELLS ON EVERYONE. THIS WILL TAKE A LITTLE WHILE SO FEEL FREE TO RELAX. BUT DON'T WANDER OFF!
I'M SORRY I MADE YOU GUYS UPSET THE OTHER DAY. I GUESS I'M JUST HAPPY THAT YOU GUYS KNOW THE TRUTH ABOUT ME AND FOUR-BLADES DAY.* I DON'T FEEL LIKE I CAN TRUST ANYONE ELSE.
THANKS, SHINJI. WE KNOW HOW YOU FEEL, BUT SOMETIMES WE'D RATHER NOT THINK ABOUT ANARCHY! WE'RE ONLY 16, YOU KNOW?
* SEE CHAPTER 2 FOR THE WHOLE STORY
FLOP
MAN, PROFESSOR QUAERO IS TAKING FOR-EVER! I WANT TO GOOOO!
AND YOU CALL ME IMPATIENT!
I KNOW! I'LL SPEED THINGS ALONG A BIT.

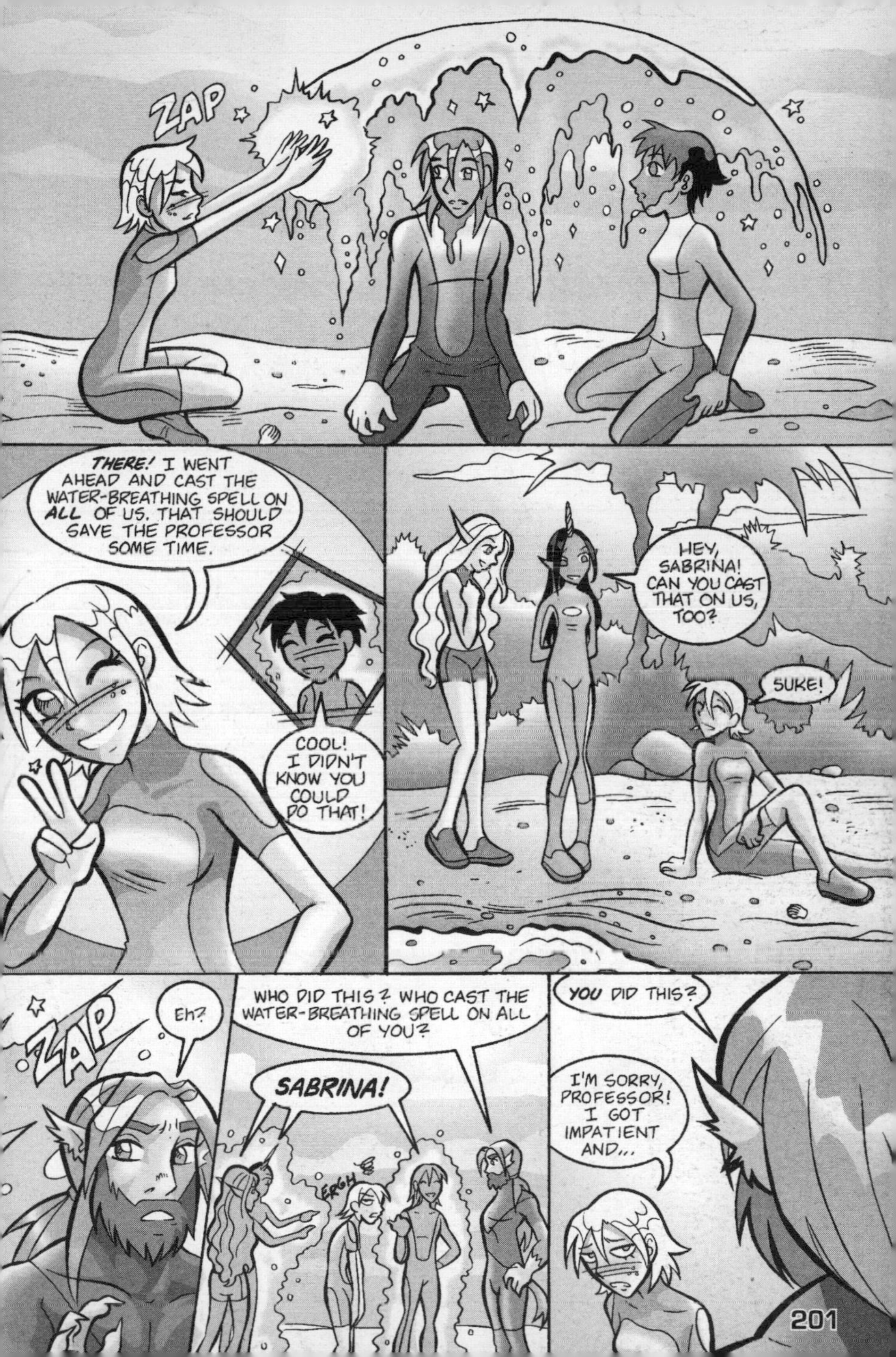
ZAP
THERE! I WENT AHEAD AND CAST THE WATER-BREATHING SPELL ON ALL OF US. THAT SHOULD SAVE THE PROFESSOR SOME TIME.
COOL! I DIDN'T KNOW YOU COULD DO THAT!
HEY, SABRINA! CAN YOU CAST THAT ON US, TOO?
SUKE!
ZAP
Eh?
WHO DID THIS? WHO CAST THE WATER-BREATHING SPELL ON ALL OF YOU?
SABRINA!
ERGH
YOU DID THIS?
I'M SORRY, PROFESSOR! I GOT IMPATIENT AND...

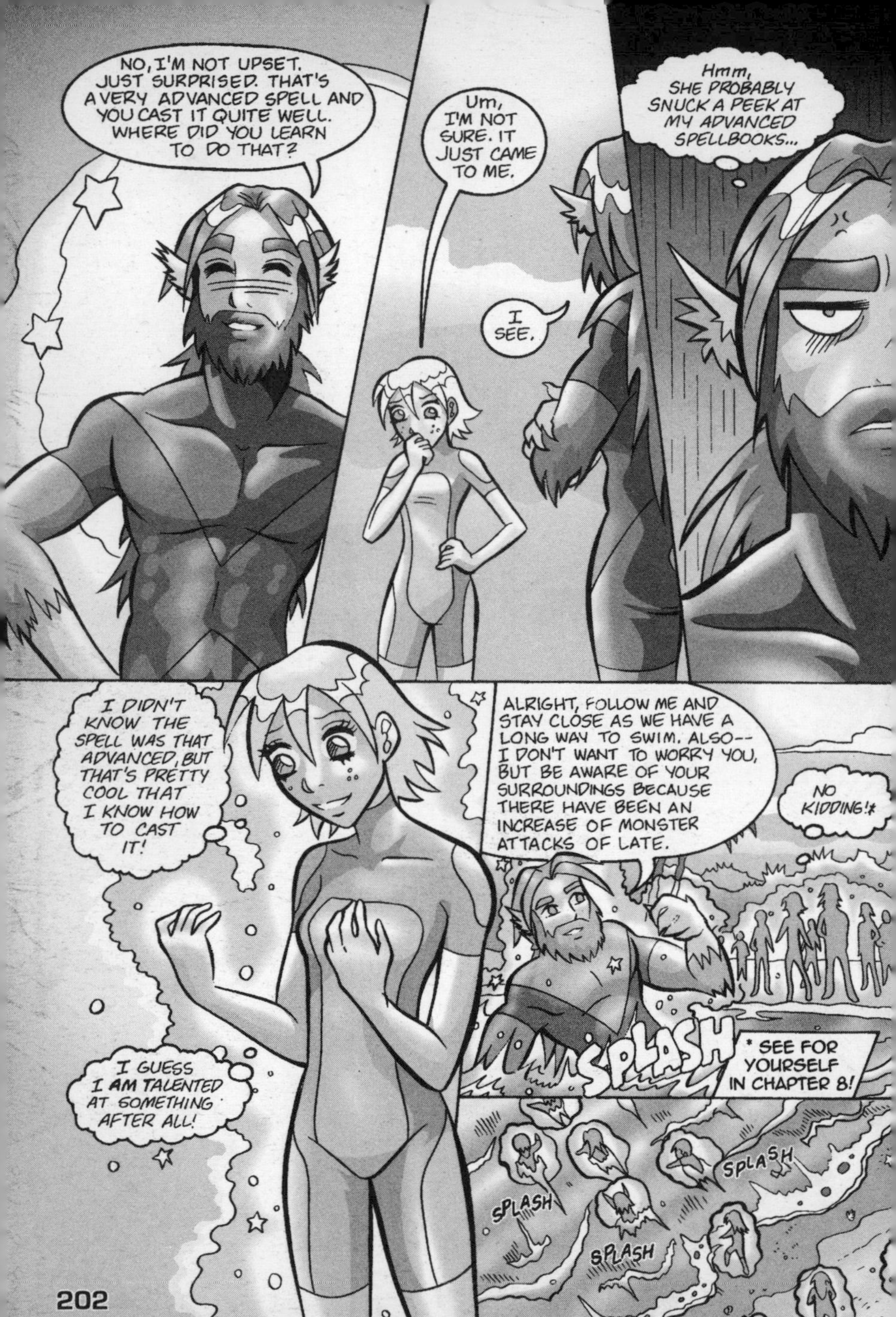
NO, I'M NOT UPSET. JUST SURPRISED. THAT'S A VERY ADVANCED SPELL AND YOU CAST IT QUITE WELL. WHERE DID YOU LEARN TO DO THAT?
Um, I'M NOT SURE. IT JUST CAME TO ME.
I SEE.
Hmm, SHE PROBABLY SNUCK A PEEK AT MY ADVANCED SPELLBOOKS...
I DIDN'T KNOW THE SPELL WAS THAT ADVANCED, BUT THAT'S PRETTY COOL THAT I KNOW HOW TO CAST IT!
I GUESS I **AM** TALENTED AT SOMETHING AFTER ALL!
ALRIGHT, FOLLOW ME AND STAY CLOSE AS WE HAVE A LONG WAY TO SWIM. ALSO-- I DON'T WANT TO WORRY YOU, BUT BE AWARE OF YOUR SURROUNDINGS BECAUSE THERE HAVE BEEN AN INCREASE OF MONSTER ATTACKS OF LATE.
NO KIDDING!*
SPLASH
* SEE FOR YOURSELF IN CHAPTER 8!
SPLASH
SPLASH
SPLASH

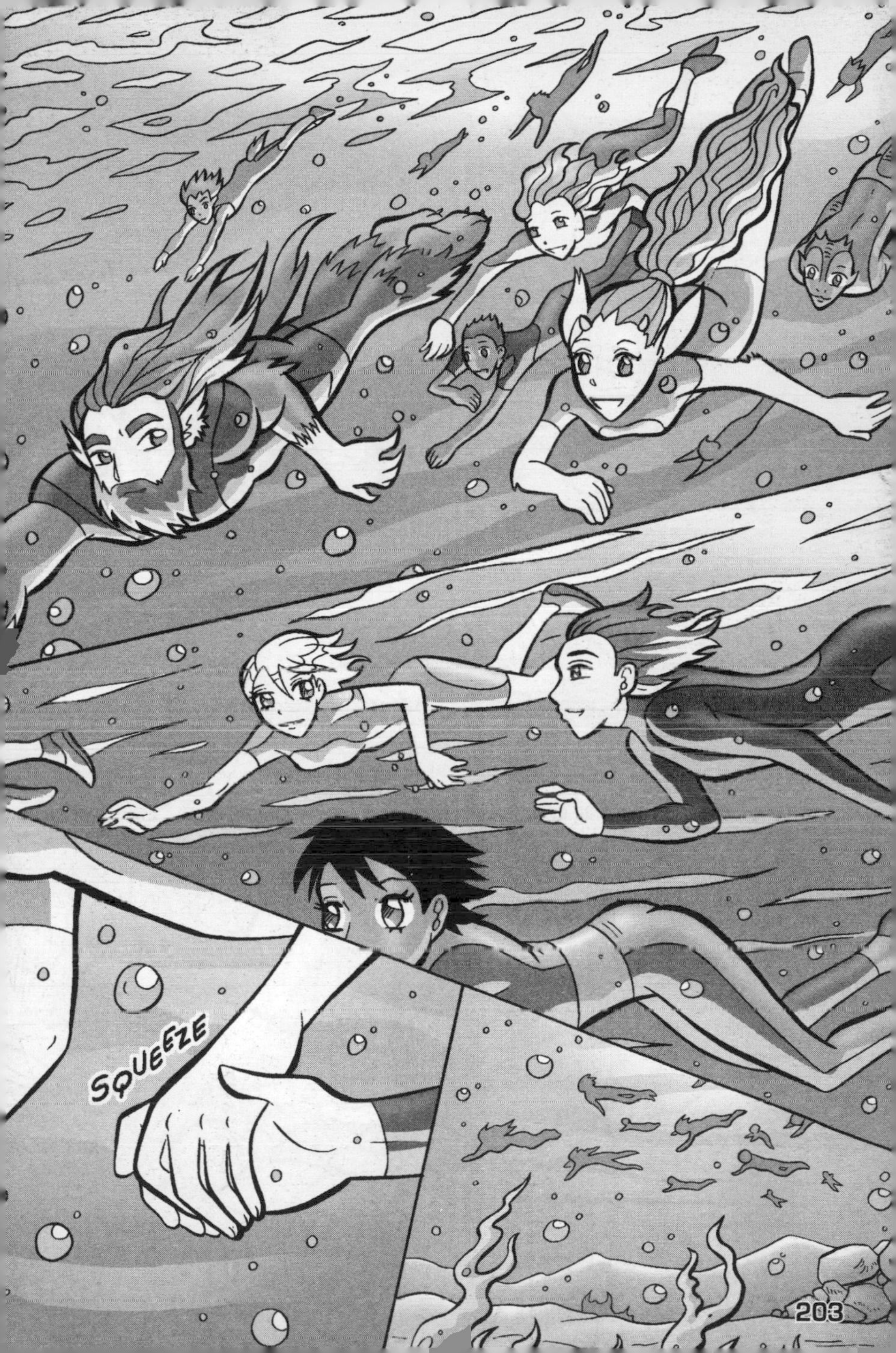
SQUEEZE

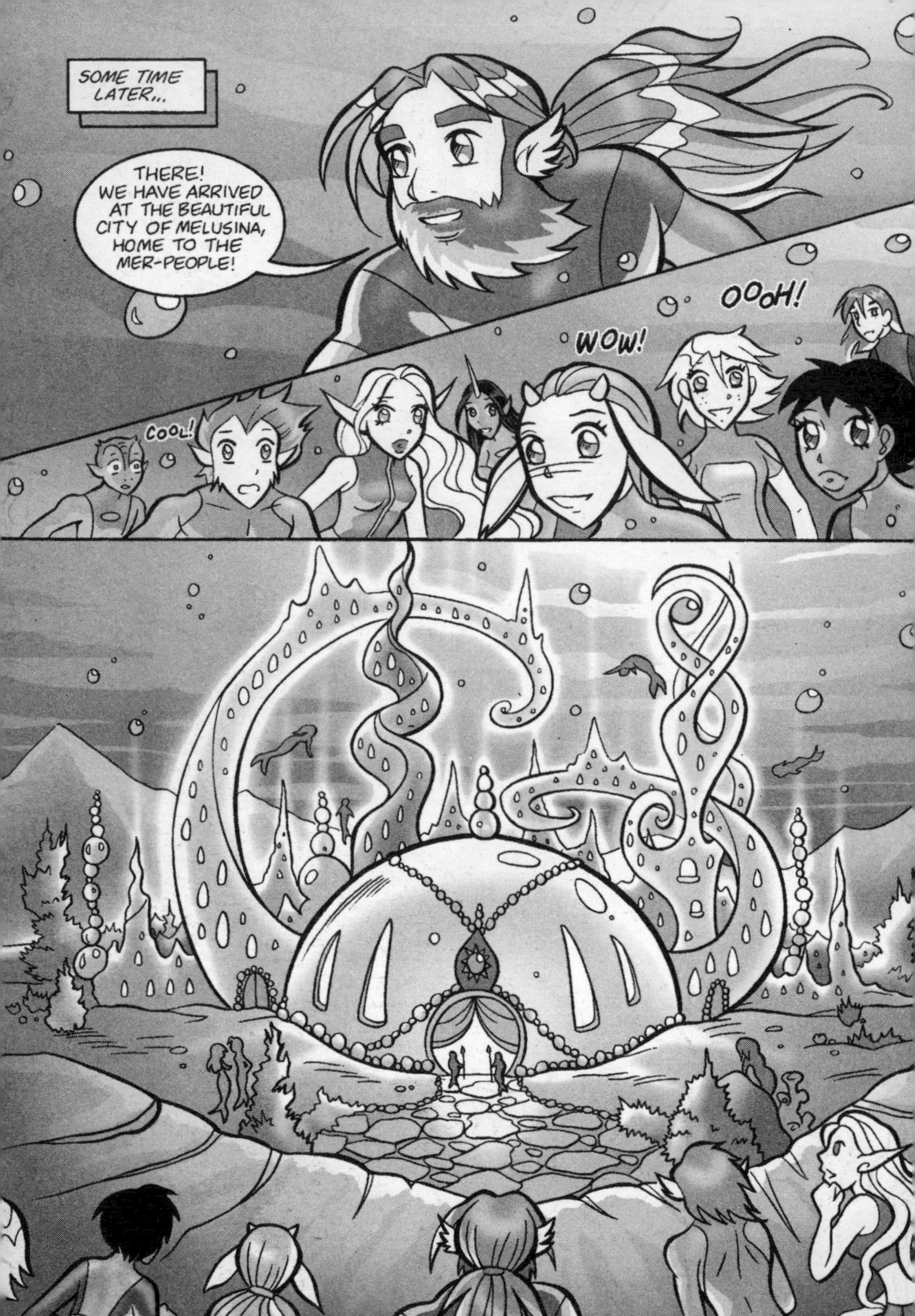
SOME TIME LATER...
THERE! WE HAVE ARRIVED AT THE BEAUTIFUL CITY OF MELUSINA, HOME TO THE MER-PEOPLE!
COOL!
WOW!
OOOH!

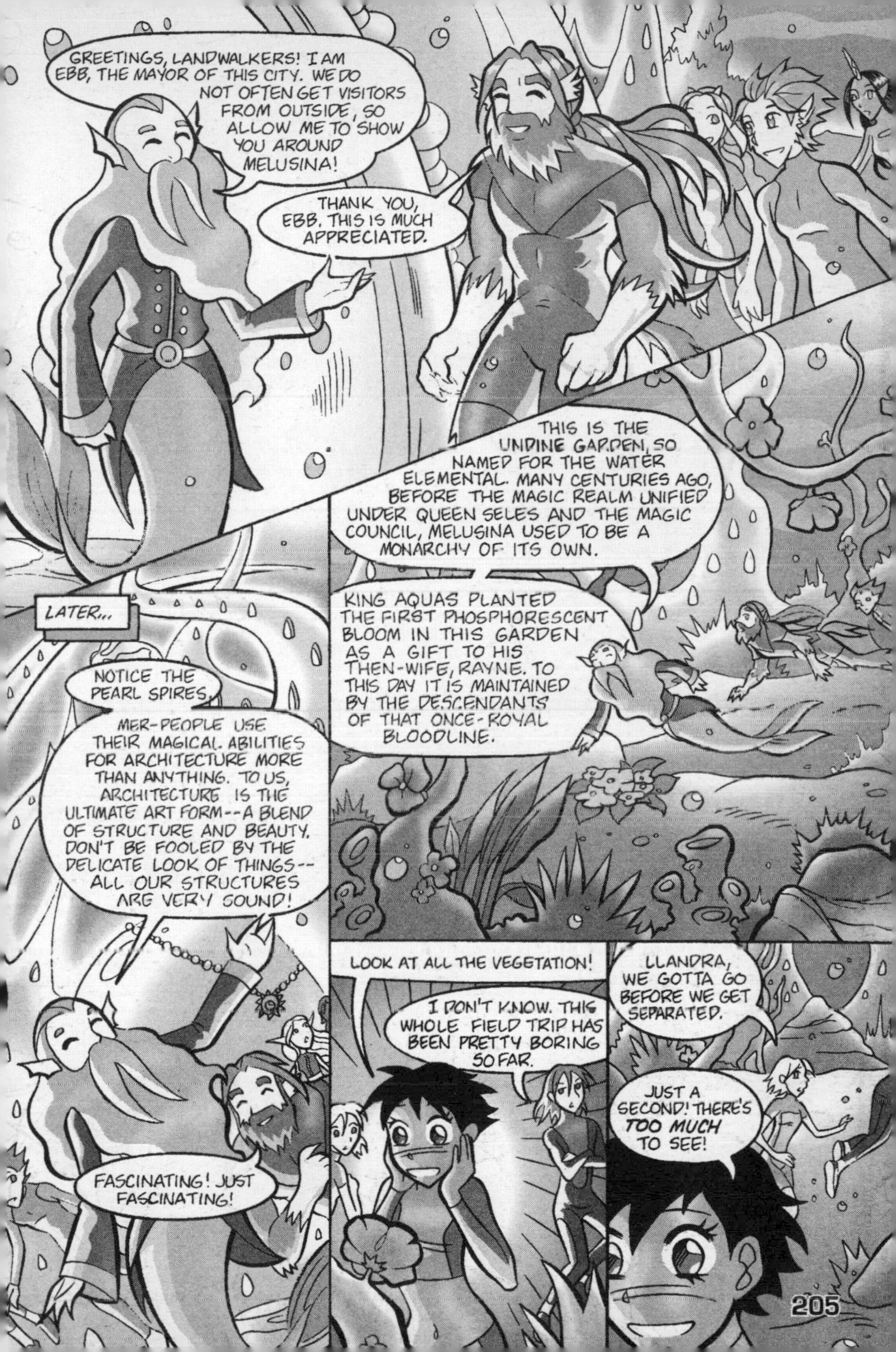
GREETINGS, LANDWALKERS! I AM EBB, THE MAYOR OF THIS CITY. WE DO NOT OFTEN GET VISITORS FROM OUTSIDE, SO ALLOW ME TO SHOW YOU AROUND MELUSINA!
THANK YOU, EBB. THIS IS MUCH APPRECIATED.
THIS IS THE UNDINE GARDEN, SO NAMED FOR THE WATER ELEMENTAL. MANY CENTURIES AGO, BEFORE THE MAGIC REALM UNIFIED UNDER QUEEN SELES AND THE MAGIC COUNCIL, MELUSINA USED TO BE A MONARCHY OF ITS OWN.
KING AQUAS PLANTED THE FIRST PHOSPHORESCENT BLOOM IN THIS GARDEN AS A GIFT TO HIS THEN-WIFE, RAYNE. TO THIS DAY IT IS MAINTAINED BY THE DESCENDANTS OF THAT ONCE-ROYAL BLOODLINE.
LATER...
NOTICE THE PEARL SPIRES.
MER-PEOPLE USE THEIR MAGICAL ABILITIES FOR ARCHITECTURE MORE THAN ANYTHING. TO US, ARCHITECTURE IS THE ULTIMATE ART FORM--A BLEND OF STRUCTURE AND BEAUTY. DON'T BE FOOLED BY THE DELICATE LOOK OF THINGS--ALL OUR STRUCTURES ARE VERY SOUND!
FASCINATING! JUST FASCINATING!
LOOK AT ALL THE VEGETATION!
I DON'T KNOW. THIS WHOLE FIELD TRIP HAS BEEN PRETTY BORING SO FAR.
LLANDRA, WE GOTTA GO BEFORE WE GET SEPARATED.
JUST A SECOND! THERE'S TOO MUCH TO SEE!

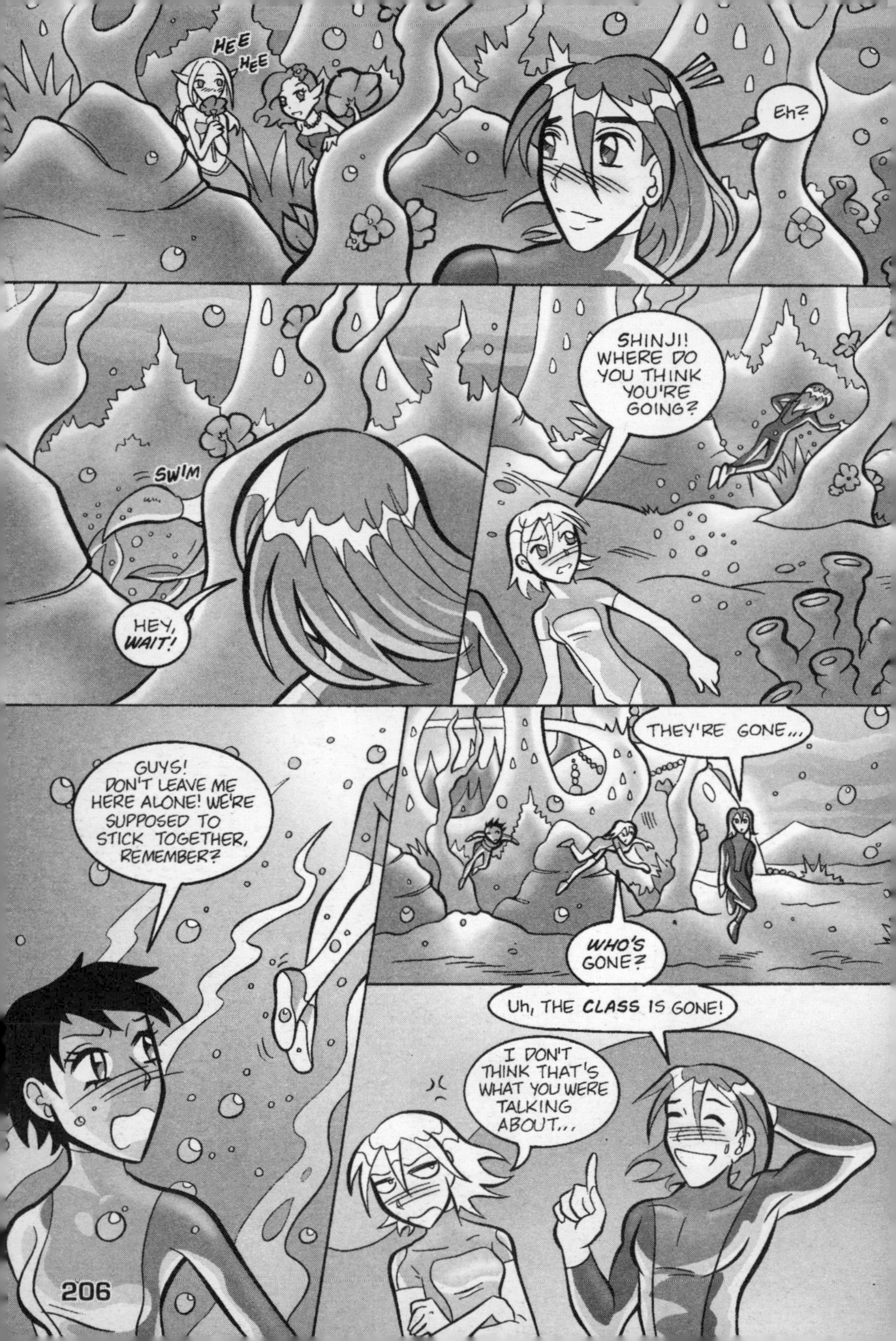
HEE HEE
Eh?
HEY, WAIT!
SWIM
SHINJI! WHERE DO YOU THINK YOU'RE GOING?
GUYS! DON'T LEAVE ME HERE ALONE! WE'RE SUPPOSED TO STICK TOGETHER, REMEMBER?
THEY'RE GONE...
WHO'S GONE?
Uh, THE CLASS IS GONE!
I DON'T THINK THAT'S WHAT YOU WERE TALKING ABOUT...

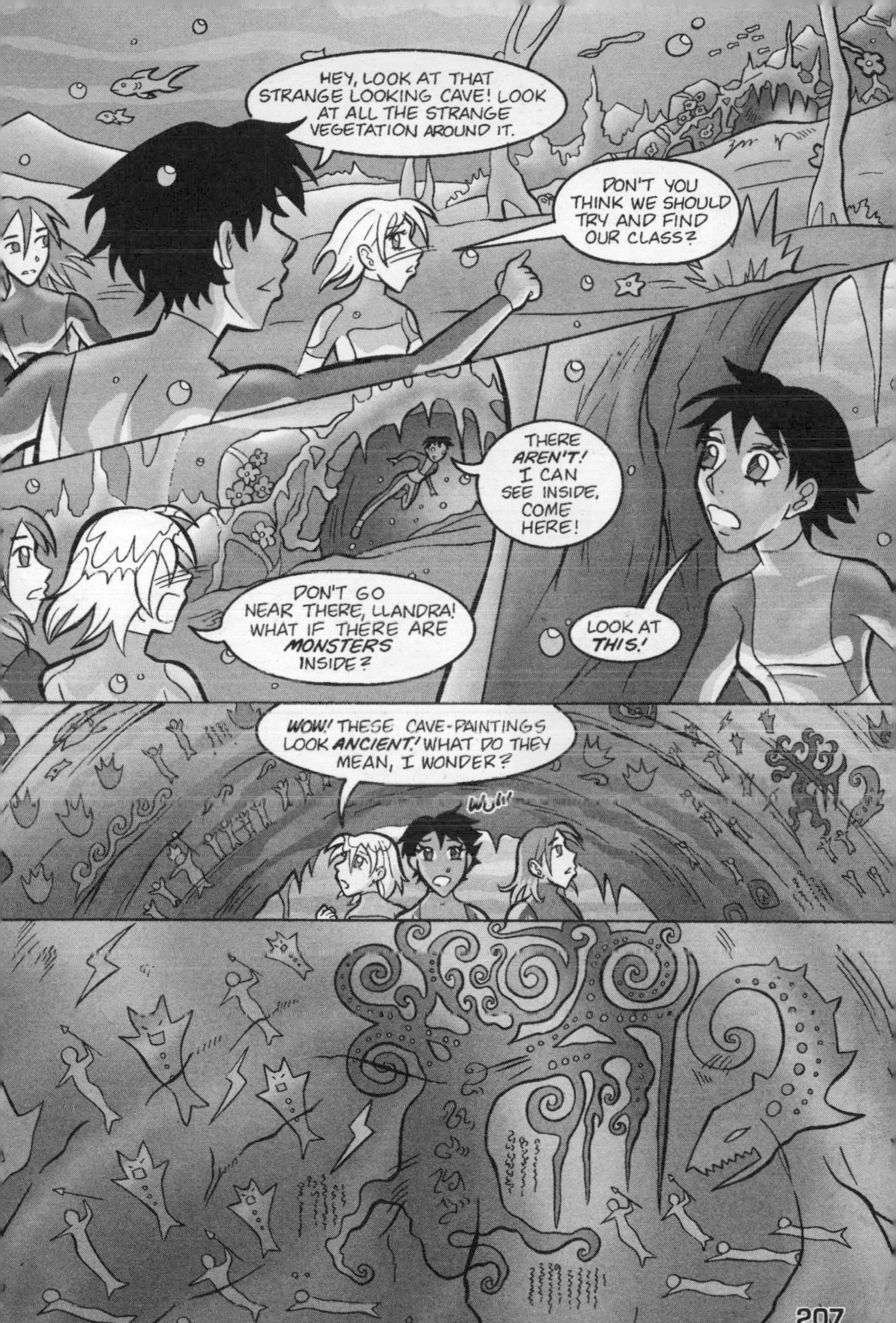
HEY, LOOK AT THAT STRANGE LOOKING CAVE! LOOK AT ALL THE STRANGE VEGETATION AROUND IT.
DON'T YOU THINK WE SHOULD TRY AND FIND OUR CLASS?
DON'T GO NEAR THERE, LLANDRA! WHAT IF THERE ARE ***MONSTERS*** INSIDE?
THERE ***AREN'T!*** I CAN SEE INSIDE, COME HERE!
LOOK AT ***THIS!***
WOW! THESE CAVE-PAINTINGS LOOK ***ANCIENT!*** WHAT DO THEY MEAN, I WONDER?

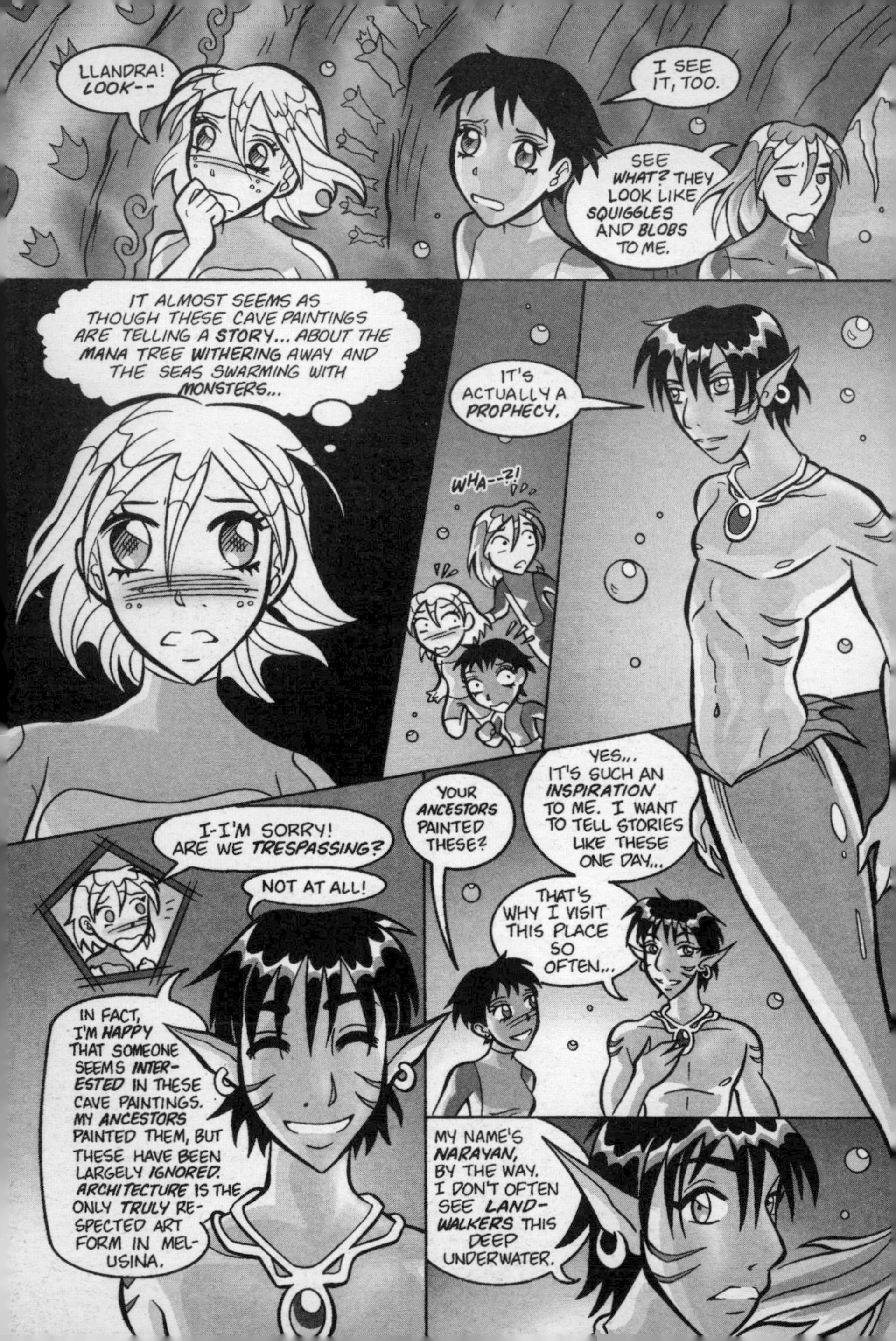
LLANDRA! LOOK--
I SEE IT, TOO.
SEE WHAT? THEY LOOK LIKE SQUIGGLES AND BLOBS TO ME.
IT ALMOST SEEMS AS THOUGH THESE CAVE PAINTINGS ARE TELLING A STORY... ABOUT THE MANA TREE WITHERING AWAY AND THE SEAS SWARMING WITH MONSTERS...
IT'S ACTUALLY A PROPHECY.
WHA--?!
I-I'M SORRY! ARE WE TRESPASSING?
NOT AT ALL!
IN FACT, I'M HAPPY THAT SOMEONE SEEMS INTER-ESTED IN THESE CAVE PAINTINGS. MY ANCESTORS PAINTED THEM, BUT THESE HAVE BEEN LARGELY IGNORED. ARCHITECTURE IS THE ONLY TRULY RE-SPECTED ART FORM IN MEL-USINA.
YOUR ANCESTORS PAINTED THESE?
YES... IT'S SUCH AN INSPIRATION TO ME. I WANT TO TELL STORIES LIKE THESE ONE DAY...
THAT'S WHY I VISIT THIS PLACE SO OFTEN...
MY NAME'S NARAYAN, BY THE WAY. I DON'T OFTEN SEE LAND-WALKERS THIS DEEP UNDERWATER.

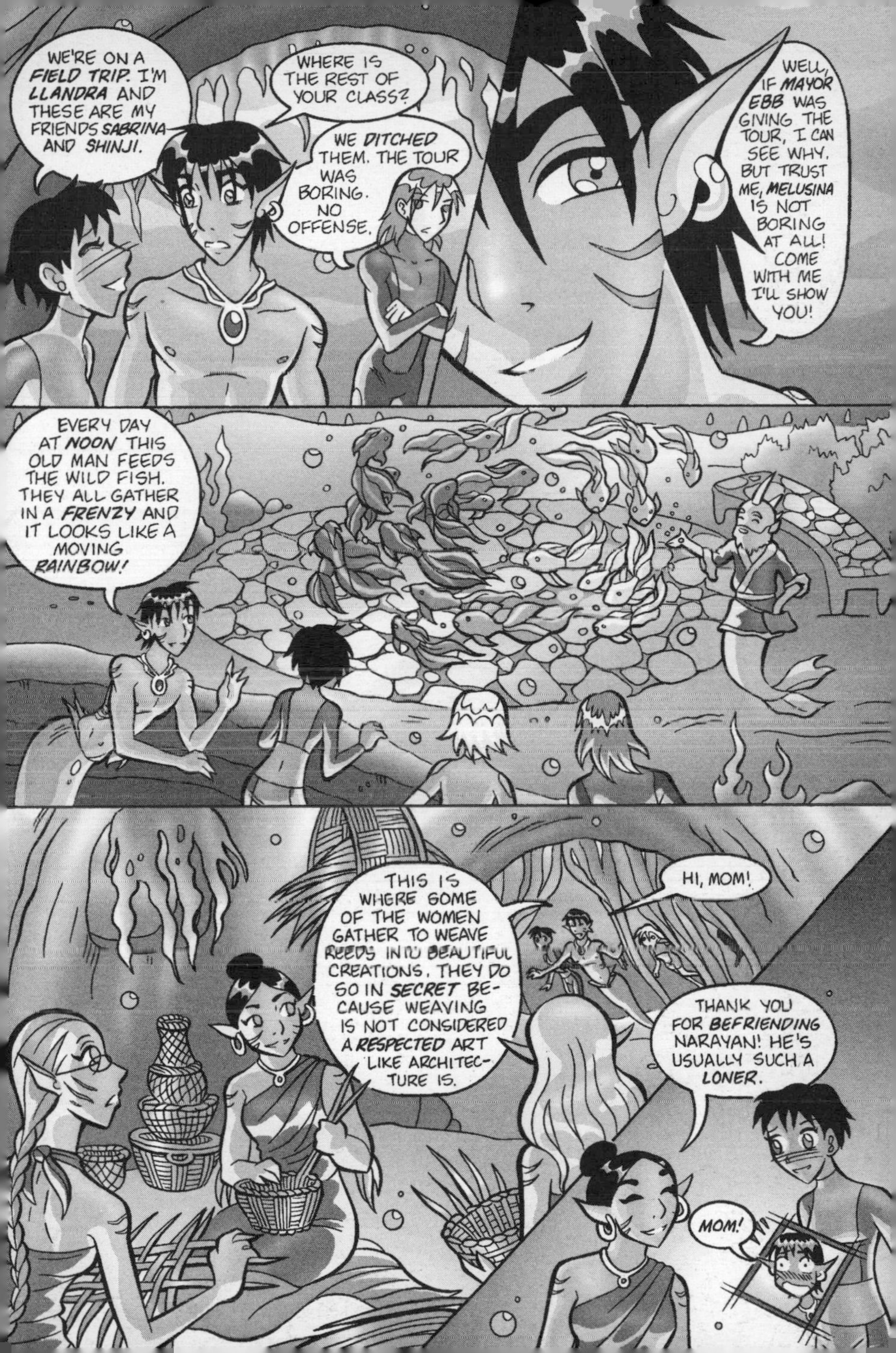
WE'RE ON A FIELD TRIP. I'M LLANDRA AND THESE ARE MY FRIENDS SABRINA AND SHINJI.
WHERE IS THE REST OF YOUR CLASS?
WE DITCHED THEM. THE TOUR WAS BORING. NO OFFENSE.
WELL, IF MAYOR EBB WAS GIVING THE TOUR, I CAN SEE WHY. BUT TRUST ME, MELUSINA IS NOT BORING AT ALL! COME WITH ME I'LL SHOW YOU!
EVERY DAY AT NOON THIS OLD MAN FEEDS THE WILD FISH. THEY ALL GATHER IN A FRENZY AND IT LOOKS LIKE A MOVING RAINBOW!
THIS IS WHERE SOME OF THE WOMEN GATHER TO WEAVE REEDS INTO BEAUTIFUL CREATIONS. THEY DO SO IN SECRET BECAUSE WEAVING IS NOT CONSIDERED A RESPECTED ART LIKE ARCHITECTURE IS.
HI, MOM!
THANK YOU FOR BEFRIENDING NARAYAN! HE'S USUALLY SUCH A LONER.
MOM!

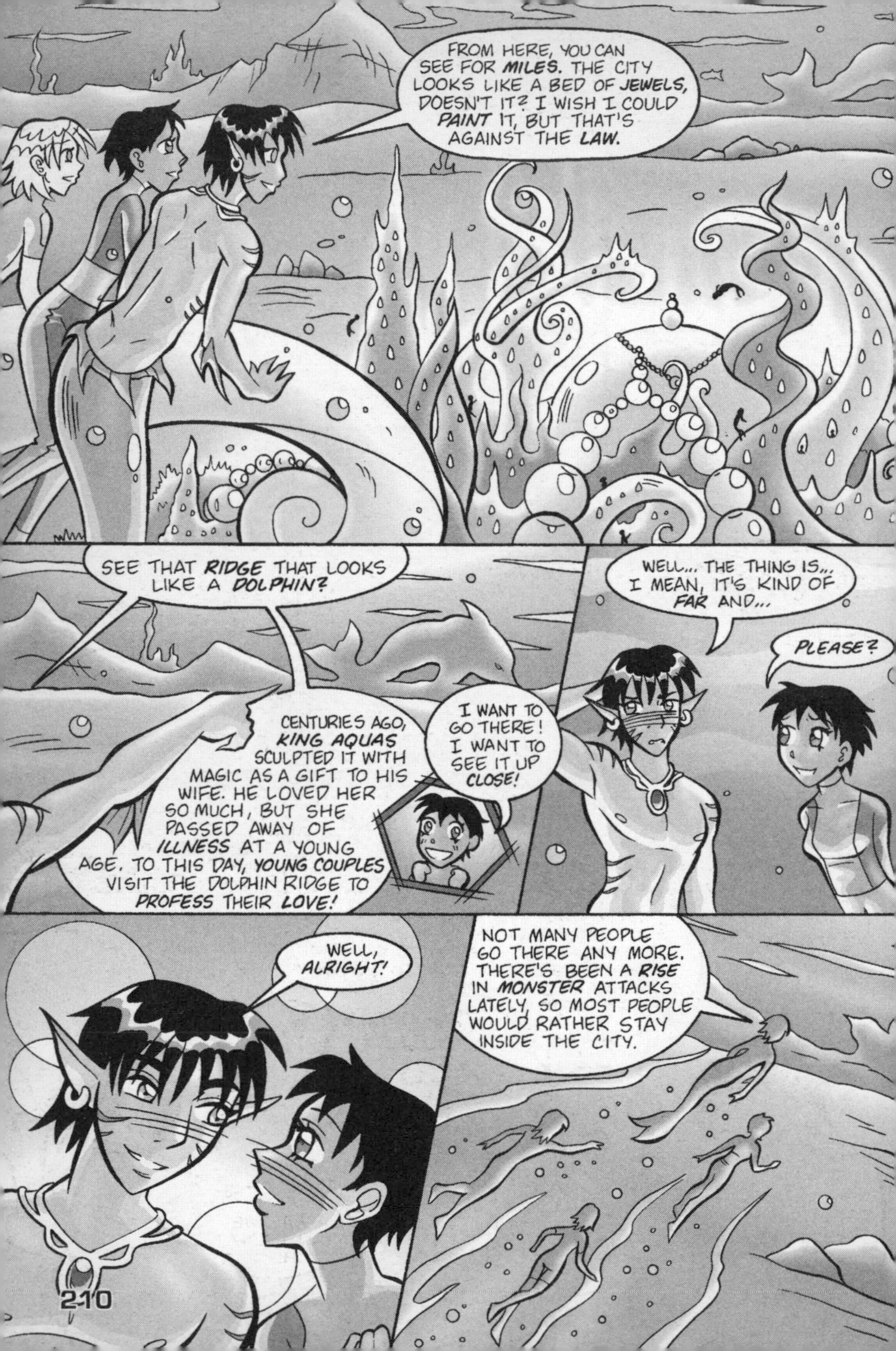
FROM HERE, YOU CAN SEE FOR MILES. THE CITY LOOKS LIKE A BED OF JEWELS, DOESN'T IT? I WISH I COULD PAINT IT, BUT THAT'S AGAINST THE LAW.
SEE THAT RIDGE THAT LOOKS LIKE A DOLPHIN?
CENTURIES AGO, KING AQUAS SCULPTED IT WITH MAGIC AS A GIFT TO HIS WIFE. HE LOVED HER SO MUCH, BUT SHE PASSED AWAY OF ILLNESS AT A YOUNG AGE. TO THIS DAY, YOUNG COUPLES VISIT THE DOLPHIN RIDGE TO PROFESS THEIR LOVE!
I WANT TO GO THERE! I WANT TO SEE IT UP CLOSE!
WELL... THE THING IS... I MEAN, IT'S KIND OF FAR AND...
PLEASE?
WELL, ALRIGHT!
NOT MANY PEOPLE GO THERE ANY MORE. THERE'S BEEN A RISE IN MONSTER ATTACKS LATELY, SO MOST PEOPLE WOULD RATHER STAY INSIDE THE CITY.

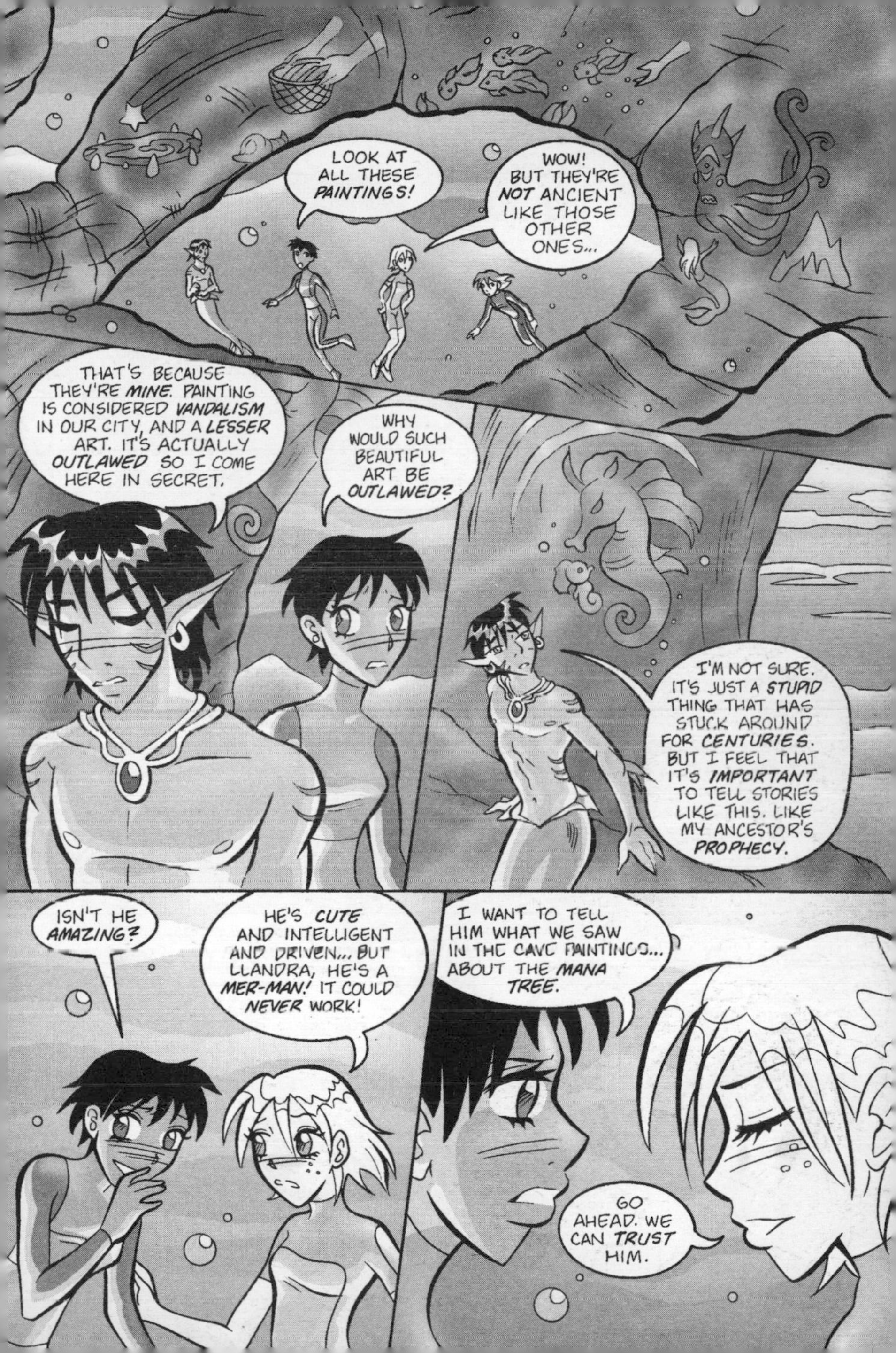
LOOK AT ALL THESE PAINTINGS!
WOW! BUT THEY'RE NOT ANCIENT LIKE THOSE OTHER ONES...
THAT'S BECAUSE THEY'RE MINE. PAINTING IS CONSIDERED VANDALISM IN OUR CITY, AND A LESSER ART. IT'S ACTUALLY OUTLAWED SO I COME HERE IN SECRET.
WHY WOULD SUCH BEAUTIFUL ART BE OUTLAWED?
I'M NOT SURE. IT'S JUST A STUPID THING THAT HAS STUCK AROUND FOR CENTURIES. BUT I FEEL THAT IT'S IMPORTANT TO TELL STORIES LIKE THIS. LIKE MY ANCESTOR'S PROPHECY.
ISN'T HE AMAZING?
HE'S CUTE AND INTELLIGENT AND DRIVEN... BUT LLANDRA, HE'S A MER-MAN! IT COULD NEVER WORK!
I WANT TO TELL HIM WHAT WE SAW IN THE CAVE PAINTINGS... ABOUT THE MANA TREE.
GO AHEAD. WE CAN TRUST HIM.

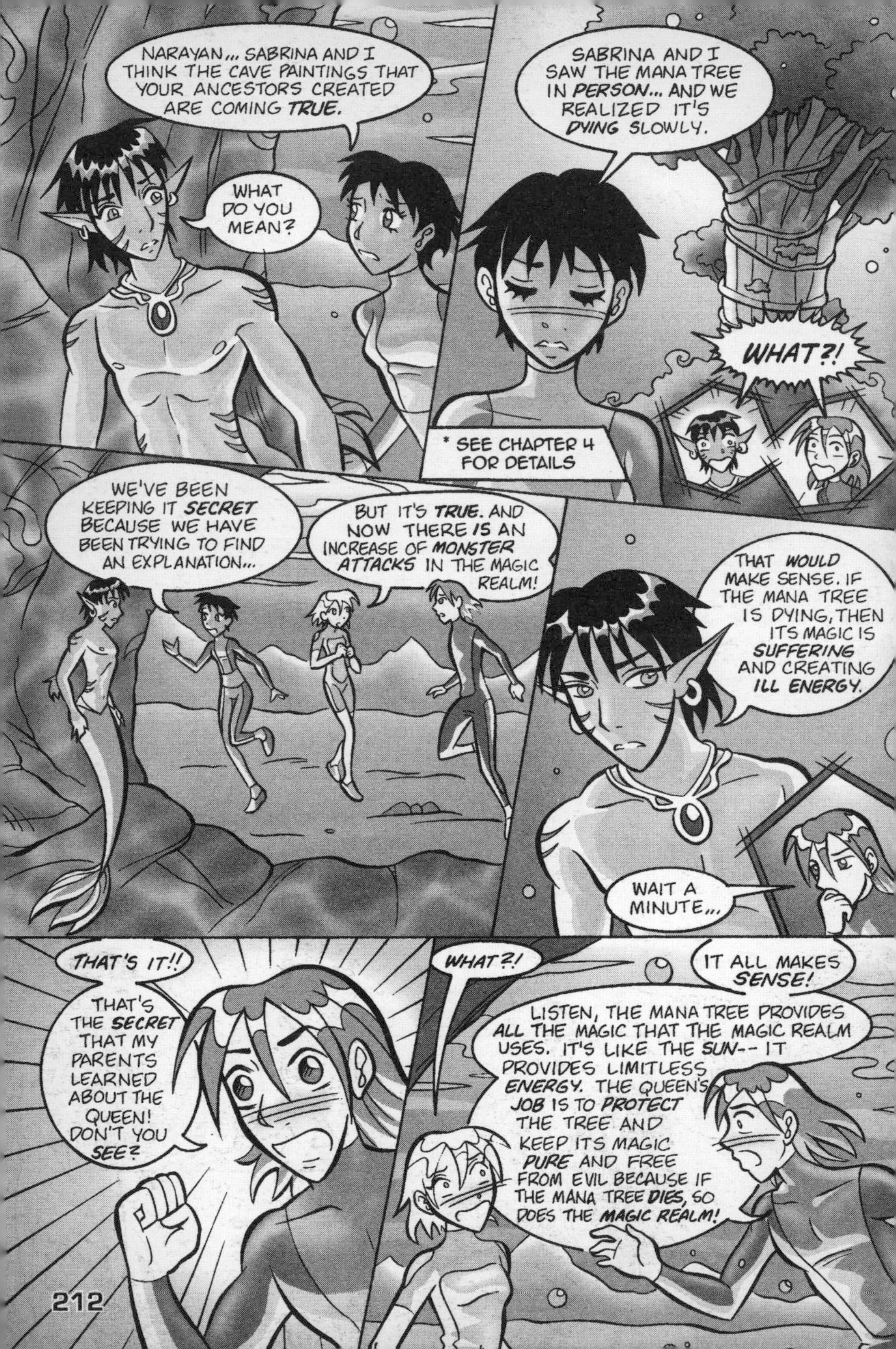
NARAYAN... SABRINA AND I THINK THE CAVE PAINTINGS THAT YOUR ANCESTORS CREATED ARE COMING TRUE.
WHAT DO YOU MEAN?
SABRINA AND I SAW THE MANA TREE IN PERSON... AND WE REALIZED IT'S DYING SLOWLY.
WHAT?!
* SEE CHAPTER 4 FOR DETAILS
WE'VE BEEN KEEPING IT SECRET BECAUSE WE HAVE BEEN TRYING TO FIND AN EXPLANATION...
BUT IT'S TRUE. AND NOW THERE IS AN INCREASE OF MONSTER ATTACKS IN THE MAGIC REALM!
THAT WOULD MAKE SENSE. IF THE MANA TREE IS DYING, THEN ITS MAGIC IS SUFFERING AND CREATING ILL ENERGY.
WAIT A MINUTE...
THAT'S IT!!
THAT'S THE SECRET THAT MY PARENTS LEARNED ABOUT THE QUEEN! DON'T YOU SEE?
WHAT?!
IT ALL MAKES SENSE!
LISTEN, THE MANA TREE PROVIDES ALL THE MAGIC THAT THE MAGIC REALM USES. IT'S LIKE THE SUN-- IT PROVIDES LIMITLESS ENERGY. THE QUEEN'S JOB IS TO PROTECT THE TREE AND KEEP ITS MAGIC PURE AND FREE FROM EVIL BECAUSE IF THE MANA TREE DIES, SO DOES THE MAGIC REALM!

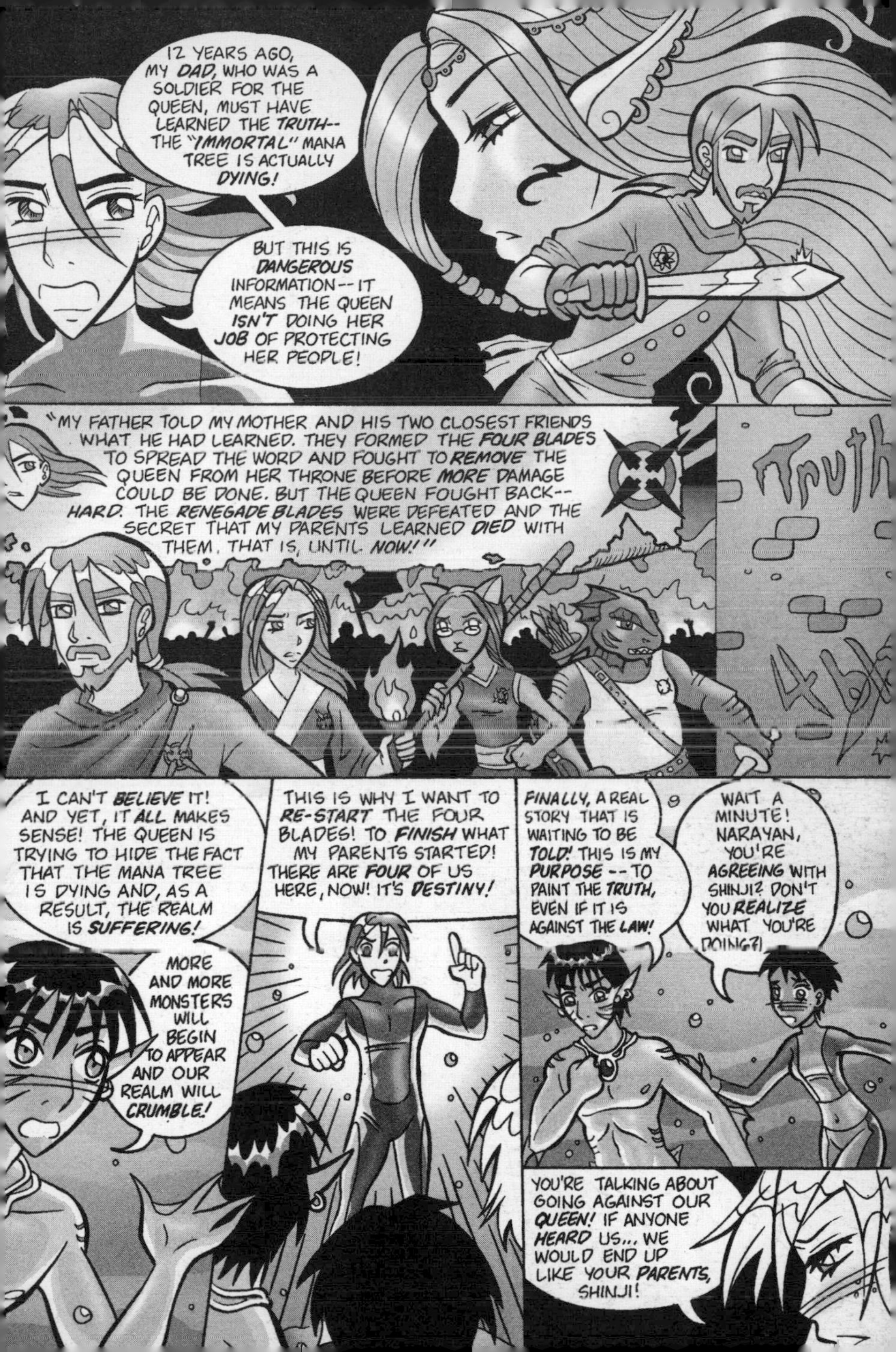
12 YEARS AGO, MY DAD, WHO WAS A SOLDIER FOR THE QUEEN, MUST HAVE LEARNED THE TRUTH-- THE "IMMORTAL" MANA TREE IS ACTUALLY DYING!
BUT THIS IS DANGEROUS INFORMATION-- IT MEANS THE QUEEN ISN'T DOING HER JOB OF PROTECTING HER PEOPLE!
"MY FATHER TOLD MY MOTHER AND HIS TWO CLOSEST FRIENDS WHAT HE HAD LEARNED. THEY FORMED THE FOUR BLADES TO SPREAD THE WORD AND FOUGHT TO REMOVE THE QUEEN FROM HER THRONE BEFORE MORE DAMAGE COULD BE DONE. BUT THE QUEEN FOUGHT BACK-- HARD. THE RENEGADE BLADES WERE DEFEATED AND THE SECRET THAT MY PARENTS LEARNED DIED WITH THEM. THAT IS, UNTIL NOW!"
Truth
I CAN'T BELIEVE IT! AND YET, IT ALL MAKES SENSE! THE QUEEN IS TRYING TO HIDE THE FACT THAT THE MANA TREE IS DYING AND, AS A RESULT, THE REALM IS SUFFERING!
MORE AND MORE MONSTERS WILL BEGIN TO APPEAR AND OUR REALM WILL CRUMBLE!
THIS IS WHY I WANT TO RE-START THE FOUR BLADES! TO FINISH WHAT MY PARENTS STARTED! THERE ARE FOUR OF US HERE, NOW! IT'S DESTINY!
FINALLY, A REAL STORY THAT IS WAITING TO BE TOLD! THIS IS MY PURPOSE --TO PAINT THE TRUTH, EVEN IF IT IS AGAINST THE LAW!
WAIT A MINUTE! NARAYAN, YOU'RE AGREEING WITH SHINJI? DON'T YOU REALIZE WHAT YOU'RE DOING?!
YOU'RE TALKING ABOUT GOING AGAINST OUR QUEEN! IF ANYONE HEARD US... WE WOULD END UP LIKE YOUR PARENTS, SHINJI!

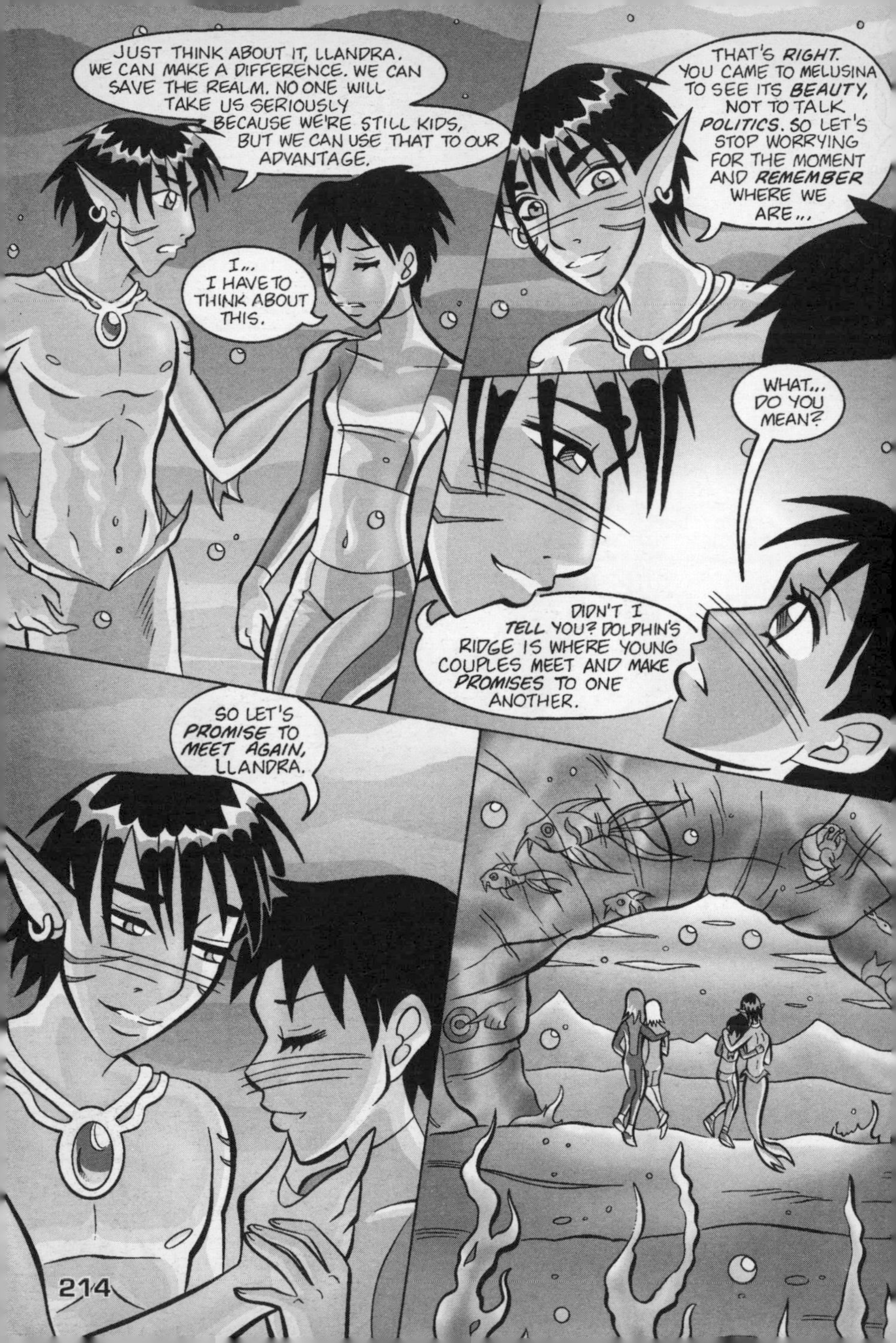
JUST THINK ABOUT IT, LLANDRA. WE CAN MAKE A DIFFERENCE. WE CAN SAVE THE REALM. NO ONE WILL TAKE US SERIOUSLY BECAUSE WE'RE STILL KIDS, BUT WE CAN USE THAT TO OUR ADVANTAGE.
I... I HAVE TO THINK ABOUT THIS.
THAT'S RIGHT. YOU CAME TO MELUSINA TO SEE ITS BEAUTY, NOT TO TALK POLITICS. SO LET'S STOP WORRYING FOR THE MOMENT AND REMEMBER WHERE WE ARE...
WHAT... DO YOU MEAN?
DIDN'T I TELL YOU? DOLPHIN'S RIDGE IS WHERE YOUNG COUPLES MEET AND MAKE PROMISES TO ONE ANOTHER.
SO LET'S PROMISE TO MEET AGAIN, LLANDRA.

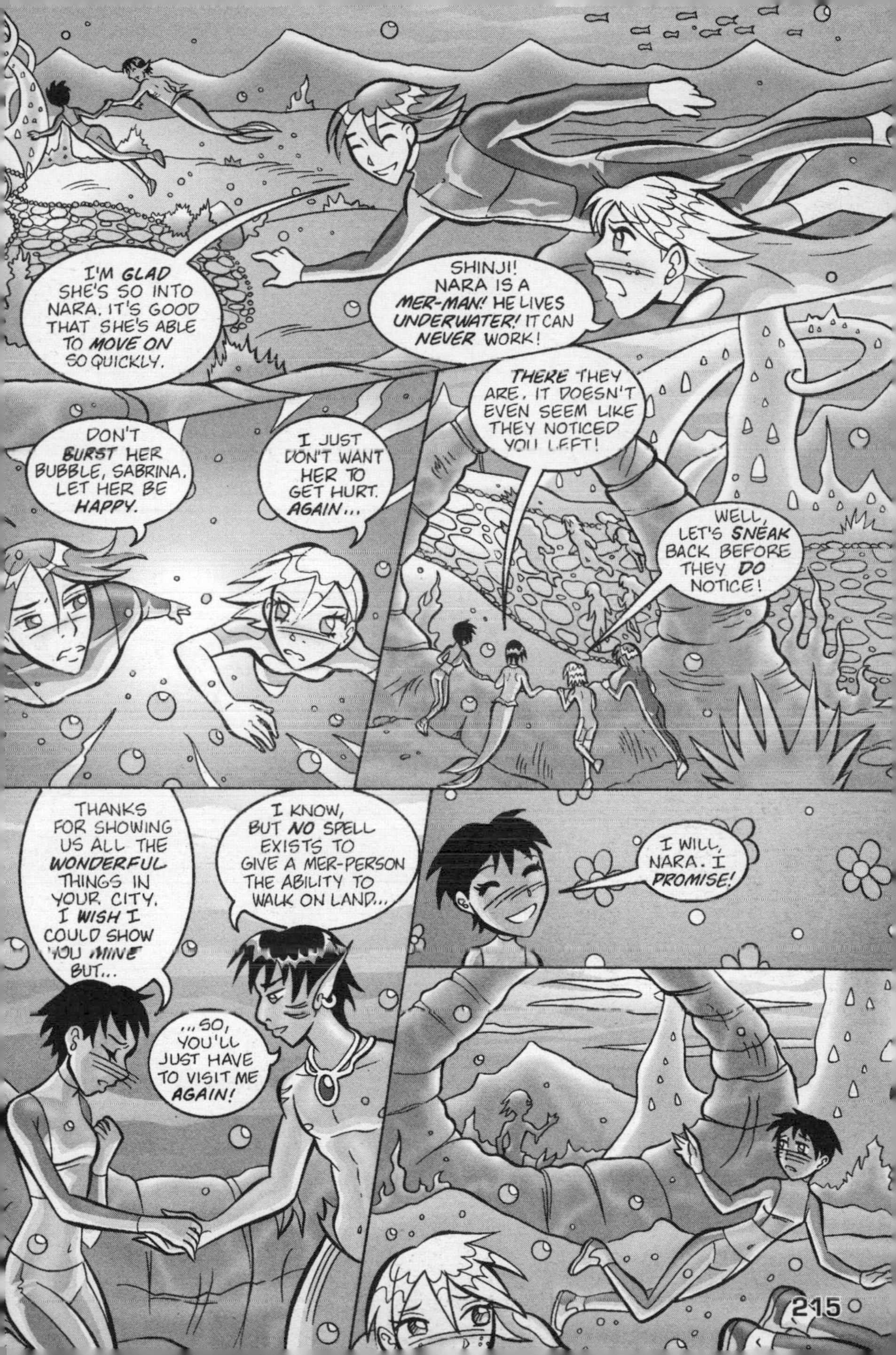
I'M GLAD SHE'S SO INTO NARA. IT'S GOOD THAT SHE'S ABLE TO MOVE ON SO QUICKLY.
SHINJI! NARA IS A MER-MAN! HE LIVES UNDERWATER! IT CAN NEVER WORK!
DON'T BURST HER BUBBLE, SABRINA. LET HER BE HAPPY.
I JUST DON'T WANT HER TO GET HURT. AGAIN...
THERE THEY ARE. IT DOESN'T EVEN SEEM LIKE THEY NOTICED YOU LEFT!
WELL, LET'S SNEAK BACK BEFORE THEY DO NOTICE!
THANKS FOR SHOWING US ALL THE WONDERFUL THINGS IN YOUR CITY. I WISH I COULD SHOW YOU MINE BUT...
I KNOW, BUT NO SPELL EXISTS TO GIVE A MER-PERSON THE ABILITY TO WALK ON LAND...
...SO, YOU'LL JUST HAVE TO VISIT ME AGAIN!
I WILL, NARA. I PROMISE!

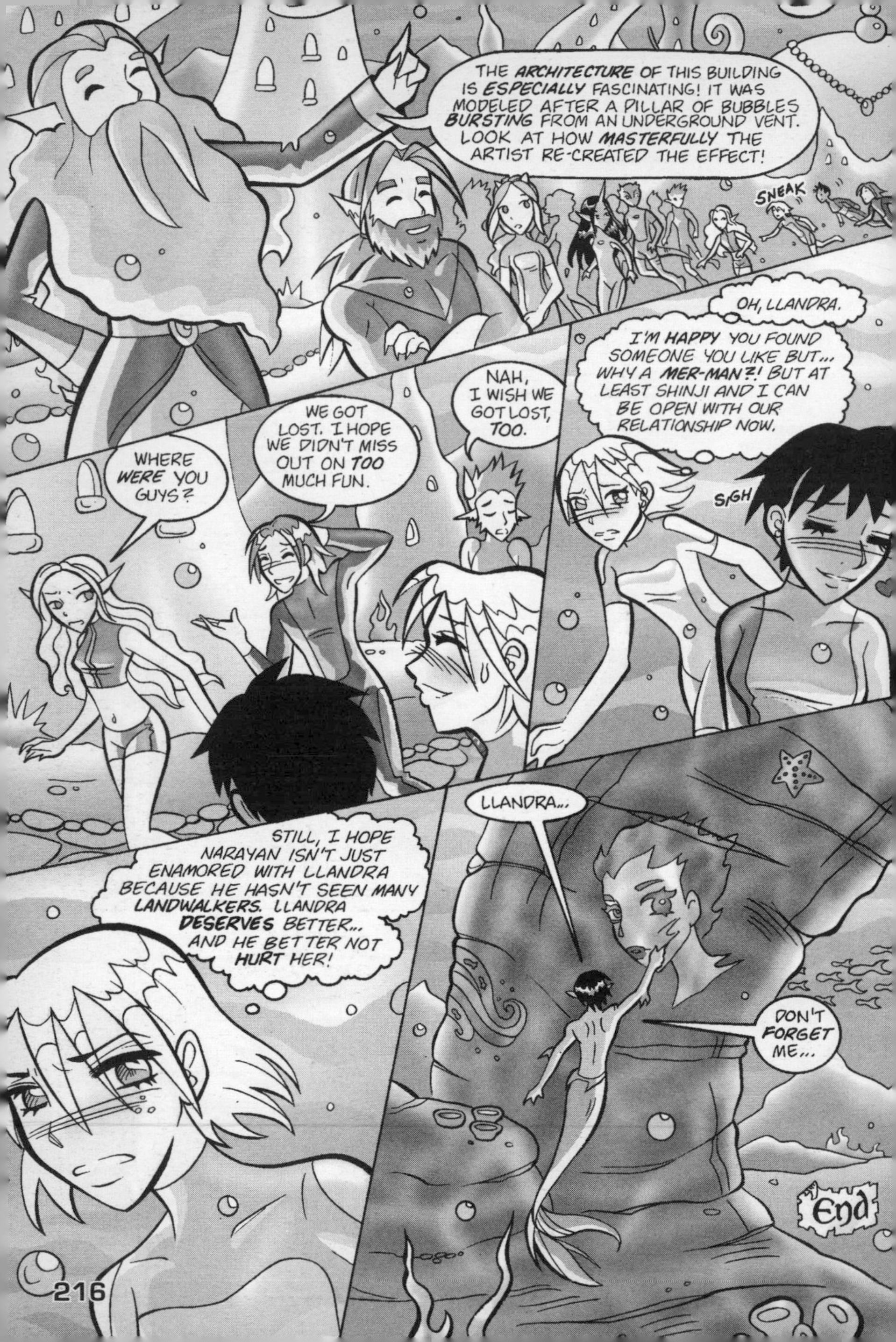
THE ARCHITECTURE OF THIS BUILDING IS ESPECIALLY FASCINATING! IT WAS MODELED AFTER A PILLAR OF BUBBLES BURSTING FROM AN UNDERGROUND VENT. LOOK AT HOW MASTERFULLY THE ARTIST RE-CREATED THE EFFECT!
SNEAK
WHERE WERE YOU GUYS?
WE GOT LOST. I HOPE WE DIDN'T MISS OUT ON TOO MUCH FUN.
NAH, I WISH WE GOT LOST, TOO.
OH, LLANDRA.
I'M HAPPY YOU FOUND SOMEONE YOU LIKE BUT... WHY A MER-MAN?! BUT AT LEAST SHINJI AND I CAN BE OPEN WITH OUR RELATIONSHIP NOW.
SIGH
STILL, I HOPE NARAYAN ISN'T JUST ENAMORED WITH LLANDRA BECAUSE HE HASN'T SEEN MANY LANDWALKERS. LLANDRA DESERVES BETTER... AND HE BETTER NOT HURT HER!
LLANDRA...
DON'T FORGET ME...
End

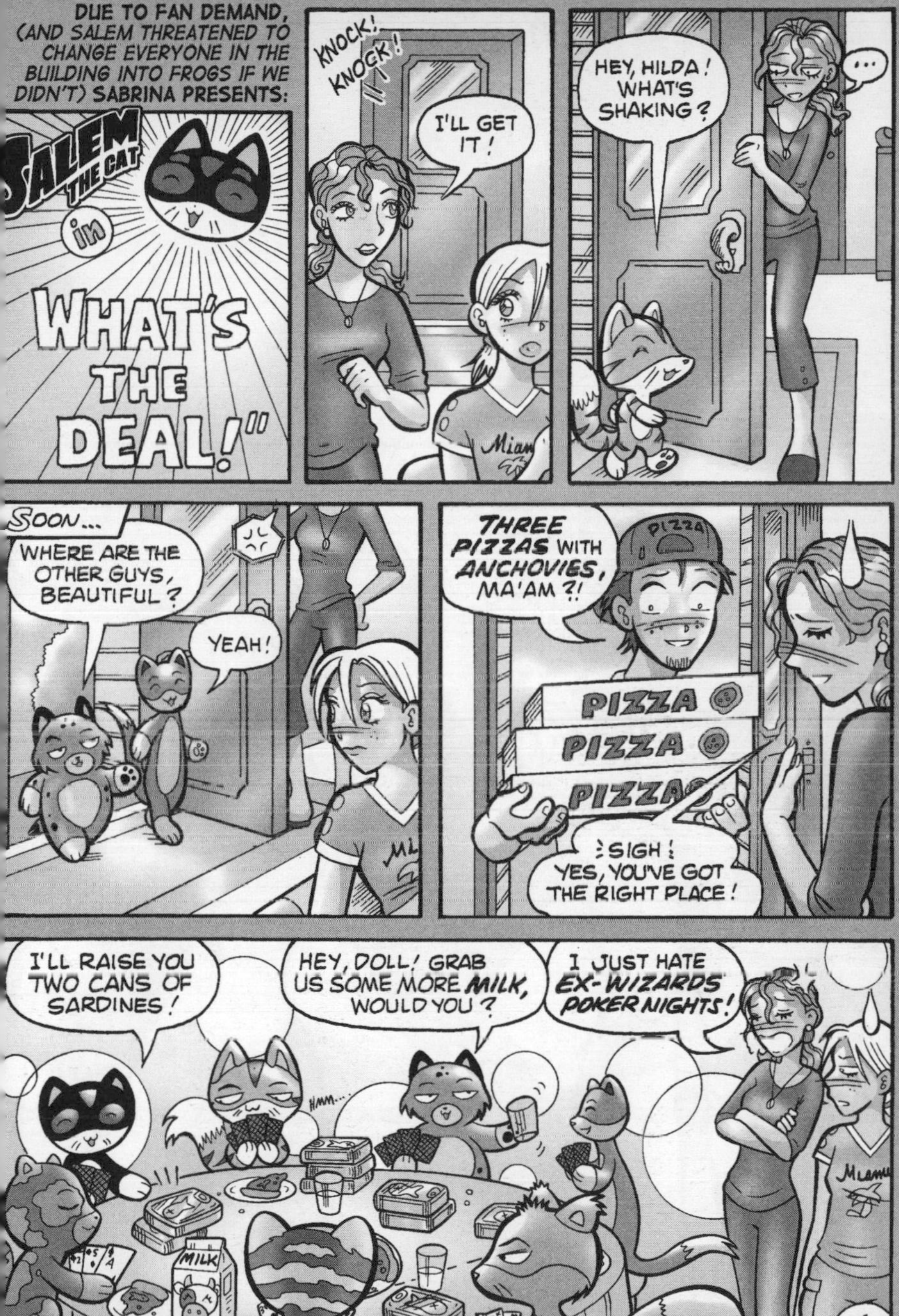
DUE TO FAN DEMAND, (AND SALEM THREATENED TO CHANGE EVERYONE IN THE BUILDING INTO FROGS IF WE DIDN'T) SABRINA PRESENTS:
SALEM THE CAT
in
"WHAT'S THE DEAL!"
KNOCK! KNOCK!
I'LL GET IT!
HEY, HILDA! WHAT'S SHAKING?
...
SOON...
WHERE ARE THE OTHER GUYS, BEAUTIFUL?
YEAH!
THREE PIZZAS WITH ANCHOVIES, MA'AM?!
PIZZA
PIZZA
PIZZA
SIGH! YES, YOU'VE GOT THE RIGHT PLACE!
I'LL RAISE YOU TWO CANS OF SARDINES!
HEY, DOLL! GRAB US SOME MORE MILK, WOULD YOU?
I JUST HATE EX-WIZARDS POKER NIGHTS!
HMM....
MILK
MOO!
THE END

Chapter 11

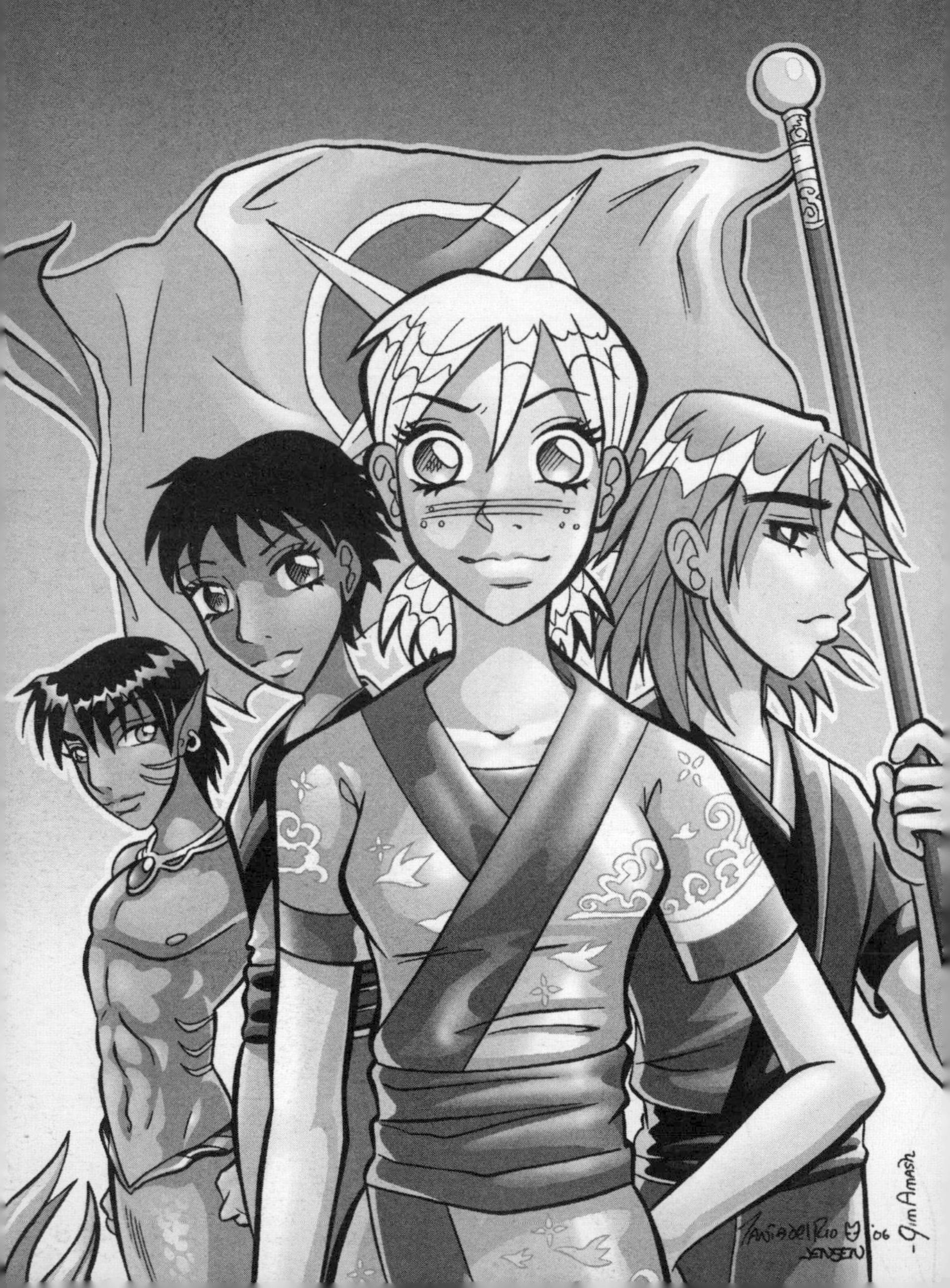

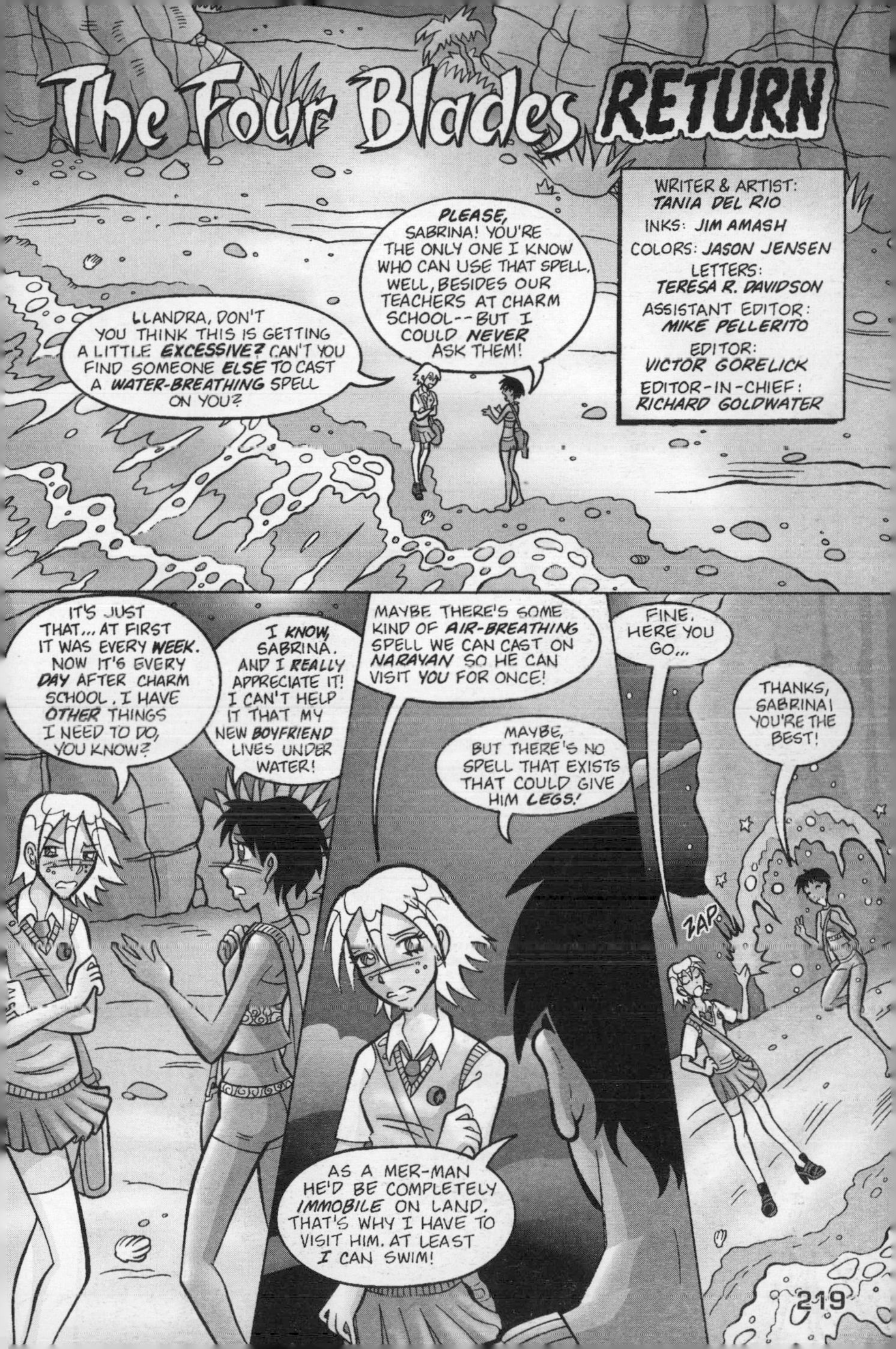

The Four Blades RETURN
WRITER & ARTIST: TANIA DEL RIO
INKS: JIM AMASH
COLORS: JASON JENSEN
LETTERS: TERESA R. DAVIDSON
ASSISTANT EDITOR: MIKE PELLERITO
EDITOR: VICTOR GORELICK
EDITOR-IN-CHIEF: RICHARD GOLDWATER
LLANDRA, DON'T YOU THINK THIS IS GETTING A LITTLE EXCESSIVE? CAN'T YOU FIND SOMEONE ELSE TO CAST A WATER-BREATHING SPELL ON YOU?
PLEASE, SABRINA! YOU'RE THE ONLY ONE I KNOW WHO CAN USE THAT SPELL. WELL, BESIDES OUR TEACHERS AT CHARM SCHOOL--BUT I COULD NEVER ASK THEM!
IT'S JUST THAT... AT FIRST IT WAS EVERY WEEK. NOW IT'S EVERY DAY AFTER CHARM SCHOOL. I HAVE OTHER THINGS I NEED TO DO, YOU KNOW?
I KNOW, SABRINA. AND I REALLY APPRECIATE IT! I CAN'T HELP IT THAT MY NEW BOYFRIEND LIVES UNDER WATER!
MAYBE THERE'S SOME KIND OF AIR-BREATHING SPELL WE CAN CAST ON NARAYAN SO HE CAN VISIT YOU FOR ONCE!
MAYBE, BUT THERE'S NO SPELL THAT EXISTS THAT COULD GIVE HIM LEGS!
AS A MER-MAN HE'D BE COMPLETELY IMMOBILE ON LAND. THAT'S WHY I HAVE TO VISIT HIM. AT LEAST I CAN SWIM!
FINE. HERE YOU GO...
THANKS, SABRINA! YOU'RE THE BEST!
ZAP

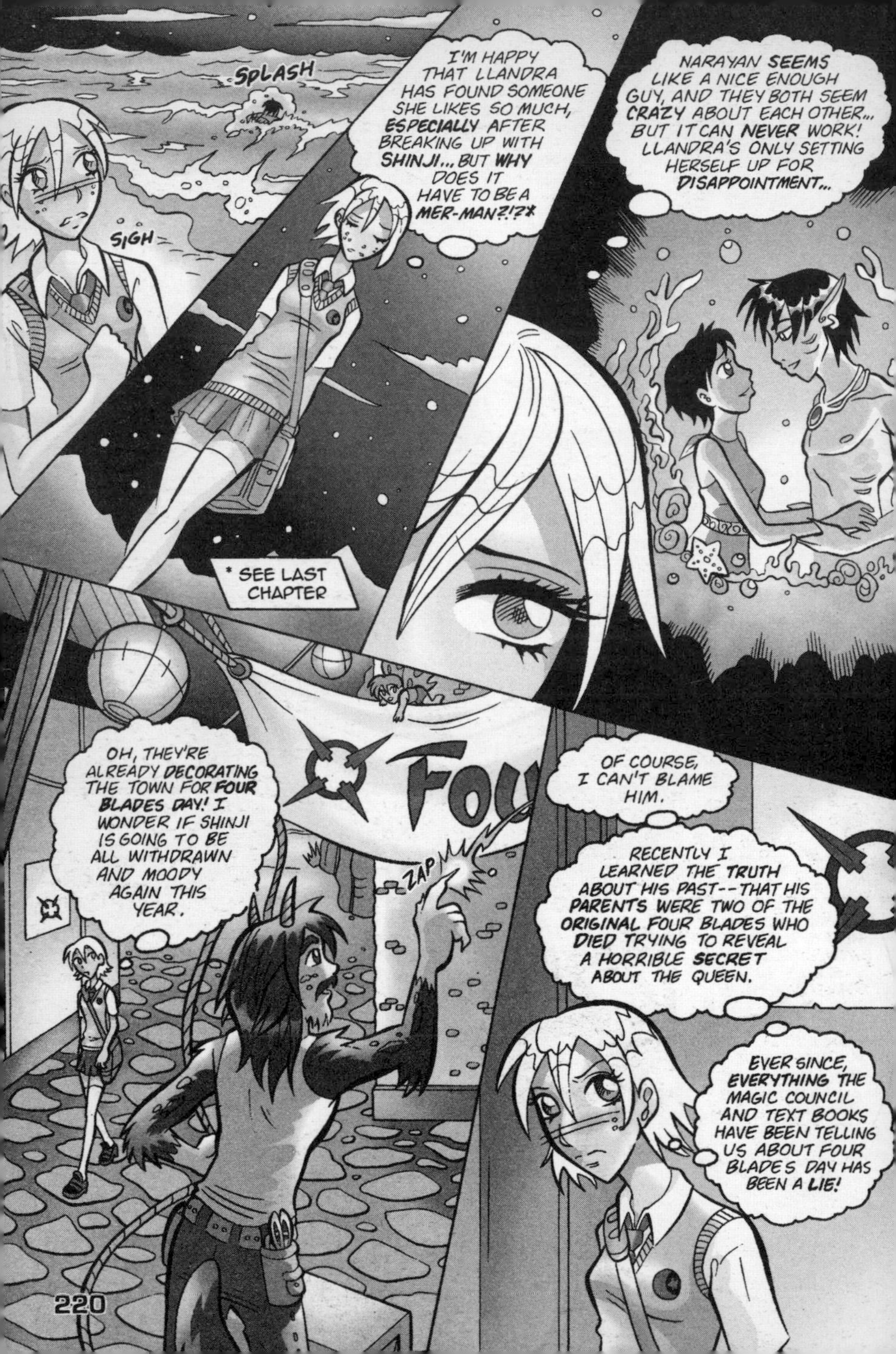

SPLASH
SIGH
I'M HAPPY THAT LLANDRA HAS FOUND SOMEONE SHE LIKES SO MUCH, ESPECIALLY AFTER BREAKING UP WITH SHINJI... BUT WHY DOES IT HAVE TO BE A MER-MAN?!?*
* SEE LAST CHAPTER
NARAYAN SEEMS LIKE A NICE ENOUGH GUY, AND THEY BOTH SEEM CRAZY ABOUT EACH OTHER... BUT IT CAN NEVER WORK! LLANDRA'S ONLY SETTING HERSELF UP FOR DISAPPOINTMENT...
OH, THEY'RE ALREADY DECORATING THE TOWN FOR FOUR BLADES DAY! I WONDER IF SHINJI IS GOING TO BE ALL WITHDRAWN AND MOODY AGAIN THIS YEAR.
FOU
ZAP
OF COURSE, I CAN'T BLAME HIM.
RECENTLY I LEARNED THE TRUTH ABOUT HIS PAST--THAT HIS PARENTS WERE TWO OF THE ORIGINAL FOUR BLADES WHO DIED TRYING TO REVEAL A HORRIBLE SECRET ABOUT THE QUEEN.
EVER SINCE, EVERYTHING THE MAGIC COUNCIL AND TEXT BOOKS HAVE BEEN TELLING US ABOUT FOUR BLADES DAY HAS BEEN A LIE!

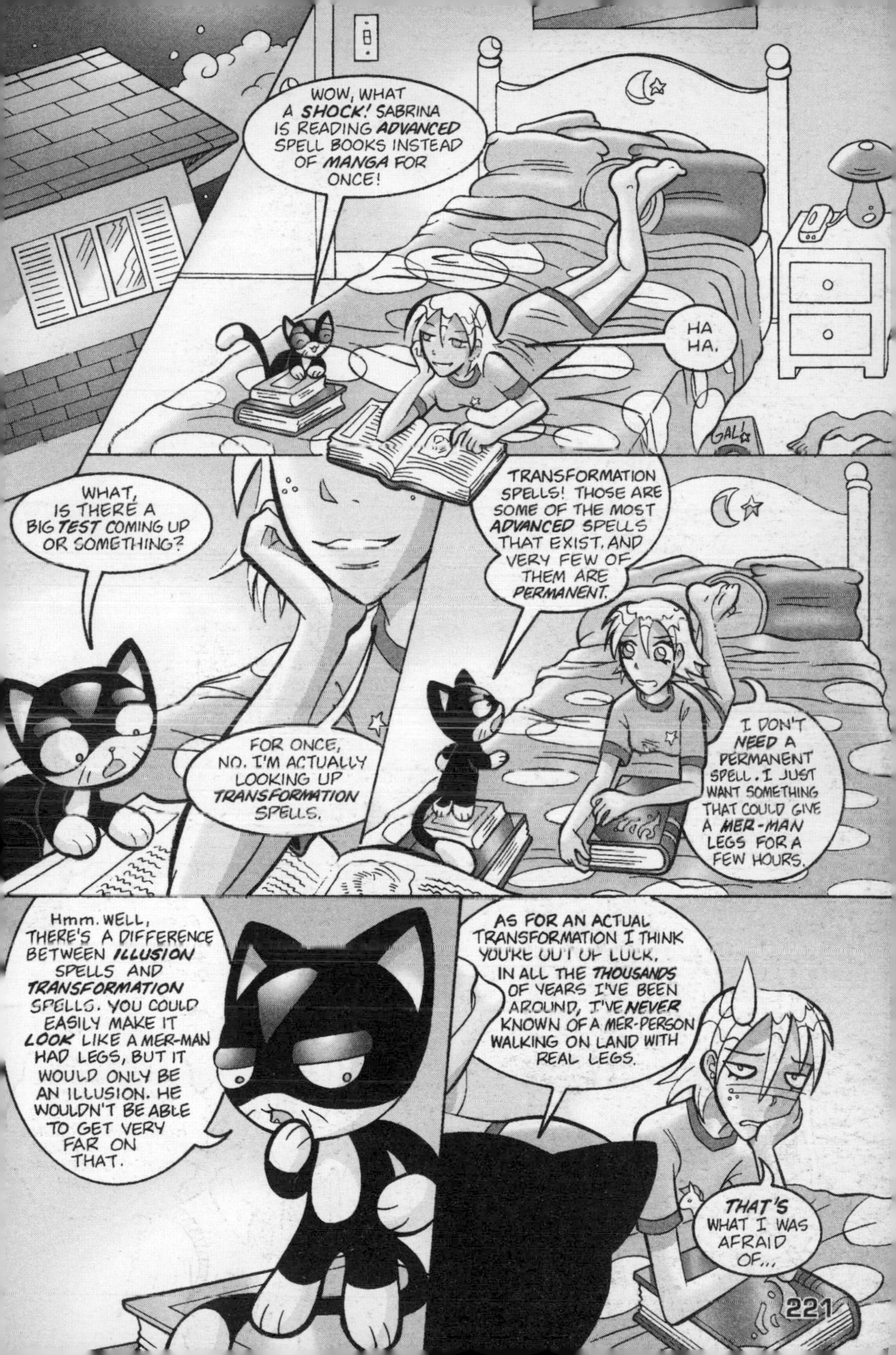

WOW, WHAT A SHOCK! SABRINA IS READING ADVANCED SPELL BOOKS INSTEAD OF MANGA FOR ONCE!
HA HA.
GAL!
WHAT, IS THERE A BIG TEST COMING UP OR SOMETHING?
FOR ONCE, NO. I'M ACTUALLY LOOKING UP TRANSFORMATION SPELLS.
TRANSFORMATION SPELLS! THOSE ARE SOME OF THE MOST ADVANCED SPELLS THAT EXIST. AND VERY FEW OF THEM ARE PERMANENT.
I DON'T NEED A PERMANENT SPELL. I JUST WANT SOMETHING THAT COULD GIVE A MER-MAN LEGS FOR A FEW HOURS.
Hmm. WELL, THERE'S A DIFFERENCE BETWEEN ILLUSION SPELLS AND TRANSFORMATION SPELLS. YOU COULD EASILY MAKE IT LOOK LIKE A MER-MAN HAD LEGS, BUT IT WOULD ONLY BE AN ILLUSION. HE WOULDN'T BE ABLE TO GET VERY FAR ON THAT.
AS FOR AN ACTUAL TRANSFORMATION I THINK YOU'RE OUT OF LUCK.
IN ALL THE THOUSANDS OF YEARS I'VE BEEN AROUND, I'VE NEVER KNOWN OF A MER-PERSON WALKING ON LAND WITH REAL LEGS.
THAT'S WHAT I WAS AFRAID OF...

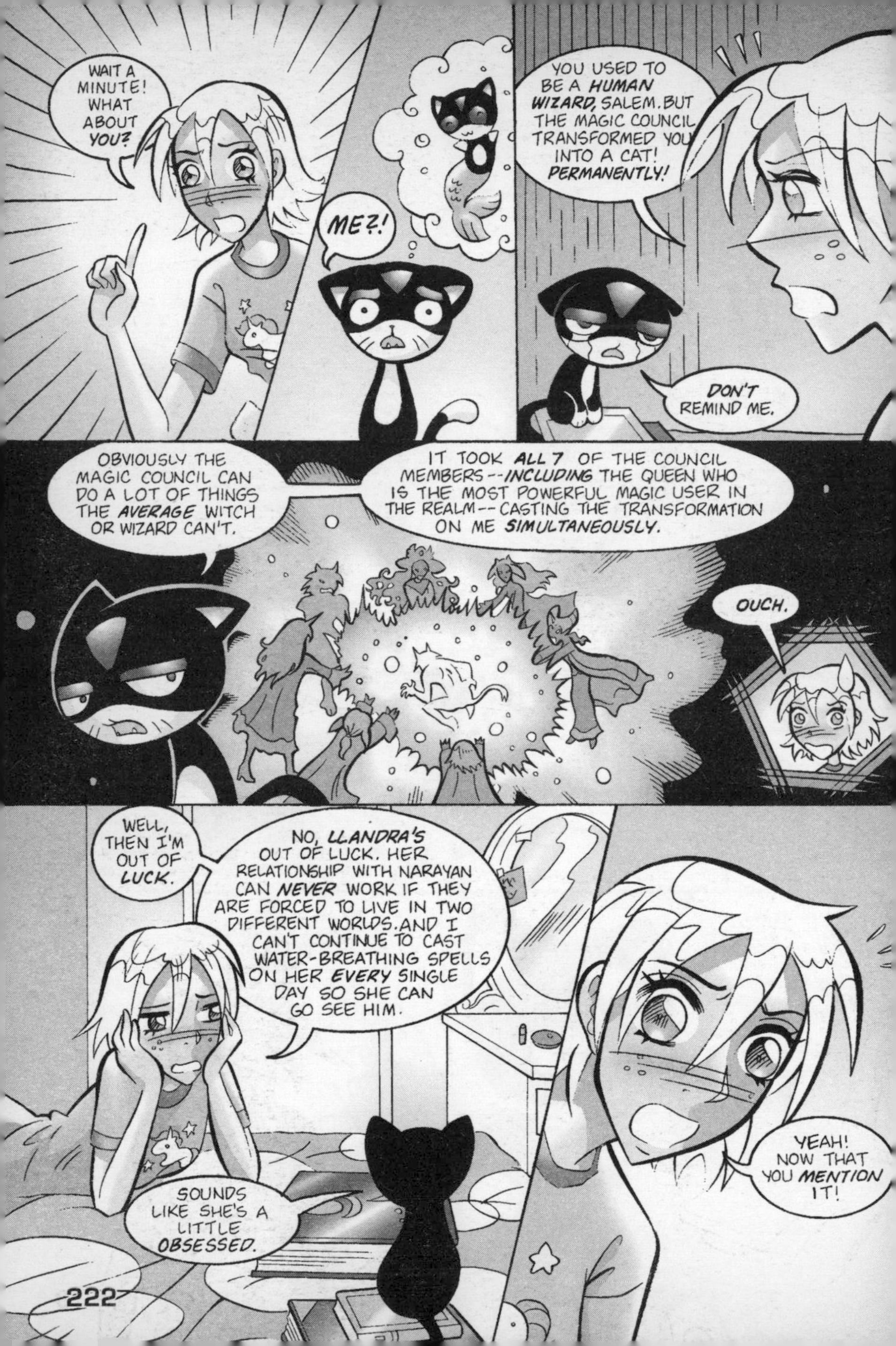

WAIT A MINUTE! WHAT ABOUT YOU?
ME?!
YOU USED TO BE A HUMAN WIZARD, SALEM. BUT THE MAGIC COUNCIL TRANSFORMED YOU INTO A CAT! PERMANENTLY!
DON'T REMIND ME.
OBVIOUSLY THE MAGIC COUNCIL CAN DO A LOT OF THINGS THE AVERAGE WITCH OR WIZARD CAN'T.
IT TOOK ALL 7 OF THE COUNCIL MEMBERS--INCLUDING THE QUEEN WHO IS THE MOST POWERFUL MAGIC USER IN THE REALM--CASTING THE TRANSFORMATION ON ME SIMULTANEOUSLY.
OUCH.
WELL, THEN I'M OUT OF LUCK.
NO, LLANDRA'S OUT OF LUCK. HER RELATIONSHIP WITH NARAYAN CAN NEVER WORK IF THEY ARE FORCED TO LIVE IN TWO DIFFERENT WORLDS. AND I CAN'T CONTINUE TO CAST WATER-BREATHING SPELLS ON HER EVERY SINGLE DAY SO SHE CAN GO SEE HIM.
SOUNDS LIKE SHE'S A LITTLE OBSESSED.
YEAH! NOW THAT YOU MENTION IT!

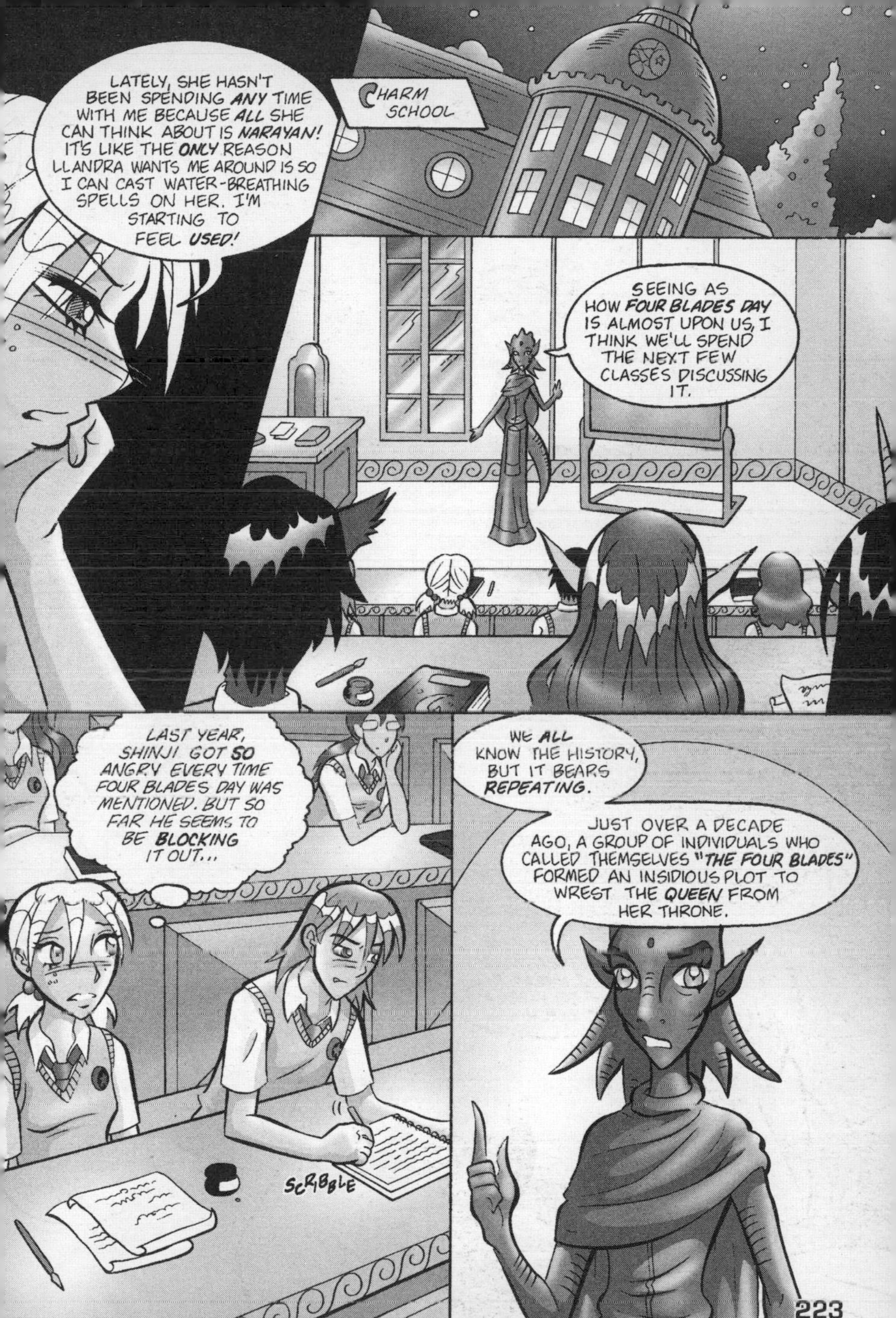
LATELY, SHE HASN'T BEEN SPENDING ANY TIME WITH ME BECAUSE ALL SHE CAN THINK ABOUT IS NARAYAN! IT'S LIKE THE ONLY REASON LLANDRA WANTS ME AROUND IS SO I CAN CAST WATER-BREATHING SPELLS ON HER. I'M STARTING TO FEEL USED!
CHARM SCHOOL
SEEING AS HOW FOUR BLADES DAY IS ALMOST UPON US, I THINK WE'LL SPEND THE NEXT FEW CLASSES DISCUSSING IT.
LAST YEAR, SHINJI GOT SO ANGRY EVERY TIME FOUR BLADES DAY WAS MENTIONED. BUT SO FAR HE SEEMS TO BE BLOCKING IT OUT...
SCRIBBLE
WE ALL KNOW THE HISTORY, BUT IT BEARS REPEATING.
JUST OVER A DECADE AGO, A GROUP OF INDIVIDUALS WHO CALLED THEMSELVES "THE FOUR BLADES" FORMED AN INSIDIOUS PLOT TO WREST THE QUEEN FROM HER THRONE.

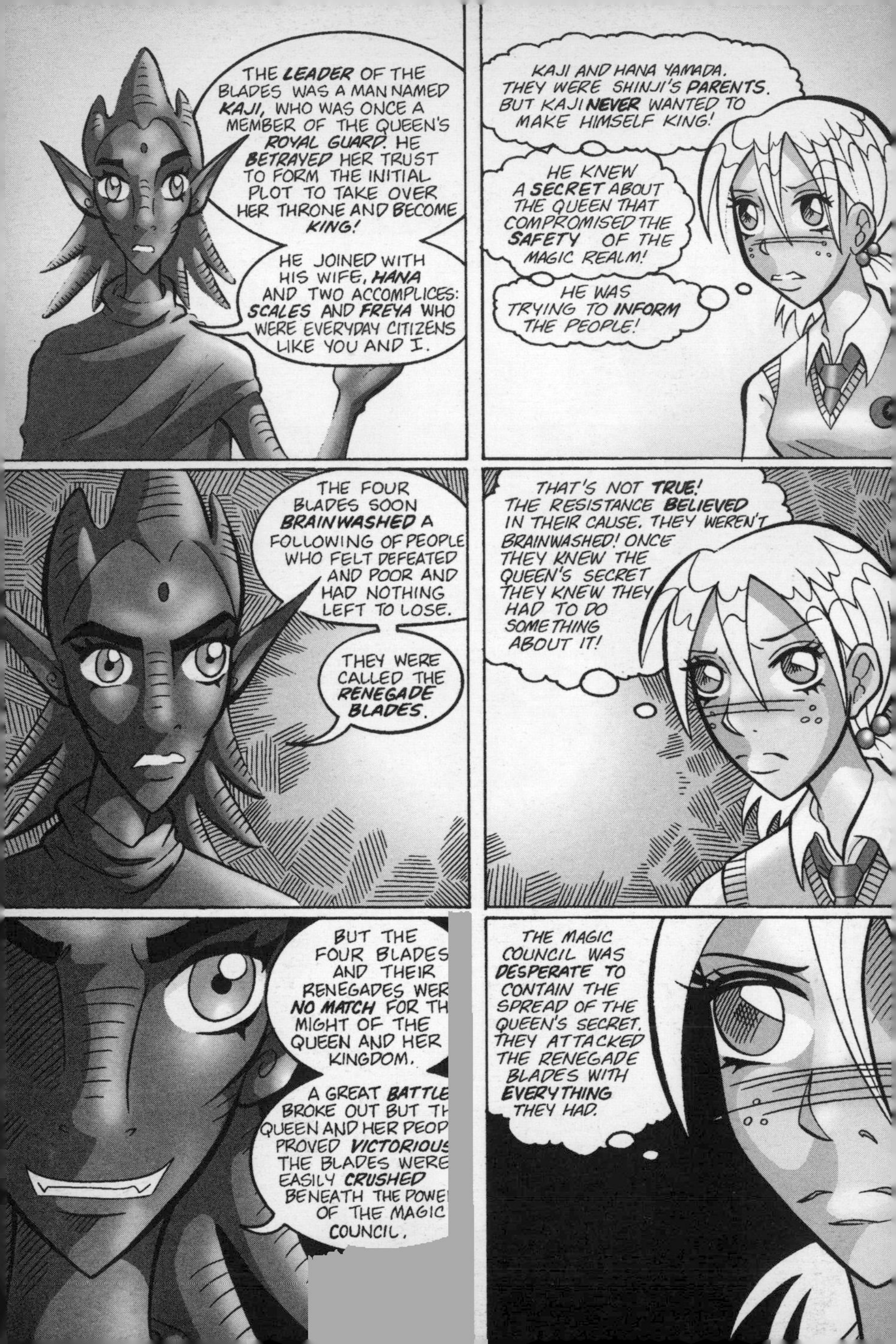
THE LEADER OF THE BLADES WAS A MAN NAMED KAJI, WHO WAS ONCE A MEMBER OF THE QUEEN'S ROYAL GUARD. HE BETRAYED HER TRUST TO FORM THE INITIAL PLOT TO TAKE OVER HER THRONE AND BECOME KING!
HE JOINED WITH HIS WIFE, HANA AND TWO ACCOMPLICES: SCALES AND FREYA WHO WERE EVERYDAY CITIZENS LIKE YOU AND I.
KAJI AND HANA YAMADA. THEY WERE SHINJI'S PARENTS. BUT KAJI NEVER WANTED TO MAKE HIMSELF KING!
HE KNEW A SECRET ABOUT THE QUEEN THAT COMPROMISED THE SAFETY OF THE MAGIC REALM!
HE WAS TRYING TO INFORM THE PEOPLE!
THE FOUR BLADES SOON BRAINWASHED A FOLLOWING OF PEOPLE WHO FELT DEFEATED AND POOR AND HAD NOTHING LEFT TO LOSE.
THEY WERE CALLED THE RENEGADE BLADES.
THAT'S NOT TRUE! THE RESISTANCE BELIEVED IN THEIR CAUSE. THEY WEREN'T BRAINWASHED! ONCE THEY KNEW THE QUEEN'S SECRET THEY KNEW THEY HAD TO DO SOMETHING ABOUT IT!
BUT THE FOUR BLADES AND THEIR RENEGADES WER NO MATCH FOR TH MIGHT OF THE QUEEN AND HER KINGDOM.
A GREAT BATTLE BROKE OUT BUT TH QUEEN AND HER PEOP PROVED VICTORIOUS THE BLADES WERE EASILY CRUSHED BENEATH THE POWE OF THE MAGIC COUNCIL.
THE MAGIC COUNCIL WAS DESPERATE TO CONTAIN THE SPREAD OF THE QUEEN'S SECRET. THEY ATTACKED THE RENEGADE BLADES WITH EVERYTHING THEY HAD.

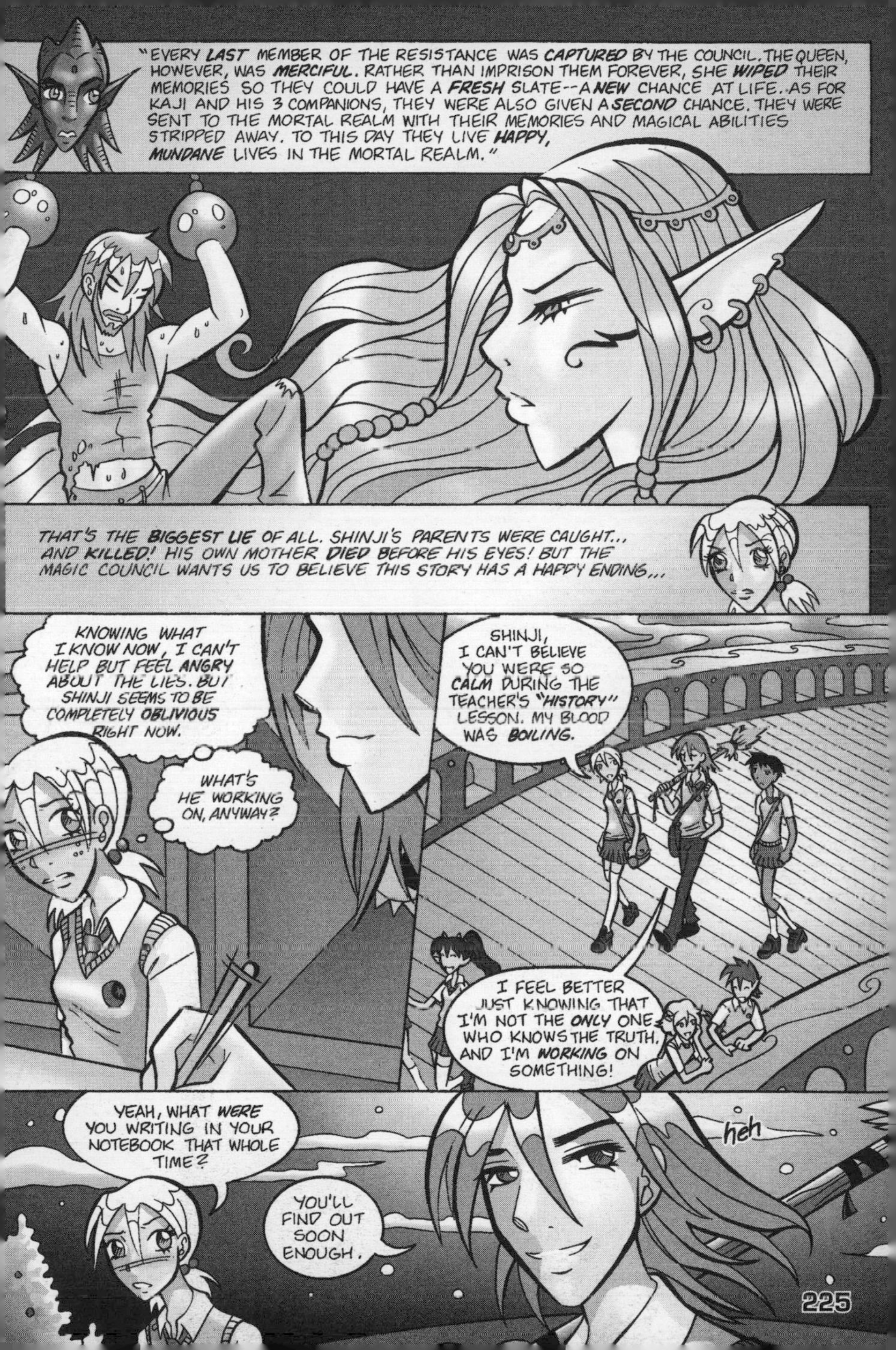
"EVERY LAST MEMBER OF THE RESISTANCE WAS CAPTURED BY THE COUNCIL. THE QUEEN, HOWEVER, WAS MERCIFUL. RATHER THAN IMPRISON THEM FOREVER, SHE WIPED THEIR MEMORIES SO THEY COULD HAVE A FRESH SLATE--A NEW CHANCE AT LIFE. AS FOR KAJI AND HIS 3 COMPANIONS, THEY WERE ALSO GIVEN A SECOND CHANCE. THEY WERE SENT TO THE MORTAL REALM WITH THEIR MEMORIES AND MAGICAL ABILITIES STRIPPED AWAY. TO THIS DAY THEY LIVE HAPPY, MUNDANE LIVES IN THE MORTAL REALM."
THAT'S THE BIGGEST LIE OF ALL. SHINJI'S PARENTS WERE CAUGHT... AND KILLED! HIS OWN MOTHER DIED BEFORE HIS EYES! BUT THE MAGIC COUNCIL WANTS US TO BELIEVE THIS STORY HAS A HAPPY ENDING...
KNOWING WHAT I KNOW NOW, I CAN'T HELP BUT FEEL ANGRY ABOUT THE LIES. BUT SHINJI SEEMS TO BE COMPLETELY OBLIVIOUS RIGHT NOW.
WHAT'S HE WORKING ON, ANYWAY?
SHINJI, I CAN'T BELIEVE YOU WERE SO CALM DURING THE TEACHER'S "HISTORY" LESSON. MY BLOOD WAS BOILING.
I FEEL BETTER JUST KNOWING THAT I'M NOT THE ONLY ONE WHO KNOWS THE TRUTH, AND I'M WORKING ON SOMETHING!
YEAH, WHAT WERE YOU WRITING IN YOUR NOTEBOOK THAT WHOLE TIME?
heh
YOU'LL FIND OUT SOON ENOUGH.

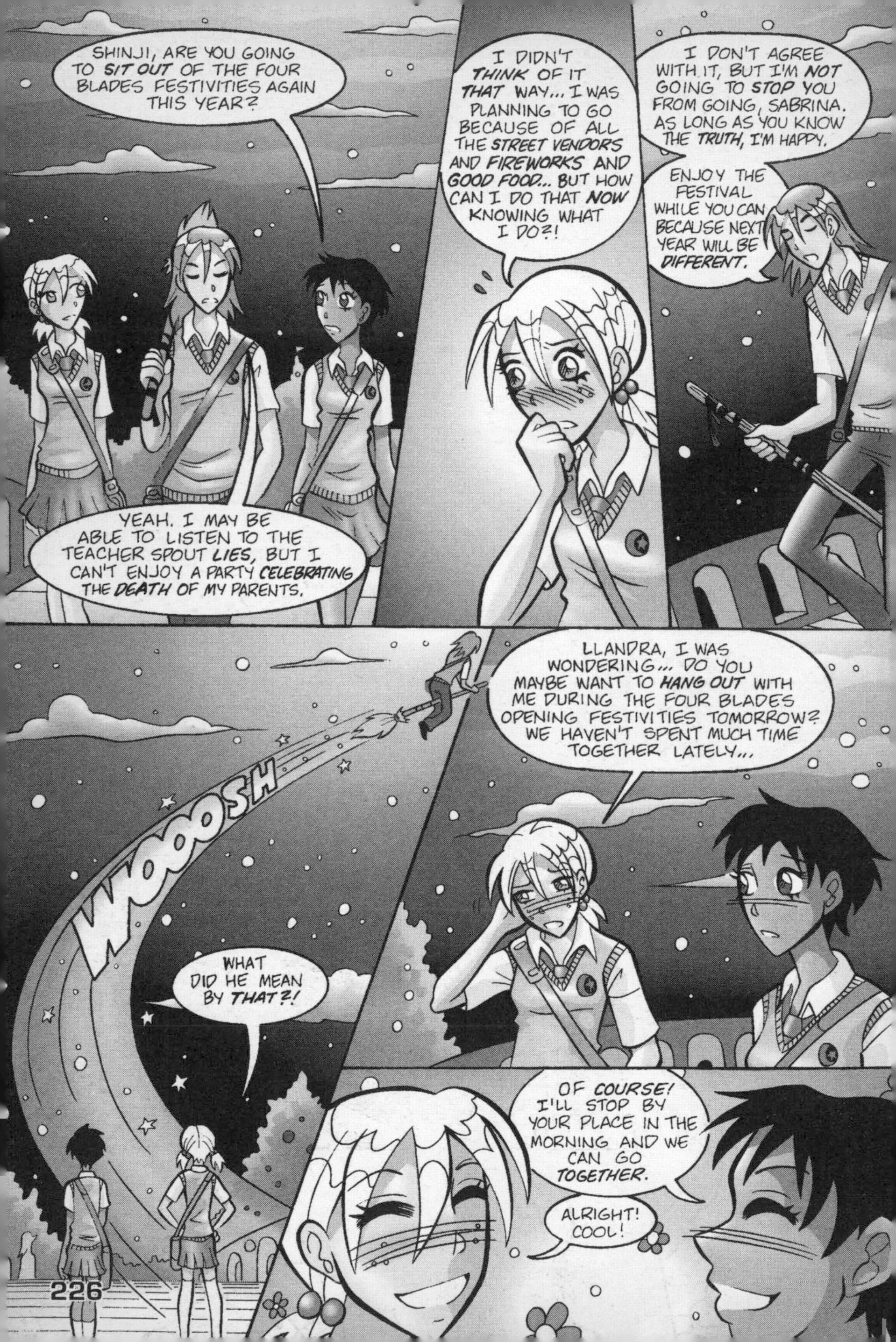
SHINJI, ARE YOU GOING TO SIT OUT OF THE FOUR BLADES FESTIVITIES AGAIN THIS YEAR?
YEAH. I MAY BE ABLE TO LISTEN TO THE TEACHER SPOUT LIES, BUT I CAN'T ENJOY A PARTY CELEBRATING THE DEATH OF MY PARENTS.
I DIDN'T THINK OF IT THAT WAY... I WAS PLANNING TO GO BECAUSE OF ALL THE STREET VENDORS AND FIREWORKS AND GOOD FOOD... BUT HOW CAN I DO THAT NOW KNOWING WHAT I DO?!
I DON'T AGREE WITH IT, BUT I'M NOT GOING TO STOP YOU FROM GOING, SABRINA. AS LONG AS YOU KNOW THE TRUTH, I'M HAPPY.
ENJOY THE FESTIVAL WHILE YOU CAN BECAUSE NEXT YEAR WILL BE DIFFERENT.
WOOOSH
WHAT DID HE MEAN BY THAT?!
LLANDRA, I WAS WONDERING... DO YOU MAYBE WANT TO HANG OUT WITH ME DURING THE FOUR BLADES OPENING FESTIVITIES TOMORROW? WE HAVEN'T SPENT MUCH TIME TOGETHER LATELY...
OF COURSE! I'LL STOP BY YOUR PLACE IN THE MORNING AND WE CAN GO TOGETHER.
ALRIGHT! COOL!

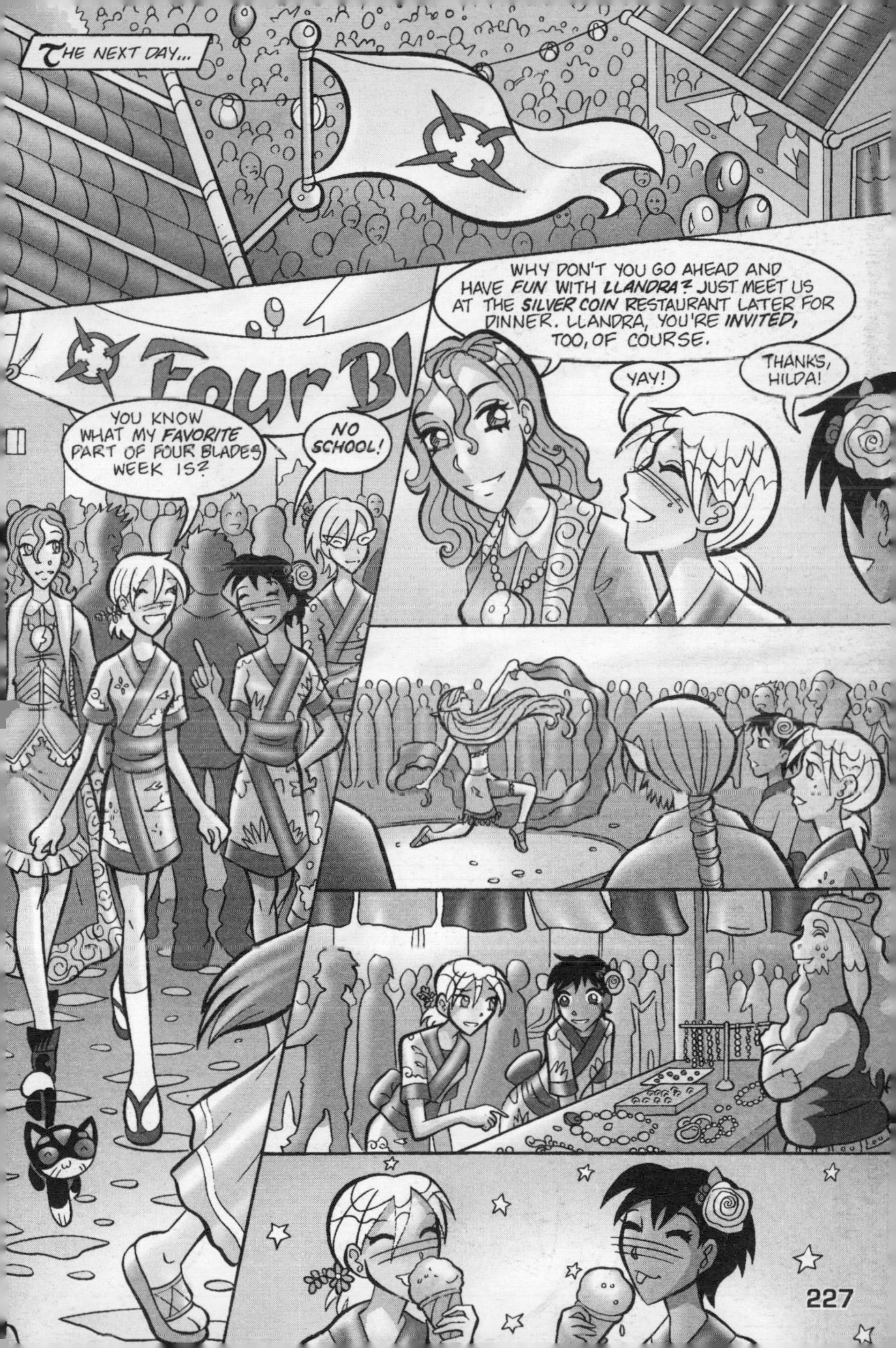

THE NEXT DAY...
YOU KNOW WHAT MY FAVORITE PART OF FOUR BLADES WEEK IS?
NO SCHOOL!
WHY DON'T YOU GO AHEAD AND HAVE FUN WITH LLANDRA? JUST MEET US AT THE SILVER COIN RESTAURANT LATER FOR DINNER. LLANDRA, YOU'RE INVITED, TOO, OF COURSE.
YAY!
THANKS, HILDA!

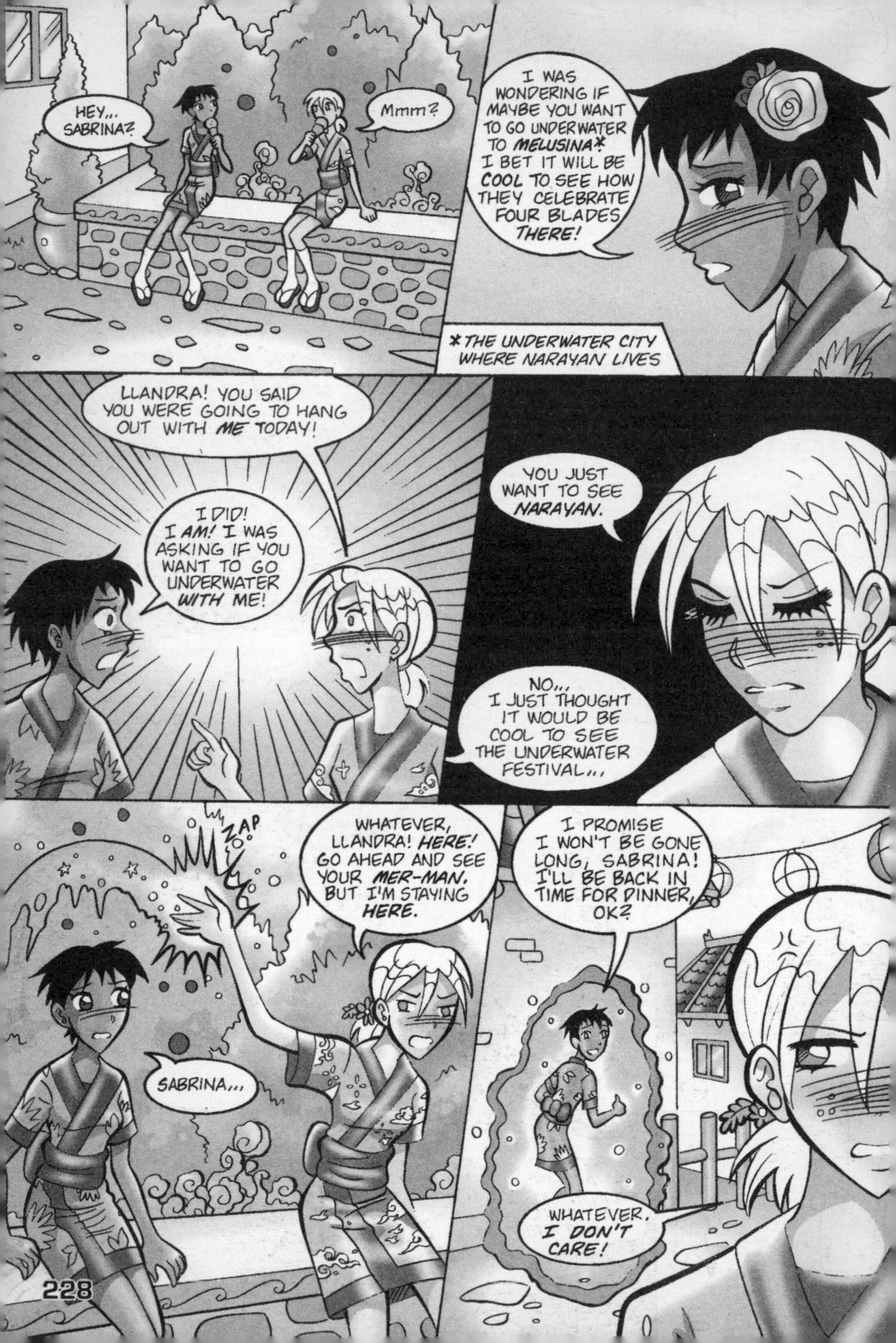
HEY... SABRINA?
Mmm?
I WAS WONDERING IF MAYBE YOU WANT TO GO UNDERWATER TO MELUSINA*. I BET IT WILL BE COOL TO SEE HOW THEY CELEBRATE FOUR BLADES THERE!
*THE UNDERWATER CITY WHERE NARAYAN LIVES
LLANDRA! YOU SAID YOU WERE GOING TO HANG OUT WITH ME TODAY!
I DID! I AM! I WAS ASKING IF YOU WANT TO GO UNDERWATER WITH ME!
YOU JUST WANT TO SEE NARAYAN.
NO... I JUST THOUGHT IT WOULD BE COOL TO SEE THE UNDERWATER FESTIVAL...
ZAP
WHATEVER, LLANDRA! HERE! GO AHEAD AND SEE YOUR MER-MAN. BUT I'M STAYING HERE.
SABRINA...
I PROMISE I WON'T BE GONE LONG, SABRINA! I'LL BE BACK IN TIME FOR DINNER, OK?
WHATEVER. I DON'T CARE!

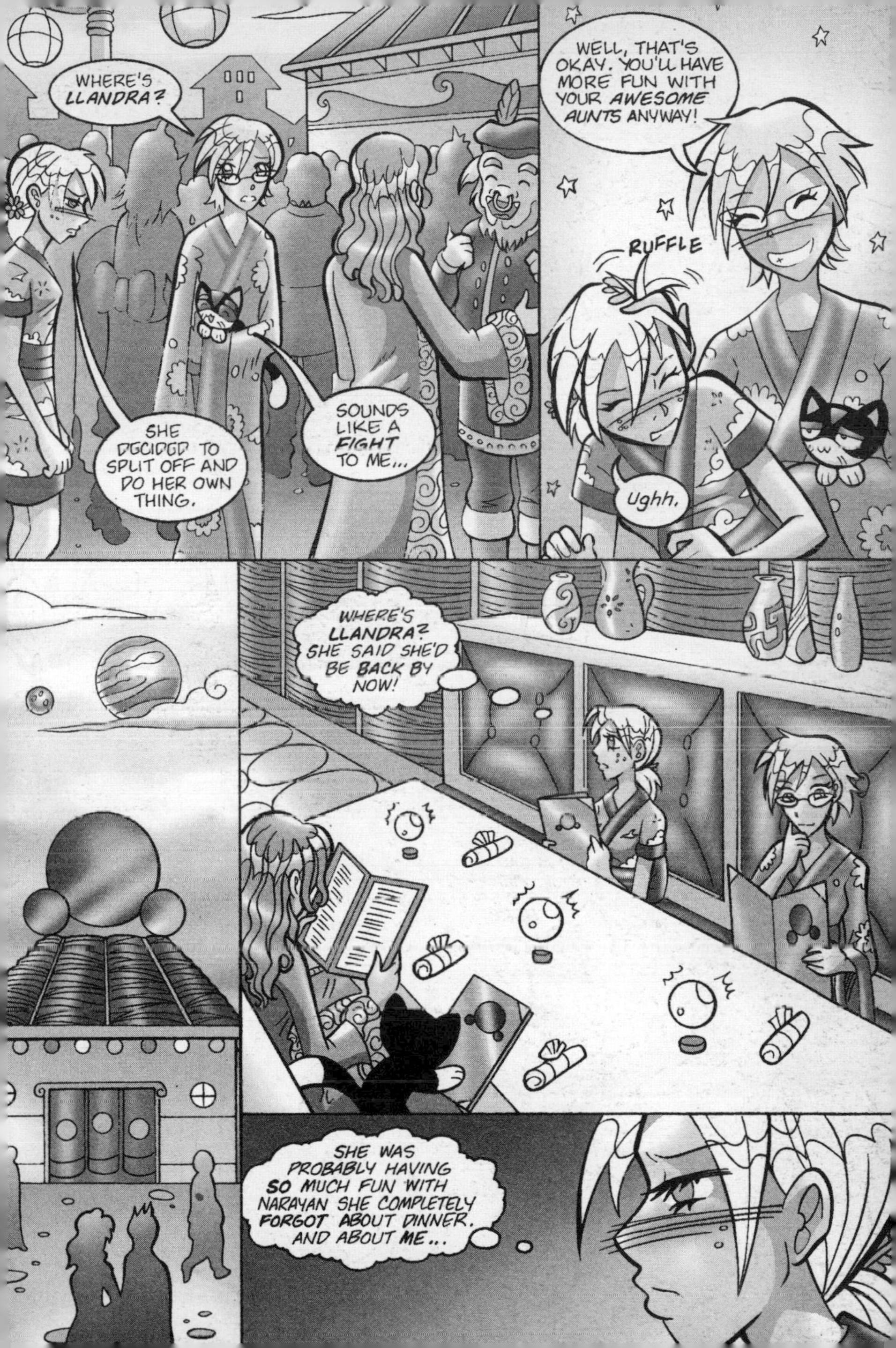
WHERE'S LLANDRA?
SHE DECIDED TO SPLIT OFF AND DO HER OWN THING.
SOUNDS LIKE A FIGHT TO ME...
WELL, THAT'S OKAY. YOU'LL HAVE MORE FUN WITH YOUR AWESOME AUNTS ANYWAY!
RUFFLE
Ughh.
WHERE'S LLANDRA? SHE SAID SHE'D BE BACK BY NOW!
SHE WAS PROBABLY HAVING SO MUCH FUN WITH NARAYAN SHE COMPLETELY FORGOT ABOUT DINNER. AND ABOUT ME...

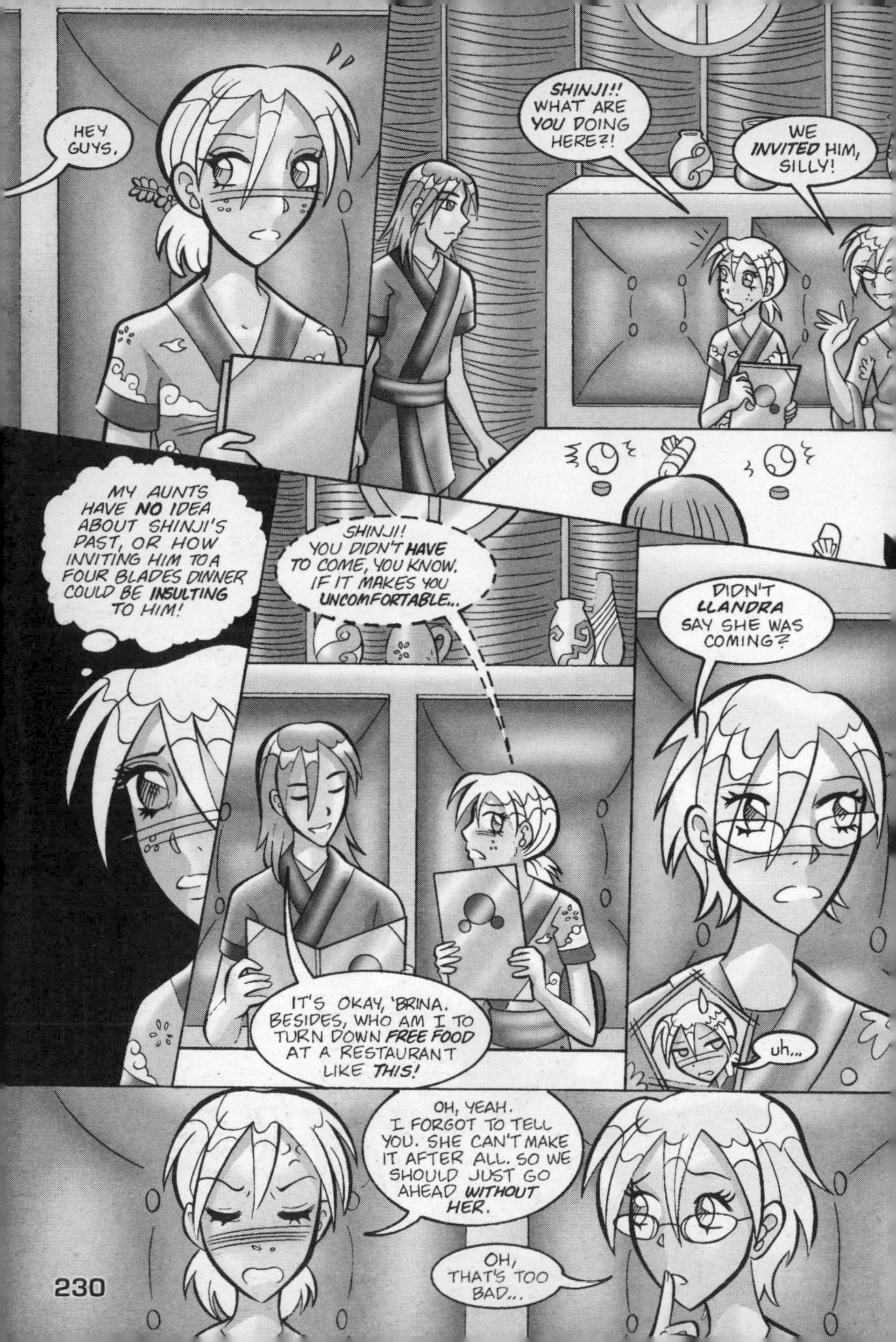
HEY GUYS.
SHINJI!! WHAT ARE YOU DOING HERE?!
WE INVITED HIM, SILLY!
MY AUNTS HAVE NO IDEA ABOUT SHINJI'S PAST, OR HOW INVITING HIM TO A FOUR BLADES DINNER COULD BE INSULTING TO HIM!
SHINJI! YOU DIDN'T HAVE TO COME, YOU KNOW. IF IT MAKES YOU UNCOMFORTABLE...
IT'S OKAY, 'BRINA. BESIDES, WHO AM I TO TURN DOWN FREE FOOD AT A RESTAURANT LIKE THIS!
DIDN'T LLANDRA SAY SHE WAS COMING?
uh...
OH, YEAH. I FORGOT TO TELL YOU. SHE CAN'T MAKE IT AFTER ALL. SO WE SHOULD JUST GO AHEAD WITHOUT HER.
OH, THAT'S TOO BAD...

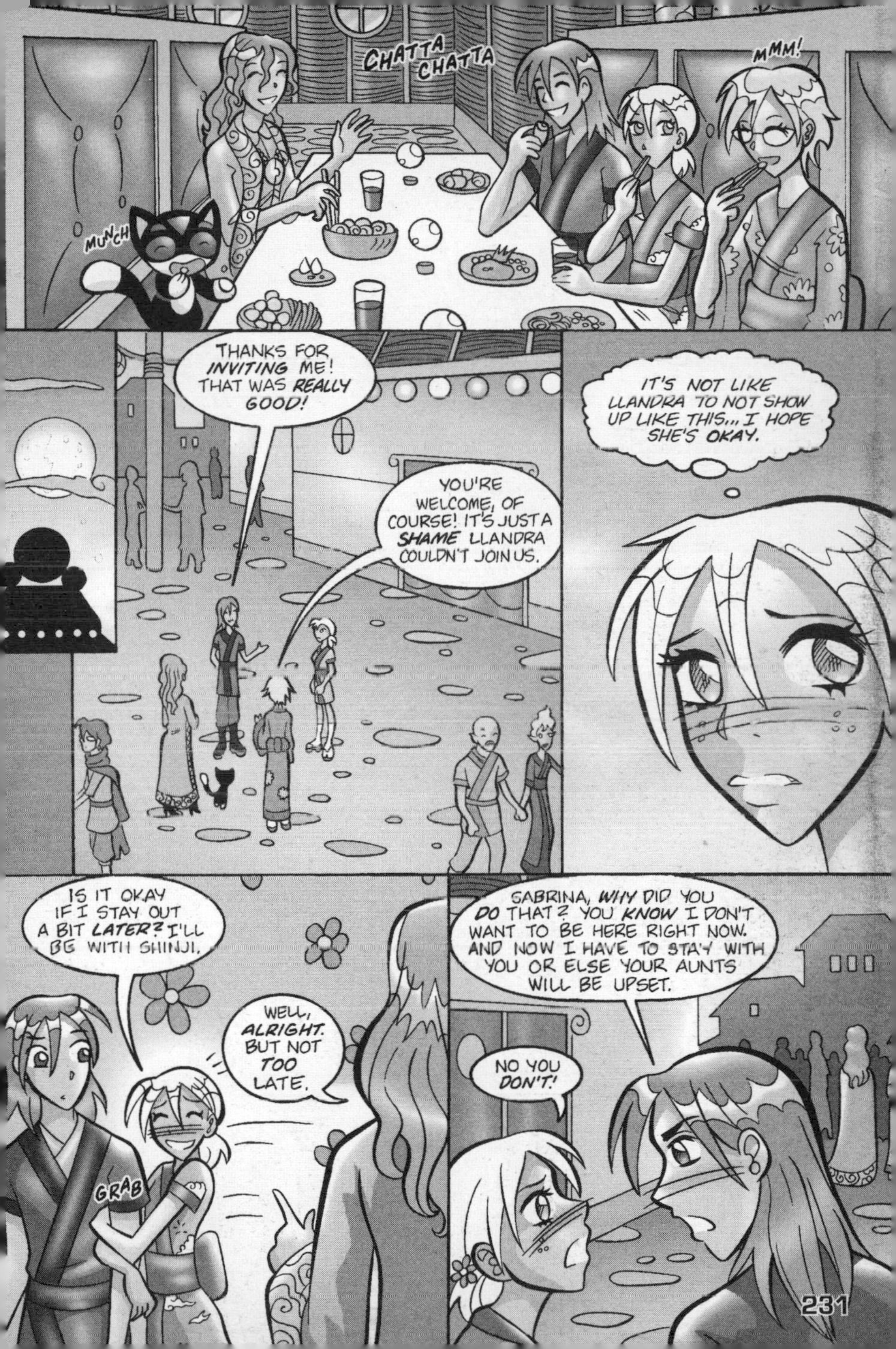
CHATTA CHATTA
MMM!
MUNCH
THANKS FOR INVITING ME! THAT WAS REALLY GOOD!
YOU'RE WELCOME, OF COURSE! IT'S JUST A SHAME LLANDRA COULDN'T JOIN US.
IT'S NOT LIKE LLANDRA TO NOT SHOW UP LIKE THIS... I HOPE SHE'S OKAY.
IS IT OKAY IF I STAY OUT A BIT LATER? I'LL BE WITH SHINJI.
GRAB
WELL, ALRIGHT. BUT NOT TOO LATE.
SABRINA, WHY DID YOU DO THAT? YOU KNOW I DON'T WANT TO BE HERE RIGHT NOW. AND NOW I HAVE TO STAY WITH YOU OR ELSE YOUR AUNTS WILL BE UPSET.
NO YOU DON'T!

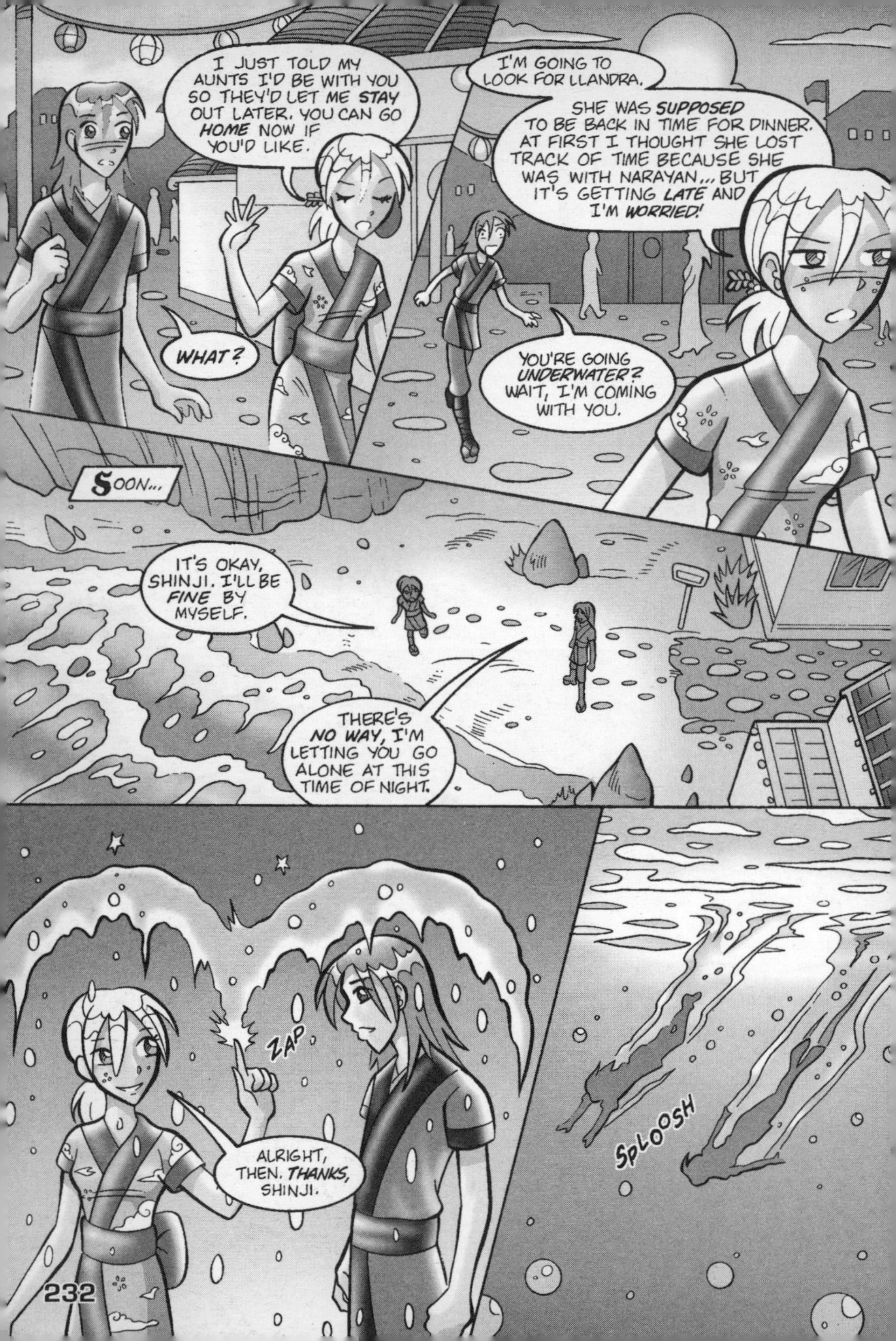

I JUST TOLD MY AUNTS I'D BE WITH YOU SO THEY'D LET ME **STAY** OUT LATER. YOU CAN GO **HOME** NOW IF YOU'D LIKE.
WHAT?
I'M GOING TO LOOK FOR LLANDRA.
SHE WAS **SUPPOSED** TO BE BACK IN TIME FOR DINNER. AT FIRST I THOUGHT SHE LOST TRACK OF TIME BECAUSE SHE WAS WITH NARAYAN... BUT IT'S GETTING **LATE** AND I'M **WORRIED!**
YOU'RE GOING **UNDERWATER?** WAIT, I'M COMING WITH YOU.
SOON...
IT'S OKAY, SHINJI. I'LL BE **FINE** BY MYSELF.
THERE'S **NO WAY,** I'M LETTING YOU GO ALONE AT THIS TIME OF NIGHT.
ZAP
ALRIGHT, THEN. **THANKS,** SHINJI.
SPLOOSH

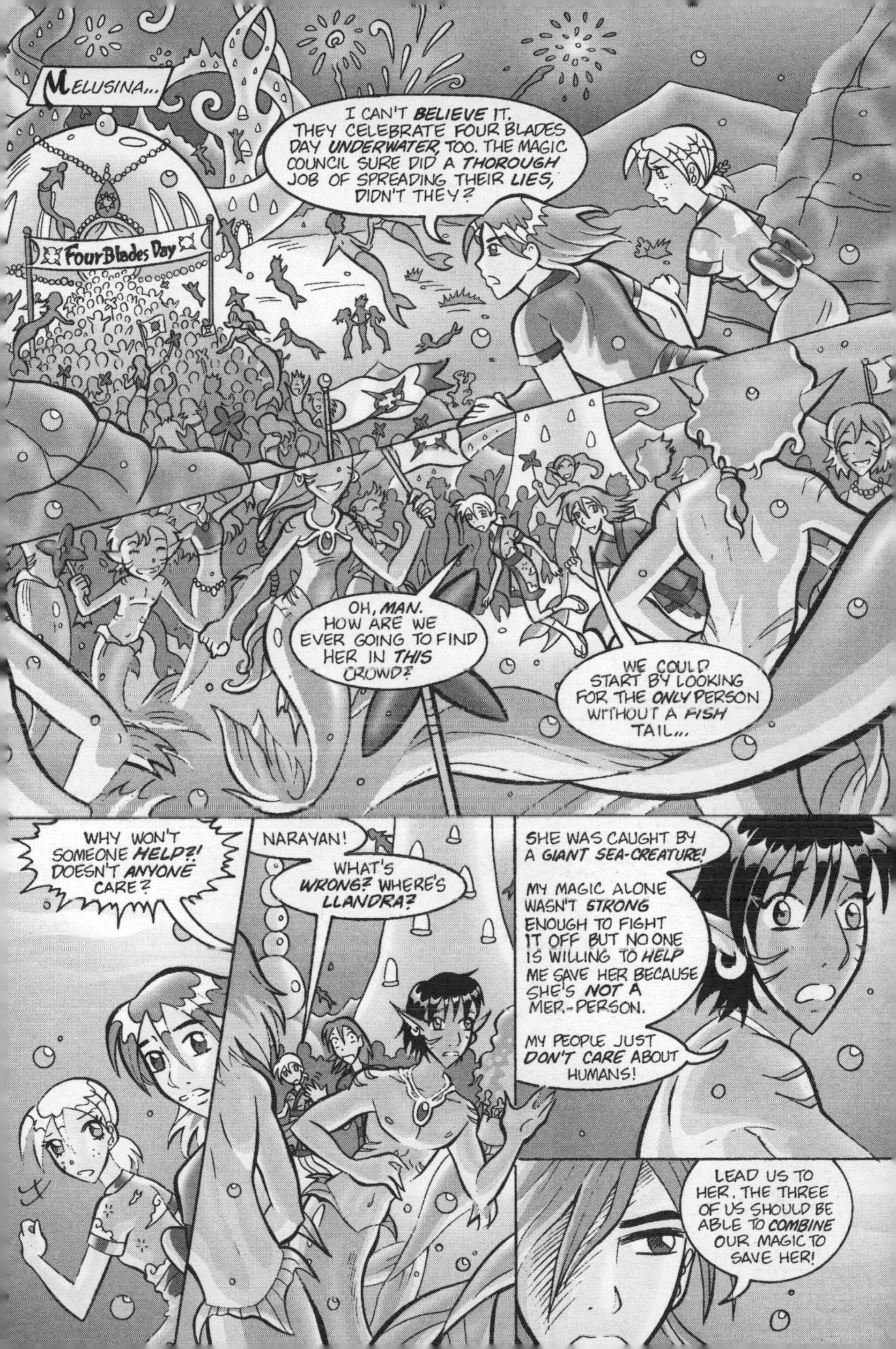
MELUSINA...
Four Blades Day
I CAN'T BELIEVE IT. THEY CELEBRATE FOUR BLADES DAY UNDERWATER, TOO. THE MAGIC COUNCIL SURE DID A THOROUGH JOB OF SPREADING THEIR LIES, DIDN'T THEY?
OH, MAN. HOW ARE WE EVER GOING TO FIND HER IN THIS CROWD?
WE COULD START BY LOOKING FOR THE ONLY PERSON WITHOUT A FISH TAIL...
WHY WON'T SOMEONE HELP?! DOESN'T ANYONE CARE?
NARAYAN!
WHAT'S WRONG? WHERE'S LLANDRA?
SHE WAS CAUGHT BY A GIANT SEA-CREATURE!
MY MAGIC ALONE WASN'T STRONG ENOUGH TO FIGHT IT OFF BUT NO ONE IS WILLING TO HELP ME SAVE HER BECAUSE SHE'S NOT A MER-PERSON.
MY PEOPLE JUST DON'T CARE ABOUT HUMANS!
LEAD US TO HER. THE THREE OF US SHOULD BE ABLE TO COMBINE OUR MAGIC TO SAVE HER!

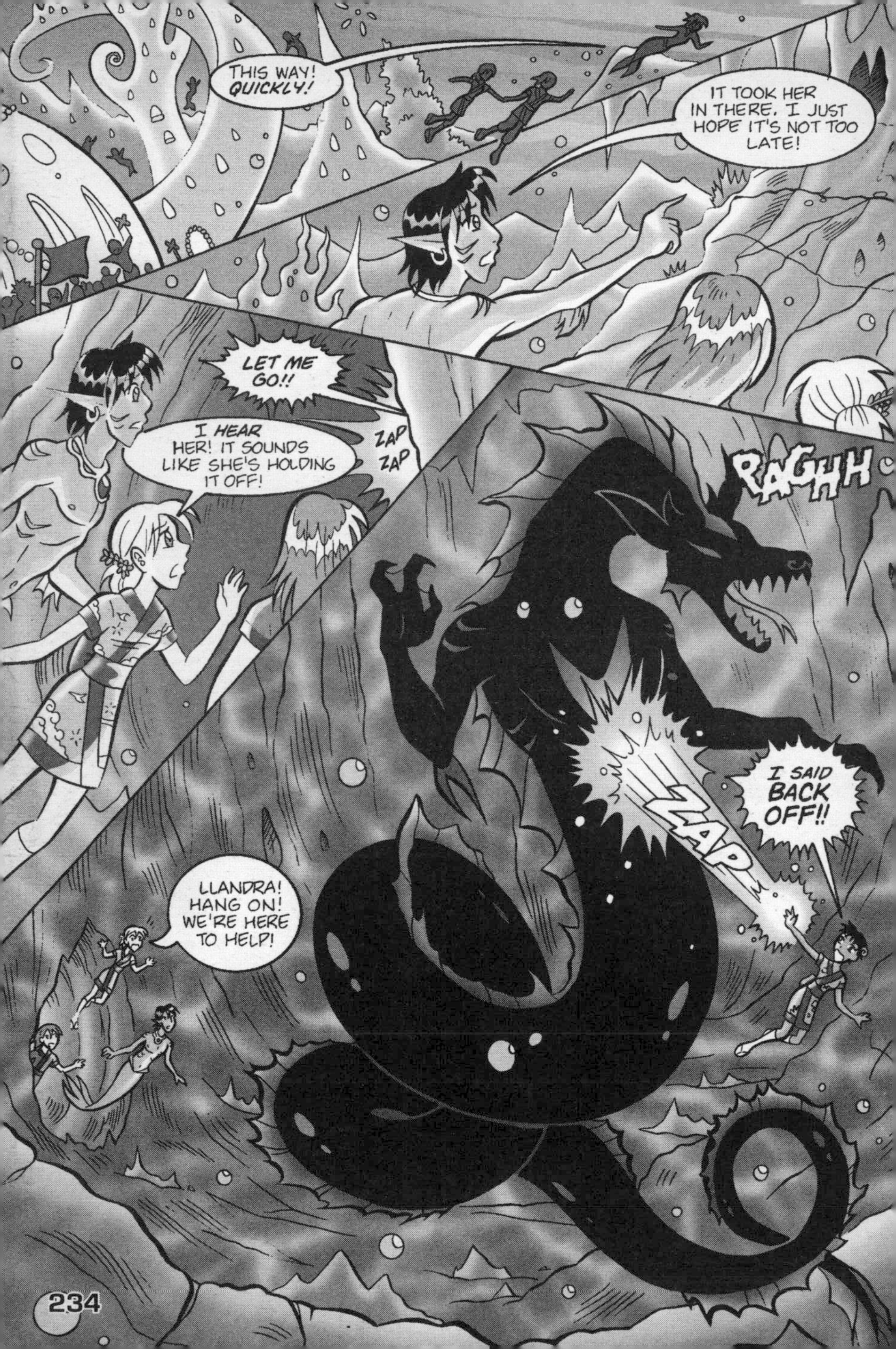

THIS WAY! QUICKLY!
IT TOOK HER IN THERE. I JUST HOPE IT'S NOT TOO LATE!
LET ME GO!!
I HEAR HER! IT SOUNDS LIKE SHE'S HOLDING IT OFF!
ZAP ZAP
RAGHH
I SAID BACK OFF!!
ZAP
LLANDRA! HANG ON! WE'RE HERE TO HELP!

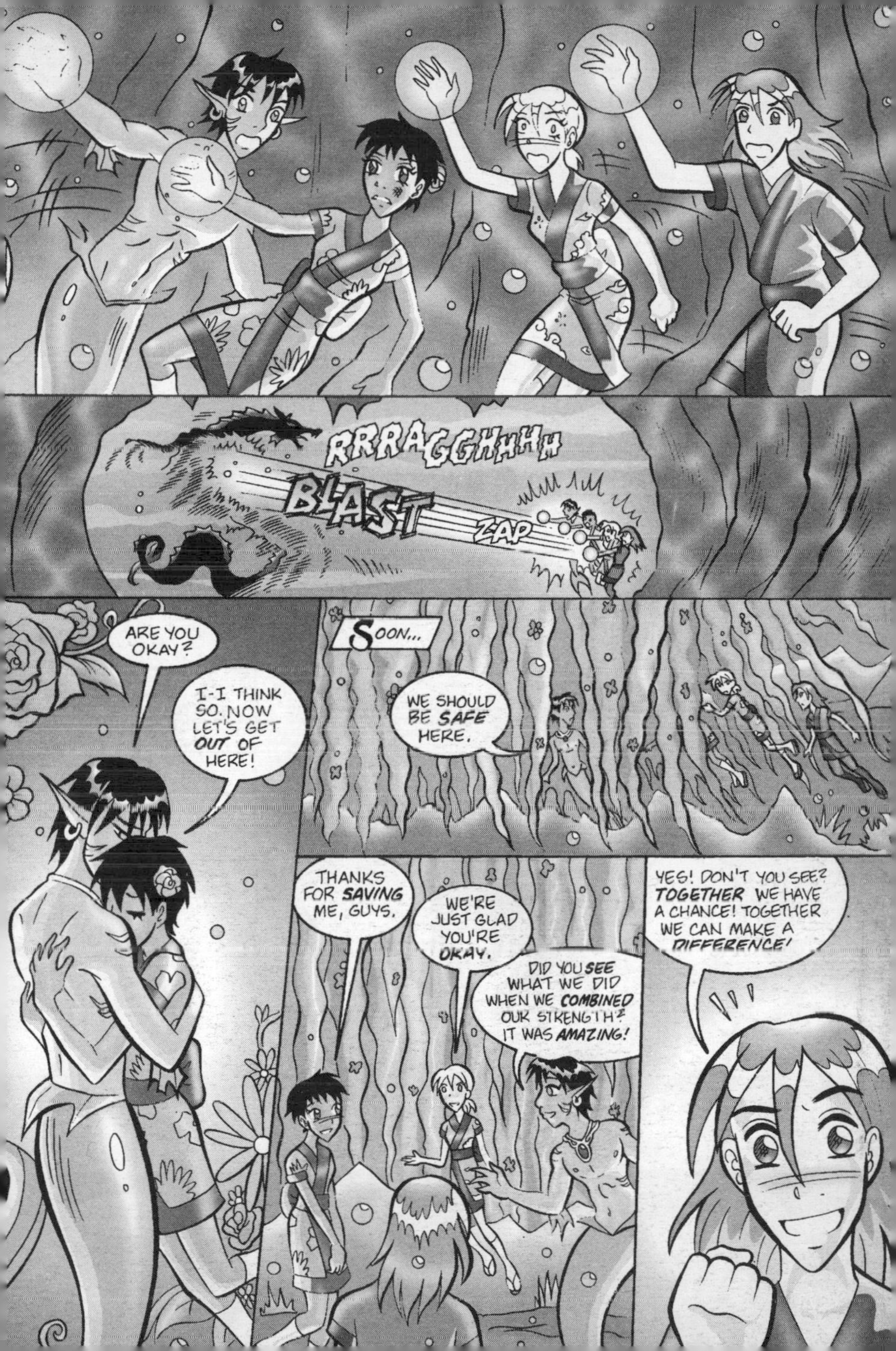
RRRAGGHHHH
BLAST
ZAP
ARE YOU OKAY?
I-I THINK SO. NOW LET'S GET **OUT** OF HERE!
SOON...
WE SHOULD BE **SAFE** HERE.
THANKS FOR **SAVING** ME, GUYS.
WE'RE JUST GLAD YOU'RE **OKAY.**
DID YOU **SEE** WHAT WE DID WHEN WE **COMBINED** OUR STRENGTH? IT WAS **AMAZING!**
YES! DON'T YOU SEE? **TOGETHER** WE HAVE A CHANCE! TOGETHER WE CAN MAKE A **DIFFERENCE!**

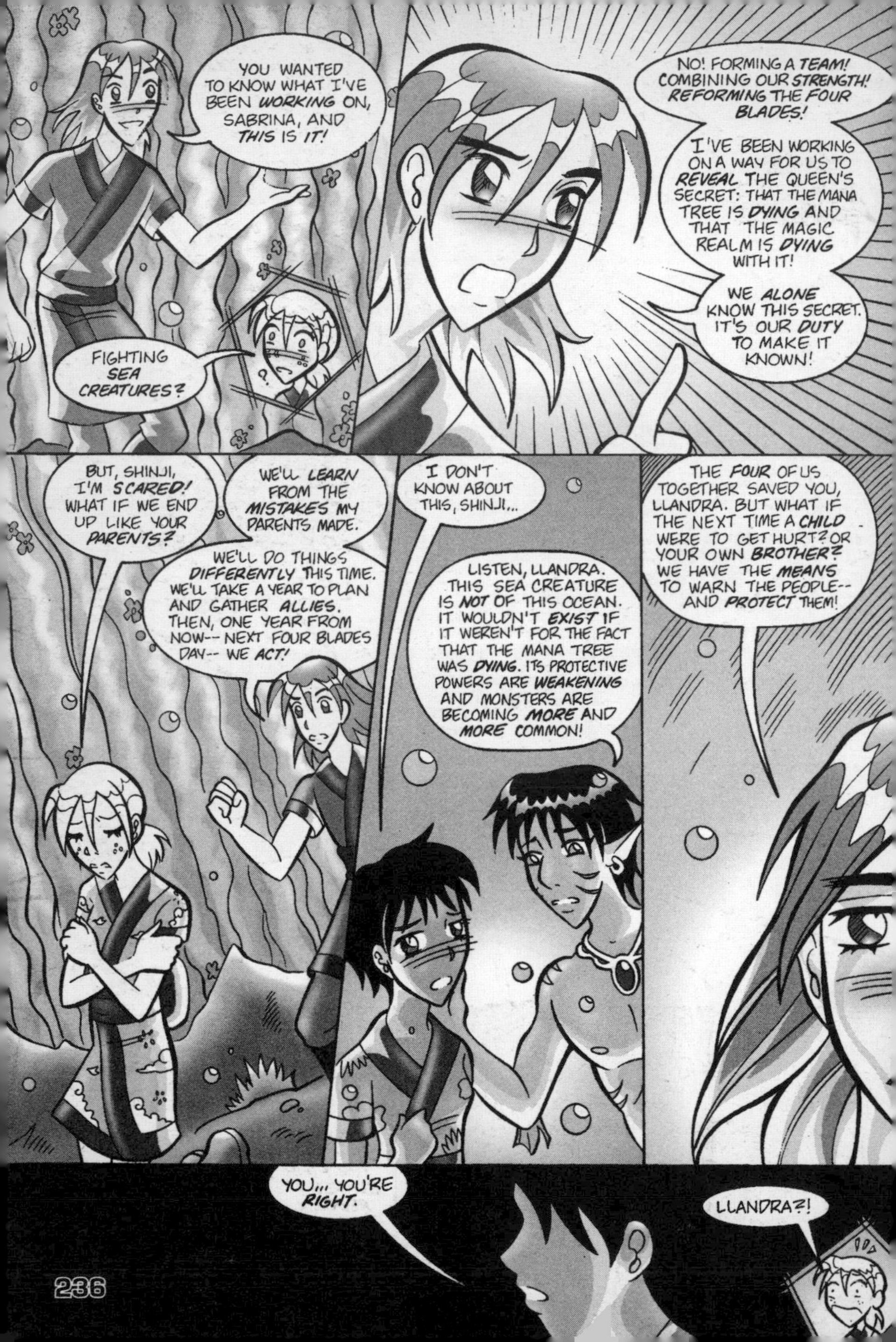

YOU WANTED TO KNOW WHAT I'VE BEEN WORKING ON, SABRINA, AND THIS IS IT!
FIGHTING SEA CREATURES?
NO! FORMING A TEAM! COMBINING OUR STRENGTH! REFORMING THE FOUR BLADES!
I'VE BEEN WORKING ON A WAY FOR US TO REVEAL THE QUEEN'S SECRET: THAT THE MANA TREE IS DYING AND THAT THE MAGIC REALM IS DYING WITH IT!
WE ALONE KNOW THIS SECRET. IT'S OUR DUTY TO MAKE IT KNOWN!
BUT, SHINJI, I'M SCARED! WHAT IF WE END UP LIKE YOUR PARENTS?
WE'LL LEARN FROM THE MISTAKES MY PARENTS MADE.
WE'LL DO THINGS DIFFERENTLY THIS TIME. WE'LL TAKE A YEAR TO PLAN AND GATHER ALLIES. THEN, ONE YEAR FROM NOW-- NEXT FOUR BLADES DAY-- WE ACT!
I DON'T KNOW ABOUT THIS, SHINJI...
LISTEN, LLANDRA. THIS SEA CREATURE IS NOT OF THIS OCEAN. IT WOULDN'T EXIST IF IT WEREN'T FOR THE FACT THAT THE MANA TREE WAS DYING. ITS PROTECTIVE POWERS ARE WEAKENING AND MONSTERS ARE BECOMING MORE AND MORE COMMON!
THE FOUR OF US TOGETHER SAVED YOU, LLANDRA. BUT WHAT IF THE NEXT TIME A CHILD WERE TO GET HURT? OR YOUR OWN BROTHER? WE HAVE THE MEANS TO WARN THE PEOPLE-- AND PROTECT THEM!
YOU... YOU'RE RIGHT.
LLANDRA?!

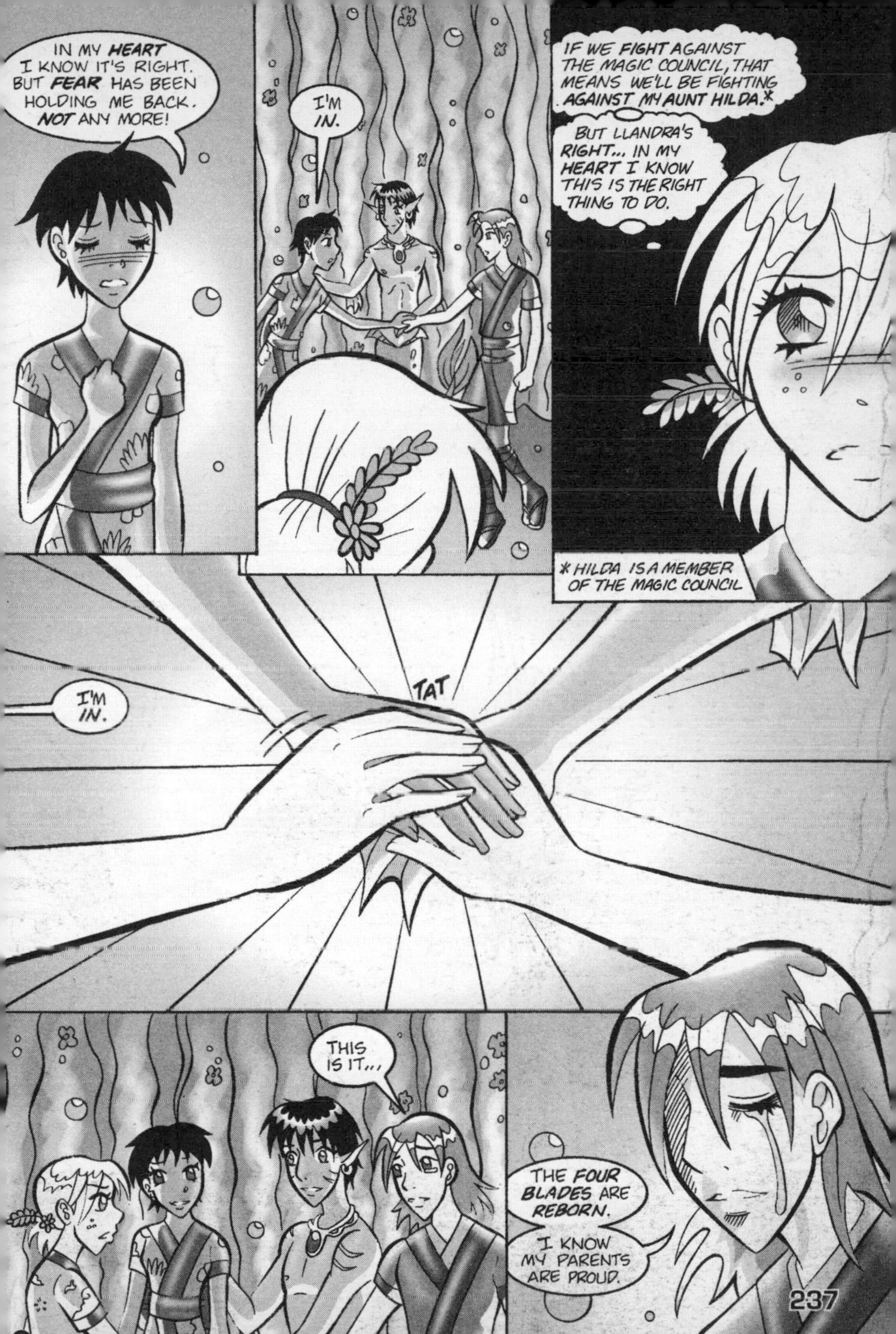
IN MY HEART I KNOW IT'S RIGHT. BUT FEAR HAS BEEN HOLDING ME BACK. NOT ANY MORE!
I'M IN.
IF WE FIGHT AGAINST THE MAGIC COUNCIL, THAT MEANS WE'LL BE FIGHTING AGAINST MY AUNT HILDA.*
BUT LLANDRA'S RIGHT... IN MY HEART I KNOW THIS IS THE RIGHT THING TO DO.
* HILDA IS A MEMBER OF THE MAGIC COUNCIL
I'M IN.
TAT
THIS IS IT...
THE FOUR BLADES ARE REBORN.
I KNOW MY PARENTS ARE PROUD.

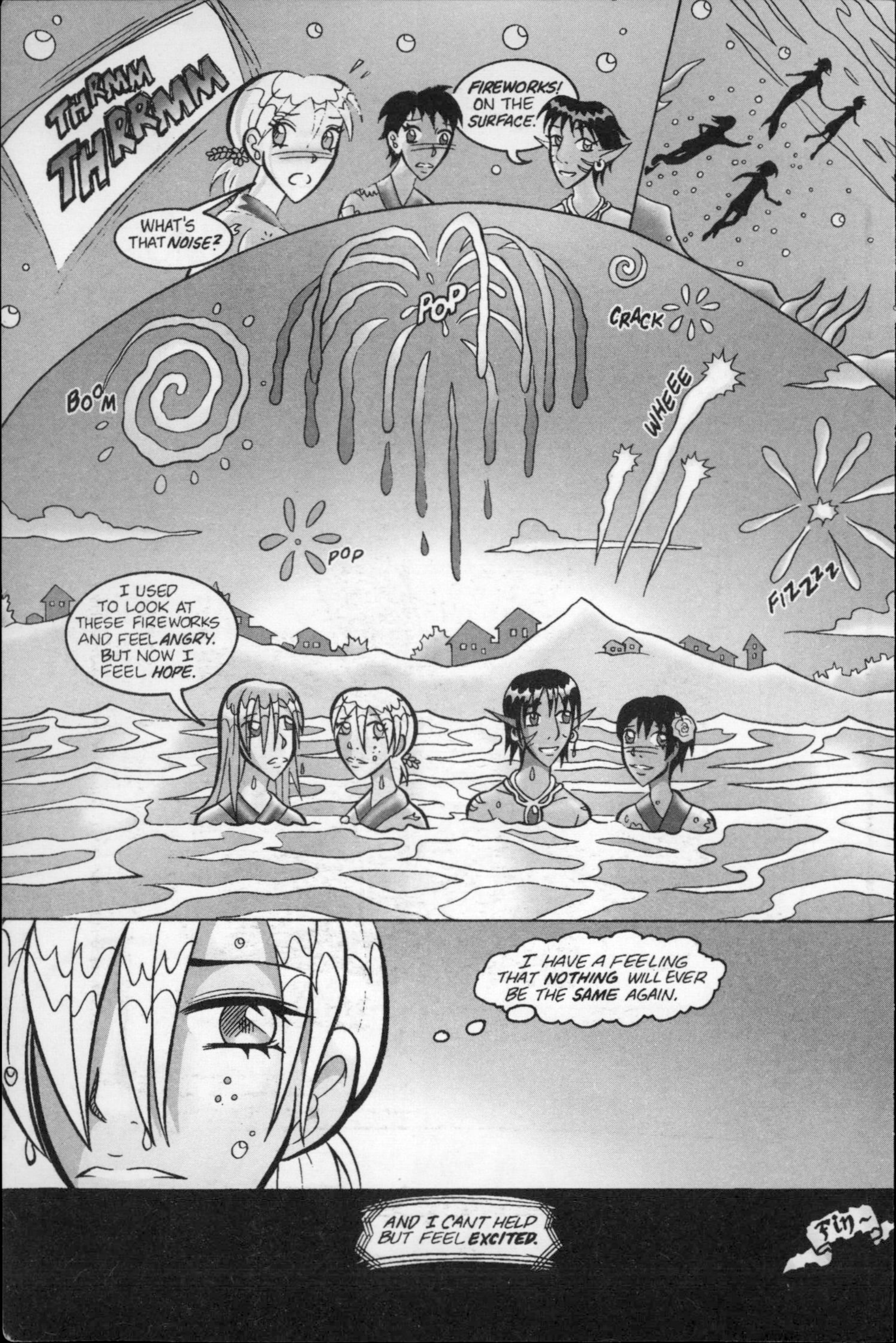
THRMM THRRMM
WHAT'S THAT NOISE?
FIREWORKS! ON THE SURFACE!
POP
CRACK
BOOM
WHEEE
POP
FIZZZZ
I USED TO LOOK AT THESE FIREWORKS AND FEEL ANGRY. BUT NOW I FEEL HOPE.
I HAVE A FEELING THAT NOTHING WILL EVER BE THE SAME AGAIN.
AND I CANT HELP BUT FEEL EXCITED.
Fin~

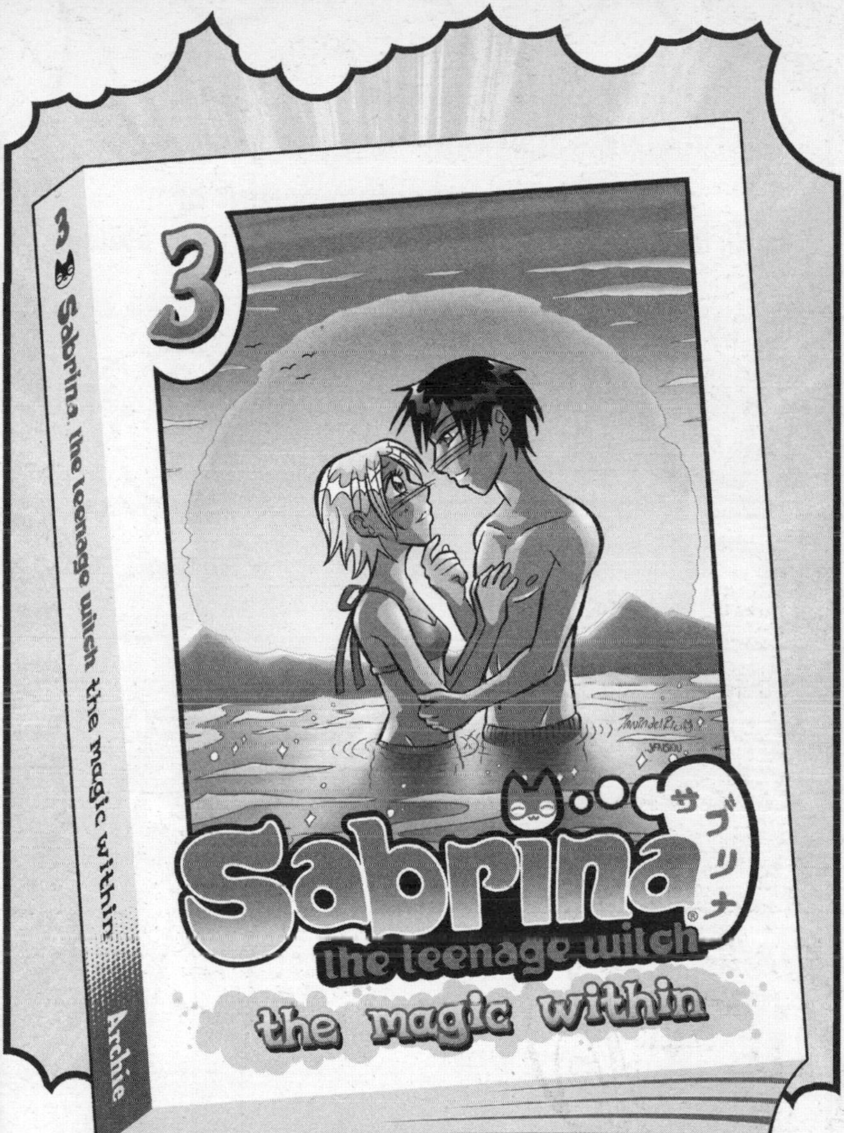
3 Sabrina, the teenage witch the magic within
Archie
3
Sabrina サブリナ
the teenage witch
the magic within

Continued in *The Magic Within 3*,

available in stores September 2013!

Collect the entire epic adventure in four magical volumes!

Don't miss a single moment of *Sabrina the Teenage Witch: The Magic Within* from Archie COMICS!

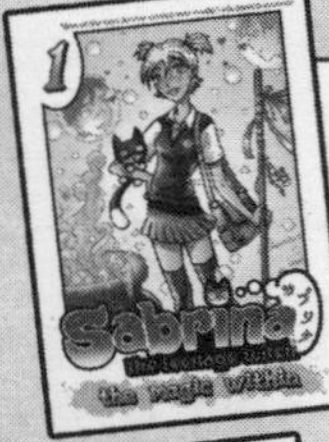
1
Sabrina
the teenage witch
the magic within

Sabrina:
The Magic Within 1

January 2013

ISBN:
978-1-879794-39-6

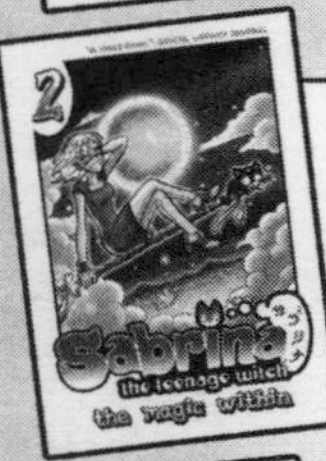
2
Sabrina
the teenage witch
the magic within

Sabrina:
The Magic Within 2

June 2013

ISBN:
978-1-879794-54-9

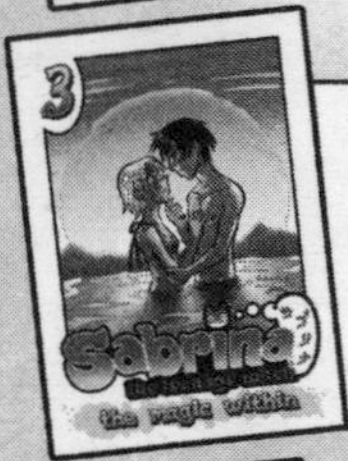
3
Sabrina
the magic within

Sabrina:
The Magic Within 3

September 2013

ISBN:
978-1-879794-60-0

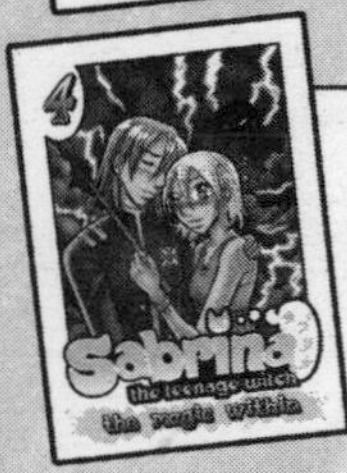
4
Sabrina
the teenage witch
the magic within

Sabrina:
The Magic Within 4

December 2013

ISBN:
978-1-879794-76-1

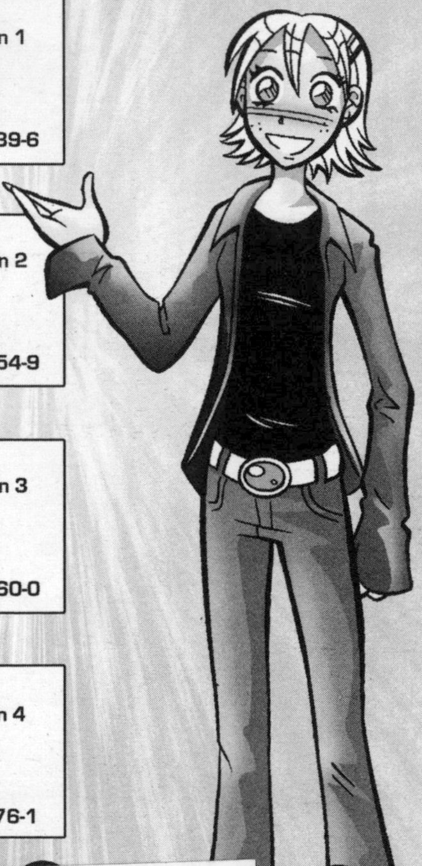

FIND THESE AND MORE GREAT ARCHIE BOOKS AT COMIC SHOPS, BOOKSTORES, AND ARCHIECOMICS.COM!

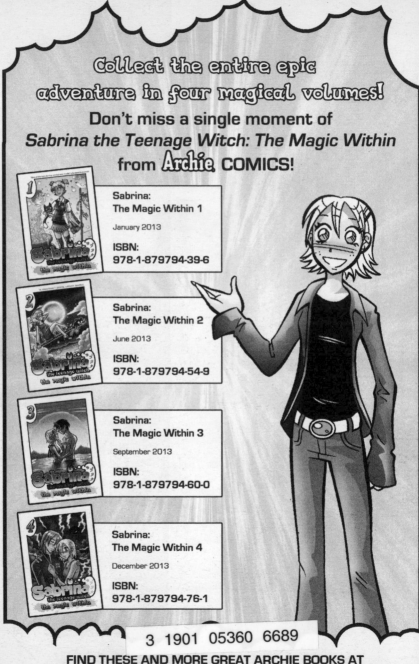